SLAVE, WARRIOR, QUEEN

ROGUE, PRISONER, PRINCESS

KNIGHT, HEIR, PRINCE

(OF CROWNS AND GLORY--BOOKS 1, 2, AND 3)

Slave, Warrior, Queen

(OF CROWNS AND GLORY—BOOK 1)

Morgan Rice

Morgan Rice

Morgan Rice is the #1 bestselling and USA Today bestselling author of the epic fantasy series THE SORCERER'S RING, comprising seventeen books; of the #1 bestselling series THE VAMPIRE JOURNALS, comprising twelve books; of the #1 bestselling series THE SURVIVAL TRILOGY, a post-apocalyptic thriller comprising three books; of the epic fantasy series KINGS AND SORCERERS, comprising six books; and of the new epic fantasy series OF CROWNS AND GLORY. Morgan's books are available in audio and print editions, and translations are available in over 25 languages.

TURNED (Book #1 in the Vampire Journals), ARENA 1 (Book #1 of the Survival Trilogy), A QUEST OF HEROES (Book #1 in the Sorcerer's Ring) and RISE OF THE DRAGONS (Kings and Sorcerers—Book #1) are each available as a free download on Amazon!

Morgan loves to hear from you, so please feel free to visit www.morganricebooks.com to join the email list, receive a free book, receive free giveaways, download the free app, get the latest exclusive news, connect on Facebook and Twitter, and stay in touch!

Select Acclaim for Morgan Rice

"If you thought that there was no reason left for living after the end of THE SORCERER'S RING series, you were wrong. In RISE OF THE DRAGONS Morgan Rice has come up with what promises to be another brilliant series, immersing us in a fantasy of trolls and dragons, of valor, honor, courage, magic and faith in your destiny. Morgan has managed again to produce a strong set of characters that make us cheer for them on every page.... Recommended for the permanent library of all readers that love a well-written fantasy."

—*Books and Movie Reviews*
Roberto Mattos

"An action packed fantasy sure to please fans of Morgan Rice's previous novels, along with fans of works such as THE INHERITANCE CYCLE by Christopher Paolini .... Fans of Young Adult Fiction will devour this latest work by Rice and beg for more."

—*The Wanderer, A Literary Journal*
(regarding *Rise of the Dragons*)

"A spirited fantasy that weaves elements of mystery and intrigue into its story line. *A Quest of Heroes* is all about the making of courage and about realizing a life purpose that leads to growth, maturity, and excellence .... For those seeking meaty fantasy adventures, the protagonists, devices, and action provide a vigorous set of encounters that focus well on Thor's evolution from a dreamy child to a young adult facing impossible odds

for survival….Only the beginning of what promises to be an epic young adult series."

—*Midwest Book Review* (D. Donovan, eBook Reviewer)

"THE SORCERER'S RING has all the ingredients for an instant success: plots, counterplots, mystery, valiant knights, and blossoming relationships replete with broken hearts, deception and betrayal. It will keep you entertained for hours, and will satisfy all ages. Recommended for the permanent library of all fantasy readers."

—*Books and Movie Reviews*, Roberto Mattos

"In this action-packed first book in the epic fantasy Sorcerer's Ring series (which is currently 14 books strong), Rice introduces readers to 14-year-old Thorgrin "Thor" McLeod, whose dream is to join the Silver Legion, the elite knights who serve the king…. Rice's writing is solid and the premise intriguing."

—*Publishers Weekly*

Books by Morgan Rice

THE WAY OF STEEL

ONLY THE WORTHY (Book #1)

OF CROWNS AND GLORY

SLAVE, WARRIOR, QUEEN (Book #1)

ROGUE, PRISONER, PRINCESS (Book #2)

KNIGHT, HEIR, PRINCE (Book #3)

REBEL, PAWN, KING (Book #4)

KINGS AND SORCERERS

RISE OF THE DRAGONS (Book #1)

RISE OF THE VALIANT (Book #2)

THE WEIGHT OF HONOR (Book #3)

A FORGE OF VALOR (Book #4)

A REALM OF SHADOWS (Book #5)

NIGHT OF THE BOLD (Book #6)

THE SORCERER'S RING

A QUEST OF HEROES (Book #1)

A MARCH OF KINGS (Book #2)

A FATE OF DRAGONS (Book #3)

A CRY OF HONOR (Book #4)

A VOW OF GLORY (Book #5)

A CHARGE OF VALOR (Book #6)

A RITE OF SWORDS (Book #7)

A GRANT OF ARMS (Book #8)

A SKY OF SPELLS (Book #9)

A SEA OF SHIELDS (Book #10)

A REIGN OF STEEL (Book #11)
A LAND OF FIRE (Book #12)
A RULE OF QUEENS (Book #13)
AN OATH OF BROTHERS (Book #14)
A DREAM OF MORTALS (Book #15)
A JOUST OF KNIGHTS (Book #16)
THE GIFT OF BATTLE (Book #17)

THE SURVIVAL TRILOGY
ARENA ONE: SLAVERSUNNERS (Book #1)
ARENA TWO (Book #2)
ARENA THREE (Book #3)

VAMPIRE, FALLEN
BEFORE DAWN (Book #1)

THE VAMPIRE JOURNALS
TURNED (Book #1)
LOVED (Book #2)
BETRAYED (Book #3)
DESTINED (Book #4)
DESIRED (Book #5)
BETROTHED (Book #6)
VOWED (Book #7)
FOUND (Book #8)
RESURRECTED (Book #9)
CRAVED (Book #10)
FATED (Book #11)
OBSESSED (Book #12)

To Storm Jensen,
a remarkable wife, mother, and hero.
Every word is a step—and you, Storm, are brave enough to start.

"Come close, dear warrior, and I shall tell you a tale.
A tale of battles distant.
A tale of men and valor.
A tale of crowns and glory."

—*The Forgotten Chronicles of Lysa*

Table of Contents

CHAPTER ONE

Ceres ran through the back alleys of Delos, excitement coursing through her veins, knowing she could not be late. The sun was barely rising, and yet the muggy, dust-filled air was already suffocating in the ancient stone city. Legs burning, lungs aching, she nonetheless pushed herself to run faster, and faster still, hopping over one of the countless rats that crept out of the gutters and refuse in the streets. She could already hear the distant rumble, and her heart pounded with anticipation. Somewhere ahead, she knew, the Festival of the Killings was about to begin.

Letting her hands drag along the stone walls as she twisted and turned down a narrow alley, Ceres glanced back to make certain her brothers were keeping up. There, she was relieved to see, were Nesos, at her heels, and Sartes, only a few feet behind. At nineteen, Nesos was just two sun cycles older than she, while Sartes, her baby brother, four sun cycles younger, was on the verge of manhood. The two of them, with their longish sandy hair and brown eyes, looked exactly like each other—and their parents—and yet nothing like her. Still, though Ceres might be a girl, they had never been able to keep pace with her.

"Hurry!" Ceres yelled over her shoulder.

Another rumble came, and although she had never been to the festival, she imagined it in vivid detail: the entire city, all three million citizens of Delos, crowding into the Stade on this summer solstice holiday. It would be unlike anything she had seen before, and if her brothers and she didn't hurry, not a single seat would remain.

Picking up speed, Ceres wiped a drop of sweat off her brow and smeared it onto her frayed, ivory tunic, a hand-me-down from her mother. She had never been given new clothes. According to her mother, who doted on her brothers but seemed to reserve a special hatred and envy for her, she didn't deserve it.

"Wait!" Sartes yelled, an edge of irritation in his cracking voice.

Ceres smiled.

"Shall I carry you, then?" she yelled back.

She knew that he hated it when she teased him, yet her snide remark would motivate him to keep up. Ceres didn't mind his tagging along; she thought it was endearing how he, at thirteen, would do anything to be considered their peer. And even though she would never admit it openly, a huge part of her needed him to need her.

Sartes gave a loud grunt.

"Mother will kill you when she finds out you disobeyed her again!" he yelled back.

He was right. Indeed, she would—or give her a good flogging, at least.

The first time her mother had beaten her, at the age of five, it was the very moment Ceres lost her innocence. Before then, the world had been fun, kind, and good. After that, nothing had ever been safe again, and all that she had to hold onto was her hope of a future where she could get away from her. She was older now, close, and yet even that dream was slowly eroding in her heart.

Fortunately, Ceres knew her brothers would never tell on her. They were as loyal to her as she was to them.

"Then it's a good thing Mother will never know!" she cried back.

"Father will find out, though!" Sartes snapped.

She chuckled. Father already knew. They had made a deal: if she stayed up late to finish sharpening the swords due for delivery at the palace, she could go see the Killings. And so she did.

Ceres reached the wall at the end of the lane and, without pausing, wedged her fingers in two cracks and began to climb. Her hands and feet moved swiftly, and up she went, a good twenty feet, until she scrambled to the top.

She stood, breathing hard, and the sun greeted her with its bright rays. She shaded her eyes with a hand.

She gasped. Normally, the Old City was dotted with a few citizens, a stray cat or dog here and there—yet today it was positively alive. It swarmed with people. Ceres could not even see the cobblestones beneath the sea of people pressing into Fountain Square.

In the distance the ocean shimmered a vivid blue, while the towering white Stade stood as a mountain amongst twisting roads and sardine-packed two- and three-story houses. Around the outer edge of the plaza merchants had lined up booths, each eager to sell food, jewelry, or clothes.

A gust of wind brushed against her face, and the smell of freshly baked goods seeped into her nostrils. What she wouldn't give for food that would satisfy that gnawing sensation. She wrapped her arms around her belly as she felt a hunger pang. Breakfast this morning had been a few spoonfuls of soggy porridge, which had somehow managed to leave her stomach feeling hungrier than before she ate it. Given that today was her eighteenth birthday, she had hoped for at least a little extra food in her bowl—or a hug or *something.*

But no one had mentioned a word. She doubted they even remembered.

Light caught her eyes, and Ceres looked down to spot a golden carriage weaving through the crowd like a bubble through honey, slow and shiny. She frowned. In her excitement, she had failed to consider that the royalty would be at the event, too. She despised them, their haughtiness, that their animals were better fed than most of the people of Delos. Her brothers were hopeful that one day, they would triumph over the class system. But Ceres did not share their optimism: if there were to be any sort of equality in the Empire, it would have to come by way of revolution.

"Do you see him?" Nesos panted as he climbed up beside her.

Ceres's heart quickened as she thought of him. Rexus. She, too, had been wondering if he was here yet, and had been scanning the crowds to no avail.

She shook her head.

"There." Nesos pointed.

She followed his finger toward the fountain, squinting.

Suddenly she saw him, and could not suppress her burst of excitement. It was the same way she always felt when she saw him. There he was, sitting on the edge of the fountain, tightening his bow. Even from this distance, she could see his shoulder and chest muscles move beneath his tunic. Hardly a few years older than she, he had blond hair that stood out amongst heads of black and brown, and his tan skin glistened in the sun.

"Wait!" cried a voice.

Ceres glanced back down the wall to see Sartes, struggling with the climb.

"Hurry up or we'll leave you behind!" Nesos goaded.

Of course, they wouldn't dream of leaving their younger brother, although he did need to learn to keep up. In Delos, a moment of weakness could mean death.

Nesos ran a hand through his hair, catching his breath, too, as he surveyed the crowd.

"So who is your money on to win?" he asked.

Ceres turned to him and laughed.

"What money?" she asked.

He smiled.

"If you had any," he answered.

"Brennius," she replied without pausing.

His brow lifted in surprise.

"Really?" he asked. "Why?"

"I don't know." She shrugged. "Just a hunch."

But she did know. She knew very well, better than her brothers, better than all the boys of her city. Ceres had a secret: she hadn't told anyone she had, on occasion, dressed as a boy and trained at the palace. It was forbidden by royal decree for girls—punishable by death—to learn the ways of the combatlords, yet male commoners were welcome to learn in exchange for equal amounts of work in the palace's stables, work which she did happily.

She'd watched Brennius and had been impressed by the way he fought. He wasn't the largest of the combatlords, yet his moves were calculated with precision.

"No chance," Nesos replied. "It'll be Stefanus."

She shook her head.

"Stefanus will be dead within the first ten minutes," she said flatly.

Stefanus was the obvious choice, the largest of the combatlords, and probably the strongest; yet he wasn't as calculating as Brennius or some of the other warriors she had watched.

Nesos barked a laugh.

"I'll give you my good sword if that's the case."

She glanced at the sword attached to his waist. He had no idea how jealous she had been when he received that masterpiece of a weapon as a birthday gift from Mother three years ago. Her sword was an old leftover one her father had tossed into the recycling pile. Oh, the things she'd be able to do if she had a weapon like Nesos's.

"I'm going to hold you to it, you know," Ceres said, smiling—although in reality, she would never take his sword from him.

"I'd expect nothing less," he smirked.

She crossed her arms in front of her chest as a dark thought crossed her mind.

"Mother wouldn't allow it," she said.

"But Father would," he said. "He's very proud of you, you know."

Nesos's kind comment took her off guard, and not knowing exactly how to accept it, she lowered her eyes. She loved her father dearly, and he loved her, she knew. Yet for some reason, her mother's face appeared before her. All she ever wanted was for her mother to accept her and love her as much as her brothers. But as hard as she tried, Ceres felt she could never be enough in her eyes.

Sartes grunted as he climbed the last step behind them. He was still about a head shorter than Ceres and as scrawny as a cricket, but she was convinced he'd sprout like a bamboo shoot any day now. That's what had happened to Nesos. Now he was a muscle-bound hunk, hovering at six foot three.

"And you?" Ceres turned to Sartes. "Who do you think will win?"

"I'm with you. Brennius."

She smiled and ruffled his hair. He always said whatever she said.

Another rumble came, the crowd thickened, and she felt the urgency.

"Let's go," she said, "no time to waste."

Without waiting, Ceres climbed down the wall and hit the ground running. Keeping the fountain in sight, she made her way across the plaza, eager to reach Rexus.

He turned and his eyes widened in delight as she neared. She rushed into him and felt his arms wrap around her waist, as he pressed a scruffy cheek against hers.

"Ciri," he said in his low, raspy voice.

A shiver ran through her spine as she spun around to meet Rexus's cobalt blue eyes. At six foot one, he was nearly a head taller than her, and blond, coarse hair framed his heart-shaped face. He smelled like soap and the outdoors. Heavens, it was good to see him again. Even though she could fend for herself in nearly any situation, his presence brought her a sense of calm.

Ceres raised herself up onto the balls of her feet and curled willing arms around his thick neck. She had never seen him as more than a friend until she heard him speak of the revolution, and of the underground army he was a member of. "We will fight to free ourselves from the yoke of oppression," he had said to her years ago. He had spoken with such passion about the rebellion that for a moment, she had really believed overthrowing the royals was possible.

"How was the hunt?" she asked with a smile, knowing he had been gone for days.

"I missed your smile." He stroked her long, rose-gold hair back. "And your emerald eyes."

Ceres had missed him, too, but she didn't dare say. She was too afraid to lose the friendship they had if anything were to happen between them.

"Rexus," Nesos said, catching up, Sartes at his heels, and clasping his arm.

"Nesos," he said, in his deep, authoritative voice. "We have little time if we are to get in," he added, nodding to the others.

They all hurried off, merging with the throng heading toward the Stade. Empire soldiers were everywhere, urging the crowds forward, sometimes with clubs and whips. The closer they came to the road that led to the Stade, the more the crowd thickened.

All of a sudden, Ceres heard a clamor by one of the booths and she instinctively turned toward the sound. She saw that a generous space had opened up around a small boy, flanked by two Empire soldiers and a merchant. A few onlookers fled, while others gawked in a circle.

Ceres rushed forward to see one of the soldiers slap an apple out of the boy's hand as he grabbed the little one's arm, shaking him violently.

"Thief!" the soldier growled.

"Mercy, please!" the boy screamed, tears streaming down his dirty, hollow cheeks. "I was ... so hungry!"

Ceres felt her heart burst from compassion, as she had felt the same hunger—and she knew the soldiers would be nothing short of cruel.

"Let the boy go," the heavyset merchant said calmly with the gesture of a hand, his gold ring catching the sunlight. "I can afford to give him an apple. I have hundreds of apples." He chuckled a little, as if to make light of the situation.

But the crowd gathered around and quieted as the soldiers turned to confront the merchant, their shiny armor rattling. Ceres's heart dropped for the merchant—she knew that one never risked confronting the Empire.

The soldier stepped forward menacingly toward the merchant.

"You defend a criminal?"

The merchant looked back and forth between the two of them, now seeming unsure. The soldier then turned and hit the boy across the face with a sickening crack that made Ceres shiver.

The boy fell to the ground with a thump as the crowd gasped.

Pointing at the merchant, the soldier said, "To prove your loyalty to the Empire, you will hold the boy while we flog him."

The merchant's eyes turned hard, his brow sweaty. To Ceres's surprise, he held his ground.

"No," he replied.

The second soldier took two threatening steps toward the merchant and his hand moved to the hilt of his sword.

"Do it, or you lose your head and we burn your shop down," the soldier said.

The merchant's round face went limp, and Ceres could tell he was defeated.

He slowly walked over to the boy and grabbed the boy's arms, kneeling in front of him.

"Please forgive me," he said, tears brimming in his eyes.

The boy whimpered and then started to scream as he tried to wring himself free from his grip.

Ceres could see the child was shaking. She wanted to keep moving toward the Stade, to avoid witnessing this, but instead, her feet stood frozen in the middle of the square, eyes glued to the brutality.

The first soldier tore the boy's tunic open while the second soldier whirled a flogger above his head. Most onlookers cheered the soldiers on, although a few murmured and walked away with heads hung low.

None defended the thief.

With a greedy, almost maddening expression, the soldier thrashed the whip against the boy's back, causing him to shriek in pain as they flogged him. Blood oozed out of the fresh lacerations. Again and again, the soldier flogged until the boy's head was sagging backward and he no longer screamed.

Ceres felt the strong urge to rush forward and save the boy. Yet to do so, she knew, would mean her death, and the death of all those she loved. She slumped her shoulders, feeling hopeless and defeated. Inwardly, she resolved to take revenge one day.

She yanked Sartes toward her and covered his eyes, desperately wanting to protect him, to give him a few more years of innocence, even though there was no innocence to be had in this land. She forced herself not to act on her impulse. As a man, he needed to see these instances of cruelty, not only to adapt, but also to one day be a strong contender in the rebellion.

The soldiers grabbed the boy out of the merchant's hands and then tossed his lifeless body into the back of a wooden cart. The merchant pressed his hands to his face and sobbed.

Within seconds, the cart was on its way, and the previously open space was again filled with people meandering about the square as if nothing had happened.

Ceres felt an overwhelming sense of nausea well up inside. It was unjust. In this moment, she could pick out a half a dozen pickpockets—men and women who had perfected their art so well that not even the Empire soldiers could catch them. This poor boy's life was now ruined because of his lack of skill. If caught, thieves, young or old, would lose their limbs or more, depending on how the judges felt that day. If he were lucky, his life would be spared and he would be sentenced to work in the gold mines for life. Ceres would rather die than have to endure being imprisoned like that.

They continued along the street, their mood ruined, shoulder to shoulder with the others as the heat grew almost unbearable.

A golden carriage pulled up next to them, forcing everyone out of the way, shoving people up to the houses on the sides. Jostled roughly, Ceres looked up to see three teenage girls in colorful silk dresses, pins of gold and precious jewels adorning their intricate up-dos. One of the teenagers, laughing, tossed a coin out onto the street, and a handful of commoners stooped onto hands and knees, scrambling for a piece of metal that would feed a family for an entire month.

Ceres never stooped to pick up any handouts. She'd rather starve than take donations from the likes of those.

She watched a young man get hold of the coin and an older man drive him to the ground and clamp a stiff hand around his neck. With the other hand, the older man forced the coin out of the young man's hand.

The teenage girls laughed and pointed fingers before their carriage continued to weave through the masses.

Ceres's insides clenched with disgust.

"In the near future, inequality will vanish forever," Rexus said. "I will see to it."

Listening to him speak, Ceres's chest swelled. One day she would fight side by side with him and her brothers in the rebellion.

As they neared the Stade the streets widened, and Ceres felt like she could take a breath. The air buzzed. She felt she would rupture from excitement.

She walked through one of the dozens of arched entrances and looked up.

Thousands upon thousands of commoners teemed inside the magnificent Stade. The oval structure had collapsed on the top northern side, and the majority of the red awnings were torn and provided little protection from the sweltering sun. Wild beasts growled from behind iron gates and trap doors, and she could see the combatlords standing ready behind the gates.

Ceres gaped, taking it all in in wonder.

Before she knew it, Ceres looked up and realized she had fallen behind Rexus and her brothers. She rushed forward to catch up, yet as soon as she did, four burly men had surrounded her. She smelled alcohol, rotting fish, and body odor as they pressed in too close, turning and gaping at her with rotted teeth and ugly smiles.

"You're coming with us, pretty girl," one of them said as they all strategically moved in on her.

Ceres heart raced. She looked ahead for the others, but they were already lost in the thickening crowd.

She confronted the men, trying to put on her bravest face.

"Leave me be or I will ..."

They burst into laughter.

"What?" one mocked. "A wee girl like you take us four?"

"We could carry you out of here kickin' and screamin' and not a soul would say nuttin'," another added.

And it was true. From the corner of her eye, Ceres watched people rush by, pretending not to notice how these men were threatening her.

Suddenly, the leader's face turned serious, and with one swift move, he grabbed her arms and pulled her close. She knew they could haul her away, never to be seen again, and that thought terrified her more than anything.

Trying to ignore her pounding heart, Ceres spun around, snatching her arm out of his stronghold. The other men hooted in amusement, but when she thrust the base of her palm into the leader's nose, snapping his head back, they went silent.

The leader placed filthy hands over his nose and grunted.

She didn't relent. Knowing she had one chance, she kicked him once in the stomach, remembering her days of sparring, and he keeled over as she connected.

Immediately, though, the other three were upon her, their strong hands grabbing her, yanking her away.

Suddenly, they relented. Ceres looked over with relief to see Rexus appear and punch one in the face, knocking him out.

Nesos then appeared and grabbed another and kneed him in the stomach before kicking him to the ground, leaving him in the red dirt.

The fourth man charged toward Ceres, but just as he was about to attack, she ducked, spun, and kicked him in the rear so he went flying into a pillar headfirst.

She stood there, breathing hard, taking it all in.

Rexus placed a hand on Ceres's shoulder. "Are you all right?"

Ceres's heart was still running wild, but a feeling of pride slowly replaced her fear. She had done well.

She nodded and Rexus wrapped an arm around her shoulders as they continued on, his full lips gliding into a smile.

"What?" Ceres asked.

"When I saw what was happening, I wanted to run my sword through each and every one of them. But then I saw how you defended yourself." He shook his head and chuckled. "They didn't expect that."

She felt her cheeks flush. She wanted to say she had been fearless, but the truth was, she had not been.

"I was nervous," she admitted.

"Ciri, nervous? Never." He kissed Ceres on top of the head, and they continued into the Stade.

They found a few spots left at ground level and they took their seats, Ceres thrilled it was not too late as she put all the events of the day behind her and allowed herself to become caught up in the excitement of the cheering crowd.

"Do you see them?"

Ceres followed Rexus's finger and looked up to see a dozen or so teenagers sitting in a booth, sipping wine from silver goblets. She had never seen such fine clothing, so much food on one table, so much sparkling jewelry in her entire life. Not one of them had sunken cheeks or concave bellies.

"What are they doing?" she asked when she saw one of them collecting coins into a gold bowl.

"Each owns a combatlord," Rexus said, "and they place bets on who will win."

Ceres scoffed. This was just a game for them, she realized. Obviously, the spoiled teenagers didn't care about the warriors or about the art of combat. They just wanted to see if their combatlord would win. To Ceres, though, this event was about honor and courage and skill.

The royal banners were raised, trumpets blared, and as iron gates sprung open, one on each end of the Stade, combatlord after combatlord marched out of the black holes, their leather and iron armor catching the sunlight, emitting sparks of light.

The crowd roared as the brutes marched into the arena, and Ceres rose to her feet with them, applauding. The warriors ended in an outward-facing circle, their axes, swords, spears, shields, tridents, whips, and other weapons held to the sky.

"Hail, King Claudius," they yelled.

Trumpets blared again, and the golden chariot of King Claudius and Queen Athena whirled onto the arena from one of the entrances. Next, a chariot with Crown Prince Avilius, and Princess Floriana followed, and after them, an entire entourage of chariots carrying royals flooded the arena. Each chariot was towed by two snow white horses adorned with precious jewels and gold.

When Ceres spotted Prince Thanos amongst them, she became appalled at the nineteen-year-old boy's scowl. From time to time when she delivered swords for her father, she had seen him speak with the combatlords at the palace, and he always carried that sour expression of superiority. His physique lacked nothing when it came to the likes of a warrior—he could almost be mistaken for one—his arms bulging with muscle, his waist tight and muscular, and his legs hard as tree trunks. However, it infuriated her how he appeared to hold no respect or passion for his position.

As the royals paraded up to their places at the podium, trumpets blared again, signaling the Killings were about to begin.

The crowd roared as all but two combatlords vanished back into the iron gates.

Ceres recognized one of them as Stefanus, but she couldn't make out the other brute wearing nothing but a visored helmet and a loincloth secured by a leather belt. Perhaps he had traveled from afar to contend. His well-oiled skin was the color of fertile soil, and his hair as black as the darkest night. Through the slits in the helmet, Ceres could see the look of resolve in his eyes, and she knew in an instant that Stefanus wouldn't live to see another hour.

"Don't worry," Ceres said, glancing over at Nesos. "I'll let you keep your sword."

"He's not defeated yet," Nesos replied with a smirk. "Stefanus would not be everyone's favorite if he weren't superior."

When Stefanus lifted his trident and shield, the crowd went silent.

"Stefanus!" one of the wealthy male youths from the booth shouted with a raised clenched fist. "Power and bravery!"

Stefanus nodded toward the youth as the audience roared with approval, and then he came at the foreigner with full force. The foreigner swerved out of the way in a flash, spun around, and slashed at Stefanus with his sword, missing by a mere inch.

Ceres cringed. With reflexes like that, Stefanus wouldn't last long.

Hacking away at Stefanus's shield again and again, the foreigner roared while Stefanus retreated. Stefanus, desperate, finally flung the edge of his shield into his opponent's face, sending a spray of blood across the air as his foe fell.

Ceres thought that was a rather nice move. Maybe Stefanus had improved in his technique since she saw him in training last.

"Stefanus! Stefanus! Stefanus!" the spectators chanted.

Stefanus stood at the feet of the injured warrior, but just as he was about to stab him with the trident, the foreigner lifted his legs and kicked Stefanus so he tumbled backwards, landing on his behind. Both hopped to their feet as quick as cats and faced each other again.

Their eyes locked and they began circling one another, the danger in the air palpable, Ceres thought.

The foreigner snarled and lifted his sword high into the air as he ran toward Stefanus. Stefanus quickly veered to the side and jabbed him in the thigh. In return, the foreigner swung his sword around and sliced Stefanus's arm.

Both warriors grunted in pain, but it was as if the wounds drove their fury instead of slowing them. The foreigner peeled off his helmet and flung it to the ground. His black bearded chin was bloodied, his right eye swollen, but his expression made Ceres think he was done playing games with Stefanus and was going in for the kill. How quickly would he be able to slay him?

Stefanus charged toward the foreigner, and Ceres gasped as Stefanus's trident collided with his opponent's sword. Eyeball to eyeball the warriors strained against each other, grunting, panting, shoving, the blood vessels in their foreheads protruding and the muscles bulging beneath their sweaty skin.

The foreigner ducked and wringed out of the deadlock, and unexpected to Ceres, he spun around like a tornado, sliced through the air with his sword, and decapitated Stefanus.

After a few breaths, the foreigner triumphantly lifted his arm into the air.

For a second, the crowd went completely silent. Even Ceres. She glanced up at the teenage boy who was Stefanus's owner. His mouth was wide open, his eyebrows knit together in fury.

The teenage boy hurled his silver goblet into the arena and stormed out of the booth. Death is the great equalizer, Ceres thought as she suppressed a smile.

"August!" a man in the crowd yelled. "August! August!"

One after another the spectators joined in, until the entire stadium chanted the victor's name. The foreigner bowed to King Claudius, and then three other warriors came running from the iron gates, replacing him.

One fight after another ensued as the day grew long, and Ceres watched with eyes peeled. She couldn't quite make up her mind whether she hated the Killings or loved it. On one hand, she enjoyed watching the strategy, the skill, and the bravery of the contenders; yet on the other, she despised how the warriors were nothing but pawns to the wealthy.

As the last fight of the first round arrived, Brennius and another warrior fought right next to where Ceres, Rexus, and her brothers were sitting. Closer and closer they came, their swords clanking, sparks flying. It was thrilling.

Ceres watched as Sartes leaned over the railing, his eyes glued to the combatants.

"Lean back!" she yelled at him.

But before he could respond, all of a sudden, an omnicat jumped out from a hatch in the ground on the other side of the stadium. The huge beast licked its fangs and its claws dug into the red dirt as it made its way toward the warriors. The combatlords hadn't yet seen the animal, and the stadium held its breath.

"Brennius is dead," Nesos mumbled.

"Sartes!" Ceres yelled again. "I said get back—"

She didn't have a chance to finish her words. Just then, the rock beneath Sartes's hands loosened, and before anyone could react, he tumbled down, over the rail, and fell all the way into the pit, landing with a thud.

"Sartes!" Ceres yelled in horror as she shot to her feet.

Ceres looked down to see Sartes, ten feet below, sit up and lean his back against the wall. His lower lip quivered, but there were no tears. No words. Holding his arm, he looked upward, his face twisted in agony.

Seeing him down there was more than Ceres could bear. Without thinking, she drew Nesos's sword and leapt over the rail, hopping into the pit, landing right in front of her younger brother.

"Ceres!" Rexus yelled.

She glanced back up and saw guards hauling Rexus and Nesos away before they could follow.

Ceres stood in the pit, overcome with a surreal feeling to be down here with the fighters in the arena. She wanted to get Sartes out of there, but there was no time. So she stepped in front of him, determined to protect him as the omnicat roared at her. It hunched low, its wicked yellow eyes fixed on Ceres, and she could sense the danger.

She whipped Nesos's sword up with both hands and clenched it tight.

"Run, girl!" Brennius yelled.

But it was too late. Charging toward her, the omnicat was now only a few feet away. She stepped closer to Sartes and just before the animal attacked, Brennius came in from the side and sliced the beast's ear off.

The omnicat rose onto its hind legs and roared, clawing a chunk out of the wall behind Ceres as purple blood stained its fur.

The crowd roared.

The second combatlord approached, but before he could cause the beast any harm, the omnicat lifted its paw and slit the man's throat with its claws. Clamping his hands around his neck, the warrior collapsed to the ground, blood seeping through his fingers.

Hungry for blood, the crowd cheered.

Snarling, the omnicat hit Ceres so hard she went flying into the air, crashing to the ground. On impact, the sword went tumbling from her hand and landed several feet away.

Ceres lay there, her lungs refusing to open up. Dying for air, her head spinning, she tried to crawl up onto hands and knees, but quickly tumbled back down.

Lying breathless with her face pressed against the coarse sand, she saw the omnicat heading toward Sartes. Seeing her brother in such a defenseless state, she felt her insides ignite with fire. She forced herself to take a breath and she discerned with complete clarity what she needed to do to save her brother.

Energy rushed through her like a flood, giving her instant power, and she rose to her feet, picked up the sword, and dashed toward the beast so fast she was convinced she was flying.

The beast was ten feet away from her now. Eight. Six. Four.

Ceres gritted her teeth and flung herself onto the beast's back, digging insistent fingers into its bristly fur, desperate to distract it from her brother.

The omnicat stood up on hind legs and shook its upper body, jostling Ceres back and forth. But her iron grip and her resolve were stronger than the animal's attempts to throw her off.

As the creature lowered back onto all fours again, Ceres seized the opportunity. She raised her sword high into the air and stabbed the beast in the neck.

The animal screeched and rose onto hind legs, as the crowd roared.

Reaching a paw around to Ceres, the creature pierced her back with its claws, and Ceres screamed from the pain, the claws feeling like daggers through her flesh. The omnicat grabbed her and hurled her into the wall, and she landed several feet away from Sartes.

"Ceres!" Sartes yelled.

Ears ringing, Ceres struggled to sit up, the back of her head throbbing, warm liquid running down her neck. There was no time to assess how serious the wound was. The omnicat was charging her again.

As the beast bore down, Ceres was out of options. Not even thinking, she instinctively raised a palm and held it out before her. It was the last thing she thought she'd ever see.

Just as the omnicat pounced, Ceres felt as if a ball of fire ignited in her chest, and suddenly she felt a ball of energy shoot out of her hand.

Mid-air, the beast suddenly went limp.

It crashed to the ground, skidding to a halt on top of her legs. Half-expecting the animal to come to life again and finish her off, Ceres held her breath as she watched it lie there.

But the creature didn't move.

Baffled, Ceres glanced at her palm. Not having seen what transpired, the crowd probably thought the beast died because she had stabbed him with her sword earlier. But she knew better. Some mysterious force had left her hand and had killed the beast in an instant. What force was it? Never had anything like this occurred before, and she didn't quite know what to make of it.

Who was she to have this power?

Afraid, she let her hand fall to the earth.

She lifted hesitant eyes, and saw the stadium had gone silent.

And she could not help but wonder. Had they seen it, too?

Chapter Two

For a second that seemed to stretch on and on, Ceres felt every eye upon her as she sat there, numb with pain and disbelief. More so than the repercussions to come, she feared the supernatural power that lurked within her, that had killed the omnicat. More than all the people surrounding her, she feared to face herself—a self she no longer knew.

Suddenly, the crowd, stunned into silence, roared. It took her a moment to realize that they were cheering for her.

A voice cut through the roars.

"Ceres!" Sartes yelled, beside her. "Are you hurt?"

She turned toward her brother, still lying there on the Stade floor, too, and opened her mouth. But not a single word came out. Her breath was spent and she felt dazed. Had he seen what had really happened? She didn't know about the others, but at this distance, it would be a near miracle if he hadn't.

Ceres heard footsteps, and suddenly two strong hands pulled her to a standing position.

"Get out now!" Brennius growled, shoving her toward the open gate to her left.

The puncture wounds in her back ached, but she forced herself back to reality and grabbed Sartes and pulled him to a standing position. Together, they darted toward the exit, trying to escape the cheers of the crowd.

They soon arrived in the dark, stuffy, tunnel, and as they did, Ceres saw dozens of combatlords inside, awaiting their turn for a few moments of glory in the arena. Some sat on benches in deep meditation, others were tensing their muscles, pumping their arms as they paced back and forth, and yet others were preparing their weapons for the imminent bloodbath. All of them, having just witnessed the fight, looked up and stared at her, curiosity in their eyes.

Ceres hurried down underground corridors lined with torches giving the gray bricks a warm glow, passing all manner of weapons leaning against the walls. She tried to ignore the pain in her back, but it was difficult to do so when with every step, the rough material in her dress chafed against the open wounds. The omnicat's claws had felt like daggers going in, but it almost seemed worse now as each gash throbbed.

"Your back is bleeding," Sartes said, a tremor in his voice.

"I'll be fine. We need to find Nesos and Rexus. How is your arm?"

"It hurts."

When they reached the exit, the door swung open, and two Empire soldiers stood there.

"Sartes!"

Before she could react a soldier seized her brother, and another grabbed her. It was no use resisting. The other soldier swung her over his shoulder as if she were a sack of grain, and carried her away. Fearing she had been arrested, she beat him on the back, to no avail.

Once they were just outside the Stade, he threw her onto the ground, and Sartes landed beside her. A few onlookers formed a half-circle around her, gawking, as if hungry for her blood to be spilt.

"Enter the Stade again," the soldier snarled, "and you will be hanged."

The soldiers, to her surprise, turned without another word and vanished back into the crowd.

"Ceres!" a deep voice yelled over the hum of the crowd.

Ceres looked up with relief to see Nesos and Rexus heading toward them. When Rexus threw his arms around her, she gasped. He pulled back, his eyes filled with concern.

"I'll be okay," she said.

As the throngs poured out of the Stade, Ceres and the others blended in and hurried off back into the streets, not wanting any more encounters. Walking toward Fountain Square, Ceres replayed in her mind all that had happened, still reeling. She noticed her brothers' sideways glances, and wondered what they were thinking. Had they witnessed her powers?

Likely not. The omnicat had been too close. Yet at the same time they glanced at her with a new sense of respect. She wanted more than anything to tell them what had happened. Yet she knew she could not. She was not even sure herself.

There was so much unsaid between them, yet now, amidst this thick crowd, was not the time to say it. They needed to get home, and safe, first.

The streets became far less crowded the further away they traveled from the Stade. Walking next to her, Rexus took one of her hands and interlaced fingers with her.

"I'm proud of you," he said. "You saved your brother's life. I'm not sure how many sisters would do that."

He smiled, his eyes filled with compassion.

"Those wounds look deep," he remarked, glancing at her back.

"I'll be fine," she muttered.

It was a lie. She wasn't at all certain she would be fine, or that she could even make it back home. She felt quite dizzy from the blood loss, and it didn't help that her stomach rumbled, or that the sun was harassing her back, causing her to sweat bullets.

Finally, they reached Fountain Square. As soon as they walked by the booths, a merchant trailed after them, offering a large basket of food for half price.

Sartes grinned from ear to ear—which she thought was rather strange—and then he held up a copper coin with his healthy arm.

"I think I owe you some food," he said.

Ceres gasped in shock. "Where did you get that?"

"That rich girl in the golden carriage tossed out two coins, not one, but everyone was so focused on the fight between the men that they didn't even notice," Sartes replied, his smile still very much intact.

Ceres grew angry and prepared to confiscate the coin from Sartes and throw it. That was blood money, after all. They didn't need anything from rich people.

As she reached to grab it, suddenly, an old woman appeared and blocked her path.

"You!" she said, pointing at Ceres, her voice so loud Ceres felt as if it vibrated straight through her.

The woman's complexion was smooth, yet seemingly transparent, and her perfectly arched lips were tinted green. Acorns and mosses adorned her long, thick, black hair, and her brown eyes matched her long brown dress. She was beautiful to behold, Ceres thought, so much so that she became mesmerized for a moment.

Ceres blinked back, stunned, certain she had never met this woman before.

"How do you know my name?"

Her eyes locked with the woman's as she took a few steps toward her, and Ceres noticed the woman smelled heavily of myrrh.

"Vein of the stars," she said, her voice eerie.

When the woman lifted her arm in a graceful gesture, Ceres saw that a triquetra was branded on the inside of her wrist. A witch. Based on the scent of the gods, perhaps a fortune-telling one.

The woman took Ceres's rose gold hair in her hand and smelled it.

"You are no stranger to the sword," she said. "You are no stranger to the throne. Your destiny is very great, indeed. Mighty will the change be."

The woman suddenly turned and hurried away, disappearing behind her booth, and Ceres stood there, numb. She felt the woman's words penetrate her very soul. She felt that they had been more than an observation; they were a prophecy. *Mighty. Change. Throne. Destiny.* These were words she had never associated with herself before.

Could they be true? Or were they just the words of a madwoman?

Ceres looked over and saw Sartes holding a basket of food, his mouth already stuffed with more than enough bread. He held it out for her. She saw the baked good, fruits, and vegetables, and it was almost enough to break her resolve. Normally, she would have devoured it.

Yet now, for some reason, she had lost her appetite.

There was a future before her.

A destiny.

⚜ ⚜ ⚜

The walk home had taken almost an hour longer than usual, and they had all remained silent the entire way, each lost in their own thoughts. Ceres could only wonder what the people she loved most in the world thought of her. She hardly knew what to think of herself.

She looked up and saw her humble home, and she was surprised she had made it all the way, given how her head and back ached.

The others had parted with her some time ago, to run an errand for her father, and Ceres stepped alone across the creaky threshold, bracing herself, hoping she did not run into her mother.

She entered a bath of heat. She made her way over to the small vial of cleaning alcohol her mother had stored under her bed and uncorked it, careful not to use so much that it went noticed. Bracing herself for the sting, she pried her shirt and poured it down her back.

Ceres cried out from the pain, clenching her fist and leaning her head against the wall, feeling a thousand stings from the omnicat's claws. It felt as if this wound would never heal.

The door slammed open and Ceres flinched. She was relieved to see it was only Sartes.

"Father needs to see you, Ceres," he said.

Ceres noticed his eyes were slightly red.

"How's your arm?" she asked, assuming he was crying from the pain of his injured arm.

"It's not broken. Just sprained." He stepped closer and his face turned serious. "Thank you for saving me today."

She offered him a smile. "How could I be anywhere else?" she said.

He smiled.

"Go see Father now," he said. "I'll burn your dress and the cloth."

She didn't know how she'd be able to explain to her mother how her dress had suddenly vanished, but the hand-me-down definitely needed to be burned. If her mother found it in its current condition—bloodied and riddled with holes—there'd be no saying how severe her punishment would be.

Ceres left and walked down the downtrodden grass path toward the shed behind the house. There was one tree left on their humble lot—the others had been chopped into firewood and burned in the hearth to heat the house during cold winter nights—and its branches hovered over the house like a protecting energy. Every time Ceres saw it, it reminded her of her grandmother, who passed away the year before last. Her grandmother had been the one who had planted the tree when she was a child. It was her temple, in a way. And her father's too. When life was too much to handle, they would lie underneath the stars and open their hearts to Nana as if she were still alive.

Ceres entered the shed and greeted her father with a smile. To her surprise, she noticed that most of his tools had been cleared from the worktable, and that no swords waited by the hearth to be forged. She couldn't ever remember seeing the floor swept this clean, or the walls and ceiling so lacking in tools.

Her father's blue eyes lit up, the way they always did when he saw her.

"Ceres," he said, rising.

This past year, his dark hair had turned much grayer, his short beard, too, and the bags under his loving eyes had doubled in size. In the past, he had been large in stature and almost as muscular as Nesos; yet recently, Ceres noticed, he had lost weight and his formerly perfect posture was sagging.

He joined her at the door and placed a calloused hand to the small of her back.

"Walk with me."

Her chest tightened a little. When he wanted to talk *and* walk, that meant he was about to share something significant.

Side by side, they meandered to the back of the shed and into the small field. Dark clouds loomed in the near distance, sending in gusts of warm, temperamental wind. She hoped they would produce the rain needed to recover from this seemingly never-ending drought, yet as before, they probably held just empty promises of showers.

The earth crunched beneath her feet as she walked, the soil dry, the plants yellow, brown, and dead. This patch of land behind their subdivision was King Claudius's, yet it hadn't been sowed for years.

They crested a hill and stopped, looking across the field. Her father remained silent, his hands clasped behind his back as he looked up into the sky. It was unlike him, and her dread deepened.

Then he spoke, seeming to select his words with care.

"Sometimes we don't have the luxury of choosing our paths," he said. "We must sacrifice all that we want for our loved ones. Even ourselves, if needed."

He sighed, and in the long silence, interrupted only by the wind, Ceres's heart pounded, wondering where he was going with this.

"What I wouldn't give to hold onto your childhood forever," he added, peering into the heavens, his face twisted in pain before it relaxed again.

"What's wrong?" Ceres asked, placing a hand on his arm.

"I must leave for a while," he said.

She felt as if she couldn't take a breath.

"Leave?"

He turned and looked her in the eyes.

"As you know, the winter and spring were particularly hard this year. The past few years of drought have been difficult. We haven't made enough money to get through the next winter, and if I don't go, our family will starve to death. I have been commissioned by another king to be his head bladesmith. It will be good money."

"You will take me with you, right?" Ceres said, a frantic tone in her voice.

He shook his head grimly.

"You must stay here and help your mother and brothers."

The thought sent a wave of horror through her.

"You can't leave me here with Mother," she said. "You wouldn't."

"I have spoken to her, and she will take care of you. She will be kind."

Ceres stomped her foot in the earth, the dust rising.

"No!"

Tears burst from her eyes and tumbled down her cheeks.

He took a small step toward her.

"Listen to me very carefully, Ceres. The palace still needs swords delivered from time to time. I have put in a good word for you, and if you make swords the way I have taught you, you could make a little money of your own."

Making her own money might possibly allow her more freedom. She had found her small, dainty hands had come in handy when carving intricate designs and inscriptions on the blades and hilts. Her father's hands were broad, his fingers thick and stubby, and few others had the skill she had.

Even so, she shook her head.

"I don't want to be a smith," she said.

"It runs in your blood, Ceres. And you have a gift for it."

She shook her head, adamant.

"I want to *wield* weapons," she said, "not *make* them."

As soon as the words had left her mouth, she regretted speaking them.

Her father furrowed his brow.

"You wish to be a warrior? A combatlord?"

He shook his head.

"One day it may be allowed for women to fight," she said. "You know I have practiced."

His eyebrows crinkled in worry.

"No," he commanded, firmly. "That is not your path."

Her heart sank. She felt as if her hopes and dreams of becoming a warrior were dissipating with his words. She knew he wasn't trying to be cruel—he was never cruel. It was just reality. And for them to stay alive, she would have to sacrifice her part, too.

She looked into the distance as the sky lit with a jolt of lightning. Three seconds later, thunder rumbled through the heavens.

Had she not realized how dire their circumstances were? She always assumed they would pull through together as a family, but this changed everything. Now she wouldn't have Father to hold onto, and there would be no person to stand as a shield between her and Mother.

One tear after another dropped onto the desolate earth as she remained immovable where she stood. Should she give up her dreams and follow her father's advice?

He pulled something out from behind his back, and her eyes widened to see a sword in his hand. He stepped closer, and she could see the details of the weapon.

It was awe-inspiring. The hilt was of pure gold, engraved with a serpent. The blade was two-edged and looked to be of the finest steel.

Though the workmanship was foreign to Ceres, she could immediately tell it was of the finest quality. On the blade itself there was an inscription.

When heart and sword meet, there shall be the victory.

She gasped, staring at it in awe.

"Did you forge that?" she asked, her eyes glued to the sword.

He nodded.

"After the manner of the northerners," he replied. "I have labored on it for three years. Indeed, this blade alone could feed our family for an entire year."

She looked at him.

"Then why not sell it?"

He shook his head firmly.

"It wasn't made for that purpose."

He stepped closer, and to her surprise, he held it out before him.

"It was made for you."

Ceres raised a hand to her mouth and let out a moan.

"Me?" she asked, stunned.

He smiled wide.

"Did you really think I forgot your eighteenth birthday?" he replied.

She felt tears flood her eyes. She had never been more touched.

But then she thought about what he had said earlier, about not wanting her to fight, and she felt confused.

"And yet," she replied, "you said I must not train."

"I don't want you to die," he explained. "But I see where your heart is. And that, I cannot control."

He reached a hand underneath her chin and lifted her head until their eyes met.

"I am proud of you for it."

He handed her the sword, and when she felt the cool metal against her palm, she became one with it. The weight was perfect for her, and the hilt felt like it had been molded to her hand.

All the hope that had died earlier now reawakened in her chest.

"Don't tell your mother," he warned. "Hide it where she cannot find it, or she will sell it."

Ceres nodded.

"How long will you be gone?"

"I will try to be back for a visit before the first snowfall."

"That's months away!" she said, taking a step back.

"It is what I must do to—"

"No. Sell the sword. Stay!"

He placed a hand on her cheek.

"Selling this sword might help us for this season. And perhaps next. But then what?" He shook his head. "No. We need a long-term solution."

Long term? Suddenly, she realized his new job wasn't just going to be for a few months. It might be years.

Her despondency deepened.

He stepped forward, as if sensing it, and hugged her.

She felt herself begin to cry in his arms.

"I will miss you, Ceres," he said, over her shoulder. "You are different than all the others. Every day I will look up into the heavens and know you are beneath the same stars. Will you do the same?"

At first she wanted to yell at him, to say: how dare you leave me here alone.

But she felt it in her heart that he couldn't stay, and she didn't want to make it harder on him than it already was.

A tear rolled down her face. She sniffled and nodded her head.

"I will stand beneath our tree every night," she said.

He kissed her on the forehead and wrapped tender arms around her. The wounds on her back felt like knives, but she gritted her teeth and remained silent.

"I love you, Ceres."

She wanted to respond, and yet she couldn't get herself to say anything—her words were stuck in her throat.

He fetched his horse from the stable, and Ceres helped him load it with food, tools, and supplies. He embraced her one last time, and she thought her chest might burst from sadness. Yet still, she couldn't utter a single word.

He mounted the horse, and nodded before signaling to the animal to move.

Ceres waved as he rode away, and she watched with unwavering attention until he vanished behind the distant hill. The only true love she had ever known came from that man. And now he was gone.

Rain started to descend from the heavens, and it prickled against her face.

"Father!" she screamed as loudly as she could. "Father, I love you!"

She fell to her knees and buried her hands in her face, sobbing.

Life, she knew, would never be the same again.

Chapter Three

With aching feet and burning lungs, Ceres climbed the steep hill as swiftly as she could without spilling a drop of water from either bucket by her sides. Normally she would pause for a break, but her mother had threatened no breakfast unless she was back by sunrise—and no breakfast meant she wouldn't eat until dinner. She didn't mind the pain, anyway—it, at least, allowed her to take her mind off her father, and the miserable new state of things since he had left.

The sun was just now cresting the Alva Mountains in the distance, painting the scattered clouds above golden-pink, and soft wind sighed through the tall, yellow grass on either side of the road. Ceres drew the fresh morning air in through her nose and willed herself faster. Her mother wouldn't find it an acceptable excuse that their regular well had dried up, or that there was a long line at the other one a half a mile away. Indeed, she did not stop until she reached the top of the hill—and once she did, she stopped in her tracks, stunned at the sight before her.

There, in the distance, was her house—and before it sat a bronze wagon. Her mother stood before it, conversing with a man who was so overweight, Ceres thought she had never seen anyone even half his size. He wore a burgundy linen tunic and a red silk hat, and his long beard was bushy and gray. She squinted, trying to understand. Was he a merchant?

Her mother was wearing her best dress, a green linen floor-length gown she had purchased years ago with money that was supposed to be used to buy Ceres new shoes. None of this made any sense.

Hesitantly, Ceres started down the hill. She kept her eyes trained on them, and when she saw the old man hand her mother a heavy leather pouch, saw her mother's emaciated face light up, she grew even more curious. Had their misfortune turned? Would Father be able to return home? The thoughts made her chest lighten a little, although she wouldn't allow herself to feel any excitement until she learned the details.

When Ceres neared their house, her mother turned and smiled at her warmly—and immediately Ceres felt a knot of worry in her stomach. The last time her mother had smiled at her like that—teeth gleaming, eyes bright—Ceres had received a flogging.

"Darling daughter," her mother said in an overly sweet tone, opening her arms toward her with a grin that made Ceres's blood curdle.

"*This* is the girl?" the old man said with an eager smile, his dark, beady eyes widening when he looked at Ceres.

Now up close, Ceres could see every wrinkle on the obese man's skin. His broad flat nose seemed to overtake his entire face, and when he took off his hat, his sweaty bald head glowed in the sunlight.

Her mother waltzed over to Ceres, took the buckets from her, and set them on the singed grass. That gesture alone confirmed to Ceres that something was severely wrong. She began to feel a panicky sensation rise in her chest.

"Meet my pride and joy, my only daughter, Ceres," her mother said, pretending to wipe a tear away from her eye when there was none. "Ceres, this is Lord Blaku. Please show your respects to your new master."

A jolt of fear stabbed Ceres through the chest. She sucked in a sudden breath. Ceres looked at her mother, and with her back to Lord Blaku, her mother gave her a smile that was as evil as she had ever seen.

"*Master?*" Ceres asked.

"To save our family from financial ruin and public embarrassment, the benevolent Lord Blaku offered your father and me a generous deal: a sack of gold in exchange for you."

"What?" Ceres gasped, feeling herself sinking into the earth.

"Now, be the good girl I know you are and show your respects," her mother said, shooting Ceres a warning glance.

"I will not," Ceres said, taking a step back as she puffed her chest up, feeling silly for not having immediately realized the man was a slaver, and that the transaction was for her life.

"Father would never sell me," she added through clenched teeth, her horror and indignation rising.

Her mother scowled and grabbed her by the arm, her fingernails digging into Ceres's skin.

"If you behave, this man might take you as his wife, and for you, that is a very lucky thing," she muttered.

Lord Blaku licked his thin crusty lips as his puffy eyes greedily wandered up and down Ceres's body. How could her mother do this to her? She knew her mother didn't love her as much as her brothers—but this?

"Marita," he said in a nasally voice. "You told me your daughter was fair, but you neglected to tell me what an utterly magnificent creature she is. Dare I say, I have yet to see a woman with lips as succulent as hers, and with eyes as passionate, and with a body as firm and exquisite."

Ceres's mother placed a hand over her heart with a sigh, and Ceres felt like she might just vomit right here. She clenched her hands into fists as she snapped her arm away from her mother's grasp.

"Perhaps I should have asked for more, if she pleases you so much," Ceres's mother said, her eyes lowering in despondency. "She is, after all, our only beloved girl."

"I am willing to pay good money for such a beauty. Will another five gold pieces suffice?" he asked.

"How generous of you," her mother replied.

Lord Blaku ambled over to his wagon to fetch more gold.

"Father will never agree to this," Ceres sneered.

Ceres's mother took a threatening step toward her.

"Oh, but it was your father's idea," her mother snapped, with her eyebrows raised halfway up her forehead. Ceres knew she was lying now—whenever she did that, she was lying.

"Do you actually think your father loves you more than he loves me?" her mother asked.

Ceres blinked, wondering what that would have to do with anything.

"I could never love someone who thinks she is better than me," she added.

"You never loved me?" Ceres asked, her anger morphing into hopelessness.

With the gold in hand, Lord Blaku waddled over to Ceres's mother and handed it to her.

"Your daughter is worth every piece," he said. "She will be a good wife and bear me many sons."

Ceres bit the inside of her lips and shook her head over and over again.

"Lord Blaku will come for you in the morning, so go inside and pack your belongings," Ceres's mother said.

"I won't!" Ceres screamed.

"That was always your problem, girl. You only ever think of yourself. This gold," her mother said, jingling the purse in front of Ceres's face, "will keep your brothers alive. It will keep our family intact, allowing us to remain in our home and make repairs. Did you fail to think about that?"

For a split second, Ceres thought maybe she was being selfish, but then she realized her mother was playing mind games again, using Ceres's love for her brothers against her.

"Do not worry," Ceres's mother said, turning toward Lord Blaku. "Ceres will comply. All you need to do is be firm with her, and she becomes as meek as a lamb."

Never. Never would she be that man's wife or anyone's property. And never would she let her mother or anyone exchange her life for fifty-five pieces of gold.

"I will never go with this slaver," Ceres snapped, shooting him a look of disgust.

"Ungrateful child!" Ceres's mother yelled. "If you do not do as I say, I will beat you so severely you will never walk again. Now get inside!"

The thought of being beaten by her mother brought back awful, visceral memories; she was taken back to that dreadful moment at five years old when her mother had beaten her until everything had gone black. The wounds from that beating and many others healed—yet the wounds in Ceres's heart had never stopped bleeding. And now that she knew for sure that her mother didn't love her, and never had, her heart split wide open for good.

Before she could respond, Ceres's mother stepped forward and slapped her across the face so hard her ear began ringing.

At first, Ceres was stunned by the sudden assault, and she almost backed down. But then something snapped inside her. She would not allow herself to cower as she always did.

Ceres smacked her mother back, across the cheek, so hard that she tumbled to the ground, gasping in horror.

Red-faced, her mother climbed to her feet, grabbed Ceres by the shoulder and hair, and kneed Ceres in the stomach. When Ceres stooped forward in agony, her mother jabbed her knee into Ceres's face, causing her to fall to the ground.

The slaver stood and watched, his eyes wide, chuckling, clearly taking delight in the fight.

Still coughing and gasping for air from the assault, Ceres staggered to her feet. Screaming, she flung herself toward her mother, driving her to the ground.

This ends today, was all Ceres could think. All the years of never being loved, of being treated with disdain, fueled her rage. Ceres smashed closed fists into her mother's face again and again as tears of fury rolled down her cheeks, sobs uncontrollably spilling out of her lips.

Finally, her mother went limp.

Ceres's shoulders shook with each cry, her insides wrung inside out. Blurred by tears, she looked up at the slaver with an even more intense hatred.

"You will make a good one," Lord Blaku said with a guileful grin, as he picked up the bag of gold from the ground and attached it to his leather belt.

Before she could react, suddenly his hands were upon her. He grabbed Ceres and climbed into the carriage, tossing her into the back in one quick motion, as if she were a bag of potatoes. His massive bulk and strength was too much for her to resist. Holding her wrist with one arm and taking hold of a chain with the other, he said, "I'm not stupid enough to think you would still be here in morning."

She glanced at the house that had been her home for eighteen years, and her eyes filled with tears as she thought of her brothers and her father.

But she had to make a choice if she was to save herself, before the chain was around her ankle.

So in one quick motion, she mustered all of her strength and snatched her arm out of the slaver's grip, lifted her leg, and kicked him in the face as hard as she could. He fell backwards, out of the carriage, and tumbled onto the ground.

She jumped from the wagon and ran as fast as she could down the dirt road, away from the woman she vowed to never call mother again, away from everything she had ever known and loved.

Chapter Four

Surrounded by the royal family, Thanos tried hard to keep a pleasant expression on his face as he gripped the gold wine goblet—yet he could not. He hated being here. He hated these people, his family. And he hated attending royal gatherings—especially the ones following the Killings. He knew how the people lived, how poor they were, and he felt how senseless and unjust all this pomp and haughtiness really was. He would give anything to be far away from here.

Standing with his cousins Lucious, Aria, and Varius, Thanos didn't make the least bit of effort to engage in their petty conversation. Instead, he watched the imperial guests meander about in the palace gardens, wearing their togas and stolas, presenting fake grins and spewing false niceties. A few of his cousins were throwing food at each other as they ran across the manicured lawn and between tables stocked with food and wine. Others were reenacting their favorite scenes from the Killings, laughing at and mocking those who had lost their lives today.

Hundreds of people, Thanos thought, and not one was honorable.

"Next month, I will purchase three combatlords," Lucious, the eldest, said in a boisterous tone as he patted drops of sweat from his brow with a silk handkerchief. "Stefanus wasn't worth half of what I paid for him, and if he weren't dead already, I would have run a sword through him myself for having fought like a girl in the first round."

Aria and Varius laughed, but Thanos didn't find his comment amusing. Whether they considered the Killings a game or not, they should respect the brave and the dead.

"Well, did you see Brennius?" Aria asked, her large blue eyes widening. "I actually considered buying him, but he gave me this conceited look when I watched him rehearse. Can you believe it?" she added, as she rolled her eyes and huffed.

"And he stinks like a skunk," Lucious added.

Everyone except for Thanos laughed again.

"None of us would have picked him," Varius said. "Though he lasted longer than expected, his form was horrible."

Thanos couldn't keep quiet another second.

"Brennius had the best form in the entire arena," he interjected. "Don't talk about the art of combat as if you know anything about it."

The cousins grew quiet, and Aria's eyes became large as saucers as she looked toward the ground. Varius puffed out his chest and crossed his arms, scowling. He stepped closer to Thanos as if to challenge him, and the air thickened with tension.

"Well, never mind those self-important combatlords," Aria said, stepping between them, defusing the situation. She waved for the boys to gather around closer, and then she whispered, "I have heard an outlandish rumor. A little bee told me the king wants to have someone of royal birth compete in the Killings."

They all exchanged an uncomfortable look as they fell silent.

"Perhaps," Lucious said. "It won't be me, though. I'm not willing to risk my life for a stupid game."

Thanos knew he could beat out most combatlords, but killing another human wasn't something he wanted to do.

"You're just scared of dying," Aria said.

"I am not," Lucious retorted. "You take that back!"

Thanos's patience was spent. He walked away.

Thanos watched his distant cousin Stephania wander about as if she were looking for someone—probably him. A few weeks back, the Queen had said he was fated to be with Stephania, but Thanos felt otherwise. Stephania was as spoiled as the rest of the cousins and he'd rather give up his name, his inheritance, and even his sword to not have to marry her. She was beautiful to behold, true—her hair golden, her skin milky white, her lips blood-red—but if he had to listen to her talk about how life was so unfair one more time, he thought he might cut his ears off.

He scurried to the outskirts of the garden toward the rose bushes, avoiding eye contact with any of the attendees. But just as he rounded the corner, Stephania stepped in front of him, her brown eyes lighting up.

"Good evening, Thanos," she said with a scintillating smile that would have most of the boys here drooling after her. Everyone but Thanos.

"Good evening to you, too," Thanos said and skirted around her, continuing to walk.

She lifted up her stola and trailed after him like a pesky mosquito.

"Don't you find it so unfair how—" she began.

"I'm busy," Thanos snapped in a tone harsher than he intended, causing her to gasp. He then turned toward her. "I'm sorry ... I'm just tired of all these parties."

"Perhaps you would like to stroll the gardens with me?" Stephania said, her right eyebrow peaking as she stepped closer.

That was the absolute last thing he wanted.

"Listen," he said, "I know the queen and your mother have it in their minds that we somehow belong together, but—"

"Thanos!" he heard behind him.

Thanos turned to see the king's messenger.

"The king would like you to join him in the gazebo straightaway," he said. "And you too, my lady."

"Might I inquire why?" Thanos asked.

"There is much to discuss," the messenger said.

Not having had regular conversations with the king in the past, Thanos wondered what that might entail.

"Of course," Thanos said.

To his great dismay, a beaming Stephania hooked her arm around his, and together they followed the messenger over to the gazebo.

When Thanos noticed several of the king's advisors and even the crown prince already sitting on benches and chairs, he found it odd that he had been invited, too. He would hardly have anything of value to offer in their conversation, as his opinions about how the Empire was ruled differed greatly from those of everyone here. The best thing he could do, he thought to himself, was to keep his mouth shut.

"What a lovely couple you make," the queen said with a warm smile as they entered.

Thanos pinched his lips shut and offered Stephania to sit down next to him.

Once everyone had settled, the king rose to his feet and the gathering quieted down. His uncle wore a knee-length toga, but where the others were white, red, and blue, his was purple, a color reserved only for the king. Around his balding temple was a golden wreath, and his cheeks and eyes still drooped even though he was smiling.

"The masses grow unruly," he said, his voice grave, slow. He slowly scanned all the faces with the authority of a king. "The time is past due to remind them who is king and enact harsher rules. From this day forward, I shall double tithes on all property and food."

There came a surprised murmur, followed by nods of approval.

"An excellent choice, your grace," said one of his advisors.

Thanos couldn't believe his ears. Double the people's taxes? Having mingled with commoners, he knew that the taxes required were already beyond what most commoners could afford. He had seen mothers mourn the loss of their children who died of starvation. As recently as yesterday, he had offered food to a homeless four-year-old girl whose every bone was visible beneath her skin.

Thanos had to look away or he would surely have to speak up against this insanity.

"And finally," the king said, "from now on, to counterbalance the underground revolution that is fomenting, the firstborn son in every family will become a servant in the king's army."

One after another, the small crowd commended the king for his wise decision.

Finally, though, Thanos felt the king turn to him.

"Thanos," the king finally said. "You have remained silent. Speak!"

Silence fell on the gazebo, as all eyes were on Thanos. He stood. He knew he had to speak up, for the emaciated girl, for the grieving mothers, for the voiceless whose lives seemed not to matter. He needed to represent them, because if he did not, no one would.

"Harsher rules will not crush the rebellion," he said, his heart thumping in his chest. "It will only embolden it. Instilling fear into the citizens and denying them freedom will do nothing but compel them to rise against us and join the revolution."

A few people laughed, while others talked amongst themselves. Stephania took his hand and tried to hush him, but he snatched it away.

"A great king uses love, as well as fear, to rule his subordinates," Thanos said.

The king gave the queen an uneasy glance. He stood up, and then walked over to Thanos.

"Thanos, you are a brave young man for speaking up," he said, placing a hand on his shoulder. "However, was your younger brother not murdered in cold blood by these same people, those who governed themselves, as you say?"

Thanos saw red. How dare his uncle bring up his brother's death so flippantly? For years, Thanos had fallen asleep to his grief as he mourned the loss of his brother.

"Those who murdered my brother didn't have enough food for themselves," Thanos said. "A desperate man will seek desperate measures."

"Do you question the king's wisdom?" the queen asked.

Thanos couldn't believe no one else was speaking up against this. Did they see not see how unjust it was? Did they not realize these new laws would breathe fire into the rebellion?

"Not for a moment will you be able to fool the people into believing you want anything other than their suffering and your profiting for yourselves," Thanos said.

There came a gasp of disapproval amidst the group.

"You speak harsh words, nephew," the king said, looking him in the eyes. "I would almost believe you mean to join the rebellion."

"Or perhaps he is already a part of it?" the queen said, her eyebrows rising.

"I am not," Thanos barked.

The air in the gazebo grew hotter, and Thanos realized if he wasn't careful, he might be accused of treason—a crime punishable by death without trial.

Stephania stood up and took Thanos's hand in hers—yet, agitated by her timing, he snapped his hand away.

Stephania's expression fell, and she looked down.

"Perhaps in time you will see the weaknesses of your beliefs," the king said to Thanos. "For now, our ruling will stand and shall be implemented immediately."

"Good," the queen said with a sudden smile. "Now, let us move onto the second item on our agenda. Thanos, as a young man of nineteen, we, your imperial sovereigns, have chosen a wife for you. We have decided you and Stephania are to be wed."

Thanos glanced over at Stephania, whose eyes were glazed with tears, an expression of worry painting her face. He felt aghast. How could they demand this of him?

"I cannot marry her," Thanos whispered, a knot forming in his belly.

Murmurs went through the crowd, and the queen shot to her feet so quickly that her chair fell backward with a crack.

"Thanos!" she yelled, hands clenched by her sides. "How dare you defy the king? You will marry Stephania whether or not you want to."

Thanos looked at Stephania with saddened eyes as tears rolled down her cheeks.

"Do you imagine you are too good for me?" she asked, her bottom lip trembling.

He took a step toward Stephania to comfort her what little he could, but before he reached her, she ran out of the gazebo, hands covering her face as she cried.

The king stood, clearly angered.

"Deny her, son", he said, his voice suddenly cold and hard, thundering through the gazebo, "and it will be the dungeon for you."

Chapter Five

Ceres sprinted, weaving through city streets, until she felt her legs would no longer hold her, until her lungs burned so much they might burst, and until she knew with absolute certainty the slaver would never find her.

Finally, she collapsed on the ground in a back alley amongst garbage and rats, arms wrapped around her legs, tears streaming down her hot cheeks. With her father away and her mother wanting to sell her, she had no one. If she remained on the streets and slept in the alleys, she would eventually die of starvation or freeze to death when winter came. Perhaps that would be best.

For hours she sat and cried, her eyes puffy, her mind muddled with despair. Where would she go now? How would she make money to survive?

The day had grown long when finally, she resolved to return home, sneak into the shed, take the few swords that were left, and sell them to the palace. They were expecting her today anyway. That way, she would have money for a few days at least until she could come up with a better plan.

She would also pick up the sword her father had given her and that she had hidden beneath the floorboards in the shed. But she wouldn't sell that, no. Not until she was staring death in the face would she give up her father's gift.

She jogged home, carefully watching for any familiar faces or for the slaver's wagon as she went. When she reached the last hill, she slunk behind the row of houses and into the field, tiptoeing across the parched earth, her eyes scanning for her mother.

A pang of guilt arose when she remembered how she had beaten her mother. She never wanted to hurt her, not even after how cruel her mother had been. Not even with her heart broken and unmendable.

Arriving at the back of their shed, she peeked in through a crack in the wall. Seeing it was empty, she stepped inside the dim shack and gathered the swords. But just as she was about to lift the floorboard where she had hidden the sword, she heard voices coming from outside.

When she stood up and glanced through a small hole in the wall, to her horror, she saw her mother and Sartes walking toward the shed. Her mother had a black eye and a bruise on her cheek, and now seeing her mother alive and well, it almost made Ceres smile knowing she had put it there. All the anger welled up again as she thought about how her mother wanted to sell her.

"If I catch you sneaking any food out to Ceres, I will flog you, do you understand?" her mother snapped as she and Sartes strode by her grandmother's tree.

When Sartes didn't answer, her mother slapped him across the face.

"Do you understand, boy?" she said.

"Yes," Sartes said, looking down, a tear in his eye.

"And if you ever see her, bring her home so I can give her a licking she will never forget."

They began walking toward the shed again, and Ceres's heart was suddenly thumping wildly. She gripped the swords and darted toward the back door as quickly and as quietly as she could. Just as she exited, the front door swung open, and she leaned against the outer wall and listened, the wounds from the omnicat's claws stinging her back.

"Who goes there?" her mother said.

Ceres held her breath and squeezed her eyes shut.

"I know you're there," her mother said and waited. "Sartes, go check the back door. It's ajar."

Ceres clenched the swords to her chest. She heard Sartes's footsteps as he walked toward her, and then the door opened with a creak.

Sartes's eyes widened when he saw her, and he gasped.

"Is there anyone there?" her mother asked.

"Um … no," Sartes said, his eyes filling with tears as they connected with Ceres's.

Ceres mouthed a "thank you," and Sartes gestured with his hand for her to leave.

She nodded, and with a heavy heart, she stole toward the field as the back door to the shed slammed shut. She would come back for her sword later.

⚜ ⚜ ⚜

Ceres stopped at the palace gates sweating, famished, and exhausted, swords in hand. The Empire soldiers standing guard, clearly recognizing her as the girl who delivered her father's swords, let her pass without questioning her.

She hurried through the cobblestone courtyard and then turned for the blacksmith's stone cottage behind one of the four towers. She entered.

Standing by the anvil in front of the crackling furnace, the blacksmith hammered away at a glowing blade, the leather apron protecting his clothing from the flying sparks. The concerned expression on his face made Ceres wonder what was wrong. A jovial middle-aged man full of energy, he was rarely worried.

His bald, sweaty head greeted her before he noticed she had entered.

"Good morrow," he said when he saw her, nodding for her to place the swords on the worktable.

She strode across the hot smoky room and set them down, the metal rattling against a surface of burnt, tattered wood.

He shook his head, clearly troubled.

"What is it?" she asked.

He looked up, concern in his eyes.

"Of all the days to fall ill," he murmured.

"Bartholomew?" she asked, seeing that the young weapon-keeper of the combatlords wasn't here as he usually was, frantically preparing the last few weapons before sparring practice.

The blacksmith stopped hammering and looked up with a vexed expression, his bushy eyebrows crinkling.

He shook his head.

"And on sparring day, of all days," he said. "And not just any sparring day." He stuffed the blade into the glowing coals in the furnace and wiped his dripping brow with the sleeve of his tunic. "Today, the royals will spar with the combatlords. The king has hand-picked twelve royals to train for the Killings. Three will go on to participate."

She understood his worry. It was his responsibility to provide the weapon-keepers, and if he didn't, his job was on the line. Hundreds of blacksmiths would be eager to take his position.

"The king won't be happy if we are one weapon-keeper short," she said.

He leaned his hands on his thick thighs and shook his head. Just then, two Empire soldiers entered.

"We are here to retrieve the weapons," one said, scowling toward Ceres.

Even though it wasn't forbidden, she knew it was frowned upon for girls to work in weaponry—a man's field. Yet she had grown accustomed to snide remarks and hateful glares most every time she made deliveries to the palace.

The blacksmith stood up and walked over to three wooden buckets filled with weapons, all ready for the sparring match.

"You will find here the remainder of the weapons the king requested for today," the blacksmith said to the Empire soldiers.

"And the weapon-keeper?" the Empire soldier demanded.

Just as the blacksmith opened his mouth to speak, Ceres had an idea.

"It is me," she said, excitement rising in her chest. "I am the stand-in today and until Bartholomew returns."

The Empire soldiers looked at her for a moment, startled.

Ceres pinched her lips together and took a step forward.

"I have been working with my father and with the palace my entire life, crafting swords, shields, and all manner of weapons," she said.

She didn't know where her courage came from, but she stood tall and stared the soldiers in the eye.

"Ceres ..." the blacksmith said, giving her a look of pity.

"Try me," she said, strengthening her resolve, wanting them to test her abilities. "There isn't anyone who can take Bartholomew's place but me. And if you lack a weapon-keeper today, wouldn't that make the king rather upset?"

She wasn't certain, but she figured the Empire soldiers and the blacksmith would do almost anything to keep the king happy. Especially today.

The Empire soldiers looked at the blacksmith, and the blacksmith back at them. The blacksmith thought for a moment. And then another. Finally, he nodded. He laid a plethora of weapons onto the table, after which he gestured to her to proceed.

"Show us, then, Ceres," the blacksmith said, a twinkle in his eye. "Knowing your father, he probably taught you everything you are not supposed to know."

"And more," Ceres said, smiling inside.

She went over each weapon, explaining in great detail their uses and advantages, how one might be better in certain types of battles than others.

When she was finished, the Empire soldiers looked to the blacksmith.

"I suppose it is better to have a girl weapon-keeper than no weapon-keeper," the blacksmith said. "Let us go and speak to the king. Perhaps he will allow it, seeing there is no other."

Ceres was so excited she almost threw her arms around the blacksmith as he winked at her. The soldiers still seemed reluctant, but with no other apparent option, they agreed to take her along.

She followed the Empire soldiers out the back door and entered the palace training ground. Ceres was used to the sound of swords colliding, of the combatlords grunting as they sparred, and of the smell of sweat mixed with leather and metal filling the air. But what was quite unique was seeing the royals practicing in the center of the yard, wearing their fancy polished armor, looking as if they needed a lesson—or a hundred—in swordsmanship. Ceres didn't feel they belonged here. No, it disgusted her to see them on the training ground, all the underlords, counts, and dignitaries watching as they ate from mounds of food and drank from golden goblets. They should go back to their lavish parties, she thought. Not feign courage and honor.

One of the royals, though, stood out from the rest: Thanos. Watching him spar, she noticed how he moved with speed, grace, and agility. To her surprise, he appeared almost as skilled as Brennius; and he wore no armor like the other royals. His hair was different from his royal peers', too; not neat and pulled back into a low ponytail, but curly, unruly dark hair flying about his face with each move.

Ceres frowned. Perhaps he knew a thing or two about combat, but he was the haughtiest of the royals, always glowering at something or someone, never seeming to want to be a part of anything.

The guards led her to the throne, and when the blacksmith presented Ceres to the king as a stand-in weapon-keeper, the king paused, and then chuckled a bit as he glanced at his advisors on either side. Ceres didn't like how he looked at her as if she were an annoyance to be rid of. But in an instant, the king's expression changed, and his face lit up as if he just had the most brilliant idea.

"Not having anyone else, I see that this must be as you say," the king said to the blacksmith. "Ceres, you shall assist Prince Thanos."

The king said it in a way that made Ceres think it was a punishment or a means to shame Prince Thanos, but she didn't care. Even though she wasn't particularly happy to be Thanos's weapon-keeper, she had been assigned, and now she could show her skills in the royal court. It was more than any girl could ever expect.

She bowed toward the king and glanced at the blacksmith as she passed him. The blacksmith nodded, an almost prideful expression on his face, and then he walked back to the chalet.

The Empire soldier escorted Ceres over to Thanos, who stood by a table, and when Thanos glanced at Ceres, his scowl intensified.

"Very well," he muttered, staring at his uncle across the yard as if daggers were shooting from his eyes. The king gave Thanos a devious smirk, affirming to Ceres that her assignment to Thanos was indeed some form of a punishment.

Thanos stepped in front of Ceres, and she noticed how the neck of his shirt was open, revealing small amounts of curly, dark hair on his muscular chest. Her breath hitched. He looked at her, and when their eyes met, she found his gaze intense—irises darker than the blackest soot. Yet, he didn't intimidate her. In fact, his bottomless eyes drew her to him, making it impossible to look away.

Once he broke eye contact, Ceres was able to take a breath and think clearly; she again resolved to show him she knew what she was doing.

"I suppose I should trust you if the blacksmith speaks so highly of you," Thanos said as she laid out the weapons one by one onto the wooden table.

Even though she was a girl, and even though Thanos was undoubtedly smart enough to figure out that what his uncle had done was more of a cruel joke than anything, it surprised her that he gave her the benefit of the doubt.

"I will do my best, sire," she said, placing a sword onto the wood.

He glanced at her, his smoldering eyes studying her too intimately for her to feel comfortable.

"There is no need for such formalities here. Thanos will do," he said.

Again, she was surprised by his casual approach. Had she read him wrong? Was he not the arrogant, self-righteous, ungrateful young man she assumed he was?

Once she had laid out all the weapons, an Empire soldier reviewed the rules of combat. First, they watched a few of the combatlords spar, and then it was the royals' turn. The Empire soldier called upon Lucious, a blond, muscular, but somewhat lanky young man, who stepped up to a combatlord. Thanos leaned over.

"I doubt Lucious will last very long," he whispered.

"Why do you say that?" Ceres asked, wondering why he would say something like that to her—a stranger—about a fellow royal.

"You'll see."

The right side of Thanos's lips rose, and Ceres liked how he spoke to her as if she were an equal.

Even before the fighting began, Ceres knew Thanos was right. Lucious's feet were too close together, his grip weak around the hilt, and his eyes too unfocused. It would be an embarrassment, to say the least, to watch him lose rather quickly to such a warrior he was facing.

With the first collision of swords, Ceres looked up and kept her gaze on the cloudy sky instead, keeping them there as she heard grunts and blades clashing. The fighting continued on for a while, and Ceres wondered if perhaps she had judged Lucious too harshly. At least Lucious was holding on, if nothing else.

But when Lucious started to scream a few minutes into the fight, and the onlookers murmured and gasped, she couldn't help but bring her eyes back onto the fighters again. Lucious was lying on the ground, holding the blade of his sword with one hand, the hilt with the other, struggling to keep the combatlord's sword away from his face. Blood ran down his arm, and he squealed, begging for the round to end.

"Enough!" the king said, and the combatlord retreated.

Lucious's weapon-keeper ran over to him and offered him a hand, but Lucious smacked it away.

"I can get up myself!" he yelled between gritted teeth, panting and spewing obscenities.

Lucious held his injured hand with the other and rolled onto his stomach before rising to his feet.

"I said I didn't want to do this!" he yelled toward the king. "And now look what happened! You have made me a fool!"

He stormed across the yard and vanished through the arching doorway into the palace. Most of the dignitaries had quieted, but some of them laughed

"Always such drama with Lucious," Thanos said, rolling his eyes.

"Next up is Thanos and Oedifus," an Empire soldier announced.

"Are you ready?" Thanos asked Ceres.

"Yes. Are you?" she replied.

He paused and gave her a sideways glance before saying, "Always. Let me start with the trident and shield."

She handed him the shield, and after he had secured it onto his arm, she gave him the trident. Her pulse rose as she watched him walk into the center of the practice arena, hoping he would win, but bracing herself in the very likely event he would lose. One did not just simply triumph over a combatlord, and especially not with as little training as Ceres assumed these royals had.

The combatlord was around Thanos's height, but his muscles were fuller, almost monstrously so, Ceres observed. His arms were covered in scars, his face disfigured from past wounds unevenly healed, and he grunted at Thanos even before the match had begun.

With Thanos's very first strike, Ceres could tell he was a marvelous warrior, and as the battle continued, as hard as he tried, the combatlord couldn't get to him. Thanos was so quick to swerve, and quick like a rattlesnake to attack, but he also possessed the strength of an omnicat. Not only did he seem to read his opponent's mind, his feet moved with the ease of a trained dancer.

The entire match, Thanos was one step ahead of the combatlord, causing the onlookers to cheer with excitement. Ceres judged the trident a great choice for him, but from the way he moved, she believed a longsword would be the weapon granting him victory.

With the next move, the combatlord crouched and whipped one leg across the sand in a circular motion, wiping Thanos's feet from under him, causing him to fall onto his back. He hopped up to his feet again, but his trident had fallen several feet away.

Faster than she could even think, Ceres picked up the longsword and yelled, "Thanos!"

He glanced at her and she threw the sword to him. Catching it mid-air, Thanos didn't miss a beat and went after the combatlord with full force. Sparks flew as metal collided with metal, and watching Thanos's face and neck muscles strain, Ceres clenched her fists as she held her breath.

Retreating, the combatlord snarled and panted, saliva gushing from his mouth, but Thanos did not withdraw. Instead, he hit the combatlord's sword out of his hand and shoved him to the ground so Thanos ended up standing above him with his blade pointed at his challenger's neck.

With eyes wide open and her heart galloping in her chest, Ceres cheered with the rest of the crowd.

Thanos looked up at the king, his face a stone, and the king squinted his eyes as he leaned over and whispered something to the advisor on his right. With the nod of his uncle, Thanos lowered his sword and stepped out of the training area.

He walked toward her, a new look of admiration and wonder in his eyes. He studied her in silence for several seconds, breathing hard. Finally, he spoke.

"How did you know which weapon to give me?" he asked, wiping the sweat from his brow with a handkerchief.

"The way you moved," she said. "It seemed a longsword would suit you."

Still panting, he watched her closely as he nodded.

Then he strode across the training ground and headed into the palace. For a moment, Ceres wasn't certain what to make of his strange behavior and his lack of further instructions. Should she stay? Should she leave? She decided to wait until she was released.

A few minutes later, and into the next round, a handler approached her.

"For you, my lady," he said, holding out a pouch. "An advance from Prince Thanos. If you accept, you have been hired as the prince's new weapon-keeper. He requests you return tomorrow an hour after dawn at this very spot."

Ceres held out her hand and after she had received the pouch, she opened it, seeing five pieces of gold. At first, overwrought with joy, she couldn't speak, but when the handler asked her again if she would accept, she said yes.

"You are at liberty to leave, my lady," he said, and then he swiveled around and walked back into the palace.

"Thank you," she said, realizing she was speaking to no one. She glanced up toward the east tower and saw Thanos standing on the balcony watching her. He nodded to her and smiled before heading inside.

With a light heart, she ran from the palace and headed home to pick up her sword. She also planned to secretly give the money to her brothers without their mother finding out, and to bid them a final farewell.

Finally, she was wanted.

Finally, she had a home.

Chapter Six

Ceres carefully peered in through the half-opened shutters, her mouth dry, eyes peeled for her mother. She had run home as nightfall descended on Delos, the clear skies above turning pink and lavender. Her eagerness to present the gold to her brothers had fueled each step. Aching with hunger, she had considered using one of the gold coins to purchase food, but was afraid to bump into her mother at the market.

With ears pinned for sounds or voices, she glanced further into the dim house. Not a soul was in sight. Where could Nesos and Sartes be? Usually, they were home at this time while Mother was away. Perhaps if she retrieved her sword first, her brothers would return by then.

Careful not to make a sound, she slunk around to the rear of the house, past her grandmother's tree and toward the shed. The door creaked when she opened it, and once inside the stuffy shack, she headed straight toward the corner. Kneeling down beside the floorboard, she lifted it up and fished out her sword. She breathed with relief to see it was still there.

For a moment Ceres sat and admired its beauty, the mixed metals, the shiny, thin, unblemished blade, the golden hilt adorned with serpents. The craftsmanship was after the manner of the northerners, her father had said. She would carry this sword with honor, always remembering the great love her father had for her.

She slid it into its sheath, secured it around her waist with a scabbard, and headed outside.

Seeing no one was there, she made her way to the front of the house again, and this time went in through the front door. The house was shadowy, the hearth unlit, and mounds of fruits, vegetables, meats, and baked goods decked the table, all no doubt bought with the gold gained by selling her life. Their savory aroma filled the room. She strode over to the food, picked up a loaf of bread, and devoured a few bites. Her stomach had churned for days.

Knowing she hadn't much time, Ceres hurried over to Nesos's bench-bed and placed the sack of gold beneath his pillow. He'd find it when he turned in for the night, and she didn't doubt he'd keep it a secret from Mother. She blinked, trying to fight back the tears while wondering if she'd ever see her dear brothers again. Her heart squeezed as she thought about Rexus. Would he forget about her?

Suddenly she jumped as the front door flung open, startling her. To her horror, in stepped Lord Blaku.

He grinned an awful, victorious grin.

"If it isn't the runaway," he said, his upper lip curled back, revealing yellowing teeth, the stench of sweat saturating the room.

Taking a few steps back, Ceres realized she needed to get away—quick. Thinking she'd be able to escape through the window in her parents' bedroom, she dropped the loaf of bread and darted toward the back door.

But just as she reached the doorway, her mother stepped into it, Ceres colliding with her.

Briefly, Ceres noted that her mother wore a new dress made of the finest silk, and that she smelled like floral perfume.

"Did you really think you could beat me bloody and blue, steal my money, and get away with it?" her mother asked in a hateful tone as she grabbed Ceres's hair, pulling it so hard Ceres let out a cry.

Steal her money? But then it all made sense. Of course her mother wouldn't be collaborating with the slaver if she knew he had taken back the gold he'd paid for Ceres. However, he probably told her mother Ceres took the gold and ran off with it. Her mother was, after all, unconscious when he snatched the pouch of fifty-five pieces.

Before Ceres could explain, her mother slapped her across the face and shoved her so she fell to the floor. She then kicked Ceres in the stomach with her new pointy shoes.

Ceres couldn't breathe. Yet she forced herself to her feet, preparing to lunge for her mother—when the slaver grabbed her from behind in a deadlock. He squeezed her so hard she was certain the wounds on her back reopened.

She kicked and screamed, wriggled and scratched, trying to wrestle her way out of the fat old man's iron grip. But it was to no avail. He carried her through the room, and toward the front door.

"Wait!" her mother yelled.

She walked over to them and wrapped covetous fingers around Ceres's sword.

"What is this?" she asked, her eyes angered.

Still not giving up the fight, Ceres kicked her mother in the shin as hard as she could muster with the slaver squeezing the life out of her.

Her mother's face turned red, and she socked Ceres in the abdomen with such force Ceres thought she might vomit up the little food she had managed to swallow.

"That is *my* sword," her mother said.

Ceres knew her mother would recognize how valuable the sword was, and that there was no way she would let the slaver take it with him.

"I paid for the girl, and whatever is on her person, I own that now," Lord Blaku sneered.

"The sword was not on her person when I sold her to you," her mother retorted, her fingers fumbling to undo the scabbard around Ceres's waist.

Lord Blaku growled and threw Ceres against the kitchen table so her head hit the corner, a sharp pain spreading across her temple. Lying on the floor, dizzy from the blow, Ceres heard her mother scream and furniture being thrown across the room. She opened her eyes and sat up and saw the slaver standing over her mother, slamming a chair against her mother's head.

"Ceres, help!" her mother yelled, but Ceres no longer had it in her.

Barely able to move, Ceres crawled on hands and knees toward the door. Once she had crossed the threshold, Ceres climbed onto her feet. But she had no time. She could feel Lord Blaku's arms reaching for her, his eyes burning at her back. She needed to hurry if she was to escape, but her body wouldn't move as swiftly as she told it to.

Her heart leapt in her chest when she stumbled across the front yard, and just as she reached the dirt road, she thought she was free.

Just then, Lord Blaku roared behind her. She heard the crack of a whip and then felt a thick leather cord wrap around her neck. Being tugged backward by the whip, throat strangled, blood pooling in her head, she crashed to the ground. Her hands reached for the cord, trying to loosen it, but it was secured too tightly. She knew she needed air or she would pass out, but a breath could not be drawn.

Lord Blaku picked her up, tossed her over his shoulder, and threw her into the back of the carriage. Slowly, her surroundings started to turn dark. Then darker.

In a rush, he chained her ankles and wrists, and then he loosened the whip from around her neck.

Wheezing and couching, she gasped for air, her surroundings becoming clear again, the slaver's stench oozing into her nose as she panted.

He tore the sword from around her waist and studied it for a moment.

"This is a very fine weapon indeed," he said. "Now it is mine, and I shall melt it down."

Ceres reached a hand out toward her father's sword, the chains rattling as she moved, but he slapped her hand away and hopped out of the carriage.

He headed back into the house and when he came back out, he was holding the sack of gold Ceres had left for her brothers.

The carriage bounced as he climbed onto it, and after he whipped the horses, the wheels creaked to a start. As the carriage drove off, she kept her eyes on the near black sky, watching as silhouettes of birds flew above. A tear rolled down her cheek, but she made no sound. She had no strength to cry. Now everything had been taken from her. Her money. Her sword. Her family. Her freedom.

And when she didn't show up tomorrow morning at the palace ready to work for Prince Thanos, she would have lost everything.

Chapter Seven

Miles and miles ago, Lord Blaku had unchained Ceres and had thrown her into an enclosed slave cart, and now she sat in the light of the moon, numb, beside dozens of girls in a cage wagon, bumping forward on the main road out of Delos.

The night had been freezing—it was freezing still—and with little protection from the rain, Ceres hadn't been able to sleep, shivering all the time. Cold hands gripping the bars, she huddled at the end of the moving prison on soggy straw that reeked of urine and rotting flesh. It had stopped raining about an hour ago, and now the moon and stars were out.

She had listened in on the guards' conversations, seated up above, and a few of them had mentioned something about Holheim, the capital of Northland, which, she knew, was several months' journey away. Ceres knew if she were taken there, she would have no chance of ever seeing her family or Rexus again. But she stuffed those thoughts deep down into the dead part of her heart. Glancing back, she noticed that the girl who had been coughing the entire trip had become silent and was now slouching in the rear corner, lifeless, lips blue, skin white.

A mother and two young daughters sat next to the corpse, oblivious to the girl's passing. All the daughters were focused on was competing for their mother's lap. Better they do that than be aware that death was their neighbor, Ceres thought.

A few girls seated against the wall opposite Ceres carried a look of fear in their defeated eyes, and a few others cried in silent sobs as they longingly gazed out through the cage. Ceres didn't feel fear or sadness. She couldn't allow herself to be afraid here. Someone might sense it and judge her weak, and then use her weakness against her. Instead, she numbed herself so completely, she almost didn't care what happened to her.

"Get out of my seat," a blonde girl shouted to another.

"I have been sitting here all along," the second girl replied, her skin smooth and olive in the glow of the moonlight.

The blonde pulled the olive-skinned girl up by her ears and threw her onto the sodden, straw-covered floor. A few of the girls gasped, but most looked away, pretending not to notice the ruckus.

"This is my cart," the blonde exclaimed. "All these seats are mine."

"No they aren't," a dark-skinned girl said, shooting to her feet, her hands on her hips.

They stared at each other for a moment, and everyone in the cart grew quiet, eyes slipping toward the rivals as they waited to see what would happen.

Hissing, the blonde shoved the dark-skinned girl, and within seconds, they were on the floor in a wrestling match, screaming at the top of their lungs as arms and legs flailed, a few eager slaves egging them on.

It was a draw. The olive-skinned girl slowly stood up and walked toward the back as her hands dappled the cage walls, blood running from her nose. The wagon hit a bump, and she wobbled as she sat down on the floor across from Ceres. Wiping the blood with her brown, threadbare, filthy sleeve, she looked Ceres in the eyes.

"I'm Anka," she said.

The moonlight shone in through the cage onto the girl's face, and Ceres thought the girl had the most peculiar eyes she had ever seen: dark brown irises with streaks of turquoise. Her hair was long, thick, and black, and Ceres guessed the girl was around her age.

"I'm Ceres."

Feeling sorry for the girl, but without any strength to become involved, Ceres looked out through the iron bars at the back of the cart, wondering if it would be possible to escape. Life as a slave was not worth living, and she'd do anything to get out, even risk her life, if it came to that.

Unexpectedly, the wagon slowed to a stop on the side of the road, as Lord Blaku yelled for his guards to break up the fight. The cart rocked as the men jumped down from the roof and into puddles of water and wet grass. His face appeared right outside the cage and Ceres heard keys rattling, his heavy breath turning into puffs of smoke.

When the door swung open, a shadow of confusion flickered across Anka's face, and when two of the five guards entered the wagon, the slaves cowered and winced. The men grabbed the wrestling girls and hauled them outside kicking and screaming.

"You're a sweet one," Lord Blaku said, grabbing Anka's arm. "Come here, girl."

Anka feverishly shook her head and scuttled backward, her eyes wide with terror, and Ceres felt a wave of nausea wash over her when she thought about what that fat, old, ugly slaver would do to the innocent girl.

Anka shrieked as Lord Blaku pulled her out.

At that moment, Ceres caught a glimpse of her sword attached around the slaver's waist, and in a split second, she saw her opportunity for escape.

Lord Blaku reached for the deadbolt, but before he could lock it, Ceres kicked the door outward and leapt out of the wagon. A few other slaves escaped and started down the street, but two guards quickly rounded up the runaways as another slammed the door to the wagon shut.

The slaver flung Anka to the ground and reached for the hilt of Ceres's sword. Ceres kneed him in the groin so he buckled forward, and before he stood up, she drew her sword and sliced his thigh, causing him to fall to the muddy road, wailing. The sword felt so light in her hand, she noticed, and the blade had cut through the slaver's thigh like butter.

Three guards threw the other slaves back into the wagon and locked it, the girls crying in disapproval.

Just as Ceres was about to pull Anka to her feet, Anka gasped and yelled, "Behind you!"

Ceres spun around to find three guards upon her. The first had his sword raised, and had Anka not warned her, Ceres would have had his blade in her back.

To her astonishment, the same power she had felt in the arena when she had saved Sartes rushed through her veins. Suddenly, she could see clearly what she needed to do in order to defeat the three guards.

She met the first guard's sword with her own several times before running her blade through him. He dropped to the side of the road in a puddle of water.

The short guard was holding a dagger, and he tossed it between his hands as he scuffled toward her. She kept her eye on the dagger for a few switches, and timing it just right, she flicked her sword between his hands so the dagger went flying into the air, landing on top of the slaver wagon.

"Let me go and I will let you live," Ceres said, so much authority in her voice, not even she recognized it.

"Anyone who captures her will receive fifty-five pieces of gold!" Lord Blaku yelled, throwing his whip toward the short guard who lost his dagger.

Ha! My mother's gold, Ceres thought, adding to her anger.

The two remaining guards inched toward her, the tall one with a patch over his eye drawing his sword, the short one cracking the whip. At the palace, Ceres had only ever fought one on one with others, and she felt uneasy having to conquer two at the same time. But then again, there, she hadn't been fighting for her life, and she hadn't felt that overwhelming surge of force she was feeling now.

The short man snapped the whip so it latched around Ceres's sword hand, and with a tug, Ceres fell to the ground, face first. She had gripped her sword so hard that it still remained in her hand, and with one hack, she severed the leather cords from around her wrist, freeing herself.

Quick as a cat, she sprung to her feet, and just as tall guard attacked, she lunged toward him, their swords colliding.

The short guard threw himself toward Ceres and wrapped arms around her legs so she couldn't move, causing her to topple over, crashing onto her back. He crawled on top of her and wrapped one hand around her sword arm, confining it, the other around her neck, choking her.

"Kill her if you must!" Lord Blaku shouted, still holding his hands around his bleeding thigh.

Ceres kicked her feet up and knocked the short guard in the head, shoving him off her as she rolled backward and up to a standing position. Seeing he was about to stagger to his feet, Ceres kicked him in the face several times until he slumped to the ground unconscious.

Just as the tall guard came at her, she swerved around him, struck his feet from under him, and once he had fallen onto his back, she sliced off his hand. He screamed as blood oozed from his stub.

She hadn't meant to be so brutal. She only wanted to harm him enough so he couldn't fight anymore and wouldn't follow her when she ran away, but the blade was exceptionally sharp and it took almost no effort to slash through his bones. Or perhaps it was this strange force that made it so effortless?

Some of girls in the wagon had climbed up the sides of the wall, rattling the cage, screaming for Ceres to let them out. Others cheered Ceres on, chanting for her to kill their captors.

"Give up your sword, or the girl dies," Lord Blaku yelled behind her.

Ceres whirled around to see Anka held at knifepoint by the slaver. Anka's bottom lip trembled, her eyes wide open, and the slaver pressed the blade into her throat, cutting her a little.

Should she try and save Anka? Ceres could just make a run for it and she would be free. But Anka's eyes pleaded with such desperation that Ceres couldn't find it in her heart to leave her to such a horrid fate. She glanced over at the girls in the wagon, who had turned quiet, realizing she could free them, too.

Ceres leaned back and threw her sword, praying her aim was true.

She watched as it spun end over end, then finally landed in Lord Blaku's face, the blade stabbing him in the eye. He fell backwards, landing flat in the mud.

Dead.

With a whimper, Anka crawled away from him, sobbing.

Ceres, breathing hard, walked forward in the quiet, pulled her sword out from the slaver's skull, and then walked over and slashed the lock off the wagon, opening the door. Shouting and sighing in delight, the women and girls streamed out of the cart one after another. A few thanked Ceres as they passed her, and the mother with her daughters embraced Ceres before turning back toward Delos.

With arms and legs feeling like they weighed a hundred pounds each, and her eyes heavy from sleeplessness, Ceres walked to the front of the wagon and cut the reins to the horses. She took a blanket, a bag of food, and a leather flask filled with wine from atop the wagon and attached it to one of the horses.

After she had removed the scabbard from Lord Blaku's carcass and secured her sword around her waist, she mounted the stout brown mare and steered it southward toward Delos. Just as she passed Anka, she stopped.

"You saved my life," Anka said. "I am indebted to you."

"You saved me first," Ceres replied. "You owe me nothing."

"Let me join you. Please. I have nowhere to go."

Ceres considered Anka's suggestion and thought it might be nice to have company on the cold, dark road back.

"Very well, Anka. We shall travel together," Ceres said with a soft smile.

She reached out her hand and pulled Anka up behind her, Anka clinging to Ceres's back as if for dear life. As lightning struck in the distance, the clouds rolling in again, Ceres prodded the horse to gallop. She would have time to spare before she needed to be at the palace, and she knew where she needed to go: to Rexus and her brothers.

Chapter Eight

The night remained brutally cold, the wind a roaring tempest, but that didn't prevent Ceres from compelling the horse forward at a furious pace, determined to reach Rexus if there was enough time. For hours, rain whipped against her like shards of ice, leaving her clothes sopping wet and her fingers frozen stiff, anger toward her mother and Lord Blaku driving her.

Finally, she sighted the capital's outer wall, and, as the rain ended, she slowed the horse to a trot. The sun crested the Alva Mountains, sparkling through dissipating clouds, and kissed the white buildings of the capital golden, and with about an hour to spare until she needed to be at the palace, Ceres hopped down from the horse and led the mare down the gently sloping gorge to the river. After she had escorted the horse to water, she unwrapped the bread and meat she had taken from Lord Blaku and portioned equal parts for Anka and herself.

She sat down on a rock and glanced at Anka, who was scarfing down the food like a ravenous animal.

"Would you like for me to take you home?" she asked Anka.

Anka paused and looked up, her eyes suddenly weary, but she said nothing.

"Perhaps now that the slaver is dead, your family—"

"My parents sold me to save their farm. Twenty pieces of gold," Anka said bitterly. "They are no longer my family."

Ceres understood. Oh, how she understood. She looked toward the Alva Mountains and thought for a moment.

"I know where you might find a new home," she said.

"Where?" Anka asked, taking a sip of the wine.

"My brothers and friends are part of the revolution."

Anka squinted her eyes, and then she nodded.

"You are my sister now and they shall be my family and friends. I shall fight by your side and belong to the revolution, too," she said.

Once they finished their meal, Ceres led the mare back onto the road and rode with Anka down the sloping hillside toward the capital's main entrance—a heavily guarded drawbridge made of thick oak. Getting in line behind other travelers and merchants, Ceres and Anka rode slowly past a soldier and onto the bridge.

They rode through the cobblestone streets, past houses and wooden shacks, and down cramped alleyways. The city began to rise, the inhabitants lining up at the living wells with buckets and vessels. Children played in the streets, their laughter filling the air, reminding Ceres of much happier, much simpler times.

Beyond acres and acres of wilted, brown plants, they arrived at the bottom of the Alva Mountains. Humble houses rested on the gently sloping hill, sheltered by jutting peaks, and a waterfall cascaded down the mountainside. From the outside, the small settlement looked like any ordinary one on the outskirts of Delos, with houses, wagons, animals, and peasants working the fields. But it was nothing but a façade to keep Empire soldiers from growing suspicious. Inside every abode, a rebellion was brewing.

Ceres had been here once before: two years ago when Rexus had shown her the growing collection of weapons stored in the cave behind the waterfall.

Outside the settlement, bordering on the sea, stood the old abandoned castle: the revolution's headquarters. Two of three towers had collapsed, and a few of the walls had been patched up with driftwood and rocks. Ceres's destination.

They dismounted and walked down the sandy pathway, the breeze from the sea tugging on Ceres's clothes. Once they arrived at the arching entryway, five heavily armored men wearing civilian clothes stopped them.

"My name is Ceres. I am here for Rexus, my friend, and Nesos and Sartes, my brothers," she said, staying the horse. "This is Anka, my friend. We want to join the rebellion."

One of the men's eyes flared a tad, as if her name held some significance. He nodded and headed into the courtyard while the other men studied the girls with distrustful glances.

Inside the courtyard, Ceres could see men and women working in a rushed, almost frantic manner. Some were training others in sword fighting; some were fashioning armor; some were making bows and whittling sticks into arrows; and yet others were sewing clothes.

A few minutes passed, and then a few more. Were Rexus and her brothers not here? Ceres wondered. Would she have to leave without seeing them? She had to see them before she left for the palace.

All of a sudden, Rexus burst around the corner.

"Ciri!" he yelled, running toward her.

Seeing his face again, Ceres felt her strength leave her, and when he wrapped eager arms around her, she broke down and sobbed. She had been strong for so long, and now standing wrapped in his safe embrace, she finally let her weakness surface.

"I thought you were dead," he said, stroking her back, squeezing her tight.

He rained kisses on her face, drying up her tears, and then he pressed his soft warm mouth to hers. But his lips were gone even before she had a chance to enjoy their first kiss.

"I was worried sick about you," he said, clutching her tightly. "Sartes said he saw you outside your father's shed, but that you vanished after that."

"Are my brothers here?" she asked.

"Not at the moment," Rexus replied. "They are on an assignment."

Ceres felt her heart sink, but she nodded and took a step back.

"This is my friend Anka," she said, placing a hand on her new friend's shoulder. "She was also in the slaver wagon. She needs a place to stay."

"In a slaver wagon? That's why you look the way you do," Rexus said, playful eyes running up and down her body.

Ceres socked him in the shoulder.

"You certainly don't look any better than me," she said with a smirk, causing Rexus to laugh.

"Please get Fausta for me," Rexus said to a guard. He turned to Ceres, a conflicted look on his face. "Are you not staying?"

Ceres was torn. Part of her wanted to stay here with Rexus and her brothers, but a huge part of her wanted to work as a weapon-keeper.

"I have been hired by Prince Thanos as his weapon-keeper."

Rexus's eyes flared, and then he nodded.

An elderly woman waddled toward them with the guard, her crinkly skin white as snow, her eyes filled with years of suffering and wisdom.

"Fausta," Rexus said. "Please see to it that Anka is given a place to stay. And make sure she has food and dry clothes."

The old woman opened her frail arms and embraced the newcomer.

"You have a new home now, and we will see each other often," Ceres said to Anka. "I owe you my life and I shall never forget you."

Anka smiled softly and nodded. She gave Ceres a hug, and then she followed Fausta into the courtyard.

Taking Ceres's hand in his, Rexus grabbed the horse's reins and escorted them toward the stable. Once there, he let go of Ceres and led the horse to the water trough.

"You have a new sword," he said, not looking back, stroking the horse's mane.

The mare whinnied in approval.

"Yes. A gift from my father," she said, her hand automatically feeling for it, a pang of sadness overwhelming her.

But she didn't want to talk about sad things.

"The rebellion seems to have grown," she said.

"Since I last brought you here, our supporters have tripled in number," he said.

It made Ceres happy to see wonderment in his eyes.

They walked outside and sat down on a wooden bench, Rexus facing her. He gently stroked her hair, and then caressed her face.

A void opened within her chest when she thought of saying goodbye, and again she entertained the idea of remaining here.

"Perhaps I will stay with you," she said.

Rexus pressed his lips together.

"I would love that, but I think the best thing is if you keep your appointment at the palace," he said.

Ceres knew he was right, but still, it hurt to hear him say she should go.

"Here, we have many supporters," Rexus continued. "But we have no one working within the palace walls."

"I don't know how much access I would have to the inside or the other royals," she said.

"If you gain Prince Thanos's trust, I'm certain he would give you access to all the rebellion needs. When the moment is right, you could lead us inside the palace, securing our victory," he said.

Ceres's stomach churned at the thought of gaining Prince Thanos's trust only to betray him. But why? Perhaps it was because he did trust her and had given her a chance where others would not. Or perhaps it was because he despised his family and what they stood for just as much as any commoner.

Either way, Rexus was right: by doing this, she could help the rebellion like no one else. In fact, her presence inside the castle walls was just what the rebellion needed, and could very well play a significant part in the downfall of the Empire.

She nodded, and for a brief moment, they held each other's eyes.

Not wanting to drag out the farewell, the sadness already overwhelming her, Ceres rose to her feet and walked into the barn. Just as she was about to mount the horse, she heard Rexus enter behind her. While securing the saddle, she glanced back.

"I must go so I am not late for the palace. Please take care of my brothers, and Anka," she said.

Rexus placed a hand on her shoulder and tingles spread through Ceres's body. Ceres thought about the kiss they had shared earlier. Had he meant to kiss her as a friend, or something more? She wanted it to be more. She knew if she turned around, she would find his eyes and his lips would meet hers. And then she wouldn't be able to tear herself away.

So without another word she mounted her horse and kicked, galloping away, far from this place, and toward the palace—determined not to look back for anything.

Chapter Nine

As the sun broke over the horizon and with hardly a second to spare, Ceres galloped through the palace gates, dropped off the horse at the royal stables, and darted toward the palace training ground. When she was almost halfway, she noticed her sword brushing against her leg, and she stopped. Would someone see her sword and perhaps even steal it from her if she brought it? She knew there was no time, and she could be fired for being late, but under no circumstances could she afford to lose this sword.

As fast as her feet could carry her, she sprinted back to the blacksmith's chalet, and finding the place empty, she climbed up the ladder to the loft. There, behind a pile of old planks and crooked twigs, she hid her sword before tearing toward the palace training ground.

When she arrived—breathless, heart thumping wildly—to her surprise, she saw that the entire court had gathered around the practice arena. The king and queen sat on their thrones, princes and princesses on chairs beneath the willow trees, fanning themselves, and the advisors and dignitaries sat on benches, whispering to each other.

In the practice arena, combatlords sparred against royals, and weapon-keepers were watching their masters, handing off swords, daggers, tridents, shields, and floggers. Since she could remember, Ceres had yearned for an opportunity like this, but now that the moment was here, she felt empty inside.

"Ceres!" Thanos yelled, waving to her.

She didn't know why, but when she saw him again, her heart stirred. Then she reprimanded herself. She had to remember why she was here, which was to befriend her enemies and gain their trust, not be amused by a handsome prince who somehow seemed to put her under his spell.

Ceres ran over to Thanos.

"Right on time," he said with a nod.

"Of course," she said as if getting here hadn't been a miracle and a half.

An Empire soldier marched to the center of the arena.

"All royal warriors, hastily line up before King Claudius, your weapon-keepers behind you," he said.

The royals stopped what they were doing and Ceres followed Thanos, taking her place behind him. She noticed that Lucious was back. Had he reconsidered? Been forced to return?

"You're wondering about Lucious?" Thanos asked, glancing back at her.

"Yes."

Ceres wasn't sure whether she hated it or liked it that he was so in tune with her thoughts.

"One doesn't say no to the king," Thanos whispered.

She wanted to ask why, but the king rose, holding a golden bowl up, and the gathering hushed.

"This dish is filled with the names of each of our royal warriors," the king said. "Today I will select three names who will fight in the Killings at noon."

The crowd gasped, each royal warrior and their weapon-keepers included.

But the Killings weren't supposed to be until next month, Ceres thought. Had the king just on a whim scheduled the Killings for today?

She glanced at Thanos, but he stood rigid as a board, his face forward so she couldn't see his expression. They weren't ready to fight in the Killings, Ceres knew. None of them were. They hadn't been given enough time to train together, to get to know each other's fighting styles.

Winding her hands tightly into fists, she focused on keeping her breathing steady. Only three of twelve would be selected, so there was still a chance they didn't have to fight today.

The king reached his chubby hand into the bowl and pulled out a slip.

"Lucious!" he yelled, an evil grin emerging on his lips.

Ceres exhaled and glanced over at Lucious, seeing that his face had turned as red as a beet. The onlookers clapped, although their applause was far from enthusiastic. Did they think this was unfair, too? Ceres wondered.

The king reached into the bowl again and drew a name.

"Georgio!" he hollered, his eyes slithering to the end of the line where Georgio waited.

A woman who looked old enough to be Georgio's mother stood up began to sob, yelling obscenities toward the king, but when she stepped onto the practice arena, she was escorted away by Empire soldiers.

Ceres huffed and kept her eyes trained on Thanos's broad back. Only one name left, she told herself. The chances of Thanos being selected were slim.

Reaching his hand into the bowl a third time, the king glanced at Thanos and the right side of his lip rose.

Ceres saw Thanos's shoulders tense, and immediately she knew something wasn't quite right. Had the king planned this? Rigged this?

Her heart nearly stopped.

"And last but not least, Thanos!" the king exclaimed with a smug smile.

The crowd went silent for a moment, but when the queen started to applaud with fervent enthusiasm, the others followed.

"The risk of death is great, my chosen ones. May you each represent your sovereign and Empire with honor and strength," the king continued.

The king sat down and an Empire soldier explained the rules of the Killings, but Ceres could hardly listen to a word he said, she was so shocked.

"Weapon-keepers who assist in the battle will be put to death … no more than three weapons on any one warrior at one time … no helping other combatlords … thumbs-up means the defeated lives, thumbs-down means the defeated must be slayed …" the Empire soldier said.

When he finished, Ceres stood frozen, staring out into thin air.

She vaguely registered that Thanos had turned around and was facing her. He grabbed her arm and shook it.

"Ceres!" he said.

Disoriented, she looked up into his face.

"Bartholomew is back. If you would like, I can have him be my weapon-keeper today," Thanos said.

At first, her heart leapt in her chest and she wanted to shout yes. Yes! But then she thought of the conversation she had had with Rexus. How would she earn Thanos's trust if she backed out now? She wouldn't.

"Is that what you want?" she asked.

"I prefer to work with you, but seeing the rules have changed, I will not hold it against you if you decide to sit this round out," he said.

She couldn't believe it. Here he was giving her freedom, and she was scheming how to best earn his trust so she could destroy him and his family. A feeling of guilt began to take root.

But then she remembered her people's suffering: the young boy who had been whipped in Fountain Square and hauled off to an unknown destination, the girl who had died in the slaver wagon alone and afraid, her brothers who never went to bed with full bellies, and her father who had to leave his family to make money elsewhere.

If she didn't stand up for them, who would?

"Then I will be your weapon-keeper today and for as long as you would have me," Ceres said.

Thanos nodded, and a hint of a smile graced his lips.

"We shall conquer together," he said.

⚜ ⚜ ⚜

With sweaty hands and an unsettled stomach, Ceres peered down the tunnel underneath the Stade. The passageway was crawling with Empire soldiers, combatlords, and weapon-keepers, weapons of every kind lining the walls, strewn across the gravel floors.

She sat down on a bench mere feet away from the iron gates, waiting for her and Thanos's turn, the crowd chanting like a dragon outside.

"Kill him! Kill him! Kill him!" they shouted.

The onlookers roared, and not a minute later, the iron gates opened, chains clattering, and in strode two Empire soldiers, each hauling mutilated, dead combatlords. They threw one corpse on top of the other onto the dirt floor right across from where Ceres sat, and then they darted back out into the arena.

Ceres startled when the iron gate slammed shut behind them, and she couldn't help but slide her eyes toward the lifeless bodies. Just minutes ago, those men had stood in front of her full of vigor, certain they would be triumphant in today's competition. Now they rested in a heap on the floor, never to rise again.

When she glanced up at Thanos, his eyes were already on her, those impossibly dark irises carrying solemnity that Ceres had only ever seen in the dying. Was he afraid like she was? she wondered.

She watched as he tightened the thick leather belt around his canvas loincloth, his rigid abdomen exposed. She could hardly believe what little protection he wore: a single leather shoulder guard covering his right arm. Most of the other warriors hid behind heavy armor and shining helmets.

Ceres had been given a uniform: a blue short-sleeved tunic that reached to her knees, a silk rope around her waist, and soft leather knee-high boots that resembled Thanos's. Although she didn't particularly like it, she was glad to be out of her old clothes that did nothing but remind her of her old life.

"Did the king set you up?" Ceres asked, remembering King Claudius's sly expression when he hand-picked the royal warriors' names from the golden bowl.

"Yes," Thanos said.

She clenched her teeth and a fire of hate burned within.

"This isn't right," she said.

"No, it isn't," Thanos said, sitting down beside her, tightening the straps on his boots. "But if there is one thing I have learned, it is that you don't refuse the king."

"Have you refused him before?" she asked.

He nodded.

"For what?"

"I wouldn't marry the princess he had chosen for me."

She stared at him for a moment, stunned. She was amazed at the courage that must have taken. Perhaps the girl was hideous, although Ceres hadn't seen any hideous princesses her entire life, all of them dressed in fine clothing, bathed in sweet-smelling perfumes, and adorned with exquisite jewelry.

She looked away, wondering who this young man really was. A rebel? Ceres had not once considered that there might be a nonconformist within the palace walls.

She had a whole new respect for Thanos. Perhaps he was not the boy she thought he was. Which made her feel even sicker to betray him.

"And what of Lucious and Georgio?" she asked.

"The king despises them for other reasons."

"But how can the king can just randomly—"

He interrupted her, his voice impatient.

"Just because I am royalty doesn't mean I have a say in my life."

Ceres hadn't thought about that. She had always assumed the royals were free to do as they pleased and that they ruled as one big enemy.

"All the pomp and haughtiness, the rules, decorum, frivolous spending… it drives me to the brink of insanity," he said, almost growling.

Ceres was taken aback that he would say such things about the royals and didn't know exactly what to say to him. Instead, she looked out the iron gates, and just as she did, she saw a combatlord stab Georgio's weapon-keeper through the abdomen.

Her hand hit her mouth and she gasped.

In her naiveté, she had assumed she was safe from other combatlords since she wasn't the one fighting. A sense of dread gripped her shoulders and she noticed how her hands shook even more than before.

An Empire soldier approached, telling Thanos it was his turn to fight next, and that he would be fighting together with Lucious against two other combatlords.

With a parched throat, Ceres said, "We have to stick together if we are to make it out alive."

Thanos nodded, a quiet understanding between them.

They stood up and walked over to the iron gates, each in their own thoughts for some time.

"I won't kill unless I have to," Thanos suddenly said.

Ceres nodded, wondering if this was one more way he planned to defy the king.

"I need to know I can trust you with my life," he said without looking away from the arena.

"You can trust me with your life," Ceres said, wondering if he heard the slight hesitation in her voice.

He closed his eyes and nodded.

"You can trust me with your life, too, Ceres," he said.

She didn't know why, but his words sank into her bones, and she felt they were true. Despite herself, she was feeling an intense bond with him.

Lucious and his weapon-keeper stepped up behind Thanos and Ceres, and Ceres noticed Lucious's shiny full body armor and visored helmet. No amount of armor will save a sloppy warrior's life, she thought.

The iron gates swung open, and in came Georgio alive, his body drenched in sweat, blood dripping from a few lacerations to his arms and abdomen. An Empire soldier dragged his weapon-keeper in behind him and flung him on top of the other cadavers on the floor.

Ceres's entire body started to shake.

"Stay close to me," Thanos said, his eyes straight forward as if in a trance, his jaw clenching.

Just as the Empire soldier nodded for them to exit, Lucious shoved Ceres out of the way and entered the arena first, his arms held high in the air as if in victory. The masses went wild, and he paraded around for a few moments, reveling in their approval.

At any other time than this very moment, his behavior would have irritated Ceres to no end, but standing here, inhaling what could quite possibly be her last breath, she paid no attention to the approval-seeking fool.

Thanos and Ceres entered the arena next, and Ceres squinted, the sun blinding her. Once her eyes had adjusted to the light, she glanced up into the audience, seeing only roughly half the seats filled.

She gazed up at the podium and saw the king sitting up on his throne, smiling glumly. How she despised him. If what Thanos said was true, he was eviler than Ceres had imagined.

"Remember, stay close," Thanos said, touching her elbow.

She nodded and then spotted the two combatlords on the other side of the arena, wearing heavy armor, each holding a sword.

When the trumpets blared, at once, a beast sprung out from one of the trap doors in the ground. It charged toward Ceres and Thanos, its grizzled black fur glistening in the sunlight, its roar echoing against the stadium walls. The dog-like creature was unfamiliar to Ceres—large body, stalky legs—and moved at a slower pace compared to an omnicat, although she didn't doubt it was just as strong.

"A wolver!" someone from the crowd yelled, and then a wave of clamors moved through the audience.

Adrenaline coursed through her, and for a moment, she didn't know where to go. But when she saw the weapons lined up against the wall, she headed toward them and waited for Thanos's command.

First, Thanos called for the trident, and she flung it to him. Good choice, she thought as she watched him catch it mid-air. She wanted to jump in and help him, but she remembered the rule forbidding a weapon-keeper to intervene.

Thanos screamed at the wolver as he jabbed the trident toward the beast, his feet moving with swiftness, his reflexes lightning quick.

From the corner of her eye, Ceres noticed one of the combatlords making his way toward Thanos. If he were smart, the combatlord would wait to strike until after Thanos had slain the wolver or the beast might attack him, too.

All of a sudden, the wolver charged toward Thanos, and Thanos jabbed it in the shoulder. The onlookers cheered in approval at the fight's first attack.

However, the wolver didn't seem to be injured in the least, only growling louder from what Thanos had done, licking its teeth, red eyes glaring at Thanos.

"Longsword!" Thanos yelled.

Right as she threw it to him, he dropped the trident to the ground and caught the longsword mid-air. But then suddenly, Ceres sensed he needed protection from fire—quick—and she yelled at him and also threw him a shield. Just as he caught the shield, the wolver inhaled, and then it spewed fire from its mouth. The onlookers gasped, and Thanos ducked behind the shield, the flames blasting against the metal surface.

Once the wolver had run out of breath, Thanos dropped his shield, picked up the trident, and hurled it at the beast's head, piercing its eye.

The animal violently shook its head as it snarled and growled, sending the trident flying halfway across the arena, Ceres saw.

Without hesitating, Thanos tore toward the wolver, leapt into the air, and lifted his sword. On his way down, he stabbed the beast in the head, and it fell lifeless onto the red sand.

But even though the audience cheered, there was no rest. The combatlord that had been lying in wait charged, his spear and sword pointed straight at Thanos.

Thanos pulled and pulled, trying to dislodge the blade from the wolver's skull, Ceres saw. But it wouldn't budge. And he already had three weapons on the field; the trident on the other side of the arena, his shield too far to reach, and the blade wedged into the wolver's skull. Ceres knew it was against the rules to throw him another one.

She held her breath. The combatlord was close. Too close. She stepped forward.

Still pulling on the blade, Thanos looked at Ceres, his eyes wide with fear, his face twisted in desperation.

He was going to die.

And there was nothing Ceres could do to prevent it.

Chapter Ten

Screaming, Thanos desperately tugged at the blade lodged in the wolver's skull, but even as fiercely as he tried, the sword would not budge in the least. Hearing the combatlord's footsteps approaching, he glanced back to see his enemy a mere ten feet away. His life depended on retrieving his sword, for he knew a weaponless warrior was a dead warrior.

Fraught, he looked to Ceres, but he knew three weapons were on the field and if she threw him another one, she would be punished.

She raised a palm toward him, and just as he heard the swooshing sound of his opponent's blade descending, Thanos's sword jutted into his hand as if by some mystical force.

Shocked at what happened but with no time to linger on it, Thanos spun and rolled on the ground, the combatlord's sword just missing him by a fraction of an inch, the crowd's roar peaking into a frenzy before retreating into a static hum.

Thanos was quick to hop to his feet, and just then, he heard Lucious calling for help. Seeing his opponent several feet away, Thanos afforded a quick glance and discovered Lucious stripped of a weapon, his weapon-keeper lying facedown in the red sand.

"Throw me something! Anything!" Lucious yelled to Ceres, his voice filled with rage. "Do it now or I'll have you skinned alive!"

As Thanos snapped his attention back towards his foe, he vaguely registered that Ceres tossed Lucious two daggers. But his irritation was replaced with alarm when he saw the combatlord hurling a spear at him.

Just as the spear approached, Thanos clenched a fist around it, stopping it from penetrating his heart, and then he whirled the spear around and flung it back at the combatlord, piercing his thigh exactly where he had meant to.

"Thanos! Thanos! Thanos!" the audience shouted, fists pumping into the air.

The combatlord fell to his feet, moaning in pain, holding his leg, the spear protruding from it.

Recognizing his opportunity, Thanos ran behind the combatlord and hit him on the head with the hilt of his sword, knocking him unconscious.

However, even before he could look to the king for acceptance of his victory, Lucious encircled him—and suddenly Lucious's combatlord attacked Thanos, forcing Thanos to continue fighting.

The scoundrel pawned his combatlord onto me, Thanos thought.

It was as he had always suspected: Lucious had absolutely no honor.

While he was battling a new opponent, Thanos could see Lucious sauntering over to the iron gate.

"Let me in or I will kill you and find your family and torture them all to death!" Lucious yelled.

Thanos heard the gate rattling as it opened, the crowed booing Lucious.

"Thanos!" Ceres yelled, holding up two daggers.

Of course. He was growing weary and needed lighter weapons. He nodded toward her, and she threw them to him.

Right away, Thanos kicked the combatlord in the chest so he flew backward. But with impeccable balance, the combatlord landed on his feet and charged toward Thanos, sword in hand. The combatlord lunged forward, thrusting his sword toward Thanos, but Thanos jumped out of the way.

As they moved around the arena, Thanos noticed that little by little, his nemesis grew exhausted, his chest heaving greatly with each breath, his movements slackening a hair. His plan was working. He didn't want to kill the man, no, only exhaust him so he could render him unconscious like he had the first one.

Right as Thanos approached his shield, he picked it up from the ground and flung it into the combatlord's face. The combatlord fell to the ground lifeless, and for the first time since he could remember since entering the arena, the spectators went silent.

Thanos panted and gazed up at the podium, awaiting the king's decision, hoping he would not be commanded to murder his unconscious adversary.

However, from what he knew about the blood-thirsty monarch, Thanos feared King Claudius would force him to do something he had worked hard to avoid—kill.

The king glowered at Thanos as if he didn't accept that the battle had ended in Thanos's favor, the tension between the two palpable, the entire Stade void of the faintest of sounds. After arising from his seat, the king walked to the edge of the platform, his hand outstretched, his thumb outstretched to the side.

Finally, the king lifted a thumb up with a frown, and the onlookers broke into applause.

Thanos couldn't believe it. Ceres and he had survived. They had survived!

He looked over at Ceres, feeling drops of sweat dripping from his hair and down his face. He nodded, and when she smiled, it was as if in that instance, the victory was complete.

He stared at her, stunned. She had saved his life more than once, and had done it in a way he did not understand.

And for the first time since he'd met her, he was beginning to wonder.

Who was she?

Chapter Eleven

A tear rolled down Ceres's cheek as her fingers carefully skimmed the weapons laid out on tables in the practice arena. Amidst the twilight she heard laughter and music spilling out from the open palace windows, every royal inside those haughty walls celebrating today's great victories. It made her feel more alone than ever. It made her miss her brothers, her father, her home, Rexus, dearly. It made her mourn for the mother she'd never had.

Ceres paused and listened to the wind sighing through the trees, as she looked up and saw a few stars twinkling down on her. She inhaled the fresh air, the scent of roses and lilies filling her nostrils. The quiet was a welcome friend after the roaring crowd at the Stade. Even if she had been invited to the feast, she wouldn't have wanted to accept, having no desire to mingle with those pompous royals who were congratulating each other for a battle Thanos and she had won.

Thanos. Her insides coiled tightly when she thought of how he hadn't even bothered to see her after the Killings. There was no "thank you." No "job well done." But she didn't need his approval or his praise, she reminded herself. She didn't need anyone.

Upset with herself for allowing such ludicrous melancholy, she wiped the tears from her cheeks, picked up a spear, and walked to the center of the practice arena.

Swinging the spear overhead, she whirled it around until a swooshing sound could be heard. She then hurled it at a training dummy, hitting it right on the center of the smallest circle. She smiled.

Feeling much lighter, she meandered over to the table again and picked out a sword—one that reminded her of her own, its blade thin and long, its hilt bronze and gold.

Lunging forward, she pretended to attack Lucious—the coward—her sword moving with deftness, her attention and anger on her imaginary enemy.

Keep light afoot. She jumped. *Attack and defend.* She lunged. *Be fluid like water, strong like a mountain.* It was what her trainers at the palace had pounded into her. And it was what she had practiced for hours and months and years.

"After today, I would have thought you'd be tucked in bed, falling fast asleep."

She turned with a start to find Thanos stepping out from behind a willow tree, smiling.

Ceres lowered her sword and turned toward him, her cheeks hot with embarrassment. She saw he wore a loose linen shirt, the neck open, and dark curls framed his face. She tried to hate him in this moment.

But somehow her heart had warmed with his presence.

"I could say the same to you," she said, raising an eyebrow, hoping he wouldn't notice her racing heart.

"I was about to—but then I heard someone practicing in the arena below my room."

She looked up the tower to the balcony, his door open, red curtains dancing in the wind.

"I'm sorry I kept you up, my lord," she said, looking back at him.

"Thanos, please," he said, bowing toward her, keeping eye contact.

He smiled and took a step toward her.

"You weren't really keeping me up. I left the party as soon as I could to look for you, and that's when I saw you from my balcony," he said.

"Why were you looking for me?" she asked, trying to ignore the nervous energy that pulsed through her.

"I wanted to thank you for today," he said.

She stared at him blankly for a moment, trying to hold onto the anger for him that was quickly vanishing.

"What brilliant skill you have," he said. "You have been taught well."

She wouldn't reveal she had been dressing up as a boy, training with the combatlords at the palace. He could report her. And he would, wouldn't he? They might be allies in the arena, but in the real world, they were enemies.

"My father was a bladesmith," she said, hoping he wouldn't pry anymore into her training.

He nodded.

"And where is he now?" Thanos asked.

Ceres looked down, thoughts of her father hundreds of miles away weighing heavily on her mind.

"He had to take work elsewhere," she whispered.

"I'm sad to hear, Ceres," Thanos said, stepping even closer.

She wished he would stay away, for when he was this close, it was hard to consider him her nemesis and to despise him so.

"And what of your mother?" he asked, watching her closely.

"She tried to sell me into slavery," Ceres admitted, thinking there was no harm in telling him the truth about her mother.

He nodded once, and squeezed his lips together.

"I'm sorry," he said.

It irritated her that he apologized for that. A prince. It was partly his fault her father hadn't been paid enough at the palace and needed to look for work elsewhere.

"How are your wounds?" she asked, walking over to the table and placing the sword on it, hoping to steer the conversation onto safer subjects.

"They'll heal," he said as he followed after her.

Standing next to her, his arms folded, he studied her face for a moment.

"How did you do that?" he asked.

"What?" Ceres said.

"Out in the arena today. First, you threw me a shield. I have never heard of a wolver, let alone that any animal could spew flames."

She shrugged her shoulders.

"I had heard of wolvers from my father," she fibbed.

"Then, my sword… it was lodged in the wolver's skull," he said, his eyes squinting. "You raised your hand and the blade jutted into my hand with this force—"

"I did no such thing!" Ceres interrupted him, backing away, afraid he was onto her.

He glanced at her with kind eyes and cocked his head to the side.

"Are you saying I imagined it?" he asked.

She balked. Was he trying to trap her? She needed to choose her words carefully or she could be thrown into prison for implying he was a liar.

"I am certain I don't know what you are talking about," she said.

His eyebrows knitted together and he opened his mouth as if to speak, but instead, he stepped toward her, placed a hand on her shoulder, and let it slide down her arm.

A delightful shiver went through Ceres, and she loathed how her body betrayed her so.

"No matter," he said. "Thank you, though. Your selections of weapons made all the difference."

"Yes, perhaps your lovely hair would have been singed off had I not offered the shield," she said with a smirk, trying to make light of the situation.

"You think I have lovely hair?" he asked.

Her breathing staggered, and she couldn't understand how she could have let such a flippant comment escape her lips.

"No," she said rather sharply, folding her arms in front of her chest.

His lips twitched.

"Well, then, I don't think you have beautiful eyes, either," he said.

"Then it's settled."

He nodded and Ceres walked over to a willow tree.

"It's getting late," she said.

"Perhaps I may escort you home?" he said, following her again.

Ceres lowered her gaze and shook her head.

"Or perhaps you need a place to stay?" he asked, his voice barely above a whisper.

Should she tell him the truth? If she didn't, she knew she would have to sleep outdoors every night.

"Yes," she said.

"There is no room for you inside the castle walls, but just down that path next to the well is a vacant summer home, and you are welcome to stay there."

He pointed to a small cottage secluded by trees, covered in vines.

"I would be very grateful," she said.

He took her arm and was about to walk her there, but then a girl emerged from the bushes. She was lovely, Ceres thought, with blonde hair and brown eyes, her skin as smooth as silk, her lips blood red. She wore a white silk dress, and when a breeze gusted against Ceres's face, she noticed the girl smelled of roses.

Feeling a bit awkward, Ceres pulled her arm away from Thanos's.

"Hello, Stephania," Thanos said, and Ceres could detect a slight irritation in his voice.

Stephania smiled at Thanos, but when her eyes reached Ceres, the girl frowned.

"Whom have we here?" Stephania asked.

"This is Ceres, my weapon-keeper," Thanos said.

"Where are you going with your weapon-keeper?" Stephania asked.

"That is none of your concern," Thanos replied.

"I am certain King Claudius would be thrilled to know you are meeting with your female weapon-keeper late at night, escorting her to unknown destinations," Stephania said.

"I'm certain the king would be equally thrilled to learn you are wandering around the palace grounds late at night in your sleepwear, unescorted by your handmaidens," Thanos snapped.

Stephania lifted her nose up, turned on her heels, and vanished down the paved walkway and back into the palace.

"Never mind her," Thanos said. "She's just upset I refused to marry her."

"It was her?" Ceres asked.

He didn't respond to her question, just jutted out his elbow, offering it to her again.

"Perhaps she was right. Maybe this is inappropriate," Ceres said.

"Nonsense," he said, and then he paused before smirking and saying, "Unless you were considering making it so?"

"Of course not," Ceres said, bothered, her cheeks flushing hot.

When she looped an arm through his to prove her point, she became irritated with herself for liking it, and immediately, she strengthened her resolve to not let the charming prince anywhere near her heart.

Chapter Twelve

Standing atop a hill overlooking Cumorla, the capital of Haylon, a remote isle in the Mazeronian Sea, Commander Akila's heart soared with joy as he watched the statue of King Claudius come tumbling down. He inhaled the air, and the sweet sensation of justice filled him, as smoke from the king's castle rose into the azure heaven above the city.

Justice, Akila thought. Justice was finally being served today. Every last royal relative of the king had been locked inside that abominable seven-spired structure, and now it had burned down.

Wind pushed at his armor as he beheld the thousands of men on the hillside, their red banners flapping for the revolution's cause. Before twilight, he would lead them into a battle that would free them, finally, from centuries of oppression. His chest swelled with pride.

The people of Haylon had suffered long enough under the rule of tyrannical kings. They had paid unreasonable taxes, sent their best warriors to Delos, and bowed their heads to the ten thousand Empire soldiers that plagued the streets day and night. His entire life, Akila had watched women and daughters raped, children flogged and arrested. The young were forced to work long days in the king's fields, returning with welts and dejected eyes. He knew it was long past since they needed to take back their freedom, to take back their lives.

A messenger approached.

"Western Cumorla has been secured, sir," he said.

"The Empire soldiers?" Akila asked.

"Fleeing to the east."

"How many civilian lives lost?"

"Three hundred, thus far."

Akila clenched his fists. It was less than expected, but each life lost was a weight on his conscience, another son or daughter dead, a mother, brother, sister, father butchered while defending this land's freedom.

He dismissed the messenger and signaled to his lieutenant to alert the final wave of militias. They would trap the invaders on the western entrance and treat them with the same courtesy with which they had treated his people. Not much would be left of them after that, and that brought great joy to Akila's heart.

Akila kicked his horse forward, leading the lieutenant and his men into battle. He rode down the hill and in through the northern city gates, past balconied passageways, closed inns, and padlocked work shacks. He passed families huddled in corners, children lying facedown on the stone streets, and horses on the run without riders. The militias followed Akila without the city walls, hiding behind trenches to await the thousands of Empire soldiers that would soon flee through the gates and try to escape toward the harbor.

Not a one must escape, Akila had told his men this morning as he had ordered hundreds of men to stand guard at the docks. For even one escapee meant word would get back to Delos—and then the king would send tens of thousands of Empire soldiers to Haylon.

Minutes passed, and minutes more, until they had been lying in wait for nearly an hour, as twilight descended.

Then, suddenly, the first Empire soldier rode out on a horse, holding the Empire ensign, Akila saw.

"Long live King Claudius!" the soldier yelled.

Three flaming arrows hit him in the chest.

He fell off his horse, into the canal below the bridge.

Three more Empire soldiers followed, all felled, too, as they rode through the gates.

Soldier after soldier then trickled out of the city gates, and a brutal battle ensued.

Akila led the way with a fierce battle cry as night fell. All around him men were losing their lives to the cause of freedom, a freedom they would never see, but that perhaps their children would.

Akila gathered his most ruthless warriors to ride with him into the city, and he looked side to side to see them now, their horses thundering in his ears. He led the group of three hundred through the southern entrance, and then as they rode split them into four groups of fifty, each to search for Empire soldiers in different directions.

With torches and swords, Akila led his men down winding streets, stopping at every house, searching—hunting high and low, not a single enemy to be found. Almost at the end of their search, they happened upon a stable behind the high priest's mansion, and Akila thought it looked like an excellent hiding place for Empire soldiers.

As he was about to command his men to search the stable, the high priest stepped out from his house.

"Have you seen any Empire soldiers this way?" Akila asked, descending his horse.

"No," the priest said, his hands clasped as if in reverence in front of his body.

But there was something unsettling in the priest's eyes that made Akila think he was lying.

"Search the stable," Akila told his soldiers, and they immediately headed toward and entered the building.

There was a sudden uproar, and when Akila turned toward the commotion, the priest took off running down the street. Akila ran after him, but when he arrived at the street, he saw the priest galloping on a horse in the direction of the southern entrance.

Akila whistled, and once his horse was by his side, he hopped onto it and rode after the escapee. Through the city gates the priest went, with Akila on his heels, but Akila couldn't quite catch up to him.

Riding eastward, Akila whipped his horse onward relentlessly, his eyes on the escapee. He passed palm trees and hopped fences, rode through grassy fields and sand dunes. Following the priest down a steep sloping hill, it was then he saw a makeshift dock, hidden below a dome of trees. None of his men had been ordered to watch this dock because no one knew it was there.

To his dread, he saw the priest push away in a small sailboat, the wind catching the red sail immediately.

Almost there, Akila wondered if his horse would make the leap from the landing pier and into the boat, the distance increasing by the second. The horse's muscles tensed beneath him, but Akila drove it forward.

The horse leapt from the dock and into the vessel, skidding as it landed on the slippery wooden deck, throwing Akila off in the fall.

Slightly dazed from the rough landing, Akila rose to his feet and drew his sword.

The priest charged immediately, his sword held high, and he lunged and stabbed with the ferocity of a man who knew his life was at stake.

Akila dashed forward and slashed his blade toward the traitor, slicing him in the face. The man growled, dropped his sword, and whipped out a dagger, flinging it at Akila. But Akila saw it coming and blocked the dagger with his blade.

The priest spun and hurled a basket at Akila, then a wooden crate. Akila hit them away. Next, the priest grabbed a net and tossed it so Akila's sword hand became wrapped in it, and then he pulled on the net, causing Akila to stumble forward.

Coming at him, the priest picked up his sword and aimed it at Akila's chest, but Akila wore heavy armor and the man's sword slid off the metal like butter, causing the priest to stumble forward.

Taking advantage, Akila shook the net from off his arm and stabbed the priest.

He collapsed to the deck, dead.

Akila pulled his blade out of the priest's limp body and cleaned it on the net before sliding it back in its sheath.

Not wasting a second, he looked to the city walls, and seeing the black sky was turning navy blue, he realized he needed to return to his men, and quick. He sailed the boat back to the dock, set the boat on fire, and rode with all he had toward the eastern entrance.

Just as he arrived, pink graced the sky. Victory was called, and a new banner was placed atop the outer walls of Cumorla.

As bells of freedom tolled through the capital, Akila rode through the city's streets with his militia, men, women, and children cheering them on.

He looked toward the north and thought of his family members in Delos, still in bondage, and he knew in his heart that freedom was coming for them, too.

For here, for the first time in history, he stood on the first free land in the Empire.

The revolution had begun.

Chapter Thirteen

Ceres felt a pang of fear as she realized someone was following her. She quickened her pace on the rocky white pathway, lit by the morning sun, winding her way amidst green lawns and endless rows of flowers, her mind still reeling from her encounter the night before with Thanos. She paused and looked over her shoulder, listening for the footsteps she knew she had just heard.

Yet there was no one in sight.

Ceres froze and listened. She didn't have time for annoying games. She needed to get to the palace training ground with the weapons in the barrow before practice started, or Thanos would be weaponless.

Who could it be?

Overheated, she glanced up into the sky as a drop of sweat rolled down her forehead. The sun was a hot glowing disk already, and just like the gardens, she was withering. The muscles in her arms and shoulders started to burn, but she couldn't afford to rest. She was late as it was.

Pushing the heavy handcart, she picked up her pace, and when the footsteps came again, and she spun and saw no one, her irritation increased.

Finally, as she neared the gazebo, the footsteps grew louder, and when she glanced over her shoulder again, this time she spotted Stephania, wearing a red silk dress, a golden wreath in her golden hair.

Of course. The snooping princess.

"Hello, weapon girl," Stephania said, a slight frown on her face.

Ceres bowed her head and turned back around, eager to get away. But before Ceres could escape, Stephania stepped in front of her, blocking the narrow path.

"How does a girl become something as lowly as a weapon-keeper, I wonder?" Stephania asked, her hand hitting her hips.

"Thanos hired me," Ceres replied. "Now if you would so kindly—"

"You will address me as your highness!" Stephania snapped.

Ceres startled and she wanted to give the spoiled girl a piece of her mind, but instead, she kept her head down, reminding herself she wasn't here to protect her honor, only to fight for the revolution.

"Yes, your highness," she said.

"It is important you know your place, would you not agree?" Stephania said.

She walked a slow circle around Ceres, eyes probing, hands clasped behind her back, and fancy shoes clicking against the bricks as she strode.

"Since the day you arrived, I have been watching you. I will *always* be watching you. Do you hear?" Stephania said.

Ceres pinched her lips together so she wouldn't be tempted to say something disrespectful in return, although it was becoming increasingly difficult to remain silent.

"I see the way you look at Prince Thanos, but you would be foolish to think he would consider you anything but—"

"I can assure you—" Ceres started.

Stephania stepped so close to Ceres's face that their noses were an inch away, and then she whispered through gritted teeth, "Don't interrupt your superior when she is speaking!"

Ceres squeezed fingers around the cart's handles, her forearms now burning.

"Prince Thanos may have hired you, but as his future wife, it is my responsibility to ensure his associations are trustworthy," Stephania said.

Now Ceres couldn't hold back anymore.

"Thanos told me he wasn't going to marry you," she said.

Stephania flinched.

"Thanos is a smart man, but he is no good judge of character. He probably failed to learn what transgressions there might be in your past before he hired you."

Did Stephania know about how she killed the slaver and his guards? Ceres wondered, now considering she could lose her position at the palace and be punished for it if it came out.

"There are no transgressions in my past," Ceres said sternly.

Stephania laughed.

"Oh, come now. Everyone has done something in the past they are ashamed of," she said.

Stephania picked up a sword from the handcart and poked Ceres's leg with it. Oh, how Ceres wanted to give the rotten princess a lesson in swordsmanship, revealing how inept her clean, dainty, little monarch hands were. But she remained immovable.

"And believe me," Stephania said as she raised the blade to Ceres's face, a hair away. "If there is so much as a sliver of a transgression in your past, I will find out, and then I will have you thrown out of the palace, headfirst."

Stephania tossed the sword onto the ground next to Ceres's feet, the blade clattering as it landed.

"Thanos is mine, do you hear?" Stephania said. "He has been promised to me by the king and queen and if you get in the way of our marriage, I will personally slit your throat while you are sleeping in my future summer home."

Stephania shoved Ceres with her shoulder as she walked by, heading toward the palace training grounds.

⚜ ⚜ ⚜

The second Ceres arrived at the practice arena, she could sense that something was wrong. It wasn't that Stephania was glowering at her from beneath the willow trees, although their conversation was still swimming through Ceres's mind, irritating her to no end. It wasn't that it seemed the day would turn into the hottest one of the year, or that Thanos wasn't here yet, practicing.

As she rolled the handcart toward their weapon table, her eyes followed Lucious in the middle of the practice arena. He was clutching a bottle of wine in one hand, a sword in the other, and his new weapon-keeper knelt before him with a worried expression, while balancing an apple on his head. The weapon-keeper had several small cuts on his face, and one on his neck, Ceres saw.

"Stay … very … still," Lucious said, closing his eyes while pointing the tip of his sword toward the weapon-keeper's head.

The other royal warriors and their weapon-keepers stood watching, rolling their eyes, arms folded across chests.

Stepping closer, Ceres could see that Lucious's face and arms were bruised, one eye swollen and red. She couldn't remember him becoming injured yesterday at the Killings. Had something happened after the event?

She walked over to the table and started laying weapons out in preparation for when Thanos would arrive. Swords, daggers, a trident, a flogger.

From the corner of her eye, she saw Lucious stagger, causing the other royal warriors and a few weapon-keepers to laugh.

Lucious touched the tip of his sword to the weapon-keeper's nose, and the weapon-keeper winced with closed eyes as a drop of blood made its way into his mouth.

"Don't move a muscle or you could lose your head," Lucious said. "And you would have no one to blame but yourself."

This was insane, Ceres thought. Couldn't someone do something? She glanced at the others, but no one said a word or seemed to have any intent on helping Lucious's victim.

Next, Lucious raised his sword, but before he swung, the weapon-keeper whimpered and the apple fell from his head and onto the ground, bouncing on impact, rolling a few feet away.

"I told you to remain still!" Lucious snapped.

"I … I'm sorry," the weapon-keeper said, cowering backward, fright in his eyes.

"Get out of my sight, you useless piece of dung!" Lucious yelled.

The young man rose from his knees and scurried over to Lucious's weapon table. Just then, Thanos arrived.

"Good morrow," he said to Ceres, not having witnessed what just happened. "I trust you slept well?"

"Yes, thank you," Ceres said, now all of a sudden feeling much lighter from his presence.

She continued to place weapons on the table, but when he remained quiet, she looked over at him. To her surprise, she found that he was studying her face with eyes that seemed to want possess her, and when she raised an eyebrow at him, his lips tilted upward into a hint of a smile.

She felt her cheeks warm.

Without a word between them, he began helping her organize the weapons.

That's odd that he would help me, Ceres thought. He's a prince. Perhaps he was trying to show appreciation in return for how she had helped him at the Killings? He didn't have to do that, Ceres knew, though she did know one thing. When he showed kindness like this, it was becoming more and more difficult to reconcile the caring man before her with the arrogant man she had always thought he was.

Ceres glanced over to Stephania, and the princess's eyes were spewing hatred toward her. Surely, it couldn't be that Stephania was jealous of her? Thanos wouldn't take interest in a commoner, would he?

Ceres shook her head and laughed a bit, throwing the ridiculous thought out of her mind.

"What is it?" Thanos asked, smiling.

"Nothing," Ceres said. "So, what happened to Lucious anyway?"

"You mean the bruises?"

"Yes."

"The king had him beaten for how spinelessly he acted yesterday," Thanos said.

Even though she, too, thought Lucious a spineless imbecile, Ceres couldn't help but feel sorry for him. She had herself been bruised and battered countless times, and it wasn't something she wished upon anyone.

All of a sudden, Lucious yelled at his weapon-keeper, and just as she glanced up, she saw Lucious punching the young man in the stomach.

"Why isn't anyone doing anything?" Ceres asked.

Immediately, Thanos strode over to Lucious, stopping a few feet away.

"What are you trying to prove?" Thanos asked.

Lucious scoffed.

"Nothing."

Thanos took a threatening step toward Lucious.

"Why would I have anything to prove to anyone? I mean, look at you, anything is better than having a ratty, thin girl as a weapon-keeper," Lucious said with a scornful laugh.

"I suggest you treat your weapon-keeper with respect, and if you don't, I'm sure the king would see nothing wrong in leaving you to fend for yourself out in the arena," Thanos said.

"Is that a threat?" Lucious asked, eyes seething.

Just then a messenger arrived and handed Thanos a scroll. Thanos read it, and looking back toward Ceres, he gave her a nod before heading toward the palace.

Had he been summoned? Ceres wondered, not too thrilled about being left without any instruction.

An Empire soldier stepped into the center of the arena and listed in which order the royals would spar, with Lucious against Argus first.

"Finally!" Lucious said.

He flung the bottle of wine onto the ground, shattering it, and his weapon-keeper offered him a sword. He snatched it, and then with contrived enthusiasm, Ceres thought, he strode onto the practice arena where Argus waited.

The Empire soldier signaled the start of the match, and the royals began to spar. Lucious's first attack ended with his sword smashing into the ground, some onlookers snickering, others rolling their eyes. Lucious used his energy unwisely, Ceres saw, his jabs and lunges careless, with far too much effort.

The contenders took their places again, blade against blade, but within seconds of starting over, only a few hits in, Argus had hit Lucious's sword out of his hands and pointed his tip against Lucious's chest.

As soon as the Empire soldier named Argus the winner, Argus lowered his sword and jogged off the practice arena.

"Come on, cousin. Give me one more chance!" Lucious yelled after him. "I wasn't even trying!"

When Lucious saw Argus wouldn't entertain him, he turned to his own weapon-keeper.

"Xavier, spar with me," Lucious said.

"S … sire?" Xavier said with a nervous stutter. "I would, my lord, but I have no skill."

Angered, Lucious darted over to his weapon table, picked up a dagger, and stabbed Xavier in the abdomen.

Ceres's hand hit her mouth, and she gasped with the others as the weapon-keeper cried and fell to the ground, arms wrapped around his waist.

"Get the runt out of my sight!" Lucious yelled.

Within a few seconds, Empire soldiers hoisted the moaning weapon-keeper onto a stretcher and carried him away.

"What I don't understand," Lucious said, making his way over to Georgio's table, "is how I always get stuck with incompetence. Georgio, friend, lend me your boy."

Georgio stepped between his weapon-keeper and Lucious.

"Lucious, you know I hold you in high regard. But this is insanity. Go home," Georgio said with a chuckle, resting a hand on Lucious's shoulder.

"Get your pretty-boy hands off me!" Lucious yelled, whacking Georgio's arm away.

Yelling obscenities, Lucious walked over to another weapon-keeper, demanding he spar with him, but his master refused, too.

"Will no one fight me?" Lucious yelled, turning in a slow circle as his eyes scanned the bystanders. "Are you nothing but pitiful chicken droppings?"

With animosity in cold eyes, he continued to scrutinize the spectators, but most turned their eyes away.

Then he saw Ceres.

A pit formed in her stomach as he stomped toward her, pointing.

"You!" he yelled. "You will fight me!"

Ceres felt she would win a match against him, yet she was reluctant to accept, fearing she might hurt him, or make him look like the incompetent warrior he was in front of his peers. And if she made him look incompetent, she suspected Lucious would make certain she lost her position at the palace.

"I mean no disrespect, but I cannot fight you," she said.

"You will!" Lucious said. "In fact, I command you to spar with me."

She glanced at the others, some of them shaking their heads, others looking away, Stephania grinned wickedly. Could she refuse him? And what would happen if she did? Would Lucious fire her? Reason told her he probably would.

"Then I must accept the command," she said, thinking it might be better to accept than refuse him.

Lucious's face lit up.

"But first, may I fetch my sword from the blacksmith's chalet?" Ceres asked, thinking of her father's sword.

"Hurry along, little rat," Lucious said.

His comment exasperated her, but she would not let insulting words from a drunken coward affect her.

Excited as a spring day to finally be able to use her sword in real one-on-one combat, Ceres ran to the blacksmith's chalet and located her sword in the loft where she had left it. She sprinted back to the practice arena and took her spot across Lucious, who was standing ready with his own sword.

Lucious took one look at Ceres's sword, and his jaw dropped open.

"Where would a rodent like you get a weapon like that?" he asked with covetous eyes.

"My father gave it to me."

"Well, what a fool he must have been," Lucious said.

"And why is that?" Ceres asked.

"Today I will triumph over you, and when I do, your weapon will be mine."

Lucious lunged at Ceres, their blades colliding. Although Lucious was rather lacking in muscularity, gangly even, he was strong. After blocking a few blows, she began to doubt whether or not she would be able to win.

He slashed again but she resisted, and sword pressing against sword, they encircled as they stared into each other's eyes. She could see his hatred for her in those hazel irises, and she wondered what she possibly could have done to deserve it.

He shoved her hard so she had to move back several steps so as not to fall, and then he hacked at her from above, as she blocked from below.

A low rumble of excitement made its way through the bystanders.

Lunging, she slashed, but he retreated and wobbled a bit, his brow misted with sweat, his shoulders tense.

But then Lucious's eyes darkened, and he swung at her, rashly. She jumped over his blade, and just as she landed, she kicked him in the abdomen so he fell onto his back.

He didn't move for a moment, and Ceres wondered if he was unconscious. But a sudden shriek spilled out of his lips and he sat up. Leaning on his sword, he climbed to his feet while mumbling something underneath his breath.

"You're better than I thought, I'll give you that," Lucious said. "But I was going easy on you. Now I'm finished playing games, and you, little rat, must die."

Sweat stung Ceres's eyes, and she raised her sword as she exhaled several forceful breaths. She could feel Stephania's glare at the back of her head, and it made her want to triumph all the more.

Coming at her, Lucious attacked with all his might. She pretended she would meet him head on, but then swerved last minute and kicked her legs between his, and he tumbled to the ground onto his belly.

His sword skidded across the ground, stopping a few feet away, and then there was utter silence.

Lucious rolled onto his back. Ceres stood above him, holding the tip of her sword at his throat, waiting for the Empire soldier to call the winner.

But the soldier remained silent.

She looked up, and the Empire soldier still said nothing, an impassive expression on his face.

Glowering, Lucious climbed to a standing position and spit on the ground next to Ceres's feet.

"I refuse to acknowledge a girl's victory," he said.

Ceres took a step forward.

"I won fair and square," she said.

Lucious raised his hand and backhanded her across the cheek, the demoralizing assault causing several observers to gasp. Without even a second thought, acting only on rage and impulse, Ceres slapped him in return.

Right as her hand hit his face, she knew it was a huge mistake; yet there was not a thing she could do to take it back. Everyone had seen it, and although she wasn't quite certain what the punishment was for striking a royal, she knew it would be severe.

Holding his cheek, Lucious looked at her with wide, surprised eyes and for a few moments, it was as if time had frozen.

"Arrest her!" he yelled, pointing at her.

Ceres faltered a few steps back, time passing as if in a nightmare. But her mind seemed to not want to function, and before she could even think what to do or what to say, two Empire soldiers had grabbed her arms.

A moment later they were dragging her away, far from here, and far from the life she had almost had.

Chapter Fourteen

"Rexus!"

Rexus turned to see a frantic Nesos sprinting toward him, and his heart flooded with dread. Nesos had been dispatched on an important mission, so his being here couldn't be good, Rexus knew.

Nesos skidded to a halt right in front of Rexus, dust stirring the air, and rested hands on knees while he panted.

"I just came… from northern Delos and… the Empire soldiers are everywhere… saying new laws are being enacted, they are hauling off… firstborn men, slaughtering… anyone who refuses," Nesos said, still breathless, sweat running down his face.

Rexus's blood curdled. He shot to his feet and took off at a run toward the main entrance of the castle. He had to warn the others.

"Next they will attack Delos east, then west…and finally south," Nesos said, trailing after him.

Rexus had an idea.

"Take with you a few men and send every dove we have to warn our supporters," he said. "Ask them to meet below North Square as soon as possible and with as many weapons as they can carry. We will free these firstborns so they can join the rebellion. I will gather the supporters here and ride out immediately."

"Right away," Nesos said.

It begins here, Rexus thought as he ran toward the others. Today they would make a stand and kill in the name of freedom.

Within moments Rexus had over a hundred men and fifty women assembled in front of the cascading waterfall, ready on horses, weapons in hand. As he explained the plan to the revolutionaries, he saw fear in their eyes. A fearful warrior would not win any battles, he knew. And so he stood before them to speak.

"I see in each of your eyes the terror of death," Rexus said.

"Fear you not death?" a man yelled from the crowd.

"Yes, I do. I have no wish to die. But more than fearing death, my deepest fear is living the rest of my life on my knees," Rexus said. "More than fearing death, I fear I will never know freedom. And these firstborn men can help us attain that."

"But we have children!" a woman yelled. "They will be punished for our rebellion!"

"I have no children of my own, but I know the fear of losing someone dear. If we win, your children and your children's children will never know oppression the way we have. And would you not rather your children follow in your example of courage than your example of fear?" he said.

The militia grew ghostly silent, and nothing but the roar of the waterfall and the occasional neighing of a horse could be heard.

"Do not fool yourselves into believing the Empire will give you liberty," Rexus said.

"I, like many here, are with you, friend," a man shouted. "But do you think we have a real chance at winning this war?"

"The war will not be won today," Rexus continued. "Not tomorrow, even. But eventually, we *will* win. A people who demands freedom will in the end claim it."

Heads nodded and a few lifted weapons into the air.

"We are few. They are many," another man said.

"We, the oppressed, outnumber the oppressors a hundred to one, and as soon as we have enough supporters, we will triumph!" Rexus said.

"They will never permit us to usurp the throne," a woman said.

"Permit?" Rexus said. "You do not need permission from any king, queen, or royal to free yourselves from the bonds of oppression. Today, and every day from now on, give yourselves permission and fight to take back your liberty!"

One by one, the rebels raised weapons into the air, soon the sound of their cheers overpowering the waterfall.

The time, Rexus knew, had come.

⚜ ⚜ ⚜

As he rode toward Delos, followed by his men, the sound of the horses galloping in his ears, Rexus's thoughts turned toward Ceres. She had looked so thin and vulnerable when he saw her last, and his heart had nearly burst with emotion. Like every time before, he had been such a fool—had only kissed her briefly when he wanted to take her into his arms and keep her there forever.

From atop his horse, he saw the palace in the distance, and it haunted him to think of her alone amidst a sea of corruption, amidst the very wolves they fought against, her life endangered at every turn. He wanted to ride like the wind and save Ceres from such a place.

Ever since he could remember, he had wanted to marry Ceres; indeed, a large part of his motivation to join the rebellion was so that their future children could live in freedom. Yet, every time he saw her, his tongue twisted into a thousand knots, and he had never been able to say those words to her. He was a fool.

Riding to an uncertain fate, he suddenly realized that it wasn't true what he had said to the rebels just minutes ago. His deepest fear wasn't living the rest of his life on his knees. His deepest fear was that Ceres would have to do that, and that they might never have the chance to be together.

⚜ ⚜ ⚜

Rexus arrived at the North Square with his troops, heavy fog a dense curtain around him, the city of Delos breathing like a ghost town. The trip had been more gruesome than he could ever have imagined—bodies lying facedown, contorted in unnatural position, mothers holding their dead children, sobbing, houses pillaged and plundered, blood flowing down the cobblestone streets.

And this, he knew, was just the beginning.

The scout he had sent out reported that there were over a thousand Empire soldiers in the piazza—though it was difficult to see clearly in such weather. At the moment, the soldiers were preparing to eat, so it would be the perfect time to attack.

Rexus glanced back at noble faces and dear friends. Not a one had proper armor like the Empire soldiers had, although most had been trained sufficiently in battle. There was no way this small army of roughly two hundred could triumph over a thousand Empire soldiers. Had he led these brave men and women into a suicide mission? he wondered.

If the doves had arrived to their destinations, a few more men and women would be on their way, he knew, perhaps adding another hundred to the militia, but that was still not nearly enough to defeat a thousand.

"But hundreds upon hundreds of young men—firstborns—are locked up in wagons in the center of the piazza," the scout told Rexus.

"Hundreds, you say?" Rexus asked, his heart growing hopeful.

The scout nodded.

Rexus named thirty men, himself included, whose main goal would be to break open the locks of the wagons and invite the firstborns to fight with them, increasing the rebellion's numbers. The other men and women would fight off the Empire soldiers, distracting them from noticing their new recruits were being stolen.

By the time Rexus had solidified the plan, more than a hundred additional revolutionaries had arrived, ready to fight with them.

Rexus ordered Nesos, the scout, and half the militia to attack from the north, and then he waited with nervous patience until the scout returned, saying the rebels had arrived safely at the other side of North Square.

This was a significant moment, he thought. For centuries, the oppression had been a curse over the land, a chain around hundreds of thousands of people's necks.

Trembling, yet resolute, Rexus raised his sword.

"For freedom!" he yelled as he led the revolutionaries into battle.

As they rode toward the square, horse hooves pounding against the rocks below, every rebel held breaths of dread, but also breaths of hope, Rexus could feel.

I must be strong for them, he thought, despite the weakness that pollutes my heart.

And so he willed his horse forward even though he feared death would take him if he didn't stop.

Rexus rode his horse as far as he could onto the battlefield, toward the wagons filled with firstborns, until the congestion of fighters prevented him from riding any further. He let out a great battle cry as he threw himself into the fray.

Rexus raised his sword and stabbed one soldier through the heart, sliced another's throat, and drove his sword through a third's abdomen, the cries of wounded men all around him.

An Empire soldier pulled Rexus from his horse and came at him with his sword, but Rexus ducked and then kicked the soldier in the knee, a sickening crack of bone.

The next Empire soldier—a monster of a man—hit Rexus's sword out of his hand. Weaponless, Rexus flung himself at the soldier, digging thumbs into the man's eyes.

The giant shrieked and socked Rexus in the stomach so he fell to the ground. Another soldier came at Rexus, and yet another.

Soon he was surrounded, three against one.

He saw his sword only a few feet away and scurried on hands and knees for it, but a soldier stood in his way. Rexus snatched the dagger from his boot and flung it into the soldier's neck before grabbing his sword and hopping to his feet.

The giant, now with a spear in his hands, sprang toward Rexus. Rexus hopped back and hacked the spear to the ground and then stepped on it, breaking it. With all his force, he kicked the brute in the abdomen. Nothing happened. Instead, Rexus stabbed his opponent in the foot, but he was punished with a fist to the side of his head, and he went crashing to the ground, his ear throbbing.

He staggered to his feet, his surroundings spinning, and suddenly, he felt a sharp pain in his arm, warm blood spilling out from the fresh wound. He cried out.

After a moment he was able to see clearly, and he plunged his sword into the giant's lower abdomen. The Empire soldier fell to his knees and Rexus stepped aside as the soldier fell forward onto his face.

Shouts caught his attention, and he looked up to see the wagons crammed with the firstborn men a mere twenty feet away. He ran over to them, slashing more Empire soldiers on the way, and slashed the lock off the first door.

"Fight with us!" he yelled as the young men streamed out. "Win your freedom!"

Rexus ran to the next wagon, and the next, smashing the locks open, releasing as many firstborns as were imprisoned, asking them to fight. Most picked up swords of fallen soldiers and joined in the battle.

As the fog lightened, Rexus was saddened to see several of his men lay fallen on the cobblestones, his allies in eternity, his friends no more. But to his great joy, many more of the Empire soldiers lay lifeless, too.

"Retreat!" Rexus cried, seeing that he had accomplished his mission.

A horn blared through the fog, echoing in the streets, and his people fled from the battle, scattering into side alleyways, vanishing down main roads, raising hands into the air, their victory cries echoing through the streets.

He looked into the faces of the living—now friends for life—and he could see a fire kindled within each of their eyes. It was the spirit of the revolution. And soon that flicker would turn into a fiery inferno that would destroy the entire Empire.

Everything was about to change.

Chapter Fifteen

Ceres sat on the cold stone dungeon floor and watched the small boy beside her, squirming in pain, and wondered if he would live. He lay there, belly down, his pale skin white in the dimness, eyes halfway open, still recovering from a flogging in the market. He was awaiting his sentence, just like everyone else in this dungeon.

Just like her.

She looked around to see the cell filled with men, women, and children, some chained to the wall, others free to roam around. It was dark in here, and the smell of urine was even more prominent here than in the slaver cart, with no breeze to carry away the stench. The stone walls were slick with grime and dried blood, the ceiling looming over them like the weight of the world, barely high enough for her to stand fully erect in, and the floor was covered in smeared feces and mouse-droppings.

Worriedly, Ceres glanced down at the boy again. He hadn't moved from his position since she had been thrown in here yesterday, but his chest was still rising and sinking with silent breaths.

With the sun beaming in through the small barred window, she saw that the wounds on his back were healing with the fabric of his tunic stuck to it. Ceres wanted to do something—anything—to relieve his pain, but she had already asked to help him several times and there had been no response, not even a flicker in his pale blue eyes.

Ceres stood and tucked herself into the corner, eyes swollen from crying, mouth and throat parched from thirst. She shouldn't have hit a royal across the face, she knew that, but when she had done it, she had only reacted.

Would Thanos come for her? she wondered. Or were his promises just as rotten as all the other royals'?

The pregnant woman sitting opposite her rubbed her swollen belly, moaning softly, and Ceres wondered if she had gone into labor. Perhaps the woman would have to give birth in this wretched hole. She looked down at the little boy again and her heart ached when she considered it wasn't many years since Sartes was that size, and remembered how she used to sing lullabies to him until he fell asleep.

She tensed up when she noticed the silhouettes of two prisoners approaching before her.

"Who is that boy to you?" a gruff voice asked.

Ceres looked up. One of the men had a dirty, bearded face with angry blue eyes, the other was a bald man, muscular as a combatlord, the skin below his eyes covered in swirling black tattoos. The robust one smashed his knuckles together and they cracked, and the chain around his ankle clattered as he moved.

"No one," she said, looking away.

The bearded man leaned hands against the wall behind her on either side, confining her, his raunchy breath wafting into her face.

"You're lying," he said. "I saw the way you looked at him."

"I'm not lying," Ceres said. "But if I were, it wouldn't make one bit of difference to you or anyone else in here. We'd still be stuck in this prison, awaiting our punishments."

"When we ask you a question, we expect an honest answer," the tattooed man said, stepping forward, his chain rattling again. "Or are you too good for us?"

Ceres knew that playing nice or trying to avoid the bullies wasn't going to make them leave her alone.

As quickly as she could, she ducked, and darted past the thugs so she could go to the other side of the room where their chains wouldn't reach. But she didn't get far.

The tattooed man lifted his leg and the chain with it, catching Ceres's legs, causing her to trip and fall on her face. The bearded man stepped on the boy's back, and the little one shrieked in pain.

Ceres tried to rise to her feet, but the tattooed man wound his chain around her neck and pulled.

"Let the boy ... go," she croaked, barely able to speak.

The boy's cries pierced straight to her heart, and she tugged on the chain, trying to free herself.

The tattooed man tugged even harder, until she couldn't breathe.

"You do care, don't you? Now, because you lied, the boy will bleed to death," the bearded man hissed.

He gave the boy a swift kick in the back, the child's cry filling the crammed cell, the other prisoners turning their heads away, some weeping quietly.

Ceres felt her body come alive, a surge of power overcoming her like a storm. Without even knowing what she was doing, she found herself strengthening her grip around the chain and snapping it in two.

The bearded man stared back at her, stunned, as if he had seen a ghost rise from the dead.

Free from the chain, Ceres stood, took hold of the chain, and whipped the bearded man, again and again, until he cowered in the corner, begging for mercy.

With her insides alight, she spun around and faced the tattooed man, the force within still feeding her body the strength she needed to stop the aggressors.

"If you touch him, or me, or any of the people in here one more time, I will kill you with my bare hands, you hear?" she said, pointing at him.

But this one growled and threw himself at her. She raised her palms, feeling the heat burning within, and without her touching him he went flying into the wall across the room with a thud and collapsed onto the ground, unconscious.

A tense silence fell, as Ceres felt all the eyes in the room on her.

"What force is that?" the pregnant woman asked.

Ceres glanced over at her, then looked at the others; everyone in the cell was dumbfounded.

The little boy sat up and winced, and Ceres kneeled by his side.

"You need rest," she said.

Now that the fabric had torn from the boy's back, she could also see puss between the blood. If his wounds weren't cleaned, he would die of the infection, she knew.

"How did you do that?" the boy asked.

Everyone's eyes were still on Ceres, wanting to know the answer to that question.

It was an answer she wanted to know herself.

"I... don't know," she said. "It just... overcame me when I saw what he was doing to you."

The boy paused and as he lay back down, with weary eyes, he said, "Thank you."

"Ceres," came a sudden whisper in the darkness. "Ceres!"

Ceres turned and looked through the bars of the cell and saw the form of a person wearing a hooded cape, the torches in the hallway illuminating the black material. Was it a servant boy sent by Thanos? she wondered.

Careful not to step on fingers and toes, Ceres made her way over to the stranger. He removed the hood, and to her astonishment and joy, she saw that it was Sartes.

"How did you find me? What are you doing here?" she asked, her hands gripping the bars, her chest brimming with joy—and trepidation.

"The blacksmith told me you were here, and I had to see you," he whispered, tears in his eyes. "I've been so worried for you."

She reached a hand through the bars and pressed a palm to his cheek.

"Sweet Sartes, I am doing well."

"This is not well," he said, his face etched with graveness.

"It is well enough. At least they haven't said anything about..."

She stopped herself from speaking the unspeakable, not wanting to worry Sartes.

"If they kill you, Ceres, I will... I will..."

"Shush, now. They will do no such thing." She lowered her voice several notches before whispering, "How is the rebellion?"

"There was a battle in northern Delos yesterday, a huge one. We won."

She smiled.

"So it has begun," she said.

"Nesos is fighting as we speak. He was injured yesterday, but not enough to keep him in bed."

Ceres smiled a little.

"Always the tough one. And Rexus?" she asked.

"He is well, too. He misses you."

Hearing Sartes say that nearly brought Ceres to tears. Oh, how she missed Rexus, too.

Sartes leaned closer, his cape covering his arm, and then she peered down when she felt a sharp, cold object against her hand—a dagger. Without a word, only the silent understanding between them, she took the dagger and stuffed it down the front of her pants and then covered it with her shirt.

"I have to go before someone sees me," Sartes said.

She nodded, and reached tender arms through the bars.

"I love you, Sartes. Remember that."

"I love you, too. Be well."

Just as he vanished down the hallway, passing him, she saw the warden approach. She huddled back in the corner next to the boy, her hand stroking his hair, and the warden unlocked the door and stepped into the prison.

"Listen up, criminals. Here are the names of those who will be executed on the day after the morrow at sunrise: Apollo."

The boy let out a gasp, and Ceres felt him start to tremble beneath her hands.

"... Trinity ..." the warden continued.

The pregnant woman cringed and swooped her arms around her swollen belly.

"... Ceres ..."

Ceres felt a sudden sense of panic overtake her.

"... and Ichabod."

A man chained to the far end of the cell buried his face in his hands and sobbed quietly.

The warden turned on his feet and exited the cell, locking it behind him, nothing but the sound of his heavy footsteps marching away.

And with those few words, her death loomed.

Chapter Sixteen

Thanos stormed into the throne room, clutching the scroll signed by the king—the abominable document which contained Ceres's execution orders. His heart was thundering against his ribs as his feet pounded the white marble floor beneath them, rage churning through him from head to toe.

Thanos had always thought this room was spacious beyond reason, the arched ceilings ridiculously high, the distance from the massive bronze door to the two thrones at the end nothing but wasted space. Or tainted space. The throne room was the place where all rules were forged, and to Thanos, this was where all the inequality originated.

Advisors and dignitaries sat between red marble pillars on intricately carved wooden seats on either side of the room, twirling their golden rings, wearing their fine apparel, proudly displaying colored sashes, which ranked them according to their importance.

The sun shone in through stained-glass windows, blinding him every few steps, but that didn't prevent him from glaring at the king who sat on his golden seat at the end of the room. Soon, Thanos stood at the bottom of the staircase below the thrones. He hurled the execution order at the feet of the king and queen, who were at the moment speaking with the minister of trade.

"I demand you recant this execution order at once!" Thanos said.

The king looked up with exhausted eyes.

"You shall wait your turn, nephew."

"There is no time. Ceres is to be executed on the morrow!" Thanos said.

The king huffed and shooed the minister away. Once the minister had left, the king looked at Thanos.

"Ceres, *my* weapon-keeper, might I remind you, was thrown in prison by Lucious, and now she is being sentenced to death?" Thanos said.

"Yes, she smote a royal, and that is, by law, punishable by public execution," the king said.

"Did you know Lucious backhanded her first? And all because she triumphed in a sword fight he demanded?"

"How does this commoner know how to wield a sword?" the queen asked. "It is against the laws of the land to do so."

The king nodded, and the advisors mumbled in agreement.

"Her father worked as a swordsmith here at the palace," Thanos said.

"If he taught her how to wield the sword, they should both be executed on the spot," the queen said.

"How can you be a good swordsmith unless you know how to wield a sword?" Thanos pressed. "Being a swordsmith is not forbidden for a woman."

"This is not about being a swordsmith, or a swordsman, Thanos. This is about a commoner assaulting a royal on royal grounds," the king said.

The queen laid a hand over the king's.

"If I didn't know Thanos was promised to Stephania, I would think he was taking an interest in this girl," she said.

"I take no interest in her other than that she is the best weapon-keeper I have had," Thanos lied.

"Stephania said she had seen you on the palace training ground with ... what was the servant girl's name?" the queen asked.

"Ceres," Thanos said.

"Yes, Ceres. And Stephania said you held her arm."

"The girl doesn't have a home, and so I offered her to stay in the southern summer cottage for the time being," Thanos said.

"And who gave you that authority?" the queen asked.

"You know as well as I do that it used to be my parents' cottage, and it hasn't been used since they passed away," Thanos said.

"Stephania is a bright young lady with dignity and integrity, and she says she doesn't trust this strange girl. Has Ceres any credentials? Any official papers? She could be an assassin working for the rebellion for all we know," the queen said, working herself into a tizzy.

"Now, dear, let's not get all carried away. Do you really think the rebellion would send a female assassin?" the king said.

"Perhaps not," the queen replied. "Or perhaps they would, thinking a gullible young prince like Thanos would fall for a feisty warrior woman who sides with him against his family."

"No matter. The girl has her sentence, and to protect Lucious's honor, it will be carried through," the king said.

"You didn't think of protecting him when you sent him to compete in the Killings!" Thanos said.

The king scooted forward to the edge of his seat and pointed at Thanos, his eyes darkened with ire.

"Boy, you live in our palace and at the mercy and generosity of the queen and me. Do you really mean to defy us yet again?" he asked.

Thanos pointed to the Empire's banner to the right of the king.

"Freedom and justice to every citizen!" he bellowed, his voice echoing through the room. "The responsibility of the country's leaders is to protect the freedom of the people and to rule in justice. This is not justice."

"Stop with this nonsense," the king said. "The decision is final, and no amount of begging or senseless reasoning from you will change that."

"Then you must also imprison and sentence Lucious to death for what he did," Thanos said.

"Although I would not mourn the loss of Lucious for one solitary second, I will follow the laws of this land," the king said. "And if you interfere with my decision in any way, you will be expelled from court. Now leave so I can use my time on matters of importance."

Fuming, Thanos turned on his heels and tore out of the throne room, his pulse in his ears.

After he had marched back outside to the practice arena, he picked up a longsword. He went at a dummy long and hard, until there was nothing left but the wooden beam holding it, and then he hacked away at that, too.

Standing with the sword in his hands, he stood frozen as he panted for a long while, and then he flung the weapon as far as he could into the palace gardens.

How could the king possibly say he was serving justice? he wondered. Justice would mean every person had the same rights, privileges, and punishments, and Thanos knew that wasn't the case in the least.

He walked to the gazebo and slumped on a bench, his temple resting against his hands.

Ceres—what was it with her? Why did he need her the way he needed air? She had come into his life a breath of fresh air, her green eyes sparkling with wonder, her pale pink lips speaking words he knew he would never tire of, a quiet strength in her lithe body laced with vulnerability. She wasn't like the girls at court who would babble on about mindless subjects and gossip about others only to make themselves look better. Ceres had a depth to her, and every part of her was genuine, not a speck of pretentiousness to be found. And it was as if she saw what he needed even before he knew it himself—a sixth sense perhaps?

He stood up and paced back and forth in the gazebo for several minutes, wondering what to do.

When they had stood below the Stade, awaiting the Killings, he had asked her if he could trust her with his life. She had said yes. And although her voice had faltered with the answer, he knew she would sacrifice herself to save him if it ever came to that.

If he saved her, he would be kicked out of the palace. If he left her to her fate, he wouldn't be able to live with himself.

He pulled his shoulders back and took a deep breath.

He knew what he needed to do.

Chapter Seventeen

Although her eyes and limbs were heavy, Ceres, despite her exhaustion, hadn't slept a wink all night. The heavens were slowly lightening, she could see from the small barred window, and how she wished they wouldn't. With morning came her last few moments, and in less than an hour, she knew, she would be dead.

"Are you afraid?" Apollo asked, his head resting in her lap as she stroked his blond hair.

She looked at him and thought of lying. But she couldn't.

"Yes. Are you?" Ceres said.

He nodded, a tear in his eye.

She could feel him quivering beneath her touch, or was it her hand that was trembling so?

The pregnant woman looked at Ceres with alarm in her eyes when the faint sound of footsteps came from the hallway. The distant noise came closer and closer until Ceres could hear nothing but the drum of marching men, and before she knew it, the warden stood before the cell, unlocking it.

"Apollo, Trinity, Ceres, and Ichabod, come with me," he said, several other Empire soldiers waiting behind him.

With hands that barely would move like she commanded them to, Ceres helped Apollo stand up. Fully erect, the boy reached only to just above her waist, Ceres noticed, and she thought it an awful shame that he would never get to grow up to be the man he might have become.

When she let go of him, his legs gave out from under him and he collapsed to the floor.

"Sorry," Apollo said with doleful eyes.

Crouching beside the boy, tears burning at the back of her eyes, Ceres shot the warden an ugly glare and helped Apollo to his feet again. Careful not to touch the wounds on his back, she supported him as they went into the dim, torch-lit hallway, the other two prisoners following behind them.

The warden jerked Apollo to the front, a soldier on each side holding the boy's arms so he wouldn't collapse. Ceres, trying to calm her shuddering legs, was next, and behind her, Trinity, and the old man Ichabod. The chains rattled when the Empire soldiers shackled Ceres's and the others' ankles and wrists, and once the prisoners had been chained, two Empire soldiers guarded each of them, one on either side. Trinity rocked back and forth, holding her belly, and then Ceres heard that she started to sing an old lullaby—the exact one Ceres used to sing to Sartes to make him fall asleep.

Ceres could no longer hold back the tears, and at the thought of her brothers, of Rexus, it was as if her heart broke in two. Never would she see them again, never would she joke with them, break bread with them, spar with them. Those had been such happy times, she remembered, even though they had been tainted by her mother's cruelty. But she loved them, and she wondered if they truly knew that.

Down the hallway Ceres walked, her feet feeling like blocks of stone as chains dragged on the floor, the beautiful tune of the pregnant woman guiding her steps. Climbing the stairs out of the dungeon, Ceres saw that it was slightly dark out, a few stars still twinkling above, refusing to give up their light in the pre-dawn heavens. An open horse-pulled wagon stood in the courtyard, and Ceres was shoved into the cart with the other prisoners, the Empire soldiers' whips causing her to cower, causing her to hate the Empire even more.

When Apollo was unable to climb into the wagon by himself, an Empire soldier picked the boy up and flung him into the cart so he hit his head against the side of the wagon, a yelp escaping his lips as his head was thrust backwards with a cracking sound.

"How could you be so cruel?" Ceres yelled at the Empire soldier, before turning her attention to Apollo.

She scooted closer to the boy, staring helplessly at the unnatural bend in his neck, and ever so carefully, she lifted his bleeding head into her lap.

"Apollo?" she croaked, dread filling her chest when she felt how lifeless his body had suddenly become.

"I can't see…" Apollo whispered with a hoarse voice, his eyes glazed with tears. "I… can't… I can't feel my legs."

She leaned forward and kissed his forehead, and seeing he was struggling to breathe, she wanted to help him. But all she could do was to take his small, cold hand in hers.

"I'm here," Ceres said, the words almost getting caught in her throat, tears dripping down onto his filthy, torn tunic.

"Promise to hold my hand… until I am… dead," Apollo stammered.

Ceres, unable to speak a word, just nodded and squeezed his hand in her own, gently stroking the blond hairs off his sweaty forehead.

His eyes fluttered before they shut, and then she noticed that his chest stopped rising and falling as his face yielded to the mask of death.

She sobbed once and brought his hand to her lips before placing it carefully on his chest. Now, at least, he wouldn't have to face decapitation, she thought. He was free.

As they rode through the crowd, she couldn't stop looking at the poor boy, his small lips, his eyelashes, the freckles on his nose. She wanted him to know she was still thinking of him and that she wouldn't leave him alone in the cart, at the mercy of the Empire soldiers that stole his freedom and his life. Perhaps she needed him in some small way, too, to remind her that there weren't only cruel people in this world, and that innocence and kindness were still more beautiful than any power on earth.

The wagon bumped past a blur of hateful words and angry faces, but she kept her eyes on Apollo's peaceful expression. Not even when a rotten tomato hit Ceres in the cheek did she tear her gaze from him.

The cart slowed to a stop in front of the wooden scaffold, and the prisoners were commanded to leave the wagon. However, Ceres refused to leave Apollo, clinging to him.

An Empire soldier, the one who had thrown him, grabbed Apollo by his legs and jerked him out of the wagon from Ceres's arms.

"Murderer!" she cried at the top of her lungs, tears spilling out of her eyes.

The soldier tossed Apollo onto a stack of hay, and then started toward Ceres, but she scuttled into the wagon's corner, refusing to get out.

Following after her, the Empire soldier that had just had his appalling hands on Apollo stepped into the wagon. She would not allow him to get away with murdering such an innocent boy. Seeing the other Empire soldiers were busy forcing the other prisoners up the stairs to the scaffold, she saw a chance to avenge him. She might die trying—but she was about to die anyway.

When the soldier leaned forward to haul her out of the cart, Ceres looped the shackles bound to her wrists around his neck and pulled with all her might.

On his back, the soldier croaked and kicked arms and legs, his filthy fingers tugging at the chain, his face turning red.

But Ceres refused to let the killer go, pulling harder until his face turned purple.

In what seemed like a last-ditch effort to save his life, the soldier's hands strained toward Ceres's neck. She blocked with her elbows, and just as she heard other Empire soldiers clamoring, scurrying toward the wagon, the man in her arms went limp.

Even after she knew he was dead, she kept the chain taut for as long as she could, until two Empire soldiers tore her out of the wagon and forced her to the bottom of the stairwell leading up to the scaffold.

One of the soldiers pulled out a dagger and pressed the tip to her back, the blade piercing her skin a little. She took a step. And then one more.

Her feet in a disoriented march, Ceres climbed the stairs after the others, the clamors of the crowd a distant tempest, and just as she arrived at the top, she was released from her chains.

Her heart hammered against her ribs, she vaguely noticed, and her throat was dry, her eyes wet. Had the crowd grown silent? she wondered, unable to tell above the roar of her trepidation.

An Empire soldier pulled her hands behind her back, tying them. She didn't resist. There was nothing more to resist now, she knew. She might as well let death take her.

The soldier shoved her in the direction of a man wearing a white hooded cloak, holding an axe—her executioner.

She was ordered to kneel before a wooden block, but when she didn't respond right away, the soldier pushed her to her knees, her head falling forward. With blurred vision, she looked up and out into the crowd, her entire body trembling, her stomach churning with nausea.

"Do you have any last words?" the executioner asked.

She remained frozen, trying to grasp this really was it. Her life, was it over? No. It couldn't be. It had gone so fast, too fast, and suddenly, there was no more time.

"Well, have you something to say, girl?" the executioner pressed.

She did have something to say, but the words would not formulate in her mind.

The crowd grew silent, all eyes on her, and then the executioner blindfolded her.

On her knees, she reached forward, feeling for the block, sensing its smoothness beneath her fingertips, and resigned to her death, she leaned forward and rested her chin on the wooden edge.

Father, she thought. Sartes. Nesos.

Rexus.

Then, to her disbelief, an image of Thanos formed in her mind, and she finally realized that even though she loved Rexus, she had fallen for Thanos, too.

And just as she grasped that, she hated herself for it. She was happy he would never find out.

She swallowed the tears back, exhaled a breath, and the crowd went silent as she waited for it all to be over.

Chapter Eighteen

Rexus was filled with rage as he lay on a rooftop and watched thousands of citizens being held captive in Blackrock Square, surrounded by Empire soldiers who encircled the outer edge of the piazza, preventing escape. Standing before them atop a platform, General Draco was reading the king's proclamation, and each word deepened the rage in Rexus's heart. They were preparing to take away more firstborns, the best men the people had to offer. He tightened his grip on his sword, preparing for battle.

Yet seeing so many Empire soldiers, Rexus began to second-guess his decision to lead the revolutionaries into yet another battle they weren't entirely prepared for. The rebellion had grown, yes, but it was still barely over a thousand men. The only way to victory today was if the citizens below joined in and helped attack the enemy.

But would they?

When General Draco finished reading, he looked up and his narrow eyes raked the crowd.

"Before we collect the firstborns—a warning. Rebellion does not come without punishment!" he yelled.

He nodded toward his lieutenant, and the lieutenant opened one of the slaver carts that stood behind the platform. Rexus squinted his eyes, wondering who could be inside.

He was stunned to see captured revolutionaries hauled out of the wagon, Empire soldiers beating them with clubs toward the podium. Rexus felt as if he were stabbed in the heart. One of the twelve groups he had dispatched had been captured.

The soldiers chained the prisoners atop the platform and gagged them, and Rexus's ire deepened as he watched them dragging a kicking and screaming Anka up to the podium, chaining her to a pole, too, her clothes bloody, her face bruised.

Rexus narrowed his eyes, the sight of Anka up there—Ceres's friend—causing his blood to boil with fury.

"Lead us to the hiding place of the rebellion, and I will let these people live!" General Draco shouted to the crowd, his voice booming through the square. "Say nothing, and after these traitors have been tortured and killed, I will seize twenty of you, and then twenty more, and yet another twenty, until someone speaks!"

Clamors of panic went through the crowd as frightened mothers embraced their children. Yet the piazza remained silent, no one willing to offer up information.

General Draco nodded, and twenty Empire soldiers marched up onto the platform, holding lit torches, taking their places beside the prisoners. When the general nodded again, the soldiers pressed the torches to the revolutionaries' faces. Each man and woman screamed, the shrieks of pain burning Rexus's ears.

The onlookers raged in disapproval, but the Empire soldiers standing amidst the crowd forced protesters into silence with clubs, spears, and whips.

Incensed, Rexus knew he could wait no longer. Ready or not, the time had come.

Rexus jumped down from the roof and mounted his horse, galloping back to where he had left his group of men.

"We attack now!" he shouted.

His men grabbed their weapons and quickly assembled, their faces hardening with fury.

Rexus dismounted and felt for the small mirror in his pocket, the same one each of the leaders of the other groups carried. He turned his mirror in the sun, catching the light, reflecting it, the sign they had made that they were ready to attack.

One after another, bright lights twinkled at him from behind houses, until he counted ten. Eleven, including his group, had made it, meaning only one hadn't.

Rexus looked back at his group and nodded, his heart racing wild.

"For freedom!" he yelled as pulled his sword from its sheath and ran into the square, the revolutionaries following at his heels. Although his hands trembled and his throat was dry, he didn't falter in the least. All around him the other groups of revolutionaries dashed out from behind shadows and buildings, their roars filling the square.

Rexus hacked his way through the wall of Empire soldiers, and then past three more inside the square, his eyes glancing at the platform when he wasn't fighting. He needed to get there before it was too late, he knew, before they lost their lives.

"Fight with us and win your freedom!" he yelled to the civilians as he worked his way through the crowd.

Slowly, he noticed that the men around him started to fight the enemy with their bare hands.

Chaos erupted.

Empire soldiers took to attacking the citizens, butchering any and all who were in close proximity. Rexus redoubled his efforts, slashing down soldiers as he went. As his men swarmed the square from all sides, he looked up to see General Draco being ushered away beneath a mountain of shields. Rexus grabbed an arrow from his quiver, aimed it through a narrow gap in the shields, and released.

A moment later, General Draco cried out and fell, and was lying on the platform with an arrow in his shoulder.

The soldiers who had protected him turned toward Rexus.

"Arrest him!" a soldier yelled.

But Rexus was quick as lightning with his bow and he shot them down so swiftly, not one reached him. He dashed toward the poles, and with the help of other revolutionaries, released the prisoners from their shackles, freeing them before it was too late.

But where was Anka? he wondered, glancing around.

There was no time to search. Rexus stood at the edge of the platform and wound his bow, killing as many Empire soldiers as he had arrows.

Finally, the wall of Empire soldiers encircling the plaza broke open on the northern side, and women and children were rushed to the side streets, leaving only men left battling against their persecutors amidst the clanging of swords and groaning of men. Men fell on both sides, piling up in the streets which ran with blood.

Rexus hopped down from the podium, slaying soldier after soldier, fully engrossed in a battle he knew would either make or break the rebellion.

His heart broke a little more each time he saw one of his men or a civilian fall. He worked himself up into such a frenzy that he imagined he might never die at the hands of an Empire sword.

But just then, two soldiers came at him at once, one stabbing him from the side, the other pounding a hammer at him from above.

The blow to the head was sudden—dizzying—the sword in the shoulder a sharp pain that made a shriek tumble from his lips as he fell to the ground.

Momentarily, he could not see. Flailing his sword out in front of him, trying to defend himself, he felt another sharp stab in the leg.

He tried to focus his eyes, everything a blur.

An outcry made him recoil into a fetal position. The echoes of the battle surrounded him.

Now, he thought, now I die.

And with that thought, he knew Ceres would never know how much he cared.

But no sword punctured his chest. No spear was thrust into his abdomen. Instead, he heard grunts as swords collided.

When Rexus was finally able to focus his eyes again, he saw Nesos going at the two Empire soldiers, carrying a sword in one hand, a spear in the other.

Slowly, Rexus rose to his feet, the wound in his shoulder stinging, the blow to his head still making him feel dizzy, and the wound in his leg screaming. He fell over once, but stood straight back up.

Nesos buried his spear in one of the Empire soldier's necks, and feeling his strength return, Rexus sunk his spear deeply into the enemy's armpit.

A horn blared through the plaza, and the Empire soldiers looked up and began to evacuate toward the side streets. Mobs of citizens followed after and killed them.

The revolutionaries cheered, Nesos included. But Rexus couldn't lift his arm and his knees felt suddenly very weak.

Nesos ran toward him, catching him in the fall, helping him onto the ground ever so gently.

As stillness settled at the piazza, Rexus lay there and looked toward the Alva Mountains, toward the cave, the castle, where he knew the bulk of his men were.

His eyes widened. His soul cried.

The castle was engulfed in a fiery inferno.

The revolution was over.

Chapter Nineteen

Ceres's hair stood on the back of her neck as she waited for the axe to descend on her. The crowd had gone silent, and she heard her executioner raise his weapon into the air.

In that moment, her entire life flashed before her.

Yet, to her surprise, the blade never dropped.

Instead, she felt arms around her waist.

And a moment later, someone was hoisting her into the air.

She landed on her stomach, hunching forward, and realized she was draped across a horse's back, her legs on one side, her head on the other. Someone hopped onto the same horse right behind her, whipping it to a sudden start, and Ceres felt a strong arm holding her around her waist, preventing her from falling. She heard arrows swooshing by, hitting against armor or a shield.

The Empire soldiers yelled, the spectators clamored, but their voices slowly vanished as the horse galloped away.

The horse stopped after riding for a while, and she felt her new captor descend the horse. Then sturdy hands grabbed her waist, lifted her off, and set her onto the ground.

She removed the blindfold from her eyes and her breath stopped when she saw Thanos's face.

"Come," he said, taking her hand, pulling her with him toward the palace.

"Wait," she said. "Why … how …?"

She noticed her hands were still shaking, and she couldn't believe she wasn't yet dead.

He dragged her into the main entrance, her knees so wobbly she could barely keep up, confusion and anger and surprise reeling through her at once.

"We must speak to the king and queen this instant before the Empire soldiers hunt us down," Thanos said.

Ceres stiffened and snatched her hand from his, the thought of seeing the king and queen petrifying.

"No! Why?" she asked. "They ordered my execution."

Thanos pulled her behind a pillar in the vestibule, gently shoving her against the cold marble, looking into her eyes.

"I meant what I said at the Stade," he said.

She narrowed her eyes.

"You can trust me with your life."

When he leaned forward and rested his forehead against hers, she became breathless.

"And … I need you," he said.

Thanos lifted his hand and looked at Ceres's mouth while tracing her lips with his fingertips, his touch as light as a feather.

She shivered in delight, his scent all around her, his face an inch away, but the war between her head and her heart caused her to stiffen. She should not, no, she would not delight in his touch, she forbade her body. He was still the enemy, and for as long as she lived, he needed to remain that.

Reaching behind her head, he pressed his cheek to hers, the tenderness causing Ceres to let out a faint sigh. She felt his hand wrap around his waist, their bodies pressed against each other, warm, tender.

"But you must tell no one," he said, pulling away. "Come. We need to see the king and queen. I have a plan."

Against her will, she let him lead her into the colossal vestibule, and they ran past massive marble pillars that reached all the way to the high ceiling. Ceres had never seen the likes of such architecture; it seemed the palace was a building made by the gods. Silk curtains, shiny chandeliers, marble statues, and golden vases adorned the interior. Having just been in the dungeon, having lived in extreme poverty her entire life, it was as if she had been transported into another world.

Arriving at the second floor, he led her to an enormous bronze door and opened it. They stepped into a huge rectangular room, and at the end of red marble pillars, and rows of seats filled with finely dressed men and women, were two thrones. There sat the king and queen.

Holding Ceres's hand, Thanos walked toward the thrones.

The king rose, his face red, blood vessels protruding from his forehead.

"What have you done?" he bellowed.

The queen placed a hand on the king's, but the king only returned her gesture with a threatening glare.

"If you promise to spare Ceres's life, I will agree to marry Stephania," he announced.

Ceres glanced at Thanos sideways, wondering what he was doing, confused about his earlier advance.

"Do you think you run this kingdom, boy?" the king said, and then turned to the Empire soldiers. "Arrest them!"

"You will not arrest me!" Thanos yelled, taking a bold step forward as he pointed at the king.

But the Empire soldiers did not heed Thanos.

The king waved his hand and with that, Ceres and Thanos were grabbed again, and this time, both were hauled off to the dungeon.

⚜ ⚜ ⚜

Ceres stood by the bars, peering out into the dungeon hallway, her disbelief slowly being replaced with hopelessness. It hadn't even been an hour, and here she was again in this rotting hole, awaiting her fate. At least now they had the cell to themselves, no thugs to fear, but other than that, she knew her circumstances were bleak. Extremely bleak.

She thought of the others she had been brought to the scaffolding with, wondering if their sentence had been completed, if they were now one of thousands of casualties at the hands of the cruel Empire.

And then there was Apollo … Tears filled her eyes and she whisked one away as it fell.

She glanced over at Thanos sitting on the filthy floor, his dignity stripped with one word from the nasty king.

"I'm sorry," he said, leaning his head backward onto the dungeon wall. "I didn't think my uncle would throw us in prison."

"You couldn't have known," Ceres said.

"I should have."

There was a long pause, for what was there to say? Ceres wondered. Examining the events that had led them here wouldn't change their circumstances.

Thanos stood up and paced back and forth a few times.

"I misjudged the queen's desire to have me marry Stephania," he said.

He kicked the wall several times and rattled the cage so hard Ceres thought he might break the bars.

"Don't blame yourself for others' cruelty," she said once he had calmed down, their eyes connecting in the dimness.

"I should have never stopped that horse."

She held his eyes, his stare intense, the memory of his fingertips on her mouth and of his body pressed against hers still resonating through her.

She heard footsteps coming down the passageway, and when she turned, she saw numerous Empire soldiers throw a young lady and several men into the cell next to them.

She gasped.

"Anka?" she said as she peered through the iron bars, recognizing her.

Anka clamped bloodied hands around the bars, her body covered in burn marks, her lovely black locks gone, shorn in uneven lengths.

"Ceres?" she said, her eyes popping.

The Empire soldiers opened the door to Ceres's cell and pulled Thanos and Ceres out, dragging them down the hallway.

"What happened? Are my brothers well? Is Rexus?" Ceres yelled back at Anka, desperate to know the answers.

"There was a battle ..." Anka started.

But they turned the corner, and Ceres could no longer hear Anka's voice over the thrashing of the Empire soldiers' heavy boots. It crushed her.

"I demand you tell me where you are taking us," Thanos said.

The soldiers remained silent and pushed them forward, and Ceres's heart was racing the way it did when she was on her way to her execution.

Down the hallway they were shoved, and once they arrived at the staircase, the Empire soldiers stopped.

"Go," one said.

Perplexed, Ceres looked to Thanos. He took her hand, and together they started to climb the stairs.

What would await them at the top? Ceres wondered, finding it impossible to believe or hope she truly was free to go. Was there a wagon standing there to take them to the scaffolding? Were a dozen Empire soldiers standing in wait, ready to shoot them down with flaming arrows?

Thanos squeezed her hand, his face appearing much calmer than the raging anxiety she felt inside, and she wondered how he could be calm at such a moment as this.

Arriving at the top of the steps, Ceres saw the queen standing in front of them, her hands clasped in front of her body.

The queen glanced down at Ceres's and Thanos's joined hands and frowned.

"I spoke some sense into the king and he agreed to set you free so long as you solemnly swear to wed Stephania," she said.

"I swear it," Thanos said, tightening his grip around Ceres's hand.

"And with that, I expect you two to cease any and all contact other than when you are training for the Killings," the queen said, her eyes narrowing into slivers.

"Understood," Thanos said with a nod.

The queen stepped forward and locked cold eyes on Ceres.

"As for you, little girl," she said, "I have plans for you, and you might think you are glad to keep your life, but soon you will regret that you weren't beheaded on that scaffolding today."

The queen turned on her heels and marched away, Ceres now realizing it was quite possibly even deadlier inside the castle walls than out.

Chapter Twenty

Ceres arrived extra early the next morning at the palace training grounds, her mind still reeling from the events of the night before, from how close she had come to death. And most of all, from thoughts of Thanos. She owed him her life. And yet she did not know if she loved or hated him. And knowing Rexus was out there, waiting for her, she hated feeling this way about anyone else.

Anxious to take her mind off of all this and resume training with Thanos, Ceres focused on her work. With great care, she laid out the weapons she thought he might use in today's practice, and then she filled the drinking bucket with fresh water.

She was focusing when suddenly, out of the corner of her eye, she saw Lucious walking straight toward her, his eyes filled with loathing, his muscles rigid with aggression. She tensed. Not a single other person was in sight, and now she wished she had not been so early.

And then, when she saw *her* sword in Lucious's hand, her heart started to race.

She knew she couldn't fight him—he might have her arrested and thrown in prison again. But she couldn't not defend herself either, knowing he would have no qualms about killing her.

Then a thought popped into her mind. Had the queen set this up?

Alarmed, she glanced around to see if anyone else might be on their way, but she heard no voices and saw no one in the distance.

Approaching, Lucious scowled and took a threatening step in her direction, his hand squeezing the hilt, the blood vessels in his forehead protruding.

"Place the sword on the table!" Ceres heard a deep voice growl behind her.

She swiveled around and saw a stranger. He was dressed in the manner of the southern isles, his longer than usual tunic similar to those she had seen from those parts. His skin was golden, his shoulder-length black hair kept in a ponytail, and his posture was an erect board.

With dark, slanted eyes, he glared at Lucious with such intensity, Ceres was convinced the stranger could kill with his eyes alone.

Lucious pinched his lips together and laid her sword onto the weapon table.

"Now leave," the man said.

Lucious gave him a disapproving look, but did as the stranger said and stomped off with a huff.

"I take it you are Ceres?" the man asked.

She hesitated to answer, wondering if this man could be trusted. Perhaps he was an assassin sent to kill her by the queen, the queen's words bouncing around inside of her skull.

"Who are you?" she asked.

"You may call me Master Isel," the man said. "I am your new fighting master."

At first, she thought she had misheard him, especially when she considered the queen's last comment to her. But the way Isel looked at her, with respect and dignity in his eyes, she almost dared to believe what he had said was true.

"From now on, for three hours a day, I will train you to become a combatlord," he said. "I will instruct you like a man, so no man can ever touch you or triumph over you. Do you accept?"

Now she believed it was true, but why? And it surprised her that he even asked that question. Was *not* accepting an option? She knew even if it were, she would be a fool to decline.

"What is the purpose of this training?" she asked.

"Thanos sent me to you. A gift to make you strong. To give you what you so craved: a chance to learn to fight. To truly fight."

A shrill of joy erupted in her chest, and for a moment she couldn't breathe.

"Do you accept, or do I need to tell him that you so respectfully declined?" he asked, a twinkle in his eye.

"I accept. I accept," she said.

"Well then. If you are ready, let us begin."

She nodded and turned toward her sword to pick it up.

"No!" Isel said.

Startled, Ceres swiveled around.

"First, you must learn how to die."

Puzzled, Ceres squinted her eyes.

"Stand in the center of the practice arena," he said, pointing his sword toward it.

Ceres followed his instructions, and once she had taken her place, he walked a slow circle around her.

"Royal combatlords are expected to behave a certain way," he said. "When you represent the king, the Empire, a standard of excellence is required of you."

She nodded.

"There are specific death rituals, and you are expected to die bravely, with no trace of fear, offering yourself to cold-blooded murder."

"I understand," she said.

He faced her, his hands clasped behind his back.

"I see a lot of fear in your eyes," he said. "Your first lesson is to eradicate any traces of vulnerability, of gentleness, and most importantly, of fear from your countenance."

He stepped closer.

"Your mind is on other things, in other places. When you are with me, no *one* and no *thing* else exists anywhere!" he yelled with passion in his voice.

"Yes, Master Isel."

"To be a contender, as a girl, you must work twice as hard, three times as hard as the men, and if they sense any weakness in you, they will use it against you."

She nodded, knowing he spoke the truth.

"Your second lesson starts right away, and it is a lesson in strength. You are skinny. You need more muscle," he said. "Come."

She followed Isel down to the ocean side and he stopped at the jutting cliffs.

For the first two hours, he had her lift heavy boulders, throw heavy rocks, and climb the steep cliff.

Just when her body begged for her to be done, for the last hour, he compelled her to performed sequences of sprints and push-ups across the sand.

By the end of Ceres's lesson, her clothes were completely drenched with sweat and her muscles trembled from fatigue, and she could scarcely manage to walk back up to the palace where the other warriors were sparring.

At the top, Master Isel handed her a wooden cup.

"You will drink this every day," he said. "It is a tonic of ashes—good for strong bones."

She gulped the foul-tasting drink down, her arms so exhausted she could barely bring the cup to her lips.

"Tomorrow, I will meet you here at dawn to continue your strength training and more," he said.

Master Isel nodded toward a hefty blonde handmaiden, and the happy girl approached.

"Until tomorrow, Ceres," he said, walking away into the gardens.

"Please follow me, my lady," the handmaiden said and started toward the palace.

Ceres didn't think she could walk another step, but somehow, when she told her legs to move, she managed to follow.

The handmaiden led her into the palace, up four sets of stairs, and toward the western tower. Up at the very top of a spiraling staircase, they walked into a room. The bed sheets were made of silk, the drapes of fine linen, and a bed as wide as it was long stood against the northern wall.

Four dresses were laid out on the bed, two made of the finest silk, and two of soft linen. In front of the fireplace, on top of a white fur rug, stood a tub filed with steaming water, iris petals floating on the surface.

"Master Isel had this food ordered especially for you, my lady," the handmaiden said.

Her stomach growled when she saw a table covered in meats, fruits, vegetables, barley, beans, and breads. She walked over to it and devoured several mouthfuls of food, washing it down with wine from a golden goblet.

"May I help you undress for the bath, my lady?" the handmaiden asked after Ceres had finished eating.

Ceres felt a sudden rush of shyness come over her. Have someone undress her?

"I..." she balked.

But before she could decline, the handmaiden was tugging the shirt out of Ceres's pants, and once she was fully undressed, the handmaiden helped Ceres into the tub, the hot water enveloping her, soothing every sore muscle.

The girl proceeded to wash Ceres's skin with a sponge, and next, she worked on Ceres's hair, detangling it with a sweet-smelling honeysuckle conditioner, turning Ceres's hair as smooth as silk.

She climbed out of the tub, and the handmaiden dried her off, after which she rubbed oil into Ceres's skin. Then the girl applied makeup to Ceres's face.

"Your dress, my lady," the handmaiden said, holding up the coral-colored one.

First, she helped Ceres into a white tunic that reached her ankles and covered her shoulders, and then she dressed her in the coral dress, securing it with a golden brooch above each shoulder.

Studying the material, Ceres saw that the fabric was embroidered with golden thread, the pattern reminding her of lilies of the valley.

Finally, the handmaiden braided Ceres's hair into a partial up-do, and on her head, she placed a thin golden headband in the shape of a wreath.

"You are lovely, if I might say so, my lady," the handmaiden said with a smile as she stood back, admiring Ceres.

There was a subtle knock at the door, and the handmaiden answered it.

Ceres looked at herself in the mirror, hardly recognizing herself, her lips stained red, her face dusted with chalk, her eyes darkened with eye makeup. Although she was grateful for the food and the warm bath, she loathed how she looked like the princesses, the very ones she had her entire life hated.

Then she had an idea and turned toward the messenger at the door.

"Will you please tell Thanos I wish to have Anka, the girl who is in prison, for my handmaiden?" Ceres asked.

The messenger bowed.

"I will relay the message," he said.

The handmaiden closed the door and walked over to where Ceres stood.

"An invitation for you, my lady," she said with a bow.

Ceres picked the note off the silver platter and unrolled it.

Ceres,

If it pleases you, I would love the honor of your company this afternoon. It would be my greatest joy if you would meet me at the library.

Sincerely,
Thanos

Ceres sat down on the bed and tried to ignore the excitement that hummed through her at the thought of seeing Thanos again—just the two of them—at the library, of all places. She loved to study, and had frequently snuck away from home to read scrolls at the library just twenty minutes from her parents' house.

I mustn't feel excited at the thought of seeing Thanos, she commanded herself, the note dropping to her side. If she allowed her affection for him to grow, deceiving him, and then betraying him, would be so very hard to do. And she loved Rexus. How could she even consider such an invitation from the enemy they a few days ago jointly despised?

Accepting Thanos's invitation was dangerous, too, Ceres knew. Just yesterday the queen had ordered they not see each other outside of practice, and here Thanos was openly defying her command. Had he no fear?

It didn't seem so.

Had he really agreed to marry Stephania to save her life? Ceres marveled. It was the kindest thing anyone had done for her. Too kind, in fact.

She should tell him it was too much of a sacrifice.

Yes, that was what she would do: accept his invitation and tell him, after which she would remind him that he had agreed not to see her.

Chapter Twenty One

This will not end well, Ceres thought as she walked down the winding staircase from her room, her handmaiden leading the way. With sweaty hands, and a heart that refused to beat at a reasonable pace, every few seconds, she'd stop and almost turn back to her chamber. There, it was safe. There, Thanos wouldn't visit her, and she wouldn't hate herself for accepting his invitation and for being untrue to Rexus.

She stopped at the bottom of the stairwell and peered down the hallway at the dozens of marble columns that lined the passage, the handmaiden continuing on. The ceilings seemed as high as mountaintops, the floor smooth as a lake on a quiet day, and the mural paintings covering the walls depicted former kings, queens, beasts, and nature.

The handmaiden, now several feet in front of Ceres, turned around and waved.

"Well, come on then," she said. "Or perhaps you are too sore?"

She was sore, yes, but that wasn't the reason she wasn't moving. However, she knew she needed to do this so she pulled her shoulders back, took a deep breath, and strode forward.

Once downstairs, the handmaiden led Ceres outside and walked her through the courtyard and to the side of the palace.

They arrived at a separate building, the face of the library having six marble columns. In front was a small fountain with a statue of the queen at the top, the queen's steely gaze looking down at Ceres.

Even here she is watching, Ceres thought.

"Is there anything else I can do for you before I leave?" the handmaiden said with a smile.

Ceres shook her head and watched as the girl sauntered off.

"Ceres?" she heard behind her.

She turned to see Thanos standing there, a white toga draped around his body, his dark curls combed back neatly. Although more formal-looking than usual, it was a good look for him, Ceres observed. She tried not to like it too much.

"I almost didn't recognize you," he said.

"I look … not like me," she said, twisting her hands into knots.

"You look exactly like you, just a little cleaner," he said, the slightest look of amusement in his face.

He leaned in and inhaled.

"And you smell good," he said.

Of all things to notice, she thought, irritated, though she couldn't stop her heart from beating a little faster.

"Did I not before?" she asked, raising an eyebrow.

"Not as much as a girl," he said.

"Well, don't get used to it. In the arena, I'll still *not* smell like a girl."

He laughed heartily, and that made Ceres even more irritated at him.

"Shall we?" he asked, holding his arm out for her to take it.

Without taking his arm, she walked right past him and up the stairs toward the library. She heard him exhaling sharply behind her.

Stepping inside, Ceres gasped when she saw thousands upon thousands of scrolls stacked into wooden shelves on every wall. She had never seen so many writings in one place—the other library she had studied at was much smaller. Oh, how she would love to sit in this room for days and weeks and months and soak up all the knowledge that was in here.

The room was hot, the scent of wood and parchment inundating the musty air, and on the sides, by wooden tables, in between marble pillars, sat scholars dressed in togas, writing. There was a hushed reverence, and Ceres felt giddy to be here.

In the center of the library an elderly man stood at a marble slab, hunched over a scroll as he read. His head was bald, making his large ears more pronounced, and he had penetrating blue eyes that sat over a long, beaky nose.

He looked up and smiled, and immediately, Ceres knew she would like him.

Thanos walked in behind her and placed his hand on the small of her back, heat collecting there as he gently pushed her forward toward the old man.

"Ceres, meet Cosmas," Thanos said. "He is the royal scholar, among other things."

"I am honored to meet you," Ceres said with a nod and a slight curtsy.

"The honor is mine, my dear," the old man replied, his smile widening as he took her hand.

"What other sorts of things?" Ceres asked.

Thanos rested a hand on Cosmas's shoulder, his eyes filled with tenderness.

"Counselor, teacher, friend, father," he said.

The old man gasped a laugh and nodded.

"Father, yes."

Cosmas rolled up the scroll in front of him, but even though Ceres itched to know what was written on it, she didn't quite dare to ask to read it, thinking it might not be acceptable.

"You would never have known it, but you should have seen Thanos when he arrived at the castle," he said in a voice that sounded like it might crack any second. "He was such a scrawny little thing, one would never have thought he would grow up to look like a god."

Ceres laughed. Thanos stepped behind the old man and tapped his ear. Ceres nodded, realizing the man was hard of hearing.

"Thanos may have told you, but he lost his parents when he was but a babe. Such nice folks they were," Cosmas said, shaking his head, his lips tilting downward.

"I'm sorry to hear," Ceres said, glancing at Thanos, but Thanos said nothing.

The old man picked up the scroll, but before he could put it away, curiosity overcame Ceres, and she pushed her hesitation aside.

"May I read it?" she asked, forcing her voice to be louder than usual so Cosmas would hear her.

Thanos's eyes widened, and he had a look of disbelief on his face.

"What?" Ceres asked, feeling a little embarrassed from his stare.

"I guess ... I just assumed you couldn't read," he said.

"Well, you assumed wrong," she retorted. "I love studying everything I can get my hands on."

Cosmas laughed and winked at her.

"Although this isn't the largest library in Delos, it is the oldest and carries the writings of the greatest philosophers and some of the best scholars in the world," Cosmas said. "You are more than welcome to study anything in here."

"Thank you," Ceres said, letting her eyes scan the scrolls. "I could live in this place."

"Hold on," Thanos said, his eyes narrowing, his expression filled with skepticism. "What is it you have you studied, exactly?"

"Mathematics, astronomy, physics, geometry, geography, physiology, and medicine, among other things," Ceres said.

Thanos nodded, a look of wonder, and perhaps even a look of pride in his eyes, Ceres saw.

"Thanos, why don't you give the dear a tour of the rest of the library, and we can study when you return?" Cosmas said.

"Would you like to see it?" Thanos asked.

"Of course," Ceres replied, bubbles of excitement rising within at the thought.

Thanos offered his arm again, but just like before, she sauntered right past him, not taking it. He rolled his eyes.

First Thanos took her to the study room, then a lecture hall and a meeting room, before finally showing her out to the library gardens.

They walked in silence on the stone path, past statues of gods and goddesses, manicured bushes, vine-covered pillars, and endless beds of brightly colored flowers. A gentle breeze delighted her face, the scent of roses stirring into the air.

At the back of her mind, she remembered there was something she had planned to say to Thanos, but with him here, she couldn't seem to recall what it was.

"I must admit, I was quite shocked when you started to list off all the philosophies you had studied," Thanos said. "I'm sorry I didn't believe you at first."

"Well, in your defense, most commoners aren't schooled, and most royals think they know everything about everyone, so how could you have known?" she said.

He chuckled at the jibe.

"I'll be the first to admit I am ignorant in many things," he said.

She glanced at him sideways. Was he pretending to be humble? She couldn't tell.

"How did you become learned?" he asked, clasping his hands behind his back as he walked.

"My father's best friend was a scholar, and the scholar would let me sneak into the library and read. And more often than not he would even sit down with me and teach me," she said.

"I'm glad there are some reasonable men out there, encouraging women to study," he said.

Ceres glanced at him again, trying to assess if he were being genuine in his remark or not, thinking he couldn't possibly be.

"Cosmas is one of those men. If you would like, I could have him continue to tutor you."

Ceres was unable to repress an ear-to-ear smile.

"I would like that. I would love that," she said.

They walked on a while longer until they came to a half-circle of marble pillars. Thanos bid her to sit on the stone bench, and after she sat down, he sat next to her. When she saw the city and the sea beyond, she sighed, for it was so beautiful.

"I didn't realize your parents died when you were young," Ceres said.

He looked out across the city, his nose wrinkling slightly.

"I don't remember them, although I have heard quite a few stories about them from Cosmas."

He paused and pressed a hand next to hers, resting on the bench, their pinky fingers touching.

She couldn't help but notice how her stomach fluttered.

"I do often wonder what they were like, and especially what it would be like to have the love of a mother," he said.

"How did they die?" she asked, her voice soft.

"It's uncertain, but Cosmas thinks someone murdered them."

"How horrible!" Ceres exclaimed, placing her hand atop his without thinking.

Realizing what she had done, she was about to pull her hand away, but Thanos grabbed it before she could and held it tight.

They sat like that for a moment that seemed to span eternity, hearts beating strong, breaths ceased.

She would not look into his eyes, she told herself, for she knew if she did, something would happen. Something terrible. Something wonderful.

He placed a hand underneath her chin and lifted it so she had no other place to look but into his eyes.

And all of a sudden it was as if all the air had vanished from around her and she felt warm, warmer than she had ever felt.

His dark eyes flicked to her lips, and some unseen force drew her to him, pulling her away from her resolve to stay away, pulling her away from Rexus and all she had ever held dear.

With a soft smile, he lifted a hand and stroked her cheek, and Ceres could not for the life of her look away. He leaned forward, his lips finding her throat, so soft.

She took in a staggered breath while her hands knitted through his thick dark curls. She found his lips, warm, soft, and she moved hers across his, slowly, tingles spreading through her, and all that had ever been and all that was, was no more.

"Thanos!" Ceres heard, a female voice, bringing her back to reality.

She turned her head to see Stephania standing there, her lips pinched together tightly, tears in her eyes.

Thanos gave Stephania a hard glare.

"The king needs to see you," Stephania snapped.

"Can't it wait?" Thanos asked.

"No, it is of an urgent matter," Stephania said.

Thanos exhaled a slow breath, an expression of disappointment in his eyes. He stood up and bowed toward Ceres.

"Until next time," he said, and marched back toward the library.

Feeling quite embarrassed, Ceres rose to her feet and was about to leave, but Stephania stepped in her way, eyes seething.

"You will stay away from Thanos, you hear? Just because you are dressed as royalty doesn't mean you are one. You have nothing but commoner blood running through your veins."

"I…" Ceres started, but she was interrupted.

"I know Thanos likes you, but soon he will grow tired of you the way he does every commoner. And once you have given him what he wants, he will throw you out of the palace just like he did the other girls."

Ceres didn't believe Stephania for one second.

"If he has so many other girls, why do you want to marry him?" she asked.

"I don't have to explain myself to a lowlife like you. Stay away from my future husband, or I will find a way to make you disappear, do you understand?"

Stephania started back toward the library, but then she turned to face Ceres again.

"And just so you know," she said, "I will be telling the queen about all that I saw."

Chapter Twenty Two

Thanos paced nervously back and forth outside of Ceres's door, his hands sweaty, his throat dry, his armor too restrictive and hot. Nothing felt right. Nothing *was* right. Although he realized he had no choice other than to accept his uncle's orders, he knew Ceres would not understand and that she would be hurt and quite possibly hate him for it. And the worst part was, she would be in the right to do so. Even he despised himself for agreeing to do as his uncle had commanded, and he wished there was some way out of this nightmare of a predicament.

Thanos wiped the sweat beading on his brow, and cursed silently.

It was idiotic to pace about here like a drunken fool, he knew, for the king had commanded him to leave immediately, so there was no time. But Ceres deserved the truth from him even if it would cause a mountain of a rift between them. Even if his greatest fear came true—that she would never want to see him again.

Never.

He squeezed his eyes shut as the horror of that thought settled in. And then he realized there was another reason he was here. A huge part of him needed to see her again, in the event he was killed.

He shouldn't think of matters he had no control over, he reprimanded himself.

He gritted his teeth and knocked on the door, and once the new handmaiden opened, he stepped inside.

Right when Ceres saw him, her face went pale.

"Thank you for freeing Anka and for allowing me to have her as my handmaiden," Ceres said.

He glanced at the girl and nodded toward Ceres.

"Of course. Ceres, may I have a word?" he asked.

Thanos noted that Ceres's shoulders went tense, and an unsettled look in her eyes verified she knew something was terribly wrong.

"Of course," Ceres said.

"Perhaps we can take a walk," he said.

They went into the hallway and climbed the stairs to the rooftop, a warm breeze tugging at his hair. From here, Thanos could see the entire capital, houses built as if on top of each other, and he could even hear the riots on the streets.

He stopped at the veranda and faced Ceres. She was so beautiful, he thought, her white dress blowing in the wind, her strawberry blonde hair moving with the breeze. But it wasn't her beauty that made him adore her so. It was her thirst for life and learning, and the passion she carried for the people and things she loved.

He took a deep breath and looked her in the eyes before he spoke.

"King Claudius has ordered the royal army to annihilate the rebellion," he said.

Her lips squeezed together ever so slightly, and she turned away from him, looking across the city.

"Was that what the note was about?" she asked.

"Yes."

"And since you are in your armor, I assume you will be one of the ones enacting the king's orders," she said.

He didn't want to say, the words feeling like molasses in his throat.

"I wish I didn't have to, but I have no choice, Ceres," he said.

"One always has a choice."

Her voice was flat, but it was greatly constrained, he could hear, and he knew with certainty all she wanted to do was scream at him.

"How can you say I have a choice? You have no idea what it's like to live beneath the king, his eyes always scrutinizing you, the threat of death always looming around the corner."

"My brothers are out there!" she yelled, tears welling up in her eyes. "My friend Rexus. Will you kill them if you see them? Will you slay the very ones I love?"

His chest filled with a dull ache, seeing her upset, when all he wanted to do was to make her smile and make her feel safe.

"I realize you are angry—" he said.

"Because they are my people!" she shouted. "They are your people, too, Thanos. Can't you see you are fighting for a corrupt king, for oppression? Is that what you really want?"

Clenching his fist, he remained silent.

"You will be fighting against exactly what it is you yourself are trying to escape. Don't you see?" she said.

He knew she was right, but he had to do this or the king would have no qualms about throwing them both back into the dungeon, like he had threatened when Thanos tried to object.

He gripped the railing, clutching until his knuckles turned white.

"I have to do what I don't want to get the things I desire more."

She stood rigid as a board, her beautiful emerald eyes widening, her mouth open in shock.

"What more could you possibly want than for your freedom and for the freedom of your people?" she asked.

"You!" he said.

Ceres's eyes turned conflicted and tears welled up in her eyes. She exhaled a breath and gazed downward, wrapping her arms around her waist as if doing so would protect her heart somehow.

"I need to leave now. I just wanted to inform you where I went before I disappeared," he said.

"Don't go. Please," she whispered, her hands falling limp at her sides, tears rolling down her cheeks.

"I'm sorry, Ceres. I have to."

Her face morphed into a dozen shades of sadness and she let out a cry.

"If you do this, I won't ever talk to you again," she said, her voice shaky and not quite certain. "That's… that's a promise!"

He watched her run away, and although Thanos wanted nothing more than to go after her and take her in his arms, kiss her tenderly, he found his feet immovable. He stood quiet for a moment, anger and shame washing through him.

In order to save himself, he was about to give up all that he loved.

Chapter Twenty Three

Thanos rode toward General Draco, passing tent after tent, passing tens of thousands of Empire soldiers peppering the Alva Mountains, and he did nothing to hide the animosity in his eyes. The despicable general stood for everything that was wrong with the Empire. In fact, he hated the corrupt man just as much as he hated his uncle; perhaps even more. It was rumored, after all, that General Draco was the one who had killed Thanos's parents.

Thanos finally arrived and dismounted his horse and strode across the scorched grass toward the silver-haired general. The middle-aged man stood in front of his tent, his red cape waving in the wind, a bandage wrapped around his muscular shoulder above his armor. He had been wounded yesterday when Blackrock Square had been stormed by the rebellion, Thanos had heard. If only that arrow had pierced his black heart.

"Come, my new lieutenant," General Draco said.

Thanos did not want that title; the king had forced it upon him. And now that the Empire stood between Ceres and him, driving a deep wedge that could destroy any chance he had at being with her, he detested it even more. However, he valued his and Ceres's life, so he would honor the title until the rebellion had been squashed.

Thanos followed the general inside the tent, where they ended standing around the massive oak strategy table in the middle of the room, a map of Delos and figurines strategically placed upon it.

"Your uncle speaks very highly of your combat and strategy skills, Thanos. I hope you will live up to your reputation." The general spoke in a rushed manner.

Thanos said nothing.

"The rebellion has grown out of hand, and we must squelch it today," General Draco said. "The rebels attacked Fountain Square today, as we suspected they would, and at this very moment, Empire soldiers are forcing them out of the piazza, northward. The instant you leave this tent, you will lead a company of one hundred and twenty men to the north side of Fountain Square, to here."

The general pointed to the map.

"You will capture or kill the leaders of the rebellion, and bring them back to camp dead or alive."

Thanos's heart groaned because he knew anyone brought back alive would be tortured to death. It would be more merciful to kill them all, he thought, although he didn't want to do that either.

"This mission must not fail, and due to the king's high recommendation, I requested you for this task," the general said.

"I understand," Thanos said.

"And just in case you need motivation, your uncle told me to inform you, if you do not succeed on this mission, he will have Ceres thrown into the dungeon, and she will be used as bait in the next Killings."

⚜ ⚜ ⚜

With one hundred and twenty Empire soldiers and four wagons of weapons in tow, Thanos arrived about a mile north of Fountain Square, at the very street where the Empire soldiers would steer the rebels. He ordered his men to stack weapons in abandoned houses, set up traps on the streets, and carry the firepots onto the rooftops.

Thanos climbed to the roof with two dozen Empire soldiers, while the others hid inside houses behind closed shutters to wait for the revolutionaries to pass by. He stood there, pacing, waiting, hating himself more with every minute that passed.

Hardly five minutes passed when Thanos heard the first set of horse hooves pounding against the cobblestones. Still fraught with conflict about his mission, detesting how he was being used as a pawn in the king's game, he lit the tip of his arrow and waited for the revolutionaries to come galloping around the corner. He could not rebel outwardly against the king, he knew; and yet he could find a way to do minimal damage to the rebels, and especially to those closest to Ceres.

Within seconds, four men on horses dashed by, their blue ensigns waving in the wind. Before they could pass, they were shot down with arrows from other Empire soldiers, and fell wounded in the street.

Thanos's arrow was still in his bow. Sweat trickled down his cheek.

Quickly, the rebels were snatched up by eight Empire soldiers and thrown into a slaver cart to be taken back to the camp for questioning.

This isn't right, Thanos thought. He knew he had no choice but to slaughter them.

Or did he? Could he save these men and women they were ordered to attack?

A group of nineteen came next, and just as they rode past Thanos, the Empire soldiers on the rooftops tilted the firepots, the hot oil drenching the revolutionaries. Their shrieks pierced Thanos's heart, and he had to look away from the writhing bodies on the streets. Once the hot oil had cooled, all nineteen were thrown into a slaver cart to be taken back to camp.

Just as the Empire soldiers had finished clearing the streets, hiding the evidence of the attack, another small group of riders came galloping toward them.

"Rexus!" Thanos heard one of the men yell.

Immediately, Thanos remembered Ceres had mentioned that name when they had spoken on the rooftop of the palace, and his gaze scanned the revolutionaries.

A muscular blond man turned his horse around and steered it to the side of the street, waving.

Behind the small group rode a slew of revolutionaries, but before they arrived at the attack site, Thanos killed the flame on his arrow, hopped down from the roof and into an alleyway, lying in wait for Rexus to pass by.

Before Rexus came close enough, a mob of Empire soldiers stormed out from the houses and started slaying the revolutionaries.

Rexus, Thanos could see, startled at the surprise attack, but quicker than eyes could follow, Rexus pulled one arrow after another from his quiver, shooting his enemies down, killing every single one he shot.

Once his arrows had been depleted, Rexus hopped down from his horse and pulled his sword, slicing Empire soldiers down left and right with the speed and precision of a combatlord, Thanos saw.

Thanos dashed out from the alleyway and tore after Rexus, his sword held high, pretending he was going to attack. He wanted to get to the young man before anyone else had a chance to slay him dead.

He snuck up behind Rexus and wrapped an iron arm around his neck, and with a hand clasped around the young man's mouth, Thanos dragged him into the dimness of the alleyway.

But Rexus was strong, and he wrestled out of Thanos's grasp, drawing his sword.

Thanos held his hands out in front of him and dropped his sword to the ground.

"I mean you no harm!" he yelled, retreating deeper into the shadows, hoping Rexus would follow.

Rexus slashed at him with a force that had Thanos hopping backwards, frightened he had made a mistake and that this could be his last hour. Rexus lunged and spun around, whirling like a tornado after Thanos, the sword slicing through the air, making a swooshing sound.

"Ceres told me you were her friend!" Thanos said. "I want to help you!"

Rexus paused for a moment, staying his sword.

"This is a trap," he said.

"No. She was worried about you. She knew I would fight, and she mentioned her brothers. She mentioned you."

Rexus hesitated.

"Stay here and you will not be killed," Thanos said.

"I won't leave my men out there to die!" Rexus growled.

Of course he wouldn't, and Thanos should have known that. But he was doing this on the fly, with no time to plan.

As quick as a flash, Thanos snatched an arrow from his quiver and shot Rexus's sleeve, the arrow wedging into the wall behind Rexus, confining him.

The distraction gave Thanos just enough time to dash behind Rexus and knock him on the head with the hilt of his sword.

Rexus fell to the ground unconscious and Thanos exhaled a breath of relief. He might not be able to save everyone, Thanos knew, but at least he had saved one of Ceres's friends' lives.

Thanos climbed back onto the rooftop and looked down toward the street. Many Empire soldiers had fallen—many more than he thought would. He saw the opportunity to save the revolutionaries, yet to make it look like he had made the best decision for his own men. No one would blame him for retreating if he judged that his men were being butchered, losing sorely.

"Empire soldiers retreat!" he shouted. "Retreat immediately!"

A few of the Empire soldiers looked up with questions in their eyes, but Thanos knew they would follow his orders. Empire soldiers were trained to obey no matter the command.

The soldiers on the rooftops trickled down one after another, heading toward the wagons, and the soldiers battling the revolutionaries in the streets and inside houses retreated toward the wagons while fighting the enemy off.

Seeing his men were safe, Thanos was just about to join them, but then a faint sound behind him caught his attention. He glanced back to see a young revolutionary, a sword in one hand, a spear in the other.

Thanos drew his sword and took a step toward the man.

"I have no desire to harm you," he said.

Screaming, the young man came at Thanos, the tip of the spear pointing straight toward Thanos's heart.

Thanos spun around and hacked the spear out of his opponent's hand. The young man slashed, but missed, and before the young man could withdraw his arm, Thanos had sliced it open.

"I do not wish to kill you!" Thanos said again, taking a cautious step back. "Walk away and you will live."

"Anything from an Empire soldier's mouth is a lie!" the young man said.

The young man cried out and his jaw clenched, and in no time he was back at Thanos, jabbing.

"I know you are Prince Thanos!" the young man said, stabbing toward him.

"Correct. And who are you?" Thanos asked, blocking.

"That I will tell you once I have run my sword through you," the young man said.

"I must warn you, I have yet to lose a duel."

The young man's eyebrows rose, no fear present in his face.

"There must always be a first!" he yelled.

The young man sped toward Thanos, their swords crashing then, a power struggle, blade against blade. Shoving with a roar, Thanos pushed him away, but the young man was at him again. He was powerful, Thanos noticed, rage, anger, and passion for his cause probably fueling his strength.

The young man stabbed toward Thanos, but missed as Thanos swerved out of the way.

Thanos didn't want to kill him, but it would seem the young man would not stop until one of them was dead. In a split second, Thanos decided he would try to outrun him.

However, before Thanos could remove himself from the duel, the young man drove for Thanos's heart, but Thanos shifted so the young man tumbled forward.

And as he did, he fell, the blade ending up buried in his own abdomen instead.

The young man fell to the roof with a grunt, and as he drew the sword out of his stomach, he screamed.

Thanos took a few steps toward his enemy.

"Kill me," the young man said, a tinge of fear in his eyes.

Thanos gazed at the young man for a few moments, a feeling of sadness overwhelming him. He slid his sword back into its sheath and turned to walk away.

"I am dying," the young man grunted.

Thanos felt overwhelmed with sadness for him. He shook his head.

"You are," he said, seeing how grievous the wound was, realizing nothing could be done for him.

"I didn't tell you my name," the boy gasped.

Thanos nodded, waiting.

"Then tell me," he said, "and I shall make sure it is known that you died an honorable death."

"My name," he gasped, "is Nesos."

Thanos stared back in horror. Nesos. Ceres's brother.

And as Nesos fell down, dead, Thanos knew his life would never be the same again.

Chapter Twenty Four

When Thanos entered the throne room, he noticed the tension right away, the king screaming at General Draco, the dignitaries arguing in their seats, gnashing teeth, and the queen spewing obscenities to an advisor. Everyone was here, he saw, even the princes and princesses who weren't usually at meetings such as this. And for good reason.

On his way back, Thanos had seen the slaughter. Houses had been burned to the ground, and citizens—men, women, and children—were left butchered in the streets, stray dogs eating at their flesh, crows pecking at bodies. A few poor souls had been nailed to the trees, while others hung from nooses. But so many Empire soldiers had died, too, and the revolutionaries weren't any kinder, torturing, desecrating bodies in vile ways and even dismembering them.

He knew this was not a war he wanted to be a part of. Not now. Not ever.

"The rebellion has grown beyond what anyone imagined it could, and now the few revolutionaries have become a monster, that if not slain soon, will vanquish the Empire," General Draco said, standing in front of the king and queen.

Once Thanos reached the bottom of the stairwell below the thrones, the room slowly grew silent.

The king did not reply to the general, but turned his attention to Thanos.

"I send my nephew out on one assignment," he said. "One measly assignment, and what happens? He fails miserably, embarrassing himself and the entire royal family in less than an hour. What have you to say for yourself, Thanos?"

Thanos pinched his lips together, in an attempt to prevent himself from telling his uncle he had failed on purpose.

"It was not just him," General Draco said. "Many failed. As I told you before, we must call in more soldiers from the north. If not, you will lose more battles and we will have a war on our hands."

Thanos was surprised that General Draco stood by him.

"If we don't keep losing, we won't have to bring in more troops," the king said.

"Perhaps, but it doesn't change the reality that we are bleeding more men than what the rebellion is birthing," General Draco said.

The king thought for a moment, running his fingers through his beard, and Thanos was glad the attention was no longer on him.

"I hesitate to call in the troops from the north. It will be days before they arrive," the king said.

"With all due respect, sire, what else can we do?" General Draco asked.

"Are there any other proposals?" the king asked, an open question to the dignitaries in the room.

"We should poison the wells in the city," one said. "And only supply water to the peaceable citizens."

"That might work, but the revolutionaries would only become angrier," the king said. "Perhaps we can offer a deal, a sign of good will, and that will calm their rage."

"Open the king's food storage vaults. Feed them," another said.

The king paused for a moment before nodding.

"Perhaps," he said. "Any other suggestions?"

"Might I speak a word?" the queen asked, eyes cunningly watching Thanos.

All gazes in the room slid toward her.

The king gestured with a hand, allowing her to speak.

"I propose a union between a commoner and a royal, a nuptial between the people and the Empire," she said.

"What did you have in mind, exactly?" the king asked.

"A marriage between Thanos and Ceres," she said.

Gasps went through the throne room, expressions of horror and disbelief painting the advisors' faces.

Thanos was stunned by the queen's suggestion as well. Of course he would have no qualms about marrying Ceres, but for political purposes and to be a puppet in the king and queen's play? He didn't like that one bit. He didn't want them to defile the one thing that was the most precious in his life.

"I think that is an excellent idea," the king said. "A union between a lowly commoner and a royal. The people will love it."

"Thanos was promised to me!" a girl's voice boomed through the room.

Thanos swiveled around, and way in the back of the room stood Stephania, her body rigid, yet her eyes wounded.

Stephania walked down the hallway toward the thrones.

"You may not approach!" the queen yelled. "Go back to your seat and close your lips for the remainder of this meeting."

Stephania stopped in her tracks and looked at Thanos, her cheeks glistening with tears, he could see.

Not until now did he feel sorry for the princess. He had never wanted to marry her, but even she was just a pawn in a game they could never escape.

Thanos nodded at Stephania and gave her as empathetic a look as he could. Perhaps now she would back away, knowing it was not Thanos's decision to wed someone else. Perhaps it would finally set her free.

Stephania turned around, her feet hesitantly taking steps away from Thanos. Then she sped up and continued out the bronze doors at the end, running, her sobs vanishing as the doors closed behind her.

"I think it will put an end to the feud. At least for now," the king said. "Are you in agreement, Thanos?"

The king stared at Thanos, his eyes intense with power, as if with a warning: if Thanos didn't accept, it would be the dungeon for Ceres and him. The king knew his weakness was Ceres, and Thanos was furious with himself for having been so open about it. He should have hidden his affection for Ceres, should have known the king would sooner or later take what was most precious to him and use it against him.

Here he was again without a choice, and Thanos's heart twisted in defiance when he nodded.

"Then let it immediately be broadcast from every watchtower across the city!" the king bellowed. "And by the gods, let us hope it works."

Thanos stood in shock. He didn't think it would be announced so soon.

"Should we not ask her first?" Thanos said.

A few of the dignitaries chuckled.

"It is not a question, but a command, but if you want to let her know before she finds out some other way, you had better run," the king said.

At once, the bells tolled through the city, signaling a royal announcement, the sound igniting Thanos to take action.

He turned on his heels and ran toward the bronze door at the end, and toward Ceres's chamber, hoping he could tell her before it was too late.

But how could he ask her for marriage when he had just slaughtered her brother?

Would he be able to keep it secret?

Chapter Twenty Five

Horrorstruck, Ceres stood by the window in her room overlooking Delos, the skyline filled with putrid black smoke rising from burning homes. Clamors filled with unspeakable pain reached all the way to her tower, and families with little ones rushed by in the street below, their faces obscured by panic.

For the past hour or so, she had done nothing but cry—cry for her people, cry for her friends, cry for her brothers, for they could be dead. And Rexus? It was more than she could bear to think about.

Unable to watch the dreadfulness unfold any longer, she walked over to the bed and sat, but just a moment later, she had to return to the window, thinking if she didn't remain there, she was somehow betraying her people.

This? This was what Thanos was fighting for? She was still as furious with him as she had been when he left. He had somehow gotten to her, weaseled his way into her heart, made her care. She had hoped he was different from all the other greedy, power-hungry royals, but when it came down to it, he was the same, and chose to fight for the inequality and injustice that cursed this land.

There was a knock at the door, and Anka opened it.

To Ceres's surprise, and great irritation, in walked Thanos.

"May I have a word in private?" he asked.

"No you may not," Ceres said, glancing back out the window again.

"Please. It is of utmost importance," he said.

After a few moments of hesitation, Ceres nodded to Anka, and the girl left, closing the door behind her.

Ceres stood immovable beside the window, her gaze still on the street below.

"Ceres," Thanos said.

Unwilling to face him, she kept looking out the window.

"What do you want?" she asked.

"I realize you are upset with me for leaving, and I remember you said you never wanted to talk to me again. But can we for just a few minutes set our differences aside?" he said.

She glanced at him, considering his comment.

"I have something important to discuss with you," he said. "What I have to say may save many lives."

"All right," she said.

She walked over to the chair in front of the fireplace and sat down, and he followed after, taking a seat straight across from her.

She could see he was anxious, his eyes shifting nervously about as if he were carefully considering what to say, but it did nothing to make her less angry with him; she simply couldn't forget that when he had left to fight, it had crushed her and destroyed all trust they had built.

"Well?" she said after he hadn't said anything for a while.

"I need you to listen with an open mind," he said. "And heart."

She stared back.

"I just came from a meeting with the king and queen, and they believe there is a way to end all the fighting."

Now her interest was piqued, although her guard was still very much up.

"They suggested a marriage between a commoner and a royal," he said.

Ceres nodded.

"I can see where that might work," she said.

Thanos's shoulders relaxed a little and his face lit up.

"You do?"

"If there is a union between the common people and a royal, perhaps the people will think there will be a change."

Ceres looked him in the eyes, and even though she was as livid with him as she had ever been with anyone, and wanted to wring his neck in a fist fight, she also wanted to be closer to him, for him to close the distance between them and kiss her on the neck the way he had before.

She looked away. Those thoughts, those feelings—she would quash them with every fiber of her being until she could no longer remember them ever being there.

"Did they have anyone in mind?" she asked, thinking perhaps Anka since she had just come from the rebellion.

"Yes," he said.

He stood up and strode two steps, vanquishing the distance between them. He knelt down before her, and it puzzled her why he would do such a silly thing.

"I have something for you," he said.

From a small leather pouch hanging around his waist he pulled out a golden bracelet with a charm in the shape of a swan. Handing it to her, he smiled softly.

"It was my mother's," he said.

Even with how mad she was, she didn't want to offend him and refuse the gift he had just offered her—it was probably the most valuable thing he owned. But did he expect her to forgive him because he gave her a present? How shallow did he think she was? How easily did he think she would forsake her principles? She would not be bought, not ever.

She opened her mouth to speak, but he spoke first.

"Ceres, it is you and I they suggested."

She stared back, floored.

"I would be honored to have your hand in marriage," he added.

She couldn't speak, for suddenly there was a lump in her throat. She would not cry, no, she would not. He might think her tears happy, when all they were, were tears of sadness and resentment, of lost trust and lost friendship. There was no way she could say yes, she knew.

She thought of Rexus, fighting for freedom, risking his life day in and day out in hopes of offering liberty to all. Thanos, he fought against all that, and she could not love someone or marry someone like him. And here Thanos was proposing to her because the king thought it would lull the citizens into believing it might lead to equality. She knew it would not.

"It is not under ideal circumstances, but you have to know, before they suggested it, I had already fallen for you," he said. "I meant what I said on the roof. More than anything, I want you."

She looked away, still hurt and unable to open her heart to forgive.

"I went out to fight, Ceres, but when I did, I couldn't get myself to kill the revolutionaries."

She glanced at him, the news melting some of her anger away.

"I saw Rexus. I pulled him into the alleyway with me and knocked him on the head so he wouldn't be killed by the Empire soldiers," Thanos said.

"Truly?" she asked.

He nodded.

"But there's more."

Ceres nodded, now willing to listen, now feeling ashamed she had been so hard on him.

"I saw your brother Nesos."

She reached for his hand and he took it.

"You did?" she asked, hope filling her chest.

"We fought on the roof top. I didn't know it was him. I didn't…"

"What happened?" she asked.

Thanos paused, and looked up at her with tears in his eyes, and she knew. She knew that look, the look of holding dreadful information from a loved one. The look of pain before it had been shared.

"He fell onto his sword and it stabbed him in the abdomen. I told him I didn't want to hurt him, but he—"

She shot to her feet so fast, the chair behind her screeched across the floor. There was simply nowhere to put the pain that was overpowering her, nowhere to contain something so mighty, nowhere to hide it or store it. It was everywhere all at once.

"MURDERER!" she shrieked, unable to stop herself from crying. "MY BROTHER!"

He stood there, looking dazed.

"I hate you, and abhor everything you stand for!" she yelled.

His eyes flinched, and he exhaled a defeated breath, the hand holding the bracelet falling into his lap.

"Now get out!" she said.

"Ceres, please don't do this," he pleaded.

"Get out!" she yelled. "I said I never wanted to see you again, and I meant it!"

Her chest tightened, her throat clenched shut. She had fallen for him, too, but her heart was foolish, she knew, and this more than anything proved it.

He rose to his feet and stood still for a moment, sorrow canvassing his face.

"I'm sorry, Ceres."

He walked away, leaving the door open behind him.

She turned to the window and wept. Nesos. Her brother. Gone forever. She could hardly breathe with grief.

Hardly had she caught her breath when she heard a sound behind her. She spun, assuming Thanos had returned, preparing to shout at him to leave—but was shocked at who she saw.

The queen.

She stared back haughtily, an evil grin upon her face.

"Hello, Ceres," the queen said, walking into the doorway, eyes rumbling with menace. "How did the proposal go?"

She grinned, stepping closer.

"As Thanos's future bride, your life belongs to the monarchy. It is my responsibility as your queen to see that you are protected. For starters, you will not leave this room unless you are permitted, and for now, I forbid it."

The queen suddenly turned, walked out, and slammed the door shut. Ceres heard a key being thrust into the keyhole.

Enraged, she ran to it and wrapped frantic hands around the door handle, pulling on it with all her might.

But it was too late. The door had been locked, and there was nothing to do but give up, she realized.

She fell to her knees with uncontrollable sobs, slamming her fists on the heavy oak, Nesos's name spilling from her lips.

And yet, amidst her cries, unbeknownst to her, she sometimes confused his name with Thanos's.

Chapter Twenty Six

Ceres didn't know exactly how long she had been sitting on the stone floor in her chamber—it could have been minutes, or hours—tear after tear trailing down her face. It was eerily quiet outside, the riots having ceased. Likely, the news of her and Thanos's marriage announcement was pacifying the leaders of the rebellion. She doubted it would last long.

Oh, how she wished she hated Thanos; and yet her heart was a villain, betraying everything she ever held dear. Sadness overwhelmed her, and she tucked her knees into her chest and sobbed quietly for a moment.

This is what I deserve, she thought as she sat up straight and wiped the wetness from her cheeks, staining the silk sleeves. She hadn't played her cards well, she realized, in this royal game of power and intrigue. And it was becoming clear that if she were to remain at the palace and marry Thanos, she would have to learn how to beat the royals at their own game.

Had she made the right choice in rejecting Thanos? She thought she had, but why then, whenever she thought about his forlorn face when she had rejected him, did it feel as if everything was wrong?

On the other side of the door, keys rattled, and then someone inserted a key into the keyhole. Expecting the queen or an Empire soldier, she scuttled away from the door on hands and knees and dried her tears.

When the door opened, Anka stood in the doorway. She strode into the room and shut the door behind her.

Ceres hopped to her feet, a feeling of elation rushing through her. She ran to Anka and threw arms around her, squeezing tightly.

"You need to get out of here before we are discovered," Anka said. "Go seek out Rexus. The rebellion's new headquarters are down by fisherman's bay, inside Harbor Cave."

Ceres knew the cave well, having played there many times with her brothers growing up. She looked at Anka, so small and lovely, and she could not bear to leave her friend here alone amidst the wolves.

"Come with me," Ceres said, grabbing her hand.

"I cannot. I must stay here until my mission is complete," Anka said. "But here, take this."

Anka slipped her gray hooded cape off and draped it around Ceres's shoulders.

"How will I ever repay you?" Ceres said, embracing Anka again.

"You owe me nothing," Anka said with a smile.

Ceres nodded, remembering speaking those exact words when she rescued Anka from the slaver cart.

"On second thought," Anka said with a smirk, "join the rebellion and make them pay for every person that was ever forced into slavery."

"I will," Ceres said.

Just before Ceres left, she snatched her sword from beneath the bed and fastened the scabbard around her waist. She drew the hood over her head and darted down the stairwell, thrilled to finally be joining the rebellion from within, to stand beside Rexus in the fight for liberty.

She ran down the corridor, eyes peeled, ears alert, her heart galloping. She knew exactly where the guards stood watch, and as she maneuvered through the palace, she made sure to avoid those areas. Moving swiftly, quietly, and above all, in the shadows, she made herself invisible. She reached the kitchen and weaved through boxes of food and past cooks and servants busily working on the royals' next meal.

Stepping into the courtyard, she slunk behind crates of wine and carts of food, passing slaves and Empire soldiers who had their attention elsewhere.

Just as she exited the side gates, she saw an Empire soldier holding up a scroll, speaking from the platform right in front of the palace, dozens of citizens huddling around.

"It has been declared that Prince Thanos will marry the commoner, Ceres. Due to this union, King Claudius and the rebellion have agreed upon a truce. All citizens are hereby commanded to cease and desist any and all opposition to the Empire, which includes…"

His voice faded as she skirted around the corner of a building.

For a few moments, Ceres became breathless, paralyzed, her heart pounding in her throat. The marriage was being publicly announced even though she hadn't agreed to it.

Ceres ran as fast as she could, sprinting down the street. Panting, lungs on fire, she flew by carnage and wreckage southward toward the ocean, the breeze streaming against her body. She cautiously followed the back roads leading to the bay.

The rocky shore was difficult to maneuver, but Ceres dashed as fast as she could towards Rexus's cave. On she ran, hopping over large boulders, stepping on small stones, the sun a globe of fire on her head, causing her to sweat. Even when her legs demanded she stop, and her mouth became parched, she continued on past fishermen and boats, the seagulls above soaring against the blue sky.

I will rest once I am at the cave, she told herself, and with every stride, the excitement in her bosom grew. So much had changed since she had last seen Rexus, and even though it had only been days, it felt as if it had been months. Would things be the same? She needed to share her mourning of her brother with someone, someone who would understand.

By the time she reached the cave the sun had started to set, and the cavern in the mountainside was a gaping black hole behind warped vines and slimy mosses. Other than a handful of scouts hiding on the cliffs and behind bushes, watching her, the outside looked abandoned.

Ceres found herself stopped by flaming arrows shot to the ground right before her feet. She looked up, irritated that they didn't recognize her.

"I am here for Rexus. Nesos and Sartes are my brothers! I am with the rebellion!" she yelled.

Two watchers climbed down from the mountainside, bows strung with arrows, approaching Ceres.

"I must search you for weapons," one said.

"I have a sword, but you will not take it from me," she insisted, opening up the cape, revealing her father's sword.

"Then you will not be allowed inside," he said.

Had they not heard her?

"My name is Ceres and my brothers, Nesos and Sartes, are with the rebellion," she said with an irritated voice. "I am with the rebellion. Rexus sent me on a mission to the palace and I am here to report. Go ask him. He will vouch for me."

"You're the girl who is supposed to marry Prince Thanos," the other watcher said, mockingly.

She didn't want to waste time explaining to them that, no, she wasn't going to marry Thanos and that she had refused him. Rexus would vouch for her once she was inside.

"Go tell Rexus I am here to report," she said, her voice stern.

One of the watchers headed inside, while the other held her at arrowpoint. After a few minutes, the watcher returned.

"Rexus will not see you. He told me to tell you to go marry your prince charming, and to stay away from the rebellion," he said.

She gasped, bursts of pain, but also wrath clenching inside. He would not see her? He thought she had agreed to marry Prince Thanos?

"I demand to see him at once!" she shouted, her body rigid.

"Get lost," one of the watchers said, nudging her with the tip of his arrow.

Ceres realized standing here and arguing would not make one difference.

She spun around, clipping one of the watcher's feet from underneath him so he fell to the rocks with a thud, and before the other watcher could react, she had already drawn her sword and knocked him unconscious with her hilt.

With not a second to waste, arrows raining down at her, she sprinted into the cave. She zoomed by dark, glistening walls, her eyes on the lit torches in the distance, her hands fumbling to get her sword back into its sheath.

"Stop!"

Yells came from behind her, but she would not stop. She would see Rexus, and as soon as she would be given a chance to explain, he would understand that she loved him, and she would know she loved him too. More than Thanos. More than anyone.

"Rexus!" she yelled, slipping on the slimy rocks.

She reached the end of the narrowing, and when she stepped into the larger space, hundreds of eyes were on her, menacing expressions causing her to want to shrink.

"Seize her!" someone yelled.

"I need to speak with Rexus!" she yelled.

A mob of men gathered around her, grabbing her arms. One took her sword and it vanished into the crowd of men and women.

"Rexus!" she yelled.

The mob opened up, and Rexus was standing there before her, his blond hair gleaming in the light of the torches. He looked so forlorn, Ceres thought.

"Rexus," she said, tears in her eyes.

She wrestled free from her captors and threw herself against his firm chest, embracing him so tightly, he grunted.

After a few moments, she noticed his arms were still by his side, limp, not embracing her in return. She pulled back a little and looked up into his gorgeous face. It was as hard and cold as ice.

"I didn't send you on a mission to marry Prince Thanos. I sent you to gain the royals' trust," he said, his eyes burning with hatred.

"I refused to marry Prince Thanos, but the queen pushed it through anyway!" Ceres said.

"What made the prince think he could marry you in the first place? Were you encouraging him?"

The crowd went silent, waiting for her answer.

"Can we please go somewhere quiet to talk," Ceres asked.

"No. I want everyone to witness this."

"Rexus, you know me. You have known me for years! Why are you doing this?" she asked.

"There must have been some reason he thought he should ask you."

"What? Rexus, I denied him!" Ceres yelled.

"Of all the people to betray me, I never thought you would."

"But I—" Ceres started.

"One of the princesses at the palace sought me out and told me she had seen you and Thanos in the library gardens, kissing," Rexus said.

"Stephania?" Ceres asked.

Rexus's eyes flared just a tad, then softened, and she hoped maybe he would finally listen.

"So it is not true?" he asked, a look of slight relief on his face.

"Stephania was supposed to marry Thanos, but when the king and queen saw their opportunity to create peace in the Empire, they broke off their engagement and—"

"First, answer my question. Did you kiss him?" he pressed.

She couldn't lie to him, but she could explain. Or at least try to.

"Yes. But—"

"And was it of your own free will and choice?" he continued.

She couldn't respond to that. She just couldn't, for so many reasons.

Rexus nodded, knowingly, his nostrils flaring, his expression hard again.

"So how can I then believe that you declined his proposal of marriage? Maybe you have even been sent as a spy here?" he said.

"No!"

"Get her out of here. And let it be known to every revolutionary that Ceres is banned from joining the rebellion forever!" Rexus said.

He swiveled around, but then stopped and glanced back at Ceres one more time, his expression disturbed.

"And I thought you should know. Nesos endured to the end. He gave his life for the rebellion while his sister was off flirting with the enemy."

She collapsed to the ground, her grief crushing her heart so thoroughly, she couldn't breathe, she couldn't see, her eyes overflowing with tears.

As the revolutionaries dragged her out of the cave, she called her brother's name again and again. Everything she had was now lost to her.

Chapter Twenty Seven

"May I have a word?" Thanos asked Cosmas in the library, his hands shaking like leaves caught in a storm.

Cosmas looked up from reading a scroll, his expression worried, but loving.

"Of course."

They walked together out into the palace gardens and sat on a bench in front of the marble fountain, beneath a cloudy sky.

"What can I help you with, son?" Cosmas asked.

Thanos huffed.

"The king and queen commanded Ceres and I to be wed to restore the peace in the land," he said.

"So I heard."

"She rejected me."

"Ah, that, too, I heard."

Thanos took a deep cleansing breath.

"I have fallen in love with Ceres, but she believes I only proposed because I was commanded to."

Cosmas nodded, paused, and brought a hand to his chin.

"Have you spoken to her, opened your heart and let her know how you feel?" Cosmas asked."

"I told her some things, but I didn't tell her I loved her," Thanos relied.

"Heavens, why not?"

She had been so angry with him, he remembered, but that hadn't been why he had held back.

"When I was on my mission, I fought with her brother and he fell onto his sword and died. I told Ceres what happened, but she was so furious with me, it was as if she believed I had killed him."

Cosmas nodded, pondering.

"You told her the truth, and she will be devastated and angry and hurt for a time. If you had remained silent, and she found out, she would never have forgiven you. You did the right thing."

"But she hates me now, even though I tried to save her brother," Thanos said.

"I have known you your entire life, Thanos. You are a good man."

Thanos moaned.

"How am I a good man when I am ready to run away and leave everything behind?"

"Running away might offer you a new start, but soon the ghosts of the past will come to haunt you," Cosmas said. "You must talk to her, and then she can decide."

"She will not speak to me." Then Thanos had a thought. "Will you try and talk some sense into her?" he pleaded.

Cosmas bushy eyebrows grew heavy and he huffed.

"Very well, but only if you promise me you will tell her you love her."

Thanos nodded. "I promise."

⚜ ⚜ ⚜

Ceres ran back through the palace, dashing up the stairs three at a time. She tore past Empire soldiers who tried to arrest her, and darted toward Thanos's chamber, her feet moving so fast they barely touched the marble floors. Thanos was the only one who could help her at this point, she knew, and if he refused, she would drag him back to Harbor Cave bound and gagged if needed. Thanos needed to tell Rexus that she indeed had declined his proposal, and to allow her a chance to join the revolutionaries.

When she stormed into Thanos's room, she was sorely disappointed to find it empty.

She sprinted toward the palace gardens, looked in the royal practice arena, and even checked the blacksmith's chalet. But he was nowhere. It was as if Thanos had vanished into thin air.

The library, of course! she thought.

As she shot back through the gardens, she saw the queen standing on the veranda, eyes like a hawk, a hint of a conniving smile on her lips. And then four Empire soldiers rushed out from behind bushes and trees, arresting Ceres, their grips around her arms so tight it was painful.

"Thanos!" she screamed, thrashing legs. "Thanos!"

But he did not come.

The Empire soldiers dragged her upstairs to the queen's chamber, and threw her onto the shiny marble floor at the queen's feet. Two stood in front of the door, blocking it, while the other two marched past the stone statue of a couple embracing, and out onto the balcony, through the open doors.

"Come with me," the queen said to Ceres.

The queen walked out through the flowing purple curtains onto the veranda, overlooking the ocean. Shaken, but still angered, Ceres climbed to her feet and followed after.

"I still don't know how you managed to get out of your room," the queen said, her steely eyes gazing into the distance, a golden wine goblet in her hand. "At first, I thought you found a way to climb out the window and down the side of the tower, but there would be no way to do that and not fall to your death."

Ceres pinched her lips, not willing to offer up that Anka had freed her.

"So someone in the palace must have opened the door for you, and when I find out who that person is, I will personally skin them alive," the queen said, her voice flat but strict.

"It's not that difficult to unlock the door from the inside," Ceres said, hoping the queen would believe she did it on her own.

The queen glanced at Ceres, squinting.

"I doubt that is what you did," she said.

The queen turned away and peered across the ocean.

"When I was your age, I thought I could do whatever I wanted, too. Youth has a way of making one naïve and irrational," she said.

"I am neither of those things," Ceres said.

The queen took a sip of wine.

"Of course, you are, my dear. Your returning to the palace proves it. You should have stayed far away, Ceres. Here, we have your entire life planned out, and it will not be to your liking."

"I won't marry Thanos, if that's what you mean," Ceres said.

"You will, and as the new princess, it will be your responsibility to produce babies. Lots and lots of babies. You will never be seen. You will never be heard. Your children will not know you, for the instant they are out of your womb, they will be ripped from your arms to be raised by a nanny, far, far away."

"I won't marry Thanos."

"You have no choice, Ceres. You *will* wed him and once you have produced enough children, you will be killed off and replaced by another girl, a woman of royal blood, someone deserving of the title *princess*."

"Thanos would never let that happen. He's not like the rest of you barbarians."

The queen chuckled.

"Do you really think he cares for you?" she said, tsking. "Oh my. You are even more naïve than I thought."

Ceres's shoulders grew tighter with the queen's words. Had he only pretended to hate his family and the royals to gain her sympathy? Had he shown affection to try and make her fall for him when in truth, he didn't care for her at all? No, she didn't believe it. His touch and his kiss had been too real.

"Thanos told me a secret, and I must say, he is even more of a barbarian than the rest of us," the queen said.

"I doubt that," Ceres said, her guard up.

"I suppose he didn't tell you he was the one who sought out and killed your brother, Nesos?" the queen said, a glib smile on her lips.

With all her might, Ceres tried to keep her face free from expressing the pang of grief she felt on the inside, tried to force her eyes not to fill with tears. But she could not hold it all inside and fell onto hands and knees as racking sobs tumbled from her lips.

"Why…why are you doing this to me?" Ceres asked, her voice cracking. "How can you hate me so much when you don't even know me?"

The queen walked toward Ceres, stepping on Ceres's filthy dress.

"I don't need to know you to realize that you are a very useful pawn to the Empire," she said.

"I will never be your or anyone else's pawn," Ceres seethed.

The queen ignored her comment.

"Because of this marriage, peace will prevail through the land, allowing the Empire to maintain power. And when you have fulfilled your purpose, make no mistake, you will be discarded."

The queen nodded toward the Empire soldiers behind her, and they grabbed Ceres's arms and pulled her to her feet.

"Take her back to her room," the queen said. "And make sure both her wrists and ankles are shackled this time."

Chapter Twenty Eight

Thanos always felt better after talking to Cosmas, and as he eagerly walked toward Ceres's chamber, he knew with every fiber of his being that the right thing was to open up to her, even if it meant she would not have him.

He marched through the palace gardens, and just as he came around the gazebo, he saw the king approaching with his advisors. His uncle must surely be the most evil man to roam the earth, Thanos thought, a cruel murderer who would go to any length to maintain his power over his subjects.

Thanos veered from the path, taking a different route, hoping the king hadn't seen him.

"Good day, Thanos," the king yelled, waving for him to come.

Thanos's skin crawled, but he approached his uncle as the advisors continued on down the path.

"Walk with me," the king said.

He strolled down the pathway beside his uncle and toward the royal practice ground, the scent of the flowers so sweet, it was nauseating. Or was it his uncle's presence that made him feel that way?

"I heard the proposal did not go as expected," the king said, hands clasped behind his back.

Of all the people in the world, the king was the absolute last person Thanos wanted to have this conversation with. But here he was, trapped, and with no choice other than to answer his uncle's prying questions.

"Not exactly," Thanos said.

The king was silent for a moment, perhaps waiting for Thanos to say something.

"I can see you care for this girl," the king finally said. "And it might surprise you to know that our stories are rather similar."

That did surprise Thanos, and his curiosity was piqued.

"When I first met Athena, she could hardly stand to be in the same room as me," the king said with a chuckle. "It was a blind marriage, one my parents had arranged in order to expand the Empire's borders. I had heard rumors of Athena's beauty and I could hardly wait to meet her, but when we met, Athena refused to acknowledge my existence in the least."

"Why?" Thanos asked, having never heard this story before.

"You see, she had fallen in love with someone else."

It was an interesting story, Thanos thought, but he failed to see how their situations were similar.

"We married, and after the first year, we became best friends, and passionate lovers," the king continued with a proud expression on his face.

"Why are you telling me this?"

The king paused, placing a fat hand on Thanos's shoulder.

"I realize our situations are not exactly the same, but I know you, Thanos. You will probably refuse to marry Ceres if she is not in agreement. And because she loves someone else, you will do everything in your power to not force her to marry you."

Thanos squinted.

"Why would you think she loves someone else?" he asked.

"We had Ceres followed when she snuck out of the palace to go visit Rexus, one of the leaders of the rebellion, and Ceres's lover," the king said.

If his uncle's words were true, it would indeed be another blow to Thanos's pride, but could he trust what his uncle was saying? Never.

"Rexus is her childhood friend, nothing more," Thanos said.

"I do not tell you this to be cruel. I tell you this so you will know the truth and not be deceived. I might be harsh on you, but I am always truthful," the king said.

Thanos slapped the king's hand away from his shoulder and took a step back.

"You lie," he snarled.

"When Ceres returned to the palace, she admitted everything to the queen. Ask Ceres yourself if you don't trust my word or the queen's," the king said.

Thanos shook his head in disbelief, but if the king were lying, why would he suggest Thanos ask Ceres in person?

He glanced up at the tower. Had he been blind? Did Ceres not return his affection? All the signs pointed to it: her snide comments, the way she maintained her distance from him, her refusal to marry him. Perhaps he had been mistaken, and now he paid the consequences: humiliation and rejection.

A surge of anger filled his chest, and he felt heat spread through his cheeks.

"In truth, Stephania is a much better match for you, Thanos. Ah, she might be a bit spoiled and full of herself, but motherhood will remedy all that."

"I don't love her," Thanos said through clenched teeth.

"I will allow you to make this decision yourself, Thanos. But know this: if you marry Ceres, it will ensure peace in the Empire and thousands of lives will be spared. If you do not, many will die on either side."

"If I agree to wed Ceres, the rebellion might die down for some time, but I can assure you they will rise again. I don't doubt you know that," Thanos said.

"Temporary or not, it would give us time to bring in additional forces from the north."

Thanos thought for a moment, but he knew he couldn't—wouldn't—marry someone who didn't love him in return.

"Think on it for a while," the king said. "In the meantime, General Draco has requested you lead a legion of men to quell the rebellion in Haylon."

At any other time, Thanos would have rejected the command without a second thought. His uncle was indeed shrewd as a serpent, he knew, offering him this opportunity now that Thanos was heartbroken. And he hated that he had been played yet again.

"When would I leave?" Thanos asked.

"Now. The ships stand ready in the harbor and the Empire soldiers are awaiting their new leader."

Thanos felt a wave of rage.

"I do not accept the position," he said.

The king smiled.

"You have no choice."

Thanos scowled.

"Then give me a chance, at least, to see Ceres before I go," he said, desperate to see her one last time, to explain to her that he might never return.

But the king merely shook his head.

"I am afraid that is impossible," he said.

And with those words, he walked away.

Thanos wanted to run to Ceres, but before he could move, a dozen soldiers surrounded him. He knew it would be no use. They would, upon the King's command, escort him to the ship, away from all of this, and to a battle that may mean his death.

Chapter Twenty Nine

Sitting on a chair by the window in her chamber, her wrists and ankles chained, Ceres finally gave up trying to escape. For hours, she had strained to get out of these shackles, to summon the supernatural strength that sometimes granted her extreme power, but she was left with nothing but bruised flesh and bloodied skin.

Unsettled, trying to hold onto the dwindling sliver of sanity she had left, she gazed out the window at the serene capital. However, seeing how peace had descended over the war-torn city was of little help for nothing but deceit had brought this peace, she knew. How many more lies were out there floating around, keeping the infrastructure of the Empire from crashing down?

Ceres heard keys clatter outside the door, and when the door opened, to her surprise, in walked Cosmas.

He froze in the doorway, gasping when he saw her, a look of horror on his wrinkled face.

"Ceres, what happened to you?" he asked, immediately making his way over to her.

"The queen felt the need to confine me to my chamber," she said.

Cosmas examined the shackles, and when he saw her blood, he walked over to the water vessel, dipped a washcloth in it, and returned to her side.

"What a despicable thing to do to a sweet dear," he said, dabbing the washcloth on her sores. "Did she say why?"

Ceres bit down, the washcloth stinging as he cleaned her wounds.

"I refused to marry Thanos and then I left the castle," she said.

Cosmas paused, his expression saddened.

"Yes, he came to me, distraught, heartbroken," he said.

She blinked, trying to keep her tears at bay.

"I never wanted to hurt Thanos," she said. "But I refuse to have the Empire use us for their own gain."

Cosmas nodded, his brows knitting together.

"The queen said that I will only be used to breed babies and then I will be killed once I am no longer of use," Ceres said.

"I hope you know Thanos would never allow that," Cosmas said, continuing to clean her wounds.

"I didn't think he would. But now I don't know anymore."

Cosmas looked at her, his crinkly eyes a question.

"The queen said Thanos sought my brother out to kill him," Ceres said, a lump forming in her throat.

Cosmas gently placed a hand on her head, stroking her hair.

"My deepest condolences for your loss," he said. "Thanos told me what happened, and he was extremely distraught. He didn't know until after he had slain the young man that he was your brother. And he did all in his power not to slay him, even though Nesos tried to kill Thanos. Your brother fell on his own sword. A tragic misunderstanding, I am afraid. I am sure that if Nesos had known then he would not have tried to kill Thanos. But for Thanos's part, there was nothing more he could have possibly done. Nesos tried with all his heart to kill him. It was only his love for you that allowed Thanos to not fight back against a man who wanted his life."

So it wasn't as the queen said, Ceres noted with relief. The news made the loss slightly less horrific, although she still felt as if her heart might burst from sadness at any moment. But now she wondered, how many more of the queen's words were spiked with lies?

Cosmas looked Ceres in the eyes with such sincerity that she found herself holding her breath.

"Thanos loves you, Ceres. He needs a good, upright woman in his life to fight for him, with him, and to be on his side. Don't let the king and queen meddle in your relationship. Don't let them destroy what beauty is between you."

"Beauty? What beauty? He hasn't even had the decency to visit me," she said, a bitter taste in her mouth.

"He was sent on a mission to Haylon. The isle overthrew the Empire, and he was sent to get it back."

"What?" she asked in horror.

"Don't believe Thanos did it because he supports anything the Empire stands for," Cosmas said. "He most certainly does not."

He stepped closer and lowered his voice, and Ceres could sense he was going to say something dangerous, the air around them becoming tense.

"I overheard something," Cosmas said. "Thanos was told lies about you, and that is why he left for Haylon, despairing. It seems someone is trying to dispatch him and wants him dead. But I am not certain who or why."

"Who could possibly want Thanos dead?" she asked, worried.

"I know not. But whisper a word of this to anyone, and all of our lives will be in danger."

He took a step back, the atmosphere in the room returning to normal.

"There must be some way to get you out of the shackles. If only I had a key," he said, glancing around. "I'd sneak you out of here and bring you to my wife. You could stay with us in our home."

"You would do that for me?" she asked, realizing he'd be risking his life.

Cosmas smiled softly, his eyes brimming with tenderness.

"Thanos is like a son to me, and he loves you. I would do anything for him, and now you, too."

That brought tears to her eyes, Ceres having felt so alone and abandoned.

"Thank you," she said.

"I will be your faithful friend forever," Cosmas said. "You don't belong here, Ceres. Thanos cares for you, but the rest of the lot are rotten and vile, and you are too innocent and good to play their games."

Then she had a thought.

"If I write a letter to Thanos, is there any way you could deliver it for me?" she asked.

"Of course. I have a few friends, and I believe they could get it to Thanos rather quickly."

She pulled out parchment and started to write. She told him about everything, from what the queen had said, to why she had rejected his marriage proposal. She even told him that she did care for Rexus, but that she was confused because she loved them both. She told him about how she knew that the king and queen were pitting them against each other, but she had no way to prove it. She told him she had learned that he had killed her brother, but knew he hadn't intended it, and that she was trying to forgive him.

And finally, she asked him to return so she could hold him, keep him close, and she asked for his forgiveness for having been so cold.

She rolled the letter up and handed it to Cosmas.

"I will make sure this gets to Thanos, and I will protect it with my life if I have to," he said.

He embraced her, and then he left, locking the door behind him.

As Ceres listened to his footsteps vanish down the stairs, she couldn't help but wonder if she had been wrong about everything. If Thanos would get her letter. If he would be killed.

And if she would ever see Thanos again.

Chapter Thirty

Ceres felt like her heart might leap out of her chest when she saw her father standing in the doorway of her chamber. He was dressed in fine clothing and his face was no longer pallid like it used to be, his cheeks rosy, his lips tilting upward. And those eyes ... How wonderful it was to see his kind, loving eyes again, the eyes she trusted and immediately soothed her frazzled nerves.

She rose to her feet to run over to him, but the shackles restrained her.

His gaze fell upon the chains, and his expression turned worried. He strode across the chamber and reached arms around her.

She squeezed him tightly, nestling her face in his chest, the warmth of his body, the tenderness of his embrace, bringing tears of joy to her eyes.

"I missed you so," she whispered.

"I love you," he said.

For one blissful moment, they held each other, and all was beautiful and Ceres felt safe and loved.

But then she felt her father shrinking in her arms, vanishing little by little, his body imploding into nothingness, and it was as if she was herself dying with his departure.

"No," she whimpered as she grasped at him, trying to make it so he wouldn't disappear.

"Father!" she cried, closing her eyes, but then he was gone.

Sunlight warmed her face and she opened her eyes to find herself standing in the arena at the Stade, seven combatlords moving in on her, the crowd chanting for her blood to be spilt. Her hands and wrists were no longer shackled, but she had no weapons to defend herself with. Petrified, she searched her surroundings for a way to escape, but seeing the combatlords encircling her, there was no way out. Weaponless, she was incapable of fighting back, and when the combatlords charged toward her, she fell to her knees, shrieking, pressing the palms of her hands to her eyes.

Ceres woke up with a scream beneath the window, her body sweating, tears in her eyes, the stone floor cold and hard beneath her. The chains clattered when she buried her face in her hands, and she let out a piercing cry into the night.

What a horrid nightmare, she thought. But what did it mean? Was it an omen of what was to come? She hugged her chest, feeling so empty, so defenseless, so raw.

She startled when the door creaked open, and for a second, when she saw a male figure standing in the darkened doorway, in her half-awakened state she thought Thanos had returned.

"Thanos?" she whispered, excitement growing in her bosom.

"Is that what he does at night, visits you?" the man said.

The hairs on the back of Ceres's neck rose when she recognized the voice as Lucious's, and immediately she knew she was in danger, unable to escape, her wrists and ankles shackled.

"I hadn't seen you in a while and was worried about you," Lucious said.

"I doubt that."

He stepped closer, and his face appeared in the moonlight.

"Leave or I will scream," Ceres said, her breathing shallow.

"And who will come and save you? Not Thanos. Not the king of queen. Not Empire soldiers."

She rose to her feet and picked up a golden goblet from the table, throwing it at him, but he veered quickly, and the cup flew out the open door and tumbled down the steps.

Lucious slammed the door shut and lunged toward Ceres, pushing her wrists into the wall behind her, rubbing his body against hers, his breath reeking of alcohol.

She screamed and kicked him in the shin, but he clasped a hand over her mouth and pressed his knees between her legs so she couldn't move them. With hasty fingers, he pulled her skirt up, and for a moment, he released her mouth and crushed her lips with his.

Bile rose in her throat, and Ceres opened her mouth, biting him as hard as she could. He pulled back and hit her across the face, fist closed, his golden ring cutting Ceres across the cheek.

She forced herself to ignore the pain and screamed as loudly as she could, but he stuffed fabric down her throat, gagging her. His hands fumbled at her skirt again, and he pressed against her with forceful hips, a wild look in his eyes, the feral gleam of a savage.

"You have given me so much trouble that you owe me a little pleasure," he hissed.

Muffled sounds escaped her lips as she fought against him with all her might, but he was too strong and she was shackled.

Suddenly, he fell to the floor behind her, lifeless. She glanced over her shoulder and was flooded with relief to see Anka standing there with a silver candleholder.

"Anka," Ceres croaked, her knees trembling so she could barely stand.

Anka ran over to Ceres and hurriedly inserted a key into the cuffs around Ceres's ankles and wrists, freeing her.

Hands shaking uncontrollably, Ceres pulled the fabric out of her parched mouth. Anka grabbed Ceres's shoulders and looked her in the eyes.

"Soldiers are coming. Run!" Anka said.

"You have to come with me this time," Ceres said.

"No, I need to stay."

Anka spun around in a flash, dashed out the door, and disappeared down the dark stairwell, her rushed footsteps gradually vanishing.

Quickly, Ceres gathered her senses, forcing herself to move even though all she felt like doing was curling up into a ball in the corner and crying. On her way out the door, she gave Lucious a swift kick in the abdomen. She had despised him before, but now her hatred would burn every time she would see him. She would remember this moment, oh, how she would remember.

With sweaty hands, she stole down the stairwell, but just as reached the bottom, a slew of Empire soldiers approached her from the right, their swords drawn.

She looked to the left, but just as many Empire soldiers were storming toward her from that direction.

Then she heard footsteps behind her, but before she could turn around, she felt a hard object hit the back of her head, and everything went black.

Chapter Thirty One

Stephania sat way in the back in the throne room and brought the fan to her lips, hiding a yawn, this dreary council of old birdbrained men and women so uninspiring she thought she might pass out from boredom. For hours, they had discussed—in that same mind-numbing monotonous tone—how the council was losing money, how the court was poorly managed, and how the rebellion, if it were to continue, would cost the Empire greatly. And as if these dignitaries couldn't grasp it, it had already been brought up *three* times that the rebellion had already drained half the king's gold.

Still, after hours of futile rambling, dozens of preposterous ideas being tossed around, they came up with no solutions. None. Stephania had sat through too many of these, and more and more, listening to these simpleminded mumbling nitwits, it just proved to her again that they were all brainless monkeys, pretending to know what they were talking about and what they were doing.

"Are there any more matters to discuss?" the king said from his throne at the front of the room.

Not a soul breathed a word, thank heavens, Stephania thought, dying to get out of this stuffy room, her bottom sore from having sat so long on this unpadded chair. Ever since the announcement that Thanos would wed Ceres, she had been demoted to sit in the back row by the exit door, next to the least important dignitary in the entire Empire, her seat the farthest from the king than anyone's.

I will climb my way back up into the king's graces, she resolved. Soon.

Just when she judged the meeting over, Cosmas, sitting at the front, rose and asked to stand before the king.

Stephania rolled her eyes. Would this day never end? She knew he was the old, senile, hard-of-hearing geriatric who cared about Thanos—a little too much, Stephania thought—but what on earth would he have to say that would warrant a single second in a council meeting such as this? All the old man did day in and day out was read scrolls in the library, stare at the stars, and talk of things that didn't really matter—not to the Empire at least.

Stephania noticed that the other dignitaries also seemed as disinterested in the old fart as her, their eyes glazing over with boredom.

Eying the floral pattern on her green silk dress, she listened with one ear, fanning herself as the ancient scholar held up a scroll toward the king.

"I was asked to deliver this letter to Thanos," Cosmas said. "It is from Ceres."

Stephania's ears perked right up. Perhaps the old scholar wasn't as much of a fool as she had thought. He had certainly misled me, Stephania thought, because she presumed the elder was more loyal to Thanos than even the king or the Empire. But perhaps she had been wrong in her assumption.

With a giddy heart, she repressed a smile. Now that commoner, Ceres, would be put to death and Stephania would marry Thanos, making everything right again. What fortune. What luck! Perhaps the gods were smiling down on her after all.

Stephania watched as the king read the letter in silence, his eyebrows sinking deeper and deeper over his fat face. When he had finished, he looked up.

"Did you read this?" the king asked Cosmas.

Cosmas stepped forward.

"Yes, and that was when I knew it needed to be brought to your attention," he said. "The girl is a lying conniving thief, a revolutionary in our very midst."

Gasps went through the chamber, and disorder erupted.

"Silence! Silence!" the king said.

"She must not marry Prince Thanos!" one advisor shouted.

"Hang the girl for treason!" another said.

The room exploded into commotion, some yelling for the king to imprison the imposter, others demanding she be put to death immediately.

"Silence!" the king yelled again, and the room settled down into a low hum of whispers. "We cannot just kill her. The revolutionaries will start rioting in the streets again and we are not ready to take upon all of them."

"But we must do something," an advisor said. "You do not mean to let a conspirator remain in our midst, leaking information to the revolutionary headquarters?"

A brilliant idea popped into Stephania's mind, and she gasped. A few heads turned toward her, and she smiled, knowing this idea would be her big chance to gain favor again. She just had to speak up.

"May I make a suggestion, Your Excellences?" she said loud and clear, rising to her feet.

The king's and queen's eyes darted to her.

"Please, it will also help to generate money for the Empire," she said, sensing their hesitation.

"Very well, speak," the king said. "But make it quick."

Stephania stepped onto the floor and walked toward the front of the room, her heels clicking against the marble floor, hundreds of eyes following her every step. She repressed a grin, bathing in the attention, elated that she had such a wonderful idea to present, when the supposed most powerful and intelligent men and women of the Empire had thought of no such thing. She knew that once she had shared with the king her idea, he would love it. And perhaps the king and queen would even give her more authority from now on—authority over Ceres.

Arriving at the bottom of the steps below the thrones, Stephania curtsied deeply before the king and queen.

"So far your excellences have done a wonderful job in using Ceres to promote and strengthen the Empire. And I see an opportunity to do it again," Stephania said.

"Well then, why don't you enlighten us," the queen said in a stiff tone.

"Don't throw Ceres out of our midst," Stephania said. "And don't execute her. Instead… use her to make the Empire wealthier than it has ever been."

The room grew silent, a few whispers throughout, and Stephania could just feel favor descending upon her again.

"And how do you propose we do that?" the king asked.

"Make her a permanent contender in the Killings," Stephania said.

Now the room had become so silent, Stephania could hear air moving in and out of her nostrils.

"She's a girl," someone yelled.

"No one would come see a commoner being butchered," another said.

Stephania was becoming impatient with these narrow-minded, short-sighted old-timers.

"Ceres is a soon-to-be royal female, a novelty, a fierce fighter in her own right," she said. "I have watched her fight, and she beat Lucious. I dare say people would travel from afar just to see her."

The king squinted, bringing a hand to his bearded chin.

"Make the spectators pay a premium to see the princess combatlord," Stephania added.

The king glanced at the queen, and the queen lifted an eyebrow.

"The princess combatlord," the king said. "I will think on it, but I do believe the idea to be excellent. Well done, Stephania. Well done."

Stephania curtsied again and walked back to her seat, extremely proud of herself for having thought of such a genius plan. Not only would her idea bring in money for the Empire, it would serve a very personal purpose, too.

Vengeance.

Finally, Thanos would be hers.

Chapter Thirty Two

What a waste of my time, Sartes thought as he sat below the willow tree in their yard, peeling potatoes for his mother, the wind pulling at his burgundy tunic in a steady stream. Sartes was too young to fight in the rebellion, Rexus had told him, and had sent him back home to sit and wait to mature, to feel useless, to ponder on Nesos's death, to sit and think of how Ceres was trapped within the walls of the palace, being abused, used, and tortured.

He tossed the potato into the pot and started to peel another one.

How was it Rexus expected him to sit here and do nothing, to suffer the consequences of the war, but to not help in any way? He wasn't too young, he knew, but the revolutionaries didn't see that. Just because he was small of build didn't mean he didn't have skills and abilities that were useful in the war against the Empire.

But no matter how much he insisted to Rexus on staying, Sartes was sent home to be with his mother to peel vegetables and wait on her hand and foot.

When he heard wheels crunching against the gravel road, Sartes looked up. The Empire's blue and gold banner waved above an enclosed wagon, dozens of Empire soldiers marching behind it in two perfectly straight rows.

The front door to the house creaked open, and Sartes's mother stepped out onto the front porch, squinting toward the cart, a hand shading her eyes, a generous frown on her face.

"Get inside the house, Sartes," she said.

"Mother—"

"Get inside the house now!" she screamed.

Sartes huffed and threw the knife into the bucket of water and potatoes. Heading toward the house, he fumed about how unfair it was that everyone treated him like a helpless child.

"And don't come out until I tell you to, do you hear?" his mother snapped.

Sartes slammed the door shut behind him and sat by the kitchen table, peering out through the partially opened shutter, seeing the Empire wagon slow to a halt right in front of their yard.

An Empire soldier hopped down from the driver's seat and approached, a scroll carrying the Empire seal in his hand.

"We are here to recruit your firstborn son for the royal army," the Empire soldier said, holding the scroll toward Sartes's mother.

Sartes saw that his mother glanced down at the scroll, but did not accept it.

"Ceres is my daughter, and as you know, she is to be wed to Prince Thanos," she said.

Sartes stood up and tiptoed to the shutter, listening intently.

"It has been ruled by the king that we recruit *all* firstborn males," the Empire soldier said.

"My eldest son is dead," she said, a tremble in her voice.

"And what of your other sons?" the Empire soldier asked.

"How dare you ask that of me?" Sartes's mother said.

"The king has not excused you or your family from serving him or the Empire. So I ask of you again, have you any other sons?" the Empire soldier continued.

"Even if I did have other sons, which I do not, he would soon be the prince's brother-in-law, and the royal army would not have claim upon him."

The Empire soldier took a threatening step toward her, and Sartes thought that he might strike his mother. He almost stormed outside, but he knew if he did, he would have to deal with his mother later, or he would be recruited to the royal army, and neither one of those options sounded tempting in the least.

"Might I assume you are with the rebellion then?" the Empire soldier growled.

"Why in heaven's name would you assume such a thing?" Sartes's mother asked.

"Because you are resisting the king's commands."

"I am not with the rebellion," she said.

"Will you obey the king's orders, then?"

"I will and I do."

"Then step aside so I can search your house."

"You have no right to search my home," she snapped.

"I have orders to kill anyone who resists!" the soldier roared. "Now stand out of my way, wench!"

Sartes gasped, realizing if he didn't get away, the soldiers would seize him and he would be forced to fight for the royal army. He started toward the back room, but as he did, he bumped into a chair, causing it to tip over with a crash. Stumbling forward, he just made it into the back room when he heard the Empire soldier kicking the front door in.

But before Sartes could escape through the window, the Empire soldier was upon him. The brute clutched Sartes's arm, pulling him out into the main room again, but Sartes grabbed a chair and swung it at the soldier, hitting him in the head so blood oozed from his brow.

The soldier cried out and fell to the floor, releasing Sartes's arm, and Sartes dashed into the back room again.

He tore open the shutters and hopped out the window, his heart pounding like a wild beast against his sternum, nothing on his mind other than getting to the field. He passed the shack, the meadow so close, but then he heard his mother screaming.

Unable to continue on, he turned around, and to his horror, he saw the Empire soldier holding a dagger up to his mother's throat.

"Mother!" he yelled, horrified.

"Please don't kill me," his mother croaked. "Sartes, you wouldn't let your mother die, would you?"

For a split second Sartes was conflicted. If he went back, he would be forced to fight against his friends, against all he believed in, freedom, prosperity, fairness. He would kill those he loved. He would be compelled to destroy all he knew in his bones and blood was the truth. But if he kept running, the Empire soldiers might catch up with him still, and his mother would be dead.

He couldn't live with himself knowing he was the reason his mother's throat had been slit by the enemy.

As three Empire soldiers ran toward him, he lifted his hands in surrender, his gaze on his mother, the relief in her eyes as the dagger was removed from her throat somewhat comforting. But also bitter.

The soldiers forced Sartes to the ground, jerking his arms behind his back, binding his wrists with rope. They pulled him up and dragged him past his mother, her eyes filled with tears.

"Sartes," she cried. "My baby."

She started after him toward the wagon, her arms longingly reaching for him, fingers straining at his shirt.

A soldier hit her across the face and she fell to the parched grass with a yelp.

The soldiers threw Sartes into the cart with three other young men and locked the door.

"I will never forgive myself for this," his mother cried. "Never!"

The driver whipped the horses and the wagon moved forward with a sudden jerk. Sartes's mother staggered to her feet and clamped her hands around the bars, eyes filled with desperation.

"Come back to me, Sartes, promise me this!"

But Sartes looked away and would not promise his mother anything. Because of her, he knew, his life was over. Because of her, he would have to fight on the side of the war that killed Nesos, on the side that stole Ceres from him, and on the side that had torn his family apart.

Chapter Thirty Three

The wind tugged at Rexus's hair as he feverishly galloped toward the palace beneath a blanket of stars, Anka sitting behind him holding on for dear life. August and Crates rode after them, their horses heavily loaded with weapons and gear hidden beneath wool throws.

Rexus hadn't been able to sleep a wink since he found out Ceres was engaged to Prince Thanos, the thoughts of them together an inescapable torment. He had judged Ceres a liar and a traitor, and had never wanted to see her again. He had never even wanted to *think* of her again either, but every thought that had occupied his mind these past days and nights had only been of her.

However, after Anka had approached Rexus in Harbor Cave earlier, everything had changed. When she had informed him that Ceres was shackled in the tower and had nearly been raped the night before last, and that Ceres had refused to marry Prince Thanos, he had felt sick to his stomach. But when Anka had told him Ceres loved him—Rexus—and that Ceres spoke of no one other than him, Rexus's heart had stopped, and he had realized with great remorse that Ceres had been nothing but loyal to the rebellion. And to him. And he had been a fool.

He swore, the pain too much to contain on the inside. He had been so hard on Ceres, had turned her away when she had begged to join the rebellion. And here she was doing nothing but supporting the revolution, fulfilling her job. He vowed that as soon as he saw Ceres again, he would beg for her forgiveness. This was entirely his fault, that she had been imprisoned. His pride had gotten in the way. He should have listened to her when she came to Harbor Cave, but like always, he was too quick to judge and was too much of a hothead.

He glanced back, seeing his friends were still right behind him. He had considered bringing twice as many men, but he figured if he brought more than two strapping young revolutionaries, the group might cause suspicion amongst the Empire soldiers who patrolled the streets of Delos at night. If he brought fewer, they wouldn't be able to ward off any potential Empire soldiers guarding Ceres's tower and the rescue mission would be a failure.

August was a new friend, young, happy, and built like a combatlord. He had joined the rebellion a mere month ago, and had told Rexus that he left his father—an advisor to the king—because of the way his father mistreated their slaves. Crates was one of August's father's slaves, and the night August left, August took him with him, making Crates a free man.

Crates was tall and lanky, but exceptional with the bow and arrow, and having lived in lack his entire life, he had a fire about him that Rexus loved, the young man embodying the spirit of the revolution.

Clouds had started to roll in when they reached the city, and as the night darkened, Rexus led them through the back streets in silence, passing crowded houses, some intact, others demolished by the Empire.

By the time they paused in an alleyway across from the palace, the heavens had cleared again, the moon and stars bringing welcome light.

Anka descended from the horse, and peeking out from behind the wall, she pointed out the tower Ceres was imprisoned in.

"I have to go back inside," Anka said. "If anyone finds out I have been gone…"

"Yes, go," Rexus said. "And Anka…"

Anka turned around and looked at him.

"Thank you," he said.

She nodded, and he watched as Anka vanished into the night down the street, around the stone wall toward the back entrance of the palace.

Rexus took a moment to study the Empire soldiers who marched around the wall, noting that they passed by approximately every five minutes. It should give them ample time to climb the wall and not get caught.

Hurriedly, they tied up the horses, took the weapons and rope, and just as the next Empire soldier marched by, seeing the coast was clear, Rexus led August and Crates toward the outer wall.

The wall was slick, but with ropes tossed over the wall, anchored in the trees on the other side, the climb took no time at all.

After they had descended the wall, making no sound as they hopped down onto the soft, green lawn, they stole toward the palace, hiding behind trees and bushes.

Once at the bottom of the tower, Rexus peered up the side of the rounded wall. The structure was higher than what he had initially thought, but he was confident he would be able to climb it and bring Ceres down with him once he had freed her. Any thought of slipping and falling he forced away, knowing uncertainty could cause him to fall.

"Wait behind the bushes while I get her," Rexus said to August and Crates. "If any Empire soldiers approach, warn me with a quail call."

He removed his cloak and handed it to August.

"Be safe," August whispered, vanishing into the shadows with Crates.

Rexus attached a rope to the end of his arrow and shot it through the partially opened shutter. He paused, looking up, hoping Ceres would come to the window, but he saw no movement.

He tugged on the rope, and seeing it was secure, he wedged his foot between two rocks and started the climb. One foot after another, pulling on the cord, he inched his way upward, his hands clamping, the muscles in his arms flexing, his feet digging into the niches of the stone wall.

Halfway up the tower there was a generous ledge, and Rexus paused to rest, panting heavily. He looked down and saw nothing but bushes and trees and shadows. August and Crates were certainly hiding well, he noted.

Once he had caught his breath, he continued to climb, and soon his heart was again pounding from exertion. Or was it from the thought of seeing Ceres?

He strained, climbing faster, just trying to reach her, to see her smile again, her beautiful eyes, feeling her soft skin.

A few inches from the top, he stopped, thinking he heard something below, but when he looked, he saw nothing.

Finally, he reached the ledge of her window and peered into the room.

"Ceres," he whispered.

"Rexus?" he heard Ceres speak, amazement in her voice.

Then he saw her face—a desperate expression—and that she wore a royal gown that was torn and filthy. When she gripped his hands, he felt how cold she was, but how strong she was, too. She pulled him inside.

"You came for me," she said, throwing her arms around him.

"I'm sorry for what I said," he said, gripping her tightly, never wanting to let go. "I love you, with all that I am."

"I love you, too," she said. "I'm sorry."

He pulled back and stroked her hair, gazing into her eyes. She rose up onto the balls of her feet and pulled at the back of his head so their lips met. He kissed her passionately, pouring all of himself, all the longing and regret, into that kiss. Her lips were soft, and he knew they were destined to be together.

They parted.

"We have to hurry," he said. "There will be time later."

She nodded.

He drew the dagger from its sheath around his waist so he could free her from the shackles.

Suddenly Rexus felt an excruciating pain in his back. He couldn't breathe.

He looked down and, to his horror, saw an arrow tip protruding from his chest, running all the way through his body.

Then, before he could register what was happening, there came another.

He was being attacked from behind, he realized. The guards below must have spotted him. He had been shot from behind.

Rexus reached out for Ceres, but his world was already darkening. Before he could sever her bonds, he found himself instead losing balance, falling backwards.

And then he tumbled out the window.

Rexus fell as if in slow motion, the wind in his ears, the sound of Ceres's scream following him, the air so thin and warm. There was no resistance. It seemed a long way down, as if he were sinking into the earth and the earth swallowed him whole. Would not the ground soon come?

The last thing he saw before he hit the ground was Ceres's contorted face, looking down, wishing, as he, that everything had turned out differently.

Chapter Thirty Four

Thanos, standing at the bow of his ship, the scent of the ocean filling his nostrils, spotted Haylon in the distance, and immediately regret brewed in his chest. With every breath he had taken on this trip, every inch he had sailed, the regret had only grown stronger. Now, with the destination in plain sight, it suddenly became crystal clear: he knew he had made the wrong decision not to take Ceres from the castle and run from his uncle, from everything he knew.

And in this moment, his regret turned to shame. Yes, he felt ashamed for letting the king play him again, this time pitting Ceres and him against each other.

Waves crashed against the ship below, drops of salt water splashing onto his overheated face. A steady stream of brisk sea breeze ran through his hair as he watched the gulls dive into the sea only to rise from the ocean with fish in their beaks.

If only I were that free, he thought.

He still felt seasick, and had since the day the ship left the shores of Delos one week earlier to sail south. Now, seeing Haylon, it made him want to jump into the ocean, swim to shore, and worship the white sandy beaches surrounding the isle. Land, solid earth, he thought. He never realized he would miss it so much.

A sense of awe went through him as his eyes scanned the paradise in the near distance. The isle, a hub of trading between all western nations, was dramatically beautiful, he could see as they approached, with towering verdurous mountains behind the city, rising from the sea, the buildings glistening golden in the evening sunlight. It was his first time here, and the closer they sailed, the more he wished his first visit were under different circumstances completely—not to kill the inhabitants, or to destroy the beautiful architecture of their most magnificent buildings.

His eyes followed the snaking road that ran from the city entrance up past domes and towers, and all the way up to the castle, resting on a hill. That was the road General Draco had described in strategy meetings, the road they would travel to seize the castle. The road where blood would flow. The road that would be unrecognizable after they had marched through it. The wall around the city was tall, but with ladders, ropes, catapults, and flaming arrows, tens of thousands of Empire soldiers attacking at once, the city would be theirs soon enough, General Draco had said. And indeed it would, Thanos knew.

When he turned around to behold his crew, the tension on board had become so thick it felt like a wall around him. Was it more than just the nerves of the warriors he was detecting? The entire trip, Thanos had sensed someone or something watching him, although when he felt eyes burning at the back of his neck, he'd turn around to find no one and no thing. He would brush it off, thinking he was growing paranoid, but just when he had forgotten about it, again, it would suddenly be as if cold fingers were creeping down his spine.

He nodded toward General Draco, who stood by a giant of a man, wearing golden armor and a visored helmet. The hulk was the tallest Empire soldier Thanos had ever seen, a true giant. The Typhoon, the rest of the men on the ship called him, although Thanos doubted that was his real name. It was rumored the Typhoon had taken on a group of twenty wild northern warriors at once, and had killed them all in under five minutes.

General Draco and the Typhoon would lead the attack on the great city, and Thanos would bring in the second group of troops once the main gates had been opened. They would attack immediately, General Draco had ordered, not give the rebels of Haylon a chance to gather their armies, although Thanos didn't doubt they had already seen their fleet of ships and that their army was more than ready to defend the city. No one would be able to defend against the numbers King Claudius had sent, Thanos knew.

Hundreds of rowboats were lowered onto the choppy azure ocean, and the Empire soldiers descended into the vessels with weapons and heavy armor. Some larger boats carried catapults and boulders.

General Draco invited Thanos into his boat, and Thanos took a seat next to the Typhoon. He felt like a dwarf next to the beast.

"Remember, the goal is to take the city in under an hour, before nightfall," General Draco said. "Kill anyone who resists."

"We will spare the women and children, correct?" Thanos said.

"As long as they obey," General Draco said. "As long as they bow before the Empire's banner and pledge to submit to the king's laws."

"I don't see how the women and children will be a threat, even if they did resist," Thanos said.

"It is the king's orders. I do not question them," General Draco snapped, glaring at Thanos.

Thanos looked away, but he made a decision to not kill women or children—not even if they rebelled.

They arrived at shore and Thanos hopped out of the boat, the warm water reaching right above his knees as he hauled the heavy oak vessel toward land with other Empire soldiers. Just as he glanced back, Thanos noticed that General Draco and the Typhoon looked at each other, and then the general nodded before heading toward the white, sandy beach.

At first, Thanos considered the gesture somewhat suspicious, but when the general turned to him and nodded, too, he thought nothing more of it.

The boats were hauled ashore, the weapons and artillery placed into wagons, and the Empire soldiers organized into twelve battalions, Thanos to lead one of them.

He took his place in front of his men and led them southward, down the coastline, wading through ankle-high water. He felt that familiar sensation running through him, a combination of excitement, fear, and adrenaline: the battle was about to begin.

Yet Thanos had not gone very far, the water still splashing on his ankles, when suddenly, without warning, he felt a shooting pain in his upper back.

He dropped to his knees, stunned, not understanding what was happening.

He felt cold metal in his back, and with a start, he realized: he had been stabbed.

He knelt there, lightheaded, not understanding. They were still far off from reaching the enemy.

Then Thanos felt the sword being pulled out of him, and he shrieked, the pain unbearable. He looked up to see the Typhoon step in front of him, wiping the blade of his sword clean of Thanos's blood.

He grinned down, and that was when Thanos realized: he was being assassinated.

And no one was turning to help him.

"Any last words?" the Typhoon asked, his voice impossibly deep.

Thanos gasped for air.

"Who sent you?" he managed to ask.

"I will tell you," the Typhoon replied. "When you're dead."

Chapter Thirty Five

Ceres sat in the dungeon on the damp floor, her back against the cold stone wall, fully defeated as an endless stream of tears trailed down her face. How—how was she to continue on? Thanos had left her. Nesos was dead. And worst of all, Rexus…

She let out a faint sob and inhaled a jagged breath as the memory came rushing back. Rexus, shot in the back, falling from her reach, backwards, out of the tower window. Torn away from her when they had been so close, so close to starting a new life together.

It was too cruel.

Ceres sobbed. There was nothing more to fear now, she realized. Not even her life mattered anymore, it seemed.

She did not know how much time had passed when she heard footsteps coming down the hallway. She didn't move. She was beyond caring what the royals did to her, so much so that if they were coming to kill her, she would welcome the merciful death.

A woman and three men appeared on the other side of the bars. Ceres refused to look up, but she knew from the overly sweet rose perfume that the woman was Stephania.

An Empire soldier unlocked the cell, but Ceres's gaze remained on the floor. She would not acknowledge them.

"You have been ordered to the Stade," an Empire soldier said.

Ceres didn't move.

"You will compete in the Killings."

Ceres felt the life rush out of her. So. They would kill her after all.

The soldier grabbed her by the arm, jerked her to a standing position, and bound her wrists behind her back. When Ceres finally looked up, she saw Stephania smiling.

Stephania stepped forward.

"Before you die," she said, venom in her voice, "I thought you might like to know something."

She leaned in close, her breath uncomfortably hot on Ceres's neck.

"I sent a messenger to Haylon," she said, "bearing a very special message. I told Thanos never to defy me. Never to make a fool of me. Now, finally, he has learned why."

She beamed, satisfied, though Ceres did not know why.

"Thanos," she said, "is dead."

⚜ ⚜ ⚜

The Empire soldiers hauled Ceres through the musty dungeon corridor and up the stairwell. They dragged Ceres outside and led her to an enclosed horse-pulled wagon. Once the door was locked and the soldiers had taken their seats at the front, the wagon rolled out of the palace courtyard and onto the streets of Delos. They passed houses, and weaved through hordes of citizens making their way to the Stade.

Ceres hardly took notice of her surroundings; everything passed by in a blur. Nothing mattered anymore. Everyone she loved was either far away or dead.

In a daze, she realized they were moving through Fountain Square, and Rexus's face flashed before her eyes. Just weeks ago they were here, happy, hopeful, free.

And just yesterday, he had been in her arms, professing his love; and a moment later, he had fallen to his death. How could a being so vibrant, so alive, now be nothing more than a memory?

Outside the Stade, the wagon creaked to a halt. An Empire soldier dragged her out of the cart and into the tunnels.

They marched past combatlords and weapon-keepers, the chants of the crowd reaching her all the way down here.

Finally, the soldier threw her into a small chamber and ordered her to change into the armor lying on the bench. He left, locking the door behind him.

Alone, Ceres undressed and slipped on the leather skirt and breastplate. They were studded with gold, and were soft and new, she could see, custom made for her, fitting perfectly. She pulled on the boots, noticing they were also her size, the leather supple, the ends of the laces embellished with gold.

All these years she had dreamt of becoming a combatlord, of wielding a sword in an arena in front of thousands of spectators.

And yet now, she hated being here. Somehow, the king and queen had stolen her dream, tarnished it, and had forced her to fight for the very people she despised.

Not a minute later, the Empire soldier returned and ordered her to follow.

They walked through the dim tunnel, past weapons, past dozens of fallen combatlords and their weapon-keepers. Arriving by the gate, Ceres heard the crowd roaring outside, and her stomach clenched tightly.

"Paulo will be your weapon-keeper," the Empire soldier said.

She turned to see Paulo, rather short in stature, nothing but a bundle of muscle with dark smooth skin. His black hair framed a heart-shaped face, and he had a few whiskers on his chin below full lips.

"It will be an honor to serve you," Paulo said with a nod, handing her a sword.

Ceres didn't want to reply. She didn't want this to be her reality.

"Ceres and Paulo are next!" an Empire soldier called.

Even though Ceres no longer feared for her life, her hands shook, as her throat dried up.

The iron gates opened with a rattle, and Ceres looked out into the arena and saw two Empire soldiers hauling a dead combatlord toward the tunnels.

Taking a deep breath, she stepped into the Stade.

The roar was deafening, the sunlight warm against her skin, the brightness stinging her eyes as she scanned the over-packed audience.

"Ceres! Ceres! Ceres!" they chanted.

As her eyes grew accustomed to the sunlight, she let her gaze wander across the arena. On the other side of the stadium stood a barbarian of a combatlord, his arms as thick as Ceres's waist, the veins in his legs bulging on top of thick, swollen muscles.

She clenched the hilt of her sword and knew that this man would kill her. She glanced at Paulo, and saw his face had fallen.

But she would not back down.

With all the courage she had inside of her, she raised her sword.

Her entire life she had been a slave. And now, even though she may very well die, that part of her life, she realized, was over.

Now, finally, she would go from Slave to Warrior.

Now, death would come for her.

And now her life would begin.

The crowd roared.

"CERES! CERES! CERES!"

Listen to THE SORCERER'S RING series in audio book format!
Now available on:

Amazon
Audible
iTunes

Download Morgan Rice books now!

KINGS AND SORCERERS

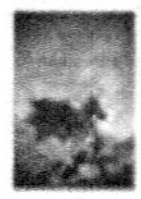

THE SORCERER'S RING

THE SURVIVAL TRILOGY

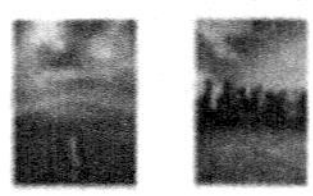

the vampire journals

ROGUE, PRISONER, PRINCESS

(OF CROWNS AND GLORY—BOOK 2)

MORGAN RICE

Morgan Rice

Morgan Rice is the #1 bestselling and USA Today bestselling author of the epic fantasy series THE SORCERER'S RING, comprising seventeen books; of the #1 bestselling series THE VAMPIRE JOURNALS, comprising twelve books; of the #1 bestselling series THE SURVIVAL TRILOGY, a post-apocalyptic thriller comprising three books; of the epic fantasy series KINGS AND SORCERERS, comprising six books; and of the new epic fantasy series OF CROWNS AND GLORY. Morgan's books are available in audio and print editions, and translations are available in over 25 languages.

TURNED (Book #1 in the Vampire Journals), ARENA 1 (Book #1 of the Survival Trilogy), A QUEST OF HEROES (Book #1 in the Sorcerer's Ring) and RISE OF THE DRAGONS (Kings and Sorcerers—Book #1) are each available as a free download on Amazon!

Morgan loves to hear from you, so please feel free to visit www.morganricebooks.com to join the email list, receive a free book, receive free giveaways, download the free app, get the latest exclusive news, connect on Facebook and Twitter, and stay in touch!

Select Acclaim for Morgan Rice

"If you thought that there was no reason left for living after the end of THE SORCERER'S RING series, you were wrong. In RISE OF THE DRAGONS Morgan Rice has come up with what promises to be another brilliant series, immersing us in a fantasy of trolls and dragons, of valor, honor, courage, magic and faith in your destiny. Morgan has managed again to produce a strong set of characters that make us cheer for them on every page.... Recommended for the permanent library of all readers that love a well-written fantasy."

—*Books and Movie Reviews*
Roberto Mattos

"An action packed fantasy sure to please fans of Morgan Rice's previous novels, along with fans of works such as THE INHERITANCE CYCLE by Christopher Paolini .... Fans of Young Adult Fiction will devour this latest work by Rice and beg for more."

—*The Wanderer, A Literary Journal*
(regarding *Rise of the Dragons*)

"A spirited fantasy that weaves elements of mystery and intrigue into its story line. *A Quest of Heroes* is all about the making of courage and about realizing a life purpose that leads to growth, maturity, and excellence .... For those seeking meaty fantasy adventures, the protagonists, devices, and action provide a vigorous set of encounters that focus well on Thor's evolution from a dreamy child to a young adult facing impossible odds

for survival….Only the beginning of what promises to be an epic young adult series."

—*Midwest Book Review* (D. Donovan, eBook Reviewer)

"THE SORCERER'S RING has all the ingredients for an instant success: plots, counterplots, mystery, valiant knights, and blossoming relationships replete with broken hearts, deception and betrayal. It will keep you entertained for hours, and will satisfy all ages. Recommended for the permanent library of all fantasy readers."

—*Books and Movie Reviews,* Roberto Mattos

"In this action-packed first book in the epic fantasy Sorcerer's Ring series (which is currently 14 books strong), Rice introduces readers to 14-year-old Thorgrin "Thor" McLeod, whose dream is to join the Silver Legion, the elite knights who serve the king…. Rice's writing is solid and the premise intriguing."

—*Publishers Weekly*

BOOKS BY MORGAN RICE

THE WAY OF STEEL
ONLY THE WORTHY (Book #1)

OF CROWNS AND GLORY
SLAVE, WARRIOR, QUEEN (Book #1)
ROGUE, PRISONER, PRINCESS (Book #2)
KNIGHT, HEIR, PRINCE (Book #3)
REBEL, PAWN, KING (Book #4)

KINGS AND SORCERERS
RISE OF THE DRAGONS (Book #1)
RISE OF THE VALIANT (Book #2)
THE WEIGHT OF HONOR (Book #3)
A FORGE OF VALOR (Book #4)
A REALM OF SHADOWS (Book #5)
NIGHT OF THE BOLD (Book #6)

THE SORCERER'S RING
A QUEST OF HEROES (Book #1)
A MARCH OF KINGS (Book #2)
A FATE OF DRAGONS (Book #3)
A CRY OF HONOR (Book #4)
A VOW OF GLORY (Book #5)
A CHARGE OF VALOR (Book #6)
A RITE OF SWORDS (Book #7)
A GRANT OF ARMS (Book #8)
A SKY OF SPELLS (Book #9)
A SEA OF SHIELDS (Book #10)

A REIGN OF STEEL (Book #11)
A LAND OF FIRE (Book #12)
A RULE OF QUEENS (Book #13)
AN OATH OF BROTHERS (Book #14)
A DREAM OF MORTALS (Book #15)
A JOUST OF KNIGHTS (Book #16)
THE GIFT OF BATTLE (Book #17)

THE SURVIVAL TRILOGY
ARENA ONE: SLAVERSUNNERS (Book #1)
ARENA TWO (Book #2)
ARENA THREE (Book #3)

VAMPIRE, FALLEN
BEFORE DAWN (Book #1)

THE VAMPIRE JOURNALS
TURNED (Book #1)
LOVED (Book #2)
BETRAYED (Book #3)
DESTINED (Book #4)
DESIRED (Book #5)
BETROTHED (Book #6)
VOWED (Book #7)
FOUND (Book #8)
RESURRECTED (Book #9)
CRAVED (Book #10)
FATED (Book #11)
OBSESSED (Book #12)

Table of Contents

CHAPTER ONE

"Ceres! Ceres! Ceres!"

Ceres could feel the chant of the crowd as clearly as her own thudding heartbeat. She raised her sword in acknowledgment, tightening her grip as she did, testing the leather. It didn't matter to her that they'd probably only learned her name a few moments ago. It was enough that they knew it, and that it was reverberating through her, so that she could feel it almost as a physical force.

Across the Stade, facing her, her opponent, the massive combatlord, paced the sands. Ceres swallowed at the sight of him, fear rising up in her, as much as she tried to suppress it. This, she knew, could very well be the last fight of her life.

The combatlord paced like a caged lion, swinging his sword through the air in arcs that seemed to be designed to show off his bulging muscles. With his breastplate and visored helmet, he looked as if he could have been carved from stone. It was hard for Ceres to believe that he was just flesh and blood.

Ceres closed her eyes and steeled herself.

You can do this, she told herself. *You may not win, but you must face him valiantly. If you are to die, you must die with honor.*

A trumpet blast rang in Ceres's ears, rising up even over the baying of the crowd. It filled the arena, and suddenly, her opponent was charging.

He was faster than she thought such a big man had any right to be, on her before she had a chance to react. It was all Ceres could do to dodge, kicking up dust as she got out of the warrior's path.

The combatlord swung his blade with two hands and Ceres ducked, feeling the rush of air as it passed. He hacked down like a butcher wielding a cleaver, and when she spun and blocked the stroke, the impact of metal on metal rang up her arms. She did not think it possible a warrior could be that strong.

She circled away, her opponent following with a grim inevitability.

Ceres heard her name mixed in with the cheers and boos of the crowd. She forced herself to stay focused; she kept her eyes fixed on her opponent and tried to remember her training, thinking through all the things that might happen next. She tried to slash, and then rolled her wrist to send her sword around the parry.

But the combatlord merely grunted as her blade took a nick out of his forearm.

He smiled as if he'd enjoyed it.

"You'll pay for that," he warned. His accent was thick, from one of the far corners of the Empire.

He was on her again, forcing her to parry and dodge, and she knew she couldn't risk a head-on clash, not with someone this strong.

Ceres felt the ground give way beneath her right foot, a sensation of emptiness there where there should have been firm support. She glanced down and saw sand pouring down into a pit below. For a moment, her foot hung over empty space, and she thrust out blindly with her sword as she struggled to keep her balance.

The combatlord's parry was almost contemptuous. For an instant, Ceres was sure she was going to die, because there was no way to fully stop the answering stroke. She felt the jarring impact of the blow against her blade. It only slowed it, though, as it slammed into her armor. Her breastplate pressed back into her flesh with bruising force, while at the spot where it ended, she felt pain flare white hot as the sword cut along her collarbone.

She stumbled back and as she did, she saw more pits opening around the floor of the arena, like the mouths of hungry beasts. And then, desperate, she had an idea: maybe she could use them to her advantage.

Ceres skirted around the edges of the pits, hoping to slow his approach.

"Ceres!" Paulo called.

She turned and her weapon-keeper threw a short spear in her direction. Its shaft thudded into her slick palm as she caught it, the wood feeling rough. The spear was shorter than might have been used in a real battle, but it was still long enough to thrust its leaf-shaped head across the pits.

"I'll take you a slice at a time," the combatlord promised, edging his way around.

With an opponent this strong, Ceres thought, her best hope was to try to wear him down. How long could someone that huge keep fighting? Already, Ceres could feel the burn of her own muscles, and the sweat that dripped down her face. How much worse would it be for the combatlord she faced?

It was impossible to know for sure, but it had to be her best hope. So she dodged and she jabbed, using the length of the spear as best she could. She managed to slip through the massive warrior's defenses, yet still, it only clattered off his armor.

The combatlord kicked up dust towards Ceres's eyes, but she turned away in time. She spun back and swept the spear low, toward his unprotected legs. He jumped clear of that sweep, but she managed to slice another wound along his forearm as she drew the spear back.

Ceres jabbed low and high now, aiming for her opponent's limbs. The big man parried and blocked, trying to find a way past the probing point, but Ceres kept it moving. She jabbed it in toward his face, hoping to at least distract him.

The combatlord caught the spear. He grabbed it behind the head, yanking it forward as he stepped aside. Ceres had to let go, because she didn't want to risk being pulled onto the big man's sword. Her opponent snapped the spear across his knee as easily as he might have broken a twig.

The crowd roared.

Ceres felt a cold sweat up her back. For an instant, she had the image of the big man breaking her body as easily. She swallowed at the thought and readied her sword again.

She grabbed the hilt with both hands as the next blows came, because it was the only way to absorb some of the power of the combatlord's attacks. Even so, it was impossibly hard. Every blow felt like she was a bell being hit by a hammer. Every one sent shockwaves running through her arms.

Already, Ceres could feel herself tiring under the assault. Every breath came ragged, feeling like she dragged it in by force. There was no question now of trying to counterattack, or do anything but step back and hope.

And then it happened. Slowly, Ceres felt the power welling up inside her. It came with a warmth, like the first embers of a brush fire. It sat in the pit of her belly, waiting for her, and Ceres reached for it.

Energy flooded through her. The world slowed, moving at a crawl, and she suddenly felt she had all the time in the world to parry the next attack.

She had all the strength, too. She blocked it easily and then swung her sword around and slashed the combatlord's arm in a blur of light and speed.

"Ceres! Ceres!" the crowd roared.

She saw the combatlord's rage growing as the crowd's chanting continued. She could understand why. They were meant to be chanting for *him*, proclaiming his victory, enjoying her death.

He bellowed and charged forward. Ceres waited as long as she dared, forcing herself to stay still until he nearly reached her.

Then she dropped. She felt the whisper of his blade passing over her head, then the rough sand as her knees touched down. She threw herself forward, swinging her sword around in an arc that slammed into the combatlord's legs as he passed.

He tumbled face first, his sword spilling from his hand.

The crowd went wild.

Ceres stood over him, looking at the awful ruin her sword had made of his legs. For a moment, she wondered if he might manage to stand even like that, but he collapsed back, turning to his back and lifting one hand as he begged for mercy. Ceres held back, looking around for the royals who would decide if the man in front of her lived or died. Either way, she resolved, she would not kill a helpless warrior.

Another trumpet blast came.

A roar followed it as the iron gates at the side of the arena opened, and the tone of it was enough to send a shiver through Ceres. In that moment, she felt like nothing more than prey, something to be hunted, something that had to run. She dared a glance up toward the royal enclosure, knowing this had to be deliberate. The fight had been over. She'd *won*. That wasn't good enough, though. They were going to kill her, she realized, one way or another. They would not let her leave the Stade alive.

A creature lumbered in, larger than a human, covered in shaggy fur. Fangs stuck out from a bearlike face, while spiny protrusions stuck out along the creature's back. Its feet held claws the length of daggers. Ceres didn't know what it was, but she didn't need to in order to know that it would be deadly.

The bear-like creature sank to all fours and ran forward, while Ceres readied her sword.

It reached the fallen combatlord first, and Ceres would have looked away if she'd dared. The man cried out as it pounced, but there was no way he could roll out of the way in time. Those giant paws smashed down, and Ceres heard the crunch of his breastplate giving way. The beast roared as it savaged her former opponent.

When it looked up, its fangs were wet with blood. It looked at Ceres, bared its teeth, and charged.

She barely managed to step aside in time, slashing with her sword as it passed. The creature gave a bellow of pain.

Yet sheer momentum tore the blade from her hands, feeling as though it would tear her arm away if she didn't let go. She watched with horror as her blade spun across the sand and into one of the pits.

The beast continued to advance, and Ceres, frantic, glanced down at the spot where the two broken sections of spear lay on the sand. She dove for them, grabbing a section and rolling in one movement.

As she rose to one knee, the creature was already charging. She couldn't run, she told herself. This was her only chance.

It slammed into her, the weight and speed of the thing lifting Ceres from her feet. There was no time to think, no time to be afraid. She thrust with the broken section of spear, striking with it again and again as the bear-beast's paws closed in on her.

Its strength was terrible, far too much to match. Ceres felt as though her ribs might burst with the pressure of it, the breastplate she wore creaking under the creature's strength. She felt its claws raking at her back and legs, agony searing across her.

Its hide was too thick. Ceres struck again and again, but she could feel the tip of the spear barely penetrating its flesh while it tore at her, its claws ripping across any exposed skin.

Ceres closed her eyes. With all she had, she reached for the power within her, not even knowing if it would work.

She felt herself surge with a ball of power. She then threw all her force into her spear, thrusting it up into the space where she hoped the creature's heart would be.

The beast shrieked as it reared back away from her.

The crowd roared.

Ceres, smarting from the pain of its scratches, scrambled out from under it and stood weakly. She looked down as the beast, the spear lodged in its heart, rolled and whined, making a sound that seemed far too small for something so large.

Then it stiffened, and died.

"Ceres! Ceres! Ceres!"

The Stade filled with cheers again. Everywhere Ceres looked, there were people calling out her name. Nobles and ordinary folk alike seemed to be joining in the chanting, losing themselves in that one moment of her victory.

"Ceres! Ceres! Ceres!"

She found herself drinking it in. It was impossible not to be caught up in the feeling of adulation. Her whole body seemed to pulse in time with the chanting that surrounded her and she spread her hands as if to welcome it all in. She turned in a slow circle, watching the faces of those who hadn't even heard of her a day ago, but who were now treating her as though she was the only person in the world who mattered.

Ceres was so caught up in that moment that she barely even felt the pain of the wounds she'd suffered anymore. Her shoulder hurt now, so she touched a hand to it. It came away wet, although her blood was still bright red in the sunlight.

Ceres stared at that stain for several seconds. The crowd was still chanting her name, but the pounding of her heart in her ears suddenly seemed far louder. She looked up at the crowd, and it took her a moment to realize that she was doing it from her knees. She couldn't remember falling to them.

From the corner of her eye, Ceres could see Paulo hurrying forward, but that seemed far too distant, as if it had nothing to do with her. Blood dripped from her fingers to the sand, darkening it where it touched. She had never felt so dizzy, so light-headed.

And the last thing she knew she was already falling, face-first, toward the floor of the arena, unable, she felt, to ever move again.

Chapter Two

Thanos slowly opened his eyes, confused as he felt waves lapping at his ankles, his wrists. Beneath him, he could feel the gritty white sand of Haylon's beaches. Salt spray occasionally filled his mouth, making it hard to breathe.

Thanos looked out sideways along the beach, unable to do more than that. Even that was a struggle, as he drifted in and out of consciousness. In the distance, he thought he could make out flames and the sounds of violence. Screams came to him, along with the sound of steel clashing on steel.

The island, he remembered. *Haylon. Their attack had begun.*

So why was he lying on the sand?

It took a moment for the pain in his shoulder to answer that question. He remembered, and winced at the memory. He remembered the moment the sword had plunged into him, lancing into his upper back from behind. He remembered the shock of it as the Typhoon had betrayed him.

The pain burned through Thanos, expanding like a flower from the wound in his back. Every breath hurt. He tried to lift his head—but he only blacked out.

The next time Thanos woke, he was face-down on the sand again, and he was only able to tell that time had passed because the tide had risen a little, the water lapping at his waist now rather than his ankles. He was finally able to lift his head enough to see that there were other bodies on the beach. The dead seemed to cover the world, stretched out on the white beaches as far as he could see. He saw men in the armor of the Empire, sprawled where they had fallen, mixed in with the defenders who had died protecting their home.

The stench of death filled Thanos's nostrils, and it was all he could do not to throw up. No one had sorted the dead into friend and foe yet. Such niceties could wait until after the battle was done. Perhaps the Empire would leave it for the tide to do; a glance behind showed blood in the water, and Thanos could see the fins breaking through the waves. Not large sharks yet, scavengers rather than hunters—but how large would they need to be in order to devour him when the tide rose?

Thanos felt a wave of panic. He tried to haul himself up the beach, pulling with his arms as though trying to climb across the sand. He cried out in pain as he pulled himself forward, perhaps half the length of his body.

Blackness swam in his vision again.

When he came to, Thanos was on his side, looking up at figures who squatted over him, close enough that he could have reached out for them if he'd had the strength left to do it. They didn't look like soldiers of the Empire, didn't really look like soldiers at all, and Thanos had spent long enough around warriors to know the difference. These, a younger man and an older, looked more like farmers, ordinary men who had probably fled their homes to avoid the violence. That didn't mean they were less dangerous, though. Both held knives, and Thanos found himself wondering if they might be as much scavengers as the sharks. He knew there were always those looking to rob the dead after battles.

"This one's still breathing," the first of them said.

"I can see that. Just cut his throat and be done with it."

Thanos tensed, his body getting ready to fight even though there was nothing he could have done then.

"Look at him," the younger man insisted. "Someone stabbed him in the back."

Thanos saw the older man frown slightly at that. He moved around behind Thanos, out of his line of sight. Thanos managed to keep from crying out again as the man touched the spot where blood still flowed from the wound. He was a prince of the Empire. He wasn't going to show weakness.

"Looks like you're right. Help me get him up where the sharks won't get him. The others will want to see this."

Thanos saw the younger man nod, and together, they managed to lift him, armor and all. This time, Thanos did cry out, unable to stop the pain as they pulled him up over the beach.

They left him like driftwood, past the point where the tide had left seaweed behind, abandoning him on the dry sand. They hurried away, but Thanos was too caught up in the pain to watch them go.

There was no way for him to gauge the time that passed then. He could still hear the battle in the background, with its cries of violence and anger, its rallying cries and its signal horns. A battle could last minutes or hours, though. It could be over in the first rush, or keep going until neither side had the strength to do more than stumble away. Thanos had no way of knowing which this was.

Eventually, a group of men approached. These *did* look like soldiers, with that harder edge that only came to a man once he'd fought for his life. It was easy to see which of them was the leader. The tall, dark-haired man at the front didn't wear the elaborately worked armor that a general of the Empire might have, but everyone there looked to him as the group approached, obviously awaiting orders.

The newcomer was probably in his thirties, with a short beard as dark as the rest of his hair, and a spare frame that nevertheless held a sense of strength. He wore a short, stabbing sword on each hip, and Thanos guessed that it wasn't just for show, judging by the way his hands hovered next to the hilts automatically. His expression seemed to Thanos to be silently calculating every angle present on the beach, watching out for the possibility of an ambush, always thinking ahead. His eyes locked on to Thanos's, and the smile that followed had a strange kind of humor behind it, as though its owner had seen something in the world that no one else had.

"This is what you two have brought me out here to see?" he said, as the two who had found Thanos stepped forward. "One dying Imperial soldier in armor too shiny for his own good?"

"A noble though," the older one said. "You can see that by the armor."

"And he's been stabbed in the back," the younger pointed out. "By his own men, it seems."

"So he's not even good enough for the scum who are trying to take our island?" the leader said.

Thanos watched as the man moved closer, kneeling beside him. Maybe he intended to finish what the Typhoon had started. No soldier of Haylon would have any love for those on his side of the conflict.

"What did you do that your own side would try to kill you?" the newcomer asked, quietly enough that only Thanos could hear him.

Thanos managed to find the strength to shake his head. "I don't know." The words came out cracked and broken. Even if he hadn't been wounded, he'd been lying on the sand a long time. "But I didn't want this. I didn't want to fight here."

That earned another of those strange smiles that seemed to Thanos to be laughing at the world even though there was nothing to laugh at.

"And yet here you are," the newcomer said. "You didn't want to take part in an invasion, but you're on our beaches, rather than safe at home. You didn't want to offer us violence, but the Empire's army is burning homes as we speak. Do you know what's happening up that beach?"

Thanos shook his head. Even that hurt.

"We're losing," the man continued. "Oh, we're fighting hard enough, but that doesn't matter. Not with odds like this. The battle still rages, but that's just because half of my side are too stubborn to recognize the truth. We don't have enough time for distractions like this."

Thanos watched as the newcomer drew one of his swords. It looked wickedly sharp. So sharp that he probably wouldn't even feel it as it plunged into his heart. Instead, though, the other man gestured with it.

"*You* and *you*," he said to the men, "bring our new friend. Perhaps he's worth something to the other side." He grinned. "And if he's not, I shall kill him myself."

The last thing Thanos felt were strong hands gripping him under his arms, yanking him up, dragging him away, before he finally lapsed back into darkness.

Chapter Three

Berin felt the ache of longing as he trekked along the route home to Delos, the only thing keeping him going, thoughts of his family—of Ceres. The thought of returning to his daughter was enough to make him press on, even though he'd found the days of walking tough, the roads beneath his feet rough with ruts and stones. His bones were not getting any younger, and already he could feel his knee aching from the journey, adding to the pains that came from a life of hammering and heating metal.

It was all worth it, though, to see home again, though. To see his family. All the time he'd been away, it was all Berin had wanted. He could picture it now. Marita would be cooking in the back of the humble wooden home, the scent of it wafting out past the front door. Sartes would be playing somewhere around the back, probably with Nasos watching him, even if his older son would be pretending that he wasn't.

And then there would be Ceres. He loved all his children, but with Ceres there had always been that extra connection. She had been the one to help out around his forge, the one who had taken after him most, and who seemed the most likely to follow in his footsteps. Leaving Marita and the boys had been a painful duty, necessary if he was to provide for his family. Leaving Ceres behind had felt as though he'd abandoned some part of himself when he left.

Now it was time to reclaim it.

Berin only wished he brought happier news. He walked along the gravel track that led back to their house, and he frowned; it wasn't winter yet, but it would be soon enough. The plan had been for him to leave and find work. Lords always needed bladesmiths to provide weapons for their guards, their wars, their Killings. Yet it turned out that they didn't need *him*. They had their own men. Younger, stronger men. Even the king who had seemed to want his work had turned out to want Berin as he had been ten years ago.

The thought hurt, yet he knew he should have guessed that they would have no need for a man with more gray in his beard than black.

It would have hurt more if it hadn't meant that he got to go home. Home was the thing that mattered for Berin, even when it was little more than a square of rough-sawn wooden walls, topped with a turf roof. Home was about the people waiting there, and the thought of them was enough to make him quicken his steps.

As he crested a hill, though, and the first view of it came, Bering knew that something was wrong. His stomach plunged. Berin knew what home felt like. For all the barrenness of the surrounding land, home was a place filled with life. There was always noise there, whether it was joyful or argumentative. At this time of year too, there would always have been at least a few crops growing in the plot around it, vegetables and small berry bushes, hardy things that always produced at least something to feed them.

That was not what he saw before him.

Berin broke into as much of a run then as he could manage after so long a walk, the sense of something wrong gnawing away at him, feeling like one of his vises clamped around his heart.

He reached the door and threw it wide. Maybe, he thought, everything would be all right. Maybe they had spotted him and were all just ensuring that his arrival would be a surprise.

It was dim inside, the windows crusted with grime. And there, a presence.

Marita stood in the main room, stirring a pot that smelled too sour to Berin. She turned toward him as he burst in, and as she did, Berin knew he'd been right. Something was wrong. Something was very wrong.

"Marita?" he began.

"Husband." Even the flat way she said that told him that nothing was as it should be. Any other time he'd been away, Marita had thrown her arms around him as he'd come in the door. She'd always seemed full of life. Now, she seemed… empty.

"What's going on here?" Berin asked.

"I don't know what you mean." Again, there was less emotion than there should have been, as though something in his wife had broken, letting all the joy out of her.

"Why is everything around here so… so *still*?" Berin demanded. "Where are our children?"

"They aren't here right now," Marita said. She moved back to the pot as though everything was perfectly normal.

"Where are they, then?" Berin wasn't going to let it go. He could believe that the boys might have run down to the nearest stream or had errands to run, but one of his children at least would have seen him coming home and been there to meet him. "Where is Ceres?"

"Oh yes," Marita said, and Berin could hear the bitterness there now. "Of course you would ask after *her*. Not how things are with me. Not your sons. Her."

Berin had never heard his wife sound quite like this before. Oh, he'd always known there was something hard in Marita, more concerned for herself than for the rest of the world, but now it sounded as though her heart was ashes.

Marita seemed to calm down then, and the sheer speed with which she did it made it suspicious to Berin.

"You want to know what your precious daughter did?" she said. "She ran away."

Berin's apprehension deepened. He shook his head. "I don't believe that."

Marita kept going. "She ran away. Didn't say where she was going, just stole what she could from us when she left."

"We have no money to steal," Berin said. "And Ceres would never do that."

"Of course you'll take her side," Marita said. "But she took… things from around here, possessions. Anything she thought she could sell in the next town, knowing that girl. She abandoned us."

If that was what Marita thought, then Berin was sure she'd never really known her daughter. Or him, if she thought he would believe such an obvious lie. He took her shoulders in his hands, and even though he didn't possess all the strength he'd once had, Berin was still strong enough so that his wife felt fragile by comparison.

"Tell me the truth, Marita! What's happened here?" Berin shook her, as if somehow that might jolt the old version of her back into being, and she might suddenly return to being the Marita he'd married all those years before. All it did was make her pull away.

"Your boys are dead!" Marita yelled back. The words filled the small space of their home, coming out in a snarl. Her voice dropped. "That's what's happened. Our sons are dead."

The words hit Berin like a kick from a horse that didn't want shoeing. "No," he said. "It's another lie. It has to be."

He couldn't think of another thing Marita could have said that would have hurt as much. She had to be just saying this to hurt him.

"When did you decide that you hated me so much?" Berin asked, because that was the only reason he could think of that his wife would throw something so vile at him, using the idea of their sons' deaths as a weapon.

Now Berin could see tears in Marita's eyes. There hadn't been any when she'd been talking about their daughter supposedly running away.

"When you decided to abandon us," his wife snapped back. "When I had to watch Nasos die!"

"Just Nasos?" Berin said.

"Isn't that enough?" Marita shouted back. "Or don't you care about your sons?"

"A moment ago you said that Sartes was dead too," Berin said. "Stop lying to me, Marita!"

"Sartes is dead too," his wife insisted. "Soldiers came and took him. They dragged him off to be a part of the Empire's army, and he's just a boy. How long do you think he will survive as a part of that? No, both of my boys are gone, while Ceres ..."

"What?" Berin demanded.

Marita just shook her head. "If you'd been here, it might not even have happened."

"*You* were here," Berin spat back, trembling all over. "That had been the point. You think I wanted to go? You were meant to look after them while I found the money for us to eat."

Despair gripped Berin then, and he could feel himself starting to weep, as he hadn't wept since he was a child. His oldest son was dead. For all the other lies Marita had come out with, that sounded like the truth. The loss left a hole that seemed to be impossible to fill, even with the grief and anger that were welling up inside him. He forced himself to focus on the others, because it seemed like the only way to stop it from overwhelming him.

"Soldiers took Sartes?" he asked. "Imperial soldiers?"

"You think I'm lying to you about that?" Marita asked.

"I don't know what to believe anymore," Berin replied. "You didn't even try to stop them?"

"They held a knife to my throat," Marita said. "I had to."

"You had to do what?" Berin asked.

Marita shook her head. "I had to call him outside. They would have killed me."

"So you gave him to them instead?"

"What do you think I could do?" Marita demanded. "You weren't here."

And Berin would probably feel guilty about that for as long as he lived. Marita was right. Maybe if he had been here, this wouldn't have happened. He'd gone off, looking to keep his family from starving, and while he'd been away, things had fallen apart. Feeling guilty didn't replace the grief or the anger, though. It only added to it. It bubbled inside Berin, feeling like something alive and fighting to get out.

"What about Ceres?" he demanded. He shook Marita again. "Tell me! The truth this time. What did you do?"

Marita just pulled away again though, and this time she sank down on her haunches on the floor, curling up and not even looking at him. "Find out for yourself. I've been the one who's had to live with this. Me, not you."

There was a part of Berin that wanted to keep shaking her until she gave him an answer. That wanted to force the truth from her, whatever it took. Yet he wasn't that kind of man, and knew he never could be. Even the thought of it disgusted him.

He didn't take anything from the house when he left. There wasn't anything he wanted there. As he looked back at Marita, so totally wrapped up in her own bitterness that she'd given up her son, tried to disguise what had happened to their children, it was hard to believe that there had ever been.

Berin stepped out into the open air, blinking away what was left of his tears. It was only when the brightness of the sun hit him that he realized he had no idea what he was going to do next. What could he do? There was no helping his oldest son, not now, while the others could be anywhere.

"That doesn't matter," Berin told himself. He could feel the determination within him turning into something like the iron he worked. "It won't stop me."

Perhaps someone nearby would have seen where they had gone. Certainly, someone would know where the army was, and Berin knew as well as anyone that a man who made blades could always find a way to get closer to the army.

As for Ceres… there would be something. She must be *somewhere*. Because the alternative was unthinkable.

Berin looked out over the countryside surrounding his home. Ceres was out there somewhere. So was Sartes. He said the next words aloud, because doing that seemed to turn it into a promise, to himself, to the world, to his children.

"I'll find you both," he vowed. "Whatever it takes."

Chapter Four

Breathing hard, Sartes ran among the army's tents, clutching the scroll in his hand and wiping the sweat from his eyes, knowing that if he did not reach his commander's tent soon he would be flogged. He ducked and weaved as best he could, knowing his time was running out. He had been held up far too many times already.

Sartes already had burn marks on his shins from the times he'd gotten it wrong, their sting just one more among many by now. He blinked, desperate, looking around the army camp, trying to make out the correct direction to run among the endless grid of tents. There were signs and standards there to mark the way, but he was still trying to learn their pattern.

Sartes felt something catch his foot, and then he was tumbling, the world seeming to turn upside down as he fell. For a moment he thought he'd tripped on a rope, but then he looked up to see soldiers laughing. The one at their head was an older man, with stubble-short hair turning gray and scars from too many battles.

Fear filled Sartes then, but also a kind of resignation; this was just life in the army for a conscript like him. He didn't demand to know why the other man had done it, because saying anything was a sure way to a beating. As far as he could see, practically anything was.

Instead, he stood up, brushing away the worst of the mud from his tunic.

"What are you about, whelp?" the soldier who'd tripped him demanded.

"Running an errand for my commander, sir," Sartes said, lifting a scrap of parchment for the other man to see. He hoped it would be enough to keep him safe. Often it wasn't, in spite of the rules that said orders took precedence over anything else.

In the time since he'd arrived there, Sartes had learned that the Imperial army had plenty of rules. Some were official: leave the camp without permission, refuse to follow orders, betray the army, and you could be killed. March the wrong way, do anything without permission, and you could be beaten. There were other rules too, though. Less official ones that could be just as dangerous to break.

"What errand would that be?" the soldier demanded. Others were gathering around now. The army was always short of sources of entertainment, so if there was the prospect of a little fun at a conscript's expense, people paid attention.

Sartes did his best to look apologetic. "I don't know, sir. I just have orders to deliver this message. You can read it if you like."

That was a calculated risk. Most of the ordinary soldiers couldn't read. He hoped that the tone of it wouldn't earn him a cuff around the ear for insubordination, but tried not to show any fear. Not showing fear was one of the rules that wasn't written down. The army had at least as many of those rules as official ones. Rules about who you had to know to get better food. About who knew whom, and who you had to be careful of, regardless of rank. Knowing them seemed to be the only way to survive.

"Well, you'd better get on with it then!" the soldier roared, aiming a kick at Sartes to get him moving. The others there laughed as if it was the greatest joke they'd seen.

One of the biggest unwritten rules seemed to be that the new conscripts were fair game. Since he'd arrived, Sartes had been punched and slapped, beaten and shoved. He'd been made to run until he felt like collapsing, then run some more. He'd been laden with so much gear that he'd felt as though he could barely stand up, made to carry it, to dig holes in the ground for no apparent reason, to work. He'd heard stories of men in the ranks who liked to do worse to the new conscripts. Even if they died, what did it matter to the army? They were there to be thrown at the enemy. Everyone expected them to die.

Sartes had expected to die the first day. By the end of it, he'd even felt as though he wanted to. He'd curled up inside the too thin tent they'd assigned him and shivered, hoping that the ground would swallow him up. Impossibly, the next day had been worse. Another new conscript, whose name Sartes hadn't even learned, had been killed that day. He'd been caught trying to run away, and they'd all had to watch his execution, as if it were some kind of lesson. The only lesson Sartes had been able to see was how cruel the army was to anyone who let it see that they were afraid. That was when he'd started trying to bury his fear, not showing it even though it was there in the background almost every moment he was awake.

He made a detour between the tents now, switching directions briefly to swing by one of the mess tents, where a day ago, one of the cooks had needed help composing a message home. The army barely fed its conscripts, and Sartes could feel his stomach rumbling at the prospect of food, but he didn't eat what he took with him as he ran for his commanding officer's tent.

"Where have you been?" the officer demanded. His tone made it clear that being slowed down by other soldiers wouldn't count as an excuse. But then, Sartes had known that. It was part of why he'd gone to the mess tent.

"Collecting this on the way, sir," Sartes said, holding out the apple tart that he'd heard was the officer's favorite. "I knew that there might not be an opportunity for you to get it yourself today."

The officer's demeanor changed instantly. "That's very thoughtful, conscript—"

"Sartes, sir." Sartes didn't dare to smile.

"Sartes. We could use some soldiers who know how to think. Although next time, remember that the orders have to come first."

"Yes sir," Sartes said. "Is there anything you require me to do, sir?"

The officer waved him away. "Not right now, but I'll remember your name. Dismissed."

Sartes left the commander's pavilion feeling a lot better than when he'd gone in. He hadn't been sure that the small act would be enough to save him after the delay the soldiers had caused. For now, though, he seemed to have avoided punishment, and had managed to get to the position where an officer knew who he was.

It felt like a knife edge, but the whole army felt like that to Sartes then. So far, he'd survived in the army by being clever, and keeping one step ahead of the worst of the violence there. He'd seen boys his age killed, or beaten so badly that it was obvious that they'd die soon. Even so, he wasn't sure how long he would be able to keep that up. For a conscript like him, this was the kind of place where violence and death could only be put off so long.

Sartes swallowed as he thought of all the things that could go wrong. A soldier might take a beating too far. An officer might take offense at any tiny action and order a punishment designed to deter the others with its cruelty. He might be pushed forward into battle at any moment, and he'd heard that conscripts went at the front of the line to "weed out the weak." Even training might prove deadly, when the army had little use for blunt weapons, and conscripts were given little real instruction.

The one fear that sat behind them all was that someone would find out he'd tried to join Rexus and the rebels. There should be no way that they could, but even the faintest possibility was enough to outweigh all the others. Sartes had seen the body of a soldier accused of having rebel sympathies. His own unit had been commanded to hack him to pieces to prove their loyalty. Sartes didn't want to end up like that. Just the thought of it was enough to make his stomach tighten over and above the hunger.

"You there!" a voice called, and Sartes started. It was impossible to shake the feeling that maybe someone had guessed what he was thinking. He forced himself to at least pretend to be calm. Sartes looked round to see a soldier in the elaborately muscled armor of a sergeant, with pockmarks on his cheeks so deep they were almost like another landscape. "You're the captain's messenger?"

"I've just come from carrying a message to him, sir," Sartes said. It wasn't quite a lie.

"Then you're good enough for me. Go find out where the carts with my timber supplies have gotten to. If anyone gives you trouble, tell them Venn sent you."

Sartes saluted hurriedly. "At once, sir."

He ran off on the errand, but as he went he did not focus on the mission at hand. He took a longer way, a more circuitous way. A way that would enable him to spy the camp's outskirts, their choke points, a way that would allow him to pry for any weak points.

Because, dead or not, Sartes would find a way to escape tonight.

Chapter Five

Lucious pushed his way through the crowds of nobles in the castle's throne room, fuming as he went. He fumed at the fact that he had to shove his way through, when everyone there should have stood aside and bowed down, making way for him. He fumed at the fact that Thanos was off getting all the glory, crushing the rebels on Haylon. Above all, though, he fumed at the way things had gone in the Stade. That wench Ceres had ruined his plans once again.

Ahead, Lucious could see the king and queen in deep conversation with Cosmas, the old fool from the library. Lucious had thought he'd seen the last of the aged scholar as a child, when they'd all been made to learn ludicrous facts about the world and its workings. But no, apparently, in the wake of the letter he had provided, showing Ceres's true treachery, Cosmas got to have the ear of his king.

Lucious kept pushing his way forward. Around him, he could hear the nobles of the court at their petty plotting. He could see his distant cousin Stephania not far away, laughing at some joke another perfectly presented noble girl had made. She looked over, catching Lucious's eye just long enough to smile at him. She really was, Lucious decided, quite an empty-headed thing. But a beautiful one. Perhaps in the future, he thought, there might be an opportunity to spend more time around the noble girl. He was at least as impressive as Thanos, by any estimation.

For now, though, Lucious's anger at what had happened was too great for even those thoughts to amuse him. He stalked to the foot of the thrones, right to the edge of the raised dais there.

"She still lives!" he blurted out as he neared the throne. It didn't matter to him that it was loud enough to carry to the whole room. Let them hear, he decided. It certainly made no difference that Cosmas was still whispering away to the king and queen. What, Lucious wondered, could a man who spent his time around scrolls possibly have that was worth saying?

"Did you hear me?" Lucious said. "The girl is—"

"Still alive, yes," the king said, stopping him with a hand held up for silence. "We are discussing more important matters. Thanos is missing in the battle for Haylon."

The gesture was just one more thing to add to Lucious's anger. He was being treated like some servant to be quieted, he thought. Even so, he waited. He couldn't afford the king's anger. Besides, it took a moment or two to digest what he'd just heard.

Thanos was missing? Lucious tried to work out how it affected him. Would it change his position within the court? He found himself glancing across at Stephania again, thoughtful.

"Thank you, Cosmas," the queen said at last.

Lucious watched as the scholar descended back into the crowd of watching nobles. Only then did the king and queen give him their attention. Lucious tried to stand straight. He would not let the others there see any of the resentment that burned through him at the small insult. If anyone else had treated him this way, Lucious told himself, he would have killed them by now.

"We are aware that Ceres survived the last Killing," King Claudius said. To Lucious, he barely even sounded annoyed by it, let alone as though he were burning with the same anger that flooded him at the thought of the peasant.

But then, Lucious thought, the king hadn't been the one who had been defeated by the girl. Not once, but twice now, because she'd bested him through some trickery when he'd gone to her room to teach her a lesson too. Lucious felt that he had every reason, every *right*, to take her survival personally.

"Then you're aware that it can't be allowed to continue," Lucious said. He couldn't keep his tone as courtly and even as it should be. "You must deal with her."

"Must?" Queen Athena said. "Careful, Lucious. We are still your rulers."

"With respect, your majesties," Stephania said, and Lucious watched her glide forward, her silk dress clinging to her. "Lucious is right. Ceres cannot be allowed to live."

Lucious saw the king's eyes narrow slightly.

"And what do you suggest we do?" King Claudius demanded. "Drag her out onto the sands and have her beheaded? You were the one who suggested that she should fight, Stephania. You can't complain if she isn't dying fast enough for your tastes."

Lucious understood that part, at least. There was no pretext for her death, and the people seemed to demand that for those they loved. Even more astonishingly, they *did* seem to love her. Why? Because she could fight a little? As far as Lucious could see, any fool could do that. Many fools did. If the people had any sense, they would give their love where it was deserved: to their rightful rulers.

"I understand that she cannot simply be executed, your majesty," Stephania said, with one of those innocent smiles that Lucious had noticed she did so well.

"I'm glad you understand it," the king said, with obvious annoyance. "Do you also understand what would happen if she *were* harmed now? Now that she has fought? Now that she has won?"

Of course Lucious understood. He wasn't some child for whom politics was an alien landscape.

Stephania summed it up. "It would fuel the revolution, your majesty. The people of the city might revolt."

"There is no 'might' about it," King Claudius said. "We have the Stade for a reason. The people have a thirst for blood, and we give them what they are looking for. That need for violence can turn against us just as easily."

Lucious laughed at that. It was hard to believe that the king really thought Delos's populace would ever be able to sweep them away. He had seen them, and they were not some blood-drenched tide. They were a rabble. Teach them a lesson, he thought. Kill enough of them, show them the consequences of their actions harshly enough, and they would soon fall into line.

"Is something funny, Lucious?" the queen asked him, and Lucious could hear the sharp edge there. The king and queen did not like being laughed at. Thankfully, though, he had an answer.

"It is just that the answer to all of this seems obvious," Lucious said. "I am not asking for Ceres to be executed. I am saying that we underestimated her abilities as a fighter. Next time, we must not."

"And give her an excuse to become more popular if she wins?" Stephania asked. "She has become beloved by the people because of her victory."

Lucious smiled at that. "Have you seen the way the commoners react in the Stade?" he asked. He understood this part, even if the others did not.

He saw Stephania sniff. "I try not to watch them, cousin."

"But you will have heard them. They call the names of their favorites. They bay for blood. And when their favorites fall, what then?" He looked around, half expecting someone to have an answer for him. To his disappointment, no one did. Perhaps Stephania wasn't bright enough to see it. Lucious didn't mind that.

"They call the names of the new winners," Lucious explained. "They love them just as much as they loved the last ones. Oh, they call for this girl now, but when she lies bleeding on the sand, they will bay for her death as quickly as for anyone else. We just have to stack the odds a little more against her."

The king looked thoughtful at that. "What did you have in mind?"

"If we get this wrong," the queen said, "they will just love her more."

Finally, Lucious could feel some of his anger being replaced by something else: satisfaction. He looked over to the doors to the throne room, where one of his attendants was standing waiting. A snap of his fingers was all it took to send the man running, but then, all Lucious's servants quickly learned that angering him was anything but wise.

"I have a remedy for that," Lucious said, gesturing toward the door.

The shackled man who walked in was easily more than seven feet tall, with ebony black skin and muscles that bulged above the short kilt he wore. Tattoos covered his flesh; the slaver who had sold the combatlord had told Lucious that each one represented a foe he had slain in single combat, both within the Empire and in the lands far to the south where he had been found.

Even so, for Lucious, the most intimidating part of it all wasn't the size of the man or his strength. It was the look in his eyes. There was something there that simply didn't seem to understand things like compassion or mercy, pain or fear. That could happily have torn them all limb from limb without feeling a thing. There were scars on the warrior's torso where blades had struck him. Lucious couldn't imagine that expression changing even then.

Lucious enjoyed watching the reactions of the others there as they saw the fighter, chained like some wild beast and stalking through them. Some of the women made small sounds of fear, while the men stepped back hurriedly out of his path, seeming to sense instinctively just how dangerous this man was. Fear seemed to push emptiness ahead of him, and Lucious basked in the effect his combatlord had. He watched Stephania take a scurrying step back out of the way, and Lucious smiled.

"They call him the Last Breath," Lucious said. "He has never lost a bout, and never let a foe live. Say hello," he grinned, "to Ceres's next—and final—opponent."

CHAPTER SIX

Ceres woke to darkness, the room lit only by moonlight filtering in through the shutters, and by a single flickering candle. She struggled toward consciousness, remembering. She remembered the beast's claws ripping at her, and just the memory seemed to be enough to summon the pain to her. It flared in her back as she half turned to her side, hot and sudden enough to make her cry out. The pain was all-consuming.

"Oh," a voice said, "does it hurt?"

A figure stepped into view. Ceres couldn't make out the details at first, but slowly, they swam into place. Stephania stood there over her bed, as pale as the shafts of moonlight that surrounded her, forming a perfect picture of the innocent noble, there to visit the sick and injured. Ceres had no doubt that it was deliberate.

"Don't worry," Stephania said. To Ceres, the words still seemed to come from too far away, fighting their way through fog. "The healers here gave you something to help you sleep while they stitched you back together. They seemed quite impressed you're still alive, and they wanted to take away your pain."

Ceres saw her hold up a small bottle. It was a dull green against the paleness of Stephania's hand, stoppered with a cork and glistening around the rim. Ceres saw the noble girl smile, and that smile felt as though it was made of sharp edges.

"*I* am not impressed that you have managed to live," Stephania said. "That wasn't the idea at *all*."

Ceres tried to reach out for her. In theory, this should have been the moment to escape. If she had been stronger, she could have burst past Stephania and made for the door. If she could have found a way to fight past the cloudiness that felt as though it was filling her head to the breaking point, she might have been able to grab Stephania and force her to help in escaping.

Yet it seemed as if her body was only obeying her sluggishly, responding long after she wanted it to. It was all Ceres could do to sit up with the covers wrapped around her, and even that brought with it a fresh wave of agony.

She saw Stephania run a finger down the bottle she held. "Oh, don't worry, Ceres. There's a reason you're feeling so helpless. The healers asked me to make sure you got your dose of their drug, so I did. Some of it, anyway. Enough to keep you docile. Not enough to actually take away your pain."

"What did I do to make you hate me this much?" Ceres asked, although she already knew the answer. She'd been close to Thanos, and he'd rejected Stephania. "Does having Thanos for your husband really matter to you this much?"

"You're slurring your words, Ceres," Stephania said, with another of those smiles without any warmth behind it that Ceres could see. "And I don't hate you. Hate would imply that you were in some way worthy of being my enemy. Tell me, do you know anything about poison?"

Just the mention of it was enough to make Ceres's heart speed up, anxiety blossoming in her chest.

"Poison is such an elegant weapon," Stephania said, as though Ceres weren't even there. "Far more so than knives or spears. You think you are so strong because you get to play with swords with all the real combatlords? Yet I could have poisoned you while you slept, so easily. I could have added something to your sleeping draught. I could simply have given you too much of it, so that you never woke up."

"People would have known," Ceres managed.

Stephania shrugged. "Would they have cared? In any case, it would have been an accident. Poor Stephania, trying to help, but not really knowing what she was doing, gave our newest combatlord too much medicine."

She put a hand to her mouth in mock surprise. It was such a perfect mime of shocked remorse, even down to the tear that seemed to glisten at the corner of her eye. When she spoke again, she sounded different to Ceres. Her voice was thick with regret and disbelief. There was even a small catch there, as if she were struggling to hold back the urge to sob.

"Oh no. What have I done? I didn't mean to. I thought… I thought I did everything exactly the way they told me to!"

She laughed then, and in that moment, Ceres saw her for what she was. She could see through the act that Stephania so carefully maintained all the time. How did no one notice? Ceres wondered. How could they not see what lay behind the beautiful smiles and the delicate laughter?

"They all think I'm stupid, you know," Stephania said. She stood straighter now, looking a lot more dangerous to Ceres than she had. "I take great care to *ensure* that they think I'm stupid. Oh, don't look so worried, I'm not going to poison you."

"Why not?" Ceres asked. She knew there had to be a reason.

She saw Stephania's expression harden in the candlelight, a frown creasing the otherwise smooth skin of her brow.

"Because that would be too easy," Stephania said. "After the way you and Thanos humiliated me, I would rather see you suffer. You both deserve it."

"There's nothing else you can do to me," Ceres said, although in that moment, it didn't feel like it. Stephania could have walked over to the bed and hurt her a hundred different ways, and Ceres knew she would have been powerless to stop it. Ceres knew the noble would have no idea how to fight, but she could have bested Ceres easily right then.

"Of course there is," Stephania said. "There are weapons in the world even better than poison. The right words, for instance. Let's see now. Which of these will hurt most? Your beloved Rexus is dead, of course. Let's start with that."

Ceres tried not to let any of the shock she felt show on her face. She tried not to let the grief rise up enough that the noble girl could see it. Yet she knew from the look of satisfaction on Stephania's face that there must have been some flicker.

"He died fighting for you," Stephania said. "I thought you would want to know that part. It does make it so much more… romantic."

"You're lying," Ceres insisted, but somewhere inside she knew that Stephania wouldn't be. She would only say something like this if it was a truth Ceres could check, something that would hurt and go on hurting as she found out the reality of it.

"I don't need to lie. Not when the truth is so much better," Stephania said. "Thanos is dead too. He died in the fighting for Haylon, right there on the beaches."

A fresh wave of grief hit Ceres, sweeping over her and threatening to wash away all sense of herself. She'd fought with Thanos before he'd left, about the death of her brother, and about what he was planning to do, fighting the rebellion. She had never thought they could be the last words she would say to him. She'd left a message with Cosmas specifically so that they wouldn't be.

"There's one more," Stephania said. "Your younger brother? Sartes? He has been taken for the army. I made sure that the draft takers didn't overlook him just because he was the brother of Thanos's weapon keeper."

Ceres did try to lunge at her this time, the anger that filled her fueling her leap for the noble girl. As weak as she was, though, there was no chance of success. She felt her legs tangling in the bed sheets, sending her tumbling to the floor, looking up at Stephania.

"How long do you think your brother will last in the army?" Stephania asked. Ceres saw her expression turn into something like a mockery of pity. "The poor boy. They are so cruel to the conscripts. They're all practically traitors, after all."

"Why?" Ceres managed.

Stephania spread her hands. "You took Thanos from me, and that was everything I had planned for my future. Now, I'm going to take everything from you."

"I'll kill you," Ceres promised.

Stephania laughed. "You won't have a chance. This"—she reached down to touch Ceres's back, and Ceres had to bite her lip to keep from screaming—"is nothing. That little fight in the Stade was nothing. The worst fights imaginable will be there waiting for you, again and again, until you die."

"You think people won't notice?" Ceres said. "You think they won't guess what you're doing? You threw me in there because you thought they'd rise up. What will they do if they think you're cheating them?"

She saw Stephania shake her head.

"People see what they want to see. With you, it seems as though they want to see their princess combatlord, the girl who can fight as well as any man. They'll believe it, and they'll love you, right up to the point where you're turned into a laughing stock out on the sands. They'll watch you torn to shreds, but before that, they'll cheer for it to happen."

Ceres could only watch as Stephania started for the door. The noble girl stopped, turning back toward her, and for a moment, she looked as sweet and innocent as ever.

"Oh, I almost forgot. I tried to give you your medicine, but I didn't think you'd knock it from my hand before I could give you enough."

She took out the vial she'd had before, and Ceres watched it tumble to the ground as she dropped it. It shattered, the pieces spinning across the floor of Ceres's room in splinters that would make it both painful and dangerous for her to try to find her way back into her bed. Ceres had no doubt that Stephania intended it that way.

She saw the noble girl reach out for the candle that lit the room, and briefly, in the instant before she snuffed it out, Stephania's sweet smile faded again, to be replaced by something cruel.

"I will be there to dance at your funeral, Ceres. I promise you that."

Chapter Seven

"I still say that we should gut him and throw his body out for the other Empire soldiers to find."

"That's because you're an idiot, Nico. Even if they noticed one more body among the rest, who's to say they'd care? And then we'd have the trouble of bringing him down somewhere they'd see him. No. We should ransom him."

Thanos sat in the cave where the rebels had holed up for the moment, listening to them argue about his fate. His hands were tied in front of him, but at least they'd done their best to patch and bandage his wounds, leaving him in front of a small fire so he wouldn't freeze while they decided whether to kill him in cold blood or not.

The rebels sat at other fires, huddling around them, discussing what they could do to keep the island from falling to the Empire. They spoke quietly, so that Thanos couldn't overhear the details, but he already knew the gist of it: they were losing, and losing badly. They were in the caves because there was nowhere else for them to go.

After a while, the one who was obviously their leader came and sat down opposite Thanos, crossing his legs on the hard stone of the cave floor. He pushed across a hunk of bread that Thanos devoured hungrily. He wasn't sure how long it had been since he'd last eaten.

"I am Akila," the other man said. "I command this rebellion."

"Thanos."

"Just Thanos?"

Thanos could hear the curiosity there, and the impatience. He wondered if the other man had guessed who he was. Either way, the truth seemed like the best option right then.

"Prince Thanos," he admitted.

Akila sat there opposite him for several seconds, and Thanos found himself wondering if he was going to die then. It had been close enough when the rebels had thought he was just some noble without a name. Now that they knew he was one of the royal family, close to the king who had oppressed them so much, it seemed impossible that they would do anything else.

"A prince," Akila said. He looked around at the others, and Thanos saw the flash of a smile there. "Hey, lads, we've got ourselves a prince here."

"We should definitely ransom him then!" one of the rebels called out. "He'd be worth a fortune!"

"We should definitely kill him," another snapped back. "Think about all his kind have done to us!"

"All right, that's enough," Akila said. "Concentrate on the fight ahead. It's going to be a long night."

Thanos heard a faint sigh from the other man as the men went back to their fires.

"It's not going well, then?" Thanos said. "You said before that your side was losing."

Akila gave him a sharp look. "I should know when to keep my mouth shut. Maybe so should you."

"You're wondering whether to kill me anyway," Thanos pointed out. "I figure that I don't have a lot to lose."

Thanos waited. This wasn't the kind of man he could push into giving him answers. There was something tough about Akila. Unyielding and straightforward. Thanos guessed that he would have liked him if they'd met under better circumstances.

"All right," Akila said. "Yes, we're losing. You Imperials have more men than we do, and you don't care about the damage you do. The city is under siege from land and from water, so that no one can get away. We'll fight from the hills, but when you can just resupply by water, there's not a lot we can do. Draco may be a butcher, but he's a clever one."

Thanos nodded. "He is."

"And of course, you were probably there when he planned all of it," Akila said.

Now Thanos understood. "Is that what you're hoping? That I know all of their plans?" He shook his head. "I wasn't there when they made them. I didn't want to be here, and I only came because they escorted me onto the ship under guard. Maybe if I had been there, I would have heard the part where they planned to stab me in the back."

He thought of Ceres then, about the way he'd been forced to leave her behind. That hurt more than the rest of it put together. If someone in a position of power was going to try to have him killed, he wondered, what would they do to her?

"You have enemies," Akila agreed. Thanos saw him clench and unclench one hand, as if the long battle for the city had started to make it cramp. "They're even the same as my enemies. I don't know if that makes you my friend, though."

Thanos looked around pointedly at the rest of the cave. At the shockingly low numbers of soldiers left there. "Right now, it looks as though you could do with all the friends you can get."

"You're still a noble. You still have your position because of the blood of ordinary folk," Akila said. He sighed again. "It looks as though if I kill you, I'm doing what Draco and his masters want, but you've as good as told me that if I ransom you, I get nothing for you. I have a fight to win, and no time to keep prisoners around if they don't know anything. So, what am I supposed to do with you, Prince Thanos?"

Thanos got the impression that he was serious. That he actually wanted a better solution. Thanos thought quickly.

"I think your best choice is to let me go," he said.

Akila laughed at that. "Nice try. If that's the best you have, hold still. I'll try to make this as painless as possible."

Thanos saw his hand go to one of his swords.

"I'm serious," Thanos said. "I can't help you win the battle for the island if I'm here."

He could see Akila's disbelief, and the certainty that it had to be a trap. Thanos went on quickly, knowing that his best hope of surviving the next few minutes lay in convincing this man that he wanted to help the rebellion.

"You said yourself that one of the big problems is that the Empire has its fleet supporting the assault," Thanos said. "I know that they left supplies on the ships because they were so eager to get on with the attack. So we take the ships."

Akila stood up. "Have you heard this, lads? The prince here has a plan to take the Empire's ships from them."

Thanos saw the rebels start to gather round.

"What good would it do?" Akila asked. "We take their ships, but what then?"

Thanos did his best to explain. "At the very least, it will provide an escape route for some of the people of the city, and for more of your soldiers. It will take away supplies from the Empire's soldiers too, so that they can't keep going for long. And then there are the ballistae."

"What are they?" one of the rebels called out. He didn't look much like a long-term soldier. Very few of those in the room did, to Thanos's eyes.

"Bolt throwers," Thanos explained. "Weapons designed to damage other ships, but if they were turned against soldiers near the shore …"

Akila, at least, looked as though he was considering the possibilities. "That could be something," he admitted. "And we can set light to any ships we can't use. At the very least, Draco would pull his men back to try to get his ships back. But how do we get these ships in the first place, Prince Thanos? I know that where you come from, if a prince asks for something, he gets it, but I doubt that will apply to Draco's fleet."

Thanos forced himself to smile with a level of confidence he didn't feel. "That's almost exactly what we're going to do."

Again, Thanos had the impression of Akila working it out faster than any of his men could. The rebel leader smiled.

"You're mad," Akila said. Thanos couldn't tell if it was intended as an insult or not.

"There are enough dead on the beaches," Thanos explained, for the benefit of the others. "We take their armor and head to the ships. With me there, it will look like a company of soldiers returning from the battle for supplies."

"What do you think?" Akila asked.

In the firelight that flickered inside the cave, Thanos couldn't make out the men who spoke. Instead, their questions seemed to emerge from the darkness, so that he couldn't tell who agreed with him, who doubted him, and who wanted him dead. Still, it was no worse than the politics back home. Better, in a lot of ways, since at least no one was smiling to his face while plotting to kill him.

"What about guards on the ships?" one of the rebels asked.

"There won't be many," Thanos said. "And they'll know who I am."

"What about all the people who will die in the city while we do this?" another called out.

"They're dying now," Thanos insisted. "At least this way, you have a way to fight back. Get this right, and we'll have a way to save hundreds, if not thousands, of them."

Silence fell, and the last question came out of it like an arrow.

"How can we trust him, Akila? He's not just one of them, he's a *noble*. A *prince*."

Thanos whirled away from the direction the voice had come from, offering up his back for anyone to see. "They stabbed me in the back. They left me to die. I have as much reason to hate them as any man here."

In that moment, he wasn't just thinking about the Typhoon. He was thinking about everything his family had done to the people of Delos, and about everything they'd done to Ceres. If they hadn't forced him to go to Fountain Square, he would never have been there when her brother died.

"We could sit here," Thanos said, "or we could act. Yes, it will be dangerous. If they see through our disguise, we're probably dead. I'm willing to risk it. Are you?" When no one answered, Thanos raised his voice. "*Are you?*"

That got a cheer in response. Akila stepped close to him, clapping a hand on Thanos's shoulder.

"All right, Prince, it looks like we're doing things your way. Pull this off, and you'll have a friend for life." His hand tightened until Thanos could feel pain shooting through his back. "Betray us, though, get my men killed, and I swear I'll hunt you down."

Chapter Eight

There were parts of Delos where Berin didn't normally go. They were parts that stank to him of sweat and desperation, as people did whatever they needed to in order to get by. He waved away offers from the shadows, giving the denizens there hard looks to keep them back.

If they'd known about the gold he carried, Berin knew he would have found himself with his throat cut, the purse beneath his tunic divided up and spent in the local taverns and gambling houses before the day was done. It was those places he sought out now, because where else was he going to find soldiers when they were off duty? As a bladesmith, Berin knew fighting men, and he knew the places they would go.

He had gold because he'd visited a merchant, taking with him two daggers he'd forged as examples for those who might have employed him. They'd been beautiful things, worthy of any noble's belt, worked with gold filigree and etched with hunting scenes on the blades. They were the last things of value he had left in the world. He'd stood in line with a dozen other people in front of the merchant's desk, and hadn't gotten half of what he knew they were worth.

To Berin, that didn't matter. All that mattered was finding his children, and that took gold. Gold he could use to buy ale for the right people, gold he could press into the right palms.

He made his way through Delos's taverns, and it was a slow process. He couldn't just come out and ask the questions he wanted to ask. He had to be careful. It helped that he had a few friends in the city, and a few more in the Empire's army. His blades had saved more than a few men's lives, over the years.

He found the man he was looking for half drunk in the middle of the afternoon, sitting in a tavern and stinking so much that he had clear space all around him. Berin guessed that it was only the uniform of the Empire's army that kept them from throwing him face first into the street. Well, that and the fact that Jacare was fat enough that it would have taken half the inn's patrons to lift him.

Berin saw the fat man's eyes lift up as he approached. "Berin? My old friend! Come and have a drink with me! Although you'll have to pay. I'm currently a little…"

"Fat? Drunk?" Berin guessed. He knew the other man wouldn't mind. The soldier seemed to make an effort to be the Imperial army's worst example. He even seemed to take a perverse kind of pride in it.

"…financially embarrassed," Jacare finished.

"I might be able to help with that," Berin said. He ordered drinks, but didn't touch his. He needed to keep a clear head if he was going to find Ceres and Sartes. Instead, he waited while Jacare downed his with a noise that sounded to Berin like a donkey at a water trough.

"So, what brings a man like you to my humble presence?" Jacare asked after a while.

"I'm looking for news," Berin said. "The kind of news a man in your position might have heard."

"Ah, well, *news*. News is a thirsty business. And possibly an expensive one."

"I'm looking for my son and daughter," Berin explained. With someone else, it might have gained him some sympathy, but he knew that with a man like this, it wouldn't have much effect.

"Your son? Nesos, right?"

Berin leaned across the table, his hand closing over Jacare's wrist as the man went to take another drink. He didn't have much of the old strength left that he'd built wielding forge hammers, but there was still enough to make the other man wince. Good, Berin thought.

"Sartes," Berin said. "My eldest son is dead. Sartes has been taken by the army. I know you hear things. I want to know where he is, and I want to know where my daughter, Ceres, is."

Jacare sat back, and Berin let him do it. He wasn't sure he could have held the other man in place much longer anyway.

"That's the kind of thing I might have heard," the soldier admitted, "but that kind of thing is difficult. I have expenses."

Berin brought out the small pouch of gold. He poured it out onto the table, just far enough from the other man that Jacare couldn't snatch it easily.

"Will this cover your 'expenses'?" Berin asked, with a look at the other man's drinking goblet. He saw the other man counting the gold, probably gauging whether there was any more to be had.

"Your daughter is the easy one," Jacare said. "She's up at the castle with the nobles. They announced that she was to marry Prince Thanos."

Berin dared to breathe a sigh of relief at that, even though he wasn't sure what to think. Thanos was one of the few royals with any decency to him, but marriage?

"Your son is trickier. Let me think. I heard that a few of the recruiters from the Twenty-third were doing the rounds down by your quarter, but there's no guarantee that it's them. If it is, they're camped a little way to the south, trying to train up the conscripts to fight rebels."

Bile rose in Berin's mouth at that thought. He could guess how the army would treat Sartes, and just what that "training" would involve. He had to get his son back. But Ceres was closer, and the truth was that he had to at least see his daughter before he went after Sartes. He stood.

"Not going to finish your drink?" Jacare asked.

Berin didn't answer. He was going to the castle.

⚜ ⚜ ⚜

It was easier for Berin to get into the castle than it would have been for almost anyone else. It had been a while, but he was still the one who had come there to discuss the requirements for combatlords' weapons, or to bring special pieces for the nobles. It was simple enough to pretend that he was back in business, heading straight past the guards on the outer gates and into the space where the fighters prepared.

The next step was to get from there to wherever his daughter was. There was a barred gateway between the vaulted space where the warriors practiced and the rest of the castle. Berin had to wait for that to open from the other side, pushing past the servant who did it and trying to pretend that he had important business elsewhere in the building.

He did, just not the kind that most of the people there would understand.

"Hey, you! Where do you think you're going?"

Berin froze at the rough tone of that. He knew before he turned that there would be a guard there, and he didn't have an excuse that would satisfy them. The best he could hope for now would be to be thrown out of the castle before he could get close to seeing his daughter. The worst would involve the castle's dungeons, or maybe just being dragged away to be executed where no one would ever know.

He turned and saw two guards who had obviously been soldiers of the Empire for a while. They had as much gray in their hair as Berin did these days, with the weathered look of men who'd spent too much time fighting in the sun over too many years. One was a good head taller than Berin, but stooped slightly over the spear he leaned on. The other had a beard that he'd oiled and waxed until it looked almost as sharp as the weapon he held. Relief flooded through Berin as he saw them, because he recognized them both.

"Varo, Caxus?" Berin said. "It's me, Berin."

The tension hung there for a moment, and Berin found himself hoping that the two would remember him. Then the guards laughed.

"So it is," Varo said, unbending from over his spear for a moment. "We haven't seen you in … how long has it been, Caxus?"

The other stroked his beard while he considered. "It's been months since he was last here. Haven't really talked since he delivered those bracers for me last summer."

"I've been away," Berin explained. He didn't say where. People might not pay their smiths much, but he doubted they would react well to him looking for work elsewhere. Soldiers didn't usually like the idea of their enemies receiving good blades. "Times have been hard."

"Times have been hard all around," Caxus agreed. Berin saw him frown slightly. "It still doesn't explain what you're doing in the main castle."

"You shouldn't be in here, bladesmith, and you know it," Varo agreed.

"What is it?" Caxus asked. "An emergency repair for some noble lad's favorite sword? I think we'd have heard if Lucious had snapped a blade. He'd probably have flogged his servants raw."

Berin knew he wouldn't be able to get away with a lie like that. Instead, he decided to try the one thing that might work: honesty. "I'm here to see my daughter."

He heard Varo suck in air between his teeth. "Ah, now that's a tricky one."

Caxus nodded. "Saw her fighting in the Stade the other day. Tough little thing. She killed a spiny bear and a combatlord. Hard fight though."

Berin's heart tightened in his chest as he heard that. They had Ceres fighting on the sands? Even though he knew it had been her dream to fight there, this didn't feel like the fulfillment of it. No, this was something else.

"I have to see her," Berin insisted.

Varo tilted his head to one side. "Like I said, tricky. No one gets in to see her now. Queen's orders."

"But I'm her father," Berin said.

Caxus spread his hands. "There's not a lot we can do."

Berin thought quickly. "Not a lot you can do? Was that what I said when you needed your spear re-hafting before your captain saw that you'd snapped it that time?"

"We said we wouldn't talk about that," the guard said, with a worried look.

"And what about you, Varo?" Berin continued, pressing his point home before the other could decide to throw him out. "Did I say that it was 'tricky' when you wanted a sword that would actually fit your hand, rather than army issue?"

"Well ..."

Berin didn't stop. The important thing was to push forward past their objections. No, the *important* thing was to see his daughter.

"How many times has my work saved your lives?" he demanded. "Varo, you told me the story of that bandit chief your unit went after. Whose sword did you use to kill him?"

"Yours," Varo admitted.

"And Caxus, when you wanted all that filigree work on your greaves to impress that girl you married, who did you go to?"

"You," Caxus said. Berin could see him pondering.

"And that's before we get to the days when I was following you all around on campaign," Berin said. "What about—"

Caxus raised a hand. "All right, all right. You've made your point. Your daughter's room is further up. We'll show you the way. But if anyone asks, we're just escorting you *out* of the building."

Berin doubted anyone would ask, but that didn't matter right then. Only one thing did. He was going to see his daughter. He followed the two along the castle's corridors, finally coming to a door that was barred and locked from the outside. Since the key sat in the lock, he turned it.

Berin's heart nearly burst at his first sight of his daughter for months. She lay in bed, groaning as she came to, and looking at him with bleary eyes.

"Father?"

"Ceres!" Berin ran to her, throwing his arms around her and crushing her tight to him. "It's okay. I'm here."

He wanted to hold her tightly and never let her go right then, but he heard Ceres's gasp of pain as he hugged her, and he pulled back hurriedly.

"What's wrong?" Berin asked.

"No, it's all right," Ceres said. "I'm fine."

"You're not fine," Berin said. His daughter had always been so strong, so if she was in pain, it had to be bad. Berin never wanted to see his daughter hurt like that. "Let me look."

Ceres let him, and Berin winced at what he saw. Tightly stitched wounds ran in parallel lines across his daughter's back.

"How did you get in here?" Ceres asked while he did it. "How did you even find me?"

"I still have some friends," her father said. "And I wasn't going to give up without finding you."

Ceres turned to him, and Berin could see the love there in her eyes. "I'm glad you're here."

"So am I," Berin said. "I should never have left you with your mother."

Ceres reached out to take his hand, and Berin had forgotten quite how much he missed his daughter until then. "You're here now."

"I am," Berin said. He took another look at her back. "They haven't cleaned it properly. Here, let me find something to help."

It was hard having to leave even for that short time. Varo and Caxus were still outside, and it didn't take much to get them to bring food and water. Maybe they saw the look on his face when it came to things that involved Ceres's well-being.

He passed her the bowl of food, and the speed with which Ceres devoured it told Berin everything he needed to know about how they'd been treating her here. He took the bowl of water, using it to clean out the wounds she'd gotten from her fight.

Ceres nodded. "I'm a lot better than I was."

"Then I don't want to think about how bad it was," Berin said.

He couldn't keep the guilt from washing up over him. If he hadn't gone, then his children would never have gone through any of this.

"I'm sorry, I should have been here."

"It might not have changed anything," Ceres said, and Berin could tell that she was trying to reassure him. "The rebellion would still have happened. I might still have fought in the Stade."

"Maybe." Berin didn't want to believe it. He knew Ceres had always had an attraction to the danger of the Stade, but that didn't mean she would have fought there. She might have been safe. "I could have protected you and your brothers."

Ceres took his hand again. "I think there are some things even you can't protect us from."

Berin smiled. "Do you remember when you were little? You used to think I was the strongest man in the world, and I could protect you from anything?"

Ceres smiled back. "Now I have to protect myself, and I'm strong enough to do it."

There was a part of Berin that was happy it was true, but he still wanted to be there for his daughter. "Either way, it's over. We'll get you out of here."

Berin thought about the guards. Exactly how much did they owe him? Exactly how much would they help before they decided it was easier to take him into custody?

"I'll find a way," Berin promised.

Ceres shook her head quickly. "No. I'm not running away."

"I know you're worried about being caught," Berin said, covering her hand with his, "but I think I have enough friends in the castle to get us both out. We could join the rebellion."

"It's not about that," Ceres said. "This is my path. I'm here to fight. I'm meant to fight."

He stared back, stunned.

"You *want* to stay here?" That was hard to believe, especially when it had taken so much to find her. It had felt obvious that if he could only get inside, he could have his family back. "I thought you'd want to go. That we could find Sartes together, and everything would be all right."

"Everything will be all right," Ceres promised him. "And you should go to find Sartes. Get him safe."

She stood and dressed in her training clothes. For a moment, Berin thought that she might come with him after all, but she showed no sign of doing so.

"What are you doing?" he asked. "If you're not coming with me, you should rest."

"I can't," Ceres said. She turned back toward him, determination set on her face. "I'm going to train. They want to kill me, but I'm not going to let them. I'm not going to give up, and I'm not going to give them the satisfaction of seeing me run away."

Berin swallowed at the strength there in his daughter. Even so, he didn't want to just leave her. "I could come with you. I could help you."

Ceres shook her head.

"It is a path for me alone, Father."

He smiled at her, and he could feel his eyes well with tears, as he saw hers well, too. He had never been more proud of her, or loved her more.

He stepped forward as she did, and they embraced for a long time.

"I love you, Ceres," he whispered, "and I always will."

"I know, Father," she replied. "And whether we ever meet again or not, you should know that I love you, too."

CHAPTER NINE

Ceres focused, dodging, weaving, gasping for breath, bruises rising from where the sticks had struck her. Master Isel faced her in the training grounds, and she stared back. As she stood there, she wondered if she had been right to request that he train her again so soon. He had seemed doubtful she was well enough, barely recovered as she was from her injuries. Yet she had insisted, determined to get back out there, to better herself, to be ready for the next match.

To go down in the Stade fighting.

The moment she'd said that she was, Isel had taken Ceres at her word, and had pushed her harder than he'd ever pushed her before. He, too, seemed to know what was at stake.

"Move!" he cried.

Ceres tried to keep up with Master Isel's instructions as she whirled on the sparring grounds. He was using a pair of long sticks against her, swinging them so that Ceres had to dodge and parry with the practice blade she held.

"Circle the other way!" he bellowed, as Ceres took a step to her right. She had to dodge back as he thrust with one of the sticks. "Don't go straight back. Do you want an enemy to chase you down? No, no, not like that!"

One of the sticks swept round, knocking Ceres's sword from her hand as it smashed into her forearm. She felt a stab of pain and watched as it landed point-first in the sand.

"Extend your sword when you are not attacking, and you will lose the arm!"

Master Isel swung around his sticks at Ceres's head to demonstrate his point. Ceres threw herself into a roll, coming up with her sword in her hand.

Ceres leaped and dodged, blocked and avoided. Even so, some of the blows got through. One knocked the air from her lungs, and she had to force herself to keep fighting. She fought until she could barely see, sweat stinging her eyes.

Finally, Isel stepped back, studying her, signaling it was time to rest.

She leaned on her sword and took a break.

Out of the corner of her eye Ceres glimpsed Lucious stepping down onto the sands to train. He strode in wearing full armor, though no one else there wore any. He looked about him, gestured to a weapon keeper, and started to spar with him, even though the weapon keeper clearly had no experience. Lucious seemed to be delighting in slamming his practice blade into his unprotected opponent.

Ceres stopped to watch when suddenly a sharp blow from one of Master Isel's sticks snapped her out of it.

"It was time to rest!" she exclaimed, indignant.

He smiled.

"Never trust your opponent."

Ceres began her dance with the constantly moving sticks again. On and on it went, until finally, Master Isel stepped back.

"That will do for now," he said with a nod. "Get water, then we go again."

Ceres walked over to where a group of the other fighters were standing around a water barrel, drinking water out of it using a ladle. Ceres was expecting to have to edge round them or wait until they were done. Instead, a combatlord with tightly corded muscles and shaved hair passed across the ladle.

"You did well," he said. "The first time Master Isel used the sticks with me, I got knocked flat a dozen times."

A shorter combatlord with thinning hair nodded. When he spoke, it was obvious to Ceres that he'd come to the Empire from the northerners' lands. "Did well with your fight too. Didn't run. A beast like that, most people back off, but you went in. Good instincts."

The others didn't speak, but they didn't need to. It was enough for Ceres that they seemed to accept her there, making room for her among them as she got the refreshment she needed.

Of course, Lucious had to be the one to spoil it for her. He pushed toward the water butt, as if he couldn't have sent a dozen servants running for refreshments.

"Out of my way, peasants," he snapped at the combatlords. Ceres thought she saw one of them smile.

"Thought I heard something," he said.

Another shrugged. "Probably just the wind."

Lucious stepped round them, and now Ceres could see his face reddening. He stood before her, and Ceres suspected that if they'd been alone he would have struck her. It was probably as well that they weren't, she decided. She would only have gotten in trouble again for striking him back.

"You think you're clever?" he asked her. "You think that you're some kind of real warrior because you survived one fight in the Stade?"

"I'm not the one who ran from the arena," she said.

That only seemed to make Lucious turn redder. He reached for his belt, where a sword sat. No, not just any sword. As he drew it, Ceres saw that it was the sword her father had made for her. She wanted to reach out and grab it in that moment, because no one like Lucious should ever get to touch something her father had made.

"Recognize this?" Lucious said. Then he did something Ceres would have thought was unthinkable: he started to strip the blade down, taking it apart to its component parts. He unwound the leather of the handle, pulling off the gold wire. He unfastened the pommel, pulling the guard free of the tang. "I'm a little bored of it."

Ceres had to swallow her own anger. She felt the hand of one of the combatlords on her shoulder, holding her back or offering support, she wasn't sure which. How could Lucious do something like that? Didn't he know how much work went into a sword like that? Scraps of metal fell to the ground, but Lucious didn't seem to care.

"Forgive me, my lord," Master Isel said, approaching. "But I think these lay-abouts have had enough of a break. Back to work with you, all of you."

Ceres wanted to ignore the instruction. She wanted to punch the smile right off Lucious's face, but she went back to the sands as Master Isel instructed.

Lucious called out to her as she went. "Train as much as you want. It won't work. Tomorrow you'll face *my* man in the Stade, and all the dancing around with sticks in the world won't save you!"

Chapter Ten

Thanos should have been used to marching at the head of units of men, leading them into battle. He was a noble, trained in violence, and had fought in the Stade.

He'd never been in a position quite like this, though.

The band at his back looked like Empire soldiers. At least, they looked as close to Empire soldiers as they'd been able to manage while taking uniforms and armor from the dead. Yet it was easy for Thanos to see that there wasn't the same rigid discipline among them, maintained by the threat of the lash or the executioner's blade. The rebels didn't quite keep step with him as they marched, and they carried their own mixture of weapons, rather than anything officially issued by the army's quartermasters.

"This had better work," Akila said as they marched into view of the army's landing craft.

"It will work," Thanos promised him. He hoped that it was true. "Just… try not to kill anyone if you don't have to."

"Want us to go soft on your Empire friends?" Akila asked. Thanos could hear the suspicion there.

"I want you to remember that these are just ordinary men."

"Who chose to attack our island," Akila pointed out.

They marched down all the beach front, where the landing boats still sat, the rowing craft dragged up above the tide line. There were guards there with them now, who looked up sharply as they approached.

"Halt, who goes!" the nearest called.

"Can't you see?" Thanos called back. It was hard to make it sound natural. "I have troops who need to resupply on the main ships."

The solider offered a hurried bow. "Forgive me, your highness, I didn't know it was you. But these ships are meant to stay here. Orders."

"Orders from someone higher than your prince?" Akila demanded, beside Thanos. To Thanos's ears, he did a perfect impression of some toady drunk on reflected glory.

"No, of course, sir."

"Then get these boats into the water!"

The guards stood back. Some of them actually helped the rebels carry the landing craft out into the breakers.

"I can't believe we've done this," Thanos heard a one of the rebels say. He shook his head.

"This part is just the start," Thanos said. "We still need the main ships."

Akila's men set to the oars, pulling back from the beach with smooth strokes that took them in the direction of the ships further out. Those cut menacing profiles in the water, bolt throwers and fire slings in their prows adding to the sense of threat they emanated. The small boats spread out, each heading for a different ship.

"If those things fire on us," Akila pointed out, "they'll sink us before we get close."

Thanos tried to project confidence. "They won't fire."

The rebel leader didn't seem convinced, but he stayed silent as they approached the ships. Thanos guessed that he didn't want to risk his fears spreading to his men. Instead, he stood there in the prow, waiting like a figurehead until the ships stood towering above them.

"Who's down there?" a sailor asked, leaning over the side. "Do you need supplies?"

Obviously, the combination of the Empire's boats and the Empire's uniforms was enough. Even so Thanos could feel the tension in the moment. He could also see Akila reaching for a knife.

"It's Thanos," he said. "Let us aboard."

The sailor stepped back, and they clambered up the netting that hung from the side of the ship exactly for that purpose, climbing onto the deck in a way they never could have hoped to if they'd been trying to board by force. The sailors would have cut them to pieces as they appeared over the gunwale, or simply shoved them overboard to drown. There weren't many sailors aboard—Thanos guessed most would have gone ashore with the landing parties—but there would have been enough.

"Prince Thanos," one asked, "do you need medical attention? You look as though you've been bleeding."

Thanos stood on the deck, looking out over the bay near Haylon. From where he was, he could see the siege of the city's waterfront, with Empire soldiers there swarming against the walls. The defenders had obviously managed to seal the city for now, but there was nowhere for them to escape to, and the attackers had the weapons on the ships with which to attack the walls. Already, parts of the city were on fire.

"No," Thanos said. "That isn't what we need."

It felt bad to have to do what he did next. This man probably had a family somewhere, and was probably only there at all because he'd been made to. The only good part about this was that at least Thanos could make sure that he came through this alive.

He struck out, catching the man on the jaw as cleanly as he could, feeling the connection as his knuckles struck home. The sailor tumbled to the deck, and Akila's people piled forward.

A sailor ran at Thanos, an awl in his hand with the sharp point set to stab downwards. Thanos ducked, catching the arm and throwing the man over his hip. He came up on top, grabbing the arm that held the weapon with both hands. He could have reached for a blade of his own, but Thanos didn't want to kill if he could avoid it. These men weren't the ones to blame. It was the ones who ruled them who had started this. Instead, he brought his elbow down in a short arc that ended with his opponent unconscious.

He looked up to find that Akila's men had already taken the rest of the ship. On the ships nearby, Thanos could see violence breaking out, although with the rebels wearing Empire colors, it was almost impossible to see who was winning.

"Do you think we're succeeding?" Thanos asked.

Akila nodded. "My men are tough. They'll signal when they have the ships."

Sure enough, one by one, men on the other ships nearby started to wave their success. Only a few of the ships on the fringes were left untaken.

"So now what, Prince?" Akila asked. "We have some ships. What do we do with them?"

Thanos nodded to the ballista that sat on the forecastle of their ship. "Now, we do what we can to stop the siege."

He hated this part. He wished that there were another way, but unless they did this, the Empire's forces would soon overwhelm Haylon. Akila and his men made their way toward the siege weapon, loading it with a bolt as long as a man was tall. They set light to it, so that Thanos could see the flames flickering as they turned it toward one of the ships they hadn't been able to take. He thought he could see some of the sailors over there moving in sudden panic as they realized that things weren't as they should be.

By then, it was already too late. Akila gestured to the firing lever. "You got us this far, Prince. We wouldn't have gotten the boats without you. You should be the one to start this."

Thanos knew it was a test. Could he do this? He looked over at the ship, where the men were still struggling to do something about the danger, then over at the city, where the Empire's soldiers were ravaging their way along the waterfront. He couldn't pretend not to know what the weapons would do. He'd helped to come up with this plan knowing all of that. Part of Thanos insisted that this was wrong, and that he would be killing his own soldiers. How many men would die if he did this? he wondered.

How many would die if he didn't? Thanos had heard General Draco. There was to be no quarter for anyone who resisted. The army in front of him was there bent on pillage and destruction, so that soon, no one in the city would be safe. He had to do this.

Thanos felt the roughness of the wood as he wrapped his hand around the firing lever, then he pulled.

The first bolt sang through the air to catch in the sails of its target. The fire caught quickly, smoke coming up from the stricken ship in moments, and flames following. Sailors ran to put the flames out, but more bolts were already flying.

They struck at the ships they hadn't been able to take first, firing in volleys of flaming bolts and ceramic pots filled with tar. Many missed. Most missed, but Thanos saw enough strike home to matter, fire after fire starting on the enemy ships. He saw sailors running about, trying to stop the fires, or fire back, or get their ships to safety. He saw more and more dive into the relative safety of Haylon's waters, preferring to take their chances with the sharks that had come there for the dead rather than risk the fire.

They turned their attention toward the city then. Thanos guessed that the troops on the waterfront would have realized that something was badly wrong, but they still seemed to be intent upon their attack. It was only as bolts started to fall among them that they started to scatter.

"Three more volleys," Akila said. "Then we have to go. My men are already getting ready to fire the ships."

Thanos nodded. He wished they could keep the ships, but the truth was that they didn't have the men to hold them, or the skills to sail them. The best they could do was to deprive the Empire of its supplies.

He made his way to one of the men he'd knocked out, shaking the man until he came awake again. The sailor thrashed in his grip, trying to break free.

"We're going to burn this ship," he yelled, as the man struggled. "You have a choice. You can stay here to fight me, or you can take your chances swimming for shore."

It wasn't a choice that took the other man long to make. The sailor took one look at Thanos and dove for the side, the splash as he entered the water sending spray up high. Already, Thanos could see Akila and the rebels firing the last of their bolts at the soldiers on the shore, while others broke open the ceramic globes holding tar, spreading it over the deck. They set light to it, and instantly, Thanos could feel the heat of the flames as they rose up to consume the ship.

"Everybody off!" Akila ordered. He clapped a hand on Thanos's shoulder. "That means you too, Prince."

Now, it didn't seem so much like an insult as it had. Thanos dropped over the side of the ship, pulling himself into the landing boat. Around him, Akila's men pressed their way into position. Thanos took an oar, hauling on it as they set the boat into motion over the waves. Behind them, the Empire's fleet was slowly turning into a bonfire.

Thanos saw him nod in the direction of the city.

"The bad news," Akila said, "is that even with their supplies gone, there's still more Empire soldiers than us. We've a lot of fighting ahead of us. Are you ready for that, Prince?"

Thanos looked out toward the waterfront, where soldiers were still attacking in scattered clumps. They were the army belonging to his land, his king. Right then, though, he had never felt more strongly that he was on the right side.

He nodded. "I'm ready."

"Well, Prince," Akila said with a smile, "looks like we're not going to be killing you after all."

Chapter Eleven

Ceres was sweating in the night air, and not from sparring, for once. Instead, she was stuck scrubbing the tiles of one of the castle's courtyards, wiping away the mud and dirt that had collected there. She had no doubt that this was Lucious's doing; just another way of him making life harder for her there, and maybe a way of wearing her down before her fight too.

Of course, she had to do her cleaning where she would have a good view of the castle's main hall, and where those within would be able to look out and laugh at her. There was a feast taking place in there, complete with dancing and lavish entertainments. Ceres could see Lucious, Stephania, and all the other royals enjoying themselves, eating delicate pastries and drinking wines that had probably been brought from all corners of the Empire. Girls in elaborate dresses danced with young men who strode around the place looking as though they'd decided they deserved all the attention in the world.

Seeing them there like that was difficult. Ceres scrubbed the tiles because she had no doubt that they'd take any excuse to punish her, but she didn't mind hard work. She'd done worse than this when her mother had set her endless chores back home. The hard part was seeing them enjoying themselves when she was stuck out here. It was the knowledge that she would never be good enough for any of them, no matter what she did.

Even if she had been there, Ceres knew, they would have treated her as nothing. She would have been just one more of the servants and slaves who moved through the hall, offering food and drink, dancing or singing for their amusement.

Thanos was the only one who treated her any differently, and now he was gone. Just the thought of that made Ceres stare up at the stars above, looking for answers among their pinpoints. How could he have died? Only the thought that Stephania might have lied to her kept Ceres going then, and the truth was that Stephania had no reason to lie. As she'd said, the truth was more painful.

Ceres sat watching the feast then. The queen sat daintily, drinking from a crystal goblet while around her, lesser nobles formed concentric rings of power and gossip. The king sat separately, at the head of the longest table, where some of the younger noblemen were already drunk enough to start making grabs for the serving girls. Just the sight of it all made Ceres sick.

I will win tomorrow, she told herself. *Whatever they throw at me.*

What would happen after that, though? Match after match in the Stade, with no time to recover from her injuries? Her back was healing well, but the physical work of scrubbing the tiles felt as though it was almost designed to open up the wounds again. How soon would there be an injury she couldn't recover from? Ceres couldn't imagine Stephania or Lucious holding back, no matter how bad things got.

Ceres could see Stephania there, dancing with Lucious. She moved with such delicate grace, like a jeweled butterfly flitting her way around him. If Lucious occasionally shot glances in the direction of the other young women there, Stephania appeared not to notice. It was hard for Ceres to guess exactly how much she saw. She certainly didn't seem to have been affected by the news of Thanos's death.

It will get worse, Ceres told herself. They will find a way to make it worse. She was certain of that much. It wasn't just about who she was now. It was about the symbol she'd become. The girl who could fight in the Stade and win. The commoner who could stand up to the power of the royals and live. She'd been the girl who was going to marry a prince, too, and Ceres knew that Stephania, at least, hated her as much for that as any of the rest of it.

They would find a way to make it worse for her. They'd treated her like a princess because of Thanos, then as a fighter because that was how they wanted her to die. Tonight proved, though, that there was nothing to stop them from treating her like much less. They would pile humiliation on top of humiliation, simply because they could, and if she fought back, they would finally have an excuse to simply execute her.

"I should have gone with my father," Ceres said, but she didn't really believe it. She couldn't run from what waited for her in the Stade, and she couldn't let her father take the risk of trying to break her out of there.

There was another option, of course. She might not be able to win, but she could deprive the nobles of their fun with her. One sweep of a knife across her wrists, and it would be over. Or she could stand there in the Stade and let it happen. She could refuse to give them the entertainment they demanded.

"Ceres?"

Ceres turned, recognizing the voice.

A woman stepped out of the darkness, and Ceres heart soared to see her old friend.

Anka. The girl she had saved from the slavers.

There appeared to be something tougher about her now that she'd joined the rebellion. Something less frightened of the world.

Ceres rushed forward to embrace her friend, the shock overcoming her.

Seeing Anka there was a shock. She'd been sure that she wouldn't see the young woman again. She was safe with the rebellion, or at least as safe as anyone could be with it. It was a good surprise though.

"How did you get here?" Ceres asked.

"It was hard getting in to see you," Anka said. "But there are things you need to know."

Something about her tone told Ceres what those things would be. "Rexus and Thanos are dead."

She said it as a fact, hoping to hear it refuted.

Anka paused. "You heard already?"

Ceres didn't want to say Stephania's name here. "One of the nobles here made sure I found out."

"That's—"

"Yes," Ceres said. "It is. You're sure though? They aren't lying?" She thought back to the moment when an arrow had struck Rexus as he was climbing, and he'd fallen through her hands, away into the depths below.

Anka shook her head. "I'm sorry, Ceres. We found the body. Rexus didn't survive the fall."

Pain shot through Ceres, clear and palpable. She should have guessed that it would be like this, but some part of her seemed to have assumed that Rexus would find a way to survive. There was something so powerful about him, so vibrant, that it seemed impossible anything could kill him.

"What about Thanos?" Ceres asked.

Anka shook her head. "We have friends around the fringes of the Empire's army. Some of them tell us that Thanos fell in the first assault on the beaches there, in the confusion as they fought to land."

That blow hurt even more than the news about Rexus. Perhaps it was just that there had been more hope. Ceres had seen Rexus fall, but Thanos… that could have been a lie designed to hurt her. Maybe it was more than that, though, and the thought of how much more made Ceres's stomach clench with the thought of it.

"It doesn't matter," she said. She shook her head. "None of it matters."

"You don't mean that," Anka replied.

"How can it matter when they're dead?" Ceres demanded. The idea that the world could go on without Rexus, without *Thanos*, just seemed impossible. "It doesn't matter. I'll be dead soon too."

Somehow, that felt like a relief. She wouldn't end things herself. No, she would do it the way that fate had set out for her. She would step out into the Stade, and she would die. She couldn't imagine it happening any other way now.

"The revolution needs you, Ceres," Anka insisted.

"No it doesn't," Ceres said. "Who has been running the revolution since Rexus died?"

"Well, I've been trying to get everyone to work together, but—"

"Then that's the answer. You don't need me, Anka."

Anka stepped back. "I don't know what to say. I never thought that you'd just give up like this."

Anger flashed through Ceres, and she welcomed it, because it seemed like the only thing that might replace the emptiness she felt right then. Her hands curled into fists. "Do you think I wanted this?" she demanded.

"Do you think I wanted any of this? Do you think I wanted the man I love…" She trailed off, realizing what she was saying.

"I'm sorry," Anka said. "I didn't want to be the one to tell you all of this. And I thought I could try to get you out of here."

It was the same offer her father had made. Anka might even have the resources to do it if she could get there without any problems. Ceres knew her answer had to be the same, though.

"I can't go."

Anka took hold of Ceres's arm, pulling her toward the shadows. "You got me out of the slaver's cage. We both know all the things you saved me from. Do you know what it's like, knowing that you're going out into the Stade tomorrow to die?"

"I have to do this," Ceres insisted. "This is what I was meant to do, Anka."

"But we could get you out of here," Anka insisted.

Ceres disengaged the other woman's hand as gently as she could. "But it's not what I want."

Ceres heard a noise from the main hall and saw one of the doors opening. It was probably one of the nobles coming out to taunt her while she worked. Anka obviously heard it too, because she turned to slip back toward the darkness, beyond the spread of lamplight from the hall.

"This is your last chance," Anka said. "Please, Ceres."

Ceres shook her head, then called out as Anka started to go. "Anka, wait. If you want to do something that will help me, there is something."

"Anything I can," Anka promised.

"Help to make sure my brother and my father are safe," Ceres said. "The army took Sartes and my father is looking for him. They're both going to need all the help they can get." She held her hands earnestly as her friend prepared to flee, and she squeezed them.

"Can I trust you?" she asked.

Anka nodded back, with all solemnity.

"With my life," she replied. "Your family is my family, and I shall not stop until I find them—and bring them to safety."

CHAPTER TWELVE

Every step brought a wrench to Berin's heart as he traveled south, in search of the soldiers who had taken his son. Every step took him a little further from his daughter, left behind in a city where she would soon fight to the death. Every time his foot hit the ground, it felt like an impossible choice, one that he made only because his daughter had insisted.

Had he made a mistake?

Berin carried whatever supplies he could with him, their weight a constant on his back. Getting out of the city was easy enough, and after that he continued on the main roads for as long as he could. The roads were there for the army to march along, after all, so sticking to them seemed like the best way to find the unit that had taken his son. He only left them when he heard others coming, hiding by the side of the road until they passed each time. He didn't want to risk running into soldiers, bandits, or worse in these troubled times.

He came to a village after hours of walking, and it was easy to see that the army had been through there. It was too quiet, the way places were quiet in the wake of a storm. Berin had seen this before, in the years when he'd followed the army to smith for it. Armies devastated the country around them through the sheer numbers of men they contained, regardless of which side it represented. They stripped it bare whenever they stayed in one place too long, leaving the locals starving. A part of Berin suspected that the Empire sent out its army to take on foreign foes simply so that it wouldn't have to support it at home.

He hated the thought of Sartes being caught up in that. He wouldn't do well in the brutality of the Empire's forces. He wasn't cruel enough, or strong enough. The sooner Berin could get his son back, the better.

Berin could see a small market in the middle of the village, although there weren't very many stalls there now. Those that there were looked as though they only had scrapings left, with as many empty spaces on barrows and under awnings as there were goods for sale. Berin stopped at the nearly empty stall of a fruit seller.

"Has the army been through here?" he asked.

"Aye. Took half my stock as well, they did."

Berin nodded sympathetically. Times would probably be hard in the village for a while now, as the traders and the smallholders tried to recover. Yet right then, it was hard for him to keep his attention on anything except what had happened to Sartes.

"Do you know which way they went?" Berin asked.

"Why? Going to join up?" The fruit seller asked that with a laugh that Berin made himself join in.

"Maybe. Although I think I'd be better off sticking to smithing."

"You're a smith?" the fruit seller said. "Then you should stay here. There would be plenty of work for you."

Berin shook his head, although there was a pang of regret that came with it. If there had been an offer like that a few months back, he might not have left his family. They could have found a spot in this village and been safe. Now, though, it was too late for that. "It's a good thought, but there are things I need to do."

He started to make his way around the rest of the market, always asking the same questions, always trying to make it sound as if he were just making conversation as he passed through. He spoke to tinkers and chandlers, butchers and farmers, getting the same picture from each of them: one of the army's units had been through a day or two ago, heading south to make camp.

Berin was asking a cheese seller if she knew anything when he saw the soldiers making their way through the market. He'd assumed that they would be long gone, but these must have been away on some errand. There were three of them, all leading horses. One wore the more elaborate armor of an officer, while the two beside him had the high boots and longer swords of cavalry. They were talking to the stall-holders, and though Berin couldn't make out the words, he could guess what they were talking about when the fruit seller pointed in his direction.

"Seems as though they're looking for you," the cheese seller asked him. "With all these questions, the others probably think that you're part of the rebellion."

"And the army left soldiers to watch," Berin said. He should have guessed that they would. His stomach knotted. He was afraid then, not for himself, but for Sartes. If he was caught, the soldiers would want to know what he was doing there, and if they found out that he was trying to get his son out of the army, then Sartes might be the one to pay the price. Berin couldn't let that happen, no matter what it took.

"Don't blame the others," the cheese seller said. "They're too afraid of the soldiers to do anything. *Are* you with the rebellion?"

To Berin, she sounded almost as though she was hoping that he was. That perhaps he was there to fight off the Empire's soldiers for them. That thought might have been laughable if the situation hadn't been so deadly serious. It was enough to make him take a risk. After all, what else did he have to lose?

"I'm trying to find my son," he said, and he saw the cheese seller's eyes widen. "He was taken away by the army as a conscript, and I want to get him back."

It was a big risk to take. He'd potentially just given this woman enough to condemn him, but some instinct made him trust her. Maybe it was just that he wanted to believe people would help, given the chance.

"I had a son once," the woman said. She nodded. "He starved two winters ago because the Empire had taken too much of our food for the city. Come with me."

She led the way away from her stall. Berin glanced back to see the three soldiers making their way across the market square, and he hurried after her. She led the way around the side of one of the village's small houses, to a space where linen hung out drying in the sun.

"Down that way," she said, pointing.

"Thank you," Berin replied. "I won't forget this."

He wanted to say more, but there was no time. Instead, he ducked amid the hanging washing, brushing it aside as he tried to lose himself in it. Somewhere behind him, he thought he heard soldiers shouting. He ignored it, concentrating on making his way through the village, staying in the shadow of the huts and outbuildings. He looked back and thought he caught a glimpse of an imperial uniform. He kept going.

Finally, Berin reached the edge of the village, where the houses gave way to the rising furrows of shared farmland. There was long grass along the side of the road, and he could have run easily then without being seen, but that wouldn't have helped him to get any closer to Sartes. Instead, Berin found a spot where he wouldn't be seen and hunkered down, putting aside the aches in his joints as he squatted there, waiting.

From his hiding place, Berin could see the soldiers out on the road. He held his breath as they looked out in his direction. If they caught him now, there would be no talking his way out of it. He'd run, and for them, that would be enough to prove his guilt. The best he could hope for would be a quick death. Berin stayed still, waiting as the men searched, then talked among themselves. After a while, they went back into the village, and one of the three came out riding his horse off at an angle from the road.

Berin started to follow the horseman, moving slowly, keeping low. When he passed out of sight, Berin switched to following the horse's tracks, and it was just as well the soldier had left a trail a blind man could follow, because Berin had never been much of a tracker. Despite the urgency of it all, he kept his head down and moved only at a walking pace. It was hard to be that cautious. Far more of him wanted to run to his son and rip him free from the army's clutches, but he couldn't help Sartes if he got himself captured, and the truth was that he couldn't keep up with the horseman even if he tried.

The flat ground gave way to a small rise with a stand of trees near the top. Berin made for them, pushing his way through the foliage and trying to watch where he put his feet so that he wouldn't make too much noise. As he reached the far side of the trees, he paused, freezing in place as he looked down.

There, spread out below, was the army camp. From up here, it was easy for Berin to see the grid pattern of the tents, the empty spaces left by the training areas and the clusters of wagons around the supply centers.

He could see the fortifications around the edges too. There were rough ditches lined with spikes and built up with earth banks, watch platforms, and posts where dogs sat chained, there to sniff out intruders. Berin found himself wondering if they were there to keep would-be attackers out, or to keep conscripts in their place.

Sartes.

His son was down there somewhere, lost in that tent city, impossible to spot when everyone in it was dressed the same way. Sartes would be down among the conscripts, mistreated casually, because that was what the army did. Berin had to find him. He *would* find him, both because he wanted his family back, and because he'd promised Ceres. He would bring his son out of there.

He took the first step, knowing he would risk his life, knowing his chances of success were slim—and knowing he had no other choice.

Chapter Thirteen

Stephania moved quietly through the castle in the early morning. She doubted any of the other nobles who had been at the party last night would be awake yet. Lucious would certainly still be snoring. Normally, even Stephania would not have woken so early. This was an hour for servants and their chores, not for those who commanded them.

Under other circumstances she would probably have had her maid beaten for waking her. Only the contents of the message she had received had her padding through the corridors now in jeweled slippers.

In a way, it was probably a good thing that no one else was awake right now. Stephania wanted to do this without too many prying eyes.

She met the woman who had come in a small receiving room, barely large enough to accommodate the couch on which she sat. Stephania couldn't see her resemblance to Ceres, but even so, her servants had assured her that this was Ceres's mother. To Stephania, she looked like any other peasant woman, her dress stained, aging and lined, made hardened and coarse by her life. At least the woman had the grace to rise and drop into a curtsy as Stephania entered. Stephania doubted that her daughter ever would, even at sword point.

"You are the woman who came to the gate, claiming to be Ceres's mother?" Stephania asked.

"Yes, my lady," she said. "Marita, my lady."

She understood proper deference, at least. Stephania wasn't sure that she could ever like someone related to Ceres, but it made this easier. Stephania gestured for her to sit, joining her on the couch without ever quite sitting close enough that she had to touch her.

"Are you here because you wish to see your daughter?" Stephania asked, watching the woman carefully. It wasn't what the note had said, but Stephania was used to people lying. If a life at court had taught her one thing, it was that everybody lied. They lied for advantage, or to say what they thought people wanted to hear, or occasionally just because they wanted to cause trouble. Stephania had learned early to watch people carefully, to work out their real motives, and never to trust anyone.

Marita shook her head sharply though, and there was something about the sense of anger there that made Stephania want to believe the denial.

"I have no wish to see that … that *creature*," Marita said. "Not when she has cost me so much."

That was interesting, and not at all what Stephania had expected, in spite of the message. Stephania had expected greed perhaps, venality, but this level of hatred was … well, it was almost in line with her own.

"What did she do to you?" Stephania asked. It wasn't that there was the feeling of a kindred soul here, obviously. This woman could never be anything like a noble such as her. Even so, she had the same sense of Ceres having done something to harm them both. With her, it had been the disruption of her plans to marry Thanos. What had it been for this woman? Stephania wondered.

"She cost me everything," Marita said. "She cost me money that should have been mine. Money I got for her fairly! Then, when my husband found out, I was left with nothing!"

Briefly, Marita started to sob. Stephania sat and watched her for a second or two, gauging her there. Then she reached out to comfort the commoner, doing what she felt was a good job of hiding her distaste. Stephania was good at hiding what she felt, and who she was.

"That must have been hard," she said. She tried to keep her tone even. "When you say you got money for her, you mean you sold her to a slaver?"

"I had to get something for all the trouble she caused over the years," Marita insisted. Stephania could hear the defensiveness there. "My husband abandoned me, and she has always been difficult."

She paused as though expecting some sharp rebuke. Instead, Stephania patted her hand.

"I understand how difficult it must have been for you."

"It was!" Marita sounded almost shocked. "No one has realized that. My husband was so cruel. He shook me, and then he abandoned me! He just wanted to know where Ceres was, and our son Sartes."

Stephania already knew where they both were. They were exactly where they needed to be. Ceres would be dying in the Stade later today, while her brother wouldn't last long as a conscript. Briefly, she considered whether it would be worth getting rid of the mother as well, but no, she decided, that wouldn't do anything to exact justice from Ceres for what she'd done, and Stephania wasn't needlessly cruel.

"It sounds terrible," Stephania said. "No one should be abandoned by the one she is promised to."

That was one element of this woman's story that she could relate to. The pain when it had turned out that Thanos had been given to Ceres had been an icicle jabbed into her heart, the cold slowly spreading through her until there was nothing left.

"Why did you come here?" Stephania asked. "You said that you had information for me. Why bring it here though?"

"I thought someone should know," Marita said.

Stephania could see, though, that it wasn't the whole story.

"What else?" she asked.

Marita paused, looking embarrassed for a second. "When the slaver left with my daughter, he took all the money he gave me … I was *tricked*."

"I understand," Stephania said. She'd brought a purse with her, even though it was early. She'd guessed that it might be necessary. Greed was one of the easier motivations to understand. It was also one of the more common ones. She pressed it into Marita's palm, closing her fingers around it. "Here. To help you now that your husband is gone."

She felt the way the other woman's hand clasped around it. Tightly, as if afraid it might be taken away at any moment. "You're too kind, my lady."

Stephania smiled back at her. "I don't think I've ever been called that before. Now, tell me what happened."

"After my husband left, I had nothing, so I went looking for Lord Blaku to see if I could get my money from him. He *owed* me." Marita had a note of determination in her voice that Stephania found quite amusing. She didn't know about this Lord Blaku, but she knew enough about slavers to guess what would have happened to this commoner if she'd found him.

"You went after him?" Stephania said. "Did you find him?"

The fact that she wasn't dead in some ditch said that she hadn't.

"I found what was left of him," Marita said. She shook her head. "He'd been killed, along with his men. At first I thought it was bandits, but bandits wouldn't leave this."

She took out a ring, more expensive than anything a commoner like her could have afforded. It had an ornate "B" insignia on the flat surface of the top, along with an insignia that might have pointed to a noble house. Stephania didn't have to ask why Ceres's mother hadn't sold it. It would be too obvious that it wasn't hers. The guards would have taken her in a heartbeat.

"That does seem unusual," Stephania said in her sweetest voice. "What would you guess happened?"

"I don't need to guess," Marita said. "I know. I asked around. I found one of the slaves they'd been transporting."

Stephania waited.

"My daughter killed Lord Blaku," Marita said. "Slaughtered him and his guards."

"Her alone?" Stephania asked. She wanted to be certain.

"That's what they said, although she must have had help," Marita said. That just told Stephania how little she knew her daughter. Stephania wasn't going to give Ceres much credit, but she could fight. If she couldn't, she would have been dead by now, and things would have been a lot easier.

"She killed Lord Blaku?" Stephania said. She lifted the slaver's ring up to eye level. Was it her imagination, or was there a smear of dried blood on it? It wasn't proof, not really, but what proof could there be for something like this? More to the point, how much proof would really be needed right now? If the story could be checked afterwards, if people could hear for themselves what Ceres had done, that might be enough.

"She did," Ceres's mother said. "I can point the spot out on a map, if you want."

"Yes," Stephania said. "I think that's a very good idea."

It shouldn't have mattered. Ceres would be dead soon anyway, if Lucious's man did his part in the Stade, but there was something unsatisfying about that. It was a heroic death, of the kind that people might talk about afterwards. Handled badly, Stephania suspected that it might even turn into a rallying cry for the rebellion.

This was potentially far better. If Ceres's mother had sold her, then she'd been a slave according to Delos's laws. If a slave killed their master, they could be killed and no one could question it. They could be flayed alive, whipped until they could stand no more of it, or simply strangled. They could take Ceres away for the kind of quiet death that would quickly fade from the mind, and any arguments could be quickly quashed.

Yes, let her have that kind of death. The kind of death that would inspire no one. Stephania stood, and Ceres's mother stood with her.

"What will you do with what I've told you?" Marita asked.

Stephania cocked her head to one side. "I'm going to make sure that your daughter gets exactly what she deserves."

Marita seemed to consider that. For a moment, Stephania thought that she might complain, or beg for some kind of leniency for Ceres.

Instead, to her shock, she nodded.

"Good," Marita said. "I should have strangled her at birth."

Chapter Fourteen

Ceres woke early, standing and stretching out her tired muscles in the morning sun, trying to pretend it was just another day.

Though she knew that it wasn't.

Her life would be at stake on this day. She would fight today, in front of thousands of spectators, against Lucious's combatlord.

That thought brought with it a kind of clarity, because it was obvious that Lucious was going to pit her against an opponent she couldn't beat. One that would ensure her death.

Ceres knew she should be afraid, but right then, she felt calmer than she'd thought she might. She half closed her eyes, feeling the warmth of the sun on her as she waited. The truth was that it didn't matter if she died today. Sartes would be safe, because her father and Anka were going to find him. Rexus was dead, but the rebellion would continue. As for Thanos…

Ceres forced herself to breathe as she thought of him being dead, letting the air out slowly as she tried to get back to the still place where she'd been. She wasn't sure she wanted to be alive in a world where he was gone.

Eventually, the guards came for her, hammering on the door in a way that made Ceres's ears ring after the silence. They put chains on her to march her down to the Stade, although Ceres had no intention of running away now. She saw the way the guards watched her now, with a kind of respect bordering on fear. They'd obviously seen her fight the first time.

She'd walked the route to the Stade plenty of times now to practice, but it felt different when it was for an actual fight. Part of that was the sound. Even here, the cheers of the crowd filtered through, making it feel to Ceres as though she was inside the belly of a living thing.

They reached the preparation room, and the guards removed her chains. To her surprise, one nodded.

"Good luck."

"Thank you," Ceres said. It was hard, sometimes, to remember that even the guards were people. Had this one seen her fight the last time? Ceres shook her head. She had to concentrate on getting herself ready for what was to come, but that felt impossible when her mind kept going back to other things. The last time she'd been in the Stade, how her father would be doing, Thanos…

Ceres stepped deeper into the preparation rooms. She didn't want to think about Thanos then, because it hurt too much. Paulo, her weapon-keeper, was waiting for her with her armor, a breastplate and kilt that left her limbs bare. Ceres knew that the idea was to have armor that protected the most vital areas of the body while still giving the crowd a chance to see blood on the sands. It made the fights last longer. As if in answer to that thought, Ceres heard the cheer that only came with the brutal end of violence. A minute later, the iron doors that led through to the Stade opened, letting guards drag a body back through. They abandoned it at the side of the room, probably expecting more to come.

"They tell me that you're fighting Lucious's man today," Paulo said.

Ceres nodded, reaching for her sword. "Do you know anything about him?"

Paulo looked uncomfortable, and Ceres could guess why he was suddenly quiet.

"It's all right," she said. "I'd rather hear it. I'm sure Master Isel would say that knowing an opponent is important."

Paulo smiled at that. "He says that you should know a foe like a brother." Ceres saw the smile vanish. "But he also says that victory is born from confidence."

Ceres understood. "It's all right. I want to know what I'm dealing with."

"The Last Breath," Paulo said, and Ceres could see the flicker of fear that crossed her weapon-keeper's face as he spoke about him. "He has been brought here from far to the south. He is larger than you, and stronger. He's fast, too."

Ceres shrugged. She'd guessed that he would be bigger than her. Most of the combatlords were. "The last man I fought was strong, too."

"Not like this," Paulo said. He shook his head. "The last time he fought in the Stade, he dropped his weapon, so he crushed his opponent's skull to finish him. But he's not just strong. The time before that, he fought Navencius. I've never seen anyone better with a trident than Navencius, but the Last Breath beat him in under a minute."

Ceres swallowed. She'd watched the killings enough to know how much that meant. Trident players were normally hard to get close to, the fights involving them becoming long games of cat and mouse. To kill one of the best with that weapon so quickly was more than impressive, it was frightening. Maybe Master Isel had been right. Maybe it was better not to know.

"So I should avoid the trident then?" Ceres joked.

Paulo didn't laugh though. Instead, he held out a sword in one hand and a long dagger in the other. "Better to stick to what you've trained with."

"A dagger though?" Ceres said. "Not a shield?"

"A shield would just make you want to stand still," Paulo said. "Trust me."

Ceres did. All the people around the Stade had become something like a second family for her, and Paulo knew what he was doing. She weighed the dagger in her hand. It was long enough to be a threat at more than close range, but short enough not to get in the way of her sword as she wielded it. It was a good choice. She waited with the weapons by her side, while beyond the preparation room, the sounds of the crowd built. Two more times, the guards came back with bodies, while three other combatlords limped back with wounds needing to be stitched.

Finally, it was her turn.

Ceres waited for the iron gates to open, then stepped out onto the sand, blinking as her eyes adjusted to the sunlight. The chanting of the crowd hit her in time to the beating of her heart.

"Ceres! Ceres!"

Last time, the words had seemed to run through her, building with her own excitement. Now, though, that excitement felt buried somewhere under everything that had happened. The feelings from the night before were still there. She was there to die. She knew it. With Thanos gone, she even welcomed it. But she wasn't going to give the royals the satisfaction of dying without a fight.

She stepped out into the middle of the Stade, looking around at the crowd. The terraced sides seemed even more crowded today than they would normally have been. Were those extra people there to see her? She looked over to the royal box, and sure enough, Lucious was there to watch. The others weren't there though, as though seeing the spectacle of her fighting were somehow beneath them.

Horns blared, and her heart froze as she saw her opponent step out onto the sands.

He was every bit as huge as Paulo had promised, his dark skin bulging with corded muscle and worked with tattoos. He wore almost no armor beyond a kilt and short greaves, as if ignoring the possibility of getting hit. For a weapon, he held a staff that had crescent-shaped blades on either end. He leaned on it without acknowledging the crowd. Even his weapon-keeper seemed to be frightened of him, following along behind at a safe distance and looking to Ceres as though he was ready to run at any moment.

On the edge of the royal box, an official in white stood and gestured for silence. In it, he boomed his announcement of the fight.

"For our next fight, we have the only woman to have ever fought in the Stade, the princess of the sands: Ceres!"

She stepped forward, waiting as the cheers rose to a crescendo. She should have been afraid, excited, something. Instead, the thoughts of what had happened to Rexus and Thanos seemed to consume everything else within her, drawing it down into some bottomless pit inside her. There was anger there though. Anger at everything the royals had done to her, and at the way this cruel world worked. A part of Ceres found itself welcoming the violence to come.

"Against her," the announcer continued, "we have Prince Lucious's greatest combatlord, the terror of the Stade: The Last Breath."

The Last Breath stood there, leaning on his weapon in what seemed to Ceres like contempt for the crowd. She wondered for a moment if he enjoyed any of this. Then he lifted his weapon and started to spin it. The bladed staff must have weighed more than either of Ceres's weapons, but her opponent twirled it as if it were nothing.

He spun it in arcs above his head, then out to either side. Ceres could hear the swish of the blades as they cut through the air, their rhythm like the scythe teams who cut meadow grass in the summer. He didn't watch the weapon as he spun it. Instead, Ceres saw his eyes fixed firmly on her. He brought the bladed staff around in one final arc, then swung it down to scatter the sand beneath his feet.

The crowd cheered at the display, but Ceres's opponent didn't react. His gaze didn't waver, and Ceres could feel the hostility there as his eyes bored into hers. She had the urge to take a step back then, or flinch, but she held herself still, concentrating on everything Master Isel had taught her. She could beat this opponent, but she had to move and keep moving.

Horns blared to signal the start of the contest. To Ceres, they seemed to come from a long way away. Even the crowd seemed to occupy a different space. There was only her and her opponent, crouched and waiting. The horn blast went on for several seconds, fading into echoes while Ceres waited.

Then the Last Breath leapt at her, almost too fast to follow, and Ceres knew the time had come to fight for her life.

Chapter Fifteen

By the time Stephania found the king and queen, they were already in the morning session of their court, listening to an argument about trading rights on the Empire's fringes. A fat merchant argued with one of the court's lesser nobles in front of them.

"And I say that I made all of the required payments," the merchant said. "But Lord Hywell has failed to pass them on to the Empire's revenue collectors."

"And is there any evidence of this?" the noble insisted. "Do you have any records of these payments?"

"Enough," King Claudius said. He pinched the bridge of his nose. "Do you think I want to listen to you prattle this early? Someone find the royal tax collector's records. If there is no record of the duty being paid, the merchant Zorat will pay it now, along with a fine of one part per hundred."

"But your majesty—"

The king's look was enough that even Stephania felt the urge to take a step back.

"You should be grateful," he said. "Trying to avoid the taxes of the Empire is normally punished with the gibbet. Which reminds me, when we find the royal tax collector, have him go through Lord Hywell's estate and find out just how much he has taken that should have been mine."

This time, it was the noble's turn to blanch. "I have always been loyal."

"Is it loyal to steal from your king?" the queen asked. "Take from the peasants if you must, but you do *not* steal from us. Now get out. Court is done for this morning."

"Wait, your majesties," Stephania called out. "I must be heard."

Almost everyone there turned to her. Most looked slightly shocked that anyone would dare to contradict the queen. Especially not when she and the king already seemed to be in a dangerous mood. Several stepped back, as though to distance themselves from whatever was going to come back.

"Stephania?" the queen said. "Do you think you can overrule our commands?"

Stephania swept down into her most perfect curtsy, keeping her eyes carefully downcast. She was sure she looked the perfect picture of elegant submission to royal authority.

"Forgive me, your majesties, but I have information that I believe you will wish to hear. Urgent information, relating to Ceres."

She looked up to see King Claudius looking straight at her.

"What about her?" the king asked. "She will die in the Stade today."

"If Lucious is right," Stephania said. She straightened up. "And even then, it is dangerous. The crowd might treat her as a hero when she dies."

Beside the king, Queen Athena drummed her fingers on the arms of her throne. "Weren't you one of the people suggesting that the Stade would be better than executing Ceres? Are you telling us that you advised us poorly, Stephania?"

Stephania thought quickly. "I argued against Ceres's execution out of hand, your majesty. The people would not stand for her simply being killed for no reason. But now, I believe I *have* a reason."

Stephania caught the change in atmosphere then. Feeling the mood of the court was an essential skill for anyone in her position. Now, she could feel it moving from being sharp edged and dangerous to something much more hopeful.

"What reason?" King Claudius asked.

Stephania took out the ring she'd gotten from Ceres's mother. She hadn't cleaned it, because the smear of blood on it seemed to make the whole thing much more convincing.

"This ring is from a slaver named Lord Blaku."

"I know of him," the queen said. "What is his role in this?"

It was a surprise to Stephania that the queen might know of a slaver, but then, the nobility made their money in all kinds of ways.

"He is dead, your majesty," Stephania said. "I have information that Ceres was the one who killed him, from the one who brought this ring."

"And who was that?" the queen asked.

"Her mother, your majesty," Stephania said. She risked a smile, because that was the part that clinched it. Anyone could make up an allegation, but for someone to be denounced by their own mother? That was practically impossible to ignore. "Ceres was the property of the slaver, and she killed him while escaping from him."

Stephania heard the faint intake of breath from some of the court. They clearly understood the seriousness of the crime. At this point, they could do almost anything they wished with Ceres and it would not matter.

King Claudius steepled his fingers. "What do you want us to do, Stephania? Wouldn't it be simpler to allow her to die in the Stade?"

"Simpler," Stephania said, "but perhaps not best."

"And you have something in mind instead?"

Stephania nodded. "I do, your majesty. The Isle of Prisoners."

That got another intake of breath and Stephania smiled at it. With all the punishments the Empire had, it seemed that the prospect of the Isle of Prisoners still had the power to shock. Stephania could understand that. It was a place of cruelty and punishment, from which few ever returned. Those who did returned broken and changed, as shadows of their former selves. Stephania looked around and watched them all start to understand.

"In the Stade," Stephania said, "Ceres is an embarrassment. At best, she is the girl we had to kill publicly because we hated her so much. She becomes a symbol that way. At worst… perhaps she will even continue to win."

"And that will become a different kind of symbol," Queen Athena said. "A symbol that people can resist us successfully. Hmm… Stephania has a point, Claudius."

The king sat there for what seemed like forever. Stephania could see him weighing it up, and someone else might have tried to say something then to push him in one direction or another. Lucious certainly would have, and Lucious would probably have found his king disagreeing with him, just to remind him of his place. Stephania had learned the lesson the noble petitioner before her hadn't. Sometimes, it was better to be patient.

"Yes," the king said at last. "I believe she does. It is a far better plan than Lucious's, at least."

Stephania smiled as sweetly as she could. "I am sure Lucious knows what he is doing."

Queen Athena regarded her carefully. "Even so, I think perhaps we have underestimated you in the past, Stephania."

"Oh, no, your majesty," Stephania said, even though it was undoubtedly true. "You have always been very kind. And this… well, Ceres's mother could have come to anyone."

"Yes, I suppose she could," the queen said.

Of course, Stephania thought, that would have required the others to pay attention and keep their ears open for useful information. Any of them *could* have done it. None of them did. But Stephania had no wish to appear too clever. It was better if they just thought she was lucky. Very, very lucky, in this case.

"What do you think should be done with Ceres once she reaches the Isle of Prisoners, though?" the king asked.

Stephania spread her hands. "A quiet death, your majesty. In whatever way pleases you most."

King Claudius nodded at that. "A quiet death, yes. A death that won't cause any more trouble."

"And a death where we can take our time," Queen Athena added. There was something cruel about the set of her features as she said it, but Stephania guessed that she could afford to be more open about it than Stephania was.

King Claudius seemed to be decided. "Yes, I like this idea. Go to the Stade, Stephania. See that Ceres is not killed where people will see her as a martyr. Let her disappear instead."

"Me, your majesty?" Stephania asked. She had expected them to send a servant, or their guards, or perhaps to go themselves. She hadn't wanted to be the one to end Lucious's fun directly. He was potentially a very useful ally.

"You are the one who suggested this, Stephania," Queen Athena said. "You should be the one to put it into practice. You will have our full authority."

And would no doubt be blamed if anything went wrong, Stephania thought. Still, the idea of the king and queen's full authority was a pleasant one. Stephania dropped down into another curtsy.

"Thank you for trusting me, your majesties. I will not let you down."

"I am sure you will not," Queen Athena said. "And if you do not, we will remember all the help you have given to us recently. Now go."

"At once, your majesty."

Stephania backed out of the smaller throne room, keeping to the courtesies required at court. It gave her enough time to enjoy the fact that things were going to go the way she wanted. When she reached the door, she turned and hurried through the corridors of the castle. The Killings would already be underway, the crowds of commoners cheering in their blood lust, and there would only be a little more time to fulfill the king and queen's orders. Stephania didn't want to think about what might happen if she failed.

Stephania went from a brisk walk to a run. She had never thought she would find herself doing this, but now she had to get to the Stade before Ceres was killed.

Chapter Sixteen

Ceres threw herself back just before a crescent-shaped blade flashed past her throat. The crowd roared, and instinct drove her to duck as the other end of the Last Breath's weapon thrust for her.

She tumbled across the sand, feeling it scrape across her skin as she came back to her feet, her adrenaline pumping with the intensity of the fight.

The crowd cheered.

Ceres stood there for a moment, trying to get her bearings as her opponent advanced on her—but there was no time. She parried another thrust with crossed blades, then felt the shaft of the staff slamming her back.

Again, the crowd roared.

Ceres retreated and circled, keeping her distance while she looked for a way past the whirling circle of half-moon edges. While those watching yelled for her to strike, she forced herself to breathe deeply, remembering her lessons.

Paulo had been right about her opponent's strength. Every time Ceres parried a stroke of the staff, the shock of it reverberated up her arms. Already, they ached with the effort of it, so that it felt as though all the strength she'd built in training was running out of her like water from a broken barrel.

She moved to her right, looking for a way to close the distance. She feinted with her sword, ducked under an answering sweep, and managed to scrape a cut across her opponent's arm with her dagger. Ceres heard the crowd chant her name.

A flash of sunlight on steel warned her about the counterstrike and she barely dodged back out of range again.

The Last Breath stood there, touched his arm, and lifted a bloody finger as if to examine it. He shrugged, and Ceres almost relaxed. Then he lunged forward again, blows coming for Ceres so fast she could barely see them.

Ceres parried the first three, tried to stab back, and felt the sudden pain along her leg as one of the blades cut across it. The clash of steel on steel came as another blow struck her breastplate, combined with an impact that spun her away, thankfully out of range of the next slash of blades.

Ceres saw the faint trail of droplets in the air as the spinning staff cast off her blood.

Ceres, desperate, kicked up sand toward the combatlord's eyes, trying to buy herself time. It rose in a cloud between them, briefly obscuring her view of her opponent. A crescent blade emerged from that cloud swinging around so fast that Ceres barely caught it.

Her sword snapped. Ceres had an instant to flinch as fragments flew; the blade sheared off just above the hilt, the shock of it sending a gasp through the crowd.

She threw the weapon at her opponent and tried to maneuver around so that Paulo could throw her a fresh weapon. The Last Breath seemed to have anticipated that, though, keeping between her and her weapon keeper, blocking any chance for Paulo to toss her the weighted net he was holding.

Ceres found herself waiting for the power that had come in her previous fights. She tried to summon it, but the truth was that she didn't have any idea how to. If she could find the power that she'd used to kill before, she might have a chance here.

But it didn't come.

For the first time in the Stade, she felt… ordinary. It was just her against this monster of a man.

The realization came to her, cold and hard in the pit of her stomach. She was going to lose. Ceres was surprised to find how much that meant to her. She'd thought she was at peace with it, ready, even eager to die.

Yet now that it looked like she might, fear coiled around her, impossible to push back.

She managed to circle enough for Paulo to toss the weighted net to her. It wasn't a battlefield weapon the way a sword was. It was something designed for use in the Stade, so in that sense, maybe it was a good choice against an opponent from so far away, who might not have seen it before. A skilled fighter with it could tangle and trip, engulf and confuse an opponent. Ceres knew the theory of it, but she'd spent far less time with it than with the sword.

She kept her distance from the Last Breath, casting her net out in arcs that she tried to match to those of his bladed staff. Her only hope now was to wear him down, tangle his blades, and pull him in close to finish him. It was a desperate plan, and as the combatlord kept attacking, Ceres found herself retreating, step by step.

Around Ceres, the crowd booed. Where they'd called her name before, now she heard them catcall and hiss. Ceres knew how much the crowds at the Stade wanted action. They hated fighters who ran, yet right then, Ceres couldn't think of a better option. The Last Breath advanced on her, twirling his bladed staff, and backing up was the only way she could find to survive.

For a moment, the staff stalled, and Ceres saw her opening. She cast out her net, throwing it underhand so that it wrapped around the haft of her opponent's weapon again and again. The weights on the net locked it in place, as tightly as if Ceres had tied it there. Wrapping the trailing rope around her forearm, Ceres set her feet and pulled, trying to yank her opponent's weapon from him.

She saw the Last Breath smile as he stood there, steady as a rock.

He pulled back, and Ceres felt herself yanked forward. Too late, she realized the danger of gripping the net so tightly. Her opponent slammed the haft of his weapon forward as she stumbled in, and the weapon caught her just above the jaw. For a moment, the world seemed to swim, and Ceres tasted the iron tang of blood.

The combatlord struck her like that again and again, using the rough wood of the staff to pummel her head and body while Ceres stood trapped by her own grip on the net. Somewhere in that assault, she lost her hold on the dagger. Then the Last Breath kicked her, knocking her sprawling. Ceres could hear the crowds cheering again now, and they weren't cheering for her.

Ceres lay on her back in the sand. She wanted to get up, but there seemed to be a gap between thinking it and doing it that was too wide to cross. Instead, she could only watch as the Last Breath stood over her, seeming to blot out the sky above as he lifted his bladed staff for a killing blow. Ceres swallowed, anticipating the moment when he would bring it down, trying not to show any fear.

She heard a horn sound as if from a great distance, and managed to look over toward the royal box. She should have guessed Lucious would want to make this decision. It would be one final reminder for Ceres that her fate was in his hands. She looked over at the royal box and saw the noble standing there, his arm outstretched, while the crowd in the Stade called for life or death.

Far too many sounded as though they were calling for her death.

There was another figure in the royal box, though. It took Ceres a moment to recognize Stephania, and to realize that she was arguing with Lucious. Lucious was bright red with anger, his features twisted into something close to fury. Slowly, with obvious reluctance, he turned his thumb up for life.

Guards rushed out onto the sand. Several guided Ceres's opponent back in the direction of the iron gates. More seized her by the arms, lifting her between them so that her feet dragged on the ground. They fastened shackles to her wrists, not seeming to care about the way the iron bit into her. Ceres wanted to struggle as they dragged her away, but right then she didn't have the strength. She heard the boos of the crowd follow her from the Stade, down so that she could still hear them as they reached the practice rooms. She half expected to be unchained there, or perhaps to be dragged back to her chambers. Instead, the guards held her in place, still in her chains, until the door to the outside opened.

Stephania and Lucious came into the room together. Lucious still looked angry to Ceres, as though he couldn't accept that he'd been cheated of his chance to see her die. Stephania looked pleased, even triumphant.

"You should thank me for your life, Ceres," Stephania said. "After all, I did just save it."

"Why?" Ceres asked. She saw Stephania nod to the guards, and they shoved her roughly to her knees.

"You will speak to me with the proper deference, peasant," Stephania said. She paused. "No, you're not a peasant are you? You're a slave."

Ceres started to shake her head, but Lucious stepped forward and struck her.

"That felt good. If we had time, I'd do a lot more, slave. I couldn't believe it when Stephania told me what you were."

"But it's true," Stephania said. "And soon, everyone will hear it. Ceres here is a slave who murdered her owner."

"I was never owned by anyone," Ceres shot back. She could feel the anger rising in her. "Lord Blaku had no right to take me."

Stephania reached out to touch Ceres's cheek. "You think any of that matters? What matters is that you killed him. What matters is what people will *hear*."

Stephania stepped back toward the door, a vicious smile on her face.

"Your death won't be quick and valiant," Stephania said. "It will be slow, and painful, and anonymous. Say goodbye to Delos," she concluded, "and enjoy your trip to the Isle of Prisoners."

CHAPTER SEVENTEEN

Thanos cut his way toward the command post of the Empire's soldiers on Haylon. A soldier swung a blade at his head and Thanos ducked, striking out with his own weapon to bring the man down. Another ran at him and Thanos disarmed him, shoving him back into the melee around him. He fought and fought, never slowing.

Beside him Akila and his men fought hard, heading for the tents the Empire had erected on the edge of the city. They were easy to make out, because the Empire's standard hung above them, along with pennants proclaiming General Draco's presence.

With the Empire's ships gone, the battle for Haylon hadn't lasted long. Thanos had been right to guess that without their supplies and their siege weapons, their opponents would be at a disadvantage. The soldiers might have had the numbers, but they had no food and no safe places to sleep. They didn't know the island, and Akila's men were experts at springing from hidden spots to attack.

"Keep forward!" Thanos shouted, and to his surprise, the rebels responded. Since the attacks on the ships, there had been no more talk about killing him. Instead, they'd trusted him like one of their own. It had helped that Thanos had fought beside them against the soldiers who still remained, in skirmish after skirmish through a long night of fighting.

Thanos brought down another soldier, doing his best not to kill the man. Even now, it felt wrong to risk killing ordinary men who probably didn't have a lot of choice about being there. It felt wrong to be killing men who, as their prince, he should have been responsible for. Yet he kept going, because to stand back and let them take the island would have been worse.

"Getting tired yet, Prince?" Akila called out with a grin.

"I can keep going if you can," Thanos replied, although the truth was that he would have liked nothing better than to stop. It had been a long night of fighting, and now his sword felt as though it had been crafted from lead rather than steel. It was getting harder to swing by the moment.

He didn't have to keep going, though. The battle ended as swiftly as a summer storm lifting. Thanos saw the few remaining Empire soldiers between the rebels and the command tents throw down their weapons and run. The rebels surrounded the command tents, and less than a minute later, they dragged two figures from them.

General Draco walked straight-backed and proud, so that to Thanos, he looked as though he was marching out for a parade. He paused as he saw Thanos, and Thanos guessed that he was surprised to see him alive. That told Thanos a lot about how much he knew of the assassination attempt. The Typhoon was bloody and bruised, still fighting, but held in place by half a dozen men.

Thanos saw Akila looking over at him.

"You understand that we can't just let these ones live?" the rebel leader said. "After everything they've done to our city, we can't let them go."

Thanos understood what Akila was saying. He obviously thought Thanos would try to save the general and the Typhoon the way he'd tried to protect others. Thanos didn't answer. Instead, he stepped up close to General Draco.

"Draco."

"Thanos," the general said. "I'm surprised to see you alive."

"I'm harder to kill than that," Thanos said.

The general shrugged. There was an edge of fatalism about it. "I take it that the capture of our ships was due to you? I heard reports, but I wouldn't have thought you'd be ruthless enough to fire on your own side. You were quite squeamish before, I recall."

Thanos's hand tightened around the hilt of his sword. "You commanded the deaths of women and children. You encouraged your soldiers to rape and pillage. I don't like killing, but the world is better off without you."

The general looked as though he might say something else, but Thanos didn't give him an opportunity. He did it quickly, before he could stop himself. He thrust up, into the general's throat and out again, stepping back while Draco stared at him in obvious shock. The general collapsed to his knees, then tumbled forward into the dirt. Thanos moved over to the Typhoon.

"Who ordered you to kill me?" he asked.

The Typhoon stared at him. "You'll let me live if I tell you?"

"No," Thanos said. "You're going to die for all the evil you've done here. You're going to die for trying to kill me. But at least you can die with some honor."

"What would you know about honor, traitor?" the Typhoon demanded.

Thanos struck out again, this time in a lateral sweep that ended with the huge soldier's head rolling to the floor. Thanos let his sword fall to land point first in the earth. He should have felt satisfaction at this, or elation at the victory, but as it was it just felt as though a grim chore was complete.

"It seems I didn't have to worry about you after all," Akila said, coming forward to clap Thanos on the shoulder. "Well done. Without you, Haylon would have fallen to the Empire by now."

That was a good thing to be reminded of as Thanos looked out over the death and destruction he'd been a part of. It meant that he could look toward Haylon, where there were fires still burning, and think that it was all worth it.

"I did what I needed to do," Thanos said.

"You did more than that," Akila assured him. "You acted the way a true friend would, and we will always think of you that way. No, as more than that. As a brother."

He embraced Thanos, and Thanos didn't know what to say. He hadn't been trying to do anything special. He'd just been trying to do the right thing for the people of Haylon. For free people.

"What now?" Thanos asked. "More ambushes?"

Akila shook his head. "If the Empire soldiers want to run, let them. As for what happens next … well, I was going to ask you that, Prince. Me and my boys owe you a lot, so what do you want to do now?"

Thanos stood there, looking over at the tents while he tried to make up his mind. The sea breeze washed away some of the smell of death that surrounded him, but not all of it. Not by a long way.

What did he want? For the past couple of days, it felt as though he'd been running on instinct. Now, though, there was a moment to think, to pause, and to feel. The last part of it was easy, at least. For what seemed like the first time in his life, he knew exactly what he felt.

He stepped forward and grabbed a handful of the Empire's standard, yanking it down.

"I want revenge," he said. "I've tried so hard to be the kind of prince the Empire needed, and they tried to kill me for it. I want to find out who ordered that."

"Is that all you want?" Akila asked him.

Thanos shook his head. It wasn't the only thing. Not by a long way. "I want to find a way to make it stop. They've spent their lives hurting the people they're meant to be ruling on behalf of, building palaces and taking from them. I want to march in there and tear it down around them. I want to change the way the regime treats the people. I want to make sure that people like you are free forever… And I want to see Ceres."

That burned brighter in him than all the rest of it put together. When he'd thought he was dying, she was what he'd thought of, and now he wanted nothing more than to be able to pull her into his arms. He didn't care what it took, he needed to get back to her.

"I want to lead your men into the middle of Delos, take the city, and not stop until we've wiped away every cruelty in the Empire," Thanos said.

"You sound determined," Akila replied.

Thanos was. In that moment, he could have torn down the entire ruling family and led the assault on Delos himself. He saw the rebel leader shake his head though.

"Even if I could persuade my lads to march on Delos now," Akila said, "it isn't the right time for it. The Empire is still strong, and the nobles' grip on it is too firm. This will take more than an army marching in to solve it."

"What will it take then?" Thanos demanded. "I can't just sit here and do nothing, Akila."

"You won't have to," Akila promised. "But perhaps you can do more good inside Delos's court than you can marching on it."

It took Thanos a moment to understand. "You want me to be a spy for you?"

Akila nodded. "You're the one man who might have a chance to work for our interests on the inside. You can tell them that you survived the fighting. It might give you a chance to find out everything you want to, and you can warn us if King Claudius wants to send more men to Haylon."

It made sense, but even so, it was hard. Thanos didn't like playing the games of court at the best of times. Being there as a spy would only make it worse. He wanted to march in and take his vengeance directly. But the truth was that he didn't even know who had ordered his death. This might give him a chance to find out, to pave the way for the rebellion…

…and to see Ceres.

That thought was the one that decided it for Thanos. If he could see Ceres again, then the rest of it would be worth it. He could put up with any amount of subterfuge and politics if she was there, and the thought of her waiting was enough to make him want to rush home.

"How will I even get back?" Thanos asked.

"Leave that to us," Akila said.

It took time, and in that time, the rebels celebrated him. They set fires where the Empire's tents had been, and those quickly became the center points of a feast. The rebels danced and drank, ate and congratulated one another. Thanos found himself at the heart of it all, unable to go more than a minute or two without one of the rebels clapping him on the back or offering him wine.

They found him a small boat, in the end, with a couple of fishermen from Haylon to crew it. The boat he'd come in on was gone, lost in the fires the rebels had set, but at least this one looked as though it could make the journey. Akila's men packed it with food and supplies, lining up on the beach to cheer as Thanos boarded.

"Thanos! Thanos!"

Thanos stood there watching them, and he would never have thought that this would feel as if he were leaving a family. He was supposedly going home, but right then, this was the place that felt like home. He watched Akila waving on the sand and Thanos saluted him with his sword, one warrior to another.

He felt the boat lurch as it started to move away. Thanos watched until Akila's men were out of sight, but quickly turned his thoughts to Delos, and everything he would have to do once he got there. It would be dangerous, perhaps more dangerous than anything else he'd done. All of it would be worth it, though, for one simple reason:

He was going to see Ceres again.

Chapter Eighteen

Ceres stumbled in blackness as they marched her toward the prison ship. Around her, she could hear the jibes and insults of the people she passed. She couldn't see them, but she could hear their sudden hate and contempt, pouring over her like water in a storm.

Ceres flinched as something struck her, bouncing off her breastplate. It might have been a piece of fruit or a stone, she didn't know which. Unable to see it and held in place as she was, there was no chance for her to dodge it. Her breastplate and kilt offered some protection, but really just meant that she was easier for the crowd to identify.

"Murderer!"

"Slave!"

The hardest part was hearing the anger in voices that had been calling her name in the Stade just a little while before. Ceres knew that the royals must have started their rumors and their announcements even before her fight in the Stade was finished, because that was the only way it could have spread so quickly.

She felt the pull of metal against her wrists as the guards dragged her along by the shackles that held her. Ceres didn't fight the movement, but she felt their sudden yanks and jerks against the chains anyway. She heard people laugh as she stumbled, and Ceres knew that was the point. They wanted her humiliated.

Finally they came to a halt, and the guards dragged the hood from her head, leaving her blinking back tears in sunlight that seemed blindingly bright after the darkness before.

A huge shape stood before her, and it took a moment for Ceres to make out the detail of the ship that sat there. It was an ugly hulk of a thing, bulky and round, tattered and with rusting fittings. The prison ship seemed to be designed to hint at the horrors to come on the Isle of Prisoners, even its gangplank seeming like the spine of some long dead creature.

They dragged Ceres up it, and she walked with shuffling steps. She had enough time to look back and see the crowds there, looking out over the sea of angry faces, all there to show their hatred of her. Was it because of the things the royals had said about her, or because she'd lost, or both? She didn't know.

The gangplank seemed to stretch out forever. Ceres thought about diving from it into the water below, but chained as she was, she would sink instantly, even if she could break away from the guards' grip.

Her footsteps seemed to shake it, and for a moment Ceres thought that she might tip in anyway. She felt the guards tighten their grips on her and throw her forward, so that she landed on the rough wood of the deck. Above her, black-stained sails lay furled on their masts, while she saw sailors lounging on the deck, watching her the way the crowds had below.

Ceres pulled herself to her feet, but the guards took a grip on her again. They dragged her toward an iron-barred hatch, open to the sky, then threw her through it, so that she stumbled down the steps below. She tried to curl and roll to keep from being hurt, but even so, the impact jarred her.

The first thing to hit her was the smell of too many people pressed together too close, the stink of it sharp and acrid with sweat. There were people huddled down there in shackles and chains. Ceres could see men, women, and children thrown together, with no apparent order or care. Some were attached together in long coffles, while others were bolted to the walls. Ceres found herself wondering where they had all come from, and what they had done.

Ceres looked up toward the hatch, just in time for one of the guards to spit down after her in contempt.

"Better get comfortable. The Isle of Prisoners will be a whole lot worse."

⚜ ⚜ ⚜

Ceres didn't dare sleep as the prison ship rolled and bucked its way across the sea. Instead, she sat watching the other prisoners there, trying to project a sense of strength that would keep the more dangerous ones at bay.

It was a cruel place. Some of those there were probably perfectly normal people: members of the rebellion the Empire didn't want to kill too quickly, people who had stolen to feed their families, or who had found themselves on the wrong side of the court's political games. There were others, though, who were far more dangerous. Since she'd been there, Ceres had heard one man boasting about the number of people he'd killed, while there had been another screaming and raging for no apparent reason. Already, Ceres had seen fights, murders, and more down there.

As far as she could tell, the guards had no interest in stopping any of it. When they brought food, they threw it out at random for the people there to fight over. Ceres managed to grab a hunk of bread that landed near her, but there were others who were not so lucky. She saw one man in the faded clothes of a noble being beaten for a crust, the gold brocade on his tunic being ripped away simply because it might have some value. This place seemed to have no rules beyond the strongest taking what they wanted. The violence of the place was enough to make Ceres feel sick that people could treat one another that way.

So Ceres forced her eyes to stay open, trying to keep her back to the bulkhead of the ship, where she could see all the others around her. She was still watching when she saw the girl.

She was young, probably around ten years old or so, and painfully thin. Her dress was torn, and her face smeared with dirt. Her sandy blonde hair was so tangled and dust streaked that it looked brown in places. She was currently crawling along, trying to snatch food from the edges of the melee without being seen.

She didn't succeed. Ceres saw a large, scarred man turn on her, raising up to his full height.

"What do you think you're doing? Give me that! Scrawny little brat, I'll kill you!"

He took a step forward, and Ceres couldn't hold herself in place. She sprang in between the girl and her would-be attacker, hands up ready to fight.

"Leave her alone," Ceres said.

"I'll do what I want," the thug said. Ceres saw him look her up and down. "To her, and you."

Ceres felt anger rising in her. Energy rose in its wake, flooding through her. Her opponent charged at her, but she was already moving. She sidestepped the thug's rush, leaving her foot out to trip him. As he went down, she was already on him, the chain that connected her shackles wrapping tight around his throat. She heard him make a gurgling sound as she strangled him, before he fell still.

She could have kept going. She could have choked him until he died, or pulled until his neck snapped. It would have been the kind of message the rest of the hold would understand. Instead, Ceres let go, kicking the man's unconscious body away.

She saw several of the hold's other denizens descend on him to rob him. Ceres held back her disgust and went back to her spot instead. The girl was there, obviously not wanting to move too far away from her. Even so, she looked frightened, as though expecting Ceres to lash out at her at any moment.

"It's all right," Ceres said. "I'm not going to hurt you. I'm Ceres."

The girl took a moment to consider that, and Ceres guessed that she was trying to work out all the ways the conversation could go. "I'm Eike."

Ceres held out a small piece of bread to her, and Eike took it, staring at it for a moment before biting down hungrily. She looked up at Ceres, as though waiting for what it would cost her. Ceres gestured to the patch of deck beside her.

"You can sit down if you like," Ceres said.

"Do I have to?" Eike asked.

"You don't have to do anything you don't want."

The girl snorted. "I know that's not true here."

Even so, she sat down. She watched Ceres with obvious curiosity.

"Is it true that you fought in the Stade?" she asked eventually.

Ceres nodded. "That's right."

"Is it true that you killed your master, too?" Eike asked. Apparently the rumors had made their way here, too. "They say that's why you're here."

"I killed a slaver who tried to capture me, and who had a knife to my friend's throat," Ceres said.

Eike stared back.

"I am here because my family joined the rebellion," she said. "When the soldiers came, they took all of us. Now"—she choked back a sob—"I'm the only one left."

Ceres put an arm around her. She felt Eike tense like an animal ready to run, and that just made her feel worse for her. No one that young should be stuck somewhere like this. Ceres didn't want to think about what they would do to the girl on the Isle of Prisoners.

She didn't want to think about what they would do to her, either. The Isle had an evil reputation as a place of torturers and cruel deaths, oubliettes and mass cages. Once there, there was almost no coming back, certainly not for anyone like her. A quick death in the Stade would have been better, Ceres decided. Far better.

"If you want to sleep, I could keep watch," Eike offered.

Ceres looked over to her. She guessed that the girl was looking for a way to make herself useful so that Ceres wouldn't abandon her. Ceres wouldn't do that, but in this place, it would be hard to convince her that anyone was capable of acting out of altruism. Besides, she was currently so exhausted that the idea of being able to sleep meant almost as much as freedom would have.

"I'd like that," Ceres admitted. "Wake me if there's trouble."

"There's always trouble," Eike said. "But I'll wake you up if anyone comes close."

It seemed bizarre to Ceres to be trusting her safety to this girl, but the exhaustion of her day overcame her, and before she could think twice, the rocking was already lulling her heavy eyes to sleep.

Chapter Nineteen

Lucious was in a mood to celebrate. He threw back a goblet of wine too fast, raising it in a mocking toast to thin air as it burned in his throat.

"To vanquished irritants!"

He tossed the goblet casually at a servant, and the man scrambled to catch it, probably terrified that Lucious would have him beaten if he let it hit the floor. Lucious resolved to have him beaten later anyway, just to keep the man on his toes.

He made his way in the direction of the throne room. Ordinarily, he found the business of the court boring, but perhaps today it would turn to more of a party atmosphere. The problem was dealt with, and soon it would be the Festival of the Moon, one of the biggest festivals in Delos's calendar. Normally, that meant days of feasting and parties, presents and enjoyment. The feasts at the castle were always a lavish affair.

Lucious was halfway to the throne room when he saw the older woman arguing with the guards.

"But Lady Stephania promised me! I was the one who gave her Ceres!"

Lucious stepped across to the argument, looking the woman over. To him, she looked nondescript and worn, not worth his interest. Only Ceres's name caught his attention.

"What's going on here?" he asked.

"She wants to speak to Lady Stephania," one of the guards said.

"I'm owed," the woman said. She held up a pouch, clutched so tightly Lucious could see her knuckles sticking out. "She gave me money for what I knew about Ceres, but now that it's let her get rid of my daughter—"

"Your daughter?" Lucious said. Despite the wine, that got through. "You're Ceres's mother?"

"I am." The woman seemed to remember herself enough to curtsy. "Marita, my lord. I provided the information that let them take Ceres."

"So you're the reason I didn't get to see her die in the Stade?" Lucious asked, letting a brief note of anger seep into his voice. That was the one part of this that still rankled. That his carefully prepared plan could be set aside, and Stephania's could work so well instead. Everybody knew that she was just a vacuous ornament at court, but through some stroke of luck she'd succeeded.

Ceres's mother looked frightened at that. She was right to be.

"And now you're here for more money?" Lucious said. He shook his head. "That's just… ungrateful."

The woman seemed to understand the position she'd put herself in at last. "I… I'll go."

"Not yet," Lucious said. He grabbed the coin pouch, ripping it from her hand and then tossing it to one of the guards.

"That's mine!" Ceres's mother insisted.

"It *was* yours," Lucious said. "Now it is this guard's."

"I earned that!" the woman insisted.

Lucious snapped his fingers. "She needs to learn the price of getting above her station. Take her outside, and take everything of value she has. Then throw her in the gutter like the trash she is."

"Yes, Prince Lucious," the guard said.

"No!" Marita screamed as the guards grabbed her by the arms. "You can't do this to me!"

It always amused Lucious when peasants tried to tell him what he couldn't do. They didn't understand how the world worked. He stood and watched as the guards dragged her outside, then called out, almost as an afterthought.

"If she resists, beat her until she learns better."

Lucious smiled then and headed for the throne room. The others were already there, and as he'd predicted, it had something of a carnival atmosphere to it. He could see Stephania at the heart of a clique of the other noble girls, with them fawning over her as usual. The king and queen sat on their thrones while before them, nobles chattered and congratulated themselves on having dealt with the crisis. Probably half of them were busy trying to claim credit for the outcome.

Lucious made his way through them, and today they mostly stepped back to give him room to get through. Many of the more minor nobles bowed or nodded, giving him the acknowledgment he deserved.

"Lucious, would you like to come to a gathering we're having for the Festival of the Moon?" one of the young noblewomen there asked as he passed. "We have a group of masked players this year who are simply delightful."

Another cut in straightaway. "Masked players are *so* last year. We have tumblers brought from the far south, and perfumers who have promised clouds of scented smoke."

"Tumblers?" the first said. "And I suppose you'll be serving the same quails and oxen as last year as well?"

Lucious forced a smile. The truth was that he would go wherever they treated him most like the prince he was on festival night. He would probably tour from party to party until they all blended into one.

"It sounds good," Lucious said. "I'll think about it."

More offers followed as he continued through the crowd.

He was almost to the front when King Claudius stood up, raising his hand for silence and instantly bringing the chattering to a halt. He stood there, and despite his age, Lucious could see the power there within him.

"Why are you all so happy?" he demanded. "Because we have gotten rid of one girl?"

"And killed the leader of the rebellion," Lucious pointed out. "Rexus is dead. Ceres is gone. The people have no one to lead them."

"That is true," Queen Athena said. "The rebellion is hurt, but that does not mean that our people will settle back into their lives easily."

"They must be *pressed* back," King Claudius said, "and firmly!"

Lucious suspected that he knew where this was going. The king and queen had ordered periods of greater severity before. Lucious had never understood why it was necessary to order it. Surely, no unrest or disobedience should ever be tolerated?

"How are they to be pressed back, your majesties?" Lucious asked. He guessed that it was the question on the minds of most of those there. Well, those who weren't preoccupied with how to host the most out of control party for the festival, at least. Stephania, for example, seemed utterly uninterested, more concerned with the attention of her coterie of noblewomen. "How much more can be done?"

Queen Athena gave him a hard look. "You don't believe that we have a plan, Lucious?"

"I'm sure you do, my queen," Lucious said. "I'm just eager to hear what it is. I'm sure we all are."

More likely, everyone there wanted to know whether it would affect them. He thought back to some of the things they had tried in the past. Those with rebel sympathies had been rounded up and either killed or enslaved. Their families had been imprisoned, their homes burned. There had been harsh taxes and harsher methods of collection. It had seemed obvious to Lucious that eventually they would realize that they were bringing such measures on themselves with their defiance, but curiously, the more rebels they treated harshly, the more there seemed to be. There was no logic to it, but then, who understood how the lower orders thought?

"I have heard you all talking about the Festival of the Moon," King Claudius said. "Well, I believe that it is appropriate that our Empire makes its rulers an offering for the festival, in reparation for all the trouble the rebellion has caused."

"What kind of offering?" Lucious asked.

King Claudius shrugged. "Whatever we desire. From now until I decide that the people of Delos have learned the price of resistance, any noble will be able to take whatever they wish from the rest. If you want their children as slaves, they are yours. If you want their last coins, or the clothes off their backs, they will give them. They say we have taken too much from them? We will move among them and show them what it is like to have *everything* taken from them."

"There will be those who resist," Lucious pointed out.

"You sound as though you're arguing against our command, Lucious," Queen Athena said.

Lucious shook his head. "Not at all, your majesties. I'm merely asking what I am permitted to do when they *do* fight back."

He heard the slap of flesh on flesh as the king slammed his fist into his palm. "Crush them. Kill any who refuse to hand over what is ours. Remind them that they only own anything in this Empire through our grace. Slaughter them, enslave their families, and have their neighbors watch as you take everything they have ever owned."

Lucious smiled at the thought of that. It was the kind of thing he'd done with Ceres's mother, only on a scale that would encompass the whole Empire. Perhaps some would argue, perhaps some would fight, but they would only serve as examples for the others.

"I would like to lead these efforts," Lucious said, thinking with relish of the possibilities.

Queen Athena smiled. "We thought you would, and we think you're the perfect choice. Go out among them, Lucious. Take our guards with you, and make them properly afraid of their rulers for once."

"With pleasure," Lucious said, and it would be a pleasure. It wasn't so much the thought of everything he could take from the peasants as the act of taking itself. He was sure that there would be the opportunity to show plenty of them their place in ways they would never forget. "When do you want me to begin?"

"At once," King Claudius said. "I want this to be a Festival of the Moon that all of Delos will remember."

"Oh, it will be," Lucious promised. "It will be."

Chapter Twenty

When Thanos returned to Delos, there were guards on the docks—indeed, there were guards everywhere. The whole city had the feel of a place under siege, making it hard to tell the difference between the Empire's capital and the way Haylon had been when it was under attack. He saw bones hanging in a gibbet over the water, the iron chain that held it creaking as it moved in the wind.

A part of Thanos wanted to avoid the guards. They reminded him too much of the soldiers he'd fought back on the rebels' island. Yet he needed to play the part of the loyal prince, returning from the war, and that meant not sneaking around.

"You there," he said to the first group he found. They appeared to be engaged in stripping a waterfront home of its contents. "What are you doing?"

"Enforcing the orders of the king," their sergeant said. "What's it to you?"

"I am Prince Thanos. You will stop this and escort me to the castle at once."

He saw the guards pale at that, but they did as he commanded. Thanos looked around as they walked with him back to the castle. In the time he'd been away, it seemed that plenty had changed. He could see other groups of soldiers looting houses, while more gibbets hung on street corners. Some of the occupants were still alive. Graffiti scrawled on the walls proclaimed the cruelty of the king among the more usual comments on the fighters in the Stade. Just the thought of them had him thinking about Ceres.

By the time he reached the castle, it was hard to concentrate on anything else, but Thanos knew he had to. He had to keep up the pretense of loyalty, the illusion of being the perfect prince. One slip could mean more than his life. It might mean defeat for the rebels' plans too. He had to find out who had ordered his death, and look for ways to help the rebels. Despite all of that, the urge to see Ceres was almost more than he could bear.

He could have gone to his old rooms and changed before heading for the throne room. Instead, Thanos strode in as he was. He wanted everyone there to see him with the dirt and blood of the conflict for Haylon on him. He wanted them to understand what had happened there. He stepped into the throne room, and heard the collective gasp from those there.

They stood in place as if frozen. Thanos walked forward between them, letting his eyes flicker left and right. He could see plenty of nobles he knew there, all looking as though they were dressed for a celebration. He spotted Cosmas in a corner, the scholar looking as though he was making mental notes on everything that was happening in the room. Lucious was off to one side, in grand armor that made him look like the general of an invading army. Stephania was holding a peach, just poised to take a delicate bite out of it. At the head of the room, King Claudius sat on his throne, while Queen Athena had moved off among the nobles to talk to them.

Thanos took all that in, and he slipped through the crowds toward the throne. Once he reached the dais, he fell to one knee, bowing his head as if in shame.

"Your majesty, I regret to inform you that the expedition to retake Haylon has not been a success."

It was an understatement. If the king knew anything about what had happened, he would know it had been a disaster. Briefly, tension clamped around Thanos. What if soldiers had escaped back to Delos? What if a dove had returned with a message? The king might already know about the part he'd played in the destruction of the Empire's forces.

The room was silent for several seconds. In it, Thanos found his thoughts of possible discovery swept away by the need to examine the others there. Someone had sent an assassin for him. He would find out who had done that.

"Thanos?" the king said, standing. He took Thanos's hands, drawing him up to his feet. To Thanos, it seemed like a surprisingly tender gesture, given how cruel the king usually was. "You're alive? We heard that you were killed by the rebels on the beaches of Haylon."

Thanos tried to listen for the nuances of that. Was the king disappointed? Had he been the one to send the Typhoon with orders to kill him?

"I was almost killed, though it wasn't by rebels," Thanos said. "One of our own soldiers stabbed me in the back."

He looked around at the room as he said it. Did anyone look shocked by the revelation? Did anyone look satisfied? How many of those here could have bribed or commanded the Typhoon? The truth was that it was too many. There was almost no one there he could trust. Every smile at his return was as likely to be fake as real.

"One of our own betrayed you?" the king said. "Why?"

"He claimed to be sent by someone at court," Thanos said. Again, he heard a gasp go around the room. "Although he wouldn't say by whom."

"How did you survive?" the king asked.

"I was left for dead," Thanos said. "Fishermen found me, and brought me back when they realized who I was. They thought there would be a reward."

It was the kind of lie he guessed the others there would believe. They understood greed far better than kindness, in Thanos's experience. He paused. It was going to be hard lying constantly. He'd tried to build his life on honesty …

… and that had nearly gotten him killed.

"And my army?" the king asked.

"I heard the fishermen talking. They said that the Imperial fleet had been burned, the land forces cut off. I'm sorry, your majesty, but I believe General Draco is dead."

King Claudius looked at him for a long time. Thanos found himself wondering how much of his story the king believed. He spent his life with courtiers telling him half-truths and outright lies. The only thing protecting Thanos now was the fact that he'd never lied to his king in the past.

"A terrible loss," King Claudius said. "But I am more concerned with the fact that you were attacked. Every aid will be provided in finding the one responsible. If there is anything you require, you have only to ask."

"Thank you, your majesty," Thanos said, although he had no intention of simply relying on the king's efforts. There was one thing the king could give him, though. "May I be permitted to see Ceres?"

That made the king's expression change. It went from something that looked like genuine concern to anger almost as fast as Thanos could blink.

"All of this, and your mind is still on that girl?"

It always would be. Thanos found himself thinking of Ceres as she'd been when he'd left, angry with him for the betrayal of fighting against the rebellion. If he could whisper the truth to her…

"I would like to see her," Thanos said.

"That is not possible," Queen Athena said. "The girl is gone."

Thanos spun to her. "Gone? What do you mean 'gone'?"

"Mind your tone, Thanos," King Claudius said. "What you have been through gives you some leeway, but remember where you are."

The queen gave him an answer, though. "Your precious Ceres turned out not to be all she seemed. She was a slave who had killed her master, not fit to live, let alone fight in the Stade. As we speak, she is on a ship headed for the Isle of Prisoners."

The queen seemed to take a certain cruel delight in telling him that. She smiled as Thanos reeled before the news, and it was all he could do not to start shouting. He wanted to demand Ceres's return; to charge down to the docks and set off after her on whatever boat he could find. As it was, he found that he couldn't bear to stay there any longer. Between the people who'd tried to kill him, the ones who'd gotten rid of Ceres, and the usual poisonous atmosphere of the court, how had he thought that he could stand to be here without exploding?

Somehow, Thanos managed to keep enough of a grip on himself to force a bow. "Forgive me, your majesties. My wound is paining me, and it has been a long journey. With your permission, I would like to retire to my room."

"Yes," King Claudius said. "Perhaps that is a good idea."

Thanos hurried from the throne room, and he saw the courtiers there rush to get out of his way. He didn't know what they saw in his face, but they stepped back quickly, leaving a clear route to the door. Thanos had made it out into an antechamber before he felt a hand on his shoulder.

He spun, his anger rising. If someone wanted to stop him now, in the moments after he'd learned that he'd lost Ceres, then—

"Prince Thanos," Cosmas said, taking a step back. The old scholar looked much as he always had to Thanos: spry despite his age, bald, with pronounced ears and a beak of a nose that only seemed to draw attention up to the intense blue of his eyes.

"Cosmas," Thanos said. The old man's presence was enough to calm him a little, but only a little. "I'm sorry. I can't talk now. Ceres—"

"I know, boy," the scholar said. "Some pains are too much to deal with all at once. You came back thinking of a happy reunion, and it hurts to have that dashed."

It did more than hurt. It felt as though something in Thanos was tearing itself apart. Even so, he nodded.

"I need some time alone," he said.

"I understand," Cosmas replied. "But when you are ready, we need to talk."

"Why?" Thanos asked.

"Because I believe I know who tried to kill you."

Chapter Twenty One

Ceres was resting when the ship lurched. She was on the edge of sleep with Eike near to her, and she barely had time to wake up before she was rolling as the ship listed. She only kept from tumbling right across the deck by grabbing for one of the long chains that bound prisoners in place.

It had to be a storm, and a big one too if it could rock the ship like this. Beside her, Eike grabbed hold of the same chain, and Ceres moved closer to wrap her arms around the girl, climbing along the chain until she could do it. As small as the girl was, there was no way she would survive if she found herself thrown across the hold of the ship.

Several of those prisoners who weren't chained down were, and Ceres heard screams and yells of surprise as they fell through the air. She heard sickening crunches as some of them hit posts or the far wall. Several didn't rise, while more screamed with broken limbs. The ones who fell into knots of other prisoners weren't much better off. Ceres heard the fights starting, and clung harder to the chain.

She just had time to wonder what kind of storm could come out of nowhere like this before the boat righted, then swung the other way. Now prisoners crashed into the wall near her, and Ceres curled around Eike, shielding her from the worst of it. For once, Ceres was glad that they'd left her armor on her when they'd thrown her in here. A crazed-looking man landed next to them and lashed out reflexively with a knife that looked like it had been made from a length of bone. It skittered off the steel, and Ceres kicked out, knocking him away.

The ship leveled out once more, but only briefly. Something slammed into the side of the ship, and for a moment, Ceres thought that they must have hit a rock. Then the side of the ship split, and a tentacle as wide as a man was tall burst through.

It seemed they weren't in a storm after all.

"Sea monster!" one of the prisoners screamed, and Ceres heard other voices join in the call.

The tentacle lashed like a whip among the prisoners, wrapping around a pair of men before jerking back. They were chained in place, but the strength of the tentacle was enough to snap them clear of it. Ceres saw one of the prisoners try to cling to the side of the hole in the ship, but the tentacle wrenched him out into the ocean.

Water shot through in a gout that swept people away, seeming to Ceres to pour in impossibly fast. She saw another tentacle punch through the wood of the hold, and then a beak like that of some giant bird of prey followed, tearing its way inside. Water followed each time, and Ceres looked down to find that it was already up to her ankles.

"We're going to sink," she said. "We need to get out of here!"

"How?" Eike asked.

Ceres didn't have an answer for that, but she still headed toward the hatch that led up to the deck. It was covered in wide iron bars, locked firmly from the outside.

"I think I can fit!" Eike said.

"Then go," Ceres replied. "You need to get off the ship!"

She might not be able to save herself, but at least she could save the girl. Other prisoners pushed up behind Ceres, crushing her against the hatch as they tried to get through, but Ceres held them back while Eike wriggled through. She scampered away and Ceres looked back at the hold.

The water was rising now. She could see those prisoners whose shackles held them to a particular spot yanking at them, trying to pull them away from their moorings. One man who had been knocked unconscious by the fall across the hold slid under the water as Ceres watched, while the tentacles of the monster continued to flail inside the hold, dragging helpless prisoners toward that waiting maw. There was nowhere to run to, and already the ship felt as though it was delicately poised, ready to tip over at any moment.

"Quick, Ceres! Up here!"

Ceres looked up and saw sunlight, unencumbered by bars. Eike was there beyond the hatch, a set of keys held proudly in one hand.

"I stole them from a guard," Eike said. "I bet one will open your shackles too!"

She grinned down at Ceres, and Ceres found herself smiling back up. She hauled herself up through the hatch, onto the deck, trying to make sense of what was going on as she took the keys from Eike and fitted them to her shackles. She hurried as much as she could. It wasn't just the rising water. Other prisoners were already pushing their way up onto the deck behind Ceres, and Ceres didn't want to have to fight them for the keys.

The ship was clearly in trouble. The monster attacking it had tentacles wrapped around the masts, tearing men from the rigging and crushing them in its grasp. Ceres saw one sweep around like a flail, knocking sailors and guards into the water like toys. Above, she saw sea raptors gathering, as though sensing the potential feast to come. She saw some of the guards jabbing at the tentacles with swords and harpoons. None of it seemed to make any difference.

She saw one of the guards look over in her direction as she succeeded in getting the shackles off.

"The prisoners are escaping!" he cried, and ran at her with a sword outstretched.

Ceres didn't have any time to think, and the terror of the monster was too great for any more fear to break through. Instead, she swung the shackles that had just confined her around as a weapon, catching the guard on the side of his head and knocking him sprawling. A questing tentacle reached out and grabbed him, dragging him screaming into the water.

More guards came her way, despite the greater threat of the monster attacking them all. Ceres tossed her keys to the prisoners coming through the hatch behind her, then struck out with her shackles at the sword a guard held, tangling it. She moved in close to rip the sword from his grasp, then kicked the guard away.

"You really were a combatlord, weren't you?" Eike said. Despite everything, she sounded surprised by it.

Ceres nodded. "Stay close to me. We have to find a way off this ship."

The ship creaked as if in response to that as the tentacled monster continued to tear through it. One of the masts shivered and fell under the power of its assault, crashing down into the water like some huge tree while Ceres held Eike and tried to keep her back from the danger. There had to be small boats for landing, didn't there? There had to be a way off the ship besides the gangplank.

Ceres barely had a chance to think that before the ship tilted, its bow plunging into the water. The world seemed to turn on its side, and for a moment, she had a view of the water below, filled with blood, struggling men, and the seething mass of the creature attacking them. She could see fins too, as sharks swam around the edges of it, looking to pick up stragglers.

Ceres had a moment to experience the full horror of it before the water came up to meet her. She clung to Eike, but the girl was ripped from her grasp as they plunged into the cold of the sea. Ceres tried to take a breath, tasted salt water, and managed to get her head above the surface for a second.

It didn't last. The weight of her armor dragged her down, and Ceres found herself dropping beneath the waves once more. She fumbled for the straps of her breastplate and iron kilt, swimming free in just her tunic and watching them tumble into the depths among the flailing tentacles and dying prisoners. She saw a whole chain of prisoners dragged down into the depths by their bonds, sharks already plunging in toward them.

She spotted Eike more by chance than anything. A tentacle had wrapped around the girl's leg, ignoring her futile efforts to kick free. Ceres dove down toward Eike, reaching out for the tentacle even though she knew there was no way she could hope to pull it clear. She silently begged for the strength to save the girl, bracing her legs as she tried to break the monster's grip.

Ceres felt the moment when the power that she'd wielded in the Stade come to her like a wave rising within her. It seemed to start somewhere deep inside her, bursting up through her and out into the tentacle that gripped Eike. The power blasted into it and the tentacle let go of the girl, jerking back the way Ceres might have from a hot piece of iron. Ceres grabbed Eike and swam upwards while her lungs burned with the effort.

They broke the surface together, not far from the upturned remains of one of the ship's boats. The rest of it was sinking rapidly, while sailors screamed in the water as they fought sharks, tentacles, or both.

"Quick," Ceres said, "get aboard."

She helped Eike out of the water, then climbed up beside her. A tentacle stretched out toward them, then pulled back, as though some part of the monster could remember what had happened the last time it had touched Ceres. Instead, it grabbed for another of the guards in the water, and the sharks followed close behind.

The feeding frenzy seemed to go on forever, while Ceres sat in the middle of it all on the hull of the small boat, her arms wrapped around Eike for protection. Nothing came close to them. Nothing seemed to dare. Even the sharks that brushed by veered away, making for other prey.

Eventually, the last tentacle plunged back into the water, and stillness replaced the violence that had come before. Ceres looked around for other survivors, but she couldn't see any. The remains of the ship had long since fallen below the water, and anyone clinging to the wreckage had been ruthlessly picked off by tentacles or sharks. Only a spread of splintered wood and supplies showed that the ship had ever been there at all.

"They're dead," Eike said in a small voice. "They're all dead."

Ceres held onto her while the girl started to cry, trying to think of a way to comfort her, even though she could barely find a way past the horror of it herself. "It's all right. I'm here. You're alive, and I'm alive. We'll find a way through this."

Yet as they drifted on the open sea, without any idea where they were, Ceres had no idea how survival would be possible.

Chapter Twenty Two

Anka kept her head down, trying not to attract attention from the soldiers of the 23rd as she walked through the city of tents. So far, she'd been lucky. She'd had nothing more than a few suspicious looks. With the way soldiers were, it could be a lot worse.

She'd managed to gain entry to the camp by dressing as one of the washer women who made their way between the campfires. There were no female soldiers in the army but there were always servants and camp followers who trailed after it as it moved. Dressed as one of them, she was as invisible as if she'd crept in under the cover of darkness.

At least, she hoped so.

She didn't want to think about what might happen to her if they caught her, or worse, what might happen to the rebellion. Since Rexus had died, she'd been the one trying to pull things together, assuring people that they could still continue, and still succeed. She'd smoothed over arguments, passed messages, and found ways to persuade their supporters that it wouldn't rebound on them.

Every second she spent away from Delos cost the rebellion dearly, but she kept picking her way through the camp, holding her bundle of washing like a protective shield. Whatever it cost, she'd promised Ceres that she would do this.

That mattered to her, more than enough for her to brave the stares and occasional catcalls of the soldiers as she passed, and to dodge past the larger groups of them. Ceres had given her back her freedom. Without her, Anka would be suffering a lot worse than this.

The hard part was finding one conscript in the middle of the Empire's vast army. Sympathizers had provided some information, bribery had gotten her more, but ultimately, Anka had found herself having to track along the route the conscript takers had followed, asking questions and hoping for the best.

She knew that wouldn't work here. Ask after Sartes, and it would bring as much trouble for him as for her. Anka looked around the army camp, trying to make sense of where she was. In the distance, she could see soldiers drilling in lines and running while officers shouted at them. Others dug ditches or cut wood for palisades.

She passed by a space between the tents where a soldier was tied to a post, being whipped for some infraction. She could hear the muffled cries as the man bit down on a leather strap to keep from screaming, while other soldiers, probably members of his unit, stood around to watch the punishment.

Anka didn't stay for it. Hating the army wasn't the same thing as wanting to see the individuals in it hurt. Instead, she headed for the larger tents near the center of the camp. The army had to keep records somewhere, didn't it? Surely there would be payrolls, or details of who served with whom? A roll call or a note of punishments dished out? Something, at least.

In her disguise, she was able to get closer to the tents than she would have believed. No one challenged her. Probably it helped that she walked briskly, trying to look as though she knew where she was going, while looking around out of the corner of her eye until she was sure that she did.

She found the tent she was looking for next to a larger commander's pavilion, and slipped in once she was sure that no one was looking. It made sense that the 23rd's commanders would want to keep their adjutants and administrators close by. Sure enough, a writing slope and parchment sat on a folding camp table, along with box after box that clearly held records.

Anka dared a glance outside before she began, wanting to make sure that no one found her. This was the most dangerous part, because no one but a spy would ever go through the army's papers. She pressed down the anxiety and started work.

Anka went as quickly as she could. She took out records, trying to make sense of the crabbed writing there as she scanned them for any glimpse of Sartes's name. If she could get some sense of where he was in the camp, that would be the best possible outcome, but even confirmation that he was really here and still alive would be enough.

She froze as she heard the sound of footsteps outside the tent, then quickly shoved the rolls back into place. She finished, grabbed her bundle of washing, and just about made it to the door when an officer walked in.

"Watch where you're going!" the officer bellowed, then paused. His hand shot out to grip Anka's shoulder. "Wait, what are you even doing here? Old Mersha handles my washing."

Anka didn't have to feign the shudder that ran through her. "I don't know, my lord. She sent me out, and I… I thought this was where I was meant to be." She grabbed for one of the names she'd seen on the papers she'd looked through. "I was looking for Captain Thero's tent?"

"Well, you're on the wrong side of the camp, then," the officer said. "He keeps his tent in the north quadrant. Don't you know anything?"

"I… I'm new, my lord," Anka said. Again, she didn't have to fake the fear. If this man guessed what she was really doing there, she would never leave the camp. "The north quadrant, you say?"

The officer waved a hand. "*That* way, you stupid girl. Now hurry. Captain Thero isn't a man to keep waiting."

Anka hurried from the tent with what she hoped was the right level of gratitude, setting off in the direction the officer had indicated but then quickly veering off in case he worked out that she wasn't all she seemed. She took deep breaths as she tried to think.

She hadn't gotten anything from the records. Sartes's name hadn't been anywhere in the ones she'd looked through, and there seemed to be no obvious way to find him without that kind of clue where he might be. Anka didn't even know for sure if he was in this camp. Everything she'd gotten from her contacts had been supposition and fragments.

The truth was that no one kept track of where individual conscripts went. The army didn't care about them enough for that, and just that fact was enough to make Anka angry. What kind of world did they live in where no one cared what happened to one boy, because he would probably be dead soon anyway?

Even if she hadn't promised Ceres to find her brother, that would have been enough to make Anka keep going. How *long* could she keep going though? she wondered. Could she really justify looking for one boy forever when the rebellion could save many more young men and women? She didn't even really know what Sartes looked like.

That thought brought despair with it, and Anka started to make her way through the tents toward the edge of the encampment. Anka had tried to tell herself that this was an easier task than trying to overthrow a whole empire, but the truth was that it was almost impossible.

In spite of her promise to Ceres, she couldn't stop herself from thinking about going home then. The rebellion needed her, and if she couldn't find Sartes here, then all she could do was get herself captured or killed. The thought of having to give up ate at her, but Anka couldn't think what else she could do. To put off the moment when she would have to make a decision, she circled back toward the command tents. Perhaps she would be able to make one more attempt to look through the army's records, although if they caught her this time…

She waited by the pavilions and marquees belonging to the army's officers, staying in the shadows and looking for an opportunity to sneak inside. She waited, trying to make it look as though she was working on something in her bundle of washing, and that was when she heard the name she'd been hoping for since she got there.

"Sergeant, I have messages I need carrying across camp. What happened to that conscript of yours?"

Anka peeked around the tent to see an officer in gilded armor talking with a burly man who was obviously of a lower rank.

"Sartes, sir?"

"How should I remember the boy's name? The one who has been so useful. Just get him."

"Yes sir."

Anka watched the whole exchange with her heart in her mouth. When the sergeant set off, she followed him, using all the caution she'd learned in Delos. It was safer doing this than waiting around the command tents, because at least she could pretend to be on an errand again.

She followed until the sergeant reached a training ring where conscripts were working on their swordplay. Already, two had deep-looking wounds, because the sharp weapons they were using had no room for mistakes. She saw the sergeant pause on the edge of the training ring.

"Sartes! Get yourself out here!"

Anka looked at the boy who disengaged himself from the melee. He had sandy hair and a wiry frame made thinner by the harshness of the army. At first glance, it was hard to see the resemblance between him and Ceres, yet there was a hint of similarity there, and this was definitely him.

"The officers have work for you, boy," the sergeant said. "Get over to the commander's tent before they have you whipped!"

Anka saw the boy take off at a dead run. She hated to see that fear there, but another emotion rose beside it: hope. She'd done what she promised. She'd found Sartes.

But now she needed to find a way to save him—before the army killed him.

Chapter Twenty Three

If they kept drifting out to sea like this, Ceres felt, they would die. Ceres was certain of it. Either the sun would bake them, or predators would come for them, realizing that Ceres no longer had the strength to fight them off.

The small boat had a piece of driftwood they could use as a makeshift paddle, but there seemed to be nowhere to paddle to. Instead, they bobbed along like some child's toy, at the mercy of the wind and the currents.

Ceres's lips cracked with thirst as they floated. She barely had the strength to lift her head and look out over the expanse of the water that stretched to the horizon in every direction.

She heard Eike moan beside her. The girl was barely conscious now, because despite the water all around them, there was none that they could risk drinking. Eike hadn't believed Ceres when she'd warned her about it, and had quickly thrown up the salt water. Ceres shook her, and her eyes barely flickered open.

Ceres looked around again, seeing the seabirds above that followed them, obviously waiting for the moment when they would finally succumb. One came close, and Ceres waved it away.

That was when she saw the island.

It appeared as a speck on the horizon at first, small enough that Ceres wasn't even certain that it was there.

As the currents carried their boat toward it though, she saw the sandy beaches and rocky rises there, leading to what looked like jungles on the interior.

And for the first time, her heart filled with hope.

⚜ ⚜ ⚜

Ceres paddled for shore with their rough wooden oar for what felt like hours. She ignored the way her muscles protested at the sudden effort after drifting for so long, keeping going until they were passing by tooth-like rocks, then on into the breakers leading to a beach.

Ceres leapt out, pulling the boat up onto the sand with Eike still in it. She lifted the girl up, helping her out and then supporting her as they set off along the beach in search of fresh water.

She didn't know what was going to happen next. She wasn't sure where they were, or what would happen to them in the next few days. She wasn't sure if she would ever see home again, and that thought was a frightening one. Right then, Ceres was just grateful to be alive.

Ceres felt the eyes on her long before anyone stepped out of the surrounding jungle. She watched the fronds near the edge, seeing some rustle in a way that might have just been the wind.

People emerged, dressed in plain tunics and dresses, supplemented by what looked like leaves and branches from the forest. Some seemed to have flowers tangled in their hair, while others wore vines wrapped around them like jewelry.

Ceres stood there cautiously. She wasn't sure how these people would react to strangers, or what was going to happen next.

It was only as they got closer that Ceres saw they weren't wearing costumes after all. Instead, she saw vines and twigs emerging from flesh, skin that had given way to the roughness of bark or the green of leaves.

Two came forward with bowls of water, and Ceres took one gratefully, before helping Eike to sip at hers. The girl seemed to regain some strength with the liquid, rousing enough to look around. Ceres saw her start at the sight of the people around them.

"What are they?" Eike asked.

"We are the folk of the forest," a voice said, and Ceres saw a man step forward from the crowd of people. "Welcome."

He was tall and slender, probably only a few years older than Ceres was, with skin that seemed to vary between delicately tanned and mossy green where it wasn't covered by a tunic. He wasn't broad across the shoulders, but Ceres could see the muscles that stood out as he moved. He had strong features, with high cheekbones and a smile that seemed to come easily. His hair was dark, cut through here and there with a tangle of flowering vines, while his eyes were such a vibrant green that Ceres couldn't bring herself to look away from him.

He seemed to be looking back at her with the same intensity.

"I'm Ceres," she said.

"I am Eoin," he replied.

"You're in charge here?" Ceres asked.

Eoin smiled. "People sometimes listen to me, but the truth is that all of us with the sickness follow the way of the forest."

"Sickness?" Ceres heard Eike ask. "You're sick?"

Eoin spread his hands. "They call it a sickness, or a curse. They send us here because they don't want us around them. We live out our time here, until the forest claims us. But you don't have to worry."

He held out a hand to Eike, and to Ceres's surprise, the girl took it.

"We'll go back to the village and talk more there," he said. Ceres saw him look over to her again. "I think there is a lot to talk about. The ocean has brought you to us for a reason."

They set off in the direction of the jungle, and Ceres followed Eoin along a trail where the trees arched over them as though forming a tunnel. She glanced up and saw a bird flit from one branch to another, and impossibly, it seemed to glow with golden light as it did so. She turned to point it out to Eike, but the girl was already staring at another part of the forest.

Ceres followed her gaze and froze in place. A horse of the purest white stood there, a horn of gold jutting from its forehead as it reared up. Ceres's breath caught at the sight. A unicorn? But they were only meant to be myths.

Eoin seemed to understand her amazement. "The creatures of magic still have places where they gather," he said. "The jungle is one of them. It isn't far now to the settlement."

They kept going, and Ceres saw the jungle open out. There were houses there, but it took her a moment to realize that they were houses, because they seemed more like giant plants, grown into their shapes rather than constructed. She saw huts and treehouses, buildings that were more like simple platforms in the branches. The only stone building she could see was a kind of ziggurat at the center of it all, and that looked as though it might have been there long before the rest of it.

There were plants there, and animals that seemed impossible. A lizard flew past Ceres's head on butterfly wings, while further over, she saw a beetle the size of a small dog. She saw trees too, warped and twisted until they almost seemed like strange sculptures of people.

"Those are the ones the curse has claimed," Eoin said.

"You mean those are *people*?" Eike said. Ceres could hear the horror in her voice. She could feel some of it herself.

"They were," Eoin said. "Eventually, the curse takes all of us, and we go back to the forest. It can't be stopped. All we can do is live our lives until then."

"That's terrible," Ceres said.

Eoin shrugged. "It is not so bad. It is beautiful here, and we have enough."

He led the way to a hut, where there was food waiting: fruit and tubers taken from the jungle. Ceres and Eike ate hungrily, while Eoin and the others joined them.

"How did you come to be here?" Eoin asked.

"It's a long story," Ceres said.

Eoin smiled. "There should always be time for stories, and we would like to hear."

Ceres did her best to explain it. She told them about what was happening in the Empire, and how she'd come to fight in the Stade. She told them about her last fight, and how she'd ended up condemned to the Isle of Prisoners.

All the while, Eoin's eyes stayed on her. It felt as though he could see right through her, looking past the surface to something else underneath. Ceres wasn't sure what it was that he could see, but right then, she'd never felt that vulnerable with anyone.

"You're a warrior?" he asked. "Perhaps that explains some of why you were sent to us."

"What do you mean?" Ceres asked.

Eoin stood, offering his hand. "Come with me. I promise that your friend will be safe here."

Ceres believed him. She'd never seen anywhere that seemed as peaceful as this hidden village. It just seemed natural to reach out and take his hand, feeling the strength there.

She let him lead her out and through the village, to a space on the far side of the ziggurat that had been cleared in a wide circle. There, she could see two young women fighting, surrounded by a small knot of villagers.

The two held no weapons, but they didn't seem to need them. Ceres could barely keep up as they blurred and spun, their hands and feet lashing out from every angle. They dodged and leapt, then came together as they tried to lock one another's limbs and throw each other to the ground. When they tumbled there together, they kept fighting, until Ceres saw one slip behind the other as quickly as a snake, her arm locking around her opponent's throat. The two got up, laughing, and began again.

It was like the training she'd done for the Stade, and yet totally unlike it. The fighting there had been brutal and efficient, while there was something beautiful about this, something that seemed to Ceres to be perfectly in balance.

"It's amazing," she said. "To be able to fight that well without weapons."

"They simply move in harmony with the world," Eoin replied. "As for weapons, we have them, but we have little need for them."

He reached around to his back, producing a dagger that seemed to be made from dark, glassy stone. He passed it to her. Ceres tested the edge, and to her surprise, it was as sharp as any steel.

"For you," he said. "You have been sent here for a reason, Ceres. I'm sure of that. I don't know what that reason is, but we will teach you what we can of our ways. If you want, that is."

Her answer was obvious.

"I want to."

Chapter Twenty Four

As he went down to the castle's gardens, Thanos found himself looking around suspiciously. The pressure of what he was doing weighed down on him now, and he found himself looking for a spot where he could just be himself for a moment without risking his life.

Everywhere else in the castle, it seemed that he had to hide what he felt and who he was. If anyone saw his anger over what had happened to Ceres, if anyone saw through the act he'd put up to his sympathies for the rebels, then he would be dead, noble of the Empire or not.

They would call him a traitor, when the truth was that they were the ones betraying the interests of their own people. They were the ones taking from their people, and Thanos had heard how much worse it had gotten since he'd left. He'd heard about the parties under Lucious's command, ravaging the countryside. Just the thought of it made him grit his teeth in anger.

He needed to find a way to stay calm, so he stood out there and looked at the blooms, imagining how Ceres might react if she were here. Would she appreciate the gentle beauty of the flowers, or would she want to be in the training pits for the Stade? Thanos smiled at the fact that he had an easier time imagining her there than here.

The smile faded as he thought about what was happening to her now. He had to find a way to help her if he could, but Thanos wasn't sure what he could do to stop Ceres being taken to the Isle of Prisoners. He couldn't just overturn the king's decision, and if he tried, he would immediately be suspect. He could try to get a message to the rebellion, perhaps, but-

"I'm not interrupting you, am I?"

Thanos turned to see Stephania approaching. She looked lovely in the night air, but then, she always looked lovely. She seemed to hesitate for a moment, then threw her arms around him, hugging him tightly. The suddenness of it caught Thanos a little by surprise, and so did the action itself. He'd always thought Stephania was too proper and reserved for such a show of emotion.

"I'm so glad that you're safe," Stephania said as she stepped back. "When I heard that you'd been killed…"

Thanos heard the catch there in her voice, and saw the faint gleam in her eyes that suggested she might be trying to hold back tears.

"It's all right," he said, reaching out to touch her arm as he tried to comfort her.

"It is now," Stephania said. "Because you're alive. Did you really survive because some fishermen found you?"

Thanos nodded. Even with Stephania, he couldn't afford to tell the truth. Maybe especially with Stephania, because it would never occur to her to keep from saying what she knew around the court. She'd always been the heart of the gossip there.

Bizarrely though, it felt wrong to be deceiving her like this.

"The fishermen saved me," Thanos said. It was true, as far as it went. Without the two men who'd found him, he would never have met Akila's rebels. "They brought me back."

"Then we all owe them a great deal," Stephania said. Thanos saw her half close her eyes. "*I* owe them a great deal. Are they still in Delos?"

Thanos shook his head. "I think they sailed back to Haylon."

"That's a pity," Stephania said. "I would have liked to reward them for bringing you back safely. Someone *really* sent the Typhoon as an assassin?"

She sounded to Thanos as though she couldn't quite believe it even now. Maybe she didn't want to believe it. Stephania was in that side of the court that was nearly oblivious to what was going on outside, not cruel the way some could be, but so self-absorbed that it seemed as though the harsh things out in the world weren't really happening.

Thanos nodded. "He stabbed me in the back on the beach. I think the idea was that it would look as though I'd been killed in the assault."

Stephania nodded. "That was what they told us here. They told us that you were the first out onto the beach, cut down by the rebels. They wanted to make us think you'd died some heroic death."

"You didn't think I could manage a heroic death?" Thanos asked, but the joke did nothing to lighten the mood.

"When I heard it, it felt as though the whole world was collapsing in on me." She looked up at him, and Thanos could see the way her breathing quickened. "Can I… can I see what they did to you? It doesn't seem real somehow without that."

Thanos only hesitated a moment before lifting his tunic to let her see. It wasn't the kind of request he would have expected from someone as proper as Stephania, but he could hear the concern there in her voice.

He saw her reach out carefully, even tenderly, to touch the spot where Akila's men had stitched him back together. He winced reflexively.

"Sorry," Stephania said. "Does it still hurt?"

"A little," Thanos said.

She paused. "You said before that you don't know who sent the Typhoon to assassinate you. Is that true, or were you just holding back so they wouldn't hear you?"

It caught Thanos a little by surprise that she would realize he might do that. It was easy to forget sometimes that Stephania had grown up in the games of the court, and that even her great beauty hadn't kept her out of them. If anything, it had probably made her a target for the jealousy of some of the others there.

"I really don't know," he admitted. "I plan to find out, though."

He saw Stephania nod at that. She seemed to consider for a moment. "I want to help you."

Thanos stared at her in surprise. "You do?"

"Of course I do," Stephania said. "It was when I thought you were gone. Seeing how close you came to dying like this… I want to find who did this to you, and I want them to pay for it."

Thanos could hear the determination there, fierce and hard behind Stephania's otherwise gentle exterior. He hadn't realized that she cared about him that much. He'd always assumed that the promise of marriage to him was purely political for her.

"I swear to you," Stephania said. "I will help you to find the person who gave the order for you to be killed."

Thanos reached out to touch her face. "You've always been so good to me," he said. "Better than I deserve."

Stephania shook her head. "That doesn't matter. You were only doing what the king and queen made you do. What matters is that you're here. You're alive, and we're going to find out who tried to do this to you."

Thanos stood back to look at her then; really look at her. It felt as though he'd never truly seen Stephania before that moment. He'd always seen her as one of the silly young women of the court, too caught up in her own luxurious lifestyle to think about anyone else. He'd assumed that she was vain, selfish, and probably only interested in the latest parties. Certainly, on a night like this, he'd have thought she'd be getting ready for the Festival of the Moon rather than seeking him out.

Yet looking at her now, it was as though he could see through all that to a core of steel underneath. She stood there in the garden, and she should have fit in with the elegance of the flowers there, but it was worth remembering how many of those flowers had thorns. It felt better than he could have imagined to have an ally like that in the court.

"I was a fool," Thanos said, shaking his head. "I should never have treated you the way I did."

"It's all right," Stephania assured him. "I understand."

"Forgive me?" Thanos asked.

"There is nothing to forgive. The only question now is how we're going to find whoever sent the assassin after you."

Thanos nodded. It was a relief to hear that from Stephania, and a weight off his conscience that she hadn't been hurt by the way he'd pushed her aside for Ceres.

"I don't know how I'm going to do it," he admitted.

"How *we're* going to do it," Stephania said. Her hand fit into his neatly, seeming so natural there to Thanos. "This isn't something you should have to do by yourself. I want you to tell me everything you find out. I want to know."

"That means a lot," Thanos said. "But we still need somewhere to start."

Stephania was quiet for a long time, and Thanos found himself wondering what she was thinking. There was obviously something that she wanted to say but wasn't. Strange that he should feel close enough to her to know that.

"What is it?" he asked.

"There … might be something," Stephania said. "I was in the stables a while ago, getting ready to go riding, and I heard one of the stable boys boasting that he was a close friend of Lucious, and that he did favors for him that no one else could."

"It sounds like empty boasting," Thanos said.

Stephania nodded. "That's what the other stable hands said at the time, but the boy showed them a dagger that he could never have afforded alone, and he was talking about taking messages to someone in the army."

"The Typhoon?" Thanos guessed.

He saw Stephania shrug. "I don't know. Not for sure. I don't think even Lucious would be stupid enough to tell a stable boy what he was planning. But it was enough to make me think of it. I don't know if it's anything, though."

Thanos put his hands on Stephania's shoulders. "Thank you for this. It's more than you think."

It was a start, at least. And if the trail did lead back to Lucious … well … then Thanos would make sure that it was an end for the prince as well.

Chapter Twenty Five

Ceres gasped for breath as water thundered down onto her. The waterfall hammered into her and she reeled with it, having to fight to keep going. She had no idea why Eoin thought that directly under one was the right place to train in the combat arts they used on the island, but right now she wished that he'd picked somewhere, anywhere, else.

Eoin, of course, stood in the shallow pool beneath it as calmly as if he were in summer rain. He barely even seemed to lift his voice to be heard above it. "This is called Clouds Weaving."

Ceres shook with the effort as she tried to copy the movements Eoin made. She tried to concentrate in spite of the relentless battering of the water, but it was almost impossible to get every detail correct, and Eoin seemed to want perfection in every motion. It seemed to be the one area where his ready smile disappeared as he made her repeat the movements over and over.

She saw him weave through it again: a complex back and forth movement of his hands that looked more like the kind of thing a dancer in the city might have done than anything to do with fighting. She tried to copy the movement and Eoin shook his head.

"Slower."

That was the hardest part of all this. She was used to the rough and tumble fighting of the Stade, but the islanders' way of fighting seemed to involve what looked to Ceres like slow motion dancing. She wanted to speed up, to *fight.*

"When can we go faster?" Ceres asked.

"When you can do it right slowly," Eoin said. He finally smiled. "You're making progress, but you have to learn to move in harmony with the world, Ceres. Learn the lessons it has to teach you."

"And what lesson does standing in a waterfall teach me?" Ceres asked, as the water continued to beat down on her.

She saw Eoin's hands flow through the movement again. "I don't know. People learn their own lessons. Maybe it will be that the softest things can become hard and relentless. Maybe it will be to let the world flow off you smoothly." His smile widened. "Perhaps that if you're going to get wet anyway, you might as well embrace it."

Ceres wanted to argue with that, and with the endless training that seemed to have so little to do with fighting. Before she could do it though, one of the other forest people ran up to them. This one was further along in the disease than Eoin was, almost as much plant as human.

"Eoin, we have people landing on the slate shore. It looks like raiders heading for the village."

Ceres heard Eoin sigh. "Will they never learn? All right, I'll come."

"Should I stay here with Ceres?" the newcomer asked.

"I should come," Ceres said. "Maybe I can help."

Eoin waved a hand in dismissal. "We can handle it. But perhaps you can learn something by watching. Follow me."

He ran along the trails that led through the jungle toward the village, and Ceres had a hard time keeping up. She was strong and fast, but Eoin seemed to flit through the trees as naturally as if he were a part of them. By the time they reached the edge of the village, Ceres was out of breath, while Eoin looked as though he could have run for another hour.

She could see men running through the village, weapons in their hands. For a moment, Ceres thought they might be soldiers of the Empire, there to hunt her, and fear ran through her. Then she saw the roughness of their weapons and the piecemeal nature of their armor. These really were pirates and raiders, not the army.

That didn't make their intentions any better. As she watched, one of the raiders rushed into a low hut, and there was a scream from within. On the edge of the jungle, Ceres looked over to Eoin.

"What do we do now?" Ceres asked.

Eoin pointed to a spot. "You wait here."

"But I can fight," she insisted. She didn't want to stand by while other people risked their lives.

Eoin shook his head. "Not yet, but you *will* be able to. For now, watch. Learn."

Ceres didn't want to hold back like that, but as she started to take a step forward, she felt the firm hand of one of the forest people on her shoulder. She stood there because there seemed to be no other choice, and she watched as Eoin ran into the village.

The forest people joined him as he ran, seeming to come from nowhere as they stepped out of hidden spots in the trees and bushes. With their curse, they blended in perfectly. They reminded Ceres of the water from the waterfall as they plunged down among the houses they were trying to defend, washing over the landing party of raiders.

In the instant before they struck, Ceres had to admit to a moment of fear. The raiders were heavily armed, strong looking and clearly dangerous. Some of the forest folk, by contrast, seemed too delicate and frond-like to do any real damage.

The moment the fight started though, it became clear that she needn't have worried. Despite their lack of weapons, the islanders moved with a deadly kind of grace, never quite there as their opponents attacked, striking back with blows that seemed languid, but which felled the raiders wherever they struck.

Ceres watched Eoin at the heart of it, and he moved like water. He swayed aside from the sweep of an ax, then brought his forearm around in a blow to the collarbone of his assailant that sent the man to his knees. He brought up his foot in a kick that seemed to be all grace and elegance until it snapped the raider's head back.

Ceres saw a swordsman move in close to Eoin and she tried to call out a warning, but she was too far away for him to ever hear it.

He didn't need the warning though. He turned instead, and his eyes seemed to fix on Ceres for an instant. Then his hands moved in a pattern that was far too familiar, because Ceres had been practicing it all morning. Eoin waved his way through the delicate movements of Weaving Clouds, and somewhere in it he twisted the sword out of his attacker's hands. The blow that he answered with only seemed to touch the raider, but the man dropped like a stone.

It took the islanders a matter of minutes to kill their attackers, and they *did* kill them. There was something unstoppably ruthless about the way they moved through the raiders, leaving none alive, letting none run back to their boats. When they were done, they carried the bodies into the jungle as gently as if they were carrying respected friends.

All Ceres could do was stand there in something close to amazement. Unarmed, sick as they were, they'd defeated a whole landing party of armed men.

Maybe there was plenty to learn here after all.

⚜ ⚜ ⚜

That night, Ceres sat at one of the fires in the village, eating the fruits of the forest while above the stars seemed to swirl as clouds passed. Eike was there beside her, while Eoin and several of the other villagers sat there too.

Eoin played a many-stringed instrument that seemed to respond to the least touch, music floating through the night air as he tapped the notes. It was so peaceful that Ceres might almost have been able to dismiss the attack earlier as a bad dream if she hadn't seen it herself.

"Do people often attack your island?" Ceres asked. She couldn't just ignore what had happened today.

"Sometimes," Eoin said. "They think that because we are cursed, we are weak. It is less common than it was. They used to raid regularly before we learned to fight back."

"How did you all get so good at fighting?" Ceres asked.

"We watched the world," Eoin said. "We learned the lessons of the forest. But we should talk of happier things. The moment for fighting has passed. You could tell us about your lives."

Ceres shook her head. "There isn't much that's happy to tell there. My father left. My mother sold me as a slave. The people I care about most are dead."

"The past can be hard," Eoin agreed. "My family cast me out when they realized I was one of the forest folk. Most of those here have a similar story."

There were nods from around the fire.

"But the future can be different," Eoin said. "Tell us about your hopes and your dreams."

Ceres tried to think. "Once, I dreamed that I would be a famous combatlord, fighting in the Stade. I guess I've already achieved that dream. Then I dreamed that maybe there could be something else for me with the man who …" She shook her head. "It doesn't matter. He died."

She heard the notes from Eoin's instrument still as he reached out to touch her hand. "I'm sorry. What now though?"

Ceres thought for a moment.

"Now," Ceres said, "there are a lot of things I want. I have a brother, and I want him to be safe. I want to get back to my father, and make sure he's found Sartes." She tightened her hands in anger. "I want revenge on the people who tried to kill me. But after that … I guess I want to change things if I can. I want to make a better world."

Eoin laughed gently. "A better world would be nice. What about you, little one? What do you dream?"

Eike looked a little surprised to be included, to Ceres's eyes.

"I don't know," she admitted, hugging her knees. "I guess I just want somewhere I'll be safe, and fit in."

"I think that might be easy enough," Eoin said, with a sweep of his arm that took in the camp. People were dancing and singing around their fires now, and Ceres could feel the pulse of it running through her. Even so, she didn't join in.

"What about you?" Ceres asked. "What do you want for the future?"

"The future is tricky for us," Eoin said, gesturing around at the island. "We know that eventually, the forest will claim us. We know that the world does not want us. We have learned to live *now,* and see what we can leave behind." He gestured to some of the others. "Jan here has his pottery. K'sala is trying to weave the perfect tapestry. Many of us try to understand the world as much as we can, or seek happiness with one another."

"And you?" Ceres asked, not willing to let it go.

"I have my music," Eoin said. "And I have the safety of the people here to think about. I want to make sure this remains a community where any of us can feel safe and happy Those are probably dreams that are big enough for one life, don't you think?"

Ceres found herself hoping that he might say more than that. "What about building a life with someone?" she asked. "What about love?"

She saw Eoin look away.

"Love would just mean someone left behind when the forest finally took me," he said.

"But it might also mean being happy until then," Ceres pointed out. She looked into the fire, watching it dance. "Maybe that's worth it."

"Maybe," Eoin agreed. "For now though, we should all get some sleep. If you want to achieve *your* dreams, Ceres, you still have a lot of training to do."

That was true, and in that moment determination filled Ceres. She had seen what the islanders could do. She was going to learn what they had to teach. She was going to return to Delos, and she was going to change things.

Whatever it took.

Chapter Twenty Six

Sartes had a plan. He reminded himself of that over and over as he started to make his way across the 23rd's camp, slipping through the early evening activity of the place like a stranger. He had a plan for his escape. Now, he had to hope that it would work.

Repeating it should have made him feel better, but instead, it just reminded him of how big the stakes were. The punishment for a conscript trying to escape was death, without exception. The best-case scenario would be a quick sword thrust as he tried to get clear of the camp. The worst… they might make his fellow conscripts do it, beating Sartes to death to prove their loyalty. He had no doubt that they would do it. They would be too frightened to do anything else.

In some ways, Sartes's plan was simple: he was going to walk to the edge of the camp, then make his way through the stakes and trip wires, pits and cordons that surrounded it. The complex part was actually doing it.

The fact that he'd managed to become useful to the officers around the camp helped. It had gotten people used to the idea that he could move around the camp, when most of the conscripts were carefully controlled. It had let him work out the timing of the guard changes and the locations of the worst traps around the camp.

"I can do this," Sartes told himself as he kept moving among the tents.

"Do what, conscript?" an officer demanded, stepping into his path. Sartes recognized him as one of the training masters. Varion, Sartes thought his name was.

"Deliver this message, sir," Sartes said, pulling out one of half a dozen he had hidden away. "The captain said it was urgent."

The training master read it through, looked at the seal on the bottom, and then shoved it back at Sartes.

"All right, get on with it, conscript."

Sartes hurried off, and he was glad right then that he'd picked one of the real messages, given the way the officer had checked the seal. He'd carefully collected messages before he'd set out, going round to as many officers as he could to gather them, because the more messages he had to deliver, the more access he had to the rest of the camp.

He'd forged more, scribbling messages on whatever parchment he could steal from the quartermaster's stores. He couldn't fight his way out of the camp, but his stock of messages and orders would let him use the machinery of the army itself as a kind of protection.

Even so, he had to hurry. There was no message or errand that would get a conscript out of the camp without at least a dozen real soldiers there to accompany him. That meant Sartes had to sneak out in one of the small windows between guard changes, when things were confused. Miss that window, and the whole escape attempt would be for nothing.

Miss that window, and he would never reach the rebellion. He might never see his family again. He would never see his sister, and the thought of that was enough to make a knot form in Sartes's stomach.

So he hurried through the camp, brandishing his sheaf of orders like a shield. He was almost to the edge when another officer stopped him.

"You, you're the boy who carries messages for the general, aren't you?"

"Yes, sir."

"Well then, I want you to go to his tent and get me the latest maps for our preparations against the rebellion. I've been sent orders, but I have no idea where I'm actually supposed to take my men. Tell them Leus sent you. Here, you'll need this."

The officer handed over a signet ring, standing there in obvious expectation. Sartes saluted, because he couldn't think what else to do. He set off back in the direction of the center of the camp for the same reason, although he veered off into the tents as soon as he could, planning to double back.

He stopped, with his hand on the rough canvas of one of the tents. He held up the signet ring, looking at the worked silver of the design. If he ran now, this might be worth something to the rebellion, giving it the chance to forge orders until the officer admitted what had happened.

But the man had talked about orders for attacks on the rebellion. The maps for that would be worth far more. Yet if he went for the maps and plans, how much time would that take? He'd planned out his escape to the last minute. Any delay, and they might find him.

That thought terrified Sartes more than anything. He couldn't go back now, and if he was caught, it wouldn't be a quick death. He couldn't afford for anything to go wrong when he'd planned it all so carefully.

Yet if Sartes ran now, and people died because they didn't know where the attacks would come, he would always feel responsible. He had to at least try to get them. He had enough time, if he sprinted. He hoped.

Sartes ran back toward the command tents, and now he must have looked like what he was: a conscript who had just been given an urgent instruction by a superior and who didn't want to waste a single instant in following it.

He made it to the commander's tent and stood panting in front of the guards for a moment, holding up the officer's ring.

"Leus wants the maps for the next attack," he managed.

"In a hurry, is he?"

"Yes, sir."

"Then you'd better get in there and grab them. The general's observing evening drill, so you'll have to find them yourself."

Sartes could barely believe his luck. He had to force himself to move into the general's tent slowly so that it would look normal to the guards. Only once he was safely inside the pavilion did he start to sort through any papers he could see, trying to work out how much he could get away with taking without the guards realizing what was happening.

In the end, he took as much as he could fit under one arm, wrapping it up in the map he'd been sent for and walking out with as much confidence as he could muster. He half expected the guards to try to stop him then, but neither even seemed to notice.

"Better run, boy," one of them joked. "You don't want to be late." "You don't know how true that is," Sartes said, and set off across the camp at a run again. Fear pushed him forward, not knowing if he'd already taken too long.

He had his route planned out already. He'd learned his way between the tents, and followed the signs and banners now. He dodged the officers and guards where he could, both because he couldn't afford any more delays and because there was too much chance of them seeing what he was carrying. Now that he'd taken the risk of getting the plans, he couldn't let them go.

He made his way to the spot he'd picked out for his escape. There was a space near one corner of the encampment where the wooden walls gave way to picket lines and there were trees not far away. The guards handed over their watch nearer the middle of the lines, before marching out, so if he'd timed it right—

"You there!" a voice called. "What are you doing there?"

Sartes looked round to see a guard approaching. The man was older than him and larger, in full armor, armed with sword, shield, and spear.

"I asked you a question, boy. What are you doing here?"

"I have orders," Sartes said automatically, but he knew it wouldn't work.

"No conscript leaves. Those are the orders that matter. Deserter!" The guard cupped his hands over his mouth, ready to call it again.

Sartes saw a figure rush out from the tents, then smash into the guard. A hammer rose and fell, once, then again. The guard went down and didn't rise. The figure straightened up, and Sartes stared at him in absolute shock.

"Father?"

He still couldn't believe it, yet it *was* his father. He stood there, looking exactly as Sartes remembered him from the days before he'd left. Sartes threw his arms wide, rushing forward to hug his father on instinct.

"Sartes!"

He felt his father hug him back, and for the first time since he'd arrived in the camp, Sartes had a moment where he felt safe.

"It's so good to see you," his father said. "I thought I'd never find you."

"What are you doing here?" Sartes asked. He shook his head. "It doesn't matter. I'm so glad to see you."

"I came looking for you. Smiths can always find a way into an army camp." His father stood back and looked at him at arm's length. "Are you all right? Have they hurt you?"

"I'm all right," Sartes assured him. "I managed to avoid the worst of it."

"I'm glad," his father said. "Ceres told me I needed to be the one to come and find you before it got worse."

"Ceres?" Sartes said. "Is she here?"

That would have been the best possible outcome. His whole family back together, all at once. The excitement that briefly rose in him sank again as his father shook his head.

"She's fighting in the Stade," his father said. "She said she couldn't run away from that. But we'll get her. We'll go back and find her if we can."

Sartes nodded. "We will, and then it will be better, right?"

"I hope so," his father said. "First though, we need to get you out of here. That shout will bring trouble."

Sartes swallowed at that thought. "I have a way out. Quick, this way."

It felt strange to be the one leading the way for his father, but Sartes was the one who knew his way through the defenses around the camp. He'd worked out his route, and now he forced himself to concentrate on it, avoiding the pits and the stakes that kept conscripts in as much as they kept others out.

"Through here," he said.

"We need to hurry," his father insisted. "What's that you have there? Leave it, we need to run."

Already, Sartes could hear the clamor in the camp. Horns sounded an alarm, and he could see soldiers running about as they tried to work out what was happening.

"I can't. I have plans showing what the Empire plans against the rebellion."

"What?" His father was the one standing there in shock now. "I'd ask how you managed that, but I don't think there's any time. They'll be coming. We need to go."

Sartes's heart felt like it was in his mouth. This wasn't how he'd planned on this. His whole escape plan had been about slipping away quietly, and being well away by the time anyone noticed. He'd figured that no one would follow if it was too much trouble.

Now, though, he could hear the sounds of hunting parties being formed. Horns sounded, and dogs barked in response. Sartes froze at the sound, but his father put a hand on his shoulder.

"We have to keep moving, Sartes."

They ran, but running hadn't been part of Sartes's plan. He tripped on one of the wires set out there, and pulled himself back to his feet only with difficulty. Somewhere behind them, he thought he could hear the sounds of the hunting party getting closer.

Sartes shook his head. "We can't outrun them. They have horses."

Already, he thought he could hear hooves. He *could* hear them, along with the whinnies of horses being pushed hard. He looked round for a stick, a stone, anything he could use as a weapon. He knew he couldn't really fight the army, but it was better to die fighting than in any of the ways he would die if they caught him.

Yet what he saw approaching was a single woman, riding one horse while leading two others. The horses looked like military mounts, complete with their riders' weapons and equipment, but the saddles were empty.

"Sartes?" she called out. "Berin?"

Sartes looked up in surprise, pressing closer to his father. "Who are you?"

"My name is Anka. There's no time to explain, but Ceres sent me. I'm with the rebellion. Quick, climb on before they realize that they're missing horses."

Sartes paused, looking back toward the camp.

"Do you want to risk them catching you?" Anka demanded.

She had a point. Even if they didn't know her, if she was claiming to be with the rebellion, then she was probably a friend. Picking one of the spare horses, Sartes climbed aboard. His father did the same with the other.

"I hope you two can ride," Anka said. "Because there's a *lot* of noise back there."

There was. On the edge of hearing, Sartes thought that he could hear more hooves, accompanied by shouts and horns. He saw Anka kick her mount into a run, and his father did the same.

Sartes took a breath. He was out. He'd found his father. He even had plans that would help the rebellion.

Now all he needed to do was survive.

Chapter Twenty Seven

Thanos resisted the urge to punch the wall of the stables, but only just.

"Tell us the truth," he demanded of the stable boy who stood in front of him and Stephania.

He would have fought any number of opponents in the practice arena rather than spend another minute in frustrating investigation. He would have given anything he had to have an opponent in front of him, a problem that he could solve in a simple, honest way, rather than by skulking around, trying to unpick the intrigues of the court.

But he *didn't* have an opponent in front of him. That was the point. He was caught up in all this, and he wasn't sure how much time he had. Eventually, he was sure, someone would work out his new role with the rebellion, and that meant he only had a little while to find the person responsible for the attempt to kill him.

"I need an answer," Thanos said.

"It's all right," Stephania said, in a much more soothing tone that made Thanos glad he'd brought her for this. "We already know that Lucious gave you that amulet, didn't he? The one you used to prove to the Typhoon that you'd been sent by him?"

The stable hand looked away, but nodded.

"At least, I think so," he said. "He sent one of his servants. I was to take the amulet and deliver a message to the Typhoon."

"What message?" Thanos asked.

The stable boy shook his head. "I don't know. It was closed tight. I didn't want the Typhoon or Prince Lucious thinking that I was spying on them."

Even so, Thanos could guess what the message would have said. It was an order for his death, delivered without question by a foolish boy determined to impress.

"What… what happens now?" the stable boy asked.

Thanos could hear the fear there. The stable boy probably thought they were going to kill him for his part in the plot. Yet the truth was that he was no more than a tool used by someone else, and Thanos wasn't like Lucious. He found himself thinking of what Ceres would have done in a situation like this. It helped, even if it brought a pang of loss to him.

"You're going to stay quiet about us coming here," Thanos said. "Then, when the time comes, you're going to tell what you know to the court."

"I… I don't know…" the stable boy began.

Stephania gave him a hard look. "You will do everything that Thanos commands, won't you?"

The stable boy hung his head. "Yes."

"Good."

The two of them left together, and once they were outside the castle's stables, Thanos let himself relax a little. He turned to Stephania.

"Thank you for coming with me for that. I don't think he would have confirmed his story if you hadn't been there."

Stephania smiled. "I'm happy to help. I take it you want me to keep quiet about this for now?"

Thanos nodded. That was the other part of this investigation that he hated. For all that the king had promised his help, the truth was that they couldn't trust anyone at court. He didn't know who was involved in trying to kill him, and he had too many secrets about the rebellion to act out in the open. They had to keep up the façade of an investigation going nowhere, while at the same time conducting a real investigation in the background.

"No one will hear about it from me," Stephania promised. "Be careful?"

"I'll try," Thanos assured her. "Although I think the most dangerous thing happening in the castle in the next few days will be parties."

"Oh, parties can be more dangerous than you think," Stephania said. "Just don't do anything foolish like confronting Lucious, I mean."

"I won't," Thanos assured her. At least, not yet. They didn't have enough yet to accuse a prince of the Empire. They needed more proof, not least about why Lucious would do something like this in the first place.

It occurred to him that there was at least one avenue he hadn't explored yet. Cosmas the scholar had said that he had information for Thanos, but Thanos hadn't followed up on it yet. The old man had always been a good friend to him, and if he said that he had something for Thanos now, then Thanos believed it.

He walked to the castle library, making his way along the twisting corridors of the castle, trying to appear calm as he passed by servants and courtiers, acknowledging their nods and trying to make it look as though nothing was affecting him.

Thanos wasn't sure whether it was the need to find the assassin's employer that had made him suspicious, or his role with the rebellion now, but either way, he saw eyes everywhere in a way he hadn't before. Every time he walked by a slave cleaning the marble of the castle floors, he found himself wondering who they reported to.

He hated the paranoia of his situation, but at the same time he needed it if he was going to stay alive here. There was so much at stake, and potentially so little time in which to do it all. He had to find out who was trying to kill him and why. He had to help the rebellion. More than all of that, he had to find a way to get Ceres back from the Isle of Prisoners. To do all of those things, he needed help.

When he made it to the library, Thanos paused. The library had always been a place Thanos enjoyed going. Its great doors were wide open, with shelves to either side, and desks set in quiet niches wherever they could fit. He found Cosmas in the library when he got there, standing in the middle of stacks of tomes, looking to Thanos like some mythical creature made of books from the waist down. Cosmas would probably consider that an improvement.

"Cosmas," Thanos said. "Are you looking for something?"

"Merely trying to undo some of the chaos that comes when the younger royals get into the library," the scholar replied. "Although it has meant I have been able to find scrolls that I haven't seen in twenty years."

Ordinarily, Thanos would have asked about them, and would probably have gotten a long lecture on some obscure subject as a result. Cosmas always seemed to learn about the oddest things. Once, Thanos had found him reading about the differences between two obscure types of beetle, neither of which was found in the Empire. When Thanos had asked why he wanted to know such a useless thing, he had answered simply that all knowledge was worth having.

Today, though, Thanos had no time for such distractions.

"You're here because of what I said to you," Cosmas said, emerging from behind his piles of books and scrolls.

"Yes, I want to know more about—"

"Wait," Cosmas said, and Thanos saw him go to the doors of the library, pushing them shut with a grunt of effort. He locked them too, using a large brass key that Thanos doubted had been used in a long time. Certainly, Thanos had never found the doors locked before.

"Now we can talk," Cosmas said. "The library is designed to be quiet. No one will overhear."

Thanos looked over to the scholar. "You said before that you knew something about who had tried to kill me and why?"

Cosmas nodded, gesturing for Thanos to follow as he headed into the shelves. "I can guess at the why," he said. "The who may come from that."

Thanos waited while the old man took out a book almost as large as he was, bound in calf-skin and edged in silver. Thanos helped him to carry it, but Cosmas was the one who fussed and cleared a space on one of the library's tables, then opened it to find the page he wanted.

Thanos looked down to find himself looking at a family tree. He recognized it instantly as the succession of the Empire. King Claudius was there, and Queen Athena. Lucious was there, with Thanos and his parents off to one side, where…

"Do you see it?" Cosmas asked.

Thanos saw it. There was an annotation in the margins.

"Ericthus, IV, 14–16? What does it mean?" he asked Cosmas. If there was anything written in the library the old man couldn't understand, Thanos hadn't found it yet.

"I believe Ericthus was a minor playwright in the reign of King Harrath," Cosmas explained.

"Two hundred years ago," Thanos said.

"Ah, so you did take in some of your studies after all."

Thanos doubted that a long dead playwright had anything to say about him, though. At least, not directly. But maybe someone was trying to say things indirectly, in a form that most people would just ignore.

"Do you have his plays here?" Thanos asked.

"Somewhere," Cosmas said, with a sweep of one wizened hand that took in the vast array of books scattered around. "I seem to remember them being next to a tome on the plant life of the outer islands."

Thanos suspected that wouldn't help much, but he set off hunting through the library anyway. Sometimes, even when a cause seemed lost, it was still worth trying. Like with Ceres. He would find a way to get her back. He had to.

For now, though, he dug through books and scrolls, trying to make sense of a system that probably only existed inside Cosmas's head. There was no method to it. He dug through works on the proper construction of aqueducts, philosophical scrolls, treatises on geometry … Finally, just as Cosmas had promised, he spotted a work on rare plants, and next to it, he saw a slender, leather-bound volume.

"I've got it!" Thanos said, holding the book aloft like it was the grand prize at the Stade after all that searching. He took it to the table, opening it to find an inscription inside.

Olivia, may you find as much happiness in Ericthus' work as I have. C.

Thanos froze at the sight of that name. His mother's name. And the initial, could that be … no, he couldn't think it.

Rather than stare at the inscription, he made himself turn to the fourth chapter, seeking out the first sixteen lines. They seemed to be a part of a speech by one of his characters, a noblewoman:

And should I hide the truth from all

That what should be done by my husband's hand
Has fallen instead to that of my king?

Thanos stared at the lines. Like the ones at the start of the book, they refused to sink in.

"This has to be some kind of joke," he managed at last.

"Not a joke," Cosmas said. "A reminder of another old story. Although this one isn't written down. King Claudius saw to that."

"What old story?" Thanos asked.

"That there was a midwife in the city who had heard things from the princess of the Empire she attended about her baby."

"You're talking about my mother," Thanos said. He'd never known enough about his mother or father to even imagine them. There were paintings in some of the galleries of the castle, but even those were stiff, formal things.

Cosmas nodded solemnly, his bald head dipping briefly so that Thanos could see the top of it.

"There have always been hints and stories," the scholar said. "But they faded, and you were just the king's nephew again."

"You're saying… you're saying that I'm the king's son." The enormity of that hit Thanos then. Everything he'd thought about the world seemed to unravel, all at once. All his life, despite everything, he'd known where he fit in, and who he was. Now, neither of those things seemed to be stable anymore.

He looked over at Cosmas, and a note of accusation crept into his voice. "If you know these stories, then you could have just told me."

"But then you would not have seen it for yourself. You do not just seek knowledge, Thanos. You seek proof."

Thanos still wasn't convinced. "You could have told me years ago."

"Some things are best left in the past. You were safer not knowing."

"But you don't think everyone has left them there," Thanos guessed.

Cosmas spread his hands. "I think someone found the book, and decided to remind themselves of their bloodline. They found a note in the margins, and they were more persistent than I could give them credit for. They learned about the old rumors. Perhaps they saw the beginnings of something they didn't want to happen."

"Who?" Thanos asked.

Cosmas smiled slightly. "You understand that I cannot say for certain. A wise man understands the limits of what he knows, and there have been many people in my library of late."

"Cosmas." That was sharper than Thanos intended. "I'm sorry, but my life's at stake."

"A lot more than your life, I think," Cosmas replied. "And to answer your question, Prince Lucious has been more diligent than usual with his studies."

Lucious again. Wherever he looked, it seemed as though Thanos was finding his name. The evidence was stacking up, but none of it seemed to be final.

"You said something about a midwife?" Thanos asked.

Cosmas nodded. "I didn't tell Lucious this part, but I was able to locate the woman. She lives in the city."

"I will need the address," Thanos said.

"Of course."

Thanos felt as though he was finally getting somewhere with his attempts to find out what was going on. He took the address from the scholar and practically ran from the library.

He forced himself to slow to a walk as he headed down to the stables, determined to ride down into the city and find the woman. He didn't want people to guess that something was wrong. He forced himself to make his way through the castle courtyard as calmly as if he were heading out for a pleasure ride, even though his every instinct said to run for the nearest horse and ride hard.

The stables were noisier than Thanos would have expected as he approached. Normally, there would have been the occasional whinny of the horses, a few good-natured shouts from the stable hands. Now, the horses sounded as though something had spooked them, clattering their hooves at the walls of their stalls, refusing to settle.

Thanos hurried to the stable doors, surprised to find them half open. No responsible stable hand would leave them like that. He looked inside, trying to make sense of it. The stables seemed to be empty of stable hands, the horses left to mill about in near panic.

In the middle of it all, Thanos saw the reason why.

"No," Thanos said, as he saw the body lying there. It was on its back, and Thanos instantly recognized the stable boy he'd interrogated earlier. The boy lay with his limbs spread wide, his eyes staring emptily upwards. There were bloody holes in the front of his tunic, but no slashes on his arms. He hadn't defended himself. Instead, someone he trusted had walked up to him and stabbed him.

No, not someone. Lucious was behind this. Thanos was sure of it. Anger rose in him, and a deep kind of sadness behind it. If he hadn't come to see this boy, would he still be alive? Had he brought this about? No, this was Lucious's fault. Everything pointed to Lucious.

Now, Thanos needed to find a way to prove it.

Chapter Twenty Eight

Ceres stared up at the ziggurat of the forest folk. It was huge and ancient, obviously built long before their village, but still looking as though it belonged there. Beside her, Eoin stood waiting.

Steps led up the side, leading to the different levels of the structure. On each, one of the forest folk stood, or sat, or moved in elaborate dance fights with the air itself.

"What am I supposed to learn here?" Ceres said, and then caught herself. "I know, I know, everyone learns their own lessons. But how does this one work?"

"It's simple," Eoin said. "When you can meet me at the top, you will be ready."

"Ready for what?" Ceres demanded.

Eoin shrugged, with a smile that was far too infuriating. "I'll tell you that at the top."

He ran up the steps and Ceres made to follow, but the woman on the lowest tier of the ziggurat moved in front of her.

"First, you have things to learn. Do you know how to kick? Kick me."

Ceres thought she did, but the moment her foot struck out, the islander parried it away almost contemptuously. Her answering kick almost knocked Ceres from her feet. Ceres struck back, and again, she found it batted aside.

"This is all you can do?"

Ceres struck out again, and again. Each time, she missed, or found it blocked. Each time, a foot or a shin struck her. Before, she'd complained about not getting to fight. About having to move slowly and practice the movements over and over. Now, with her arms throbbing with bruises,

Ceres was starting to wish for the dancelike slowness of the training before.

"Concentrate!" the forest woman in front of her snapped, making her point with a kick that whipped up to ruffle Ceres's hair.

Ceres guessed that she was supposed to copy and react, but when the forest folk were so much more skilled than her, it felt as though all she could do was get hit. A sideways kick slammed into her stomach, and Ceres gasped for air.

"How am I supposed to learn all this?" Ceres demanded. "You're not even showing me what you're doing."

"We show you every time we move," the woman countered. She spun, her foot flicking up again, and Ceres barely leaned back out of the way in time. "The world shows you with every breath."

Ceres did her best to copy, throwing kick after kick. She tried to mimic the form of it, but that didn't seem to be enough for her opponent.

"The outer skin of it doesn't matter," she snapped, kicking out at Ceres again. Ceres forced herself to push harder, hoping it would be enough.

Eventually, reluctantly, the woman let her pass. By the time she did, Ceres felt as though she could barely stand, and the act of pulling herself up to the next step took all she had. She wasn't even sure how much she'd learned from the endless, exhausting repetition.

And that was just the first step.

There was a man on the next who jabbed at the body's vulnerable points with bark-covered fingers. Ceres threw one of the kicks she'd learned at him, and he struck down painfully on her knee.

"That is not what you are here to learn."

So she had to start again, with the only way to learn her own pain. She copied as best she could, but it still seemed like forever before she could haul herself to the next tier, then the next. There was a woman who threw her effortlessly to the ground, a man who struck with his elbows and knees, impossible to retreat from.

She didn't see the point of it. She couldn't learn all this in one attempt, no matter how much she'd been training with Eoin. All she was doing was getting so bruised that she could barely make it from one tier to the next.

She stood, ready for her next opponent, her next teacher, and found herself facing a girl barely older than Eike, so deeply enmeshed in the islanders' curse that her skin seemed more bark than flesh.

"I'm supposed to fight you?" Ceres asked.

The girl laughed. "It's not about fighting, silly. No wonder you're getting hit so much. It's about understanding. You know, I bet I could push you right off this ziggurat if I tried."

She tried, and Ceres had to dodge out of the way of the push. Then the girl caught her arm, twisting, and Ceres had to roll to take the pressure off.

"Can you feel the forest?" the girl asked, in between pushes. "Eoin says you will, but I don't know. You're getting hit a *lot*."

She kept attacking, in a strange mixture of pushes, trips, and twisting joint locks that meant Ceres could never quite get her balance, never quite attack.

"You've got to learn the lessons the world has," the girl said, with another laugh. "You've got to be part of it. Relax."

Ceres did her best, even though it seemed strange to take lessons from someone so much younger than her. She managed to twist out of the way of the next push, but the one after that caught her, sending her to the edge of the step she was on. For a moment, she teetered on the edge, looking out over the village and the jungle below. It was a surprise to see just how high she'd climbed by then, with the rest of it spread out like some green carpet.

She felt the breath of the wind there, seeming to hold her against the side of the ziggurat as it came in off the jungle. It felt as though the whole thing was breathing like one giant organism, pulsing with life.

"Don't think, move," the girl said, and aimed a push at Ceres that would have sent her off the edge to tumble to the forest below if she hadn't stepped aside.

She was so tired by now that she did it without thinking, energy rising within her automatically. It felt then as though she could feel everything around her. She could see the flow of the next push, timed in rhythm with the endless pulse of the jungle. Ceres fit into the flow of that push, moved neatly into the space it created, and timed a push of her own that sent the girl spinning and laughing.

"Good. You can go up."

The next step had a massive man whose legs were halfway to being tree trunks, and who threw punches Ceres suspected would have killed her if she hadn't been flooded by the power that lay within her. She struck back, and although her opponent didn't move, he seemed satisfied.

The one after that was a woman who grabbed Ceres, dragging her to the ground. Ceres felt the opening and rolled, coming up behind her, throwing an arm around her opponent's throat and squeezing.

On and on it went. Each of the forest folk seemed to have a different skill, but Ceres was starting to see that they weren't so different after all. Whether they punched or kicked, danced around her or charged forward to grapple with her, all of the islanders moved in tune with the world around them, no thought or form to it beyond that of the moment. With energy flooding through her, Ceres found it easy to relax into the same moment, and one by one they let her rise up the slopes of the ziggurat.

Finally, Ceres climbed to the top of the structure, where Eoin was waiting. Up here, Ceres could see a ribbon of water that poured down the rear slope of the ziggurat, coming from a spring that arched over a block of stone, tumbling down in a waterfall easily as powerful as the one they'd trained beneath before. Ceres couldn't see beyond that curtain of water, but she was certain there was something.

Eoin stood before the wall of water. He stood there looking as perfect as a statue.

He gave her a questioning look. "Do you understand yet? Can you feel it, Ceres?"

Ceres nodded. She could feel the whole world around her as she stood up there. She could see the island spread out below them too, looking even more beautiful from here than it did at ground level. She could see the streams and lagoons there, the inlets and the beaches that edged onto the jungle. This high, she could feel the wind whipping around her too, swirling as they stood there together.

"The first time I saw you, I knew you had power," Eoin said. "I thought that our ways might lead you to it." He smiled. "And now I see that I was right."

Ceres stood there, and she could feel the energy pulsing from within her.

"There are some things that cannot be controlled," Eoin continued. "You might as well try to control the jungle. But you do have a choice. You can choose to develop the power within you. Or you can choose to let it disappear."

Ceres frowned at him then. "Why would I do that?"

Eoin sighed.

"Because the power within you is a dangerous one," he said. "It is a very old gift, and if you choose to accept it, it will grow within you. You will hurt or kill all those who attempt to harm you. Anyone who touches you with malice will turn to stone."

Ceres thought back to the moments in the Stade when her power had come to her, killing creatures that had been on the verge of tearing her to pieces. She thought of the creature that had attacked their ship, and the way it had recoiled from her.

"That doesn't sound like a bad thing," she said.

"Perhaps not," Eoin replied. "But it is like keeping a wild animal to protect yourself. It might be fiercely loyal, but you will not be able to hold it back from others. It will strike at anyone who touches you in anger, whether you want them to be hurt or not. It could hurt those you love. And once your power has been revealed, it cannot be contained."

That was a harder thing, and it was enough to make Ceres pause.

"Do I have to do this?" she asked.

Eoin shook his head. "You've already learned a lot about fighting from us. Perhaps that's what you were brought here to do. Perhaps it's *all* you were brought here to do."

"But you don't believe that," Ceres guessed.

Eoin held out his hand to her. Ceres took it, feeling the mossy smoothness of his skin where they touched.

"I think that there are many places you could have learned to fight, but very few where you can go deeper. Where you can learn to understand what lies within you. I think you were brought here for a reason."

She stood there, her heart pounding, fearing to embrace her power—yet craving it.

Eoin stepped back.

"The decision is yours."

Ceres stood, looking out over the village. She looked further out, to where the ocean lapped at the edges of the island. Somewhere beyond it, her family was waiting. She wanted to get back to them. She wanted to have the strength to protect them. The rebellion was out there too. They needed her to have the strength to make a difference.

But did it need her to unleash something like this? How many people might she hurt? How many people might she kill? This was a decision that couldn't be undone. The kind of decision that might affect her whole life.

She saw Eoin step through the wall of water at the top of the ziggurat, disappearing beyond it. His voice carried back.

"Follow me if you dare, Ceres."

Ceres stood there for a long time. She thought of the rebellion, and of all the people who had been taken away by the Empire. She thought of her family. Then she thought of Thanos, dead because of all this madness. Madness that she might finally have the power to stop if she accepted this.

Ceres felt the water thunder down on her as she stepped through it.

Chapter Twenty Nine

Thanos walked down into the poorest districts of Delos, trying not to let the pity he felt at the state of this quarter of the city show on his face. He kept his cloak wrapped around him so that no one would see who he was. He doubted that being a prince would carry much weight here amongst those so poor they couldn't even afford food.

The houses down here barely even merited the term. They weren't so much discrete units as agglomerations of wood and plaster, one shack flowing into the next until Thanos couldn't tell where the buildings started and stopped.

There were beggars on the street, and Thanos guessed that there would have been thieves too if anyone had possessed anything worth stealing. He kept a wary eye on the alleys he passed while he tried to find the one that matched the address he had for the midwife.

He looked behind him too. It wasn't just thieves he had to worry about. After what had happened to the stable boy, he didn't want to risk bringing death down on anyone else.

Even with the address Cosmas had given him, it took time to find the right place. The address was for a house in one of the city's poorest neighborhoods. Thanos slipped down there in the early morning light, wrapping himself in his cloak so he wouldn't attract attention.

He found the house after more than an hour of searching. It was ramshackle and dilapidated, looking to Thanos as though the spider webs were the only things keeping one of the walls standing. There was a faint smell of rot there as he got closer, and it was so quiet that Thanos wasn't sure whether it was empty or not.

He knocked anyway, and was a little surprised when a woman his own age answered the door.

"I'm looking for the woman who was a midwife up at the castle two decades ago," he said. The young woman looked as though she might bolt, but when Thanos threw the hood of his cloak back, she seemed to freeze in place. She obviously recognized him.

"Please," he said. "It's important."

She stood there considering him for a moment. "You're…"

"Yes," Thanos said with a nod. "I am."

"You want my mother. Come with me."

Thanos followed her into a shack that didn't look much better on the inside than the outside. The little furniture that there was looked as though it had been there a long time. It certainly didn't look like the home of a midwife successful enough to be summoned to the palace.

In a back room, he found an old woman sitting on a chair that looked as though it might fall apart at any moment. As soon as he saw her hands, crabbed with arthritis, Thanos understood why the two weren't living anywhere better.

"Be gentle with Mother," the young woman said. "Her memory isn't what it was. She hardly speaks now."

Thanos made his way over. There was no response from the old woman. He crouched down beside her, but her expression didn't change.

"I need your help," Thanos said. "I found a reference in the castle library, in a genealogy. I'm trying to find out why."

There was no response from the woman.

"It was to a collection of plays," Thanos tried. Still, there was no response.

"Please," Thanos said. "People have been trying to kill me, and I think this has something to do with it. I need to understand the reason why."

There wasn't any answer from the old woman. There barely seemed to be any spark of life there, so that it seemed to Thanos as though he might be talking to an empty shell.

The seconds stretched out, turning into minutes. He looked into the woman's eyes, silently pleading for something.

"Please," he said. "I just want to understand who I really am."

This was hopeless. He would never find out what he needed to know.

He stood with a sigh. "I'm sorry to have bothered you. I'll go."

He turned, and found a hand clamped onto his arm. The old woman's fingers felt fragile around his wrist, but Thanos could feel the strength there too.

Thanos saw her eyes lock onto his as he turned back. "The son of the king."

Thanos shook his head. "I'm sorry, but I'm the king's—"

"Son," the old woman said, cutting him off in a voice that sounded rusty with lack of use. "The girl pretended that you weren't at first, but he was right there outside the room, pacing the way only a father can."

"You're sure?" Thanos asked.

The former midwife nodded. "She told me, because there wasn't any-one else to tell."

Thanos swallowed as he tried to make sense of it. Even though he'd guessed at this with Cosmas, it was still a shock to hear it like this, from a woman who'd been there. There was a part of him that still wanted to say that it was a lie, but it made more sense than he'd thought it would. The shock still hit him like a falling boulder, but there was something about it that seemed right too.

He stood there while the pieces fell into place. If this old woman was telling the truth, then he really was the heir. And that gave Lucious more than enough reasons to want him dead.

Anger rose in Thanos then, hard edged as diamond. He'd put up with so much of what Lucious had done over the years. He'd stood by while he'd been the worst kind of noble, while he'd put Thanos down, even while he'd attacked Ceres. Well, no more.

"Thank you," Thanos said to the old woman. "I have to get back to the castle."

"Don't thank me, boy," he heard her say. "There's some news that brings no one happiness."

⚜ ⚜ ⚜

Thanos stormed his way back to the castle, ignoring the guards who tried to challenge him at the gates. He made his way along the corridors, heading back to his rooms only because it would give him a chance to fetch his weapons and armor. Right then, he could have walked up to Lucious and ripped him in half with his bare hands, after all he'd done.

He threw open the doors to his rooms, and was surprised to see Stephania sitting in there on a couch, obviously waiting for him. She stood with a frown as soon as he came in.

"Thanos? What's wrong?"

"How did you get in here?" Thanos asked. Too much of his anger came through in that.

"A servant let me in," Stephania said. "There were things I needed to tell you, and I thought it was better to wait for you in here. But that can wait. What's happened?"

Thanos stood there, with his hands balled up. "I found out the truth."

"What truth?" Stephania asked.

Thanos paused for a moment before he told her, but he had to say this to someone. "Lucious is the one who tried to kill me."

"Oh, Thanos," Stephania said, and Thanos saw her raise her hand to her mouth. He knew how she felt.

"I'm going to kill him," Thanos said. "After everything he's done, I'm going to kill him, Stephania."

She stepped between him and the door.

"Don't try to stop me," Thanos said.

"It's not that," Stephania replied. "It's … I have some news."

"It can wait."

He saw her shake her head. "It *can't* wait. It's about Ceres."

That was enough to stop Thanos in his tracks. He stood there in silence.

"You should come and sit down," Stephania said, moving back to the couch and gesturing for him to join her.

Thanos didn't want to. He wanted the news now, whatever it was, but it seemed clear that Stephania wasn't going to say anything until he joined her. He sat down carefully, feeling the hardness of the couch beneath him.

"Don't tell me …" Thanos began.

"They were taking her to the Isle of Prisoners on a prison ship. That ship never arrived."

Thanos thought of all the possibilities. Maybe the rebellion had intercepted the ship. Maybe Akila's people had captured it. Maybe Ceres had orchestrated an escape.

"When a boat passed close to their path, they found wreckage," Stephania said. "They say there must have been a storm. The ship was torn apart. There were … I'm sorry, Thanos, but there were no survivors."

"No," Thanos said, shaking his head. He stood up. "No, it can't be."

Ceres couldn't be dead. She *couldn't* be. If she was dead, then nothing else made sense. Thanos felt tears welling up in his eyes, impossible to stop no matter how hard he tried. He made to turn away so that Stephania wouldn't see, but she was there in front of him anyway.

She wrapped her arms around him, holding him close enough that he could smell the soft, floral scent of her.

"I'm sorry," she said. "I wanted to be the one to tell you. I didn't trust anyone else to do it."

"It's …" He didn't know what to say next. He just didn't know. It felt as though the world had come to a jarring halt, caught between one moment and the next. It felt as though he'd breathed out, and fresh air refused to come into his lungs, leaving him as some kind of gasping wreck.

Stephania was there in that space, holding onto him, feeling like an anchor to the world when so much of Thanos felt as though he was floating free. Her hand felt so small and delicate in his, but there was strength there as she held onto him. She was there while his grief washed over him, building in waves that he wouldn't have wanted anyone else to see.

Stephania held onto him through all of it, and Thanos found himself more and more grateful for the fact that she was there. She was right; there was no one else there who could have told him something such as this. There was no one else he would have trusted to hold him like this.

And he *did* trust her. Stephania had been there to help him through his investigation. She'd put aside the way he'd treated her, and she was there now in the darkest moment of his life. She didn't say anything. She didn't need to. She was simply there, waiting while Thanos's grief burned itself out. He was surprised to find what was there as the initial rush of it passed.

He'd never thought he could feel anything for someone like Stephania, but now, looking at her, it was impossible not to. She was perfect in so many ways, but this moment just went to show exactly how deeply he understood her.

Thanos realized how close they were then. Close enough that it would have been nothing to close the distance between them. It would have been so easy to kiss her then, and maybe that would have helped. Maybe, he thought, it would be enough to make him feel something, anything, instead of the awful emptiness that yawned inside him.

Instead, he felt her fingers touch his lips.

"Don't," Stephania said. "Not like this. You're upset. I don't want it to be just because of that, and it's not why I'm doing this. I'm here because you're my friend, and because I care about you."

The amazing thing was just how much he cared about her too. It felt like it had crept up on Thanos, feelings for Stephania building up within him almost imperceptibly the more time he spent with her. He'd gotten to see who she really was, and it was someone he could easily find himself falling in love with.

Someone he could find himself being with forever.

"You need to concentrate on the important things," Stephania said. "Like what you're going to do next."

"That part's simple," Thanos said. "I'm going to deal with Lucious."

Chapter Thirty

Sartes clung to the horse tightly as they raced toward the city, terrified that he might fall off if he didn't. Just as terrified that he might drop the precious plans he held. He reined in his horse, and beside him, Anka and his father did the same.

"Anka, we have to go slower," he said. "I can't risk dropping these."

"What's more important than your life?" Anka called back.

"Sartes has plans taken from the Empire's command tents," his father said, answering for him.

Sartes saw Anka stare over at him in obvious surprise.

"Really? You have their plans?"

Sartes nodded. "One of the commanders wanted them so he could see where he was supposed to go. I took everything I could."

"Then we can't just take you into the city the normal way," Anka said. "Follow me."

She heeled her horse into a gallop and Sartes did his best to follow. He dared a glance back, and now he could see horses on the horizon, dust flying from their hooves. They'd spent too much time talking. The soldiers were in sight.

Sartes did his best to stay on the horse as Anka led the way down back trails and over broken ground. He looked over to see his father urging his horse on, and tried not to show how scared he was then. If the soldiers could see them, it had turned from a hunt into a race, and he didn't know if he could win it.

Sartes followed Anka along a twisting series of trails that led through a stand of trees and past a spot where two boulders stood at either side, almost blocking the path. It seemed to Sartes that it was a route designed to confuse and distract those following, but it meant that he was jolted with every rut and shift of ground.

"Not far now," he heard Anka call. "We'll have to let the horses go when we get to the city, but our people have a way in."

Our people. Sartes liked the sound of that. He'd wanted to be a part of the rebellion since the first time he'd heard about it. He'd wanted to be there for the attack on Fountain Square. If he'd been older…

…then maybe he would have ended up dead, like Rexus and his brother. He'd been too young to do anything for the rebellion before, but maybe he could now.

He saw a creek ahead, steep sided and too fast flowing to risk plunging into, especially with the plans. Anka's horse jumped it easily, and Sartes saw his father follow. His horse seemed to know what was required of it without being told, giving Sartes no time to think about just how wide the gap was, or how cold the water would be if he fell.

He felt the muscles of the horse bunch beneath him and he gripped it with his thighs as it leapt. For a moment, everything felt weightless, then the ground came thundering up to meet them, and Sartes was almost jarred from the saddle. He felt the plans he held shifting, grabbed for them, and managed to keep them from falling as his horse surged forward again.

In the distance, Sartes saw the walls of Delos. Given the misery of the city, he had never thought he would be so grateful to see them again. The three of them rode toward the walls, and Anka angled a mirror toward the sun in a pattern that seemed to repeat as they got closer.

They rode in through a side gate and Sartes dared another glance back. The soldiers chasing them were closer now, swords out ready to fight, their horses straining as they charged after the three of them.

They raced through the streets, to a crossroads thronging with people. To Sartes's surprise, one waved.

"Dismount here!" Anka said, practically leaping off her horse.

Sartes and his father followed her lead, and almost before he was off the horse, Sartes found the reins being taken by a man in simple clothes, the hilts of weapons just visible as they moved. Another man threw a worn and filthy cloak his way.

"Put it on!" Anka ordered, donning one that was almost identical.

Wearing them, Sartes, his father, and Anka looked to Sartes like a group of beggars making their way through the city. The crowd closed around them and he saw the soldiers riding through, shoving people out of the way. Briefly, Sartes's heart was in his mouth. What if their disguise didn't work? What if the men spotted the three of them?

But they rode past, while Sartes and the others made their way along the city's streets. Anka led the way, taking twists and turns that seemed to make no sense until they reached a space with a walled courtyard. Anka headed inside, then up into a building that mixed stone and timber, more solid than most of those around it.

Sartes followed. His father put a hand on his shoulder.

"We did it. We actually got away."

Sartes nodded, and relief flooded through him. "You saved me."

His father shook his head. "Anka saved both of us."

"And now maybe we can repay her," Sartes said, fingering the maps he still held.

He followed while Anka led the way up to an attic-level room where more than a dozen people were waiting for them. They stood around a large table, the space lit by guttering candles.

The surprising thing to Sartes was how ordinary they all looked. He'd heard so many stories of the rebellion that he was expecting something… more. Perhaps an army of combatlords, each ready to take on a horde of the Empire's soldiers. Skilled assassins, cloaked in black and armed with rare poisons. Heroic leaders like Rexus.

Instead, they just seemed to be normal people. People like his father. People like him. They didn't seem happy.

"Anka, what were you thinking riding in here in such a hurry?" one man asked. He had the broad shoulders of a farmer, and a rough beard. "You could have compromised everything here."

"Were you followed?" a shorter man asked. He fingered the hilt of a knife. "Will we need to fight?"

"We weren't followed," Anka assured him. "And there was no time for anything else. We have something to show you."

Sartes let her take the plans from him, then helped her to spread them out on the table.

"As you know, I've been looking for Ceres's brother Sartes," Anka said.

"Wasting time," a woman said, "when everyone's sons and brothers are at risk."

It was hard for Sartes to like someone who thought finding him was a waste of time.

"Not wasting time, Hannah," Anka shot back. "I found him. And he brought us these. Plans showing the Empire's intentions. They show which of our bases they know about, and which they intend to move against. We even have the orders to tell us when they plan to get there."

"So we have plenty of time to evacuate our people," the first rebel to speak said.

"That's one possibility," Anka said.

"What's the alternative?"

Sartes understood, even if the others didn't. "We could ambush them."

"You're Sartes?" Hannah asked.

Sartes nodded.

"So we owe you a great deal for getting these papers, but that doesn't mean you know about tactics or strategy."

Sartes shrugged. "Only as much as I learned in the army."

"As a conscript," the woman countered. "I doubt they teach you much about planning."

"They teach you how to stay alive," Sartes said. "You learn about your enemies. You guess what they're going to do before they do it, so that they can't hurt you."

He paused as he realized that everyone's eyes were on him. He almost couldn't keep going, but then he felt his father's hand on his shoulder. That presence was enough to give him the confidence to keep going.

"I know what the army is like better than any of you," Sartes said. "I can tell you which of the officers will rush in, and which will be cautious. I can tell you that the conscripts will run, if you give them any real prospect of escaping. We can ambush them. We can win."

"It's what we need to do," Anka said, adding her voice to his. "We can't fight them head on, so what's left? We either sit back and wait to be destroyed, or we take chances like this one."

"Do we have enough people?" one of the rebels asked.

"We have some," Anka said.

"You'll have more if you free the conscripts," Sartes said. "They hate the Empire. The ones who don't fight for you will run."

"And we fight smart," Anka insisted. "Look here. If they want to get to our people to the north of the city, that means going through the burial grounds here and here. We know there are catacombs to strike from where they can't see us. And if we do it here, we have the ruins of the old mausoleums to use. We could bring walls down right on them. Then we have tripwires, pits… we could halve their numbers before it even came to fighting."

"They're still better armed and armored than us," Hannah insisted.

Sartes pointed to his father. "My father is the best smith you will ever meet. He can help you to make all the weapons you will ever need."

Sartes saw his father nod. "That's true. Give me metal, a fire, and enough people to help, and I can produce whatever you need."

"How quickly?" Anka asked.

His father seemed to consider for a moment. "That will depend on what kind of resources you can give me. But if you give me enough people, I can equip you as well as the army. Better."

"And we don't need enough to take them all on at once," Anka pointed out. "We just need enough people and weaponry to hit the weakest forces. We can hit supply centers to take more. Look. We could evacuate the people in the old quarter, leave traps behind, and hit their supply train while they're still looking for us."

She started to outline her plans, and Sartes had to admit he was impressed. He'd expected things to be difficult for the rebellion without Rexus there, but Anka seemed to understand every detail. In some ways, Sartes thought, she was an even better choice than Rexus. Where the rebels' former leader might have charged in, Anka seemed more cautious, wanting to plan everything as carefully as possible to ensure that their people weren't hurt.

Somewhere in all the planning, Sartes drifted to the back of the room. His father was there, and he put an arm around his son's shoulders. For the first time since the soldiers had taken him as a conscript, he actually felt safe.

"It sounds as though there's going to be a lot of work to come," his father said.

Sartes nodded. "I don't mind that. I *want* to help the rebellion."

"Are you sure?" his father asked. "It's already cost me one son. You could go and be safe."

"Would you go?" Sartes asked.

His father shook his head. "They need me to make weapons for them. But you could get away."

"Where?" Sartes asked. "Where is there that's safe? Anywhere I go, the army could come and take me, or kill me just because they feel like it. The only way to be safe is if we help everyone, and I *want* to help everyone. There are still plenty of others like me stuck in the army, or getting attacked every day out there."

His father nodded. "I'm proud of you, son, and you're right. We have to make this better. I guess I can do that making weapons."

"And I'll do whatever I can to help," Sartes said.

He wasn't sure what he would do yet, but he was sure of one thing: this time, when the time came to fight the Empire, he wanted to be there.

Chapter Thirty One

The wall of water gushed over Ceres, so cold that it made her shiver. As it poured across her, it felt as though it was washing away some block or barrier, letting something open up inside her like a flower.

She'd passed the islanders' test. She'd learned the lessons they wanted her to learn. Even now, she could hear the whisper of the island in the background, pulsing like one living thing. For a moment, her own power pulsed in response, and the strength of it was enough that Ceres couldn't concentrate.

Only Eoin's voice brought her back to herself, letting Ceres see that she was in a stone-walled tunnel, which sloped down sharply in a long spiral. She couldn't tell if it was natural or if it had been carved out by the hands of the islanders.

"This way," Eoin said, and Ceres could see him a little way ahead.

She followed him down it by the faint sunlight that seemed to reflect from the walls. The tunnel twisted and turned, so that soon, Ceres wasn't sure if they were still under the ziggurat, or somewhere else entirely.

Ahead, Ceres thought she could see a square of sunlight, with Eoin briefly silhouetted against it as he stepped out into it. Ceres followed, stepping through another curtain of water, this one a trickle compared to the previous one.

She stepped out onto grass, into a giant, bowl-shaped depression. Trees hung over the rim at improbable angles, clinging to the rock as they stuck out. Ceres found herself wondering how many were forest folk who had succumbed to the curse.

There were forest folk there, building a bonfire at one side of the open space with driftwood and deadfall. There were others setting out food and drink, obviously preparing a feast from forest fruits and fish from the shores.

"We shall celebrate your accepting your power," Eoin said.

"And afterwards?" Ceres asked.

Eoin held out a hand for Ceres to take. "That is up to you. You can stay with us for as long as you wish. You can return to the Empire to fight. Or you can go another way if you choose. We will help you, wherever you want to go."

At the very center of the bowl-shaped depression, there was a ring of what looked like wooden posts, surrounding a plinth. Yet, as she got closer, Ceres could see the eyes in the posts, moving even though the rest of them couldn't.

"In the last stages before the curse claims them fully, our people are connected to the jungle more than ever," Eoin said. "They see things that the rest of us don't. We come here for the most important decisions."

Ceres walked with him into that circle, feeling the eyes upon her. The forest folk gathered around now, their bonfire burning in the background.

There was a bowl on the plinth. Eoin lifted it, offering it to her. It was sweet smelling and sticky looking. He pressed it into her hands.

"If you want to accept the power within you, drink. Drink and see."

"Drink and see what?" Ceres asked.

Eoin spread his hands. "Everything."

She took the bowl and sipped at it, then drank it down swiftly. No one there was going to try to hurt her. At least, not in ways that didn't involve the normal rough and tumble of fighting. The drink was sticky and thick, tasting of sweet berries and the sap of jungle plants as she drank it.

"What's in this?" Ceres asked, but Eoin just smiled. Ceres looked around, and the flames of the bonfire seemed to swim.

She heard a repetitive thudding, and for a moment she thought that maybe a drummer had started to play. Then she realized that it was the rhythmic pounding of the forest folk's feet, stamping in perfect time. It seemed to join with the ever louder beating of her heart.

It seemed impossibly slow, but then, so did the rest of the world. It seemed to Ceres as if the dancers were drifting along like leaves in the firelight, every movement so slow and precise that it felt as though they were barely dancing at all.

The world seemed to swim, and Ceres felt herself falling. Eoin was there beside her, laying her down gently on the jungle floor.

"Sleep, Ceres," he said. "Sleep, and dream."

Ceres stared up at him for a breath or two longer. It was a good last sight before she closed her eyes.

Delos spread out below her like some child's toy. It seemed as though she was drifting toward the city, down and down, ever closer. Ceres could feel the rush of the air through her fingers, but she didn't feel as though she was falling. She certainly didn't feel in any danger.

She fell closer, and she realized that she was falling toward her former home. Almost as soon as she realized that, the scene shifted, and she found herself looking at two people it took her a second to recognize.

Her mother and father looked so much younger there; younger than Ceres had ever seen them. She could see a tiny boy toddling about, and knew it had to be her older brother, Nesos. The two of them were looking down into a crib.

"What have you done?" her mother asked.

"What I had to do," her father replied.

"If you think that we're going to take in some brat, then—"

"That's exactly what we're going to do," her father insisted. "We will raise her as our own, and never give her any reason to think otherwise."

Ceres wanted to look closer, but the images in front of her shifted again.

Now, there were armies clashing around her, the clash of blades mixing in with the screams of the dying and the thud of armored bodies slamming into one another. She saw people struggling against each other, stabbing and slashing as they fought for room.

She saw herself at the heart of it, dressed in gold-edged armor, wielding a sword and shield. A man ran at her and she stepped aside, slicing with her sword. She heard herself shouting orders over the chaos of the melee, and to her surprise, those around her listened. They reformed, charged, and fought again.

Ceres saw herself at the heart of the fight, her opponents falling until finally they turned and ran, the rout spreading out from the point where she fought until it encompassed all of the opposing forces. Ceres heard the battle cry of her soldiers repeated over and over.

"Ceres! Ceres!"

Ceres stood there, not understanding. What was happening? Were these just random images, or was there more to them?

"You know what they are, Ceres."

Ceres turned, and she wasn't standing in a battlefield anymore. She might have been back on the island again, but this island was different. Where the forest folk's home was covered in the green of the jungle, here rainbow marble stood up in spires and arches above flat meadows.

A woman stood there, or at least the vague impression of a woman. She wore what looked to Ceres like a cloak at first glance, but it was more than that. It was like a haziness she couldn't quite see through; a gap in the vision that she couldn't pierce.

"Who are you?" Ceres demanded. "What are you?"

"A vision, an image," the woman said.

"An image of what?" Ceres wasn't going to let it go.

The woman tilted her head to one side, the cowl over it shifting in response.

"Of your mother."

The woman reached out toward her, and Ceres stood still as she touched Ceres's brow. The power within her flared with that touch, and Ceres felt it like a living thing inside her. In that moment, it seemed to burst up through her, pouring out of her like dark smoke until it hung above her in a cloud.

The female figure seemed to regard it. She reached out, shaping the smoke between her hands like clay, twisting it into strands and reshaping it into something else. It seemed to grow as she did it, becoming something different, something more.

"Do you choose this?" the female figure asked.

Ceres nodded. "Yes."

"Then be what you should be."

It poured back into Ceres then, and now it seemed to fill her to bursting point. It was there in her, and it was her, all at once. The power of it seemed to overwhelm her in that moment, and Ceres fell. The hidden woman caught her, laying her down gently.

"When you wake, come and find me," she said.

"Where?" Ceres asked.

"The Isle Beyond the Mist."

Ceres wanted to ask what she meant, and where it, was, but in that moment she felt the vision starting to fade. She dropped back into wakefulness, and realized she was lying on the grass by the bonfire.

She saw Eoin looking down at her, in obvious concern.

The aches and pains of her fights had faded, the power within her just below the surface. She let Eoin help her up.

She still stood within a circle of the forest folk, and she could see the way they watched her now. She knew that they could see the new power within her, the same way that she could feel them all joined in their connection with the island.

Slowly, they started to chant, and it took Ceres a moment to realize what it was that they were chanting, slow and solemn, as if a great leader were amongst them.

"Ceres, Ceres, Ceres!"

Chapter Thirty Two

Thanos had made his way to the king's chambers many times in his life, but he doubted he'd ever felt as much as he did now. Anger, betrayal, but also a strange sense of having found some kind of completion. All of them vied for space within him as he strode toward the entrance.

The doors there were extravagant things, like so much of the rest of the castle, covered in painted carvings depicting scenes of battle and judgment. When he was younger, Thanos had traced them with his hands, imagining all the great deeds of kings long dead. Now, he saw them for what they were: a boast, a message.

A guard stood at either side of the doors, in armor that practically dripped in gold, given their status as royal bodyguards. One raised a hand as Thanos approached.

"I'm sorry, your highness, but the king is not receiving visitors."

Thanos fixed him with a look. Normally, he would have argued or tried to persuade. He understood that this man was just trying to do his job, but right then, nothing was going to keep him from speaking with King Claudius.

With his father. Just the thought of that was enough to send a fresh wave of emotion running through him.

"Step aside," Thanos said, and the guards must have heard something in his voice, because they hurriedly moved out of the way. That was good. In spite of everything, Thanos didn't want to hurt *them*.

He pushed open the doors. Inside, he found King Claudius drinking, attended by serving girls while he chewed on a chicken leg. He sat on an elegantly carved chair in front of a roaring fire, with a gaming board in front of him, the counters there suggesting a game already in progress.

Thanos saw the king look up as he entered. He saw the initial flash of anger soften at the sight of him, and now Thanos could guess why.

"Thanos, I thought I said I wasn't to be disturbed. But no matter. Join me. Normally, the only way I can get a good game is to play myself."

Thanos stood there, looking around at the servants. "Everybody get out." When they didn't move, he raised his voice. "Leave, I said."

He watched the servants run for the door, then waited for the thud of it swinging shut. King Claudius stood, and for the first time in a while Thanos looked, really looked, at him. He found himself searching the king's face, picking out features and looking for similarities. Was the arch of that brow the same as his? The slight raise of the cheekbones?

Right now, it seemed as though the main thing that they had in common was their anger. King Claudius was reddening with it, and Thanos saw his arm sweep out to knock away the gaming pieces.

"How dare you dismiss my servants? Have you forgotten who is the king here, Thanos?"

"I have not forgotten," Thanos said. On another day, he might have bowed or knelt, but not today.

"And storming in here. Who do you think you are to do such a thing?"

"I think I am your son," Thanos said, and each word felt like a stone slab being put down. He hadn't been sure how he would say it, but now that he had, it couldn't be taken back.

The energy of the anger seemed to drain from the room as quickly as it had come. If Thanos hadn't already had confirmation of who he was, that would have done it, with no need for the king to say anything. Even so, he wanted to hear King Claudius admit it.

The king staggered back into his chair, falling there as heavily as if Thanos had shoved him. He reached for his wine cup, then threw it into the fire. Thanos heard it clatter against the coals, the wine hissing as it steamed.

"What have you heard?" King Claudius demanded. "*Where* have you heard it?"

Thanos thought of the midwife, then of the dead stable hand. He wasn't going to bring trouble to anyone else. Even Cosmas might be in danger if Thanos explained too much about how he'd learned the truth.

"Does that matter?" Thanos countered. "What matters is that I'm your son. Aren't I?"

King Claudius looked down at the remains of his game for what seemed like a long time before he finally answered.

"Yes. Your mother… she was so beautiful. When I learned that she was pregnant, I was so happy, but I couldn't admit it. Neither of us could. It would have torn things apart. Instead, we hid things."

Thanos thought of the references left in the book of genealogy. The king might have ordered it hidden, but his mother had clearly intended that it should come out at some point. That, or she simply wanted the comfort of being able to put the truth down somewhere.

"So, I am your son," Thanos said. "Your eldest son."

"And my finest," King Claudius said. "You are all that I could have hoped you might be. You are clever, skilled in war, diligent, able to command those around you. You were victorious in the Stade when Lucious ran, and I couldn't have been prouder of you then. When I thought you were lost in the war, something broke inside me. When you came back, it was like the sun returning after a long winter."

Thanos wasn't sure what to say to that. He hadn't heard the king speak that warmly of him in a long time, and King Claudius had been the one to send him to war in the first place. It meant a lot to be the king's son, but he still wasn't sure *what* it meant, because this man was still cruel, still a tyrant to his people.

"I'm glad that I finally know the truth," Thanos said. "I feel like I know who I am for the first time."

"You have always been my son," the king said. "Even though you didn't know it, you have always been a man I could have wished to be."

Thanos was more than that though, wasn't he? "If I'm your son, am I your heir?"

King Claudius nodded. "And that is one reason we couldn't speak of it. It would have torn the Empire apart."

"The Empire is tearing itself apart," Thanos pointed out, but this wasn't the time for that argument. There was too much to think about before any of that. Too much to process all at once. Everything he'd thought about himself had changed. He didn't even know where he fit into the Empire now.

The king seemed to be having as much trouble with it all as Thanos was. He sat there, looking out around the room as though seeking an answer somewhere there.

"I'm glad you know," King Claudius said. "I didn't think I would be. I've spent so long hiding this from you, but now that you know, it feels as though a weight has been lifted from me."

"It's not the only thing I know," Thanos replied. "I know who tried to have me killed."

That brought the king back to his feet again. "You do? Who? I'll have them hanged. I'll have them—"

"Lucious," Thanos said simply.

He saw the change in the king's expression at once. When he'd told King Claudius that he knew the secret of his birth, Thanos had seen pure shock. Now, the surprise was back, but this time it wasn't anywhere near as great. Why would it be? They both knew that Lucious was more than capable of it.

"No," King Claudius said, but there wasn't certainty there.

"Yes," Thanos insisted. "He sent a message to the Typhoon, and had him try to kill me. He followed the same clues that I did about my birth, and he wanted me dead because of it. He *wants* me dead."

"Lucious is a prince of the Empire too," King Claudius said, as though that made it impossible that he would do something like this.

"Which explains why he found it so easy to get the Typhoon to do the job," Thanos insisted. "I found the boy he sent to carry the message. Lucious gave him an amulet to identify the message as coming from him."

"And you have this boy? He will swear to this?"

Thanos gritted his teeth. "He was murdered shortly after I spoke with him."

And Thanos thought that the king would have heard of something like that happening in his own castle. Did he really not care what happened to the people who spent their lives serving him?

"He found out what was happening," Thanos insisted. "He sent the boy. Who else could? He should be executed for this!"

"I will not execute Lucious," King Claudius snapped back. "Do not even suggest it."

"Imprison him then," Thanos said. "Put him where he can't do any more harm. You must know what he's like. I thought you were only keeping him around because of his status, but if I'm your son—"

"Lucious has his uses," King Claudius said. "He has a role to play, even if you don't understand it right now."

"What's to understand?" Thanos demanded. He could feel the anger rising in him, overwhelming the strange kind of rightness he'd felt on hearing the king admit who he was. "He tried to kill me. He *did* kill that boy. He needs to be stopped."

"He will do exactly what he needs to do," King Claudius said.

"And you won't do anything to punish him?"

Thanos saw him shake his head.

"Come, Thanos," King Claudius said. "This should be a happy moment. I have a son who knows who I am again. Sit with me, eat."

"Suddenly, I've lost my appetite. Please excuse me, your majesty."

"Thanos," King Claudius said. "Don't do anything foolish."

Foolish? Thanos wasn't going to do anything foolish. He was going to do something he should have done a long time ago. If his newfound father wouldn't do anything about Lucious, then he would.

Chapter Thirty Three

Lucious liked wine, so it seemed obvious to take a vineyard. When the king had given him license to take what he wanted to show the peasants their place, why shouldn't he?

Not just any vineyard, of course. There were more than enough around Delos producing slop he'd flog a servant for putting in front of him. The Cervin vineyard, though, was worth taking. Not only did it produce wine worth drinking, but its owners sold wine from across the world to every noble Lucious knew. The money from it would be a useful addition to the royal coffers. Lucious would certainly enjoy owning it.

He and his men rode through the fields, probably looking like a band of noble knights out to slay some monster. He saw the workers scatter before them and run. Briefly, Lucious thought about chasing them down for the sport of it, but it was better to do what they'd come to do. They didn't look like slaves, so maybe it was better if they ran, anyway. Lucious didn't want to have to pay workers on his new vineyard.

"Remember what we're here to do," Lucious said, looking around at the men with him. He'd picked them himself, selecting only the hardest, toughest members of the army for the job. He'd wanted men who wouldn't shy away from what was needed. "Let's show Delos the price of rebellion!"

The men roared their response. There had been a couple who had expressed qualms in the last couple of raids. Lucious had ordered them to the front to fight against the rebels there. He had no time for weakness. The men who were left had proven themselves willing to follow any order. Most of them seemed to enjoy it.

They approached the farmhouse at a full gallop, and Lucious casually kicked aside a boy who ran out too close to them, sending him sprawling in a tangle of broken bones. Lucious didn't give him a second look.

The farmhouse was bigger than most around Delos, probably thanks to the money from the wine. It was a hovel compared to the castle, of course, but it wouldn't take much to remodel it for guests or hunting. Perhaps even as a place to keep a noble mistress. He'd had his eye on Stephania for a while now, but there were plenty of others.

Wealthy or not, these people were still peasants, without a drop of noble blood. If anything they were the worst of the lower orders, thinking that the ability to make good wine made them somehow better than all the rest. Maybe even almost as good as those they should serve. Just the thought of that made Lucious glad he'd picked this place.

They stopped outside the door, and Lucious handed his reins to one of the men. He didn't bother knocking, but instead waited while another of his men kicked the thing back against the wall. The man stepped through and Lucious followed.

Inside, he saw a high ceilinged hall, dominated by a long table with silverware set out on it, while a wide staircase stood at the side, hung with trophies the way a noble's home might be. Lucious had been right about these wine makers getting ideas above their station.

There was a fat peasant man with graying hair wearing enough velvet and silver that he could have been a noble. There was a woman the same age, dressed in just as foolish a fashion. A younger man was wearing rough work clothes, but Lucious could see the resemblance between him and his father. There were two younger women, one heavily pregnant and possibly the wife of the young man, the other probably his sister.

The fat man was already rising from the table as Lucious entered.

"What is this?" the wine merchant thundered. "What do you think you're doing, bursting into my home like this? By what right do you—"

Lucious drew his sword in one smooth movement and stabbed the fat man in his ample stomach. He was so huge that the blade didn't even come out of the other side.

"I think I am your prince," Lucious snapped, then stepped back to let the man fall. "And this house is mine now."

"Father!" the younger man cried out. He drew a sickle from his belt, running at Lucious. The blade clattered from the steel of Lucious's armor as he stepped back, then the prince swept his sword across at throat height. He was aiming for a neat beheading, worthy of the warrior he was, but instead, his sword only made it about halfway through the man's throat. He felt it dragged from his hand as the young man collapsed.

"Honestly, can't you peasants even *die* properly?" Lucious demanded. He put a foot on the man's chest and yanked at his sword, only getting angrier as he tried to pull it free. Finally, it came loose.

"You saw them resist," Lucious said to his men. "The families of traitors are forfeit. The young one goes to the slave pits. Hang the others when you're done with them. Find any servants and get them ready to sell if they're worth anything. Kill the others. Then I want this house stripped of anything of value. What are you waiting for? Go!"

His men rushed forward, and the women screamed as they dragged them away. Lucious sat down at the table, enjoying the start of the violence. There was a bottle of wine on it, so he helped himself, drinking straight from it as around the house, more screams sounded. It wasn't the best vintage, but it was more than passable.

He looked around, imagining what he would do with the space as the looting began. The silverware would be worth a decent amount, while the space might be good for parties. Yes, he decided as the body of a servant came tumbling down the stairs, this was a good place to take.

He stepped out into the sunlight, where his men were binding servants on their knees. Lucious strode along the line, silently picking out whether any were worth keeping. One was arguing with his men as they dragged him toward a noose.

"You need me," he said. "Now that the master vintner is dead, I'm the only one who knows all the details of his business."

Lucious stepped in. "Wait. He's right. We do need to know these things."

He heard the servant sigh with relief. Lucious smiled at that.

"So make sure you only kill him once you have beaten every detail out of him," he finished.

He walked on, finding the boy he'd knocked down before. Lucious watched him trying to crawl away, his leg obviously broken, then moved to crouch beside him.

"You might as well stop," he said. "I could catch you any time I wanted."

"Please," the boy said. "Please don't kill me."

"What's your name, boy?" Lucious asked.

"V-Vel."

"Do you know who I am, Vel?" Lucious asked.

"You're Prince Lucious," the boy said.

"And do you know what's happened here?"

"You… you killed them."

"Yes," Lucious said. "Because they were traitors who wouldn't give up what belonged to their betters. Because there is a price to pay for rebellion, and you're all going to pay it until the rebellion stops. It's their fault that this is happening. Do you think you can remember all that?"

The boy nodded.

"Good. I won't have to kill you then. One of my men will splint your leg, and then you can hop your way to Delos. On the way, you will tell anyone you meet all of it, do you understand?"

The boy nodded. "Y-yes."

"Yes what?" Lucious demanded, his voice sharp again.

"Yes, your highness."

"That's better," Lucious said. At least one peasant had learned his proper place today.

It was a start.

CHAPTER THIRTY FOUR

Sartes huddled in amongst the statues and mausoleums of the burial ground, listening to the leaders of the rebellion argue. They'd gathered around one of the slabs there, the map spread out upon it, with Anka at the heart of a cluster of the rebellion's more senior figures. Sartes was that close only because Anka had insisted on it.

"We don't know that they'll come through here, not for sure," a large man who looked like a wharf hand insisted. "We could be committing all our people for no reason."

"Not for no reason, Edrin," a younger man insisted. He looked like a fighter. "To stop the Empire from capturing, torturing, and slaughtering our people."

"You're always taking Anka's side," Hannah said. She'd been at the meeting when they decided on this.

Sartes was starting to get a better sense of who the rebels were. The younger man was Oreth. As Anka struggled to hold the rebellion together, he seemed to be serving as a kind of deputy. The big man, Edrin, was solid but obviously suspicious of whether Anka could do the job. Sartes didn't like Hannah, because it seemed too much like she was more interested in her own place within the rebellion than anything else.

"We're in the right place," Anka said, pointing to the map.

"Then where are they?" another man asked. He was called Yeralt, and Sartes had heard that he was the son of a merchant, probably wealthier than the rest of the rebellion's people. "I don't want to argue, Anka, but our people are getting worried, just waiting like this. They think it's going wrong."

"Then I'll speak to them," Anka said. She looked around, and to Sartes's surprise, he saw her eyes settle on him. "Come with me, Sartes. Let's show them what they're fighting for."

Sartes followed as Anka stepped out onto the road that ran through the burial ground. Around them, rebels slipped out of hiding places in pits and behind statues to listen.

"Listen to me," Anka said. "I know you're scared. I know there are some of you who think that we shouldn't be doing this at all. That we should be running and evacuating our people. The truth is that we could do that." She raised her voice. "We could do that, and the army would march straight through here. It would descend on towns and villages, looking for us, but that would be all right. We wouldn't be there."

"Ordinary people would," Anka went on. "We've all seen what the army can do. It will go into those towns and it will murder people. It will drag them out and torture them. It will conscript young men like Sartes here. It will enslave those who can't fight for them. We could run away, but we won't. We won't, because the people of Delos need us."

That got a cheer from the surrounding rebels, and Sartes couldn't help joining in. Above it, he heard a rumble. Oreth ran up.

"They're coming!"

Sartes saw Anka nod. "Everybody to your places! Remember the plan!"

Sartes ran back to his spot by the statue, and saw the others take up their positions. They practically disappeared back into the landscape of the burial ground once they were there. Sartes watched the approach of the Empire's soldiers from around the arm of a marble figure. His stomach knotted at the thought of what was about to happen, but he didn't move. He didn't run.

Instead, he thought of how brave Ceres would have been if she'd been here. He clutched his sword tighter. His father had made it, and it fit his hand perfectly, in a way that the practice swords the army gave to conscripts never had. In his other hand, he held a horn ready to blow. He wore the uniform that they'd made him wear in the army, because they needed that for the plan.

Around him, Sartes could see the other members of the rebellion. They waited in their hiding places, armed with the armor and weapons they'd started to produce under his father's instructions, positioned exactly according to Anka's instructions throughout the burial ground and the ancient ruins within it.

She stood beside him, and Sartes could see the way she kept her features blank as she tried not to show any fear. She kept looking around, though, and Sartes guessed that she was going over and over the preparations they'd made.

"You didn't miss anything," Sartes whispered. He'd never seen anyone so thorough. "You thought of everything."

"I hope so," Anka whispered back.

Sartes watched the column of soldiers as they got closer. He could see horsemen at the front, armed with swords and short bows, there to serve as scouts or rapidly moving archers. They carried chains on their saddles, and Sartes guessed that they were there to seize prisoners and slaves too. Behind them, he saw the conscripts, easy to recognize in their ragged armor. The regular soldiers followed them, as if to sandwich them in so that they couldn't escape. Sartes could see officers and elite soldiers among them, resplendent in engraved or gilded armor, marked out by red or gold cloaks. At the back of the column came a group in darker colors: slavers and torturers, not there for whatever raid the army was going to conduct, but for its aftermath.

Sartes wet his lips, lifting his horn ready to blow when the time came.

"Not far now," Anka whispered beside him. "Wait for it."

Sartes waited, although that was hard, when the column of soldiers was walking past so close. At any moment, one of the soldiers could have looked round and spotted them, even though they were well hidden amongst the monuments of the burial ground. Any one of them could have seen what was coming and shouted a warning. Then the rebellion would have to withdraw, or risk a much more dangerous battle.

But they didn't look round. They kept going. The soldiers kept marching, the conscripts kept being pushed forward, and Sartes held his breath as the horsemen continued to lead the way.

"Now," Anka whispered, and it almost took Sartes by surprise when she did.

He had to lick his lips again before he could blow his horn, but he managed it. A single high note rang out around the burial ground, and for a moment, everything was still. Then rebels burst from their hiding places ahead of the column, readying bows and firing stones from slings. Sartes saw one hit a horse, so that it reared, throwing its rider from the saddle.

The others drew their blades in response, spurring their horses forward. Sartes swallowed at the sight of the charging war horses and the thundering sound of their hooves. It seemed obvious that they would ride down their attackers, who suddenly seemed too few, and too ill prepared.

Then the horses hit tripwires that Sartes and the others had prepared earlier, and the riders screamed as they fell.

Their horses tumbled, sending riders careening over their backs as they crunched into the ground. Some tried to ride around, only to hit pits lined with spikes. Soon, the riders were trying to leap over their own comrades, and the rebels were shooting at them as they did it. Behind them, Sartes could see the soldiers standing as if they didn't know what to do next.

"Again," Anka said.

Sartes nodded and blew his horn once more.

Now, the burial ground burst into motion. Rebels who had been hiding behind the walls of the ruins pushed at them together using long spars of wood, shoving against spots they had weakened in the night. Stones came tumbling down onto the heads of the soldiers at the edges of the lines, forcing the others to crowd together.

The rebels flung fire pots into the middle of their lines, and they scattered again. Without a solid shield wall, they weren't able to defend against the arrows and stones that rained down on them.

"Now," Anka said, and Sartes blew his horn a final time.

He saw rebels rush from their hiding places. Some rose up from covered pits that looked like freshly dug graves until they struck from them. Others came out of the entrances to the burial ground's catacombs, charging into the sunlight. He saw his father among them, wearing a mail shirt and wielding a hammer large enough to crush through any shield.

All the while, those already in place continued to fire stones and arrows down into the mass of the Empire's soldiers.

Now it was time for Sartes to do his part.

He stepped out in front of them, not knowing if any of them would recognize him. They didn't have to, so long as they listened. He raised his voice over the sounds of the battle.

"Conscripts! My name is Sartes. I escaped from the army to join the rebellion. We are here to rescue you. Join us to fight, or run to safety. You will not be harmed!"

An arrow came toward him, and Sartes dodged to the side, repeating his message. Some of the conscripts looked confused, but at least they weren't joining in the fight while the rebels attacked the main body of soldiers. He saw some break and run, while others threw down their weapons. A few even plunged into the fray, striking at one of the slavers there and dragging him to the ground.

Sartes hung back. Both Anka and his father had been clear on that, but he'd already done his part. Without the conscripts, the Empire's force was far smaller, already crumbling under the assault by the rebels. Taken by surprise, they had no chance to mount a real defense, or reorganize from the long lines of their column into something that could protect their flanks. He saw his father hammering at the shield of an officer, buckling it under the weight of his blows.

Sartes saw a soldier running at him from the battle. For a moment, he thought that maybe one of the conscripts was running to him to get clear of the violence, but the man's sword was out, and he wore the armor of an officer.

"I might die, but at least I'll kill you, traitor!" the officer yelled.

He swung his blade at Sartes, and it was probably ironic that if it hadn't been for his training in the army, Sartes would probably have died right then. As it was, he brought his own sword up, parrying and backing away into the rows of statues.

"You can't run forever, runt," the officer said.

"He doesn't have to," Anka said, stepping in from the side. She thrust a long dagger in past the officer's guard, catching him in the throat. The officer tried to turn to stab her, but Sartes grabbed his arm, holding on until the man fell between them.

"Thank you," Sartes said.

"You're one of us, Sartes," Anka replied. "We look out for one another."

Sartes looked around for another place to help. He saw one of the conscripts who'd joined their side in trouble, frantically defending himself against a pair of slavers armed with clubs. Sartes charged forward.

"This is for my brother!" he yelled, and stabbed the first slaver as he turned. The second swung a set of shackles at his head, then jabbed with his club as Sartes ducked. Sartes cut across the man's leg, then thrust into his chest as he fell.

The rest of the battle didn't take long. With an ambush like that, it was never going to be drawn out, because the rebellion didn't give the Empire's soldiers a chance to fight back the way they were used to. In a matter of minutes, the only soldiers Sartes could see who weren't dead were either freed conscripts or running away.

He looked around at the aftermath of it. He hadn't seen a battle with the army, so he hadn't known what to expect. The reality was hard to look at. There were so many dead bodies there on the ground, piled together so that it was hard to believe that minutes ago they had all been people, walking and breathing. There were dead and injured horses there, brought down by the tripwires, or fallen into pits.

There were members of the rebellion dead too, although there were very few of them, thanks to Anka's plans. Sartes could see injured men and women there, being helped to their feet by their colleagues, and stretchers being brought out of hiding places. Anka had obviously planned for this part too.

It was sickening to see so much death and destruction there. Already, the smell of it was awful, and Sartes knew it would only get worse. It was hard to comprehend the idea of so many people being killed in such a short space of time. Only the thought that if they hadn't done this, these same soldiers would have marauded through a rebel area made it any easier to bear.

"We have to go," Anka said. "Tell the conscripts that they can either scatter or come with us, but they have to decide now. They'll listen better if it comes from you."

Sartes nodded, and stepped out in front of the remaining conscripts to deliver the message. A few more ran off, but the majority stayed. He couldn't decide if that was because they genuinely wanted to join the rebellion, or if they simply didn't have anywhere else to go.

They stood there at the heart of the burial ground, and once more Anka addressed them.

"My friends, today we have won a victory. It has cost us. There is no such thing as a pretty, painless fight. But we must remember what that victory means. It means that young men captured by the Empire now walk free! It means that people who would have been tortured, enslaved, and murdered are safe. Above all, it means that the Empire is one step closer to falling. We have won a victory today, but it won't be our last!"

Sartes was the one who started the chant. It seemed like the obvious thing to do.

"Anka! Anka!"

At first, he was the only one shouting it. Then he heard other voices join his. His father's, Oreth's. The conscripts'. Eventually, the chant reverberated around the burial ground, filling it completely.

They'd found a true leader.

Chapter Thirty Five

Thanos was armored for war, and more than ready to kill.

He had his full armor from the Stade in place, his sword at his side, and a shield on his arm. He had a throwing spear strapped to his back and a dagger in his boot. Even his horse was armored, the barding that would protect it from an errant sword stroke shining in the castle courtyard's sun as he tightened the straps on its saddle.

A second horse held his supplies, although the truth was that Thanos doubted this would last long. He would go out, do what was necessary, and return. Or not. Perhaps he would die doing it. Perhaps he would go and join the rebels on Haylon again. It would be hard to come back here after he had killed a prince of the Empire.

"You're going after Lucious, aren't you?" Stephania said. Thanos looked across as she hurried out into the courtyard. Thanos had been hoping to avoid her, if only because he'd known that this would happen, and because she was the one person there it would be hard to leave.

"What are you doing here?" Thanos asked. "You shouldn't be a part of this."

"Did you think you could slip off without me noticing?" Stephania countered. "The servants do occasionally tell me things, you know."

She looked as beautiful as ever, perfectly poised even with a look of worry that seemed out of place with the rest of her. Was she worried about him?

"I'm doing what I need to do," Thanos said.

"Because he tried to kill you," Stephania said. She reached out to put a hand over his as he cinched his saddle tight.

"Not just that," Thanos said. "He's responsible for Ceres's death. He killed that stable hand. Even now, he's out ravaging the countryside, and King Claudius won't do anything about him."

"You can't expect him to execute Lucious," Stephania said. "It's too much to ask."

"He won't even lock him away," Thanos replied. "If you have a mad dog biting people, even if you used to love it, you put it down."

"And you're going to do that, are you?" Stephania shot back. "What if he kills you?"

Thanos had been hoping that Stephania wouldn't ask that question, because there were no easy answers.

Thanos forced a smile. "I can outfight Lucious. He's never come close to beating me in a practice match."

"And what if he gets lucky?" Stephania asked. "What about all the men he'll have with him? What if he shoots you with a hunting bow from a nice, safe distance, and claims the rebels did it? He gets to be rid of you and have another excuse to go after them."

"I'll be okay," Thanos insisted.

Stephania stepped between him and his horse. "No you *won't*. Even if you do this, you won't be able to come back. And I want you to come back."

That was enough to make Thanos pause. The sheer closeness of Stephania to him had a lot to do with it, but so did the passion he could hear there in her voice. He could hear how much she cared, and the truth was, he felt the same way. If he could have, he would have stayed there with her.

But wanting something and it being possible weren't the same thing.

"I have to do this," Thanos said. "Lucious has to be stopped. He has to *die*."

"Then we'll make sure that happens," Stephania said. "But there are better ways to do it. Smarter ways."

"What do you mean?" Thanos asked.

He felt the brush of Stephania's hand as she reached out to touch his face, then she did something he'd been dreaming about her doing ever since that moment in his rooms. She kissed him. Her lips touched his, and there was something so sweet about her there that he couldn't help kissing her back.

It was a gentle kiss, a delicate one, there and gone too soon, but it was still amazing. It left Thanos breathing quickly as they parted, and he could see the slight parting of Stephania's lips as she looked at him.

"I need you to trust me," she said. "You *do* trust me, Thanos?"

He nodded. There was no one in the castle he trusted more. There was no one there he cared about more.

"Then trust me to do this," Stephania said, putting a hand on Thanos's chest and gently pushing him back from his horse. "I will find a way. A way that doesn't put you in danger, that means that you can still be here. With me."

That part was hard to ignore.

"I'd like that," Thanos said. He looked at Stephania again. It was so hard for him to take his eyes off her. Every small movement she made seemed to draw his gaze, so that it felt as though the whole world consisted of her. "I was so wrong about you before."

"You were," Stephania said with a smile, "but I'm hoping that you'll have plenty of time to learn everything there is to know about me."

There was something about the way she said it that made Thanos tilt his head to one side. "What do you mean?"

Stephania paused, taking a step back. "I thought… oh, I've got it wrong, haven't I? No, it's a stupid idea. I should have known—"

"What, Stephania?" Thanos said.

She seemed to collect herself. "I thought maybe, with the way you were talking, that you might want to go through with the wedding they planned for us both."

That caught Thanos a little by surprise. He hadn't thought that Stephania might still feel that way after everything that had happened with Ceres. He hadn't dared to.

Thoughts of Ceres made Thanos pause. If she'd still been alive, he wouldn't be thinking like this at all. He would have been trying to save her and be with her. But since her death, he had started to realize how much Stephania really meant to him. Stephania had been the one who was there for him since her death. She'd been the one he'd felt his feelings blossoming for.

"But I know," Stephania went on, "it's too soon, and you have a lot to think about, and—"

Thanos caught her by the arms. "I think that's a wonderful idea, Stephania."

She shook her head. "You're just saying that. You don't have to do this just because you think you ought to, Thanos. You don't know what you're saying."

"I do," Thanos insisted. On impulse, he took one of Stephania's hands in both of his, dropping down to one knee. He wanted her to see just how serious he was about this. Yes, Ceres's death still hurt. He suspected that it would never stop hurting. But Stephania made it feel better, and he wanted this.

"Oh, Thanos, stand up," Stephania said with a laugh.

"Not until I've done this," Thanos said. "Stephania, you've been so good to me, and I've started to realize just how much you mean to me. Maybe if all this hadn't happened, we would have already been married, and right now, I can't think of anything else I want. Will you marry me?"

Stephania paused as if she couldn't quite believe that he'd actually said it. Perhaps she couldn't think what to say. Perhaps she was already having second thoughts.

"Yes," she said, throwing her arms around him. "Yes, of course I'll marry you."

Thanos stood, lifting her up, and Stephania laughed. Right then, Thanos felt like doing the same. Everything else in his life was so complicated, so difficult, but this one thing felt so bright and wonderful.

Stephania was like a point of light in the dark, leading him onward.

Chapter Thirty Six

Stephania spent the next few hours in preparations, both for the wedding and … otherwise.

She spent most of it considering the joy of marrying Thanos, the dress that she would wear, the feast that would take place, and what it would be like appearing at court on his arm. She worked on how they would announce it to the other nobles, and of course on all the things that would happen afterwards. Her maids and the ladies of the court bustled about her, seemingly delighting in the news even more than she did. In the midst of it all, she sent one with a quiet message.

"Enough of this for now," she said with a carefully exasperated smile. "I think I'm going to walk the gardens. If I'd known that marrying would involve so much, I wouldn't have gotten Thanos to ask me."

They all laughed along with her, of course. Partly, Stephania knew, that was because they'd learned that it was better to laugh at her jokes. Partly, it was because there wasn't a single one of them who could imagine not wanting to marry someone as handsome and powerful as Thanos. Probably a few laughed at her joke that she could make a prince of the Empire do anything.

She had though. The right touches and looks, being there at the right moments… Her show of timidity in the courtyard had been perfectly judged so that he asked her. Stephania wanted Thanos to remember it as his idea, as much as hers.

Now for other business. She walked gracefully along the corridors of the castle, attended by no more than the bare minimum of ladies-in-waiting and noble friends. She smiled and listened to their gossip as she walked, mentally parsing it into the useful and the unlikely easily enough that she barely had to pay attention to it at all.

The talk of Thanos asking her to marry him brought talk of other proposals: the noble girl who was marrying one brother of a family out on the borders while secretly in love with the other, a union between two merchant houses sealed by an arrangement between two nobles still little more than children, a high-born wife who had deserted her husband as he went to war. Stephania made all the appropriate sympathetic noises as they made their way toward the gardens. She carried a wine bottle with her, along with two glasses.

"All this talk has given me quite a headache," Stephania said as they approached. "Might I beg a moment or two of solitude?"

They agreed, of course. No one there was important enough to disagree with anything Stephania suggested, and they knew it. The ones who didn't had been quietly weeded from her social circle a long time ago, or taught appropriate lessons. They probably didn't all believe her about the headache, given the wine, but even those probably only thought that she was saying goodbye to an admirer now that she was to be married. After all, it was what they would do.

It meant that Stephania was able to step into the gardens alone. She had to admit that the palace gardens were beautiful. There was something about the way the blooms hid their thorns that she found particularly appealing.

Her favorites were the long-stemmed white roses, so delicate looking and carefully cultivated that they seemed almost fragile in comparison to other plants, yet more than capable of twisting around them and strangling them if they took up too much space. Stephania reached out to pluck one, ignoring the thorns and lifting it so that she could drink in the heady scent of it.

The man she sought stood at the far end of the garden. He was in his thirties, with slender features and a pointed beard that only added to the effect. His clothes were of high quality, but less grand than those of the best nobles. If Stephania hadn't known what he was, he might have put her in mind of one of those minor nobles who dabbled in poetry or song, using them as an excuse to tour the great houses and court a wealthier wife, engaging in assignations wherever they could in the meantime.

Probably even her maid believed it was something like that. Stephania hoped so. It would be unfortunate to have to make the girl disappear.

"Xanthos," Stephania said, and stepped forward.

"My lady," he said as she came closer. He had a trace of an accent, but Stephania had never quite been able to work out where it was from. Possibly it was feigned, like so much else about him. "Your radiance outshines the sun itself today. You have another task for me?"

Stephania smiled.

"What happened with Thanos?" she asked. "Why did you fail?"

Xanthos swallowed, seeming suddenly nervous.

"I cannot be held responsible for the Typhoon's failures," Xanthos said. "I told you that things would be uncertain within a battle."

He grinned.

"Besides," he added, "it seems to have worked out for the best."

She had to admit he had a point. Things had worked out for the best, after all. Thanos was not dead, but now he was *hers*. And perhaps, after all, that was just as good.

"Perhaps you're right," she said.

She saw him relax and she uncorked the wine, pouring out two glasses. The wine shone clean and pure in the sunlight of the garden.

She lifted her glass. "To success."

"To us," Xanthos countered, and drank his with such speed that it was obvious he wanted to get through this part of it as quickly as possible.

Stephania sighed, and poured hers out into the nearest bush.

"What are you doing that for?" Xanthos asked, and then shocked realization crossed his face. "No, you didn't, you—"

He gagged, clutching his throat and taking a step toward Stephania. His hand fastened on her dress, clutching weakly. Stephania pulled it away. She watched as foam rose at the corners of his mouth, and he fell to his knees.

"I can't afford loose ends, Xanthos," Stephania said. "As far as the world knows, I love Thanos. I have always loved Thanos. I'm sure you understand."

She watched him fall, and stood there, watching, laughing, until finally his body stopped twitching.

Chapter Thirty Seven

Ceres stood above one of the island's many bays, feeling the wind ruffle her hair as she stood atop the cliff overlooking it. It felt like there might be a storm coming, but for the moment at least the day was perfect.

She could feel the power thrumming within her, in time to the wind and the rhythms of the island. It seemed to push up against the limits of her skin, filling her in a constant roil of energy that seemed to want to crackle out from her with every touch.

She'd felt the power come to her before, she knew what it felt like, but it had always drifted away again in the past, leaving her feeling ordinary again, human again. Now, it sat there even though there was no danger, and Ceres found herself having to adjust with every movement, accustoming herself to the new strength of her body.

She felt like a different person as she stood there on the cliff edge. Whatever had happened to her after walking through the wall of water, after taking the sacred drink, had changed something within her. It had burnt away whatever it was within her that had been blocking this energy from emerging, had left her moving through the world in a new way. Even the way she responded to it was different

She could feel the wind now breathing against her skin, and the whole island was there behind it if she wanted it. She could understand the islanders' connection to their home now, and the way they tried to fit in with what was around them.

But it wasn't her home, and there were things in the world that were worth trying to change. She couldn't sit back and let the Empire do what it wanted to its people, or let those who ran it get away with sending

Thanos to his death. She wanted to see her father and her brother again, too.

Below, Ceres could see the forest folk preparing the vessel that was going to carry her to the Isle Beyond the Mist. They were coming together to craft it, and Ceres could see Eike there among them, joining in where she could. Ceres knew without being told that she wouldn't be taking the girl with her on her voyage. While Ceres had been trying to find a way to control her powers, Eike had found a home to replace the one she'd lost. Ceres couldn't take her away from that.

The way the forest folk crafted her boat kept Ceres watching. Where boat builders back in the Empire would have worked with saws and axes, rivets and tar, the people of the island seemed to be growing a vessel from the living wood of the island. They coaxed and worked, touched the wood and seemed impossibly to stretch it, bringing it together the way a weaver might have spun strands of wool.

They created the boat as Ceres watched, making it rise from the water with smooth, rounded sides and rigging that seemed to be made from creepers. Ceres heard Eoin approaching before she saw him, and the fact that she could hear him when he moved so quietly just showed how in tune with the island she was right then.

He stepped up next to her, and Ceres couldn't help watching him. He stood there with her at the edge, looking as if he could have been rooted in the edge of the cliff.

"It will not be long before your boat is ready," Eoin said. "Our curse has a lot of downsides, but we can work with wood."

"It's incredible," Ceres said. "If you wanted to, you could craft a fleet that could rule the world."

"And why would we want to do that?" Eoin asked. "We're not the Empire, Ceres, to want to rule over others. And we only have so much time in this world, thanks to our curse."

That was a sobering thought. Looking at Eoin there, so strong and so perfect, it was easy to forget that eventually the jungle would claim him as it had claimed so many of the others. Of course he wouldn't want an empire. He had his music, and his people, and that was enough.

"Will you miss me when I'm gone?" Ceres asked.

"Why would I miss you?" Eoin asked with a smile that broke into a laugh at the change of Ceres's expression. "I am with you in spirit."

Ceres's heart rose with those words. She'd thought, in their time on the island, that there had been something there between them. Perhaps if she managed to come back, she could find out.

"I wish that I could journey with you," Eoin said. "But this is a journey for you alone."

Ceres felt a thread of worry at those words. "I don't know the way."

"Your power will set you on the right course," Eoin promised. "You have seen it, after all."

Ceres had, but she'd seen a lot of other things too. She'd seen the violence to follow. And she had seen countless masses chanting her name. Had seen herself as queen.

Queen.

First she had been a slave.

Then a warrior.

And then, one day, somehow, queen.

It did not seem possible.

"Are you ready?" Eoin finally asked, breaking the silence.

Despite all the time she'd spent on the island, it felt to Ceres as though things were moving quickly. She'd expected to have more time. The world seemed to be moving at its own pace, and it wasn't one Ceres was sure she could keep up with.

Even so, Ceres took the first steps down toward the beach. She had a journey to make, and she *did* have to make it. Despite all the power, despite the war, despite everything, only one thing mattered now.

She was going to discover who she really was.

She was going to meet her mother.

Listen to THE SORCERER'S RING series in audio book format!
Now available on:

Amazon
Audible
iTunes

Download Morgan Rice books now!

KINGS AND SORCERERS

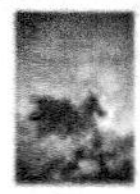

THE SORCERER'S RING

THE SURVIVAL TRILOGY

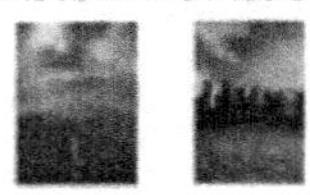

the vampire journals

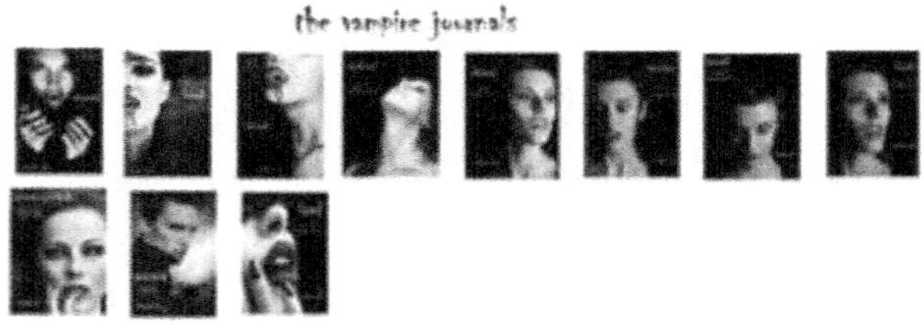

Knight, Heir, Prince

(OF CROWNS AND GLORY—BOOK 3)

Morgan Rice

Morgan Rice

Morgan Rice is the #1 bestselling and USA Today bestselling author of the epic fantasy series THE SORCERER'S RING, comprising seventeen books; of the #1 bestselling series THE VAMPIRE JOURNALS, comprising twelve books; of the #1 bestselling series THE SURVIVAL TRILOGY, a post-apocalyptic thriller comprising three books; of the epic fantasy series KINGS AND SORCERERS, comprising six books; and of the new epic fantasy series OF CROWNS AND GLORY. Morgan's books are available in audio and print editions, and translations are available in over 25 languages.

TURNED (Book #1 in the Vampire Journals), ARENA 1 (Book #1 of the Survival Trilogy), A QUEST OF HEROES (Book #1 in the Sorcerer's Ring) and RISE OF THE DRAGONS (Kings and Sorcerers—Book #1) are each available as a free download on Amazon!

Morgan loves to hear from you, so please feel free to visit www.morganricebooks.com to join the email list, receive a free book, receive free giveaways, download the free app, get the latest exclusive news, connect on Facebook and Twitter, and stay in touch!

Select Acclaim for Morgan Rice

"If you thought that there was no reason left for living after the end of THE SORCERER'S RING series, you were wrong. In RISE OF THE DRAGONS Morgan Rice has come up with what promises to be another brilliant series, immersing us in a fantasy of trolls and dragons, of valor, honor, courage, magic and faith in your destiny. Morgan has managed again to produce a strong set of characters that make us cheer for them on every page.... Recommended for the permanent library of all readers that love a well-written fantasy."

—*Books and Movie Reviews*
Roberto Mattos

"An action packed fantasy sure to please fans of Morgan Rice's previous novels, along with fans of works such as THE INHERITANCE CYCLE by Christopher Paolini .... Fans of Young Adult Fiction will devour this latest work by Rice and beg for more."

—*The Wanderer, A Literary Journal*
(regarding *Rise of the Dragons*)

"A spirited fantasy that weaves elements of mystery and intrigue into its story line. *A Quest of Heroes* is all about the making of courage and about realizing a life purpose that leads to growth, maturity, and excellence .... For those seeking meaty fantasy adventures, the protagonists, devices, and action provide a vigorous set of encounters that focus well on Thor's evolution from a dreamy child to a young adult facing impossible odds

for survival….Only the beginning of what promises to be an epic young adult series."

—*Midwest Book Review* (D. Donovan, eBook Reviewer)

"THE SORCERER'S RING has all the ingredients for an instant success: plots, counterplots, mystery, valiant knights, and blossoming relationships replete with broken hearts, deception and betrayal. It will keep you entertained for hours, and will satisfy all ages. Recommended for the permanent library of all fantasy readers."

—*Books and Movie Reviews*, Roberto Mattos

"In this action-packed first book in the epic fantasy Sorcerer's Ring series (which is currently 14 books strong), Rice introduces readers to 14-year-old Thorgrin "Thor" McLeod, whose dream is to join the Silver Legion, the elite knights who serve the king…. Rice's writing is solid and the premise intriguing."

—*Publishers Weekly*

BOOKS BY MORGAN RICE

THE WAY OF STEEL
ONLY THE WORTHY (Book #1)

OF CROWNS AND GLORY
SLAVE, WARRIOR, QUEEN (Book #1)
ROGUE, PRISONER, PRINCESS (Book #2)
KNIGHT, HEIR, PRINCE (Book #3)
REBEL, PAWN, KING (Book #4)

KINGS AND SORCERERS
RISE OF THE DRAGONS (Book #1)
RISE OF THE VALIANT (Book #2)
THE WEIGHT OF HONOR (Book #3)
A FORGE OF VALOR (Book #4)
A REALM OF SHADOWS (Book #5)
NIGHT OF THE BOLD (Book #6)

THE SORCERER'S RING
A QUEST OF HEROES (Book #1)
A MARCH OF KINGS (Book #2)
A FATE OF DRAGONS (Book #3)
A CRY OF HONOR (Book #4)
A VOW OF GLORY (Book #5)
A CHARGE OF VALOR (Book #6)
A RITE OF SWORDS (Book #7)
A GRANT OF ARMS (Book #8)
A SKY OF SPELLS (Book #9)
A SEA OF SHIELDS (Book #10)

A REIGN OF STEEL (Book #11)
A LAND OF FIRE (Book #12)
A RULE OF QUEENS (Book #13)
AN OATH OF BROTHERS (Book #14)
A DREAM OF MORTALS (Book #15)
A JOUST OF KNIGHTS (Book #16)
THE GIFT OF BATTLE (Book #17)

THE SURVIVAL TRILOGY
ARENA ONE: SLAVERSUNNERS (Book #1)
ARENA TWO (Book #2)
ARENA THREE (Book #3)

VAMPIRE, FALLEN
BEFORE DAWN (Book #1)

THE VAMPIRE JOURNALS
TURNED (Book #1)
LOVED (Book #2)
BETRAYED (Book #3)
DESTINED (Book #4)
DESIRED (Book #5)
BETROTHED (Book #6)
VOWED (Book #7)
FOUND (Book #8)
RESURRECTED (Book #9)
CRAVED (Book #10)
FATED (Book #11)
OBSESSED (Book #12)

Table of Contents

Chapter One

Even without every noble in Delos staring at him, Thanos would have felt the nerves of a groom on his wedding day. He stood by the altar that had been set up in the castle's largest feast hall, and somehow he managed to stand perfectly still—but only because his soldier's training kept him from showing any fear. Standing out in front of all of them, he could feel his stomach knotting with the pressure of it.

Thanos looked about while awaiting his bride. The feast hall swam in white silk and shone with diamonds, hardly a surface there that didn't glitter. Even the servants attending the nobles wore clothes that would have shamed most merchants. As for the nobles themselves, today they looked like something out of a bard's tale, dressed in silk and velvet, dripping with gold and silver.

To Thanos, it was far too much; yet he hadn't exactly been given a say in it. Delos's royals had gotten the wedding the king and queen decided they should have, and anything less than perfection would have disappointed his bride. He glanced over and saw them: King Claudius and Queen Athena, sitting together on thrones carved from ironwood and covered in gold leaf. They sat proudly, obviously delighted by his decision to accept their choice of bride.

The high priest, decked in a robe of gold reflecting the rays of the sun, stood beside him. He seemed like a kindly man, and Thanos, feeling more alone than ever, wanted to take him aside and ask him: *What do you do when you aren't sure that you belong somewhere?*

Yet he could not.

It wasn't just that Thanos was nervous about the wedding. It was so many other things as well. There was the fact that back on Haylon, the rebels there were relying on him to help them to free the Empire. That thought brought a flash of determination with it, because he *would* help them, whatever it took. Yet here he stood in this hall, surrounded by the enemy.

There was also the fact that Lucious was here, standing in the corner, dressed in royal purple and silver, smirking as he eyed the serving girls. Thanos had to fight to keep from walking over there and strangling him with his bare hands.

And then there was the thought that would not let him be:

Ceres.

That brought with it a spike of pain that felt, even now, as though it might burst through his chest. He could still barely believe that she was dead and gone, lost on a prison ship while he'd been on Haylon. Just the thought of that threatened to drag him back toward the darkness that had consumed him when he'd heard the news.

Stephania had pulled him out of that. She'd been the one shining point in it all, the only person in Delos who had brought him any happiness when he had wanted to end it all, when he could not envision a life without Ceres.

It was not that he did not love Stephania; he did. He had come to love her. It was, rather, that he could not let himself forget Ceres. It was as if the two loves still co-existed in his heart. He could not understand it all. Why had Ceres been meant to come into his life only to leave it? Why had Stephania been meant to come into his life at the moment she had? Had Ceres come to him to somehow prepare him to accept Stephania? Or had the two nothing to do with one another?

Music stirred. Thanos turned and his heart caught to see Stephania arrive to the strains of lyre music. His heart beat faster as she walked, all the nobles standing as she went, accompanied by handmaidens who threw rose petals and rang bells to drive away any lingering bad luck. Her dress was a pure, elegant white that made it look as though the whole room had been designed around it. She wore a diamond-studded caul over her golden hair, flowers worked into it with elaborate grace. The veil that covered her face shimmered with silver thread and tiny sapphires that mirrored the shade of the eyes beneath.

Thanos felt his fears melt away.

He watched as she approached, seeming to glide her way through the hall to the altar. She stood before him, and Thanos lifted the veil from her features.

He felt his breath catch. She was always lovely, but today she looked so perfect Thanos could barely believe that she was real. He stood staring at her for so long that he barely heard the priest begin the ceremony.

"The gods have given us many feasts and ceremonies in which to reflect on their glory," the high priest intoned. "Of these, marriage is the most sacred, for without it there would be no continuation of humankind. This marriage is an especially glorious one, between two of the great nobles of this realm. Yet it is also between a young man and a young woman who love one another deeply, and whose happiness should find a place in all our hearts."

He paused to let the words sink in.

"Prince Thanos, will you present your arm to be bound to this woman for all time? To love her and honor her until the gods take you from one another, and to see your families made one?"

He'd hesitated before, but now he didn't. He extended his arm toward the high priest, palm up. "I will."

"And Lady Stephania," the high priest continued, "will you present your arm to be bound to this man for all time? To love him and honor him until the gods take you from one another, and to see your families made one?"

Stephania's smile was the most beautiful thing Thanos had ever seen. She placed her hand in his. "I will."

The high priest wrapped a length of pure white cloth around and around their arms, the wrapping both traditional and elegant.

"Bound together in marriage, you are one flesh, one soul, one family," the high priest said. "May you be happy together always. You may kiss."

Thanos didn't need to be told. It was awkward, bound together like that, but that was always one of the minor amusements of a wedding feast, and they found a way. Thanos tasted Stephania's lips against his, melting into her, and for a moment at least, he could put aside all the other concerns in the world and just be there with her. Even thoughts of Ceres faded into the background, consumed in Stephania's touch.

Of course, Lucious would be the one to break the magic of the moment.

"Well, I'm glad that's done," he said over the silence of the crowd. "Can we start the party now? I need a drink!"

⚜ ⚜ ⚜

If the wedding ceremony had been opulent, the feast that followed was spectacular. So much so that Thanos found himself wondering about the cost of it. It looked as though half the profits from the latest raids had gone into it, with no expense spared. He knew that the king and queen were paying, as a way of showing how happy they were about the wedding, but how many families in the city could something like this have fed?

A glance around let him see tumblers and dancers, musicians and jugglers entertaining knots of nobles. Nobles danced together in swirling circles, while food was spread out in what seemed to Thanos like small mountains of pastries and sweetmeats, oysters and rich desserts.

There was wine, of course, enough that as the festivities continued, things grew wilder. The dancing sped up, with people spinning between partners almost faster than Thanos could follow. The king and queen had already retired, along with some of the older nobles, leaving the room. It was like a signal to the partygoers to put aside those inhibitions that remained.

Stephania was currently being whirled around in the traditional farewell dance, where the bride danced quickly between all the eligible young men in the room, before she would head back to Thanos's arms at the finish. Traditionally, it was a way for the bride to show how happy she was with her choice compared to all she was rejecting. More informally, it gave the young men a chance to show off to any of the other young noble women watching.

To Thanos's surprise, Lucious didn't join in the dance. He'd half expected the prince to do something foolish like trying to steal a kiss.

Although, compared to the part where he'd tried to have Thanos killed, that would have been relatively innocuous.

Instead, the prince swaggered over while the dance was still in progress, pushing his way through the crowd with casual arrogance as he held a crystal goblet of the finest wine. Thanos looked at him and tried to find any similarity between them. They were both the king's offspring, but Thanos could never imagine being anything like Lucious.

"It's a beautiful wedding," Lucious said to him. "All the things I like best: good food, better wine, plenty of serving girls around for later."

"Watch yourself, Lucious," Thanos said.

"I have a better idea," Lucious countered. "Why don't we both watch that lovely bride of yours, spinning between so many men? Of course, with it being Stephania, we could have a small wager on which of them she's slept with."

Thanos's hands clenched into fists. "Are you just here to cause trouble? Because if so, you can get out."

Lucious's smile widened. "And how would that look, you trying to throw out the heir to the throne from your wedding? That wouldn't go well."

"Not for you."

"Remember your place, Thanos," Lucious snapped back.

"Oh, I know my place," Thanos said in a dangerous voice. "We both do, don't we?"

That got a faint flicker of reaction from Lucious. Even if Thanos hadn't known it, it would have been confirmation: Lucious knew about the circumstances of Thanos's birth. He knew they were half-brothers.

"Curse you and your marriage," Lucious said.

"You're just jealous," Thanos countered. "I know you wanted Stephania for yourself, and now I'm the one marrying her. I'm the one who didn't run away in the Stade. I'm the one who actually fought on Haylon. We both know what else I am. So what's left for you, Lucious? You're just a thug the people of Delos need protecting from."

Thanos heard the crack as Lucious's hand tightened around his crystal goblet, squeezing until it shattered.

"You like to protect the lesser orders, don't you?" Lucious said. "Well, think about this: while you've been planning a wedding, I've been crushing villages. I will continue to do it. In fact, while you're still in your marriage bed tomorrow morning, I'll be riding out to teach another bunch of peasants a lesson. And there is *nothing* you can do about it, whoever you think you are."

Thanos wanted to hit Lucious then. He wanted to hit him and keep hitting him until there was nothing left but a bloody smear on the marble floor. The only thing that stopped him was the touch of Stephania's hand on his arm, approaching as her dance ended.

"Oh, Lucious, you've spilled your wine," she said with a smile that Thanos wished he could match. "That won't do at all. Allow one of my attendants to fetch you more."

"I'll get my own," Lucious replied with obvious bad grace. "They got me this one, and look what happened to it."

He stalked off, and only the pull of Stephania's hand on his arm stopped Thanos from following.

"Leave it," Stephania said. "I told you there are better ways, and there are. Trust me."

"He can't just get away with all he's done," Thanos insisted.

"He won't. Look at it this way though," she said. "Who would you rather spend the evening with? Lucious, or me?"

That brought a smile to Thanos's lips. "You. Definitely you."

Stephania kissed him. "Good answer."

Thanos felt her hand slip into his, pulling him in the direction of the doors. The other nobles there let them pass, with occasional laughs about what would happen next. Thanos followed as Stephania led the way to Thanos's rooms, pushing the door open and heading in the direction of the bed chamber. There, she turned to him, throwing her arms around his neck and kissing him deeply.

"You don't have any regrets?" Stephania asked, as she stepped back from him. "You're happy you married me?"

"I'm very happy," Thanos assured her. "What about you?"

"It's all I ever wanted," Stephania said. "And you know what I want now?"

"What?"

Thanos saw her reach up, and her dress fell from her in waves.

"You."

⚜ ⚜ ⚜

Thanos woke to the first rays of sunlight spilling through the windows. Beside him, he could feel the warm pressure of Stephania's presence, one of her arms thrown across him as she slept curled against him. Thanos smiled at the love welling up inside him. He was happier right now than he had been in a long time.

If he hadn't heard the clink of harness and the whinnying of horses, he might have curled up against Stephania again and gone back to sleep, or woken her with a kiss. As it was, he rose, heading over to the window.

He was just in time to see Lucious leaving the castle, riding at the head of a group of soldiers, pennants flying in the wind as if he were some knight-errant on a quest rather than a butcher preparing to attack a defenseless village. Thanos looked out at him, then over at where Stephania was still sleeping.

Silently, he started to dress.

He couldn't stand by. He couldn't, not even for Stephania. She'd talked about better ways of dealing with Lucious, but what did they involve? Politeness and offering him wine? No, Lucious had to be stopped, right now, and there was only one way to do it.

Quietly, taking care not to wake Stephania, Thanos slipped from the room. Once he was clear, he ran for the stables, shouting for a servant to bring him his armor.

It was time for justice.

Chapter Two

Berin could feel the excitement, the nervous energy palpable in the air the moment he stepped into the tunnels. He weaved his way underground, following Anka, Sartes by his side, passing guards who nodded with respect, rebels who hurried every which way. He walked through the Watcher's Gate and felt the turn the Rebellion had taken.

Now, it seemed, they had a chance.

"This way," Anka said, waving to a lookout. "The others await us."

They walked down corridors of bare stone that looked as if they had stood forever. The Ruins of Delos, deep underground. Berin ran his hand along the smooth stone, admiring them as only a smith could, and marveled at how long these had stood, at who had built them. Maybe they even dated back to the days when the Ancient Ones had walked, long before anyone could remember.

And that made him think, with a pang, of the daughter he had lost.

Ceres.

Berin was yanked from that thought by the clang of hammers on metal, by the sudden heat of forge fires as they passed an opening. He saw a dozen men toiling away as they tried to produce breastplates and short swords. It reminded him of his old smithy, and brought back memories of the days when his family hadn't been torn apart.

Sartes seemed to be staring, too.

"Are you all right?" Berin asked.

He nodded.

"I miss her too," Berin replied, putting a hand on his shoulder, knowing he was thinking of Ceres, who always lingered by the forge.

"We all do," Anka chimed in.

For a moment the three of them stood there, and Berin knew that they all understood how much Ceres had meant to them.

He heard Anka sigh.

"All we can do is keep fighting," she added, "and keep forging weapons. We need you, Berin."

He tried to focus.

"Are they doing everything I instructed?" he asked. "Are they heating the metal enough before quenching? It won't harden otherwise."

Anka smiled.

"Check for yourself after the meeting."

Berin nodded. At least in some small way he could be useful.

⚜ ⚜ ⚜

Sartes walked by his father's side, following Anka as they continued past the forge and deeper through the tunnels. There were more people in them than he could have believed. Men and women were gathering supplies, practicing with weapons, pacing the halls. Sartes recognized several of them as former conscripts, freed from the army's clutches.

They finally came upon a cavernous space, set with stone plinths that might once have held statues. By the light of flickering candles, Sartes could see the leaders of the rebellion, awaiting them. Hannah, who had argued against the attack, now looked as happy as if she'd proposed it. Oreth, one of Anka's main deputies now, leaned his slender frame against the wall, smiling to himself. Sartes spotted the larger bulk of the former wharf hand Edrin on the edge of the candlelight, while Yeralt's jewels shone in it, the merchant's son looking almost out of place among the rest as they laughed and joked among themselves.

They fell silent as the three of them approached, and Sartes could see the difference now. Before, they'd listened to Anka almost grudgingly. Now, after the ambush, there was respect there as she walked forward. She even looked more like a leader to Sartes, walking straighter, appearing more confident.

"Anka, Anka, Anka!" Oreth began, and soon the others took up the chant, as the rebels had after the battle.

Sartes joined in, hearing the rebel leader's name echo around the space. He only stopped when Anka gestured for silence.

"We did well," Anka said, with a smile of her own. It was one of the first Sartes had seen since the battle. She'd been too busy trying to arrange to get their casualties away from the burial ground safely. She had a talent for seeing to the details of things that had blossomed in the rebellion.

"*Well?*" Edrin asked. "We smashed them."

Sartes heard the thud of the man's fist against his palm as he emphasized the point.

"We destroyed them," Yeralt agreed, "thanks to your leadership."

Anka shook her head. "We beat them together. We beat them because we all did our parts. And because Sartes brought us the plans."

Sartes found himself pushed forward by his father. He hadn't been expecting this.

"Anka is right," Oreth said. "We owe Sartes our thanks. He brought us the plans, and he was the one to persuade the conscripts not to fight. The rebellion has more members, thanks to him."

"Half-trained conscripts though," Hannah said. "Not real soldiers."

Sartes looked around at her. She'd been quick to argue against him taking part at all. He didn't like her, but it wasn't about that in the rebellion. They were all a part of something bigger than themselves.

"We beat them," Anka said. "We won a battle, but that isn't the same thing as smashing the Empire. We still have a lot ahead of us."

"And they still have a lot of soldiers," Yeralt said. "A long war against them could prove costly for all of us."

"You're counting the cost now?" Oreth countered. "This isn't some business investment, where you want to see the balance sheets before you get involved."

Sartes could hear the annoyance there. When he'd first come to the rebels, he'd expected them to be some big, unified thing, thinking of nothing but the need to defeat the Empire. He'd found out that in a lot of ways they were just people, all with their own hopes and dreams, wishes and wants. It only made it more impressive that Anka had found ways to hold them together after Rexus died.

"It's the biggest investment there is," Yeralt said. "We put in all we have. We risk our lives in the hope that things will get better. I'm in as much danger as the rest of you if we fail."

"We won't fail," Edrin said. "We beat them once. We'll beat them again. We know where they're going to attack and when. We can be waiting for them every time."

"We can do more than that," Hannah said. "We've shown people that we can beat them, so why not go out and take things back from them?"

"What did you have in mind?" Anka asked. Sartes could see that she was considering it.

"We take villages back one by one," Hannah said. "We get rid of the Empire's soldiers in them before Lucious can get close. We show the people there what's possible, and he'll get a nasty surprise when they rise up against him."

"And when Lucious and his men kill them for rising up?" Oreth demanded. "What then?"

"Then it just shows how evil he is," Hannah insisted.

"Or people see that we can't protect them."

Sartes looked around, surprised they were taking the idea seriously.

"We could leave people in the villages so that they don't fall," Yeralt suggested. "We have the conscripts with us now."

"They won't stand against the army for long if it comes," Oreth shot back. "They'd die along with the villagers."

Sartes knew he was right. The conscripts hadn't had the training that the toughest soldiers in the army had. Worse, they'd suffered so much at the hands of the army that most of them would probably be terrified.

He saw Anka gesture for silence. This time, it took a little longer in coming.

"Oreth has a point," she said.

"Of course you'd agree with *him*," Hannah shot back.

"I'm agreeing because he's right," Anka said. "We can't just go into villages, declare them free, and hope for the best. Even with the conscripts, we don't have enough fighters. If we join together in one place, we give the Empire an opportunity to crush us. If we go after every village, they'll pick us apart piecemeal."

"If enough villages can be persuaded to rise up, and I persuade my father to hire mercenaries…" Yeralt suggested. Sartes noted he didn't finish the thought. The merchant's son didn't have an answer, not really.

"Then what?" Anka asked. "We'll have the numbers? If it were that simple, we would have overthrown the Empire years ago."

"We have better weapons now thanks to Berin," Edrin pointed out. "We know their plans thanks to Sartes. We have the advantage! Tell her, Berin. Tell her about the blades you've made."

Sartes looked around to his father, who shrugged.

"It's true I've made good swords, and the others here have made plenty of passable ones. It's true that some of you will have armor now, rather than being cut down. But I'll tell you this: it's about more than the sword. It's about the hand that wields it. An army is like a blade. You can make it as big as you want, but without a core of good steel, it will break the first time you test it."

Maybe if the others had spent more time making weapons, they would have understood how seriously his father meant his words. As it was, Sartes could see they weren't convinced.

"What else can we do?" Edrin asked. "We're not just going to throw away our advantage by sitting back and waiting. I say that we start making a list of villages to free. Unless you have a better idea, Anka?"

"I do," Sartes said.

His voice was quieter than he intended. He stepped forward, his heart pounding, surprised that he had spoken. He was all too aware that he was far younger than anyone else there. He'd played his part in the battle, he'd even killed a man, but there was still a part of him that felt as though he shouldn't be speaking there.

"So it's settled," Hannah started to say. "We—"

"I said I have a better idea," Sartes said, and this time, his voice carried.

The others looked over at him.

"Let my son speak," his father said. "You've said yourselves that he helped to hand one victory to you. Maybe he can keep you from dying now."

"What's your idea, Sartes?" Anka asked.

They were all looking at him. Sartes forced himself to raise his voice, thinking about how Ceres would have spoken, but also about the confidence Anka had shown before.

"We can't go to the villages," Sartes said. "It's what they want us to do. And we can't just rely on the maps I brought, because even if they haven't realized that we know their movements, they will soon. They're trying to goad us out into the open."

"We know all this," Yeralt said. "I thought you said you had a plan."

Sartes didn't back down.

"What if there were a way to hit the Empire where they don't expect it and gain tough fighters into the bargain? What if we could make people rise up with a symbolic victory that would be bigger than protecting a village?"

"What did you have in mind?" Anka asked.

"We free the combatlords in the Stade," Sartes said.

A long, stunned silence followed, as the others stared at him. He could see the doubt in their faces, and Sartes knew he had to keep going.

"Think about it," he said. "Almost all combatlords are slaves. The nobles throw them in to die like toys. Most of them would be grateful for the chance to get away, and they can fight better than any soldiers."

"It's insane," Hannah said. "Attacking the heart of the city like that. There would be guards everywhere."

"I like it," Anka said.

The others looked at her, and Sartes felt a rush of gratitude for her support.

"They wouldn't expect it," she added.

Another silence fell over the room.

"We wouldn't need mercenaries," Yeralt finally chimed in, rubbing his chin.

"People would rise up," Edrin added.

"We'd have to do it when the Killings were on," Oreth pointed out. "That way, all the combatlords would be in one place, and there would be people there to see it happen."

"There won't be more Killings before the Blood Moon festival," his father said. "That's six weeks. In six weeks, I can make a lot of weapons."

This time, Hannah fell silent, perhaps sensing the tide turn.

"So we're agreed?" Anka asked. "We'll free the combatlords during the Blood Moon festival?"

One by one, Sartes saw the others nod. Even Hannah did, eventually. He felt his father's hand on his shoulder. He saw the approval in his eyes, and it meant the world to him.

He only prayed that his plan would not get them all killed.

CHAPTER THREE

Ceres dreamed, and in her dreams, she saw armies clashing. She saw herself fighting at their head, dressed in armor that shone in the sun. She saw herself leading a vast nation, fighting a war that would determine the very fate of mankind.

Yet in it all, she also saw herself squinting, searching for her mother. She reached for a sword, and looked down to see it was not yet there.

Ceres woke with a start. It was night, and the sea before her, lit by the moonlight, was endless. As she bobbed in her small ship, she saw no sign of land. Only the stars convinced her that she was still keeping her small craft on the right course.

Familiar constellations shone overhead. There was the Dragon's Tail, low in the sky beneath the moon. There was the Ancient's Eye, formed around one of the brightest stars in the stretch of blackness. The ship that the forest folk had half built, half grown seemed never to deviate from the route Ceres had picked out, even when she had to rest or eat.

Off the starboard side of the boat, Ceres saw lights in the water. Luminous jellyfish floated past like underwater clouds. Ceres saw the faster figure of some dart-like fish slipping through the shoal, snapping up jellyfish with every pass and hurrying through before the tendrils of the others could touch it. Ceres watched until they disappeared down into the depths.

She ate a piece of the sweet, succulent fruit the islanders had stocked her boat with. When she'd set off it had seemed as though there was enough to last for weeks. Now, it didn't seem like quite so much. She found herself thinking of the leader of the forest folk, so handsome in a strange, asymmetrical way, with his curse lending him patches where his skin was mossy green or roughened like bark. Would he be back on the island, playing his strange music and thinking of her?

Around Ceres, mist started to rise up from the water, thickening and reflecting fragments of the moonlight even as it blocked out her view of the night sky above. It swirled and shifted around the boat, tendrils of fog reaching out like fingers. Thoughts of Eoin seemed to lead inexorably to thoughts of Thanos. Thanos, who'd been killed on the shores of Haylon before Ceres could tell him that she hadn't meant any of the harsh things she'd said when he left. There in the boat alone, Ceres couldn't get away from just how much she missed him. The love she'd felt for him felt like a thread pulling her back toward Delos, even though Thanos was no longer there.

Thinking of Thanos hurt. The memory felt like an open wound that might never close. There were so many things she needed to do, but none of them would bring him back. There were so many things she would have said if he were there, but he wasn't. There was only the emptiness of the mist.

The mist continued to coil around the boat, and now Ceres could see shards of rock sticking up out of the water. Some were razor-edged black basalt, but others were in rainbow colors, seeming like giant precious stones set in the roiling blue of the ocean. Some had markings on them that swirled and spiraled, and Ceres wasn't sure whether they were natural, or if some long distant hand had carved them.

Did her mother lie somewhere beyond them?

The thought brought a thrill of excitement in Ceres, rising up through her like the mist that swirled around the boat. She was going to see her mother. Her real mother, not the one who had always hated her, and who had sold her to slavers at the first opportunity. Ceres didn't know what this woman would be like, but just the opportunity to find out filled her with excitement as she guided the small boat along past the rocks.

Strong currents pulled at her boat, threatening to pull the rudder from her hand. If she hadn't had the strength that came from the power within her, Ceres doubted that she would have been able to hold on. She pulled the rudder to the side, and her small boat responded with an almost living grace, slipping past one of the rocks almost close enough to touch it.

She sailed on through the rocks, and with every one she passed, she found herself thinking about how much closer she was getting to her mother. What kind of woman would she be? In her visions, she'd been indistinct, but Ceres could imagine, and hope. Maybe she would be kind, and gentle, and loving; all the things she'd never had from her supposed mother back in Delos.

What would her mother think of her? That thought caught at Ceres as she guided the boat onward through the mist. She didn't know what was ahead. Maybe her mother would look at her and see someone who hadn't been able to succeed in the Stade, who had been nothing more than a slave in the Empire, who had lost the person she loved most. What if her mother rejected her? What if she were harsh, or cruel, or unforgiving?

Or maybe, just maybe, she would be proud.

Ceres came out of the mist so suddenly that it might have been a curtain lifting, and now the sea was flat, free of the tooth-like rocks that had jutted from it before. Instantly, she could see that there was something different. The light of the moon seemed brighter somehow, and around it, nebulae spun in stains of color on the night. Even the stars seemed changed, so that now, Ceres couldn't pick out the familiar constellations there had been before. A comet streaked its way across the horizon, fiery red mixed with yellows and other colors that had no equivalent in the world below.

Stranger than that, Ceres felt the power within her pulse, as though responding to this place. It seemed to stretch within her, opening out and allowing her to experience this new place in a hundred ways she'd never thought of before.

Ceres saw a shape rise from the water, a long, serpentine neck rising up before plunging back beneath the waves with a splash of spray. The creature rose again briefly, and Ceres had the impression of something huge swimming past in the water before it was gone. What looked like birds flitted through the moonlight, and it was only as they got closer that Ceres saw that they were silvery moths, larger than her head.

Her eyes suddenly growing heavy with sleep, Ceres lashed the tiller in place, lay down, and let sleep overcome her.

⚜ ⚜ ⚜

Ceres woke to the shriek of birds. She blinked in the sunlight as she sat up, and saw that they weren't birds after all. Two creatures with the bodies of great cats wheeled overhead on eagle-like wings, raptor beaks wide as they called. They showed no signs of coming closer though, merely circling the boat before flying off into the distance.

Ceres watched them, and because she was watching them, she saw the tiny speck of an island they were heading for on the horizon. As quickly as she could, Ceres raised the small sail again, trying to catch the wind that rushed past her to push herself toward the island.

The speck grew larger, and what looked like more rocks rose out of the ocean as Ceres got closer, but these weren't the same as the ones that had been there in the mist. These were square-edged, built things, crafted in rainbow marble. Some of them looked like the spires of great buildings, long sunk beneath the waves.

Half an arch stuck out, so huge that Ceres couldn't imagine what might have passed beneath it. She looked down over the side of the boat, and the water was so clear that she could make out the sea bed below. It wasn't far to the bottom, and Ceres could see the wreckage of long past buildings down there. It was close enough that Ceres could have swum down to them just by holding her breath. She didn't, though, both because of the things she'd already seen in the water and because of what lay ahead.

This was it. The island where she would get the answers she needed. Where she would learn about her power.

Where she would, finally, meet her mother.

Chapter Four

Lucious swung his blade overhand, exulting in the way it glinted in the dawn light, in the instant before he cut down the old man who had dared to get in his way. Around him, more commoners fell at the hands of his men: the ones who dared to resist, and any stupid enough to simply be in the wrong place at the wrong time.

He smiled as the screams echoed around him. He liked it when the peasants tried to fight, because it just gave his men an excuse to show them how weak they really were compared to their betters. How many had he killed now in raids like this? He hadn't bothered to keep count. Why should he save the least speck of attention for their kind?

Lucious looked around as peasants started to run, and gestured to a few of his men. They set off after them. Running was almost better than fighting, because there was a challenge to hunting them like the prey they were.

"Your horse, your highness?" one of the men asked, leading Lucious's stallion.

Lucious shook his head. "My bow, I think."

The man nodded and passed Lucious an elegant recurve bow of white ash, mixed with horn and set with silver. He nocked an arrow, drew back the string, and let it fly. Away in the distance, one of the running peasants went down.

There were no more to fight, but that didn't mean they were done here. Not by a long way. Hiding peasants, he'd found, could be as amusing as running or fighting ones in their way. There were so many different ways to torture the ones who looked as though they had gold, and so many ways to execute the ones who might have rebel sympathies. The burning wheel, the gibbet, the noose … what would it be today?

Lucious gestured to a couple of his men to start kicking open doors. Occasionally, he liked to burn out those who hid, but houses were more valuable than peasants. A woman came running out, and Lucious caught her, throwing her casually in the direction of one of the slavers who had taken to following him around like gulls after a fishing vessel.

He stalked into the village's temple. The priest was already on the ground, holding a broken nose, while Lucious's men gathered gold and silver ornaments into a sack. A woman in the robes of a priestess stood to confront him. Lucious noted a flicker of blonde hair straying from under her cowl, a certain fine-featured resemblance that made him pause.

"You can't do this," the woman insisted. "We are a temple!"

Lucious grabbed her, pulling away the hood of her robes to look at her. She wasn't the double of Stephania—no lower-born woman could manage that—but she was close enough to be worth keeping for a while. At least until he got bored.

"I have been sent by your king," Lucious said. "Do *not* try to tell me what I cannot do!"

Too many people had tried that in his life. They'd tried to put limits on him, when he was the one person in the Empire on whom there should be no limits. His parents tried, but he would be king one day. He *would* be king, whatever he'd found in the library when old Cosmas thought he was too stupid to understand it. Thanos would learn his place.

Lucious's hand tightened in the hair of the priestess. Stephania would learn her place as well. How dare she marry Thanos like that, as if he were the prince to be desired? No, Lucious would find a way to make that right. He would split Thanos and Stephania as easily as he split open the heads of those who came at him. He would claim Stephania in marriage, both because she was Thanos's and because she would make the perfect ornament for someone of his rank. He would enjoy that, and until then, the priestess he'd grabbed would make a suitable substitute.

He tossed her to one of his men to watch, and set out to see what other amusements he could find in the village. As he got outside, he saw two of his men tying one of the villagers who'd run to a tree, arms spread wide.

"Why have you let this one live?" Lucious demanded.

One of them smiled. "Tor here was telling me about something the northerners do. They call it the Blood Eagle."

Lucious liked the sound of that. He was about to ask what it involved when he heard the shout of one of the lookouts, there to watch for rebels. Lucious looked around, but instead of an approaching horde of common scum, he saw a single figure riding on a mount easily the size of his own. Lucious recognized the armor instantly.

"Thanos," he said. He snapped his fingers. "Well, it looks as though today is about to get more interesting than I thought. Bring me my bow again."

⚜ ⚜ ⚜

Thanos spurred his horse forward as he saw Lucious and what his half-brother was doing. Any lingering doubts he'd had about leaving Stephania behind burned away in the heat of his anger as he saw the dead peasants, the slavers, the man tied to the tree.

He saw Lucious step out and raise a bow. For a moment, Thanos couldn't believe that he would do it, but why not? Lucious had tried to kill him before.

He saw the arrow fly out from the bow and raised his shield just in time. The head struck the metal facing of his shield before clattering off. A second arrow followed, and this time it punched through, stopping only inches from Thanos's face.

Thanos forced his horse to a charge as a third arrow whizzed past him. He saw Lucious and his men diving out of the way as he careened through the spot where they'd been standing. He wheeled and drew his sword, just as Lucious regained his feet.

"Thanos, so fast. Anyone would think you were eager to see me."

Thanos leveled his sword at Lucious's heart. "This stops now, Lucious. I won't let you kill any more of our people."

"Our people?" Lucious countered. "They are *my* people, Thanos. Mine to do what I wish with. Allow me to demonstrate."

Thanos saw him draw his sword and start toward the man tied to the tree. Thanos realized what his half-brother was going to do and set his horse in motion once more.

"Stop him," Lucious commanded.

His men leapt to obey. One stepped toward Thanos, jabbing a spear up toward his face. Thanos deflected it with his shield, hacking the head from the weapon with his blade and then kicking out to send the man sprawling. He stabbed down as another ran at him, thrusting down through the shoulder of the man's mail and drawing his blade out again.

He forced himself forward, through the press of opponents. Lucious was still advancing on the victim he'd chosen. Thanos swung his sword down at one of Lucious's thugs and hurried forward as Lucious drew his own blade back. Thanos barely managed to interject his shield as the blow came in a ring of metal on metal.

Lucious grabbed his shield.

"You're predictable, Thanos," he said. "Compassion was always your weakness."

He pulled, hard enough that Thanos found himself yanked from the saddle. He rolled in time to avoid a sword blow, and pulled his arm free from the straps of his shield. He took a two-handed grip on his sword as Lucious's men closed in again. He saw his horse run clear, but that meant that now he didn't have the advantage of height.

"Kill him," Lucious said. "We'll blame it on the rebels."

"You're good at trying that, aren't you?" Thanos shot back. "It's a pity you aren't any good at finishing the job."

One of Lucious's men rushed him then, swinging a spiked mace. Thanos stepped inside the arc of the blow, cutting diagonally, then spinning away with his sword extended to keep the others at bay.

They came in quickly then, as if knowing that none of them could hope to defeat Thanos one on one. Thanos gave ground, putting his back against the wall of the nearest house so that his opponents couldn't surround him. There were three men near him now, one with an axe, one with a short sword, and one with a curved blade like a sickle.

Thanos kept his sword close, watching them, not wanting to give any of the mercenaries a chance to tangle the blade long enough for the others to slip in.

The one on Thanos's right tried a thrust with his short sword. Thanos partly parried it, feeling it clatter off his armor. Some instinct made him spin and drop, just in time for the left-hand man's axe to pass overhead. Thanos slashed at ankle height to bring the thug down, then reversed his blade and thrust backward, hearing a cry as the first man ran in.

The one with the curved blade attacked more cautiously.

"Attack him! Kill him!" Lucious demanded, obviously impatient. "Oh, I'll do it myself!"

Thanos parried as the prince joined the fight. He doubted that Lucious would have done it if there hadn't been another man there to help him, and maybe there would be more on the way. Really, all Lucious had to do was delay things, and Thanos might find himself overwhelmed by sheer numbers.

So Thanos didn't wait. Instead, he attacked. He threw blow after blow, alternating between Lucious and the thug Lucious had brought with him, building the rhythm of it. Then, suddenly, he paused. The sickle wielder parried empty air. Thanos cut into the gap, and the man's head went flying.

He was on Lucious in an instant, binding blade to blade. Lucious kicked out at him, but Thanos swayed aside from the blow, reaching over the guard of Lucious's sword to get one hand onto the pommel. Thanos yanked upward and wrenched the blade from Lucious's hands, then struck sideways. His blade clanged from Lucious's breastplate. Lucious drew a dagger and Thanos changed his grip on his blade, swinging low with the hilt end so that the cross-guard hooked around Lucious's knee.

He pulled and Lucious went down. Thanos kicked the dagger from his hand with crunching force.

"Tell me again how compassion is my weakness," Thanos said, lifting the point of his sword over Lucious's throat.

"You wouldn't," Lucious said. "You're just trying to frighten me."

"Frighten you?" Thanos said. "If I thought frightening you would work, I'd have scared you half to death years ago. No, I'm going to end this."

"End it?" Lucious said. "This doesn't *end*, Thanos. Not until I've *won*."

"You'd be waiting a long time for that," Thanos assured him.

He raised the sword. He had to do this. Lucious had to be stopped.

"Thanos!"

Thanos looked over at the sound of Stephania's voice. To his astonishment, he saw her approaching, riding alone at a full gallop. She wore a riding outfit that was a long way from her usual elegant dresses, and from the disheveled state of it, it looked as though she'd thrown it on in a hurry.

"Thanos, don't!" she cried as she got closer.

Thanos gripped his sword tighter. "After all he's done, do you think he doesn't deserve it?"

"It's not about what he deserves," Stephania said, dismounting as she got closer. "It's about what you deserve. If you kill him, they'll kill you for it. That's how it works, and I will *not* lose you like that."

"Listen to her, Thanos," Lucious said from the ground.

"Be quiet," Stephania snapped. "Or do you want to goad him into killing you?"

"He has to be stopped," Thanos said.

"Not like this," Stephania insisted. Thanos felt her hand on his arm, pushing the sword away. "Not in a way that gets you killed. You swore you would be mine for the rest of our lives. Did you really mean for it to be so short?"

"Stephania—" Thanos began, but she didn't let him finish.

"And what about me?" she asked. "How much danger will I be in if my husband kills the heir to the throne? No, Thanos. Stop this. Do it for me."

If anyone else had asked, Thanos might still have gone through with it. There was too much at stake. But he couldn't risk Stephania. He thrust down into the dirt, missing Lucious's head by an inch. Lucious was already rolling away, running for a horse.

"You'll regret this!" Lucious called back. "I promise you'll regret this!"

Chapter Five

Thanos saw the guards awaiting him on the long run into the city gates, as he and Stephania returned home. He raised his chin and kept on riding. He had expected this. And he wouldn't run from it.

Stephania obviously saw them too. Thanos saw her stiffen in the saddle, going from relaxed to prim and formal in an instant. It was as though a mask had slid down in front of her features, and Thanos found himself reaching out automatically to slide a hand over hers as she held the reins.

The guards crossed their halberds to bar the way as they approached, and Thanos drew his horse to a halt. He kept it between Stephania and the guards, just in case Lucious had somehow bribed men to attack him. He saw an officer step out from the knot of guards and salute.

"Prince Thanos, welcome back to Delos. My men and I have been instructed to escort you to see the king."

"And if my husband does not wish to travel with you?" Stephania asked, in a tone that could have commanded the whole Empire.

"Forgive me, my lady," the officer said, "but the king has given us clear orders."

Thanos raised a hand before Stephania could argue.

"I understand," he said. "I'll go with you."

The guards led the way, and to their credit, they managed to make it look like the escort they claimed it was. They led the way through Delos, and Thanos noted that the route they picked was one through the most beautiful parts of the city, sticking to the tree-lined avenues that held noble houses, avoiding the worst parts even when they formed a more direct route. Perhaps they were simply trying to stick to the safer areas.

Perhaps, though, they thought that nobles like Thanos and Stephania wouldn't want to see the misery elsewhere.

Soon, the walls of the castle towered above. The guards led the way through its gates, and grooms took their horses. The walk through the castle felt more confined, with so many guards surrounding them in the narrow spaces of the castle corridors. Stephania took Thanos's hand, and he squeezed it gently in reassurance.

When they reached the royal apartments, members of the royal bodyguard blocked the way at the door.

"The king wishes to speak to Prince Thanos alone," one said.

"I am his wife," Stephania said in a tone so cold Thanos suspected most people would have stepped aside instantly.

It didn't seem to affect the royal bodyguard at all. "Nevertheless."

"It will be all right," Thanos said.

When he stepped inside, the king was waiting for him. King Claudius stood, leaning on a sword whose hilt formed the tentacles of a twisting kraken. It came almost to the level of his chest, and Thanos had no doubt that the edge would be razor sharp. Thanos heard the click of the door shutting behind him.

"Lucious told me what you did," the king said.

"I'm sure he came running straight to you," Thanos replied. "Did he also tell you what he was doing at the time?"

"He was doing what he was commanded to," the king snapped, "in order to deal with the rebellion. Yet you went out and attacked him. You killed his men. He says you defeated him through trickery, and would have killed him too if Stephania hadn't intervened."

"How does butchering villagers stop the rebellion?" Thanos countered.

"You're more interested in peasants than in your own actions," King Claudius said. He lifted the sword he held as though weighing it. "It is treason to attack the king's son."

"*I* am the king's son," Thanos reminded him. "You didn't execute Lucious when he tried to have me killed."

"Your birth is the only reason you are still alive," King Claudius replied. "You are my son, but so is Lucious. You do *not* get to threaten him."

Anger rose up in Thanos then. "I don't get anything that I can see. Not even the acknowledgment of who I am."

There were statues in one corner of the room, depicting famous ancestors of the royal line. They were out of the way, almost hidden away, as if the king didn't want to be reminded of them. Even so, Thanos pointed to them.

"Lucious can look at those and claim authority going back to the days when the Empire first rose," he said. "He can claim the rights of all those who gained the throne when the Ancient Ones left Delos. What do I have? Vague rumors about my birth? Half-remembered images of parents that I'm not even sure are real?"

King Claudius strode to the spot in his rooms where his great chair sat. He sat upon it, cradling the sword he held across his knees.

"You have an honored place at court," he said.

"An honored place at court?" Thanos replied. "I have a place as a spare prince no one wants. Lucious might have tried to have me killed on Haylon, but you were the one who sent me there."

"Rebellion must be crushed, wherever it is found," the king countered. Thanos saw him run his thumb along the edge of the sword he held. "You had to learn that."

"Oh, I've learned," Thanos said, moving across to stand in front of his father. "I've learned that you would rather be rid of me than acknowledge me. I am your eldest son. By the laws of the kingdom, I ought to be your heir. The eldest son has been the heir since the first days of Delos."

"The eldest surviving son," the king said quietly. "You think you would have lived if people knew?"

"Don't pretend you were protecting me," Thanos replied. "You were protecting yourself."

"Better than spending my time fighting on behalf of people who don't even deserve it," the king said. "Do you know how it looks when you go around protecting peasants who should know their place?"

"It looks as though someone cares about them!" Thanos shouted. He couldn't keep from raising his voice then, because it seemed like the only way to get through to his father. Maybe if he could make him understand, then the Empire might finally change for the better. "It looks as though their rulers aren't enemies out to kill them, but people to be respected. It looks as though their lives mean something to us, rather than just being something for us to throw aside while we have glittering parties!"

The king was silent for a long time after that. Thanos could see the fury in his eyes. That was fine. It matched the anger Thanos felt almost perfectly.

"Kneel," King Claudius said at last.

Thanos hesitated, only for a second, but it was apparently enough.

"Kneel!" the king bellowed. "Or do you wish me to have you made to? I am still the king here!"

Thanos knelt on the hard stone of the floor before the king's chair. He saw the king raise the sword he held with difficulty, as though it had been a long time since he'd done it.

Thanos's thoughts went to the sword at his own side. He had no doubt that if it came to a battle between him and the king, he would be the winner. He was younger, stronger, and had trained with the best the Stade had to offer. But that would mean killing his father. More than that, it really would be treason.

"I have learned many things in my life," the king said, and the sword was still poised there. "When I was your age, I was like you. I was young, I was strong. I fought, and I fought well. I killed men in battle, and in duels in the Stade. I tried to fight for everything I believed to be right."

"What happened to you?" Thanos asked.

The king's lip curled into a sneer. "I learned better. I learned that if you give them a chance, people do not come together to lift you up. Instead, they try to tear you down. I have tried showing compassion, and the truth is that it is nothing more than foolishness. If a man stands against you, then you destroy him, because if you do not, he will destroy you."

"Or you make him your friend," Thanos said, "and he helps you to make things better."

"Friends?" King Claudius raised his sword another inch. "Powerful men have no friends. They have allies, servants, and hangers-on, but do not think for a moment that they will not turn on you. A sensible man keeps them in their place, or he watches them rise up against him."

"The people deserve better than that," Thanos insisted.

"You think people get what they deserve?" King Claudius bellowed. "They get what they take! You're talking as if you think the people are our equals. They aren't. We are raised from birth to rule them. We are more educated, stronger, better in every way. You want to put pig farmers in castles beside you, when I want to show them that they belong in their sty. Lucious understands."

"Lucious only understands cruelty," Thanos said.

"And cruelty is what it takes to rule!"

Thanos saw the king swing the sword then. Perhaps he could have ducked. Perhaps he could even have made a move for his own blade. Instead, he knelt there and watched as the sword swept down toward his throat, tracking the arc of the steel in the sunlight.

It stopped short of cutting his throat, but not by much. Thanos felt the sting as the edge touched his flesh, but he didn't react, no matter how much he wanted to.

"You didn't flinch," King Claudius said. "You barely even blinked. Lucious would have. Would probably have begged for his life. That is his weakness. But Lucious has the strength to do what is needed to hold our rule in place. *That* is why he is my heir. Until you can carve this weakness from your heart, I will not acknowledge you. I will not call you mine. And if you attack my acknowledged son again, I will have your head for it. Do you understand?"

Thanos stood. He'd had enough of kneeling to this man. "I understand, Father. I understand you perfectly."

He turned and walked for the doors, not waiting for permission to do it. What could his father do? It would look weak to call him back. Thanos stepped out, and Stephania was waiting for him. She looked as though she'd maintained her image of composure for the benefit of the bodyguards there, but the moment Thanos came out, she hurried forward to him.

"Are you all right?" Stephania asked, raising a hand to his cheek. It dropped lower, and Thanos saw it come away with blood on it. "Thanos, you're bleeding!"

"It's only a scratch," Thanos assured her. "I probably have worse from the fight earlier."

"What happened in there?" she demanded.

Thanos forced a smile, but it came out tighter than he intended. "His majesty chose to remind me that prince or not, I am not worth as much to him as Lucious."

Stephania put her hands on his shoulders. "I told you, Thanos. It was the wrong thing to do. You can't put yourself at risk like that. You have to promise me that you will trust me, and never do anything so foolish again. Promise me."

He nodded.

"For you, my love, I promise."

He meant it, too. Going and fighting Lucious in the open like that wasn't the right strategy, because it didn't achieve enough. Lucious wasn't the problem. The whole Empire was the problem. He'd briefly thought that he might be able to persuade the king to change things, but the truth was that his father didn't *want* things to change.

No, the only thing to do now was to find ways to help the rebellion. Not just the rebels on Haylon, but all of them. Alone, Thanos couldn't accomplish much, but together, they might just bring down the Empire.

Chapter Six

Everywhere Ceres looked on the Isle Beyond the Mist, she saw things that made her stop and stare at their strange beauty. Hawks with rainbow-colored feathers spun as they hunted things below, but were in turn hunted by a winged serpent that eventually settled on a spire of white marble.

She walked over the emerald grass of the island, and it seemed as if she knew exactly where she had to go. She'd seen herself in her vision, there atop the hill in the distance, where rainbow-colored towers stuck up like the spines of some great beast.

Flowers grew from the low rises on the way, and Ceres reached down to touch them. When her fingers brushed them, though, their petals were of paper-thin stone. Had someone carved them that fine, or were they somehow living rock? Just the fact that she could imagine that possibility told her how strange this place was.

Ceres kept walking, heading for the spot where she knew, where she hoped, her mother would be waiting.

She reached the lower slopes of the hill and started to climb. Around her, the island was full of life. Bees buzzed in the low grass. A creature like a deer, but with crystal tines where its antlers should have been, looked at Ceres for a long time before springing away.

Yet she saw no people there, despite the buildings that dotted the landscape around her. The ones closest to Ceres had a pristine, empty feel, like a room that had been stepped out from only moments before. Ceres kept going, up toward the top of the hill, to the spot where the towers formed a circle around a broad area of grass, letting her look out between them over the whole of the rest of the island.

Yet she didn't look that way. Instead, Ceres found herself staring at the center of the circle, where a single figure stood in a robe of pure white. Unlike her vision, the figure wasn't fuzzy or out of focus. She was there, as clear and real as Ceres was. Ceres stepped forward, almost to within touching distance. There was only one person it could be.

"Mother?"

"Ceres."

The robed figure threw herself forward at the same instant Ceres did, and they met in a crushing hug that seemed to express all the things Ceres didn't know how to say: how much she'd been looking forward to this moment, how much love there was there, how incredible it was to meet this woman she'd only met in a vision.

"I knew you would come," the woman, her *mother,* said as they stepped back, "but even knowing it is different from actually *seeing* you."

She pulled back the hood of her robe then, and it seemed almost impossible that this woman could be her mother. Her sister, perhaps, because she shared the same hair, the same features. It was almost like looking into a mirror for Ceres. Yet she seemed too young to be Ceres's mother.

"I don't understand," Ceres said. "You *are* my mother?"

"I am." She reached out to hug Ceres again. "I know it must seem strange, but it's true. My kind can live a long time. I am Lycine."

A name. Ceres finally had a name for her mother. Somehow, that meant more than all the rest of it put together. Just that was enough to make the journey worth it. She wanted to stand there and just stare at her mother forever. Even so, she had questions. So many that they spilled out in a rush.

"What is this place?" she asked. "Why are you here alone? Wait, what do you mean 'your kind'?"

Lycine smiled and sat down on the grass. Ceres joined her, and as she sat, she realized that it wasn't just grass. She could see fragments of stone beneath it, arranged in mosaic form, but long since covered over by the meadow around them.

"There's no easy way to answer all of your questions," Lycine said. "Especially not when I have so many questions of my own, about you, about your life. About everything, Ceres. But I'll try. Shall we do this the old way? A question for a question?"

Ceres didn't know what to say to that, but it seemed her mother wasn't done yet.

"Do they still tell the stories of the Ancient Ones, out in the world?"

"Yes," Ceres said. She'd always paid more attention to the stories of combatlords and their exploits in the Stade, but she knew some of what they said about the Ancient Ones: the ones who had come before humanity, who sometimes looked the same and sometimes looked like so much more. Who'd built so much and then lost it. "Wait, are you saying that you're—"

"One of the Ancient Ones, yes," Lycine replied. "This was one of our places, before… well, there are some things that it is still best not to talk about. Besides, I'm owed an answer. So tell me what your life has been like. I couldn't be there, but I spent so long trying to imagine what it would be like for you."

Ceres did her best, even though she didn't know where to start. She told Lycine about growing up around her father's forge, about her brothers. She told her about the rebellion, and about the Stade. She even managed to tell her about Rexus and Thanos, though those words came out choking and fractured.

"Oh, darling," her mother said, laying a hand over hers. "I wish I could have spared you some of that pain. I wish I could have been there for you."

"Why couldn't you?" Ceres asked. "Have you been here all this time?"

"I have," Lycine said. "This used to be one of the places of my people, in the old days. The others left it behind. Even I did, for a time, but these past years it has been a kind of sanctuary. And a place to wait, of course."

"To wait?" Ceres asked. "You mean for me?"

She saw her mother nod.

"People talk about seeing destiny as if it were a gift," Lycine said, "but there is a kind of prison to it, too. Understand what must happen, and you lose the choices that come with not knowing, no matter how much you might wish…" Her mother shook her head, and Ceres could see the sadness there. "This isn't the time for regret. I have my daughter here, and there is only so much time for you to learn what you came for."

She smiled and took Ceres's hand.

"Walk with me."

⚜ ⚜ ⚜

Ceres felt like days had passed while she and her mother walked the magical isle. It was breathtaking, this vista, being here with her mother. It all felt like a dream.

As they walked, they spoke mostly of the power. Her mother tried to explain it to her, and Ceres tried to understand. The strangest thing happened: as her mother spoke, Ceres felt as if her words were actually imbuing her with the power.

Even now, as they walked, Ceres felt it rising up inside her, roiling like smoke as her mother touched her shoulder. She needed to learn to control it, she'd come here to learn to control it, but compared to meeting her mother, it didn't seem important.

"Our blood has given you power," Lycine said. "The islanders tried to help unlock it, didn't they?"

Ceres thought of Eoin, and of all the strange exercises he'd had her doing. "Yes."

"For people not of our blood, they understand the world well," her mother said. "But there are things even they can't show you. Have you made anything stone yet? It's one of my talents, so I would guess it will be one of yours."

"Made things stone?" Ceres asked. She didn't understand. "So far, I've moved things. I've been faster and stronger. And—"

She didn't want to finish that. She didn't want her mother to think badly of her.

"And your power has killed things that have tried to harm you?" Lycine said.

Ceres nodded.

"Do not be ashamed of that, daughter. I have only seen a little of you, but I know what you are destined to be. You are a fine person. All that I could hope. As for making things stone…"

They stopped in a meadow of purple and yellow flowers and Ceres watched her mother pluck a small flower from the meadow, with delicate, silken petals. Through the contact with her mother, she felt the way the power flickered within her, feeling familiar but much more directed, crafted, shaped.

Stone spread across the flower like frost over a window, but it wasn't just on the surface. A second after it had begun, it was over, and her mother held one of the stone flowers Ceres had seen lower on the island.

"Did you feel it?" Lycine asked.

Ceres nodded. "But how did you do it?"

"Feel again." She plucked another flower, and this time it was impossibly slow as she turned it to something with marble petals and a granite stem. Ceres tried to track the movement of the power within her, and it was as though her own moved in response, trying to copy it.

"Good," Lycine said. "Your blood knows. Now you try."

She passed a flower to Ceres. Ceres reached down, concentrating as she tried to grasp the power within her and push it into the form she'd felt her mother's take.

The flower exploded.

"Well," Lycine said with a laugh, "*that* was unexpected."

It was so different from the way the mother she'd grown up with would have reacted. She'd beaten Ceres for the least failure. Lycine just passed her another flower.

"Relax," she said. "You already know how it should feel. Take that feeling. Imagine it. Make it real."

Ceres tried to do it, thinking about what she'd felt when her mother had transformed her flower. She took the feeling and filled it with power the way her father might have filled a mold at the forge with iron.

"Open your eyes, Ceres," Lycine said.

Ceres hadn't even realized that she'd closed them until her mother said the words. She forced herself to look, even though right then she was afraid to. Once she'd looked, she stared, because she could barely believe it. She held a single, perfectly formed, petrified bloom, transformed into something like basalt by her power.

"I did that?" Ceres asked. Even with everything else she could do, it still seemed nearly impossible.

"You did," her mother said, and Ceres could hear the pride there. "Now we just need to get you to do it without your eyes closed."

That took longer, and a lot more flowers. Yet Ceres found herself enjoying the practice. More than that, every time her mother smiled at her efforts, Ceres felt a burst of love expanding through her. Even as the minutes spilled into hours, she kept going.

"Yes," her mother said at last, "that's perfect."

It was more than that; it was easy. Easy to reach out and pull power from inside her. Easy to channel it. Easy to leave behind a perfectly preserved stone flower. It was only as the rush of doing it faded that Ceres realized just how tired she was.

"It's all right," her mother said, taking her hand. "Your power takes energy and effort. Even the strongest of us could only do so much at once." She smiled. "But your power knows what it is for now. It will rise up when someone threatens you, or when you summon it to you. It will do more, too."

Ceres sensed a flicker of power from her mother, and she could see the full potential of her power. She saw the stone buildings and gardens in a new light, as things that had been built with that power, crafted in ways no human could understand. She felt full, somehow. Complete.

Some of the happiness seemed to fade from her mother's expression. Ceres heard her sigh.

"What is it?" Ceres asked.

"I just wish that we had more time together," Lycine said. "I would love to walk you through the towers here and tell you the history of my people. I would love to hear all about this Thanos you loved so much, and show you the gardens where the sun has never touched the trees."

"Then do it," Ceres said. She felt as though she might have stayed there forever. "Show me all of it. Tell me about the past. Tell me about my father, and what happened when I was born."

Her mother shook her head though.

"That is one thing you aren't ready for yet. As for time, I told you before that destiny can be a prison, darling, and you have a bigger destiny than most."

"I've seen flashes of it," Ceres admitted, thinking of the dreams that had come to her again and again on the boat."

"Then you know why we can't stay here and be a family, no matter how much either of us might wish it," her mother said. "Although maybe the future holds time for that. That and more."

"First, though, I have to go back, don't I?" Ceres said.

Her mother nodded.

"You do," she said. "You must return, Ceres. Return and free Delos from the Empire, as you were always meant to do."

Chapter Seven

It was hard for Stephania to believe that she'd already been married to Thanos for six weeks. Yet with the feast of the Blood Moon here, that was how long it had been. Six weeks of bliss, every one as wonderful as she could have hoped for.

"You look amazing," she said, looking over at Thanos in the rooms they now shared in the castle. He was a vision in deep red silk, set off with red gold and rubies. She could hardly believe that he was hers, some days. "Red suits you."

"It makes me look as though I'm covered in blood," Thanos replied.

"Which is rather the point, given that it's the Blood Moon," Stephania pointed out. She leaned in to kiss him. She liked being able to do that when she wanted. If there were more time, she might have taken the moment to do a lot more.

"It hardly matters what I wear though," Thanos said. "There's no one in the room who will be looking at me when you're there beside me."

Perhaps another man could have put the compliment more elegantly, but there was something about the earnest way Thanos said it that meant more to Stephania than all the perfectly judged poems in the world.

Besides, she *had* worked rather hard on picking out the most beautiful dress in Delos. It shimmered in shades of red like a flame wrapped around her. She'd even bribed the dressmaker to ensure that the original, destined for a minor noblewoman lower in the city, was irretrievably delayed.

Stephania offered her arm, and Thanos took it, escorting her down toward the great feast hall where they'd had their wedding. Was it already six weeks that they'd been married? Six weeks of more bliss than

Stephania could have believed, living together in apartments set aside for them by the queen within the castle. There were even rumors that the king was planning to bestow a new estate on Thanos, a little way from the city. For six weeks, they'd been the most watched couple in the city, lauded wherever they went. Stephania had enjoyed that.

"Do remember not to punch Lucious when you see him tonight," Stephania said.

"I've managed to keep from doing it so far," Thanos replied. "Don't worry."

Stephania did worry, though. She didn't want to risk losing Thanos now that she had him as her husband. She didn't want to find him executed for attacking the heir to the throne, and not just because of the position it would put her in. She might have set out to acquire him for a husband for the prestige it would bring, but now … now she was surprised to find that she loved him.

"Prince Thanos and his wife, Lady Stephania!" the herald at the door announced, and Stephania smiled, leaning her head against Thanos's shoulder. She always loved hearing that.

She looked around the room. For their wedding, it had been arranged in white, but now it shone in red and black. The wine in the glasses was a thick blood red, the feast tables had meat left just on the edge of bloody, and every noble in the place wore the colors of the shifting moon.

Stephania walked on Thanos's arm, parsing the relationships there, keeping track of the latest intrigues even as she simply enjoyed being seen. Was that Lady Christina, slipping off into the shadows to talk to a merchant prince from the Far Islands? Was Isolde's daughter wearing fewer jewels than usual?

Of course, she saw Lucious drinking too much, eating too much, and eyeing the women. Briefly, Stephania thought his eyes flickered to hers, his look one that would have guaranteed a fight if Thanos had seen it. It was a pity, really, that her attempt to poison him at the wedding feast had gone so badly. If Thanos hadn't made him so angry that he'd crushed his wine glass, then Lucious would have gone to sleep that night and not woken. It would have been done.

Since then, there had been no opportunity to deal with him. The usual people she might have employed were being more cautious now that the one she'd used for Thanos had gone missing, and the trick with killing was never the act of it; it was always doing it in such a way that people didn't suspect. There had simply never been a chance to get close to Lucious without it being obvious.

"Ah, Prince Thanos," a white-whiskered man said, approaching them both, "Lady Stephania. You make such a wonderful couple!"

Stephania searched her memory for the man, coming up with the answer effortlessly. "General Haven, you're too kind. How is your wife doing?"

"Happy enough to spend my gold on new necklaces. I take it you'll be keeping Prince Thanos from the new expedition to Haylon?"

"There's a new expedition?" Thanos said. Stephania could hear the curiosity there. It was obviously the first her husband had heard of it.

"Heading out tomorrow," General Haven said. "I tried to persuade his majesty to let me head this one, but he decided on Olliant instead."

Probably because the man was capable of organizing something more than a long-winded speech. Stephania had heard that Haven had once been a competent general, but now he hung onto his role only through his connections.

"Well," Stephania said, "I'm sure your wife will be happy to have you home. I know I'm glad that Thanos isn't going anywhere."

The old man drifted away, and Stephania turned to Thanos.

"We should go and mingle," Stephania said. "I should go and hear all the gossip the women of the court have to tell, and tell them how glorious their choices of dress are. *You* should go and pay your respects to the king. People have been muttering about how little you've been there for formal audiences lately."

"I've just been busy," Thanos said. "Enjoying married life, for a start."

Stephania knew her husband better than that. She still laughed though. "I've been enjoying it too, but you know you can't afford to offend the king. Think of it as a game, Thanos. A big game, where the prize is getting to live happily, and where you don't get a choice if you play."

"Is that what you do?" Thanos asked.

Stephania spread her hands. "Why do you think I'm about to go and tell General Haven's wife how lovely her new necklace is?" She kissed his cheek. "Please, Thanos. I love how honest you are, but whatever happened when you spoke to the king, you can't get on his bad side."

"I'll try," Thanos said, heading off in the direction of the king and queen.

Stephania watched him go. She loved watching him. Even as she started making her way through the room, she kept glancing back to keep an eye on where Thanos had gotten to. She'd never thought that she would be like this, giddy as a milkmaid swooning over him. But that was love, and Stephania wasn't going to allow anything to jeopardize things.

"Do we have any information on the boy, Sartes, yet?" Stephania asked one of her handmaids in a whisper. She made sure that none of them ever knew all of her affairs, but she also made sure that she picked clever girls, drawn up from the lower end of the acceptable classes. Girls who would owe her everything, in other words.

"We know that after his escape from the army, he joined up with the rebellion," the handmaid said. "I believe I know which group, my lady."

"Well done," Stephania said, with a brief touch of her hand bestowed like a blessing. "Go to Captain Var and tell him that I want the boy in chains."

"Yes, my lady."

The girl hurried off. Captain Var was a necessary evil. The mercenary was a lecher and a torturer, but curiously, he was surprisingly loyal, and he was good at the… specialized jobs Stephania had him perform. Probably it helped that Stephania was in a position to outbid everyone else for his services. At least one would-be rival had found herself disappearing into the slave pits thanks to the good captain's graces.

Stephania continued her smiling way around the feast, sampling a bite of food here, a sip of wine there as she moved from acquaintance to rival to would-be friend, never stopping long in one place, never letting her eyes stray from Thanos for long.

Perhaps she shouldn't be making such an issue of Ceres's younger brother. If he hadn't already died in one of the rebellion's raids, he almost certainly would soon. Even if he lived, did it really matter?

It did. Just the thought of it was enough to make Stephania dig her nails into her palms, bringing with it a sharp stab of pain. The boy was no threat in himself. Stephania bore him no ill will, but just the fact that he existed was a connection to the memory of Ceres. Stephania could *not* allow her to intrude on her marriage. Not in life, and not in death. No, she had to be certain, whatever it took.

Stephania looked over to Thanos again. He seemed to be done with the king, and she wanted to dance with him now. She wanted to draw him close to her and feel the strength of him pressed up against her. She wanted to remind all those there that she had gained the greatest prize worth taking. Above all, she wanted to fill his thoughts so full of her that there could never be any room for Ceres ever again.

She started to make her way over toward him, but she only got a little of the way there before she started to feel so sick that her head swam. Had she been poisoned? No, she couldn't have been. She was always careful about what she ate and who she took it from. She consumed antidotes every morning, and she knew better than anyone what to taste and smell for.

Even so, she found herself stumbling in the direction of the courtyard. One of her maids helped her, and Stephania found herself leaning on the girl more than she would have liked. The night air was cool, but it didn't really help.

"Are you all right, my lady?" the maid asked as they got out there.

Stephania wanted to snap that of course she wasn't, but her body chose that moment to betray her and she vomited. It tasted foul, but Stephania was mostly just glad that she'd gotten out of the hall before anyone saw. Her maid held her hair back.

"I don't know what's happening," Stephania said. "It can't be poison. It *can't*."

"My lady," the maid said, "is it … is it possible that you're pregnant?"

Stephania wanted to tell the girl not to be stupid, but it fit, didn't it? Could she be? Was it possible? She stood there in shock, trying to think as she cleaned herself up with her maid's help. It had never occurred to her that she might be pregnant. It had just seemed so much more obvious in her world that she might have been attacked by some enemy.

"Tell no one about this," Stephania said. "Go back to the feast. If anyone asks you where I am, say that I felt unwell and returned to my rooms. Fail and I'll have you skinned, do you understand?"

"Yes, my lady," the girl said, looking frightened.

Stephania offset that with a hug. "Thank you. I should have thought of it myself."

She hurried through the castle, but even so, it took her a while to find the chambers of the royal apothecary. In general, if Stephania needed a potion or a poultice, she was more than capable of putting it together herself. Yet this wasn't something she kept the materials for, and she didn't want to waste her time with the toads and rabbits of so-called wise women.

Of course, when Stephania got there, the door was locked, the apothecary away. Thankfully, the lock was a poor one, easy to force open even though Stephania rarely stooped to such things for herself.

She made her way inside, looking through the jars of powders and herbs. It was dangerous, working with someone else's stocks, but Stephania thought that she could recognize what she needed. There were enough ladies of the court having enough affairs to need to know these things, and it seemed the apothecary kept vials made up.

Stephania found one and used it, ignoring the embarrassment of doing so in the middle of the place. She stared at the clear solution with impatience, waiting to see what would happen next.

When it slowly shifted to blue, Stephania felt a rush of feelings spreading through her. Shock, because she'd never expected this. Apprehension for all that might happen next. Above all, though, there was joy. Joy for one simple fact:

She was having Thanos's child.

Chapter Eight

The morning after the feast, Thanos rose quietly and sneaked his way through the rooms he shared with Stephania. He'd learned to be careful after she'd followed him to hunt Lucious.

"Let her sleep," Thanos said to one of Stephania's maids as he passed. "I'm just going down to the training ground ahead of the Killings later, and Stephania looked a little tired after the feast last night."

"Yes, Prince Thanos," the maid said.

Thanos set off in the direction of the training grounds, because that was a believable place for him to go this early. He needn't have worried. The castle was quiet. Servants bustled about their work, but the nobles who might have been in a position to question him were all still in bed. After the feast last night, it was exactly what Thanos had been hoping for.

Because of what he'd heard last night. What General Haven had said was just the start. With the wine flowing and so many nobles gathered in one place, Stephania hadn't been the only one listening to gossip. The only difference was that Thanos had been listening with a point, taking in anything that might help the rebels.

He hurried along the corridors of the castle, heading for the offices of the royal chamberlain. They had probably been grand once, but were now piled so high with records and missives that the only effect was of chaos. There was a minor official sitting at a table there, but no sign of the man himself. He was probably sleeping off the effects of the feast like everyone else.

"Can I help you, Prince Thanos?" the official asked.

Thanos silently apologized for how difficult he was about to make the other man's day. It was the only way he could think of.

"Where is the Lord Chamberlain?" Thanos demanded in his best "spoiled noble" voice. He'd modeled it on Lucious.

"Forgive me, but his lordship is feeling a little ill this—"

"I didn't ask how he was," Thanos snapped. "I asked *where* he was. I need to discuss details of the estates the king is considering giving to me and my wife, because I want to make sure that it's suitable for Stephania."

"Perhaps I could—"

"Are you the Lord Chamberlain?" Thanos asked, then paused. "I'm sorry. It's just that I want this to be perfect before Stephania hears the details. Would you please fetch him?"

The official hurried off. Thanos hoped he wouldn't hurry too much as he shut and locked the door behind him, because he needed the time.

As quickly as he could, he found pen, ink, and parchment, trying to remember what he could of the usual forms. His Majesty, King of Delos, ruler of the Empire… Thanos did his best to keep the letters sharp and official looking. How long would he have to write everything he needed?

He found the chamberlain's copy of the royal seal, and set wax to melt. Thanos could imagine the official running, the Lord Chamberlain dressing in a hurry. Even so, he couldn't rush the writing more. It had to look just right. The king did not rush commands like this. He sent them with full majesty, knowing that others would wait for him.

Thanos could hear footsteps now, along with arguing voices. He reached for the seal, dripping wax down onto the parchment.

"You couldn't deal with this yourself?"

"The prince insisted!"

"Even so, you could have found a way! And now the door is shut. The key."

Thanos pressed the seal down into the soft wax, putting it back into place as quickly as he dared. There was no time to do more. He just had time to hide the parchment he'd worked on before the Lord Chamberlain came blustering in, smiling with the lack of warmth of a man who had just been roused from his bed too soon.

"Prince Thanos, it is an honor. What can I do for you this fine morning?"

The hardest part was spending fifteen long minutes discussing details of estates and stables, farms and river rights, when Thanos knew just how little time he might have before it was too late. Finally, it felt as though he was able to smile and make his exit.

"Thank you for all this," he said. "Now that you've gone through it with me, I see that there was no reason to worry. I will leave you to your work."

He forced himself to walk as made his way through the castle, heading for the tower where they kept their messenger birds: rock doves and homing pigeons, ravens and occasional larger birds. Every outpost of the Empire regularly sent its birds, well trained to know where their homes were. There was no one minding the entrance yet, but Thanos was still cautious. There might be someone above by now.

He crept up among the birds, moving quietly, with every creak of the boards below his feet making him pause. Thanos hoped that no one was up there feeding the birds, because he wasn't sure what lie he would be able to tell them. There wasn't, though, and Thanos made his way over to the cages where the birds for Haylon, large black ravens, were kept. They looked as though they hadn't flown in a while.

Thanos picked one out and attached a message to its leg. It wasn't much more than a hurried warning, along with a promise to do what he could. He didn't dare sign it, but hopefully, Akila and the other rebels would know who it was from and trust it.

Now for the more dangerous part of his plan, and the one where he had to hurry the most. Thanos practically ran in the direction of the stables, saddling his horse and riding toward the docks at a full gallop. Around him, the city was already waking up. Servants and wives were emptying chamber pots into the streets, hawkers were calling out their wares, while carts were making their way through the streets.

Thanos had to dodge them all as he raced down over the cobbles, following the scent of sea air. The docks were busier than the rest of the city put together. Fishermen were landing their catches or heading out. A merchant ship was unloading with the aid of a string of porters.

And what was left of the Empire's navy sat low in the water, laden down with troops. It was a motley collection of ships compared to the first invasion force, hastily repurposed pleasure craft and cargo ships obvious among the war galleys. Thanos ran his horse down to the water's edge. This was more public than he wanted, but it couldn't be helped.

"Where is General Olliant?" he called out to a group of soldiers. When they pointed to a ship still being loaded by the docks, he handed his reins to one of them and ran up the gangplank. Sailors started to move in front of him, but they obviously recognized Thanos, because they quickly stepped back.

Thanos spotted the general by his golden armor and hurried over to him on the top deck. The general saluted.

"Prince Thanos," the general said. "I wasn't aware that you were to travel with us."

"I'm not," Thanos said. "But it seems you aren't going anywhere either, General."

He held out the parchment he'd prepared. He only wished he'd had more time to work on it. Was the ink even dry yet?

"What's this?" General Olliant asked.

"New orders," Thanos said. "General Haven is to be given command of this expedition."

"Haven?" The shock in the general's voice was obvious. Thanos could understand it. Haven was a long way from the dynamic, ruthless general that would be needed to crush Haylon. That was the point. "This is my expedition!"

"The king requires you elsewhere, General."

The general tore open the orders Thanos had forged, staring at them. Thanos's heart beat faster as he did it, tracking every movement of the man's eyes. Thanos saw him trace the outline of the seal.

"This is still warm," General Olliant said, "and why is the king sending you with messages, your highness?"

Thanos could hear the suspicion there. At any moment, the man might decide to send a runner to the castle to find out what was happening. Thanos couldn't let that happen.

"That just shows how urgent it is," Thanos said. He lowered his voice. "And there's more to it. Do you trust the men around you?"

The general glanced around, then took a step back from his men before dropping his voice to match Thanos's. "What is it?" he demanded. "What is this all about?"

"You're not going to Haylon because the king has a crucial task for you," Thanos said. "We think we know where the leaders of the rebellion are going to be meeting, but we need a general with the skills to handle the task."

He saw General Olliant's eyes shine with interest. "I'll go back to the castle then, and gather—"

"There's no time," Thanos said quickly. "If you have men here you can trust, take them, but unless we act now, we'll miss them. There's a force waiting for your orders in the Glass Spur pass, but if you don't ride hard, you'll never get there before the leaders move on from their meeting."

"I'll go at once," General Olliant promised, and he was almost faster down the gangplank than Thanos was. Thanos knew it was the desire for glory that had him moving so fast, not the thought of new orders, but it was enough.

Thanos rode back in the direction of the castle. Now he just had to tell General Haven about his new position, but he suspected that wouldn't be a problem. After all, the man had already hinted that he wanted this. It would simply look as though Thanos had interceded.

As he rode, his mind went to the risks he'd taken this morning. Could he ensure that no one found out? The army was about to take off in the direction of Haylon, and so those who had seen him at the docks wouldn't be able to talk about what he'd done. Of course, there was the problem of what might happen when General Olliant discovered there was no force of soldiers waiting for him, but maybe Thanos could kill two birds with one stone there. Maybe he could send the rebellion news of where one of the Empire's generals was going to be relatively unguarded. He was almost back at the castle. Now he—

"Thanos? Is that you?"

Thanos cursed silently as he turned in the saddle to see Lucious walking out of one of the side streets near the entrance, along with a small group of hangers-on.

"Lucious," Thanos said, forcing a smile. "You're up early."

"Up early?" Lucious countered, and now Thanos could hear the faint slur to his words. "A real man doesn't sleep on a festival night! At least, not in his own bed. Talking of beds, have you tired of the lovely Stephania already? Or maybe she's tired of you? Maybe she's gone out looking for a real man, and you're going after her?"

His cronies laughed along with him, of course.

"Just out for a morning ride, Lucious," Thanos said. "You should try it."

"As I recall," Lucious said, "the last time you went out for a morning ride, you ended up betraying the Empire for some peasants. What are you up to this time?"

"Oh, go get some sleep," Thanos snapped back, but inside, his stomach knotted. "You're too drunk to be worth talking to."

"You're hiding something, and I'll find out what," Lucious promised.

Thanos waved it away, but it was probably just as well Lucious was drunk, or he'd see the way Thanos paled.

"I'll see you at the Killings later, Lucious. For now, I have better things to do."

Like persuading an incompetent general to take over the Empire's biggest military operation, telling the rebels about General Olliant, and finding a way to do it all without Lucious finding out more than he should.

Chapter Nine

Anka forced herself to stay still and watch while below, in the Stade, men died in honor of the Blood Moon. Two muscled southerners fought, their blades flickering, while the crowd bayed with every spray of red that stained the sands.

There was more red spread throughout the terraces. People wore whatever they had in the Blood Moon's colors, and some threw red dust and dye into the air, covering even those who'd come in normal clothes. Anka had plenty on her, but she was already wearing an elaborate red costume, complete with long-nosed mask.

It made it easier to hide the weapons.

Below her, the fight continued out on the sands, with the clang and clash of blades lost in the shouts of the people around her. There were only a few nobles up in the royal enclosure today, dressed in ways that made the simple red tunics of most of the crowd look like children copying their parents. They wore silk and rubies, reclined on deep red couches, and drank red wine from crystal goblets. It was a pity there weren't more. If the king had been there, they could have brought down the Empire.

Anka signaled to other figures costumed in the colors of the Blood Moon, watching them start to slip through the crowd around her. They all had their jobs. Anka had planned every step of this, but there were some things you couldn't account for, especially in a place like this.

"Hey, watch yourself!" a man said as Anka started to push her way through the crowd. He reached out for her, and Anka felt him pull back as she drew a knife. There wasn't any time for trouble. She had to keep moving.

"Sorry, excuse me," Anka said, picking her way through. She could see the others moving and pick out the patterns there. She just hoped that none of the guards in the Stade could.

Ahead, she could see the gates that led down underneath the Stade, into the spaces where the combatlords were kept. There were large guards on the door, there to keep the crowds back. One put a hand up as Anka approached.

"Get back," he said. "If you want to see the combatlords, you'll have to wait, the same as anyone else."

"Get out of my way, and you won't be harmed," Anka said.

"Won't be harmed?" the guard said with a laugh. "What do you think you're going to do?"

"This," Anka said, and pulled away her costume, revealing the armor underneath. "For the rebellion!"

"For the rebellion!" voices called around her. "Down with the Empire!"

Other figures rushed forward, casting off their disguises, drawing daggers and clubs. They overwhelmed the guards at the gate in seconds. Berin was there with Sartes, breaking open the locks with forge hammers and rushing inside. Anka went with them, down into the space beneath the Stade, rushing for the next set of gates, the next group of guards.

Those stood just beyond another set of iron doors, armed with the clubs and whips and swords they would need to control unruly combatlords. Anka could see the dank, cruel conditions beyond, and guess at some of the horrors there. It gave her the strength she needed to lift a crossbow and fire through the bars.

Others fired with her, and the guards went down. She saw Oreth working on the lock, and then they were inside. Now they had to fight, because the Empire wasn't going to leave just a few guards to control so many dangerous slaves. A guard ran at her, sword cutting down, and Anka barely sidestepped in time.

He cut again, and Anka managed to get the body of her crossbow in the way. She stabbed with the knife in her other hand, moving in close as she struck once, then again. She felt the blade go into her attacker, and he fell. She saw Sartes and Berin struggling with another guard, bringing him down with hammer blows.

Around her, guards were dying. The space under the Stade was formidable, the guards strong and powerfully built, but their whole system was designed for controlling threats from the inside, not keeping out attackers from the world beyond. Who would want to attack a space full of combatlords? Who would want to free slaves?

Anka would.

She strode into the space beneath the Stade and looked around at the combatlords there with their weapon carriers and trainers. Some were in their armor, some were in chains, while a few were receiving massages as their trainers sought to prepare them. They were pampered in some ways. Anka was just hoping that they understood that freedom still mattered more.

Berin spoke first. It was what they'd agreed; the only way this might work. "Listen up, lads. You all know me. I made weapons for you long enough. Now, I'm bringing you something better: the chance of freedom. All you have to do is listen."

He stepped aside, and it was time for Anka to step forward.

"I am Anka, the leader of the rebellion," Anka said as she stepped into the middle of them. She could see them sizing her up, and a flicker of fear passed through her at the thought of what might happen if these men decided that she was somehow unworthy.

"What are you doing here?" one asked. He was a black-bearded giant of a man, thick with muscle.

"We're here to free you," Anka said.

"Free us?" the combatlord countered. "*You're* here to free *us*?"

He laughed, and Anka knew she had to act fast.

"Maybe you don't want to be free," she said, raising her voice. "Maybe you like your time here. Maybe you like having everything you want provided for you, with nothing to do but train, and fight…" She paused for a second. "And die, of course."

She looked around at them. At all of them down there in the cool half-dark. "That's what it means, being a combatlord. You fight, and you're told it's for honor or for glory, but deep down, you know the truth.

You fight because you aren't given a choice. Even the ones of you who are free don't really have the choice to walk away, because there's too much riding on every match."

"And you're going to give us more?" the bearded combatlord asked.

Anka shook her head. "You're going to take it for yourselves. The nobles above treat you like playthings. They wager on you and they sell you, they take the applause when you win and cast you aside the moment you lose. They might give you a few luxuries, but let's not pretend they care about you."

"So what do you want us to do?" another combatlord asked.

Anka smiled, because she knew she had them. "Rise up. Fight for *everyone*. It's what they've trained you to do, but they've never given you anything worth fighting for. Fight with us, and that's what you'll have. You can fight to be free. You can fight for all the people out there. With us, you can fight to bring down the Empire!"

That brought a cheer from the men there, and several were already reaching for the weapons they would have used in the Stade.

"More guards are coming," Oreth called from near the doors. "It looks as though they know what's going on."

"Let them come," one of the combatlords said, but Anka didn't want to fight there. This whole space was designed to put those within at a disadvantage.

"Up!" she ordered. "Up to the Stade!"

To her astonishment, even the combatlords did as she said, pouring up toward the sands together. They burst out onto the floor of the Stade, but Anka didn't waste any time blinking in the sunlight. Instead, she raised her dagger, hoping it caught the sunlight.

"People of Delos! We are the rebellion, and we are here to free you!"

There was no time to say more than that, because guards were already pouring onto the sands of the Stade from the other side. There were so many that Anka could barely count them all; far more than their own small force. It might have been some horribly mismatched contest in the Killings, except this was about more than the entertainment of the crowd. Much more.

There was no time for clever planning, and they couldn't sit there waiting for the soldiers to attack them in perfect formation, so Anka did the only thing she could do.

"Charge!"

She ran at the head of the group, not knowing if anyone would follow her. She closed in on the guards there, who stood with shields up and spears extended. Anka could imagine herself impaled on those spears all too easily.

Then the combatlords surged past her, and she got to see firsthand that Sartes had been right. They were better than any soldier could have been. Anka had seen them fighting one another before, and the evenness of it had disguised just how dangerous they were. Against anyone normal, they seemed barely human.

She saw one leap over the wall of shields, stabbing downward as he passed over a guard. Another spun spiked chains, ripping spears out of the hands of their wielders. The bearded fighter struck with a trident, thrusting it through one soldier before knocking another back with the haft.

Anka found herself plunged into the middle of the fight, and it was chaos. A soldier got near her, so she stabbed at him, but the fight swept them apart again. A sword came at her head, and she found a sword interposed. Sartes nodded to her as Anka stabbed at the soldier who'd struck.

The combatlords were like whirlwinds in the middle of the fight. Each fought alone, an island of violence surrounded by opponents, but it didn't seem to make any difference. The rebels fought like small fish following in the wake of sharks, darting in and out of the fight, filling in the gaps left by their mayhem. They were more evenly matched with the soldiers, but with the combatlords there, it seemed to be enough.

For now, at least. Anka knew there would be more coming. She pulled back from the fight, standing on the sands and staring up at the crowd.

"We are the rebellion, but so are you!" Anka called out. "If you want to be free, you must take that freedom!" She pointed at the balcony where the nobles were already starting to flee. "Look at them! The Empire has oppressed you for too long! Help to fight it now!"

Many people kept staring down as though it was all a show, but many more responded. The crowd surged as people started toward guards at the gates, or struggled to get to the nobles above. Anka saw people starting to fight; against guards, against those who wanted the Empire to stand, or simply to get away.

She threw herself back into the fight in the Stade as she saw Edrin struggling with a soldier. She kicked out, knocking the man off balance, and Edrin lashed out with his sword. Anka saw a group of guards trying to re-form their shield wall, and she didn't have the strength to do more than point, charging again and knowing this time that the others would follow.

The battle swirled around Anka like a living thing. She did what she could, looking for openings to attack even though she knew she could never keep up with the capabilities of the combatlords. She saw people fighting and dying in every direction, men and women, combatlords and soldiers, rebels and people who had joined them from the crowd.

Above it all, Anka heard one noise she had hoped not to hear when she arrived: the sound of horns. It meant that they'd run out of time. They'd done what they'd come there to do, but now they needed to find a way out of there before it fell apart around them.

The Stade was in uproar now, with the people there in full revolt. It should have been a sight to fill Anka with hope.

Even so, the sound of the horns only brought dread with it.

More soldiers were coming, more than they could ever dream to battle.

And they had no way out.

Chapter Ten

Ceres left the Isle Beyond the Mist behind with a heavy heart. She didn't want to go, however much she might need to, however much her destiny might lie on the mainland. Her mother was on the island.

But her mother had been the one to insist that Ceres go, even if there had been tears in her eyes while she did it. She'd been the one to load fresh supplies onto Ceres's boat, and to point her on the bearing she needed to take to return to the mainland. She'd stood on the beach, not waving, but watching, while Ceres sailed off. She'd been there as a tiny figure on the beach until finally Ceres had been too far away to make her out. Possibly she had still been there even when the mist closed around her.

The journey back through the mist was less eerie than it had been coming there, but this time, Ceres could feel the power in the fog surrounding her. Eoin had said that this was somewhere for her to go alone. *Could* anyone else have made it through with her? How many people blundered into this barrier and didn't come out?

When she made it through, it was daytime, but somehow the world didn't seem quite as vibrant as it did on the other side. It was like stepping into another, slightly more leaden, reality, where the glorious homes of the Ancient Ones couldn't be imagined except as stories.

She sailed on, keeping the tiller of her small boat lashed to the course her mother had set and focusing on catching the wind with the boat's sail. There was a fresh breeze behind her, pushing her along, but even so, Ceres didn't know how long it would take her to return.

She thought of everything that might be waiting for her there. The rebellion was there, and she didn't know how well it was doing. Perhaps it had already won, or already been wiped out. That thought made her chest tighten, because her father and her brother would be with the rebellion, if they were anywhere. No, she had to believe that they were all right.

Ceres wasn't sure what she was going to be able to do once she got there. She knew more of who she was now, but not everything. She had more control of the powers within her. Would it be enough? Ceres thought of Thanos, dead on the beaches of Haylon, and of all the people who suffered under the Empire. She would *make* it enough, even if she had to walk into the throne room of the Empire and turn the king to stone in front of everyone.

Ceres watched the waves around her boat for a while, and she realized that they were growing, forming into a swell that buffeted the small craft despite its construction. The boat was moving faster too, and Ceres could feel the wind ripping at the sails, shoving her craft along roughly through the peaks and troughs of the water.

She looked ahead, and her heart pounded as she saw a storm brewing.

It began as a patch of bruised sky on the horizon. It spread, seeming to fill everything ahead, and Ceres knew that there would have been no way to sail around it even if she had dared to deviate from the course her mother had set. It seemed to fill the world.

The wind soon raged in her ears, and she clutched the wood, knowing the only thing to do was hold on and hope that it wouldn't be too bad.

It was.

The first band of rain hit Ceres as solidly as a river. It pummeled her from above, while around her the rising wind howled. The first cracks of thunder sounded, deafening against the quiet of the sea, and lightning flickered among the clouds. It arced down too, and Ceres saw the water steam where it struck.

Her boat's sails billowed madly, and Ceres fought to get them down before they tore to shreds. She should have done it as soon as she saw the storm, but somehow it had felt right to press on in spite of the danger. She hauled at the ropes, using all of the strength that her blood gave her, and even then, it was a fight to keep the boom of the mast from breaking free of her grip.

In the distance, she thought she could see a waterspout rising. It spun wildly, and Ceres hoped desperately that it wouldn't come close. Her head whipped around as it stalked along like some living thing, passing close enough that Ceres could feel the massive pull of the air there.

Just that moment of distraction was enough. Ceres felt the ropes in her hand pull free fast enough to burn, and she cried out as they ripped through her palm. She heard a crack that drowned out even the thunder, and slowly, so slowly that it might have been a huge tree falling, her mast toppled into the waves.

Ceres looked at it in despair. Her boat had no oars, no way to control it without the sail, but there was nothing she could do to get it back. Tossed by the waves, without even a mast now, all she could do was hold on—as the waves grew ever higher.

A massive wave suddenly lifted her fifty, a hundred feet high. She looked over the precipice and screamed, as her entire world came crashing down.

Mother, she thought. *How could you let me die like this?*

⚜ ⚜ ⚜

Sharpness poked at the edge of Ceres's consciousness, and she woke slowly, struggling out of the depths of exhaustion into which she'd fallen. How many days had it been now? How long had she drifted? Heat and a lack of fresh water had glued her tongue to the roof of her mouth, while her eyes felt so heavy it seemed like an impossible task to open them.

Something jabbed at her again, and Ceres managed to open her eyes this time. She found herself looking up at the features of a man whose hair had been styled into elaborate spikes that were probably there to make him look more terrifying. He wore a kind of half armor of leather scraps, and the curved sword in his hand explained the sharp pain that had dragged Ceres from her sleep.

There were half a dozen more like him on her small boat, rooting through it for any scrap that might be of value. They were wild-looking men, covered in tattoos and bangles, their clothes gaudy wherever they didn't form armor. To the starboard side of Ceres's boat, the hull of a much larger galley rose like a wall punctuated by oar ports. Symbols promising pain and death were daubed on the side in paint the color of blood, leaving Ceres in no doubt about the kind of men who had woken her.

Pirates.

"She's awake," the one who'd prodded her said. "Looks like she might be worth hauling out of this boat after all."

"Could be fun for a while," another agreed. "Been a long time at sea."

"It'll be a longer time for her," a third pirate said with a laugh that made Ceres shiver.

Ceres looked up and saw more men leering over the side of the ship. Some of them catcalled and made lewd gestures. She cringed back.

"Eventually, we'll sell you to a slaver," the first pirate said with a laugh. "Eventually. And in the meantime, we're going to keep you chained in the galley for any man that wants you."

"I'll … kill you," Ceres managed through cracked lips.

That just got another laugh from him. "Oh, it's fun when they have fight in them. Hey, Nim, do you remember that barbarian woman we took? Had to tie her to the prow like a figurehead in a storm to break her. I doubt it will take that much with this one, though. Probably just a good whipping or two."

He reached down for Ceres, and she felt his hand close over her arm, hauling her to her feet. She tensed to fight, even though there were probably too many of them to fight all at once, given how weak she felt.

"Not so tough now, are you?" the pirate asked, casually backhanding her. Ceres tasted blood.

She also felt the power in her rising up, lashing out like a whip through her. She remembered the way she'd shaped it before, with her mother in the meadow. She felt her power jump out through the contact between her and the pirate, and she saw the stone creep out over him.

It rippled across his flesh like one of the waves around her, and he barely even had enough time to look surprised before the flow of the stone passed across his face. One moment, Ceres was faced with a pirate who wanted to attack her; the next there was a statue there that seemed like a perfect replica of the man.

It felt no different from the moment when she'd done it with the flower, but it *was* different, because until a second ago this had been a human being. Ceres had been staring into the man's eyes when the stone took them, and now they were orbs of blank marble, veined in red and looking as though they could have been carved by the greatest sculptor who ever lived.

A brief, pure sense of horror passed through Ceres at what she had just done, and yet, hadn't this man deserved it? She forced herself to composure, and looked up at the rail of the pirate vessel as she disengaged her tunic from the cold, dead grip of the statue.

The men above were staring down open-mouthed, silent now where before they had called down obscene suggestions. Ceres looked around until she found the cargo netting the men had used to clamber into her smaller boat, and climbed up it a little at a time. She still felt starved and thirsty beyond endurance, but with her power flowing through her, she more than had the strength to make the climb.

She hopped onto the deck of the pirate galley, standing in the middle of an expanding circle of the thugs there. None of them seemed to want to be the first to step toward her.

"Who leads here?" Ceres asked, finding the strength to make the words seem powerful.

"I do!" a man said, stepping forward with a sword in his hand. "And the others might be scared of your witchcraft, but I'm not."

He stepped forward, hefting the sword as if to strike at Ceres. The skills the forest folk had taught her made it easy to step aside and kick his feet from under him.

"I'll kill you," he promised. "I'll do it so slowly you beg for death."

"How many people have you hurt?" Ceres asked. "How many boats have you attacked? How many have you sold into slavery?"

She stepped aside from another blow, bringing her hand up. This time, she called the power, and the stone flowed over the pirate leader, spreading out from her hand in ripples. Before, she'd been horrified by it, but every evil thing the others there had done, this man had ordered. There were some people even Ceres couldn't feel pity for.

"Who leads here?" Ceres asked again, and the silence among the pirates was answer enough. The first of them to kneel was a relatively young one, but the others soon followed, falling down to the deck in obvious fear.

"You lead," one of the pirates said. "We'll do whatever you want."

Whatever she wanted. That was a long way from what they'd been threatening only a minute or two ago. A part of Ceres wanted to punish these men for what they were, and what they did, but she pushed down that urge. She wasn't going to do that, even if they did deserve it.

Besides, her ship was ruined.

"Take me to Delos."

Chapter Eleven

Thanos had decided not to attend the Stade for the Blood Moon festival. The sight of the Killings would only have brought back too many memories of Ceres, and that wouldn't have been fair to Stephania. A man should concentrate on his wife, not on the dead.

Besides, there was too much of a chance that Lucious would be there, and after this morning, Thanos wanted to avoid his half-brother even more than usual.

That was why he was in the castle when the guards started rushing about. Thanos knew fighting men. He knew the difference between the speed that came with a hurried order from a superior and a genuine emergency. One look at the guards rushing to get their weapons in order, looking around as though not knowing what to do, told him which this was.

"What is it?" Thanos asked, stopping one of them. The man had the look of a city guard, not one of the castle contingent. His uniform was less pristine, and there wasn't the flash of a royal insignia at his shoulder. "Calm down. Tell me what's happening."

"Prince Thanos." The man sounded breathless, as though he'd run all the way from the city. "Thank the gods you're here. We've been trying to find someone senior to take charge, but Prince Lucious isn't here, and in the wake of the Blood Moon festivities..."

All the others who might have done so were probably too hung over to be useful, Thanos thought. He'd sent away the two generals who'd been there.

"You've found me now," Thanos said. "What's the emergency?"

"It's the Stade, your highness," the guard said. "The rebellion has attacked the Stade!"

A flicker of interest and hope flared in Thanos, but he did his best to disguise it.

"What do you mean, soldier?"

"In the middle of the Killings, your highness," the guard said. "They attacked the Stade and freed the combatlords. Now … now the whole area around the Stade is rioting! They're in open rebellion, and we don't know what to do!"

Inwardly, Thanos cheered in joy at the audacity of the move. It was brilliant, in its way, striking at the heart of the Empire while acquiring truly dangerous fighters for the rebellion. The rioting around the rest… handled properly, it might turn into full rebellion in the city.

He'd just been handed the opportunity to do it.

"Right," he said. "From this moment, I'm in command. What's your name?"

"Gil, your highness."

"Well, Gil, you're with me. I hope you know how to ride."

Thanos raced for the stables, saddling his horse as quickly as he could and ordering the stable hands to fetch one for the soldier while he grabbed his weapons. Together, they rode down into the city, and it probably looked to the guard as though Thanos was hurrying to try to put down the rebellion. Instead, Thanos wanted to get there so that he could see it for himself and look for ways to fan the flames.

There were *real* flames as the two of them rode down into the city. People had set fires in some of the poorest areas, and Thanos could see smoke rising in curls while guards, looters, and rioters fought on the streets.

"Noble scum!" A man ran at Thanos, a knife in his hand. Thanos kicked him away and kept riding.

"You don't want to stop and finish him, your highness?" Gil asked. "Prince Lucious would—"

"There's no time," Thanos said, cutting him off. It wasn't the real reason, but it was one a guard might believe. "Where are the officers currently in charge?"

"We're not sure *who's* in charge, your highness, but a few of the officers have found a spot in one of the old towers overlooking the Stade."

"Then that's where we need to go," Thanos said, spurring his horse forward. The streets were closing in now, and in the side streets, he could see groups of people gathering. Most of them looked as though they were just standing around, as though they wanted to know what was going on.

If he'd had more time, Thanos might have gone to them and urged them to revolt with the others. As it was, he rode in the direction of the Stade, and even from here, he could see the signs of violence. There were groups of guards in the streets, and even as he watched, a cluster of them set off after a running man.

"Leave him!" Thanos ordered. "I need you with me."

He and his group of guards advanced through the streets. In one, he saw a group of what were clearly looters smashing their way into houses. He saw them dragging a man and a woman from one. It was obvious that they intended to rob them, and probably murder them, taking advantage of the call to rebellion to steal or settle some old score.

"With me!" Thanos said and charged forward. He drew a sword and struck out, making a man fall back as he clutched a bloodied stump of an arm. He parried a blow from a club, then kicked another man back. The guards were there then, fighting off the others and setting them to flight.

"Are you all right?" Thanos called down to the man and woman who had been dragged from their home.

"I—" the man began, "they were going to kill us. Thank you."

Thanos pointed to the guards accompanying him. If he had them to command, he should at least use them in a way that protected the people of the city. "These men will stay here and make sure that they don't come back. Stay inside. It will pass soon."

Except that Thanos was hoping it wouldn't. He was hoping it would turn into something more as he set off toward the Stade again. Far more.

The Stade was ahead, and so were the old towers. They were so ancient they had probably been there as long as the city, reaching up in pure white marble so high that they almost rivaled the castle's bastions or the spires of some of the city's temples. Normally, they were empty, but now Thanos could see the guards standing around the base, obviously unsure what to do next.

Inside, there was a spiral staircase running around the wall of the tower, leading up to a level far above. Thanos ran, ignoring the burning in his muscles as he made it to the top level. There, he found half a dozen men in the uniforms of guard captains, soldiers and royal guards, all arguing and shuffling orders.

"And I say that we need to move now, Maximus," one said. "Without waiting for orders."

"And risk angering the king, Pullo?" another countered.

Thanos decided to take charge. "What move were you thinking of making?"

The men there stared at him. The one called Pullo bowed low.

"Prince Thanos. We hadn't expected that *you* would come."

"I hadn't expected to be here," Thanos said. From the top of the tower, there was a good view out over the Stade and the rest of the city. From there, he could see the violence in the Stade, and it was chaos.

There were fights in every corner of it. Thanos could see knots of guards in the colors of the city, engaged in outright battle with rebels, with combatlords, or simply with people in the stands. The combatlords were easy to make out even from up here, standing proud in the chaos, whirling and leaping, killing almost effortlessly. There were fires in the Stade too, burning in the stands where people had set light to whatever they could.

"Look at them," Maximus said. "Animals."

Thanos shook his head. "Just desperate people. How bad is it?"

"There are riots in the Stade and all the surrounding streets," Maximus explained. "We have lost—"

"Temporarily," another of the soldiers interjected.

"We have temporarily lost control of half of the lower district next to it."

Thanos tried to think. Could this be turned into the loss of the entire city? Could this be the moment when things changed in the Empire? Below, the violence certainly felt as though it might never cease. There were guards down there, but too few to ever fully contain the chaos. Thanos felt as though he was floating above it up here, but even so, the violence felt almost close enough to touch. In a nearby street, he could see men and women ripping up the cobblestones with their hands, flinging them in the direction of an advancing group of guards.

"What are you doing to regain control?" Thanos asked. "*Can* you regain control, or do I need to evacuate my wife from the castle?"

His throat tightened at that thought. He wanted the rebels to succeed, but he also knew the kind of violence that could accompany a revolution. He would not allow Stephania to be caught up in that. He needed to find ways to help the rebels, but if they were already winning, he would ride back to make sure that Stephania and any other innocents in the castle got out of the city safely. He'd already seen what the mob in the city could be like.

"There should be no need for that, your highness," Pullo said. "We have more than a thousand good soldiers in place outside the city gates, ready to advance at your command."

"Our thought was to advance and surround the Stade," Maximus said. Thanos could practically hear his need for royal approval. "We can trap the rebels and the combatlords in there, then tighten the ring like a noose. We can attack them from all sides and end this. Maybe we can even capture some of the leaders of the rebellion."

Thanos had to admit that it was a good plan. It was simple, but there was a kind of strength in that. There was nothing to go wrong, only a constant kind of pressure that would crush the rebels under the weight of numbers.

Thanos had to find a way to stop it.

"No," he said. "We can't do that."

"Why not?" Maximus demanded, then seemed to realize what he was saying. "Forgive me, your highness. I don't mean to speak out of turn, but I'm not sure you understand everything that might be at stake."

Thanos tried to think, and one hard, harsh truth rose up in him like bile: this wasn't going to be the moment when the rebellion overthrew the Empire, or even the city. There were too many soldiers waiting. Even if this thousand didn't put down the revolt, there would be more to follow.

All he could do now was try to salvage some kind of victory for the rebels, even though the thought of what he would have to do was pure pain. He had to choose, right now, which lives to spare and which to take.

"It's you who don't understand what's at stake," Thanos said, trying to put as much authority into his tone as possible. "Do you think the Stade matters at this point?"

"Your highness," Pullo said, "that's where the rebels *are*."

"There are rebels in every corner of the city," Thanos snapped back. "You, Gil, didn't we have to fight a group of them on the way here?"

"Well, I suppose so," the guard who'd brought him said.

Thanos went on before anyone else could argue or contradict. He changed his tone to that of a general giving a speech before a battle.

"The truth is that the rebels are in the city. There are fires spreading, and riots growing in every district. A thousand men sounds like a lot, but it will barely be enough to control the whole city. I want the soldiers divided up, with city guards running each group. I want patrols on every major street. I want the fires controlled, and any looting stopped. We go out and we show the people that we control every street. Where there are rebels, we engage them, but the priority is showing that the city belongs to us."

Maximus still looked skeptical. "What about the Stade?"

"We put in a cordon around the Stade," Thanos said. "Two hundred men."

"Two hundred? That—"

"You will do as I have ordered," Thanos said. Two hundred was far too few to stop the rebels slipping out. There would be holes in the line. There would be escape routes. "I will not take the Stade while hordes of rebels march on the castle to kill my family and my wife! We will hold the city until the battle in the Stade burns out, and then we will move in to take what's left."

And in the meantime, soldiers would be putting down the revolt everywhere else. It would have happened anyway, but now that Thanos had given the order, everything the soldiers did would be down to him. Every death, every beating, would be because he had given this order. Here at the top of the tower, he wouldn't see the executions, but he would know they were happening.

He just had to hope that the rebels in the Stade would make it.

CHAPTER TWELVE

Lucious wandered through the aftermath of the revolt in the city while the soldiers swept away rioters. No one challenged him. They knew who he was, and the men around him were hard men, tough men, whom it was better not to ask questions of.

It wasn't the same as his raids had been, though, because the guards were being far too restrained by comparison. No gibbets, no whippings in the street. Hardly even any executions. It was almost as if they didn't want to clamp down on the city where their friends and families lived. He made a mental note to look into bringing in mercenaries from the further corners of the Empire. Men who wouldn't hold back.

On another day, he would have ensured it happened in Delos. He and his men would have gone on a binge of violence through the city, paying back the rioters and the rebels for daring to rise up. On another day, he would have been the one there when they wanted a commander for their forces, rather than his brother, Thanos.

His brother. Just the thought of that made Lucious curl his lip in anger. He was the heir. Delos was *his*, whatever the books said.

"Just down this way, your highness," Vrek said.

Lucious had brought a quartet of guards with him, replacements for the ones he'd lost to Thanos. Vrek was a former bandit, who had joined the army because it offered better pickings. Quellon and Fen were both equally massive. They looked like they might be brothers, although that was hardly a thought to calm Lucious right then. Justino was whip thin and good with knives.

"You're sure this is where the people I want will meet?"

The former bandit shrugged. "This is Delos. These kinds of people aren't hard to find."

The tavern was a long way from anywhere Lucious would normally have chosen to drink, even on one of his forays into the city with the other young nobles. There were places that held the dashing hint of danger, and then there were places like this.

It was stone built, but probably only because the patrons would have burnt down anything wooden. The doors were iron bound and the windows had bars, making the place look more like a fortress than just a place to drink. Instead of a sign, a ram's skull hung above the door. From inside, Lucious could hear the sounds of people drinking and yelling to one another, shut in while the rest of the city fought.

"I'd have thought that people in a place like this would be out looting," Lucious said.

"Begging your pardon, your highness," Vrek said, "but looting is a mug's game at a time like this, and people in here will know it. Stuff you could steal any day of the week, with a whole army's worth of soldiers out to kill you if they so much as see you outside."

Lucious shrugged off the familiarity for now. "I don't need a lecture on the finer points of reaving etiquette. Just get me *inside*."

It took his men perhaps a dozen blows before the door's lock broke open. Lucious stepped into a room that had long since fallen silent. Rough-looking men stood frozen, halfway to standing, obviously caught off guard by the sight of their prince entering the room. Many of them wore cloaks, their features hidden under the cowls. Lucious found himself wondering if they'd done that when his men started pounding on the door, or if they actually drank there like that. He strode over to the tavern's bar and put down a coin, spinning it so that the gold gleamed in the sunlight.

"Wine," Lucious said, "and this will pay for the door."

The barkeep snatched up the coin as Lucious let go of it, coming back with a skein of wine. Lucious held it, but didn't drink it. Behind him, he heard the sound of men settling back into their seats. He didn't look round. These peasants wouldn't dare to attack him.

"I'm looking for information," Lucious said. He took out another coin and spun it. "My men told me that this might be the right place to come."

"Maybe your men didn't hear right," a voice from the back called out.

Lucious turned and nodded. Vrek and Justino moved forward and dragged out one of the cloaked figures while the two brothers watched the rest. Some looked like animals tensed to spring, but they didn't. Perhaps they could guess what would happen if they attacked the heir to the throne.

Lucious stood and pulled the cowl from the man's head. He had probably been a strong man once, but now the years were taking their toll.

"My men hear very well," Lucious said. He struck out, catching the man in the stomach with his fist, hard enough to knock the breath from him. "Mostly because they know when to be quiet and listen."

Lucious went and sat down again. He went back to spinning his coin.

"I've seen things," he said to the room. "I want to know what they mean, and that means asking you. Believe me, I wouldn't be here if I didn't have to be."

Given the choice, he would have burned this place down with everyone there still in it, but sometimes it was necessary to do unpleasant things like associating with this scum.

"I saw Prince Thanos this morning," Lucious said.

"Most of us did," another of the tavern's patrons said. "He was the one putting down the riots."

"Before that," Lucious said, pushing down his anger for the moment. "I saw him riding back toward the castle early this morning. He's been sneaking about. I want to know why."

"Then why not ask him instead of interrupting our drinking?" another of the men there asked.

Lucious sighed and drew his sword, laying it down on the bar. He looked over to his men. "You see what happens?" he asked. "I try to be reasonable, and people just throw it back in my face."

He sprang forward, snatching up his blade and swinging it in one motion. Blood sprang from the inn patron's throat as Lucious cleaved through it. He died as easily as any other peasant. Strange; Lucious had expected more.

Now the other patrons reacted, and for a moment Lucious felt real fear. They sprang up from their seats, knives and clubs clearing their sheaths. His men moved into formation around him, and just for a second, Lucious thought that maybe he'd miscalculated. Then he remembered who he was.

"Harm me, and you'll watch your families flayed before they finally impale you," Lucious said. He drew a pouch from behind his back. "On the other hand, if you help me, it could be very profitable for you all."

He threw it into the blood on the table, and the clink of it cut through the silence. Slowly, Lucious felt the tension in the room dissipate.

"Never did like Eskrin much anyway," one man muttered, and that seemed to be the cue for the others to sit down again, even if they kept their weapons on the tables.

"Always did have a big mouth on him," another agreed.

The first man shrugged. "Not a problem anymore."

Lucious went back to his seat. Now, he *did* sip the wine. He needed it after how close that had been. It was vile stuff, watered and sour from being left out too long.

"Thanos," he said, letting the words sit. "I want to know anything you've heard about him. I want to know why he's sneaking about. And don't tell me that you haven't heard anything. There's always something. There had better be, anyway, if you want the soldiers to give this sty a miss."

The men there looked at one another before looking at one of their number in a corner, a small man nursing a glass in both hands. Lucious saw him swallow as the eyes turned to him, and when Lucious nodded, his men brought him out.

"Your friends seem to think you know something," Lucious said. "Now, as you may have noticed, I don't have a great deal of patience, so I'd advise you to say what it is."

The man stood there, opening and closing his mouth. To Lucious, he looked like a fish.

"Justino here is quite good at getting information from people, I hear," Lucious said. "He can do things with knives that—"

"There are rumors," the man said.

"There are always rumors," Lucious said.

"These are about Haylon."

That was enough to catch Lucious's interest. Absently, he wiped the blood from his still wet sword blade.

"What's your name?" Lucious asked.

"Alexander, your highness."

"Well, Alexander, what about Haylon?"

"I… I don't know much," the man admitted. "I just… know people who know people. People who claim to be in the rebellion. People who've been to Haylon. I've only heard a few things."

"And what are they?" Lucious asked as he put his sword away.

"Just that things weren't as they seemed there with the first expedition," Alexander said. "That the story Prince Thanos told about it wasn't the real one."

"So what is the truth?" Lucious asked.

"I don't know," Alexander admitted. Lucious saw him pale. "But I… I could find out. I know the right people."

Lucious smiled slowly. Today was proving more interesting than he'd expected. "Then I think you should ask them, don't you?"

"Y-yes, your highness."

Lucious saw him squirm in place. "What is it?"

"It's just… the people I'll have to ask… it's not the sort of information that comes cheap."

Lucious took another pouch from his belt, flinging it down alongside the first.

"Consider that a down payment," he said. He looked around the room. "No. Consider it a retainer, for all of you. From this moment forward, you're my men." He held up a hand as some of those there started to mutter. "I know, I know, you're all busy with your own little 'business enterprises.' I have no interest in interfering with that. If you want to steal or kill or sell the weak, that's your business. *My* business is the truth about Thanos. Help me with my business, and you'll find it easier to go about *your* business."

"You're offering us protection?" one of the patrons asked.

Lucious gestured to the thugs he'd brought with him. "I look after my men," he said. "Ask them if you like. Ask how good the pickings are, and how much freedom there is to do what they like. So long as you also do what *I* like, you'll never have to worry about the guards again."

"And there will be gold?" one of the others asked. "You're still offering us gold, right?"

"I'm offering you a choice," Lucious countered. "I'll pay you for what you do. If you need to bribe informants, or buy secrets, I'll pay. If you give me information, I'll pay. If you give me enough to have Thanos's head… I'll give you your weight in gold. Of course, you could choose to ignore all that. You could try to walk away, or to cross me."

He walked over and drew his finger through the blood of the man he'd killed. Peasant blood, but he'd gotten used to the feel of it.

"If a man chooses that, he becomes my enemy. I'll hunt him down. You'll all get coin for any betrayers you find for me. Then… well, there are torturers in the castle who can keep a man alive for weeks if they want. Long enough to see everyone he loves executed, at least."

Lucious wiped his hand on the dead patron's tunic.

"But it's your choice, of course. I wouldn't want to pressure you. Now, if you'll all excuse me, I'm going to enjoy the Blood Moon while there's still some of the festivities left."

He walked from the tavern, his men falling in behind him. Lucious didn't have to wait to know what decision these peasants would make. He would go back to the castle, and soon enough, one of these men would deliver Thanos to him. Thanos would die, Stephania would be begging at his feet to be his, and the world would be as it should be.

Chapter Thirteen

Ceres stood at the prow of the pirate ship as it bore down on a harbor village far to the north of Delos, and her heart filled with the sight of home. The village wasn't a large one. It had a natural harbor, wooden buildings clustered around a central square, and fish dried in the sun on racks, prior to smoking.

Tears came to her eyes. After all these moons, she would be home at last. She thought of her family, of the rebels, of the destiny awaiting her—and her heart quickened.

On the shore, she could see people running around in response to the approaching ship. This close, she could hear the tolling of an alarm bell, and she could see guards in the uniforms of the Empire forming up, ready for battle. At least a few people were riding clear on horseback, and Ceres couldn't help a moment of regret at that. She didn't want to scare them, but the pirate ship was the best way for her to reach the mainland again.

Ceres saw a spiked chain rise from the water, lifted across the harbor by the villagers. Obviously, they'd had to deal with pirates before. She felt the stilling of the ship's rhythm as the oarsmen struggled to bring it to a halt, caught up on the chain.

"This is as far as we can go," one of the pirates told her, and Ceres could hear the note of fear then. He didn't even suggest being allowed to raid the village.

"Then I'll make my own way to shore," Ceres replied. "You have small boats?"

"Two, my lady."

"Then any man you've taken for the oars who wishes to leave is to be allowed to do so."

"But we can't sail the ship at full speed if—"

"It will move a lot slower if it's stone," Ceres replied, her tone hardening as she cut him off. Life on the boat was hard. The only way to keep respect was to show no weakness. "Now do it."

While she waited for them to obey, she went through the ship, taking what she needed. There was no armor that would really fit her there, but she managed scraps and fragments of it, piecing them together in a way that felt vaguely reminiscent of the Stade. She still had the stone dagger Eoin had given her on the forest folk's island, but to it, Ceres added one of the curved swords of the pirates, and a pair of etched steel bracers that ended in gauntlets of metal scales.

"When I'm gone," Ceres said, "put back out to sea. If you've any sense, you'll stop robbing people. I've spared you once, but if I catch you again…"

She let that hang while she watched the boat go down into the water with more than a dozen men aboard. Ceres could have gone with it, but she could see an easier way to the shore. With the lightness and balance the islanders had taught her, she walked her way along the chain the villagers had raised, hopping lightly onto the shore.

She watched the contingent of Empire soldiers as she approached. There were probably twenty of them, arranged in a square. They stood as if not knowing what to do. They'd probably been expecting to have to deal with a boat's worth of pirates, not one woman. Ceres walked up to them as calmly as she could.

"Halt!" the leader of the soldiers called. "Who are you? What are you doing here?"

"I don't want trouble," Ceres said. "I'm just passing through here."

"And those pirates just happened to give you a ride?" the officer demanded. Ceres saw a soldier beside him touch his shoulder. "What is it, Rikard?"

"Sir, it's her, sir!"

"Who?"

"Ceres! The rebel! I saw her at the Stade when I was south in the city, carrying messages."

"You're sure? I thought she was dead."

Ceres drew her blades, holding them out to either side, feeling the weight of them. She could have lied about who she was, but the Empire needed to understand what was coming for it.

"I'm not dead," she said. "And you should run."

"Run?" the officer said. "There's twenty of us! No one can beat twenty armed men. Not the greatest combatlord who ever lived. Certainly not some girl who played at it. So here's what's going to happen. You're going to surrender or we'll beat you senseless. Then we'll take you in chains down to the city."

"Not to Lord West?" the soldier who'd spoken before asked.

"Lord West?" the officer countered. "The man's halfway to being a rebel himself. The only reason he doesn't join the rebellion is because he's worried about losing his lands. No, we'll take this one where she belongs. Grab her."

The soldiers broke ranks as they started forward, and that was when Ceres attacked. Their officer had been right. The greatest combatlord couldn't have fought twenty men. They would have been rushed and brought down in seconds, but she was more than just a combatlord. She had the training of the forest folk. She had the power that came from the Ancient Ones' blood. Put together, it was as though her attackers were corn waiting for the scythe. The only reason she didn't turn them all to stone was because she suspected the effort of it would be too much for her.

She cut down one with a sweep of her curved blade, stepped through the line of men and stabbed out at another with her dagger. She spun and kicked, smashing away a soldier who tried to grab her and continuing to move.

A club came at Ceres's head. She ducked underneath it and answered with a sword stroke, then parried another attack with her bracers, ripping a weapon from its wielder's hand. She leapt, clearing the heads of two men who tried to tackle her, landing lightly.

She kept moving, because stillness was the one thing that could bring her down now. There were still enough soldiers to simply pile in and bring her down in a scrum of flailing limbs, so Ceres didn't give them the chance. She was so much faster than they were, so much stronger, that it was easy to keep the soldiers in one another's way. She stepped out of the way of another rush, stabbed one man with her dagger, and slammed another soldier into the frame of a door hard enough to crack it.

The strangest part about it wasn't the speed or strength with which she moved. She'd experienced that before in the Stade, in flashes. The part that went beyond it was the way it felt like a part of her now. It felt natural. Indeed, the whole fight felt like some bloody dance in which Ceres already knew the steps. She'd been opened up to the power within her, but she'd learned more than that. She'd learned to fit in with the world around her. She opened herself up to the battle, and let it tell her exactly where she needed to move.

Ceres swayed back from a slash, parried a thrust, and countered with a blow that took an Empire soldier in the leg. She spun and she struck, her blades always moving, always intercepting or striking, shoving away or cutting through. She felt the warmth of breath behind her, and was already ducking as a soldier moved in to grab her. Ceres sent him sprawling into the dirt.

The moments blended. There were so many swords around her, so many attackers, and yet Ceres didn't feel the fear that she should have at it. Instead, she felt almost serene. There was something beautiful about the act of moving with a blade in her hand, even if the consequences of it were so terrible.

Her bracers caught the sun, shining as they deflected blades, reflecting the uniforms of men as her fists slammed into them. The soldiers got in one another's way as Ceres kept moving, never still for long, never pausing to let them regain the formation they'd given up.

Maybe if they'd managed to circle her, and strike at her from all sides, they might have had a chance. Maybe if they'd been more than just ordinary soldiers, barely trained and used to peasants who didn't fight back, they'd have been able to slip past the whirling circle of her blades.

As it was, man after man attacked, and then fell. They started to push to keep out of Ceres's way, to not be the one to have to fight her next. Ceres felt as though she was pushing through trees in a forest, except that these were trees lined with blades, any one of which could still hurt her or kill her.

Suddenly, Ceres found herself in clear space, facing off against the officer who'd ordered her taken. She could tell just from the way he stood that he'd had more training with a blade than most of his men. Certainly, the sword he held was finely worked, honed to a razor's edge.

He thrust and Ceres parried, keeping her distance. She had to keep moving, because there were still other men around her. None seemed to be attacking now, and Ceres guessed that they were hoping their officer would deal with her where they couldn't, but she still couldn't afford to let her guard down. She moved around the officer, continuing to parry.

"You might be able to best these scum, but I was first sword in my unit, back in Delos. They used to give me criminals still armed, when they wanted it to look as though they'd died fighting."

Ceres didn't reply. Instead, she continued to circle. She tried a cut, and the riposte was fast enough that she was grateful for the speed her power gave her. She leaned away, pushing aside the thrust, but it seemed to embolden the officer.

"Look at you," he said, striking and striking again. "You're not so dangerous. You're nothing. Probably only got into the Stade because you were trying to seduce—"

Ceres struck while he was still mid-sentence. The officer's sword came up to parry, and she rolled her wrist around it, her blade cleaving down through his armor from shoulder to mid-chest. She let go of the hilt and let him fall, already looking for the next threat.

There wasn't one. Half a dozen soldiers were running by now, but that was all that was left of them. The rest lay in a broad circle around her, dead, unconscious, or simply wounded too badly to run.

The adrenaline of the fight passed in a rush, and Ceres stood shaking as the scale of what she'd done hit her. Fourteen men. She'd cut down fourteen men. Men who would have happily killed her, but that did nothing to clean away the blood from the village square around her, or from her armor. She'd cut them down easily, thanks to her training, and her powers.

It had felt as natural as breathing. Now, Ceres had to remind herself to do that, catching the iron tang of the blood in the air while she stood and waited for her heart to return to normal.

Ceres could see the people looking out from their houses, as though wondering what she was. Ceres had an answer to that at least. She was of the blood of the Ancient Ones. On the island with her mother, she'd started to get a sense of what that meant. Now, with so many people staring at her over the bodies of the dead, she felt as though she'd learned another side of it.

She heard the sound of hooves over the silence of the square. She looked up to see horses approaching; so many that it seemed like half an army. Easily a hundred men, all armored in mail, all carrying long spears for throwing or jabbing down with at full charge. Ceres doubted that even she could survive if they attacked.

One had a pennant attached to his lance, marked with a stylized weather vane, being blown by the west wind. He rode forward from the mass of them, stopping short of her and raising the visor of a helm in the shape of a boar's head. The face beneath was surprisingly young.

"What happened here?" he demanded. Ceres could hear the note of fear there.

"They attacked me," she said, as if it explained all of it. In a way it did.

"And you killed that many men?" He sounded as though he couldn't believe it. Ceres didn't blame him. She could barely believe it herself. Even now, the violent beauty of it seemed like some kind of dream. Some kind of nightmare, but she couldn't let them see that. She had to be more than just a girl standing in a square then. She had to be a symbol.

She stood as openly as she could, trying to wear the blood that covered her more like a badge than it felt.

"I fought in the Stade. I was cast out by the Empire. I survived their prison ships. And yes, I killed that many men, but only because I will not let the Empire control my life any longer."

"I must bring you to Lord West, ruler of these lands, and allow him to decide your fate."

He squinted into the light.

"What is your name?" he asked, as if beginning to recognize her.

"I am Ceres," she said proudly.

A gasp erupted from the crowd.

"That is not possible," he said. "Ceres is dead."

For the first time, she allowed herself to grin.

"Not anymore."

Chapter Fourteen

Thanos stood in the king's council chambers while around him, the senior nobles of the Empire stood and applauded. He clutched a scrap of paper deep in his fist, clinging to it while the noise rang around him. At the head of the great oval table, his father sat impassively next to Queen Athena, but Thanos searched his face. Even now, even hating all that this man represented, he wanted to find some hint of pride there.

At the back of the room, he could see Lucious watching. Lucious wasn't applauding with the others. Instead, his expression was intense, following every movement Thanos made.

"Well done, Prince Thanos," the master of the king's forests said. "Without you, we would be having our throats cut by rebels even now!"

"I think the royal guards would have handled it," the captain of the royal bodyguard replied.

The master of coin shrugged. "I'm grateful that we don't have to find out."

King Claudius stood. "Enough of this. I want to know what happened today. How did things get so out of hand? Naymir, you're meant to have control of the Stade."

Thanos saw a sweating nobleman take a small step back.

"Who would have thought that rebels would attack *there*, your majesty?" the man said.

"No one here, apparently," Queen Athena said with obvious disdain. "And as a result, how many were harmed in the Stade?"

"We don't have full numbers yet," Thanos said. "We don't know how many people were killed on the on the Stade floor, and as for the streets around it—"

"How many *nobles*?" Queen Athena said, cutting in. "Who cares about a few dead peasants?"

"Perhaps if we'd cared more," Thanos pointed out, "it wouldn't have come to this."

"Oh, poor Thanos," Lucious said. "Still with a heart bleeding for the peasantry."

Thanos might have argued, but the captain of the royal guard chose that moment to speak.

"There were perhaps a dozen minor nobles at the Killings, your majesty," he said. "Four were killed, two suffered injuries serious enough to require the healers, and the others escaped with cuts and bruises."

"Were they anybody important?" King Claudius demanded. "No? Then we have more important things to consider. Like how this happened. I thought we were crushing the rebellion, piece by piece."

If he thought that, Thanos thought, then he really didn't understand how these things worked. He created more rebels with every act of cruelty. The Empire was like a drowning man who needed to swim but instead only thrashed.

"I have been attacking rebels wherever we can find them," Lucious said. "Applying pressure to force them into submission. Eventually, we will crush them."

Thanos saw King Claudius shake his head.

"I don't care about 'eventually.' I care about what happened at the Stade. Thanos, you're here to report, so report."

Thanos gripped the paper in his hand tighter at the casual way his father treated him. As though he were just some officer to be commanded.

"The commanders down by the Stade sent a runner as I was returning from a morning ride," Thanos said.

"You're fond of those," Lucious muttered in the background. Thanos ignored him.

"He reported that there was violence around the Stade, and that no one was available to take control of the situation." Now he did allow himself a pointed look in Lucious's direction. "He'd been trying to find Lucious, but he wasn't there."

"Enough squabbling," the king said. "Why was the runner not able to find one of my generals? General Olliant might have left for Haylon, but Haven should have been around."

Thanos looked around, hoping that no one caught his look while he tried to see if anyone was suspicious.

"The old fool has probably wandered off," Queen Athena said. "He's well past his usefulness. Honestly, husband, can you imagine the mess he would have made of this?"

"Possibly," King Claudius said, but he looked thoughtful. "Go on, Thanos. What about when you got to the Stade?"

"The captains there reported on the situation," Thanos said. "And I saw that the biggest risk was of the situation spreading beyond the Stade. I deployed troops to the streets to ensure that didn't happen."

King Claudius steepled his fingers. "I have spoken to the captains, Thanos. They said that they urged you to surround the Stade and move in to take it. Is that true?"

"It is," Thanos said, because there was no way he could deny it. "They didn't grasp the full situation."

"As far as I can see," Queen Athena put in, "the situation was that you had a chance to capture the leaders of the rebellion, and you failed to take it. You do know that they escaped?"

"I know," Thanos said. He tried to fill his voice with regret. He wasn't made for this, for politics and secrecy, but he had to do it. "I also know what would have happened if rebels had reached the castle."

"From what I hear," Lucious said, "the real rebels weren't in the streets. That was just a rabble."

"You weren't there!" Thanos snarled back, grateful that Lucious made it so easy to be angry. "I was. I heard that there was violence on the streets. I *fought* rioters, and I had to make a choice. I had to choose between crushing the Stade and risking that coming here. Here, where my wife was still in our bed. Where all of you were. Where *you* Lucious, were presumably still sleeping off the festivities!"

"And if I hadn't, do you think the rebels would still be free? I don't take things so gently."

"You might think I made the wrong choice out there," Thanos replied, "but that's the point. I was the one who was there to make the choice, and I made the one that would keep my family safe." The nobles there probably thought that he just meant Stephania. The king and Lucious would probably be wondering. "I won't be questioned on that."

He turned and made for the door. No one stopped him, which was probably as well. He was running out of answers. He'd bought some time by making his actions look like an emotional outburst, but there would still be questions.

He didn't have time to answer questions, because of the scrap of paper in his hand. It had come by raven this morning. Just six words.

The sculpture garden. Noon. Meet me- A.

⚜ ⚜ ⚜

The sculpture garden was an ode in stone to Thanos's ancestors, yet he couldn't feel comfortable there. Carved images of kings since the start of the Empire stared down, along with their wives, children, generals, and favorites. The first king, Ullian, sat atop a rearing marble horse, the broken granite body of a creature that could only have come from the depths of the artist's imagination beneath the hooves. After all this time, the marble features atop the horse were weathered to the point where Thanos couldn't make them out. Would he have seen a resemblance there if they hadn't been?

"The Great King Ullian, crushing the Ancient Ones," Akila said, stepping from behind another statue. The rebel leader looked a little more battle worn than he had back on Haylon, but he was still spare-framed and dark-haired, with a short beard and a tinge of dark humor in his expression. As always, he wore two short stabbing swords at his waist.

"It probably didn't happen like that," Thanos said. "Cosmas, the royal scholar, is always saying history is more complicated than you think."

"No? It's the story I heard. The founders of the mighty Empire, freeing humanity from the yoke of the Ancient Ones, bringing fair and just rule to all." That brought with it one of the sardonic smiles that the rebel leader seemed to specialize in. "Of course, for an Empire supposedly founded on rebellion, you and your family seem remarkably resistant to it now."

"I'm surprised to see you here," Thanos said. "I wouldn't have thought you could leave the rebellion just to talk to me."

"I needed to see if another story was true," Akila said. He didn't draw either of his swords, but his hands rested on the hilts.

"Akila?" Thanos said with a frown. "What's going on?"

"You tell me," the rebel leader snapped back. Thanos saw him take a step forward. "I let you go because of how much you helped us on Haylon. You swore brotherhood to us."

Thanos didn't give ground. "And I've been working to help you. I sent you a warning of the attack on Haylon."

"An attack they're saying you ordered," Akila snapped back, and now one of his swords did clear its sheath. "We captured soldiers and they were talking about how you rode down to the docks to appoint the general attacking us."

"Because he's incompetent!" Thanos retorted. He took a step back now, and found himself pressed against the statue of Ullian, literally depending on his ancestors for support. "I only found out the morning that they sent the fleet. I had to forge orders to stop it from being commanded by one of our greatest generals."

"Our greatest generals?" Akila said. He moved forward, his sword pressing to Thanos's throat. Thanos shoved the other man away.

"You know what I mean," Thanos said. He didn't draw his own blade, but he wasn't just going to let Akila murder him. "You know I'm on your side."

"Do I?" Akila demanded. "This general of yours is a long way from incompetent. He's plodding, but plodding is dangerous when you have the men. Now, I hear that you commanded a force that put down a rebellion here."

Thanos shook his head. "I was trying to ensure that it succeeded."

"By sending troops into the city?"

"The troops were coming anyway!" Thanos insisted. "All I could do was ensure that the leaders of the rebellion had enough time to get away."

He saw Akila stalk among the statues. The rebel leader lashed out, hacking a chip out of a marble figure's arm.

"You have all the answers, don't you?"

"If I had *all* the answers, I would have found a way to bring down the Empire by now," Thanos said.

"Would you?" Akila asked. "You'd bring down the nobility, and all the cruelty that goes with it? Then why did you marry one of them?"

Thanos thought of Stephania, and of all the joy he'd had with her. He wouldn't let even Akila make him feel bad about loving her.

"You wouldn't understand," Thanos said. "Stephania and I are happy together."

"So why should I believe that you want to disrupt all of that?" Akila demanded. "You know why I came here? Why I took a boat in the middle of defending my home? Because if anyone was going to kill you for betraying us, I swore it was going to be me. I was going to look you in the eye, and if you'd betrayed us, I was going to do the job myself."

There was a time, after Ceres's death, when Thanos might have let him do it. Now, though, there was too much to fight for. Too much still to do.

"I haven't betrayed you," Thanos said. He could feel Akila's gaze on him. "You told me to come here and do this, when I wanted to fight."

"I think you actually believe that," Akila said. "You really believe you're doing what we want. If you hadn't sent that warning, you'd be dead by now. As it is… I don't know what to make of you, and I don't have enough time to waste working it out. Thanks to you, I have an island to defend from a plodding general who has seen every trick before. Thanks to you, the rebellion here has been set back by who knows how much. I'm not going to kill you, Thanos, but you aren't one of us either, not really."

"I'm risking everything for you," Thanos said.

"We're *all* risking everything," Akila replied. "But some of us do it in ways that don't involve marrying nobles and having rebels butchered." He shook his head. "I have to get back. Thank you for your warning, but if this is your idea of helping, we can do without it."

Thanos watched him walk back among the statues, quickly disappearing among the still marble figures. He couldn't believe that Akila had come. More than that, he couldn't believe that Akila didn't trust him, after all he'd done.

He would find a way to do more. He had to.

Chapter Fifteen

Stephania walked the grounds of the castle, searching for her husband and taking a moment to enjoy the sunlight. Down in the courtyard, where servants and soldiers bustled about their duties, the world seemed brighter today, and had ever since she'd learned the news at the feast.

It was still hard to believe that she was really pregnant, but just the thought of the tiny life growing inside her filled her with joy. She hadn't told anyone, and it was far too early for the pregnancy to show, but right then she wanted to shout the news to the world.

Not until she'd told Thanos though. So far, Stephania hadn't even told her maids for certain. She wanted Thanos to be the first to hear the news, and to learn about the child they would be bringing into the world.

Stephania allowed herself a moment to daydream about what it would be like. Thanos, she had no doubt, would be a wonderful father, doting on his son or daughter, kind and protective, loving and strong. Stephania would need to ensure that their child got the core of ruthless steel that would see them through the world, but Thanos would be the one to try to ensure they never needed it.

Stephania loved him for that, and for so much else besides. Soon, their lives would be as close to perfect as Stephania could imagine.

She was drawn from her reverie by the sight of a man making his way across the castle's courtyard. He was grubby, dressed in the uniform of a soldier, but looking nothing like the pristine guards of the castle. Stephania wouldn't have given him a second look, might even have called for the guards to remove him, except that she recognized him.

"Fikirk, what are you doing here?"

The man looked around, and yes, it was definitely him. The same harried look, as though constantly expecting to be attacked. The same collection of scars, collected more in barroom brawls than in the wars he claimed. He was the kind of man Stephania would normally never admit to knowing, but he'd been a useful informant over the years, providing information from within the armies of the Empire that most of its generals could only wish for.

She normally communicated with him at second- or third-hand, or occasionally by meeting in secluded spots. She certainly hadn't summoned him to the castle today.

"My lady," he said, with an attempt at courtly manners that was frankly embarrassing. "I hadn't expected to see you today."

"If you hadn't expected that, then what are you doing here, Fikirk?" Stephania shook her head. It had to be important, whatever it was. The man wouldn't have come if it weren't crucial, and she wasn't about to let the man get away without telling her. "Come with me."

"My lady..." Fikirk said with a glance around. He was obviously looking for a way out.

"Do you want me to be seen out here with you?" Stephania demanded. "More to the point, do you want to continue receiving the stipend I send your way?"

She saw the man swallow, but he went with her. She led the way to a small side chamber. Not one of her own rooms, of course. That would have created too much of a chance of being seen. Instead, she picked a room that was probably used for storage, filled with sacks and crates that had probably been taken from peasants' homes.

She carefully propped the door shut so that no servant would dare to interfere, then returned her attention to the informant.

"Do you understand the difficulty you've created for me by coming here unannounced?" Stephania demanded. "If people see you here meeting with me, then they'll know that you're one of my informants."

"Maybe they'll think I'm a lover," Fikirk joked, and just the thought of it was enough to make Stephania feel ill. Or maybe that was just the pregnancy. "That was the story they told about old Xanthos. Haven't seen him in a while. Was he really in your bed?"

The way he said that made Stephania pause. Her informants weren't supposed to know about one another. They certainly weren't meant to know about the people who arranged more dangerous matters for her, or to make guesses about what had befallen one who had become too dangerous.

"Wouldn't you like to know?" Stephania countered with a forced laugh.

"Oh, are you shocked that I know about him?" Fikirk asked. He tapped his nose. "I work things out, I do. Wouldn't be much use otherwise, would I?"

"I think you'd better prove yourself *very* useful right now," Stephania said. "You obviously came here to tell me something."

To her surprise, Fikirk looked down at his boots like some naughty child caught out stealing sweetbreads.

"Not to see ... *you* ... as such, my lady."

Stephania sighed. She should have guessed that this would happen. That was the problem with informants. They had no sense of loyalty.

"Who then?" Stephania demanded.

"Well, you see, it's tricky—"

"You'd best make it a lot less so quickly, if you want to continue working for me," Stephania said.

The soldier took a look around the storeroom and spat. Stephania saw a rat scurry away across the floor. It seemed that even his own sort wanted nothing to do with Fikirk.

"Well, I guess I have been working for you for a while," Fikirk said, "but Prince Lucious wasn't exactly what you'd call subtle in his recruiting strategy, you know?"

"Lucious? You're here to see *Lucious*?" Stephania asked.

"Not exactly," Fikirk said.

"His people, his thugs, whatever he wants to call them," Stephania said, waving that away. The point was that her informants were working for a man she'd assumed to be too arrogant and stupid to employ any at all. Lucious was the kind of man who assumed he knew everything anyway, so why would he employ informants now?

"Well, it was Prince Lucious who set me off looking, but what I found…" Stephania waited out Fikirk's pause. "I think I might go straight to the king with this. Isn't as though Lucious will pay me what he says."

"And what does he say he'll pay?" Stephania asked, taking out a small pouch of gold. "Maybe I can outbid him?"

The soldier shrugged. "It would take more than that. This information is worth a man's weight in gold."

"And maybe you'll get that from the king," Stephania said, "but this is what I have now. Think of it as me paying for a preview."

Even with that, the man seemed reluctant. Was he really that ungrateful after all the time he'd spent working for her?

"I don't know, Lady Stephania. You might not like what I have to hear."

"All the more reason for me to hear it then," Stephania snapped. Why was she spending all this time in a dank storeroom? Only some sense that this was truly important kept her pushing. She had gotten where she was today by never letting things happen without her knowledge. She drummed her fingers on the edge of a crate, then decided to try a different approach.

"You aren't thinking this through, Fikirk. You've come here because you don't trust Lucious to pay you. Maybe the king won't either. You're already a part of his army."

"I have the proof stashed," Fikirk said. "Well, more or less."

"And you think that will matter?" Stephania countered. "Tell me now, and you can still try to get what you can, but you'll at least have something for the information."

"Hmm…"

Stephania knew she had him with that small sound. It was just a matter of waiting.

"All right," he said at last. "But like I said, you won't like it. You're going to have to work out what to do about your husband. Prince Thanos is a traitor."

Maybe he put it that bluntly because he wanted to see the look of shocked disbelief rise up to overtake Stephania's features. She could already feel her mind racing, grasping for any explanation, any straw.

"No," she said. "He's a prince of the Empire!"

"And he's working with the rebels," Fikirk insisted.

Stephania shook her head so hard she thought it might fall off.

"Oh, not those here," she heard Fikirk say, and it seemed as though it was coming from a distance. "Didn't you ever wonder what happened to him on Haylon?"

Of course she had. She'd wondered, because somehow her attempt at revenge had gone wrong.

"Fishermen found him," Stephania said.

"Rebels found him," Fikirk insisted. "Ever wonder why Thanos was one of the lucky ones? They took him in as a prisoner, and he helped them to beat Draco's men. Then today, I heard he helped replace Olliant with old Haven for the new expedition."

It couldn't be true. It had to be some lie, made up to discredit Thanos. Except… Stephania had seen him fight Lucious to protect the common folk. She knew he'd argued with the king, and she'd heard the rumors about what had happened in the Stade. That he'd had a chance to crush the rebels and hadn't. She'd assumed that it was just Thanos not wanting to risk the people of the city, but what if it was more?

"Is that all of it?" Stephania asked.

"It's enough, I reckon," Fikirk said.

It was. It was enough that Thanos would find himself branded a traitor, regardless of who he was. And that would mean only one thing, because the king didn't allow rebellion. Thanos would die.

"No," Stephania whispered to herself. "No."

Stephania tried to compose herself, but she couldn't stop the feelings welling up inside her. She was so used to being in control. She planned things well in advance, but there was no way to plan around this. How could she not have known all this about Thanos? How could she have been so stupid, not to learn it earlier?

Why didn't it make a difference to her?

She should have been planning then. She should have been thinking about ways to extricate herself from this, maybe even about bringing the information forward herself. But she couldn't. Not when it was the father of her child. Not when it was Thanos.

"Well, that's all I know," Fikirk said. "So I guess it's time to pay me so we can see how the king likes it."

Thanos was a traitor. Stephania knew it, deep in her bones, but the truth was, she didn't care. She didn't care if she had to kill half the Empire to keep him safe, either. The only thing that mattered was that he was hers, and nothing, *nothing* was going to destroy that.

"Yes," Stephania said, hefting the bag of gold. She threw it, lobbing it high and to the right of the soldier. He had to reach out wide to grab it, half turning to snatch it out of the air with a grin.

That was when Stephania stabbed him.

She hadn't planned it. She'd never stabbed anyone herself. Poison was so much neater. So much cleaner. But she didn't have time for poison, or even to think. All she had was the small knife that she kept for eating, like everyone else. It barely seemed like enough to kill someone with.

It still slid up under Fikirk's ribs easily enough, jabbing upward toward the heart as his blood spattered. Stephania pulled back in disgust at the wet heat of that, trying to wipe herself clean while the guard staggered, trying to grab his own blade. He fell to his knees, and Stephania simply stared at him.

"You can't… stop this," he managed, and Stephania stepped in to stab him again, then again. She didn't stop until she was certain he was dead on the floor in an expanding red pool.

Chapter Sixteen

Ceres stared up at Lord West's fortress home with a deep sense of foreboding. She had agreed to come along on the ride, willing to at least hear what this lord had to say before, if need be, fighting to the death. After all, she was back in her homeland now, and nothing, no lord, would stop her.

Lord West's castle was craggy and gray, with a keep sitting on a hill above a larger enclosure, only the presence of flowers growing around the walls offsetting the forbidding look of it.

She rode closer on a horse one of Lord West's men had loaned her. The creature was pale and skittish, so that Ceres spent as much time comforting the horse as looking at the castle around her. Even so, she could see the difference between this and the castle at the heart of Delos. That was a place designed to terrify the local populace into submission. This had more of a strong, protective feel to it. There were plenty of ordinary people living within the protective outer walls, in slate cottages that made the lower section seem like a village in its own right.

She had heard much of Lord West over the years and had heard, as far as nobles went, he was a fair one. But she still wasn't taking any chances. She eyed all possible exits in case she had to fight her way out of there, to the death, and flee on foot or on horseback.

The horsemen around her dismounted, and Ceres walked with them up the slope to the central keep. At least they gave her the respect of not trying to detain her. She went through the large entrance gate, following the warriors' leader through into a hall dominated by long tables. The warriors spread out around them, taking places that looked as though they were long established.

Another table sat at the front, and at it, Ceres saw a man in his forties working on documents with the aid of a pair of clerks.

"If the Empire's men have burned the fields, then I'm not going to expect them to provide grain, but my men still need to be fed. For the winter, give them work helping in the weavers' workshops while they replant. We can trade the extra for spelt from the hill farms."

"Yes, Lord West."

He looked up, and Ceres stared right back at him.

Ceres saw a man with shaggy, graying hair, a neatly trimmed beard, and deep brown eyes that seemed to take in everything about her at a glance. His clothes were finely made, but they were not the silks and fripperies of Delos's court, and they looked well worn.

"Gerant," he said, with the faint burr of a North Coast accent, "I sent you out because the riders from the Empire's contingent said there was a threat of pirates landing in the village, yet you seem to have brought back a single young woman with you. Please explain."

"She was what I found when I got there, uncle," the young man who'd led the warriors said. "A few other men alighted from the pirate ship, but they were clearly freed slaves. This was the only armed person there."

"If she's a pirate, hang her," Lord West said. "You know I won't allow any harm to befall my people."

"She isn't a pirate," the young man, Gerant, said.

"Then what is she?"

Ceres took a step forward. "Why don't you ask me that yourself?"

She heard a faint intake of breath from the soldiers around her as Lord West stood up and walked down to her. He was taller than she was, with the slightly bulky frame of a once strong man who now spent too much time indoors.

"I am Lord West of the North Coast," he said. "My family was given these lands as stewards in the days when the Ancient Ones still walked. My line is longer than that of the current king. Who exactly are you, young lady?"

"I'm Ceres," she said, trying to match the confidence in the nobleman's voice. "I fought in the Stade. I joined the rebellion. The Empire tried to kill me and failed."

Ceres thought she saw Lord West blink at that.

"When I heard who she was," Gerant said, "I thought you would want to speak with her, uncle."

"Do we have evidence that she is who she claims to be?" Lord West asked, never taking his eyes from Ceres.

"When I found her in the village," Gerant said. "I found her surrounded by the bodies of Empire soldiers. She'd fought twenty of them and won."

"Twenty men?" Lord West said. "That isn't possible."

Ceres made herself shrug as if it were nothing. "It's possible for me. There's a reason I fought in the Stade, and I've learned a lot since then."

She watched the older man's face.

"If you are who you say you are," he said at last, "then by the loyalty I have sworn to the Empire, I should put you in chains."

There was something about the way he said it that made it into a question. A man like this would know that Ceres must have come to his home for a reason, and now he was asking why.

"You owe them no loyalty," Ceres said. "When I came in here, you were talking about them burning your fields and killing your people. You're obviously a man who cares about those he rules."

"Enough to avoid getting them into wars they cannot win," Lord West said. "Yes, I have seen the things the Empire has done, but that does not mean I must throw away my people trying to change it all."

"If you don't, who will?" Ceres insisted. "It's easy to sit back and look after your little corner of the world, but if everyone does that, when will things ever get better? The Empire is stronger than any one of us, but it is not stronger than *all* of us."

"Ah, so you want us to join your rebellion," Lord West said. "You want me to join with people who would probably gladly see me thrown off my lands, my family and friends cast out."

"It isn't about that," Ceres said. "It's about overthrowing a tyrant, not overturning the world. You must have seen the things that are done in the Empire's name. If you put your own interests ahead of stopping it, then they're being done in your name as well." She had a question she wanted to ask. "Why do your men not wear the uniforms of the Empire's army?"

"Because then they would have to take the orders of the Empire's generals, even if that means burning villages," Gerant said beside Ceres. "My uncle would never allow that."

"But he can speak for himself," Lord West said. "My nephew has made some of the same arguments to me. But there is another reason why my men wear my colors. It is to show that they are *my* men. That we are not the Empire. That we exist to protect the people, not to command them. But by the same token, we will not come just because someone else calls."

"Then protect your people," Ceres said. "I have traveled to places and seen things that I never thought I would see, but all the time, I was thinking about the way things were back in the Empire. I was thinking about everything it has taken from me: my brother, my family, the man I loved—"

Thoughts of Thanos still brought the ache of loss with them. For all the things Ceres had learned, she hadn't found a way to shut that pain away. She shook her head.

"Again and again, the Empire has hurt me," she said. "It put me in the Stade to die, and I didn't. It put me on a ship to the Isle of Prisoners, and I survived. But how many more are not surviving? How many people die every day because we do nothing to stop it?"

"Many," Lord West said. For a moment, a note of sympathy crept into his voice. "And I can understand why you have every reason to hate the Empire. I have more than a few reasons of my own."

For a moment, Ceres thought that she had him.

"Then act on those reasons," she said. "Lend me your men."

"However, the fact remains that my family swore to serve the Empire, and I will not be the man to betray that. Honor matters. Loyalty matters. No, I'm sorry," he said. "Unless you can give me a better reason, I will be forced to take you prisoner. I have no choice."

"And hand me over to the Empire?" Ceres said.

She saw Lord West shake his head. "You will remain here. I can do that much, but no more."

"The Empire did not give your family its lands," Ceres pointed out. "The Ancient Ones did."

She heard a small sound of annoyance from Lord West. "And if you can produce one of them to command me, I will obey. Until then, though, you are merely wasting both of our time. Gerant, please escort the young lady to the north tower and secure it."

Ceres stood, summoning the power that lay within her. Before in the Stade, she'd managed to pull a weapon into Thanos's hand. Now, she reached out for the sword at Gerant's belt, wrapping her power around it and pulling with it. She wasn't sure it would work, but she wouldn't turn the men around her to stone. They weren't pirates or soldiers of the Empire, and they'd been nothing but courteous to her. She reached out with her power…

…and a second later, she was holding the sword belonging to Lord West's nephew.

Ceres heard men rising to their feet in a rush of armor, the scrape of blades clearing sheaths filling the hall. She knew she had to act fast, because if she didn't take advantage of this moment, she was simply someone who'd ended up holding a weapon in front of their lord.

"I don't need to produce one of the Ancient Ones," Ceres said, "because I *am* one."

She saw Lord West hold up a hand to halt his men. He stood there, staring at Ceres as though he couldn't quite believe what he'd seen.

"You're truly one of them?" he asked at last, in a tone so filled with awe it hardly seemed like the same man.

She held out the sword, closed her eyes, and wrapped her fingers around the blade. She felt them turn to ice, and felt the power flowing through her.

She opened her eyes and saw the sword in her hand turned to stone.

More than that, she saw the horrified looks of the warriors all around her, looks of fear, which slowly morphed to awe.

Lord West, most of all.

She dropped the sword, and the stone shattered, skidding across the floor in pieces. One stopped at Lord West's boot.

Lord West stood there for several more seconds. Then, using the table for support, he did the one thing Ceres hadn't expected.

He knelt.

"We are sworn to serve the Ancient Ones," he said. "All of us."

One by one, the other warriors followed his lead and knelt.

Ceres surveyed the room. She took a deep breath, feeling her destiny manifest within her. She had seen this moment, in a dream or in some other dimension, she could not be sure.

"The time has come to undo some of the evil the Empire has been bringing with it. Will you lend me your soldiers, Lord West?"

"There is nothing to lend," Lord West replied. "If you are one of the Ancient Ones, then they are yours by right. I will send messengers to all who owe me fealty, and they will send whatever soldiers they have."

Ceres reached out a hand, helping the older man to his feet. She turned back to the room.

"You've already heard what I have to say," she said. "I want to take you south, all of you. I want to join up with the rebellion, and fight against the tyrant who has oppressed all of us for far too long. Lord West says that you will go with me, but I know it is him you owe your loyalty to, not me. So I will not command you to go with me. I will simply ask it. Will you travel with me? Will you strike at the heart of the Empire, and overthrow the king who has your lands burned and your people killed? Will you fight?"

At first, Ceres thought she hadn't persuaded them. She'd been expecting some great cheer. Instead, she got silence, but it was a silence that came to be filled with a dull thudding that grew piece by piece. She realized that it was the sound of the men banging their sword hilts on the table, the rhythm of it filling the hall.

And she knew that war was on its way.

Chapter Seventeen

Thanos crept his way along tunnels by flickering candlelight, wheeling along a box on a two-wheeled trolley more normally used for transporting sacks of grain. The squeak of the wheels was the only sound he could hear down there. The candle stub he held gave off a firefly glow of orange, illuminating walls to either side, close enough that he could have reached out and touched them both.

It hadn't been easy to find this place. Just to keep slipping from the palace was getting harder, because Thanos had to do it in a way that Stephania wouldn't notice, and Lucious seemed to be taking far too much of an interest in his movements too. Doing it with the box he wheeled had been even harder.

Then he'd had to bribe people in some of the poorest parts of the city, and that hadn't been easy when his face was so well known. He'd had to come down into the slums wrapped up in an old cloak, being careful never to let anyone glimpse his features.

The entrance had been at the back of a butcher's yard, behind sides of beef and pork hanging on hooks. Thanos had felt the eyes on him as he descended into the depths of the tunnels beneath the city, and seen the cleavers close to the hands of the men there. He had a sword and dagger under his cloak, but he'd come without armor. He wasn't there to fight.

He kept wheeling his box down the tunnels, and now, Thanos thought he could hear sounds ahead. There was the clang of hammers, and a faint feel of greater heat, mixed in with a deep orange glow that might have come from fires somewhere nearby.

The tunnel he was in opened out a little, and there was the sense again of eyes watching him as he made his way through the tunnel system. Thanos didn't know if he was going the right way, but he could at least follow the sounds of the hammering and hope that it led him to what he was looking for.

The rebellion.

Akila's words had stung. Thanos had thought of the man as a friend, as something close to a brother. Yet the rebels on Haylon didn't believe that he was doing all he could, and Thanos could understand why. So he was going to do more, and if the rebels on Haylon wouldn't take his help, he would do it for those in Delos instead.

Thanos found an opening in the tunnel he was walking along, which gave way to a room where hammering seemed to dominate everything else. Thanos saw men and women hammering away on anvils and working metal in forges. The sound, heat, and rhythm of it were almost overwhelming.

When it stopped, the silence was worse.

"Who's that?"

"I don't know him."

"What's he doing here?"

Thanos saw the smiths and workers grabbing for hammers or recently finished weapons, hefting them as they tried to decide if they should be attacking him or not. Thanos looked around and saw men coming into the cavern behind him, armed with a variety of weapons that could only have come from the Stade. He saw a woman with them, thin and tough looking, but more than that, he saw the way they looked to her as though waiting for orders.

He threw back the hood of his cloak, hoping that this wouldn't be the last thing he ever did.

"I know him," a man called, and Thanos recognized a combatlord when he saw one. "It's Prince Thanos!"

"A royal? Kill him!"

Thanos saw several of them start forward, and braced himself for what was to come. He couldn't hope to fight all of them, even if he wanted to.

To his astonishment, a young man, still just a boy, really, stepped in front of them all. To his even greater surprise, they stopped.

"You're right," he said, "that's Thanos, which means he does more for the people around Delos than any other royal. It means my sister, Ceres, loved him. We shouldn't kill him."

"Your sister?" Thanos said. "That means you must be Sartes."

The boy nodded. "Come on, all of you. If you were a combatlord, you've trained with him. You know what he's like."

Thanos heard a murmur of assent go around the room.

Sartes went on. "It isn't *Lucious* standing there."

"Maybe it's worse," the woman from the doorway said, and Thanos could hear the authority in her voice. "Lucious is an evil thug who doesn't know any better, but it wasn't Lucious leading the attack on Haylon. It wasn't Lucious who put down the riots in the street a few days ago. It wasn't Lucious who sent General Olliant looking for us, or who got Ceres killed because she loved him!"

The last point seemed almost to make her angrier than the rest of it. Thanos guessed that she'd been close to Ceres, whoever she was. Even so, he couldn't keep himself from snapping back.

"And I loved her!"

"We should at least hear him out," he heard Sartes say. "Please, Anka."

Thanos had heard that name. The mysterious head of Delos's rebellion. The woman who had replaced Rexus. Strange, he'd been expecting someone… different. Older, stronger, more dangerous looking. Maybe she'd found herself having to grow into a role she hadn't expected, the same way he had when he'd learned who he was.

"You think I was behind the attack on Haylon?" Thanos said. "I joined the rebels there. I helped them to fight off the attack. Since I got back, I've been looking for information to pass on to them. I warned them of the new attack, and I even switched the generals so that Olliant wouldn't be descending on the island with a massive army."

"Instead, you sent him looking for us," Anka said.

"You killed him?" Thanos asked.

"We have him," Anka said.

Thanos nodded. "Good. That was the idea."

He saw the rebel leader cock her head to the side. "It's easy to say that now."

"Just as it's easy to say that I'm the one who allowed you all to escape the Stade," Thanos said. "It doesn't make it any less true."

He heard another murmur go around the room. He saw one of the former combatlords there thump his chest.

"Allowed us to break out, boy? We *fought* for the freedom we had. There were hundreds of the Empire's men there."

"Two hundred," Thanos agreed. "Two hundred men holding a cordon around the Stade, when there should have been a thousand closing in on it. I sent the others to hold the city, because it was the best move I could make to give you all a chance."

"Do you have any proof of that, either?" Anka asked.

"You're still here," Thanos pointed out. "You heard about the troops in the city. Ask questions, and you'll soon find out what the captains wanted to do."

To Thanos, Anka looked thoughtful. He could see her looking around the room as though trying to guess at the feelings of the others there.

"Why would I have come alone?" Thanos asked. "If I could find this place, then I could have brought troops with me. I could have filled this place with soldiers, but I'm here alone for a reason."

Thanos saw an older man step out of the crowd. He was wearing a blacksmith's apron, but he wasn't carrying a hammer or a weapon right then. Instead, he walked over to Thanos, holding out a hand for him to take. Thanos grasped it, feeling the strength there and seeing the assessing look in the other man's eyes.

"I'm Berin, Ceres's father. They say my daughter loved you," he said.

Thanos met his gaze. "More than you could ever know. If I hadn't been sent to Haylon—"

He saw the other man nod. "If I hadn't gone looking for work. Or if I hadn't left her in the Stade while I tried to free my son. There are a lot of ifs in this world. You married a princess quickly enough after my daughter died, though."

There was a challenge in that. Thanos could hear the question the older man was really asking: had he truly loved his daughter, if he'd been able to move on so soon?

"Stephania helped me through it when I was … broken," Thanos said. "It was as though my heart had been ripped out of me, and she found a way to fill that hole. She was the woman I was always supposed to marry, but that doesn't mean I don't think about Ceres every day."

"We both do," Berin said, pulling him into a bone-crushing hug.

That seemed to be enough for Anka. "All right. I believe you." She raised her voice. "No one is to hurt Thanos. It seems that we owe him a lot. But there's still the question of what you're doing here, Prince Thanos."

"I'm here to help you," Thanos said as Berin pulled back from him. That got some looks of surprise from around the cavern, in spite of all that he'd just said. "A … friend told me that I should be doing more than I am."

"What did you have in mind?" Anka asked.

Thanos looked around the underground forge. "I can see that you're trying to produce weapons and armor, but what if I had a way for you to take enough to supply an army?"

"Unless you're planning to help us raid the royal armories …" Anka began, and she obviously caught Thanos's expression. "You are, aren't you?"

"Not the castle," Thanos said, "but the army has staging posts and warehouses where weapons and armor are gathered together before they're sent out to the army."

"They do that in secret," Anka said. "And never in the same place twice. But that doesn't matter, does it?"

Thanos shook his head. "I know where. The next shipment will be going out from a warehouse on the north side of the city, supposedly used for bolts of cloth. There will be guards, but not many, and disguised as private thugs because their best defense is secrecy."

"So that's what you're here to bring us?" a woman toward the back asked. "A tip that might just as easily be a trap?"

"That's enough, Hannah," Anka said. "This could be a huge moment for the rebellion."

"We need more than just weapons," the woman continued. "We have the combatlords, but we need more people. We need resources."

A young man in richer clothes than the others nodded. "We need to be able to hire tradesmen and soldiers," he said. "My father's money will only go so far. We need to be able to spread the rebellion to every corner of the Empire, and even with the most audacious raids, we can't do that one move at a time."

"Trust you to be thinking about money, Yeralt," said a man who seemed to be armed mostly with knives.

"The world runs on money, Oreth," the other man countered. "The Empire continues because no one has the resources to stop it."

"It continues because we don't work together to fight it," Thanos said. "But you're right, gold matters. Which is why I brought this."

He kicked over the box that he'd brought, letting the lid fall open and the contents spill out onto the floor. Coins glinted gold in the forge light, while the gems amongst them seemed to have an inner fire of their own.

"They won't miss this from the royal treasury," Thanos said. "Or, if they do, they'll assume it went to the army."

He saw Anka smile at that. "We're going to fight the Empire using its own gold?"

"You're going to do more than fight," Thanos said. "You're going to win."

He'd taken a risk, getting the gold like this, but it would be worth it if the rebels could make use of it to support their cause. With this much gold, they could hire mercenaries, or they could buy horses. They could acquire ships or find more smiths. They could buy food, supplies, whatever they needed.

With this much gold, the rebellion could build an army.

She stepped forward and clasped his arm, and slowly, she grinned.

Chapter Eighteen

Lucious stalked into the throne room with bad grace, barely looking round at the empty spaces where there would normally have been assembled ranks of nobles forming phalanxes to either side and leaving a clear path to the thrones his mother and father occupied. When he stopped before the dais, his bow was perfunctory at best.

He had better things to do than be there.

"Ah, Lucious," King Claudius said. "I trust we didn't drag you away from anything important?"

His tone said quite clearly that he doubted it. Probably, he thought that Lucious had been busy drinking or hunting, sleeping or running down the peasantry. Even his own father didn't take him as seriously as he should.

"I came as quickly as I could," Lucious replied.

In fact, he'd spent days working his way through reports and rumors, half truths and untruths. He'd listened to idiots droning on about things they'd heard, or thought they'd heard when it came to Thanos, only to find that they'd been making it up as they went in the hope of getting gold out of him. His only consolation had been the things he'd been able to do with them in the dungeons after they'd disappointed him.

"I'm sure you did," his mother said. "We have important news."

Lucious wondered if he should tell her what a dangerous profession that was at the moment. Curiously, he hadn't been the only one getting rid of informants. In the last few days, it seemed that there had been almost a quiet epidemic of deaths, by poison, by stabbing, by apparent accident. It looked almost as if someone was trying to deprive Lucious of the use of his newly acquired network.

And now that it seemed there might finally be some answers from it, he found himself summoned here, in front of the court, to stand uncomfortably amidst the Great Hall and wait for his father to declare whatever it was this time. So long as he didn't actually recognize Thanos, Lucious didn't care. Although Thanos didn't seem to be here today, which suggested something else entirely.

"What is it you require, your majesties?" Lucious asked. Well, he couldn't just tell them to get on with it, could he? "If you want me to crush the rebellion more thoroughly, I will need more men, and permission to—"

He saw his father wave that away. "Forget that. We have bigger concerns than simply taking more from ungrateful commoners."

There was something about his tone that made Lucious pause. "What is it?"

It was his mother who answered. "We have reports in from the north. Birds came today from one of our garrisons on the edge of Lord West's lands. There is an army heading south, towards Delos."

An army? Lucious couldn't keep the shock off his face. The Empire did not get attacked by armies, not this close to home. It had to deal with small forces of rebels, or threats on its farthest borders. It didn't have to worry about armies advancing on its greatest city.

"Lord West is leading an army?" Lucious said. He shook his head. "I don't believe it. The old fool is loyal. He'd cut his own head off if you commanded it."

"The army contains Lord West's men, but he is not the one leading it," the king said. "He and all the old lords of the North Coast have joined under a different general."

"Who?" Lucious asked.

"Ceres."

Lucious could feel the blood draining from his skin, although whether it was in anger or fear, he couldn't say. Both seemed to be competing for top position within him, swirling round and round without any resolution.

"What? I thought she was dead!"

His father held up a hand before he could go on to rail at the unfairness of it all. "We all did, and for now, it will remain a secret that she has survived at all. It would disturb the people to hear it."

"The people, or Thanos?" Lucious asked.

He saw a flash of annoyance cross his father's face. "Do not go against me on this. Do you want to risk the commoners rising in revolt?"

"They wouldn't dare."

"Wouldn't they?" Queen Athena asked. "If they heard that a girl we built into a symbol of the rebellion so we could kill her is back, that she *isn't* dead… it would be a powerful blow to us, my son."

Perhaps they would rise up after all. Lucious had to admit that he had no idea how the lower orders thought.

"We want no one to hear of her return, least of all Thanos, until we are able to say for certain that she is dead again," King Claudius said.

"And where do I fit into this?" Lucious asked.

The king smiled. "You're going to lead the army to deal with her."

Now fear won out over the anger. Lucious didn't mind dealing with unruly peasants, but Lord West commanded a powerful collection of horsemen, and Ceres… His mind went back to the times she'd beaten him far too readily.

"Me?" Lucious said. "Don't we have generals for this sort of thing?"

"Apparently not," King Claudius said. "Olliant is still busy on Haylon, although we haven't heard much from him. Who knows where Haven is? I will not put the army under Thanos, for obvious reasons."

Like the part where he would probably rush into Ceres's arms in the middle of a battle. Even so, Lucious found himself scrambling for alternatives. The sensible thing to do in a situation like this was not for the heir to the throne to go out to meet the enemy in open battle. It was for him to sit nice and safe behind thick walls while others undertook the dangerous work.

"Surely we can recall one of the generals?" Lucious said. "Or if not them, what if—"

"You will lead this force, Lucious," the king said, and suddenly there was steel in his voice. "You've been happy enough to lead when it just involved butchering rebels. Well, these are also rebels, and they must be dealt with."

"But Father—"

"No," King Claudius said. "No more arguments. You will do this. I keep giving you chances to show that you are a man, Lucious. You ran away in the Stade. You shy away from real work. You must show the people of the Empire, show *me*, what a great king you could someday be! That means crushing this army yourself, not leaving it to someone else. People respect strength, so it is time for you to show some."

Lucious looked to his mother, his jaw already growing tight with the need to say something, but there was no help to be found there.

"You will make us proud, Lucious," she said.

Lucious mostly felt like running away, but he couldn't say that. Instead, he gave a stiff bow.

"As you command, your majesties."

"The closest legions of the army have been gathered outside the city," the king said. "They will expect you there with them by sundown. Do not disappoint me, Lucious."

There was something about the way he looked at Lucious that said Lucious already had. That said he would much rather Thanos were the one standing there. Maybe that was the point of this. Maybe his father secretly hoped that Lucious fell in battle, so that the king could say that actually, there was another heir. Or that he ran, so that he could be disinherited. Lucious wouldn't put it past him.

Well, Lucious would do it. He would go, and he would crush the army, and he would bring Ceres back impaled on a spear for all to see. Before that, though, he had business to attend to. Business that would hopefully ensure Thanos was never a threat again.

⚜ ⚜ ⚜

The upper rooms of the Ram's Skull tavern were, if anything, worse than the one beneath. Lucious looked around with disgust at the splintered floorboards, the soiled bedclothes, and the mold growing from the walls. There was a door on the far side, connecting to another room that would no doubt be even worse. If he could have risked meeting somewhere better, he would have, but there had been no time. As it was, he and his bodyguards had been forced to race across the city to get here.

The man they were there to meet was hardly much better than the room. To Lucious, he looked like the kind of beggar who might have occupied any street corner in Delos: straggle-bearded and wild-eyed, filthy and rag covered.

"You said you had information?" Lucious said. "I find it hard to believe a man like you has information about anything but bedbugs."

"Mad Fal sees a lot of things," the beggar said. "He finds things."

"I bet you see things," Lucious said. "Probably after drinking too much."

"Mostly because people think I'm stupid," the beggar said, his voice changing and suddenly sounding as though he could have been from any of the richer sections of the city. "But I've found what you're looking for."

"And that is?" Lucious asked.

The beggar pushed open the door to the adjoining room. In it, a man sat who had burns down one side of his body, his beard giving way to the scar tissue where the two crossed. He wore the clothes of a sailor or a porter, but on the stand beside the bed, Lucious saw the flash of the Empire's insignia.

"This is Todol. He was on Haylon."

"You were one of the soldiers in the attack?" Lucious asked.

The man looked up as though only just realizing that Lucious was there. His look was so blank that Lucious might have thought he was some kind of empty shell, but he nodded.

"Todol doesn't say much," the beggar said. "Not after the fire on his ship. But Mad Fal, he knows how to get him talking, he does."

The beggar gave the bearded man a drink. Lucious could probably also think of a few other ways, depending on how well this went.

"And what does he have to say?" Lucious asked. He turned to the man. "What did you *see*?"

The man's mouth cracked open. "Thanos. Prince Thanos betrayed us."

They were the words Lucious had been hoping to hear. "Go on."

"He went over to the rebels. He led them onto our ships. He shot burning oil at the shore, then he fired our ships so we couldn't get around the rebels. I was on one. I only survived because I threw myself overboard. Others did too, but the sharks—"

"Yes, yes," Lucious said, with a hint of impatience. "I'm sure it was terrible. But you survived."

"Barely. The rebels hunted us down one by one. I thought it was just because they hated us, but no. It was so we couldn't tell stories of the spy they'd sent back. So we couldn't say what Prince Thanos really was. I got back by hiding on a boat and then killing the crew."

"But you didn't come forward before this?" Lucious demanded. "I might almost think that you're only saying this because I'm offering the reward."

He saw the man gesture to his scars. "Do you think I did *this* for the reward? I tried to say nothing. I tried to hide and stay safe. Now, it seems like they're killing anyone who knows. I told a man I used to be in the army with. He went to the palace and didn't come back. I need a way to stay safe."

"I can provide that," Lucious promised. He would have promised anything right then for the information he needed. "Just tell me all of it. And quickly."

He sat, and he listened. He didn't even have to feign interest. When the former sailor was done, Lucious smiled to himself.

"If you repeat this when I tell you to, you'll be a rich man."

"And me?" Fal the beggar asked.

"You'll be paid, don't worry."

The beggar nodded at that. "Then I have some other information you might like too."

Lucious raised an eyebrow. "All of this, and there's more?"

"As I said, Mad Fal sees things. You know Lady Stephania pays the informers?"

"I know that," Lucious said.

"Well, would you like to know *everything* she's done?"

Lucious thought, but only for a moment. He put an arm around the beggar, even managing not to wince while he did it.

"Why yes, Fal. I think I would."

Chapter Nineteen

Ceres sat high in the saddle of her horse as they rode south toward Delos, grateful that the horse was a fine one. Otherwise, she would never have managed to keep up with the riders of the North Coast around her. They rode in a horde of shining mail shirts and gleaming spear tips, banners rising over their horse backs to proclaim the subdivisions of their houses. Lord West and his nephew rode beneath their weathervane banner, but Ceres knew that it was *her* they were following. She just hoped that she could live up to their expectations.

The moment she'd revealed her Ancient One ancestry, it had been as though she'd been in some kind of dream, because things had happened so smoothly. Lord West had sent out messages, and riders had come in response almost too quickly for Ceres to believe. She didn't know if they had come from hatred for the Empire, loyalty to the lord of the North Coast, or some distant memory of the times when the Ancient Ones had ruled, but they had come in the hundreds.

Then thousands. More than two thousand horsemen now rode at Ceres's back. An army, and one to be feared thanks to the easy way they sat in the saddle. Some were minor nobles or the sons of old families. Some were their retainers or soldiers who had wanted a better path than joining the Empire's main army. All were well armed and steel armored. Some had spears, others hunting bows they could fire from the saddle. Ceres had already seen them do it, bringing down rabbits or birds to cook at their campfires.

"We will be at Delos soon, my lady," Lord West said, riding close to Ceres. It was strange to hear the note of deference in his voice. The older man treated her the way Ceres saw others treat him: with deference and a sense that of course she would know the correct thing to do. He'd rejected any suggestion that he should stay behind, and now sat wearing mail armor reinforced with plates that he didn't look entirely comfortable with. Even so, he sat comfortably in the saddle, and if his swords sat uncomfortably on his hip, Ceres still had no doubt that he knew how to use them.

Ceres tried to look as confident as he felt. That was one of the strange parts of this. She was as much a symbol as a leader, and she couldn't afford to show any weakness. She kept riding, keeping pace with the others along forest trails and across open ground. Her horse never seemed to tire, keeping going so that its strides seemed to eat up the ground in front of her.

She and the others rode up a rise, and at the top, Ceres raised her hand to bring the army behind her to a halt. Delos lay ahead in the distance.

How long had it been now since she'd been there? Weeks, at least, possibly longer. So much had changed that it seemed like a lifetime ago. She hadn't seen her family since her father had sneaked in to visit her in Delos's castle. They probably didn't even know if she was alive now, and the thought of that made her feel sick, but she had no idea how best to contact them.

"Tell the men to get whatever rest they can," Ceres said, while she looked down at the city.

Lord West nodded. "I'll have them make camp."

Delos didn't shine, except around its castle. There were too many slums, too many areas of the city that were barely scraping by, for that. With the wind blowing toward them, Ceres could already make out the stink of the city, of too many people crammed into too small a space. She could see the Stade there, and the castle, the walls that looked like those of a prison holding in the inhabitants.

And she could see the trenches set out on the plain before the city, too.

There was an army there, the uniforms of the Empire a bloody red in the sun. Its men were spread out before the city, obviously there to intercept Ceres's advancing army. The trenches looked freshly dug, broad and lined with spikes, obviously designed to stop horses.

Ceres sat there looking down at it, watching the way the soldiers moved. She was no expert on battle tactics, but she could see the way the Empire's army was laid out. The trenches were designed to stop horses, or at least slow them down. Meanwhile, the strongest soldiers would probably be on the edges of the line, there to swing around and crush any force coming into the middle.

If her army did what it was designed to do and charged, it would be carnage. If they could persuade the Empire's forces to move ahead and try to attack, it would work far better, but Ceres couldn't imagine them giving up their position like that. What was left? A long, drawn-out game of archery and hitting at the edges? No, because Ceres suspected other Empire forces would be marching this way.

So, what did that leave? Ceres looked down again at the forces below. She could see a figure in golden armor leading them, shining like a beacon among a horde of officers, hangers-on, and toadies.

Even at this distance, she recognized Lucious.

A part of Ceres wanted to charge down regardless of the trenches, just leap across them and cut Lucious down for all he'd done. If she killed him, though, it wouldn't make things better. It would only remove one fragment of the Empire's evil, not change things completely.

What if it could though? An idea came to Ceres, one that might get them around the trenches and the armies. That might solve this directly, *and* give her the revenge she wanted when it came to Lucious.

"Lord West," she said. "Can you fetch a flag of truce?"

"Truce, my lady?"

"Don't worry, I didn't ride all this way to give up," Ceres assured him. "But I *do* want to talk to them."

In the end, Ceres rode down onto the plain before the city with a dozen men. Lord West wasn't among them, but his nephew was, a white pennant tied to his spear. The others were all volunteers, there to ensure that if this went wrong, Ceres might still get back to the army. They stopped halfway to the Empire's army, and at Ceres's signal, Gerant stuck the pennant in the ground.

They waited, and waited. Ceres could feel the tension building amongst the others there. There was no way of knowing how the Empire's army would react. Only the fact that she knew Lucious let her sit there on horseback with confidence. There were only two ways this would go. Either he would come to talk to them, or he would send his army forward to try to capture them, letting hers charge it once it was beyond the trenches. This was the best move they could make.

Finally, a group of soldiers rode forward from the Empire's lines. Lucious was at their head. Ceres forced herself to remain in place rather than charging forward to attack him. There would be time for that later. For now, she had a battle to win, and possibly a war, so she settled for glaring at Lucious as he came closer.

He drew his horse to a halt, looking every inch the noble prince as he sat there in his golden armor. Only the collection of rough-looking thugs he rode with belied it.

"It seems a long way to come just to surrender," Lucious said with a laughing gesture at their flag.

"Maybe I'm offering you a chance to surrender," Ceres countered. "Yield now, and I'll see that you get a fair trial for the things you've done, Lucious."

She saw Lucious sneer. "I'd say I'd missed you, Ceres, but I try not to think about peasants. You should have known when to stay dead. Did you want something, or are we just here to exchange pleasantries?"

Ceres gestured to the horsemen behind her. "You can see I didn't come back alone," she said. "Step aside. Remove your army from the field. There doesn't have to be bloodshed. We both know that you're too much of a coward to want to risk your skin."

"Watch your mouth, girl," Lucious snapped back. "The only skin at risk is yours when we catch you. Maybe I'll have it removed bit by bit and hung up in one of the galleries as a warning."

"You'd have to have it done," Ceres said. "You certainly don't have the fighting skills to ever best me."

"Still challenging your betters?" Lucious retorted. "I could cut you down any time I chose."

Maybe he actually believed it. Certainly, Ceres knew, Lucious would never admit to anything else. In fact, she'd been counting on it.

"Then why don't you prove it?" Ceres said. "Let's settle this one to one. No armies, just single combat. If I win, your army moves out of the way and lets us take Delos."

"And when I cut you down?" Lucious asked.

"Mine turns around and goes home," Ceres said. "You get to be the prince who saved Delos without bloodshed."

Lucious looked as though he was looking for a way out then. He was good at making threats, but he had to know by now that Ceres was the better fighter. She'd bested him before, after all.

"If you refuse," Ceres said, "I'll have men shout the same challenge loud enough that your whole army can hear it. They'll know they're fighting for a coward. What do you think that will do for their morale?"

She saw Lucious flush then, but she still doubted that he would do more than storm off. This wasn't about that. This was about riling him. She wanted to anger him, and taunt him. Anything to get his army to move out of its defensive position to attack hers.

To her surprise, though, Lucious nodded curtly.

"Very well," he said. "Sundown. Single combat. The loser's army to disband. Though I make no promises about what will happen after that. If I can hunt your rabble down, I will."

"You have to beat me first," Ceres said. "I'll see you at sundown."

Chapter Twenty

"It's a lot of people to bring in at once," Anka said, as she walked the corridors of the rebellion's current hideout. She was trying her best to keep her anger in check, and to get Yeralt to see her point of view, but so far, the argument wasn't going well.

"You wanted more people," Yeralt countered, "so I *found* more people."

"You hired them, you mean?" Anka shot back. "You threw Thanos's gold around and let in anyone who showed up?"

Anka guessed that the merchant's son probably wouldn't see the difference. There was no doubting his commitment to overthrowing the Empire, but he often didn't seem to understand how things really were for the poorest of Delos.

"If you want people who know how to fight, you have to pay for them," Yeralt said, as if it were obvious.

Anka saw Sartes ahead in the press of bodies that now filled the underground hideaway. The sight of him calmed her a little. In spite of his age, he seemed to understand the realities of life better than some of the others there. Maybe it was because of the time he'd spent as a conscript. Certainly, his idea to attack the Stade had been a good one. The combatlords were already teaching the others there more about fighting than they could ever have learned otherwise.

"Sartes," Anka said in exasperation. "Explain to Yeralt why it's a bad idea to simply hire in all the fighters we need."

"Where did you get them?" Sartes asked, walking up to the pair.

It was the right question. The sensible question. One that the merchant's son didn't seem to have asked, and that Anka should have.

"My father has people he hires when he wants caravans protected," Yeralt replied, "and I know where to look to find fighting men."

"So they're mercenaries?" Sartes said.

"Or tavern grade thugs," Anka put in.

"Does it matter what they are if they'll fight?" Yeralt said. Anka could hear the annoyance there now. "We give them gold, they fight the Empire. It's easy."

"Until someone comes along with more gold," Anka tried to explain.

She saw the merchant's son shake his head. "You worry too much, Anka. We've grown more in the last few days than in the year before it. Edrin says that the raid on the warehouse went well. Oreth will find us ships. Hannah has been talking to whole networks of informants we didn't know about, now that we have the gold to spend loosening tongues."

"Discreetly, I hope," Anka said.

Yeralt sighed, and Anka knew she'd gone too far. "Of course discreetly. Look, Anka, the others think this is a good idea. We're sick of waiting and being cautious. When a business doesn't expand, it stagnates, or worse, it collapses."

"A lot more's at stake than coin here," Anka said. She tried to be a little more conciliatory, but it was probably too late for that. "I'm not saying we sit and do nothing. I'm saying that we have to do this *right*."

"And we are," Yeralt said. "We know how to do this, and we've decided. Now, I have to get back before I'm missed. I'm going to try to find another route into the city for supplies. There are too many to funnel through my father's caravans."

Anka watched the merchant's son go, trying to contain her frustration. There was a point past which she couldn't afford to be angry. She had to hold things together. Bizarrely, her time in the slaver's pen had helped her with that. It had taught her not to show what she felt. It had taught her that there were worse things than any petty issues that might come. It had shown her what was at stake.

"He doesn't get it," Anka said, when Yeralt was gone. "For all his businesses, he doesn't understand. Please tell me you do, Sartes."

Sartes nodded. "There are too many people to be sure who they all are. Mostly, they'll all be people who want to help the rebellion. Maybe people who always wanted to but weren't sure of the best way to do it."

"But some of them won't be," Anka said, grateful that someone else got the danger. "When the rebellion was still fairly small, I could know who everybody was. If I didn't know, at least one of the people I knew would. Now, people walk past me and I just have to accept that they're with us. That they aren't spies or criminals or worse."

Sartes shrugged. "Part of what makes the rebellion great is that it does accept anybody. We don't turn people away because of their past. This only works if we make it a movement for everyone, until one day the Emperor wakes up and he's the only one not in the rebellion."

Anka smiled at that. "I like that idea, although I'm not going to let Lucious into the rebellion."

"No one's asking you to," Sartes said. "I don't think he's the joining type."

"But plenty of others are," Anka said. "Come with me, would you? I want to see what we're getting for Thanos's gold."

She led the way up through the tunnels, out of an exit that led into a tenement building. There were people waiting there, training with weapons or simply sitting around with nowhere else to go. There was a bench in one corner, where men and women were lining up to receive weapons and gold.

Anka walked across, regarding the man who stood at the front of the line coolly. He had the scars of a man who'd been in a lot of fights, and the slightly ruddy skin of a man who drank too much. There was something about him that set Anka's teeth on edge.

"What's your name?" Anka asked.

"What's it matter to you?" the prospective recruit countered.

"It matters because I'm trying to decide if I want you in my rebellion," Anka said. "I'm Anka. You ask around here, and you'll find out who I am. I want to know who you are so I can ask about *you*."

"I'm Hern, out of the fifteenth regiment. I deserted and came back to the city, joined one of the gangs. That what you want to know about me, girl?"

Anka tried not to match the tone of hostility there. "You say you were in a gang? What were you? A thief? A murderer?"

"What I am is willing to fight the Empire," he replied. "I used to be an enforcer for the Second Streets. Is that good enough for you?"

Anka wanted to say no, but instead, she just gestured him forward to the table. She walked away with Sartes at her side.

"Where do we draw the line, Sartes?" she asked. "We know we wouldn't let the likes of Lucious in, so there are some people we won't tolerate, but who? Criminals? We're all criminals by the Empire's definition. Soldiers? You're a former soldier, and so are all the conscripts who joined us. Yeralt's right, we need all the people we can get, but mercenaries and thugs? We can't trust them."

"So don't trust them," Sartes said, and he made it sound so obvious. "You can't question everyone who wants to join personally, but you can ask someone to vouch for them before they join. You can make sure that only the people who need to know things are told them."

"You're too young to have so little trust in people," Anka said.

Sartes shrugged. "There are plenty of people I trust. I trust you."

"It seems as though a lot of people are trusting me these days," Anka said. "I have to make the right decisions, or it could mean people's lives."

"You've been making the right calls so far," Sartes said. "You organized the ambush in the burial ground and the freeing of the combatlords. We have the army's weapons and Thanos's gold."

"You played a pretty big role in those too," Anka said. "How's the weapon sorting going?"

Sartes shook his head. "My father says that the Empire needs to employ better smiths. He also said I might be able to help you more here."

Anka smiled. "He's probably right. It looks as though I could use all the help I can get."

She stood there, and Sartes could hear something left unsaid in the silence.

"What is it?" Sartes asked. "I mean, if you can tell me."

"I'll always be able to tell you things," Anka said. "If there's one person in the rebellion I *don't* have to worry about being a spy, it's you. It's not that."

"Then what?" Sartes asked.

"Sartes, I have news." Anka stood there, uncertain for a moment, standing next to a window and looking out on the city. Should she say this now? "You were talking about things people need to know. Well, I don't know if I should tell you this, because it's just a rumor, and I didn't even believe it when I heard it."

"What is it?" Sartes asked. "Is it about the army?"

"In a way," Anka said. There were enough rumors about the army outside the city that Sartes must have heard some of them. "I've spent the morning listening to what's happening out there, piecing things together. The army formed up in front of the city yesterday, because it had heard that there was a force coming under Lord West."

"So there's going to be a battle?" Sartes asked.

Anka spread her hands, trying to think of the best way to say this. "We thought so, but there's been an offer of single combat to settle it. Lucious has sent a champion, and on the other side … I can hardly believe I'm saying it."

"What is it?" Sartes asked.

"It's Ceres," Anka said, and she could see the shock on Sartes's face even as she said it. "Ceres is the one fighting on the other side."

She took his shoulders in her hands.

"She is alive, Sartes."

Chapter Twenty One

With sundown looming, Ceres prepared herself. She sharpened her sword, made sure the dagger Eoin had given her was still strong, went through the motions of the islanders' way of fighting, stretched her muscles, and waited.

No one disturbed her.

They all seemed to know instinctively to leave her in peace for it.

Finally, sunset came.

Down below, Ceres could see men coming out from the Empire's army, moving out to the center of the plain. For a moment, she thought that perhaps Lucious might be trying a surprise attack—but they came out with spades and rushes, digging a series of pits that they filled and then set light to, illuminating a section of the field even as the sun faded.

They were making a ring to fight in.

"It's time," Ceres said, mounting her horse. "Lord West, if this goes wrong—"

"It won't," he replied. "Remember who you are. *What* you are."

Ceres nodded. Heart pounding, feeling the eyes of thousands of men upon her, she mounted her horse, kicked, and rode.

Around her, her army formed, lifting banners high in a kind of salute, cheering as she rode through the pathway they created. She felt as if she were back in the Stade, with the crowd roaring in appreciation as she stepped onto the sands.

She rode down in the direction of that impromptu arena, and some of her men followed her. Not many. Not enough that it would look like an attack, but enough to form a crowd. Enough to prevent an attack on her by Lucious's forces.

Ceres dismounted by the edge, hobbling her horse. She stepped between two of the fires, into the brightly lit space beyond. Then she waited.

She saw Lucious ride forward at the heart of a cluster of men to match her own. Another horse beside him carried a servant or weapon carrier wrapped up in a thick cloak.

When they reached the ring, though, it was the servant who dismounted, not Lucious.

Ceres felt a hint of outrage rise in her chest.

This was replaced with dread as she saw the size of the servant, who stood far taller than she did, far taller than Lucious.

"What's this?" Ceres demanded.

She heard Lucious laugh.

"I'm a prince, you stupid peasant. You think I fight my own battles? I have champions for that! Don't worry, though, I've brought you an old friend."

His "servant" threw aside the cloak then. Ceres saw dark, muscled skin, criss-crossed by scars and tattoos and only partly covered by armor. The man there held a staff with crescent blades at either end, but it was his dead, baleful gaze that held her attention most.

Ceres heard the intake of breath from the crowd around her. They knew who this was, just as she did. The only man to ever best her in the Stade. The one who'd been about to kill her when they'd dragged her away to the prison ship.

The Last Breath.

The combatlord known as the Last Breath stepped into the circle of flames, and while the fire reflected from his dual-bladed weapon, Ceres heard Lucious laugh.

Ceres felt a thrill of fear as the Last Breath stood there before her. She found herself remembering the sight of him standing over her, his weapon poised for the final blow that had never come in the Stade.

It was obvious that her opponent remembered it too.

"I kill my enemies," he said, sending his bladed staff into a contemptuous spin. "All of them, except you. This time, I make that right."

Ceres pushed back the residue of fear, remembering the things that had happened to her since. She'd learned all the islanders had to offer, but more than that, she'd learned who she was.

"You won't find it that easy," she promised him. "I've learned a lot since then."

She heard him laugh, and the sound was like a boom of thunder in the dusk. Midway through it, the Last Breath attacked, and the crowd roared.

Ceres was ready for it this time in a way she hadn't been in the Stade. There, her powers had deserted her. Now, energy flooded through her, lending her the speed to flow out of the way of a kick that would have sent her back into the fiery ring.

She parried and dodged, moving aside from the Last Breath's strikes. He was still frighteningly fast for such a big man, but this time she was as fast as he was, and she wasn't going to be overwhelmed the way she had been in the Stade.

She could see the patterns now, understand the furious malice behind it, seeing it like sharp spikes at the edges of her awareness. She sank into the feeling of the fight, letting herself go the way Eoin and the others had taught her.

She leaned back from a sweep of the crescent blades, dropped further to avoid a swinging kick, and then rolled smoothly back to her feet. She struck out with her long blade, forcing the Last Breath to parry, then stepped back to avoid the counter.

She kept moving, feeling the heat of the fires at her back as she went. The Last Breath rushed her, obviously trying to force her back into that heat, and Ceres dodged, bringing her blades together to block a stroke that tried to catch her as she angled away.

She cut out, drawing a line of blood on the Last Breath's arm.

He stared at it in fury, and Ceres knew he would be thinking back to what had happened after she'd cut him in their fight in the Stade.

Sure enough, he came at her then, swinging his staff in blow after blow.

Part of his skill, Ceres realized now, was in not having an obvious rhythm to his attacks. Most fighters struck and moved in clear beats, and anyone else using a weapon like the one the Last Breath did would have swung it back and forth, back and forth. He seemed to instinctively realized the danger of that, the blades never quite there when they should have been.

For a moment, Ceres felt herself falling out of the place where the power flowed into her. It was as though the world around her sped up, and suddenly the Last Breath was everywhere. Ceres parried one blow, felt another graze through the flesh of her side, and then found herself caught across the back of the legs by the haft of her opponent's weapon.

Ceres lay on her back for a moment or two, looking up as the Last Breath stood there, his weapon raised high. The firelight glinted from the steel, the flames seeming to reflect in his eyes. It was too close, far too close, to the way things had been in the Stade.

Only this time, there wouldn't be any reprieve. There was no one to heed the calls of the crowd, or to decide that it would be better if she died quietly, away from other eyes. Stephania wasn't there this time, but Lucious was, looking on with obvious glee from the sidelines.

"Ceres! Ceres! Ceres!" she heard the men on her side chanting, as if trying to revive her just with the calls.

"This time," the Last Breath said, "you die."

Except this wasn't the Stade. Ceres understood the power that lay within her now. It wasn't some strange, unknown thing that came and went as it wished. It was a part of her. It was a part of who she was.

So when she called it up within her again, it was there waiting.

She rolled smoothly, moving out of the way of the Last Breath's blow and kicking out to force him back.

Ceres leapt back onto her feet and then went on the attack. She thrust with her dagger and cut with her sword, never staying in one spot, never giving the Last Breath a chance to settle. She spun inside the arc of his weapon, opening another wound on her opponent then moving out again.

She saw a moment of balance and seized the opening. Ceres kicked out at the haft of the Last Breath's weapon, lifting her leg high and catching it in the middle. Before, such an attack might not have done anything, but now Ceres heard the crack as the pole arm gave way beneath her strike. She saw the Last Breath stare at it as though Ceres had just killed the only thing he had cared about in the world.

He roared, clutching one half of the broken weapon and swinging it in a figure eight like an axe. He swung at Ceres's head and she ducked, cutting with her dagger as she moved past him. The Last Breath swung again and Ceres leaned back, slicing another cut into his arm.

The Last Breath didn't have an obvious rhythm to his attacks, but there *was* a rhythm to it, hidden under the fury and the cunning. It was hummingbird fast, varying and shifting, but it was there.

Ceres would never have been able to pick it out if she hadn't spent so long with the forest folk trying their different skills on her. She would never have been fast enough to keep up with it if she hadn't learned to accept what she was.

As it was, she fit in with it as smoothly as a dance.

She spun and ducked and leapt, always a beat ahead of the Last Breath's furious swings. With each movement, she struck out, wounding him again and again, wearing him down the way a hunter might wear down some great beast. It wasn't cruelty; it was simply that, even now, Ceres knew that trying to finish things would only open her up to a lightning fast riposte.

The Last Breath feigned a stumbling step, but Ceres saw it for what it was. She took a half step forward, then pushed back, dodging as the combatlord threw himself forward in a desperate strike. Ceres struck with both her swords, catching the Last Breath across his back.

She saw him stumble, his weapon falling from his hand. Even so, he stood, somehow defying the wounds that would have killed another man.

"Yield," Ceres said. "Let this end. Don't let Lucious keep using you."

The Last Breath shook his head and leapt at her.

Ceres reached out, and her power flowed from her into the Last Breath.

She watched the shock in his eyes as stone flourished in place of his skin, freezing him in place. The stone was as thick and dark as his skin, basalt and obsidian, matching every scar and nick on him.

Ceres could have left him like that, but some part of her didn't trust the combatlord even as a block of dark granite. She kicked out and set the statue rocking back and forth on the hard earth.

It toppled almost slowly, and when it hit the ground, Ceres heard the crack as it shattered, breaking into a dozen or more pieces.

Ceres stood, making sure that both armies could see her there as she called out.

"You've lost, Lucious! Surrender the city, or be branded the oath breaker you are!"

Something flew at Ceres from out of the dark. She dodged on instinct, and an arrow whispered past her cheek before thudding into the dirt. Ceres ran forward, leaping over the nearest fire, setting off in pursuit of Lucious.

He was already riding away, pushing his horse to greater speed than Ceres could hope to match. She could hear him shouting out what sounded like orders as he rode, although she couldn't make out the words from there.

Behind her, she saw her army advancing. Lord West had obviously seen Lucious's betrayal, and wasn't about to risk leaving Ceres to face the Empire's whole army. The horsemen of the North Coast charged in a long line, apparently not caring about the danger of the Empire's trenches if it meant keeping Ceres safe.

Yet the Empire's army didn't move to attack. Nor did it stand ready to receive the charge. Instead, while Ceres watched, its phalanxes wheeled and started to march back through the open gates of the city.

"Quick!" Ceres called to the approaching riders. "We have to catch them before they get inside."

They could win it here. Even if Lucious wouldn't keep his word, if they could hit their army from behind while it was on the move, they had a chance to break its ranks. Her riders thundered down toward Ceres, and they didn't slow. Instead, she saw Gerant leading a spare horse, and Ceres understood.

She caught the reins as it rode past her, leaping up and hauling herself into the saddle. She kicked her horse on, trying to make it to the Empire's ranks before they could enter the city. There was no way they could all make it inside now, and some of them seemed to have gathered by the trenches.

Except they didn't form defensive ranks. Instead, Ceres saw the flicker of flaming torches. They threw them into the trenches, and fire roared up.

There must have been oil in the pits. That was the only explanation for the great walls of flame that surged up in front of her charging army. Even as far away as she was, Ceres could feel the heat of it.

So could the horses, it seemed. Ceres saw them shy away, the charge faltering. Many reared up, and it was only the riding skills of her men that kept them from falling from the saddle. Around her, Ceres heard men trying to calm their horses, and horses snorting in fear at the flames ahead. She had to lean down, gripping her own reins tightly as she pulled her horse to a halt.

There was no way past the flames. Even where there had seemed to be thin bridges of land between the trenches before, there were no gaps now. Oil had obviously been spread over the ground too. All Ceres could do was sit there in the saddle, watching the fires burn.

There was the whir of arrows in the night, and somewhere beside her, Ceres saw a man fall. Other arrows thudded into shields. One caught a horse, and the beast went down, taking its rider with it.

"Pull back," she called. "We're in bow shot here. Pull *back*!"

Her army retreated, away from the trenches, back up the hillside they'd come from. All Ceres could do up there was watch as the fires burned down to embers, their orange glow spreading over the ground before the city.

They illuminated its gates perfectly. Those were massive, stone built, and very firmly shut now behind Lucious's army. Above them, Ceres thought she could see a flash of gold illuminated in the firelight: Lucious looking out, probably feeling very pleased by it all.

Ceres turned to Lord West, and she could see he was thinking the same thing as she.

"Make camp and set watches on all of the city's gates," she said. "We're going to have to take Delos by siege."

Chapter Twenty Two

Lucious waited in front of the throne like a condemned man while his father bellowed.

"A *siege*?" the king demanded. "How could you let it come to a siege?"

Right then, standing before the court with most of the nobles of Delos watching, Lucious had never felt so angry with them all. He was still wearing his golden armor, still carrying the sword he'd worn on the battlefield, and a part of him wanted to rush among them then, cutting them down just for daring to be there while his father tried to humiliate him in front of them.

But he didn't do it. Instead, he stood there, his armor spattered with mud, looking far from his glorious best in the throne room while his father the king shouted. The nobles around him were silent, as though sensing that any sound might bring royal wrath down on them.

"You were supposed to go out and give battle to them, you stupid boy!"

"We might have lost if we'd done that," Lucious countered. "There were more of them than we anticipated, and Ceres—" He didn't finish that, even though he could see the nobles leaning in, looking for news of the girl. He still wasn't sure *what* had happened with Ceres. What he'd seen her do there in the ring of flames made no sense.

"You might have crushed them as you were supposed to!" King Claudius said, bringing his hand down hard on the arm of his throne. The one beside it was empty; Lucious couldn't look to his mother for help tonight. Indeed, many of the ladies of the court were absent, as if this were beneath them to see. "When you had the fire pits dug, I thought it was a sign that you were maturing as a leader, but they were meant to cut off your foes' escape, not give you time to run!"

"I ran because there was no other option!" Lucious insisted, raising his voice to match his father's. How *dare* he treat Lucious like this in front of all the others? "After they saw the Last Breath lose, the men wouldn't have stood and fought."

Lucious could practically feel the tension in the nobles around them. Men shifted in place, as though wishing they could be anywhere else. Cowards.

"You mean that you wouldn't," the king said. "As for this business of single combat, you should have thought about the implications of it before you accepted the challenge from that girl."

"She was supposed to *lose*," Lucious snapped back. There was just the faintest intake of breath from those around them.

"Watch your tone, boy," his father said. "Remember who is king here."

Lucious remembered, just as he reminded himself that sooner or later, his father would die, and he would be king in his turn. Then there would be no one to talk to him like this.

"Ceres had already lost to the Last Breath once," Lucious said. "He should have beaten her easily, and then probably that fool Lord West would have disbanded, because he believes in honor so much. At the very least, we would have been able to parade what was left of her through the streets to break the rebellion's spirit."

"All of which sounds like a fine plan," his father said. "Except for the part where she cut your man to pieces."

"She used some trickery, or magic, or something to do it," Lucious insisted. "How was I to know that she could do something like that?"

"A good commander learns the facts of the situation before he acts," the king said. "Didn't I provide you with enough warning? Didn't I tell you what you needed to do? You were to go out and meet them. If you'd judged it right, you could have ambushed them as they made their way to the city; cut them down before they even got close. Instead, you stood and waited beneath the safety of the walls."

Fury rose in Lucious then, sweet and hot, but explosive too. The words poured out before he could stop them. "Maybe you should have gotten someone else to command the army then! Oh, no, wait, you couldn't, could you? You were too busy sitting here, your generals are missing, and as for Thanos—"

"Enough!" King Claudius roared. "I have defended you at every turn, Lucious. I gave you this command because I thought you might be the one to put down this rebellion the way it deserves to be put down. But it seems you weren't capable of dealing with it, and now *I* must be the one to deal with our city being under siege."

"Not Thanos?" Lucious said with a smirk. "It's almost as if you don't trust him when it comes to Ceres, or something, Father."

"Thanos is as loyal as any man," the king declared. "And at least he knows how to command properly. He survived Haylon, and the Stade. Give me one good reason, Lucious, why I shouldn't send you from this room in disgrace and give him your command under me."

Lucious almost didn't say anything, but his anger had gone from something burning red to something cool and white and dangerous. He'd spent a lot of gold learning everything he knew, and to miss an opportunity this good would be far too foolish.

"I think you might want to reserve judgment, my king," Lucious said. "At least until you've heard what I have to tell you."

"And why would I do that?" his father said.

"Because then, you might change your mind about who you want in charge of your armies, and who you trust."

⚜ ⚜ ⚜

Thanos sat, looking at his wife, feeling amazed that his life could have taken the turns it had. She'd said she had things to tell him tonight, and he was trying to guess at what they might be. He knew Stephania liked to collect secrets.

He was still wondering about it, dining quietly with Stephania, when the servants hammered on the door to his rooms.

"Prince Thanos, come at once. The king requires your presence on an urgent matter."

"Ignore them," Stephania said, reaching out to close her hand over his arm as if to hold him there. "There are things I need to talk to you about, and tell you."

Thanos heard more thudding fists on the door. "Prince Thanos, the king said that there can be no delay."

Thanos made a face and leaned over to kiss his wife. "I don't think we're getting a choice in this. It's probably to do with whatever's got the army in front of the city. And you keep saying that I can't afford to anger the king."

"No," Stephania agreed. "Try to remember that." She looked down at her relatively simple day dress. "Give me a chance to dress properly, and I'll come with you."

Thanos waved that away. "You shouldn't have your evening ruined for this." He took her hand and kissed it. "I'll be back soon, then you can tell me whatever your news is. I bet it will be better than the king's."

"It will," Stephania promised.

Thanos rose and headed for the door. He wasn't really dressed for an audience with the king, in just a relatively simple tunic and breeches, but it sounded too urgent for anything more formal.

The men outside weren't servants, but members of the royal bodyguard.

"What's this?" Thanos said.

"It's a vital matter," one of the men said. "We need to hurry."

So Thanos hurried, half expecting to be led in the direction of the king's private chambers. Instead, though, he saw that they were heading in the direction of the throne room, hurrying along at something just short of a run.

"Is it something to do with the army?" Thanos asked, hoping to understand what was going on. He figured that fighting men might at least give him a clue.

"Forgive us, Prince Thanos," the bodyguard said, "but the king said he would explain once you got there."

Thanos wasn't sure what to make of that, but he knew there was no point in testing the loyalty of the royal bodyguard. Besides, thanks to the speed they were walking at, they would be at the throne room soon enough.

They reached it, and the guards at the doors let them inside. Thanos could feel straightaway that something was wrong. There was a hush there that there shouldn't have been, even if the king had demanded quiet. The nobles there looked shocked, even angry, as they stood to either side of the hall. He heard the sound of the doors slamming shut behind him like a tombstone falling over.

Something had gone wrong.

"What is it?" Thanos demanded. "What's happened?"

Then he saw Lucious's face; saw the look of triumph there, and he understood. By that point though, the royal bodyguards had already formed up around him with their swords drawn. There would be no chance to run, and unarmed, even Thanos couldn't fight so many.

King Claudius sat perfectly still, and to Thanos, he seemed caught halfway between anger and sadness. "What happened? What happened is that you betrayed us."

"And who says that?" Thanos countered. It was his only chance now. "Lucious? You know he'd say anything to cause trouble. He's probably just looking for revenge for beating him senseless, still."

"That's what I suspected," the king replied. He gestured to one side of the court. "Until Lucious brought me this man."

A ragged-looking man stepped forward from the crowd, wearing a soldier's uniform. It was too new to be original, and Thanos guessed Lucious had given it to him for effect.

"Say again what you told us," the king said. "*Say* it."

"Prince Thanos joined the rebels on Haylon," the man said. "He helped them to burn our ships and attack our men. Do I … when do I get my reward?"

"You hear that?" Thanos said. "He's only saying it because Lucious paid him."

"That is possible," the king said, "but when he came forward, others brought forward their suspicions. A guard mentioned that you had requisitioned gold from the treasury for the army, but there is no record of it reaching them. A bird from Haylon has arrived informing me of General *Haven's* progress there, when I'm sure I sent Olliant. At the same time, a junior member of my chamberlain's staff tells me that you were in his office the morning that fleet sailed, and Lucious says he saw you out there. Of course, I will have this wretch tortured to ensure he is telling the truth, but we both know what he will say, *don't we?* After all, you have already tried to murder my son!"

The king stood then, and with the added effect of the dais, he loomed over Thanos.

"You are a traitor, Thanos. Admit it. Or maybe I'll make you watch the torture. You're soft enough that I'm sure you wouldn't want that."

"I'm soft?" Thanos said. "Maybe it's just you who's forgotten what it's like to have any humanity. You ordered General Draco to slaughter men, women, and children on Haylon. You've had Lucious butchering your own people in the name of putting down the rebellion. It's evil, and it needs to be stopped!"

"So you've been helping to stop it?" the king demanded.

Thanos stood proudly, because there was no point in trying to deny it anymore. "Yes. Yes, I have. And you might kill me for it, but there will be a dozen more to take my place. A hundred. The more brutal you try to be, the more the rebellion will rise up, until you and everyone like you are swept away!"

Thanos saw the king, his father, bring his hands together, looking down as though searching for some kind of answer. Then he shook his head.

"A fine speech, but an empire like this exists only because there is order within it. Only because it is strong. I tried to explain that to you once before, and you failed to learn the lesson. I gave you a chance, and you have thrown that chance back in my face! Even now, I suspect that you would cut me down if I gave you the opportunity."

Thanos looked him squarely in the eye. "If it is the only way to stop you."

"Then you are the one who must be stopped," King Claudius said. "Take Thanos to a cell. Tomorrow, he will be taken by boat to the Isle of Prisoners. Once he is there, I will decide a suitable way for him to die."

Thanos tried to struggle, because he couldn't *not* struggle. He swung a punch at one royal bodyguard, then tried to grab a weapon from another. There were too many, though, and they piled in together, dragging him to the ground. Even some of the nobles joined in, as though wanting to show their loyalty. They punched and kicked at him: people he'd known, former friends.

Then Lucious was there, holding a weighted club. "I've wanted to watch you fall for a long time. Now I get to."

He swung it, and darkness exploded through Thanos's skull.

Chapter Twenty Three

The nobles of the North Coast had looked at Ceres with respect before, but now it felt more like awe as she sat amid the campfires and the hastily erected tents. Half of them didn't seem to dare to speak to her after what she'd done to the Last Breath, while the other half treated her as if she were something far more than human.

Then again, she supposed she was. It was just that it took some getting used to.

Right now, she was sitting around a fire with Lord West and a few of his men. The fire wasn't anywhere near as intense as the flame-filled trenches had been, but even so, it was a reminder of them. The lord of the North Coast had fetched Ceres a platter of trail bread, venison, and beans himself, and had tasted it before he'd handed it to her.

"You don't have to do that," Ceres tried to tell him, but the older man shook his head.

"I do," he insisted. "My family swore to lay down their lives if necessary for your ancestors, and there are more than enough poisoners around Delos for it to be a risk. We cannot afford to lose you."

"These are your men," Ceres said. "They fight for you."

That just got another shake of Lord West's head. "They fight because you are here, my lady. Because you have shown them that there are powers out there greater than the strength of the Empire."

"It's not as though I could take on the Empire alone though," Ceres said. It might have been nice if she could have turned all of their opponents to stone, taken all the risks for herself rather than pulling others into it, but her powers didn't work like that. They took effort. "We've only come this far because you're all here."

"I just hope the rebellion is waiting for us," Lord West said. "We cannot afford a long siege."

"Lucious won't dare bring his men out to face us now," Ceres said. "Trust me, he's a coward at heart. He's nice and safe behind a wall, and he'll stay there until someone pries him out."

"With respect, my lady," Lord West said. "That's all he needs to do. We are horsemen. On open ground, we can run down the strongest foes, but horses cannot climb walls. And they need to eat, just as their riders do."

Ceres understood then. "Lucious has been ravaging the countryside for a long time now. There won't be any food to find. I'm sorry, Lord West. I've fought in the Stade, but I'm not used to how armies work."

Lord West gestured to the others there. "You've got us this far, and you *did* best Lucious's man. If he'd taken the challenge himself, we might not have this problem now. But if you wouldn't mind my saying, my lady?"

"You don't have to ask, Lord West," Ceres said, taking a bite out of her food. After all that had happened today, she was ravenous. "I don't want to be someone like King Claudius. Someone people are afraid to say things to in case they don't like them."

"That's good," Lord West said. "Then you have to understand that there are more problems than just the food, although that is significant. Delos *can* outwait us. And when it comes to winter, it will be hard. But it might not last that long. My hope was that the rebellion would rise up when we reached the city, and we would have it in our possession before any of the other legions of the Empire's army could come to reinforce it."

"But now, with us stuck outside the city, we're easy prey," Ceres said. "Caught between the hammer and the anvil."

"Exactly," Lord West said. "My men have shot down what messenger birds they could, but we cannot be certain they got them all, and we do not control the docks."

"They could simply send a messenger that way, or even bring reinforcements back by boat," Ceres said. She understood the magnitude of the situation now. They needed to take the city quickly. "All the gates will be well guarded, so we can't just slip into the city, but—"

"What is it?" Lord West asked.

"There might be a way," Ceres said. "The rebellion has always had secret ways into the city, and I know some of the old ones, from when Rexus was alive."

"We wouldn't be able to sneak the army that close to the walls," Lord West said. "With this many men and horses, someone would spot the movement, and doing it by night is dangerous anyway, simply with the numbers of the men."

Ceres stood. "I'm not talking about sneaking the whole army in," she said. "Just me."

"You?" Lord West shook his head. "What if something were to happen? No, we need you."

"To sit out here with you until the rest of the Empire's army arrives?" Ceres said. "No. I got you into this. I should be the one to get you into the city, too."

"You're too valuable," Lord West said.

"We've already established that I don't really know how to command an army," Ceres said. "But I *do* know the ways into the city, and there will be people in the rebellion who trust me." She thought of her brother, and her father. Of Anka. "Hopefully, people I've wanted to see for a long time now. They'll listen to me, but if you or one of your men goes, what will they see? A noble trying to give them orders? I'm the best person for this job, while *you're* the best person to ensure that when I get one of the city's gates open at dawn, your men are ready to respond."

"I still don't like this," Lord West said. "I should send men with you."

"You know that would only increase the risk," Ceres said. "The best thing you can do right now is trust me. It's not as though you can stop me, unless you're going to have me guarded day and night."

Lord West hesitated for several seconds and then stood, clasping her hand. "Very well. But if you're not back by noon, my lady, I will assault the walls to get you back."

"You've already told me that horses can't climb," Ceres pointed out.

"They can't," Lord West said. "So you'd better make sure that you succeed."

Ceres crept toward the city's walls with only the faintest points of light to guide her. There were the dying embers in the fire pits outside the walls, the pinpricks of starlight above, and the glow of torches belonging to the sentries the Empire had set on Delos's walls. Ceres was grateful for the last of those, because at least it told her where the watchers were likely to be.

She was grateful that it was a moonless night, too. It meant that, wrapped in a cloak, she barely left a trace as she crept across the open ground between her camp and the city. She hoped that any watcher would just see one more shadow against the grass, and not catch any glimmer from the armor that lay beneath.

She'd padded that so it wouldn't make a sound as she moved. The last thing Ceres wanted was to be all but invisible, but to make so much noise that the Empire's sentries could find her anyway. She picked her steps as carefully as she could too, feeling for twigs or broken ground that might give her away.

"I just hope there's someone there when I get there," Ceres murmured to herself.

When Rexus had led the rebellion, there had been set points where its members would look out for people who wanted to enter the city secretly, and set signs to let them know that a friend was approaching. Ceres had known all of them, because Rexus had made sure that she knew.

Now, though, Ceres had no way of knowing if the spots were still the same. The signals might have changed, or worse, the Empire might have found some of the routes and started watching them, capturing any rebels foolish enough to still use them. When Rexus had been in charge, they'd had to change several of the routes for exactly that reason. Ceres had no way of knowing which ones were still current.

She kept on toward the walls. Perhaps someone else could have done this, in spite of what she'd said to Lord West, but the truth was that she was the one with the best chance to persuade the rebellion.

Ceres skirted around the edge of one of the fire pits, and heard a noise somewhere above. On instinct, she threw herself flat.

"What's that?" someone said from a spot on the wall that had seemed dark and empty a moment before.

"Probably nothing," another voice said. "You've been jumping at shadows all night."

Ceres saw a guard then, lighting a previously cold torch. She could imagine him looking out over the grass beyond the walls, and tried to stay as still as possible, hoping that the darkness of her cloak would hide her.

"You see? There's nothing there. Now, we need to get back to our patrols. The captain will kill us if he catches us playing dice."

Ceres dared to move again as she saw the light move off, but she didn't move quickly. Instead, she crawled her way toward the base of the wall, not caring how long it took. She couldn't afford any more risks.

It seemed to take forever before her fingers touched stone and mortar, and even longer before Ceres found the spot she wanted. Above, there was a section where a gate for goods might once have been that now looked walled up. The bricks could still be moved from inside though, and when she'd left, the rebellion had sent people to watch it at night.

Ceres whistled, following a pattern of long and short notes she hoped she'd remembered correctly. The noise seemed far too loud against the silence of the night air. Ceres waited, pressed flat against the wall, hoping that none of the guards had heard.

She kept on waiting, counting her heartbeats, trying to get some sense of the time that was passing. At least a minute went by with no sound from above, and now, along the wall in the distance, Ceres could see the steady light of a torch moving in her direction. She didn't think it was because someone had heard. It wasn't moving fast enough for that, but the light would still be enough to see her by.

She had to make a choice. She could run back into the night, but that movement risked being seen, and she might not get another shot at this. Or she could whistle again. She did, and halfway through she realized that she'd been whistling the wrong sequence. Quickly, she changed it.

The light was moving toward Ceres quicker now. Obviously the guard had heard, but Ceres could hear something too: the scrape of stones moving, followed by the quiet slap of rope falling against stone. A rope ladder came down beside her, and Ceres didn't hesitate.

She clambered up, forcing herself to concentrate on the climb rather than on the light that signaled a rapidly approaching guard. She hurried up the ladder, hauling herself into a small, dimly lit space that was little more than a gap left over by new building and forgotten about. She watched as a man in a rough tunic pulled the stone façade back into place.

He turned to her and drew a knife.

"Who are you, and why are you using out-of-date signal codes? If one of the others had been watching, they probably wouldn't even have recognized them."

Ceres stepped into what little light there was, watching the shock spread across the features of the watcher as she did so.

"My name is Ceres," she said. "And I have returned to lead you."

CHAPTER TWENTY FOUR

Stephania was spending the coin of favors as fast as she dared. Faster, because what she was doing right now might very easily get her killed. When she'd heard what had happened to Thanos, she'd sent her handmaidens out to look for details at once. She'd dressed as carefully as she could, and she'd set out to free him as surely as a warrior in full armor might have set off after some fair maiden in a story.

Except that this wasn't a story, and her husband, the man she loved, was in danger.

Stephania had always told herself that love was a trap; that the only love worth having was for oneself. Now, she was doing things that might get her killed, and all for a man who was trying to bring down the very Empire that had given her such a good life.

It was a kind of madness, but a madness that made so much more sense now. Finally, she was starting to understand what true love meant, and it wasn't what she had thought. It wasn't about possessing another. It wasn't about hurting them when they refused you. It was this… this willingness to give anything for them.

"Even my life," Stephania whispered.

"What's that, my lady?" one of her handmaids asked.

"Nothing," Stephania said. "Milla, I need you to go and find Captain Delvar. Take him this note. If he argues, remind him who saved his head when the father of his last lover wanted to take it. If *that* doesn't work, remind him that I know he hasn't paid the king his cut of the slaving operations he conducted among the Isles of Teeth."

"Yes, my lady."

So many secrets, so many strings of knowledge and obligation that she'd hoarded like a miser. Now, Stephania was running through them almost too fast to keep track of. There had been the secrets spent to find out exactly what had happened in the throne room. There had been the attempts to find out how Lucious had found this soldier, when Stephania thought that she'd disposed of the only link to him. She'd used a noble lady's former indiscretions to find out which part of the dungeons Thanos had been sent to, and a guard captain's dangerous habits to secure access to the upper layers of them.

Now she was walking through them, past cells holding rebels and dissidents, thieves and murderers. They were mostly thrown in together, and Stephania could see men and women huddled in barred spaces seemingly at random. She could practically smell the despair there, mixed in with the sweat and human waste of the place. Would she end there, if this went wrong, or would they simply kill her out of hand?

"This way, my lady," one of the jailors said. His price had been the location for a daughter long believed lost. It was a surprisingly maudlin thing, Stephania thought, for such a rough-looking man. "Ignore all them. They're just not looking forward to what's coming to them."

That was probably death or torture, mutilation or shipment to the Isle of Prisoners. Stephania didn't particularly care which. They didn't matter. Only Thanos mattered to her right then. She would see every one of her servants and friends impaled or tied to an execution pyre before she lost him.

She would even risk it for herself.

Stephania swallowed as she walked down through the dungeons, tasting the scent of the guttering torches that lit it as much as smelling them. She could hear screams, only partly muffled by thick doors, and she guessed that was deliberate, designed to put fear into the prisoners yet to suffer.

"Oh, don't worry," the jailor said, and he seemed to be enjoying Stephania's discomfort far too much. "We won't be working on your husband. Not when there's the Isle of Prisoners waiting for him."

If the circumstances had been different, Stephania would have seen that the man suffered for that comment. As it was, she merely nodded and kept walking. Their route headed down, always down, until it seemed that they must be deep underneath Delos, in a space that sunlight never touched.

"This is as far as I go," the jailor said, pointing. "His cell's that way."

"That wasn't our agreement," Stephania snapped back.

"Well, I want to live to see my daughter, and those royal bodyguards—"

"*What* royal bodyguards?" Stephania asked.

"You didn't think they'd leave him unguarded, did you?" the jailor countered, already walking away.

Stephania stood there and fumed. She hadn't prepared for this. She hadn't planned for this, and she should have. An idiot could have guessed that there might be extra guards at a time like this, but Stephania had been too busy thinking about Thanos. Love could make a fool out of anyone.

She pulled her favorite necklace from around her neck. It was a thing of heavy white gold, dripping with emeralds and sapphires. At least she could plan now. She took a small vial from her dress, carefully avoiding contact with the stones as she dripped the contents on them.

She kept walking and found a door at the end of the corridor, attended by a royal bodyguard seated on a chair, his gilt-edged armor reflecting light from a torch and a naked blade sitting across his knee. Stephania saw him rise as she approached.

"Forgive me, my lady, but the king said that Prince Thanos was to be kept secluded."

"I merely wish to see my husband," Stephania said.

"The king's orders were very clear."

"My *husband* has been accused of being a traitor and dragged away to a cell without my even getting to say goodbye. I would give anything … *anything,* just to be able to speak to him for a moment or two."

"Anything?" the guard asked, and Stephania knew she had him. The royal bodyguards were supposedly incorruptible, but in her experience, no one was. No one except Thanos, perhaps.

Stephania held up the necklace. It was worth more than a man like this would see in his lifetime. Stephania dangled it in her hand.

"Would this be enough?" Stephania asked. "Not even to do anything much. Just to walk away for a few minutes while I speak to the man I love. You can understand love, I'm sure."

"I prefer the kind I can buy," the guard said. His fist closed around the necklace. "But this buys a lot."

He walked away, tossing a key to Stephania as he went. She hurriedly fit it into the lock. Thanos was in there, looking bruised as he sat in a bare stone cell. Stephania ran to him, putting a hand to his cheek.

"Thanos," she said. "How could you be so foolish as to get caught?"

He smiled up at her. "I thought you'd be angry with me for helping the rebels. I thought you'd hate me."

"I could never hate you," Stephania said. "I love you."

After all the lies she'd told in her life, that one truth felt oh so sweet. She kissed him then, long and deep.

"It isn't safe for you to say that right now," Thanos said. "It isn't safe for you to be here, Stephania."

"I don't care," Stephania said.

"You should," Thanos replied. "You should get as far away from my cell as you can and pretend that you hate me, even if you don't. You should be the first to condemn me whenever they speak about me. That way, they won't think you're a traitor along with me."

Stephania smiled at that. Almost no one else who had ever been in her life would have put her first like that. They wouldn't have decided, in a moment when their own life was at stake, that Stephania's life was worth more. It just showed how special Thanos was.

"It's probably a little late for that," Stephania said, pulling Thanos to his feet. "For one thing, I'm carrying your child."

Thanos stopped, stepping back and staring at her in obvious disbelief. "You're pregnant?"

Stephania bit her lip as she nodded. "I'm pregnant."

The world seemed to light up with Thanos's smile. "That's incredible. It's wonderful news!"

Stephania found herself folded into a hug, and she wished that she could stay there like that with Thanos forever. She felt safe like that with him. Wanted. Loved. She could feel tears beginning to roll down her cheeks, because she'd never had anything like this in her life before. She was surprised when she stepped back and found similar tear tracks on Thanos's cheeks.

"We're really going to be parents?" Thanos asked, taking her hands.

Stephania could feel the strength in his touch, but also the gentleness there. "We really are, and I don't care if you have been helping the rebels. None of that matters."

"It matters if they take me away and kill me for it," Thanos said. "Or worse, if they kill you just for being married to me. And what about our baby? Even if they leave it be, it will grow up being taught that its father was a traitor. Or worse, they might decide that no one with my blood can be allowed to live. That they're too much of a threat."

Stephania didn't want to think about that, although she also wasn't sure why Thanos's bloodline would be a threat. If she had decided to join in the condemnation of him, she had no doubt that the child would have been welcomed, simply because of its obvious nobility. Now, though… now, things would be more complicated.

"None of that is going to matter," Stephania said. "Because we're going to get you out of here."

That seemed to get an even bigger look of surprise than the fact that she was pregnant.

"What? How? Stephania, you can't take that much of a risk!"

Stephania shrugged. "It's a better risk than the risk of not having you, and it's already done. I've bribed the people I needed to bribe, and my maids will be putting sleeping draughts in the beer of any guards along the way."

Although what she'd smeared on her necklace hadn't been a sleeping draught. She hadn't had anything that gentle at hand, and she hadn't been willing to risk the guard going back on their deal. There was nothing, *nothing* she wouldn't do for Thanos.

"So you see," Stephania said, "I'm committed. They'll kill us both if they catch us now."

"I won't let that happen," Thanos said, and Stephania smiled at the thought that even here, even now, he wanted to protect her.

"*I* won't let that happen," Stephania corrected him. She held out her hand. "We have to hurry though."

She felt Thanos's hand slide into his. He looked so strong like that, and she passed him a short dagger.

"Just in case," she said.

Thanos looked at it and nodded. Stephania could see the determination there.

"Are you sure we'll be able to get out of here?" he asked.

Stephania kissed him. "Trust me. You're good at fighting those who need fighting. I'm good at… arranging things."

Maybe one day she would even be able to tell him about some of the things she'd arranged to keep him safe. Then again, maybe not. Thanos might have helped the rebels, but in some ways he was too pure, too innocent, for the things Stephania had done to protect him.

"We'll need to get out of the castle," Thanos said. "After that… I don't know. Perhaps the rebellion will have a way out of the city. If we can find them, maybe—"

"It's all right," Stephania said, cutting him off with a kiss. "I have this covered."

She led the way up through the dungeons, pulling Thanos along past the spots where there were screams or people crammed in together. She knew her husband would want to save them, but right then, that would only attract attention. And if others had to suffer so that the people she loved would be safe, Stephania didn't care.

She found guards slumped here and there. Her maids had done their jobs. She thought she glimpsed the body of the royal guard off to one side, but there was no time to check. They'd already spent too long there.

"We'll get out of here and head for the docks," Stephania said. "There will be a boat there waiting for us. After that… we'll find somewhere to go."

"Haylon," Thanos said. "We'll be safe on Haylon."

Perhaps, or perhaps Stephania would be able to think of somewhere better. The important part was that they would be together.

All they needed to do now was reach the docks.

Chapter Twenty Five

Ceres didn't know the route that the rebel led her along. She traced her hand along the stone of the walls, feeling the strangeness of it. That strangeness, more than anything, told her how long she'd been away from the rebellion. So did the fact that Anka was now leader of the rebellion. It seemed like too much for the former slave to be running, because it seemed like too much for anyone to run by themselves.

In the passages and hidden spaces the rebels had carved out, Ceres saw more people than she could have believed. There were people training and working, laughing and sleeping. There were storerooms and workrooms, hallways and forges…

"Who all is leading you now?" Ceres asked as they walked.

"Besides Anka?" the rebel replied. Ceres could hear the respect there. From the moment she'd announced herself, he'd been as deferential as he might have been with a returning hero. "There's Edrin and Hannah, Berin and Sartes and—"

Ceres didn't listen beyond that. In that moment, none of the rest of it mattered.

"My father and my brother are here? Now? Take me to them!"

He led her to one of the sleeping spaces near the forges, and Ceres heart soared as she saw her father, sitting near a small bed—and her brother beside him.

"Father? Sartes?"

Her father looked up as though he'd seen a ghost. He paled, seeming overcome with disbelief, joy, relief. He stood there staring, as if not daring to hope that this might really be happening.

Ceres could understand the feeling. She felt equally shocked, and elated.

She saw Sartes sit up in the bed and clamber from it, rubbing sleep from his eyes.

"Ceres?" he said, and he sounded as shocked as her father looked. "You're alive?"

He stood there as though not knowing what to do, looking her up and down as though trying to make sure that it was really her, and not some imposter.

Ceres looked him up and down, trying to guess at all that had happened to him in the time she'd been away, but right then, she was just glad he was there. She opened her arms wide, and her brother ran to her, holding onto her tightly. He was a little taller than Ceres remembered, and stronger, too.

"You're *alive*!" Sartes said.

"We thought you were dead," her father said, moving to join in the hug. "I thought… I thought we'd lost you."

Ceres could hear notes of old grief there. She clung to them then, wanting to reassure them both that this was real.

"I've missed you both so much."

It seemed then as if the moment might never end. Certainly, Ceres didn't want it to.

"Where have you been?" her father asked. "What happened to you?"

"I washed up on an island," Ceres said. "There were people there who helped me to learn a lot of things about myself."

Her father's look changed a little. "What kind of things?"

"They taught me more about the power inside me," Ceres said. "And they led me to my mother."

This time, she saw Sartes frown. "Your mother? But our mother—"

Ceres put a hand on his arm. "Is still your mother, but not mine."

"You mean we're not family?" Sartes said. There was surprise there, but also a kind of fragility Ceres never wanted to hear in her brother.

Ceres hugged him again. "We will *always* be family, little brother, no matter who my parents turn out to be."

Her father held her at arm's length. "What did you think of your mother?"

Ceres thought for a moment or two. "She was… strange. Beautiful. Kind. I liked her, but she also seemed… sad. It must be hard for her, alone on the Island Beyond the Mist. How did you meet her?"

Her father shook his head. "That's a story for another time. What matters now is that you're here. It's *all* that matters."

"Are you with the army that's come?" Sartes said. "We can't find out what's happened."

Ceres smiled. "I'm *leading* the army. And we're going to take Delos from the Empire."

"I'd like to hear how you plan on doing that," Anka said from the doorway.

Ceres looked around at her, pausing as she saw her. She'd heard that Anka was in charge, but it was a very different thing to see it. She stood there, watching the way people reacted to her, seeing that it really was true.

Anka looked different from how she had in the slaver's cage. Different even from how she'd looked in the courtyard of the castle. Ceres could see the worry etched in her features, but also the sense of strength there.

Ceres hurried and they embraced. She could feel the strength in Anka's arms and shoulders.

"It's good to see you again. It looks as though you're doing a bit more than just holding things together now."

Anka spread her hands. "It turns out I had a talent for it, and I've had a lot of help. Sartes has done a lot. And of course, I would never be alive if it weren't for you."

They shared a look of mutual admiration.

Anka led them all away from the space by the forge through to a larger spot that had probably once been a storeroom, but was now filled with people.

Ceres could hardly believe how large the rebel army was now.

"Anka?" a woman asked. Ceres recognized her as Hannah, who'd been with the rebellion from the start. "Is that… Ceres? How is she alive?"

Ceres waited while Anka walked into the middle of the room, following her into a clear space there and letting her speak. Ceres could feel the way that people were looking at her. They knew who she was. They'd seen her in the Stade, or they'd heard about her role in the army.

"Those of you who've been in the rebellion long enough will recognize Ceres," Anka said. "Maybe some of the rest of you will as well. She fought in the Stade, and she is the reason why many of us are still here today."

Anka gestured for Ceres to step forward.

She did so, feeling the weight of the many eyes upon her. Most of these people would know who she was, some would even know her, but many wouldn't.

"I'm guessing that you have heard about the army besieging the city." She took a breath. "I am leading it."

Gasps arose from the crowd.

"You've brought an army to attack our city?" a man asked Anka.

She could see their confusion.

"We are not trying to destroy the city or hurt its people," Ceres said. "I've brought an army to *help* the rebellion."

"And how do we know that?" someone called from the crowd. "I saw the banners out there. Those are Lord West's men. Why would a lord help the likes of us, common peasants?"

"Because he hates the way the Empire rules," Ceres explained. "He just needed the right prodding to rise up against it."

"And we're supposed to believe that?" Hannah asked. "For all we know, he's just planning to replace the king with himself, and nothing will change. He could be duping you, Ceres."

"*Everything* will change," Ceres said. "And even if you don't trust Lord West, trust me."

"It's not about trusting you," Edrin said. "It's—"

"It's about trying to *win*!" Anka said. "Listen to yourselves. You're so worried about what might come next that you're not paying attention to what's happening now. We have a chance to crush the heart of the Empire. We have to take it. I trust Ceres. We should listen to what she has to say."

Ceres looked around at the people there.

"I understand that you're scared. You've been working for the overthrow of the Empire, but even so, this must feel like a huge step. I'm asking you to make the stand you've been preparing for. I'm asking you to take a big risk. I know that."

She waited for a moment or two, letting it sink in.

"But there comes a time when you have to stop preparing and *act*," she continued. "We have a chance to take Delos, but that chance will pass far too quickly. I have an army waiting out there, but when the rest of the Empire's forces get here, it will be caught between them and the city. If we attack the walls, we'll be slaughtered. But if we can take the city quickly, we can hold it against anyone."

"So you want us to do all the fighting for you?" one of the combatlords there asked.

Ceres shook her head. "You know me better than that. You've trained beside me, haven't you?"

The combatlord admitted: "You didn't shy away from the fights in the Stade."

"And I'm not going to run from this one," Ceres said. "I don't want you to win the city for me. I want us to win it together. My army can't get into the city, so I want us to open a gate where they can get inside without being cut to pieces. You wouldn't be fighting the whole of the Empire, just a few guards."

All of them fell silent. She understood. Someone would have to volunteer for the risky assignment of emerging from these tunnels and seeking out the least-guarded gate. It was a life and death task, and no one wanted it.

"I shall do it," came a voice.

Ceres turned, and her heart fell to see Sartes, standing there proudly.

"I can find the least defended gate," he said. "I'm the best placed to do it. No one would suspect me."

Ceres felt a wave of pride and fear for her brother. She didn't want to put her brother in danger, but no one else had volunteered. And he had a point.

"Sartes is right," Anka said. "And he is brave." She then turned to the crowd. "Will you be as brave? Once we find this gate, will you open it for Ceres and her army?"

A silence lingered, as a few nodded.

"And then you shall storm in?" Edrin asked.

Ceres nodded.

"And then we fight together," Ceres said. "Together, we can do this. Together, we can take Delos. Together, we can overwhelm the Empire and hold the city against the world. Together, we can forge a new world, but only if we do this now. Are you with me?"

There was silence, but that silence was quickly broken by a low chanting. Sartes started it, but the others soon took it up, one word rising until it filled the room.

"Ceres! Ceres!"

Chapter Twenty Six

Sartes moved carefully through the city streets in the hour before the dawn. He was watchful as he darted from doorway to alley mouth, clambered up stacked pallets, and blended in as best he could with those people who were out on the streets in spite of the early hour.

This being Delos, there were more than a few of those. It didn't matter that there was an army outside the city; its business still had to go on. That meant fishermen and merchants rising early to catch the tide out of the docks. It meant traders and food sellers setting up their stalls in the streets. It meant the night people coming back from whatever jobs they'd been doing by starlight, legal or otherwise.

It meant guards too, which was why Sartes was being careful. The Empire hadn't tried to impose a curfew on the city, presumably because everyone knew it would be unworkable, but Sartes still couldn't afford to be seen too openly. There was too much of a chance that someone might recognize him from the army, and then he would be taken as a deserter or a rebel.

Even so, he had better odds than most of the rebellion, which was why he was the one doing this. To any guard who *didn't* recognize him, Sartes would just look like an urchin worth no more attention than it took to kick him out of the way, or perhaps like an apprentice late to start work in his master's shop. Either way, it was easy enough to blend in with the people around him, to keep moving, making his way toward the city's gates.

Ceres undoubtedly had a harder job. While Sartes got to walk along safe streets, she had the job of sneaking back out to her waiting army to direct their attack. Sartes didn't want to think about the danger his sister might be in. He knew that she was a great fighter, but right then, one mistake and she would find herself facing the whole of the army within the city alone.

He couldn't do anything to help her, though. He just had to trust her, and make sure that he did his part.

He walked in the direction of one of the smaller gates first, the Dead Gate, where bodies were taken out on their way to the burial grounds. He ducked in behind a water butt while he watched the guards there. Too many, but more than that, the ground in front of the gate was too open. The guards would see any attack coming, and that would make it harder to succeed. No, he needed a better—

"Hey, what are you doing there, boy?" a guard demanded.

Sartes thought about running, but running would only prove that he was doing something wrong. He thought about the knife strapped to the small of his back, but that was a last resort. Sartes looked up at the guard, looking for any spark of recognition. That *would* have him reaching for the knife, because at that point, it would be the only way he lived.

"I… I'm sorry," Sartes said, thinking quickly. "I just thought if I could get close to the walls, I might be able to see the army. My friend Julin said that there were horsemen as far as the eye could see, and I wanted to look for myself, because I think he's lying."

The guard shook his head. "He's not lying."

"Could I… could I get up on the wall and see them?" Sartes said. It would let him see more of the defenses, and perhaps pick out the right spot to attack.

"No, you can't," the guard snapped back. "Do you think I'm running some kind of tour here, boy?"

"I'm just—" Sartes didn't have to fake his fear, although the guard probably wouldn't guess the reason for it. "We're going to be safe, aren't we? I mean, they aren't going to get in and kill us all, are they?"

"Don't be stupid, boy," the guard said. "Our walls are high, they aren't equipped for a siege, and the gates are strong. Why, the dockside gate is so well defended that half a dozen men can defend it, firing bolts through the murder holes until reinforcements arrive."

It seemed that Sartes had his gate, but he needed to be sure. He'd have to see it for himself.

"You should run along. A boy like you probably has chores to get to."

"Yes, sir," Sartes said, and ran, exactly as the soldier had commanded.

Perhaps it was because he was moving so fast that he got the sense that someone was following him. He was moving far faster than the crowds now, running from hiding place to hiding place because there was no time to waste. But there was someone else moving as fast. Sartes caught glimpses of them, or at least of the disturbances in the crowd behind him. He saw people moving out of the way of someone moving too quickly. He heard the beginnings of an argument, quickly cut off. On a stretch of cobbles, he thought he heard the slap of a pair of hobnailed boots.

Sartes headed for a deeper patch of crowd, householders and servants out looking for bread and meat even before it got fully light. He followed the flow of the crowd, forcing himself to wait even though there wasn't much more time for his scouting mission to continue. He thought he caught sight of a dark cloak as someone slipped through the crowd, obviously looking for him.

Sartes moved away carefully, waiting until he was well clear of the crowd before he started running again. He couldn't afford to waste time now. He had to check the gate and get back to the others. They were relying on him. *Ceres* was relying on him.

He sprinted to the dock district, sticking to the back streets and keeping his ears pricked for any continued pursuit. When he got to the dock gate, he looked around for a hiding spot and settled in on the fringes of a group of porters, obviously waiting for a ship that needed loading. They didn't seem to care about him. Possibly they thought he was waiting for the chance of easy coin like the rest of them.

Sartes watched the dockside gate. The guard he'd met had been right: there were almost no soldiers there. There didn't need to be, because the gates there were massive, solidly built with a portcullis behind them. There were stone towers above, crenulated on top, with a small catapult set there where it could do damage to anyone attacking. There was an alarm bell too, and Sartes guessed that it would summon soldiers from all across the district.

But there were ways to deal with it. What had once been clear routes to let the guards see threats coming were now cluttered with crates and sacks, ropes and barrels ready for loading or moving to warehouses. All of it would provide cover for the rebellion as its people moved closer. If they disguised themselves as dock workers, they might even be able to sneak right up to the guards before they attacked. They might be able to take the gate without losing anyone.

And then they would be able to let the army in. Sartes was a little nervous about that in spite of everything Ceres had said. He'd seen what armies were like when he'd been a conscript. Possibly Lord West's men would be more disciplined, and he knew that Ceres would never allow the kind of wanton destruction the Empire sanctioned, but even so, there would be violence. People would get hurt.

"It will be worth it," Sartes told himself. When they took the castle and brought down the king, it would be worth it. "Think of all the fighting it will stop."

Potentially, it could stop a wider war. The Empire's army attacked because the royals told it to. Take away the king and his cronies, and the army had no one to command it. From what Sartes had seen, half the men in it would desert at once, while the others would be cautious about fighting on for a lost cause. At a stroke, they could end this.

This was the gate. Sartes could feel it, just as he could feel the excitement building in him at the thought of what was going to happen next. They could do this. They could really do this.

First, though, he had to get back to the others, and he had to hurry, because dawn was coming far too fast.

Sartes ran back through the city's streets, over cobbles and dirt, gravel surfaces and evenly laid stone. Hardly anyone gave him a second glance. He saw a gang of slaves in the street, repairing a patch of broken cobbles under the supervision of armed guards. It was enough to remind him that no matter what happened in the attack, people would be better off. This was the only way to really change things in the Empire.

Sartes tried to imagine what it would be like once the Empire was gone. It was hard to think that far ahead. They'd all spent so long now working for it, but Sartes almost hadn't dared to think past the rebellion to what might lie beyond it. He'd been thinking perhaps that there would be time with his father, time for a normal life. Now, with Ceres back, he was already thinking of how much better things might be.

Ahead, he could see the entryway to the rebellion's tunnels, disguised as a half-forgotten stairway, hidden behind an overgrown arch. He crouched there, making sure that the coast was clear.

The others would be as excited to hear about the gate as he was to have found it. Anka would be pleased that she'd sent him, and grateful to know that she could trust him. The others would gain hope from it, because he'd given them the ideas that had worked in the burial grounds, and the Stade. His father would be proud of him, and Ceres—

Sartes caught a flicker of movement and half turned, but he was too slow. He just had time to see the cloaked figure running toward him before it slammed into him, sending the two of them tumbling to the ground in a scrambling sprawl of limbs.

Sartes twisted, reaching down to the small of his back for the knife he'd hidden there. Nothing was going to stop him from getting back to the rebellion now. His hand closed around the hilt and he drew it, but it seemed that his attacker had been expecting the move, because Sartes found the weight of a shin bearing down on his forearm, hard enough to make him cry out. A brutal twist of his wrist later, and the knife was skittering off across the cobbles.

Sartes hit out with his free hand but the figure grabbed his free wrist, using it to lever him over onto his belly, where Sartes quickly found his wrists bound with loops of cord. He tried to cry out, and tasted cloth as a rag was stuffed into his mouth.

"Lady Stephania sends her regards."

Chapter Twenty Seven

From the top of the tenement building, Anka watched the rising sun, tracking its progress with growing trepidation. Across from her, she could see Berin, his fingers tightening on the forge hammer he held. Anka could understand it far too easily.

"Sartes should have been back by now," she said, although she said it softly. She didn't want the others there to see how nervous she was right then. Far too many of them were new recruits, who needed to believe that their leader knew what was going on if they were going to do this.

"He should," Berin agreed. "But Sartes is resourceful. He survived the worst the army could throw at him."

To Anka, it sounded like a man trying to convince himself, and Anka wasn't going to puncture it with too much reality if she didn't have to. For one thing, she hoped that the old smith was right. She didn't want to think about the possibility of Sartes being lost to them.

"We helped him then," she said, "and we'll help him now if he needs it. But probably, he doesn't. He's probably just holed up somewhere because he can't get back. Or he's still looking for the right opportunity."

Or he was dead or captured, having been caught by the soldiers Anka had sent him to spy on. If that proved to be the case, she wasn't sure that she would be able to forgive herself. Sartes was so eager to help sometimes that it was easy to forget that he was just a boy.

"He wants to do this," Berin said, as if guessing Anka's thoughts. "You didn't make him do it, and you know he's the best choice for it."

Anka guessed that was his way of saying that he didn't blame her. Anka would rather that Sartes was safe, though, and that there was nothing to blame her for.

"What do we do now?" Berin asked.

Anka shrugged. "We wait as long as we can for Sartes to come back. After that… I don't know. We think of something."

"Ceres is relying on us," Berin said.

Anka nodded. "And we're relying on her. A lot of things have to go right today."

And already, they were starting to go wrong. Sartes really should have been back by now with details of the best gate to target and the best way to go about their attack. He'd proven so effective in the past, providing them with the idea to take the Stade and the one to free the conscripts. Anka had come to rely on him as much as anyone.

Yet now, with the sun almost fully up, he wasn't there. Anka didn't know what to make of it.

Oreth came in, his knives strapped into place and a leather jerkin thrown on over his normal clothes. He looked ready for war, almost impatient for it.

"Do we know yet?" he asked.

Anka shook her head.

"Well," she heard him say, "we need to know soon. The combatlords are getting restless. So are the mercenaries Yeralt hired."

Either one would have been a problem. Both together were something more than that. The combatlords were strong, tough men, but they didn't take orders well. They were too used to fighting on their own terms against a single opponent, and cautious battle tactics were something that just didn't come into it. They would fight as long as they respected the people they were fighting for, and being kept waiting was not something they liked.

The mercenaries were a little more disciplined, but they didn't have the same commitment to the cause. Yeralt might believe they would stay there as long as they were paid, but Anka knew better. Mercenaries would only stay as long as they believed that there was a good chance of winning. They needed to believe that their commander was competent, or they would start to desert, or worse.

"We need to hurry," Oreth said. "If we hit them while they're changing guards, it will be twice as difficult."

Anka knew it was true, but there had to be a way.

"Ask around. Ask if anyone else has information on the gates. We can't wait for Sartes."

She saw Oreth nod. "I'll try to be discreet."

The wait was the hardest part. Every moment, Anka could see the sun rising higher. It was getting late. Maybe too late.

When Oreth returned, it was with a man who looked more like a beggar than one of the usual members of the rebellion. Anka didn't know his name, but that was far too common these days. He was probably one of the ones they'd brought into their rebellion in the last few days.

"This is Ralk," Oreth said. "Ralk, tell Anka what you told me."

"I've seen all kinds of things the last day or two," the beggar said. "Including which gates they're pulling men from to protect the others. There's a gate on the east side that we could take."

"You're sure?" Anka asked.

"I'm sure," Ralk replied. "It might be hard to get there, but once you're there…"

Anka wished she had more information, but forced herself to look confident. It was part of what being a leader *meant*. "We knew that wherever we attacked, it wouldn't be easy, so let's do it."

She led the way down into the tenement, where her people were waiting for her. She could feel the mixture of nerves and eagerness there in the habitual sharpening of weapons, the constant movement to no purpose.

She had to be clear now. "You all know why we're here. We're going to end this. We're going to open the eastern gate."

That got a cheer from some of those there. Others had the set faces of men and women who knew about the violence that would be coming.

"We'll go out in two waves," Anka said. "I'll lead the first wave, and Oreth will lead the second. The job of those of us in the first wave will be to take the guards on the gate by surprise and get it open. The second wave will come in after that to hold the gate until Ceres's army can arrive, rising up in the city to take it. The element of surprise is crucial here, so keep weapons out of sight until we're ready to act. Does everyone know what they need to do?"

Anka went through the room, picking out the people she needed. She picked some of the core of the rebellion, but also plenty of combatlords and mercenaries. This was a job for fighters. She checked their disguises like a mother ensuring her children were wrapped up against the cold, then headed out into the streets with them at her back. Berin was beside her, and Anka could see the head of his forge hammer in the palm of his hand, the haft hidden away up the sleeve of a long coat.

There were enough people in the streets that they could just about pass for the normal flow of the crowd. Even so, Anka could see people hurrying back inside their homes, shutting their doors as the rebellion passed. That was probably a good thing. The fewer people there were in the street, the less chance there was of ordinary people being hurt.

They walked in the direction of the gates, down through the poor districts and the merchant districts, keeping to the back streets and keeping their weapons out of sight. Anka held her breath as they walked past a squad of guards loitering at the side of a street, yet they didn't give the rebels a second look, and Anka didn't order her people to attack. There was no need, and the worst thing they could do right then would be to get caught up in fighting in the streets. Even with the hundreds, the thousands who would rise behind them, they couldn't afford to give away what they were doing.

She looked up to see more of her people following across the rooftops, making their way over flat roofs and between gaps. She hoped that no one else would dare to look up then, because if they did, it was over. It would be open fighting, and the task of opening the main gates would be many times harder.

Anka signaled for the figures above to keep lower, and Oreth signaled back before slipping out of sight behind a roof edge. She kept going, making her way along the roads that skirted the city's east-west processional way. That, more than anything, convinced her that the gate was the right one to try for. With it open, Ceres's forces would be able to ride down the broad expanse of the street almost all of the way to the castle. The invasion of the city would be over almost before anyone knew what was happening.

In the distance now, Anka could see the gates. They were imposing things, covered in metal, embossed with scenes of the Empire's triumph. The stone bastions around them were solid enough that siege engines would probably barely scratch them. The walls were high and strong, with watchers set every hundred paces or so.

Yet Ralk had been right: there wasn't a whole army there on the walls. Those soldiers there were seemed to be loitering in the space in front of the gates, waiting for any move from beyond the walls. That made sense to Anka. They couldn't stand at full readiness all the time. Of course they would wait there until there was some sign of threat. The trick would be to get the gates open before they realized that there was anything wrong.

"We'll go in pretending to be a group of disgruntled traders," Anka said, keeping her eyes on the gates. "If we make enough noise about it, the soldiers will be too busy arguing with us to see the real threat."

"Or they might decide to attack to teach us a lesson," Berin pointed out.

"If that happens, Oreth will bring his group in to back us up," Anka assured him. By now, she knew how the other members of the rebellion would react. "Either way, it will look like a scuffle rather than a real attack. Half of them won't bother joining in until it's too late."

She turned back to the others. She could see the nerves there. Several of the newer members of the group were fingering their hidden weapons, obviously ready for action.

"Stay calm," Anka said. "And keep those blades hidden until I make my move. When we go up there, we're just slightly stupid traders who want to know why a little thing like an army is getting in the way of us getting to make our living, all right? We're going to go up and demand that they open the gates for us. If we're really lucky, they might even let us do it, just so that they can think about shutting us outside. Is everybody ready?"

Anka saw the members of her little group nodding to one another. The mercenaries crowded to the back, but that was only to be expected with their sort.

"Then let's go," she said, turning back to the gate. She waved to where she thought Oreth was waiting above, but there was no response.

Anka looked around for him, because this needed to be coordinated, but there was no sign of him. She kept going anyway, because it was too late for anything else, and it was only as she set off that she saw the one thing she'd hoped not to see: figures struggling on the rooftop. Oreth was fighting against a pair of figures, silhouetted against the morning sun. She saw the flash of a blade as it plunged into him.

It was only as she saw that the figures were wearing the colors of the rebellion that Anka understood.

She heard the snick of blades clearing scabbards. Instantly, she spun back, but it was already too late. She saw her people there in the hundreds, and the mercenaries, the new recruits, had them. Berin had a blade pressed to his throat. One of the combatlords was on his knees, blood pouring from a wound. Three mercenaries had swords leveled at Anka.

She tried to think of something to do, something to say, but there was nothing. She'd warned the others about the dangers, and now it had come to pass.

They'd been betrayed.

Chapter Twenty Eight

Thanos looked back over Delos as he rode down toward the docks, tension there with every stride of the creature as the dawn rose. At any moment, he expected to see guards appearing behind them, riding him and Stephania down.

"It will be all right," Stephania said from beside him. "By the time they realize that you've escaped, we'll be long gone."

Thanos nodded. Stephania knew him better than he could have believed.

"It's strange to think this might be the last time we see Delos," Thanos said, looking back at the city. In spite of the squalor of the docks, the destitution of the city, it was still difficult to be leaving it like this.

"It doesn't matter," Stephania said, reaching out for his hand without slowing down. "So long as we're together."

It did matter, though. It didn't feel right that because of the evil of the Empire, he and his wife were being forced to flee the place where they'd been planning to build their lives.

"Do you really think they'll take us in on Haylon?" Stephania asked him.

Thanos nodded, trying to look confident in spite of the argument he'd had with Akila. "When they hear what's happened, they'll help us."

They had to. It was the only place they had left to go. Now that the Empire had condemned him, surely that would be enough to prove to the rebels that he was on their side.

"And we'll be stuck on an island that's under attack," Stephania pointed out.

Thanos wanted to reassure her. He wanted to make things so much better for her. "Haylon is beautiful," he said. "The Empire can't touch us there, and it doesn't have to be forever. Sooner or later, the Empire will fall, and we'll be able to go anywhere we want. You, me, and our child."

"Just you, me, and our child," Stephania said. Thanos saw her smile. "Put that way, I think we'll be fine wherever we go. We need to hurry though. This captain will carry us for coin, but the boat won't wait long."

They rode to the docks as quickly as they dared. Ahead, Thanos could see a boat waiting. It wasn't as large or grand as some of the galleys the Empire used, but it had the sleek look of a ship well used to keeping ahead of pursuers.

"A smuggling boat?" Thanos said, as they got closer.

"I've always tried to find friends in strange places," Stephania replied.

Thanos dismounted and helped her down. He slapped the rumps of their horses, setting them running. The more he and Stephania could disguise their trail, the better it would be, for them and for anyone who had helped them.

They stepped toward the waiting boat, and it was only then that Thanos saw the figure slip from the shadow of a stack of crates. He carried the markings of a royal messenger, and he thrust a scroll into Thanos's hand, and then did not wait as he turned to go.

"From Lucious, my lord," he said. "You may want to open it."

And without another word, he hurried off, disappearing into the darkness.

Thanos stared at Stephania, who stared back at him, each of them floored. Lucious knew they were here; and yet he had not come. He could have had them imprisoned if he'd wanted. Then why hadn't he? Thanos wondered. And then he realized there could only be one reason: whatever was in this scroll was so damaging, he did not have to appear.

That, and perhaps because Thanos would kill him on the spot.

Thanos studied the scroll with a new interest. It was genuine, the messenger was genuine, and the wax seal was genuine. It was definitely from Lucious.

"What are you doing?" Stephania asked, examining it with disgust. "Who cares what that beast has to say? Discard it at once!"

But Thanos shook his head.

"No, my lady," he said. "We must know what he knows before we embark. This vessel, after all, may be a trap."

He looked back up at the smuggling ship, the hardened faces of its men, now unsure of anything.

Slowly, Thanos broke the seal, his heart pounding, bracing himself as he did. He read aloud, so Stephania could hear.

Thanos,

I would have come myself. But if I bring you back, then there's always a chance you could talk your way back into the king's good graces. So I believe this scroll shall suffice to serve my purpose.

I hear things now, brother. And I thought you might like to hear some of them before you leave. If you choose to leave.

Ceres is alive.

Thanos lowered the scroll, his heart slamming, disbelieving, trying to process what he was reading. His world reeled at the news, and he felt it spinning out from under him.

Ceres was alive? Thanos's heart leapt at the prospect, but he didn't dare to believe it. Not when it was Lucious saying it.

He continued reading:

If you don't believe it, ask your lovely wife. She knows all about what happened to Ceres. After all, she was the one who arranged for Ceres to be sent to the Isle of Prisoners.

Thanos looked up at Stephania, expecting to see her deny it, but instead, her face was reddening.

His heart dropped at her expression.

Could it be possible?

"Stephania?" he asked, his heart broken.

"I… she would have been dead in the Stade if I hadn't," Stephania said. "I saved her."

Now Thanos reddened. He could hardly believe his ears.

"No more!" Stephania cried. "Read no more!"

She reached out, as if to rend the scroll, but Thanos, intrigued, pulled it back and read fervently.

But this should come as no surprise. Stephania, after all, is the one who arranged to have you killed. Who do you think hired the Typhoon?

Thanos turned back to Stephania, expecting her to tell him that it was all lies. Instead, she just stood there, looking torn, looking guilty.

"Stephania?" Thanos said.

"I… I don't want to start off our new life together by lying to you," Stephania said. "I love you, Thanos. I never thought I could love anyone like I love you."

"What are you saying?" Thanos asked, feeling his world melting around him.

Suddenly, she burst into tears, rushing in to hug him.

"You were supposed to be mine," Stephania said. "You said it yourself. You cast me aside for her, for Ceres. So I sent a message to the Typhoon. If I couldn't have you—"

She wept and wept.

"I know how it sounds. It was awful. I should never have done it. I just couldn't bear the thought of losing you. And I didn't love you then like I do now. I am so ashamed of it. Please believe me. So ashamed. I beg God every day for forgiveness. I am begging for your forgiveness. Now, I would give my *life* for yours."

Thanos couldn't believe what he was hearing. He stared at Stephania as though only just seeing her for the first time. Perhaps he was.

"It was *you* who tried to have me killed," he said, incredulous. His voice sounded flat, even to himself. It felt right then as if his emotions hadn't caught up with the rest of him. "*You.* The woman I love most of all. The only one in this court I trusted."

"I love you, Thanos," she said through her tears. "I've loved you even when I didn't know what love was."

He didn't know what to think right then, what to feel. Ceres was alive, and Stephania had tried to kill him. She had tried to kill Ceres, too.

And yet Stephania was pregnant with his child, she claimed to love him, she'd married him. And she had risked her life to break him out of jail.

But she'd also tried to have him killed, and she'd sent Ceres away to die. He should have felt angry, but instead, he simply felt as though the world had been turned on its head. He didn't know what to feel.

How could he ever trust her? How could he ever know who Stephania truly was? Did she even know who she was?

"You went around with me, looking for the killer," Thanos said. "You pointed me at Lucious. You led me to the stable boy and then you had him killed."

He could feel the anger rising up in him at that. Stephania had been willing to sacrifice innocents in her efforts to protect herself, and to blame Lucious.

Stephania reached out for his shoulder, and Thanos shook her off.

"No," he said. "I can't. I thought you loved me."

"I *do* love you," Stephania insisted. Thanos could see the tears in her eyes. The hard part was that he had no way of knowing if they were genuine now. He didn't want them to be, because even now, he couldn't bear the thought of Stephania in pain.

Thanos shook his head. "I don't think you know what love really means."

"I risked *everything* for you," Stephania said. "If that's not love, I don't know what is. I need to spend my life with you. I've *killed* people to keep you safe."

She wept and hugged him and he stood there, numb, not knowing what to say or think.

"I only tell you all this because I've changed," Stephania insisted. With the tears in her eyes, a part of Thanos wanted nothing more than to comfort her.

He reached out for her automatically, and he saw the hope in her eyes.

"I … I wouldn't have married you if I didn't love you, Stephania. But I still don't think you understand."

"I shouldn't have tried to kill you," Stephania wept softly.

She kissed him then, and Thanos could taste the sweetness of her lips as she did it. He wished that things could be this easy. Just kiss, and everything would be better. Just pretend that none of it had happened. He wished he could do that. Maybe it would hurt less then.

Finally, Thanos pulled away.

"Do you remember the name of the stable boy you had killed?" Thanos asked. "Do you remember the name of the isle to which you sent Ceres off to live a tortured life?"

Stephania paused, looking stricken. "What? I… Thanos, this is about us."

Thanos slowly shook his head.

He stepped toward the ship. When Stephania went to follow, he put a hand up to stop her.

His heart broke even as he did it. It was the hardest thing he'd ever had to do.

"I am sorry, Stephania," he said. "I have grown to love you. I truly have. And yet… I can't… I can't be with you after this. However much I want to."

"But Thanos, please, you can't—"

"No," Thanos said. He tried to keep his voice steady. "It's not even the fact that you tried to kill me. We could get past that. It's what you've done to everyone else."

"No one but you matters," Stephania said.

"Yes, they do," Thanos countered. "They matter as much as either of us. More sometimes. If you can't see that …"

Finally, Stephania's eyes squinted in a slow rage.

"You're going to find her, aren't you?" Stephania demanded, and Thanos could hear the anger there, the jealousy. "You're going to run back to her."

He hadn't thought that far ahead, but now, he knew he was.

"I do love you, Stephania," Thanos said. "But yes, I will find Ceres. I have to. I never left her. I had been told she was dead."

"They'll kill me if I stay here," Stephania said. He could hear the pleading note there. "They'll execute me. Thanos," she said, her voice sounding as though it might crack at any moment.

He knew she was right. They would. And that broke his heart most of all. Especially as she had just risked it all to save his life.

And yet, he could not be with her. Not anymore.

Thanos was already making his way onto the smugglers' vessel. He looked back and watched, with a broken heart, Stephania slump in place there, sobs wracking her body. It took everything Thanos had not to run back to her.

The captain met him on the deck, looking him over. Thanos saw him frown slightly.

"Where to?" the captain asked.

Thanos replied without looking back, his voice cold and hard and determined:

"The Isle of Prisoners."

The captain's eyes widened, whether in fear or awe, Thanos did not know.

"Get a move on, you dogs!" the captain called out to his crew. "Soldiers are coming. And I don't like soldiers! We need to be away from here."

Thanos stood there as the boat lurched into motion, slipping through the dock smoothly. He looked back at Delos, in what might be his last view of the city. It had been his home for so long, and now it felt like ashes to him. On the docks, getting smaller, he could see Stephania crumpled there.

She looked up and reached out for him, sobbing.

"THANOS!" she shrieked. "NO!"

He closed his eyes and heard her shriek rolling off the rising fog, and he knew it was a sound that would reverberate within him forever.

The only thing that made it bearable was the thought of what he might be sailing toward.

Ceres was alive out there.

And he would find her.

Chapter Twenty Nine

Ceres sat atop her horse, watching the walls of the city as the sun rose. She forced herself to remain still, but her horse was skittish.

Something was wrong.

"Still no news from the other gates?" she asked Lord West.

The nobleman shook his head. "You will know as soon as there is a signal, I promise you."

"In the Stade, the waiting was always the worst part," Ceres said. "Listening to the fighting outside."

"Most of war is waiting," Lord West said. "Waiting, or camping in the rain, or marching through mud. When I was a young man like Gerant, I used to dream of glorious clashes and charges. No one tells you about the mud."

"Or the blood," Ceres said. "Or the death."

"You're too young to have seen so much," Lord West said.

"In Delos, I think there are plenty of people my age who have seen violence," Ceres pointed out.

"But none with the blood of the Ancient Ones," Lord West said. "And maybe this will change things." He looked as though he might say more, but he broke off, pointing. "Look there, below!"

Ceres followed the line of his finger, and she saw a gate opening at the side of the city. Not one of the largest gates, a merchant gate meant for moving goods in, but still more than big enough for what they wanted.

"They've done it," Ceres said. "The rebellion has given us our way in."

Lord West nodded, then yelled to his men. "Form up!"

Horns sounded, and the horsemen of the North Coast gathered together in a great wedge, their horses whickering as they held in place, obviously sensing some of what might come next.

"When you're ready, my lady," Lord West said, "just give the order."

Ceres paused, but not for long. She could only guess at the fighting that had to be taking place below as the rebellion struggled to hold the gate. Even if they'd managed to open it by stealth, there would still be guards coming to investigate soon. They had to act.

"For Delos," she called out. "Charge!"

She heeled her horse forward, and the riders of the North Coast went forward. Their wedge felt like an arrowhead now, fired by some great invisible bow toward the waiting roundel of the city. There were so many of them there, but even so, they felt like one coordinated thing in that moment. One entity, following behind Ceres, matching her stride for stride.

She saw Gerant there, his spear flying his uncle's pennant. Around him were other young men, other pennants reflecting other nobles, but they were all following Ceres because of what she represented and what she wanted to achieve. Together, they thundered down toward the city, the sound of their hooves so loud that Ceres imagined the king being able to hear them in the castle.

Good, she thought, let him know what was coming for him.

They reached the open gates of the city, powering in through the wide space left there for goods and carts. Ceres had her sword in her hand then, fully expecting to find herself in the middle of a fight between the rebellion and the army. Yet as far as she could see, the streets beyond the gates were empty.

Something felt wrong again, but Ceres couldn't simply bring her horse to a halt. Not with so many men piling into the city behind her. Instead, she had to raise her hand to get them to slow, trying to call out over the sound of horseshoes on cobbles.

"Stop! Everybody stop! There's something wrong."

Lord West's men were well trained, but even so, it took them time to come to a halt. They swirled around in a great open space intended for merchants and their teams of oxen. Ceres knew it well. She'd been to it plenty of times with her father, and normally by this hour it was bustling with the sounds of people haggling and arguing, straining and trying to get animals to go the way they wanted.

Instead, it was so silent that Ceres could make out the cawing of the crows that had settled on one nearby rooftop.

"This is wrong," Ceres said, looking around. "There should be people here."

"Perhaps they fled indoors when the rebellion took the gates?" Gerant suggested.

"Then where are the rebels?" Ceres demanded. "They should be here."

"I agree," Lord West said, riding up beside her. "But we cannot let this chance pass for a feeling." He called out to his men. "Be on your guard."

They rode forward, and still, everything was too quiet. Unnaturally so. There had been more noise in some of the woodland they'd passed through on the way there. This had the carefully still silence of too many people making no sound.

Then they passed a side street, and Ceres saw the carts that had been brought up there, blocking the way. She heard the crows again, and this time they took to the air, scattering as someone moved near them.

"Back!" she yelled. "Back! It's an ambush!"

They'd been betrayed. That much was obvious, although Ceres didn't want to guess who had done it. The Empire had known they were coming though. More than that, they'd known enough of their plan to emulate it, and draw them into a trap that they couldn't resist.

"We need to get away!" Ceres called again. "Scatter. All of you, scatter!"

There were too many men, though, and too many horses. They crowded the square beyond the merchants' gate, filling it until it seemed impossible that they might be able to turn around. With the side streets blocked, they couldn't even flee that way, and half of the men seemed not to understand what was going on in any case.

Ceres leaned over to Gerant to order him to sound the retreat on his horn. To shout it if he couldn't do that. Anything that might get them out of the killing ground of the square. Even as she did it, though, she heard another horn sound, in a note that was deep and harsh, different from anything Lord West's men carried.

There was metallic crash as a portcullis came down across the merchants' gate. Above them, figures appeared in the armor of the Empire, armed with bows, slings, and javelins.

Feathers seemed to sprout from Gerant's open visor. For a moment, Ceres stared at him, unable to comprehend the oddity of it. Then she saw the rest of the arrow's haft, and she watched as the young nobleman tumbled slowly from the saddle.

She barely had time to look up as arrows darkened the sky, hundreds of them, thousands, as the Empire's men opened fire.

As she fell with the men all around her, one final thought ran through her mind:

So this is what death looks like.

Now Available!

REBEL, PAWN, KING
(Of Crowns and Glory—Book 4)

"Morgan Rice has come up with what promises to be another brilliant series, immersing us in a fantasy of valor, honor, courage, magic and faith in your destiny. Morgan has managed again to produce a strong set of characters that make us cheer for them on every page.... Recommended for the permanent library of all readers that love a well-written fantasy."

—Books and Movie Reviews, Roberto Mattos
(regarding Rise of the Dragons)

REBEL, PAWN, KING is book #4 in Morgan Rice's bestselling epic fantasy series OF CROWNS AND GLORY, which begins with SLAVE, WARRIOR, QUEEN (Book #1).

17 year old Ceres, a beautiful, poor girl from the Empire city of Delos, wakes to find herself imprisoned. Her army destroyed, her people captured, the rebellion quashed, she has to somehow pick up the pieces after being betrayed. Can her people ever rise again?

Thanos sails for the Isle of Prisoners, thinking Ceres is alive, and finds himself in a trap of his own. In his dangerous voyage he remains tormented by the idea of Stephania, alone, with his child, and feels torn over his life's path. Yet as he struggles to return to Delos, to find both of his loves, he encounters a betrayal so great, his life can never be the same again.

Stephania, a woman scorned, does not sit idly back. She turns all the power of her fury on the ones she loves the most—and her treachery, the most dangerous of all, may be what finally brings the kingdom down for good.

REBEL, PAWN, KING tells an epic tale of tragic love, vengeance, betrayal, ambition, and destiny. Filled with unforgettable characters and heart-pounding action, it transports us into a world we will never forget, and makes us fall in love with fantasy all over again.

"An action packed fantasy sure to please fans of Morgan Rice's previous novels, along with fans of works such as The Inheritance Cycle by Christopher Paolini .... Fans of Young Adult Fiction will devour this latest work by Rice and beg for more."

—The Wanderer, A Literary Journal (regarding Rise of the Dragons)

Book #5 in OF CROWNS AND GLORY will be released soon!

REBEL, PAWN, KING
(Of Crowns and Glory—Book 4)

Listen to THE SORCERER'S RING series in audio book format!
Now available on:

Amazon
Audible
iTunes